THE SEAGULL READER

Stories

Second Edition

W. W. Norton & Company, Inc., also publishes

THE SEAGULL READER: POEMS, Second Edition

THE SEAGULL READER: ESSAYS, Second Edition

THE SEAGULL READER: PLAYS

THE SEAGULL READER: LITERATURE

THE SEAGULL READER

Stories

Second Edition

edited by Joseph Kelly

College of Charleston

W. W. Norton & Company, Inc. • New York • London

Manufacturing: Haddon Craftsmen, Inc./RR Donnelley.
Book design: Chris Welch.
Production manager: Jane Searle.

Library of Congress Cataloging-in-Publication Data

The seagull reader. : Stories / edited by Joseph Kelly. — 2nd ed.
p. cm.
Includes bibliographical references.
ISBN 978-0-393-93091-7 (pbk.)
1. Short stories, American. 2. Short stories, English. 3. Short stories—Translations into English. 4. College readers. I. Kelly, Joseph, 1962–

PN6120.2.S39 2008
813'.0108—dc22

2007019244

ISBN 13: 978-0-393-93091-7 (pbk.)

W. W. Norton & Company, Inc., 500 Fifth Avenue, New York, N.Y. 10110
www.wwnorton.com
W. W. Norton & Company Ltd., Castle House, 75/76 Wells Street,
London W1T 3QT

9 0

✶

Contents

Acknowledgments

I would like to thank Susan Farrell, whose support throughout the production of this volume was invaluable. And I thank John Alvarez, whose student I was long ago: encouragement that he must have considered unremarkable was not.

Along with the publisher, I am happy to thank the following for their assistance during various stages of this project:

James Andres, Harper College; James J. Badal, Cuyahoga Community College; Peter J. Bailey, St. Lawrence University; Jane Bernstein, Carnegie Mellon University; Franz Blaha, University of Nebraska-Lincoln; Robert Boswell, New Mexico State University; Mary Jane Brown, Miami University, Middletown; Stuart Burrows, Brown University; Vivian Casper, Texas Woman's University; Lawrence Coates, Bowling Green State University; Jane Creighton, University of Houston Downtown; Natalie Daley, Linn Benton Community College; Jane Delury, University of Baltimore; Shannon Dobranski, Georgia Institute of Technology; Lisa Ede, Oregon State University; Cai Emmons, University of Oregon; Grace Epstein, University of Cincinnati; Grace Farrell, Butler University; Nate Gordon, Kishwaukee College; Paul Graham, St. Vincent College; Jacqueline Gray, North Carolina State University; Susan Hagen, Riverland Community College; Sean Henne, West Shore Community College; Clinton S. Hirst, University of Detroit, Mercy; Helen Houston, Tennessee State University; Priscilla Jackson, Dominican University of California; Patrick Keyes, Kirkwood Community College; Susan Kress, Skidmore College; Cynthia Kuhn, Metropolitan State University; Jun Liu, California State University, Los Angeles; Agnetta Mendoza, Nashville State Community College; Madonne Miner, Texas Tech University; Chris Moylan, New York Institute of Technology; Lara Narcisi, Regis University; Caroline Nobile, Edinboro University; Jolynn Parker, Syracuse University; Pedro Ponce, St. Lawrence University; Paul M. Puccio, Bloomfield College; John Samson, Texas Tech University; Karen Schneider, Western Kentucky University; Heidi Sjostrom, Marquette University; S. L. Stafinbil, Marquette University; David Stevenson, Western Illinois University; Kremena Todorova, Transylvania University; Lucilia Valerio, Clark University; Charles Watson, Syracuse University; Gary Williams, University of Idaho; Allen Woodman, Northern Arizona University; Patricia A. Young, College of St. Scholastica; Thomas Zelman, College of St. Scholastica.

INTRODUCTION

*

What Are Stories?

We can't escape stories. We read them in the newspaper; we see them on television; and over lunch or coffee or on the phone we tell each other stories about ourselves, our friends, our enemies, our heroes. Stories keep us afloat. We need to both hear and tell stories to make sense of the world and our place in it.

There's that story your roommate told you last week about his old girlfriend: she was a fine person, but he left her for selfish reasons and feels guilty about it now. Or the one you told your parents about why you got a D in your first semester at school: it had something to do with a crooked-faced teacher who had it in for you. We tell stories to define and judge character, and there's hardly a more interesting topic in the world. Our own characters have fascinated us since before the first scribe thought to write down the heroic tales he heard told 'round the fire, and we're no less spellbound today. **Short stories** are nothing more than these tales told by men and women who have studied the art of telling, refined it through long practice, and adapted it to the demands of a sophisticated reading—as opposed to a listening—audience. As a result, short stories tend to be more complex and sophisticated than the anecdotes we tell one another. Even so, fundamentally, short stories are no different from the anecdote you heard this morning while walking to class.

You have probably already mastered every element of the short story simply by growing up in society. *Point of view, character, plot, setting, symbols, motifs, theme*—these are some of the terms critics use to break stories down, and each of these terms refers to some thing or things with which you already are familiar. You might not realize that you're an expert, but you are. Already, you probably interpret each of these elements intuitively whenever you hear or read a story. The purpose of this introduction is to bring what you do intuitively into the light of your consciousness so that you can interpret stories more confidently and accurately, so that your interpretations will gain sophistication, and so that you can understand sophisticated stories.

How Do You Read Stories?

In each section below I discuss an element of short stories. These discussions are in no particular order. You do not necessarily need to analyze point of view before character, or character before symbols. Analyzing a short story is a more organic, sloppy affair. It is an art, not a science. You will consider these elements as your needs demand. You might puzzle over a strange ending, and then think about who was telling the story. You might get bored in a long description of place and wonder why the writer put it there. If you are reading a story for pleasure—that is, outside the context of school—you might never bother to define in your own mind who the protagonist is, but you would sense it intuitively. Or you might interpret a symbol without consciously recognizing that it is a symbol. In the context of school, however, you should at some time consider each of these elements formally.

Point of view

Every story has its teller. For example, when you listen to one friend bad-mouth another, you tend to take into account the source of the gossip: Does the teller have an ax to grind? Is he capable of lying? Will she distort the truth? Is he too dull to take into account the full picture? Every person has his or her own **point of view,** and the same event will sound different when reported by different people. Sometimes these differences will be dramatic—each driver in a car crash might hold the other at fault, for example. More often the differences will be more subtle. Ask two people long married about their first date, and though the facts might remain the same, each will color the event with his or her own perceptions, which derive from his or her own prejudices. This is natural. Everyone has a particular version of events.

We call the person who "tells" a story the **narrator.** When the narrator is a character in the story, whether he or she is involved in the events or merely reporting them from the sidelines, we are usually pretty aware of the point of view. We know that the narrator has witnessed the events from his or her own perspective. This type of narrator is called a **first-person narrator** because he or she uses the first-person pronoun: "I" or "we." If the story is told from the periphery of the action, the narrator is a **first-person observer:** "I saw the thief run off with the queen's jewels." If the narrator is in the midst of the action, he or she is a **first-person participant:** "Just as I ran off with the queen's jewels, I realized that I'd been seen." If we have reason to doubt the information we're getting, if the narrator is naïve or dim-witted or mentally handicapped or dishonest or extremely prejudiced, we call the narrator **unreliable.** Clearly, all first-person narrators are unreliable to some degree, since they all have their own perspectives and therefore cannot present a purely objective reality, but we reserve the term *unreliable* for those few narrators who severely distort the tales they're telling. When reading a story by such a narrator, part of the reader's pleasure comes from piecing together a more reliable account of the events.

The point of view of a story is less obvious when the narrator is not a character at all. Such narrators are called **third-person narrators** because they do not refer to themselves as "I": "Completely unobserved, the thief made off with the queen's jewels." No one was in the room to see the thief, yet his action is reported to us, almost as if the narrator were a fly on the wall. Often, the perspective of a third-person narrator does not seem to belong to a real person. The narrator gives us information no human could. He might tell us about events that occur in different places at the same time or about the biographical histories of unrelated characters, or he might enter into the thoughts of different characters. If there is no limit to what the third-person narrator knows, if he can eavesdrop on the minds of characters and reveal their unspoken thoughts, we call him **omniscient.** If there are limits—for example, if the narrator tells us the thoughts of only one character but not the thoughts of others—he has what we call **limited omniscience.** With all third-person narrators, you can be pretty certain that the information you get is trustworthy. To put it more precisely, the author does not intend for you to question the narrator's perspective. The author expects you to regard the narrator's information as objective, undistorted truth, even the narrator's value judgments. If the narrator tells you the day was dreary, the day was dreary. If the narrator says this character is evil and that one is good, then it is so. For example, if the narrator says, "The good-hearted thief stole the queen's jewels out of devotion to his own wife," we can be sure that the author thinks the thief is a good man. Sometimes third-person narrators get heavy-handed in their value judgments. For example, the narrator might address readers directly: "Now we mustn't judge our thief too harshly. His disrespect for private property is more than amply compensated for by his love of humanity. He is the type of person whom any of us would cherish as a friend." This is called editorializing. Of course, we do not have to accept the third-person narrator's point of view. We might decide the narration is distorted by the author's prejudices or by the prejudices of the time or place in which the author wrote. But within the fictional world of the short story itself, a third-person narrator is generally reliable. (The use of a central consciousness, which is discussed below, is one significant exception to this rule.)

(I should note that I have been using the pronoun "he" when discussing the third-person narrator. Normally, I would substitute "she" now and then, but I haven't here because I do not want to imply that third-person narrators are sometimes male and sometimes female. They are neither, typically. "It" would be a neutral pronoun, but "it" denies personhood, and it is best to think of a third-person narrator as being a person. So we are stuck with the unsatisfactory, old use of "he," meaning "anyone.")

About a hundred years ago, writers began experimenting with a narrator who combined aspects of the first and third person. This narrator never uses the personal pronoun "I"; he is not a character in the story; and if you don't read closely, he might seem to be a third-person narrator with limited omniscience, for his knowledge is limited to the thoughts and perceptions of a single character. But more careful attention reveals that everything this type of narrator says comes to us as if filtered through the consciousness of that one particular character. The perceptions of the events given voice by the narrator are the perceptions of the character. This type of narrator is called the **central consciousness.** Though the narrator seems to be third person, we must take into account the distorting prejudices of the central consciousness just as we would take into account the prejudices of a first-person narrator.

Use of the central consciousness was the first step toward the development of a radical method of narration perfected by James Joyce and Virginia Woolf: **stream of consciousness.** The American psychologist William James coined the term *stream of consciousness* to describe the flux of thoughts—many of them preverbal—that run through our minds when we are awake. If you have ever tried to capture even a couple of moments of your own consciousness, you know how idiosyncratic and various and layered our thought patterns are. A writer using stream of consciousness approximates the thoughts of a character in a technique called **interior monologue.** The narrator is not precisely third person, because it is as if we were witnessing the thought process of one character—so we will see the word "I." Even so, the character is not telling a story. Instead, we are witnessing the story through the character's mind. All the events, then, are conveyed to us through a lens even more distorting than the lens of an unreliable first-person narrator. In stream-of-consciousness style, the story of the thief that I've been using as an example might read like this: "Dark. Darker than I thought it would be. Wait a minute. There. Shapes emerge. A bureau. Right where they're supposed to be, the whole lot of them. These pearls on Jenny. How she looks in that dress. The sunlight on her, that day on the seashore, how she said she would. I could still turn back. Pocket them and I'm a thief forever after. No—already if someone turns on the light and me standing here in the room where I'm not supposed to be in these clothes, the necklace hanging in my fingers, I'm a thief already. Explain I decided not to? Just putting them back. On my way out. Don't you believe me?" As you can see, with stream of consciousness, it is difficult to make out what exactly is literally happening.

Both central-consciousness and stream-of-consciousness narratives reflect the shift toward psychological drama in literature that took place around World War I. Few writers today use either type of narrative.

Character

The purpose of stories is to reveal **character.** The focus might be human character in general or the character of particular individuals, but either way, everything in a story serves this end. The main character of a story, the person you would say the story is about, is called the **protagonist**. Protagonists do not need to be good people; generally they are a complex mix of good and bad. But typically a story will make us sympathize and perhaps also identify with its protagonist and perhaps also identify with him. In most short stories, the protagonist will face some physical or psychological challenge, usually a moral choice, and grappling with that challenge will change her. Protagonists, then, are usually **dynamic characters:** they change.

Most other characters in a story do not change: they are **static.** Folklorists have developed catalogs of the different types of static characters, what we might call "stock" characters, who are defined by the roles they play in stories. But the most important character besides the protagonist is the **antagonist.** This is a character who opposes or impedes the protagonist. Not all stories have an antagonist. In many of the psychological stories written in this century, protagonists struggle against themselves, instead of against another person.

In stories, character is revealed in the same way it is revealed in real life. What a character says, what others say about him, physical descriptions, items (such as clothes) associated with the character, and what a character does all contribute to our understanding of that character. Some narrators provide even more information: what is going on in a character's head, for example. You judge characters, then, the same way you judge people. Though some English teachers tend to discourage simple questions such as, "Do you *like* this guy?" or "Would you like to *be* this woman?" they are actually very useful. Questions like these activate the very skills of interpretation you will need to use. Characters who appeal to us and have our good wishes are called **sympathetic characters,** and perhaps the most fundamental question to ask yourself about any character, especially a protagonist, is "Is she *sympathetic?*" Then you should figure out what in the story made you react the way you did: Why is the character sympathetic or unsympathetic?

One warning about this last bit of advice: sometimes our reactions to stories can be idiosyncratic. I might like a character, despite his faults, while my wife thinks he is a jerk. Our reactions might also be affected by our background—class, race, education, etc. Therefore, a more sophisticated way to think about character is to ask: "Does the author *want* me to find this character sympathetic?" You might find that Hemingway wants the reader to sympathize with a character whom you detest, or that Hawthorne wants you to disapprove of someone you admire. When you analyze a story, you are seeking to determine not only what you think but also what the author wants you to think.

If you don't react to a character the way you think the author meant for you to react, it could be because the writer is not very good at his craft. Or it might be because you are not the audience the writer had in mind when she wrote the story. If you find your own judgments differing from those you think the writer wanted you to make, you should try to figure out whom the writer expected to read the story. Generally, writers tend to write for people like themselves, so a little biographical information—the kind provided in the headnotes and in the biographical sketches in this volume—can tell you a great deal.

Your consideration of character should go well beyond this initial question of whether a character is sympathetic or not. You should define the protagonist's character as thoroughly as you can. What motivates him to do what he does? Why does she hesitate when she ought to act? How does he change? These and similar questions—the kind you might ask yourself about someone in real life—will help you understand each character. The discussion in the next section will also help you to analyze and understand characters.

Plot

Critics have developed a wide array of terms to help them analyze **plots.** Most of the terms were first used to describe the plots of plays, but they can be adapted to analyze the plots of short stories also. As you learn to apply these terms, don't lose sight of why you're analyzing plot: to help you understand the characters. The various elements of stories described below, then, are not ends in themselves; they are crucial to understanding character.

There is a difference between a plot and a mere recitation of incidents. Consider this example made famous by the English novelist E. M. Forster: the queen died; then the king died. No connection is made between these events; they are coincidental. So this is not a plot. A plot is a series of incidents that are unified: the queen died; then the king died of grief. In this case, the incidents are not coincidental. They are united by the king's love for his wife. The second event *results* from the first event.

A plot, then, is a linked chain of events. Sometimes—perhaps most often—these events are not presented to readers in chronological order. The story might begin *in medias res*—that is, in the middle of the plot. Or the narrator might begin at the end and relate the story through **flashbacks.** But if you rearranged the incidents into chronological order, you would find that every story begins in a situation of **equilibrium:** the protagonist's life is in a state of relative order and calm. Something then happens to disrupt that order. Consider, for example, the biblical story of the Prodigal Son:

There was a man who had two sons; and the younger of them said to his father, "Father, give me the share of property that falls to me." And he divided his living between them. Not many days later, the younger son gathered all he had and took his journey into a far country, and there he squandered his property in loose living. And when he had spent everything, a great famine arose in that country, and he began to be in want. So he went and joined himself to one of the citizens of that country, who sent him into his fields to feed swine. And he would gladly have fed on the pods that the swine ate; and no one gave him anything. But when he came to himself he said, "How many of my father's hired servants have bread enough to spare, but I perish here with hunger! I will arise and go to my father, and I will say to him, 'Father, I have sinned against heaven and before you; I am no longer worthy to be called your son; treat me as one of your hired servants.' " And he arose and came to his father. But while he was yet at a distance, his father saw him and had compassion, and ran and embraced him and kissed him. And the son said to him, "Father, I have sinned against heaven and before you; I am no longer worthy to be called your son." But the father said to his servants, "Bring quickly the best robe, and put it on him; and put a ring on his hand, and shoes on his feet; and bring the fatted calf and kill it, and let us eat and make merry; for this my son was dead, and is alive again; he was lost, and is found." And they began to make merry.

Now his elder son was in the field; and as he came and drew to the house, he heard music and dancing. And he called one of the servants and asked what this meant. And he said to him, "Your brother has come, and your father has killed the fatted calf, because he has received him safe and sound." But he was angry and refused to go in. His father came out and entreated him, but he answered his father, "Lo, these many years I have served you, and I never disobeyed your command; yet you never gave me a kid, that I might make merry with my friends. But when this son of yours came, who has devoured your living with harlots, you killed for him the fatted calf!" And he said to him, "Son, you are always with me, and all that is mine is yours. It was fitting to make merry and be glad, for this your brother was dead, and is alive; he was lost, and is found."

The state of equilibrium in this story is a time we must infer, because it exists before the story actually begins. There is a rich man who has two sons grown to young adulthood living under his roof. They are prosperous, and everything is fine.

This status quo is disrupted when the younger son demands his inheritance. Such a disruption is called a **complication.** A complication introduces the story's **conflict,** which is a struggle between the protagonist and some other person (the antagonist) or force. You may have seen some list of possible conflicts before: man versus man, man versus nature, man versus society, man versus himself. This list suggests just how wide is the range of things that the protagonist might struggle against. It could be nature, even human nature; it could be an unjust society; it could be a part of herself. It is crucial that you be able to define this conflict. Make sure you can answer the question, What does the protagonist struggle against?

In the Prodigal Son, the conflict is between the younger son and his father: the son wants to live a life that he cannot live while he's under his father's roof and authority. The subsequent events in the story—the squandering of the inheritance, the famine, the job feeding pigs—are parts of the **rising action.** They raise the tension in the conflict to a breaking point. The father is not present in the foreign country, so the son is not struggling against him *literally*. But we know that his dissolute life is a rebellion against his father, especially when we reach the **climax** of the story, which is the point in a story where the conflict is decided. In other words, the climax decides who wins. Sometimes, you will sense when the tension has reached its peak. But be aware that though the climax is sometimes the emotional high point of a story, sometimes it is not. Rather than looking for your own heightened emotion, look for the point when the conflict disappears. Often the climax requires the protagonist to make a decisive choice. In the Prodigal Son, the climax is the moment the son decides to return to his father and beg his forgiveness. At this moment, the conflict ends. The father has "won," so to speak, and the son, with his dissolute ways, has lost.

But the end of the conflict is not the end of the story. Following the climax is a **resolution,** or **denouement.** A new situation of equilibrium is established, often quite different from the state that existed before the initial complication. Sometimes, the resolution is a **reversal** of fortunes. In a tragedy, the plot resolves itself with the protagonist's fall from prosperity to poverty. This situation is the opposite in a comedy: the protagonist begins in a state of figurative or literal poverty and ends up in prosperity. But these terms—tragedy and comedy—apply to plays more readily than to stories. In stories, the change revealed in the resolution is often more subtle than these obvious reversals.

In the Prodigal Son, the son expected a reversal. Instead, he was surprised to find his original status restored by his forgiving father. This is a good example of why you cannot automatically equate the emotional high point of a story with its climax. I feel a flush of emotion not when the son has made his decisive choice to again live under his father's authority, but when the father rushes to welcome his returning son. My own emotion at this point comes from the father's unexpected generosity: the prodigal son's final status is equivalent to the initial state of equilibrium.

Or it is nearly so. The last episode in the story, which reveals the jealousy of the older brother, indicates that despite his father's forgiveness, the prodigal son's brief life of debauchery does have permanent consequences. It has altered his relationship with his brother, and it has altered the older son's relationship with the father. But as strained as the relations within this house are, the conflict is resolved: we have returned to a state of relative order and stability.

Not all stories have plots that can be mapped out so neatly. For example, many writers in the early twentieth century, influenced by the rise of psychology, wrote plots that took place entirely inside the main character's psyche, and these can be harder to analyze. These usually are the man-versus-himself (or man-versus-human nature) plots in which two aspects of the protagonist's psyche struggle against each other. Because there is no antagonist, you might find it hard to identify the complication and rising action, and the climax in these stories is often nothing more dramatic than a personal insight that comes upon the protagonist suddenly. The insight might be about human nature in general, though usually it is about the protagonist's own self. These types of climaxes are called **epipha-**

nies, and a good example is the conclusion to James Joyce's "Araby," in which the protagonist suddenly recognizes that he is "a creature driven and derided by vanity."

But even in modern stories, you will probably find it useful to summarize the plot. A plot summary should identify each of these elements: initial equilibrium, complication, conflict, rising action, climax, and resolution. If you can identify these, you have gone a long way toward understanding the protagonist.

Setting

The **setting** is the locale in which you find the characters. If the story were performed on stage, the setting would be the scenery and the stage props, the landscapes or cityscapes, or the rooms in which the characters move. You might think initially that setting is neutral so far as a story's meaning goes. After all, there has to be ground on which the characters walk; the ground doesn't *mean* anything. Sometimes, this might be true. The setting is so spare in the story of the Prodigal Son that we probably cannot glean any meaning from it. But if the setting is described in a story, you can be pretty well assured that it has some meaning. Short stories are such an economical art form that they leave little room for neutral details. If the ground is mentioned, you can mine it for meaning. For example, a description of the setting can establish the **atmosphere** or **mood** of the story, the emotional state the writer wants you to be in while you read the story. This technique is most obvious in ghost stories, in which the setting—for example, a giant, ramshackle old house on a rainy night—makes you feel apprehensive and vulnerable. Though it might not be so obvious as it is in horror fiction, setting is a feature of nearly all short stories. Usually in the opening pages of a story you will find some description of the setting, and that description will establish the story's atmosphere.

Setting might also serve as a window into the emotional state of a character. This technique is called **projection** because the writer projects onto the setting the emotions of the character. If we were to slip some projection into the Prodigal Son, we might use the setting to communicate the father's joy at seeing his son return. The time of day would be morning; the sun would have just burst from the horizon, banishing the last darkness of night; birds would be singing in the trees; and the air would be fresh and bracing.

In some stories, the setting alludes to events in the world beyond the little circuit of the characters. The drama of the protagonist's story might be surrounded by a larger drama involving all society. There might be a war going on or some other social unrest. Just as the protagonist's state of equilibrium has been disturbed by a complication, so the wider world may be convulsed in some conflict. Such a conflict is called an **enveloping action.** The dominance in literature of internal, psychological drama during the last hundred years means that few modern stories contain an enveloping action, but those stories that do will tend to use that action to comment on the smaller plight of the protagonist. The larger social events will probably parallel or contrast with the protagonist's difficulties, either trivializing them or making them seem more profound.

Symbolism

A **symbol** is an object that represents something else, sometimes another object but more often an abstraction. For example, consider General Robert E. Lee's surrender to Ulysses S. Grant at Appomattox. One object represented another: Lee stood for the defeated Army of Northern Virginia, and by surrendering himself to Grant he surrendered his entire command. So he dressed in his last clean uniform and belted on his sword in order to present his ragtag army in the best possible light. Grant might have taken Lee prisoner, but he didn't. He refused, even, to confiscate Lee's sword. In this context, the sword represented a number of abstractions, not the least of which was Lee's honor. Grant's refusal to take the sword communicated his esteem for Lee and for the soldiers who had until that minute been his enemies.

Some things, usually things in the natural world, carry the same symbolic meaning in just about any culture. The sunrise will probably call to mind birth or new beginnings no matter where you go, just as the sunset seems to naturally represent death or an ending. These symbols are perceived in Bali just as they are in Belgium.

Similarly, ferocious predators might represent evil in many different cultures, and a dense forest might symbolize the unknown. These are **universal symbols.**

Other objects carry meaning only in the context of a particular culture. You're driving across the United States, and in St. Louis you see a giant, soaring arch towering over buildings and trees and silhouetted against the blue sky. It's the gateway to the West, and it calls to your mind the American conquest of the Great Plains in the nineteenth century. You might feel a mix of respect for the accomplishment, regret for the people displaced by the migration, and all the ambivalence that usually accompanies thoughts of Progress. Citizens of St. Louis probably take the arch as a symbol of their city and enjoy some degree of civic pride whenever they see it. Other travelers, those unfamiliar with American monuments, would puzzle over its significance. The arch might have no meaning for an Australian touring the States by bus. The symbol is not universal: it is a convention contrived by a particular population of people. Such symbols are called **conventional symbols.**

Sometimes it is obvious that the symbolic meanings of conventional symbols are contrived. The regalia of clubs and political organizations are good examples. The mascot of a sports team is chosen by the team's owner or by a committee of professional marketers, and thereafter the Major League Baseball team in Arizona is symbolized by a rattlesnake. A flag is sewn by Betsy Ross and adopted by a committee, and instantly it symbolizes a nation.

But most conventional symbols have an anonymous genealogy. It is impossible to say who created them. It is as if they arose out of the culture itself. Who can say when apple pie came to symbolize the values of Middle America? Did any one person decide that the Midwest would represent wholesomeness and naïveté? Or that the American West would symbolize rugged individualism? Show almost anyone who grew up in American culture a picture of John Wayne on a horse in a Western landscape, and he will understand the symbolism. In fact, many people around the globe would recognize it too, for the icon of the American cowboy, and the notions of self-reliance and freedom and violence that he represents, is one of our cultural exports, courtesy of Hollywood. But show the picture of John Wayne to a farmer in rural China, and he would see just a man on a horse. No one person or committee decided that these objects would convey symbolic meaning in our culture; nevertheless, they do. And outside our culture they are meaningless.

A **literary symbol** is an object with symbolic meaning limited to the very narrow context of a particular work of literature. Outside the short story, the object does not mean what it does inside the short story. A literary symbol is authored neither by nature nor by a culture, but by a writer. As with a conventional symbol, when you take a literary symbol out of its original context, it stops being a symbol. In John Steinbeck's "The Chrysanthemums," for example, chrysanthemums represent a number of things, including the love and care and kindness of the protagonist. But outside the story they carry no such meanings.

So far I've only discussed the different types of symbols. It takes a good deal of interpretive skill to recognize that an object in a story is not just its literal self but also represents something else. Identifying literary symbols is an art, but there are a few tricks you can count on to help you. If the title of a story is an object, you can be pretty sure it also symbolizes something—thus the symbolic meaning of the chrysanthemums in John Steinbeck's story. By calling attention to the chrysanthemums in the title, Steinbeck alerts us to their importance. On even your first reading of the story, you should be asking yourself, What could the chrysanthemums represent? But for the most part, it is impossible to teach someone a foolproof way to recognize which objects are symbolic and which are not. You have to trust your own gut feelings. If you find your attention drawn to an object, if you suspect that something might have more than literal significance, you're probably right. The text will itself call attention to its literary symbols. Even if Steinbeck had called his story "A Day in California," we could still have figured out that the chrysanthemums were symbolic because the story itself draws our attention to them.

After you've identified which objects might be symbols, you still have a tougher task—figuring out what the objects represent. Again, this is a skill impossible to teach. You have to trust your instincts. Read the story a few times and an idea will more than likely come to you: the object represents love; it represents death; it represents the American dream; it represents hope. Usually, a symbol represents abstractions: love, death, dreams, hopes. Trust your gut. Even so, be prepared to revise your gut feelings. If you try to interpret an object symbolically and it just does not seem to work, maybe you were wrong. To quote Sigmund Freud, "Sometimes a cigar is just a cigar." Maybe the object is not a symbol. Or maybe you were wrong about what the object represents. Keep revising and refining your ideas until you think you get it right.

After you have done all this, there is one thing left to do. To fully interpret the symbol, you must follow what happens to the literal object in the story and then apply that to whatever the object represents. I don't want to ruin Steinbeck's story for you by telling you how it ends, but when you read it, be sure to note what happens to the chrysanthemums. What happens to them also happens to love and care and kindness.

Allegory is a special use of symbolism. In an allegory, characters or objects have a one-to-one correspondence with whatever they represent. Often in allegory, all the characters participate in a web of symbolism; one character might represent Sin, another Virtue, and yet a third Mercy. In allegory, the literal level is much less important than the symbolic level. The literal objects or characters are merely devices by which the writer explores the abstractions they represent. Allegory was popular in the Middle Ages, but current tastes, which tend to demand a high degree of realism, make it rare today.

Motifs

A **motif** is an image, object, character, situation, theme, even a word that the writer uses repeatedly throughout a work. For example, there is a motif of decay in William Faulkner's "A Rose for Emily." Emily decays, her house decays, her entire way of life decays, and something else decays too, though I won't ruin the story by telling you ahead of time. This motif helps give you, the reader, a sense of the story's unity. More important, it tips you off to an important theme—maybe the most important theme—in the story.

Recognizing motifs draws your attention toward something important to a story, and that attention will help you understand the story. For example, if an object keeps popping up again and again, you will know that the writer is calling your attention to it. To use a famous example, if you see a gun in the opening scene of a story, safely holstered and out of the way, you might think it is just part of the setting, but if it turns up a second time, you should begin to suspect it is a motif. Probably, you will begin to suspect that someone will shoot it by the end of the story, and the motif will thus contribute to the rising sense of tension as you approach the climax of the story.

If the motif is an object, more than likely that object will, by the end of the story, carry symbolic meaning. Dirt and dust crop up again and again in Katherine Ann Porter's "The Jilting of Granny Weatherall," so we suspect that they might represent something. In fact, dust is a conventional symbol: it represents our mortality, as when a minister on Ash Wednesday says, "for dust thou art, and unto dust shalt thou return." If dust were not a motif in the story, we might hesitate to equate it with mortality, and with a host of other meanings Porter might have given it. But because it is a motif, we read great meaning into Granny's persistent housework. We ask ourselves, "Why does she struggle so hard against the dust?"

Sometimes a particular motif might be characteristic of stories within a subgenre or a particular period. Detective stories, for example, often end with the variety of suspects gathered in one room to hear the sleuth unravel the mystery and identify the guilty party. That scene is a motif of mysteries. Similarly, the isolated, intelligent, lonely protagonist trying to overcome his feelings of alienation is a motif common to stories written in the modern period, in the years just before and after World War I. To recognize these motifs, you will have to become familiar with a lot of stories—far more than are represented in this volume. Your instructor can help you.

Theme

A story's **theme** is what that story is about, though not in a literal sense. Literally, the story of the Prodigal Son is about one man who chooses a wayward life and ends up begging forgiveness from his father. Themes are more universal: prodigality, remorse of conscience, mercy. In a larger sense, the Prodigal Son is about these abstractions. It has something to say about prodigality, remorse, and mercy—and jealousy too; it teaches us something about these themes.

Theme is one thing that distinguishes fictional stories from most of the stories you read in newspapers. A newspaper will tell a story merely because it happened: a plane crashed and everyone on board died; the president gave a speech in a nearby city; a famous actor got married. These stories generally do not have any larger thematic significance. Sometimes they do. When the "unsinkable" *Titanic* sank on its maiden voyage, many saw the sinking as an enormous reminder of the puniness of humans as compared to nature or God and as a rebuke of our pride. But most stories you read in the papers do not explore abstract themes. They are written simply to tell us what happened yesterday, and we read them because they are "news." Just think how stale yesterday's paper is, or last week's. Fictional stories last longer because their themes broaden their scope.

Nevertheless, we do not read short stories to extract a moral, as we would when reading a fable. Short stories do not offer some universally applicable lesson that can be easily paraphrased, such as "Slow and steady wins the race," which is the lesson of Aesop's story of the tortoise and the hare.

But short stories, like fables, are about more than just the particular characters who enliven them. Frank O'Connor's "Guests of the Nation," for example, is not just about a couple of IRA members during the Anglo-Irish war; it is about war in general and its effects on soldiers. To interpret the story, to comprehend its meaning, you have to draw some conclusion about the story's theme. You have to ask—and answer—questions such as, What does Frank O'Connor have to say about war?

Conclusion

Ultimately, this is why we analyze stories. We examine point of view and consider symbols and root out motifs so we can better understand what a story tells us about its themes. You might instinctively shy away from analysis because you're afraid that it ruins the story. After all, any reader who feels a visceral emotion at the end of "Guest of the Nation" *gets* the story. You don't need to analyze the story to feel the emotion swelling in your throat. That instinct against analysis is a good precaution. It *is* irreverent to ignore your visceral response in order to pursue questions about, say, narrative point of view with the clinical attitude of a scientist dissecting a cadaver.

But rather than letting that precautionary instinct turn you away from analysis altogether, you should let it lead you back to the story, back to the coherent whole story, *after* you've taken it apart in analysis. You will find that detailed analysis doesn't ruin a story. It increases the intensity of your unreflecting response. And added to the impossible-to-articulate meaning that a good story injects into your blood will be the intellectual pleasure of understanding.

THE SEAGULL READER

Stories

Second Edition

Chinua Achebe
b. 1930

Achebe is a Nigerian writer who grew up listening to the old Igbo stories told by his mother and reading the literature of Britain, which ruled Nigeria as a colony until 1960. Like the cultures of many colonized peoples, Achebe says, the Igbo culture "had been branded as inferior and bad by British oppressors, when they did not say it was non-existent. It appeared to be a vital cultural necessity to fight and rebel against that view." "Uncle Ben's Choice" explores this conflict between native beliefs and customs imposed by colonialism, but Uncle Ben himself is unusual because he peaceably combines Igbo and Christian beliefs. Achebe regrets that modern Nigeria has lost the magic of tales told and retold orally, and here he tries to approximate that tradition. Reading a story cannot replace listening to a storyteller, according to Achebe, but the writer can try to minimize what is lost.

Uncle Ben's Choice

In the year nineteen hundred and nineteen I was a young clerk in the Niger Company at Umuru. To be a clerk in those days is like to be a minister today. My salary was two pounds ten. You may laugh but two pounds ten in those days is like fifty pounds today. You could buy a big goat with four shillings. I could remember the most senior African in the company was one Saro[1] man on ten-thirteen-four. He was like Governor-General in our eyes.

Like all progressive young men I joined the African Club. We played tennis and billiards. Every year we played a tournament with the European Club. But I was less concerned with that. What I liked was the Saturday night dances. Women were surplus. Not all

1. Yoruba (Nigerian language and people) term for freed British and American slaves resettled in Africa via Sierra Leone who eventually made their way back to their ancestral homelands in southern Nigeria.

the waw-waw women[2] you see in townships today but beautiful things like this.

I had a Raleigh bicycle, brand new, and everybody called me Jolly Ben. I was selling like hot bread. But there is one thing about me—we can laugh and joke and drink and do otherwise but I must always keep my sense with me. My father told me that a true son of our land must know how to sleep and keep one eye open. I never forget it. So I played and laughed with everyone and they shouted "Jolly Ben! Jolly Ben!" but I knew what I was doing. The women of Umuru are very sharp; before you count A they count B. So I had to be very careful. I never showed any of them the road to my house and I never ate the food they cooked for fear of love medicines. I had seen many young men kill themselves with women in those days, so I remembered my father's word: Never let a handshake pass the elbow.

I can say that the only exception was one tall, yellow, salt-water girl like this called Margaret. One Sunday morning I was playing my gramophone, a brand-new HMV Senior. (I never believe in second-hand things. If I have no money for a new one I just keep myself quiet; that is my motto.) I was playing this record and standing at the window with my chewing-stick in my mouth. People were passing in their fine-fine dresses to one church nearby. This Margaret was going with them when she saw me. As luck would have it I did not see her in time to hide. So that very day—she did not wait till tomorrow or next tomorrow—but as soon as church closed she returned back. According to her she wanted to convert me to Roman Catholic. Wonders will ever end! Margaret Jumbo! Beautiful thing like this. But it is not Margaret I want to tell you about now. I want to tell you how I stopped all that foolishness.

It was one New Year's Eve like this. You know how New Year can pass Christmas for jollity, for we end-of-month people. By Christmas Day the month has reached twenty-hungry but on New Year your pocket is heavy.[3] So that day I went to the Club.

When I see you young men of nowadays say you drink, I just laugh. You don't know what drink is. You drink one bottle of beer

2. *Possibly:* women who complain.
3. The pocket is "heavy" because it is payday.

or one shot of whisky and you begin to holler like crazeman. That night I was taking it easy on White Horse. *All that are desirous to pass from Edinburgh to London or any other place on their road, let them repair to the White Horse cellar.* . . . God Almighty!

One thing with me is I never mix my drinks. The day I want to drink whisky I know that that is whisky-day; if I want to drink beer tomorrow then I know it is beer-day; I don't touch any other thing. That night I was on White Horse.[4] I had one roasted chicken and a tin of Guinea Gold.[5] Yes, I used to smoke in those days. I only stopped when one German doctor told me my heart was as black as a cooking-pot. Those German doctors were spirits. You know they used to give injections in the head or belly or anywhere. You just point where the thing is paining you and they give it to you right there—they don't waste time.

What was I saying? . . . Yes, I drank a bottle of White Horse and put one roasted chicken on top of it . . . Drunk? It is not in my dictionary. I have never been drunk in my life. My father used to say that the cure for drink is to say no. When I want to drink I drink, when I want to stop I stop. So about three o'clock that night I said to myself, you have had enough. So I jumped on my new Raleigh bicycle and went home quietly to sleep.

At that time our senior clerk was jailed for stealing bales of calico and I was acting in that capacity. So I lived in a small company house. You know where G. B. Olivant is today? . . . Yes, overlooking the River Niger. That is where my house was. I had two rooms on one side of it and the store-keeper had two rooms on the other side. But as luck would have it this man was on leave, so his side was vacant.

I opened the front door and went inside. Then I locked it again. I left my bicycle in the first room and went into the bedroom. I was too tired to begin to look for my lamp. So I pulled my dress and packed them on the back of the chair, and fell like a log into my big iron bed. And to God who made me, there was a woman in my bed. My mind told me at once it was Margaret. So I began to laugh and touch her here and there. She was hundred per cent naked. I

4. Brand of Scotch whiskey associated with the White Horse Inn, the starting point of the stagecoach trip from Edinburgh to London.

5. Brand of cigarettes.

continued laughing and asked her when did she come. She did not say anything and I suspected she was annoyed because she asked me to take her to the Club that day and I said no. I said to her: if you come there we will meet, I don't take anybody to the Club as such. So I suspected that is what is making her vex.

I told her not to vex but still she did not say anything. I asked her if she was asleep—just for asking sake. She said nothing. Although I told you that I did not like women to come to my house, but for every rule there must be an exception. So if I say that I was very angry to find Margaret that night I will be telling a white lie. I was still laughing when I noticed that her breasts were straight like the breasts of a girl of sixteen—or seventeen, at most. I thought that perhaps it was because of the way she was lying on her back. But when I touched the hair and it was soft like the hair of a European my laughter was quenched by force. I touched the hair on her head and it was the same. I jumped out of the bed and shouted: "Who are you?" My head swelled up like a barrel and I was shaking. The woman sat up and stretched her hands to call me back; as she did so her fingers touched me. I jumped back at the same time and shouted again to her to call her name. Then I said to myself: How can you be afraid of a woman? Whether a white woman or a black woman, it is the same ten and tenpence. So I said: "All right, I will soon open your mouth," at the same time I began to look for matches on the table. The woman suspected what I was looking for. She said, "Biko akpakwana oku."

I said: "So you are not a white woman. Who are you? I will strike the matches now if you don't tell me." I shook the matches to show her that I meant business. My boldness had come back and I was trying to remember the voice because it was very familiar.

"Come back to the bed and I will tell you," was what I heard next. Whoever told me it was a familiar voice told me a lie. It was sweet like sugar but not familiar at all. So I struck the matches.

"I beg you," was the last thing she said.

If I tell you what I did next or how I managed to come out of that room it is pure guesswork. The next thing I remember is that I was running like a crazeman to Matthew's house. Then I was banging on his door with both my hands.

"Who is that?" he said from inside.

"Open," I shouted. "In the name of God above, open."

I called my name but my voice was not like my voice. The door opened very small and I saw my kinsman holding a matchete in his right hand.

I fell down on the floor, and he said, "God will not agree."

It was God Himself who directed me to Matthew Obi's house that night because I did not see where I was going. I could not say whether I was still in this world or whether I was dead. Matthew poured cold water on me and after some time I was able to tell him what happened. I think I told it upside down otherwise he would not keep asking me what was she like, what was she like.

"I told you before I did not see her," I said.

"I see, but you heard her voice?"

"I heard her voice quite all right. And I touched her and she touched me."

"I don't know whether you did well or not to scare her away," was what Matthew said.

I don't know how to explain it but those words from Matthew opened my eyes. I knew at once that I had been visited by Mami Wota,[6] the Lady of the River Niger.

Matthew said again: "It depends what you want in life. If it is wealth you want then you made a great mistake today, but if you are a true son of your father then take my hand."

We shook hands and he said: "Our fathers never told us that a man should prefer wealth instead of wives and children."

Today whenever my wives make me vex I tell them: "I don't blame you. If I had been wise I would have taken Mami Wota." They laugh and ask me why did I not take her. The youngest one says: "Don't worry, Papa, she will come again; she will come tomorrow." And they laugh again.

But we all know it is a joke. For where is the man who will choose wealth instead of children? Except a crazy white man like Dr. J. M. Stuart-Young. Oh, I didn't tell you. The same night that I drove Mami Wota out she went to Dr. J. M. Stuart-Young, a white

6. A legendary seductress in West African mythology who brings wealth to her lover but prevents his fathering children.

merchant and became his lover. You have heard of him? . . . Oh yes, he became the richest man in the whole country. But she did not allow him to marry. When he died, what happened? All his wealth went to outsiders. Is that good wealth? I ask you. God forbid.

1966

Sherman Alexie
b. 1966

While most of his memorable characters are Native Americans, Alexie challenges the typical myths about Indians that are still abundant today. For example, in response to the popular belief that Native Americans have a natural or special connection to the land, that they're naturally environmentalists, he describes growing up with "aunts and uncles and cousins throwing cans out the window." Many writers produce Indian literature, he explains, by throwing in "a couple of birds and four directions and corn pollen." In contrast, Alexie wants to write about "the daily lives of Indians," which are not as romantic as the myths would have us believe. "What You Pawn I Will Redeem" was first published in The New Yorker *in 2003 and later that year in a collection called* Ten Little Indians.

What You Pawn I Will Redeem

Noon

One day you have a home and the next you don't, but I'm not going to tell you my particular reasons for being homeless, because it's my secret story, and Indians have to work hard to keep secrets from hungry white folks.

I'm a Spokane Indian boy, an Interior Salish, and my people have lived within a hundred-mile radius of Spokane, Washington, for at least ten thousand years. I grew up in Spokane, moved to Seattle twenty-three years ago for college, flunked out after two semesters, worked various blue- and bluer-collar jobs, married two or three times, fathered two or three kids, and then went crazy. Of course, crazy is not the official definition of my mental problem, but I don't think asocial disorder fits it, either, because that makes me sound like I'm a serial killer or something. I've never hurt another human being, or, at least, not physically. I've broken a few hearts in my time, but we've all done that, so I'm nothing special in that regard. I'm a boring heartbreaker, too. I never dated or married more than one woman at a time. I didn't break hearts into pieces overnight. I broke them slowly and carefully. And I didn't set any land-speed records running out the door. Piece by piece, I disappeared. I've been disappearing ever since.

I've been homeless for six years now. If there's such a thing as an effective homeless man, then I suppose I'm effective. Being homeless is probably the only thing I've ever been good at. I know where to get the best free food. I've made friends with restaurant and convenience store managers who let me use their bathrooms. And I don't mean the public bathrooms, either. I mean the employees' bathrooms, the clean ones hidden behind the kitchen or the pantry or the cooler. I know it sounds strange to be proud of this, but it means a lot to me, being trustworthy enough to piss in somebody else's clean bathroom. Maybe you don't understand the value of a clean bathroom, but I do.

Probably none of this interests you. Homeless Indians are everywhere in Seattle. We're common and boring, and you walk right on by us, with maybe a look of anger or disgust or even sadness at the terrible fate of the noble savage. But we have dreams and families. I'm friends with a homeless Plains Indian man whose son is the editor of a bigtime newspaper back east. Of course, that's his story, but we Indians are great storytellers and liars and mythmakers, so maybe that Plains Indian hobo is just a plain old everyday Indian. I'm kind of suspicious of him, because he identifies himself only as Plains Indian, a generic term, and not by a specific tribe. When I asked him why he wouldn't tell me exactly what he is, he said, "Do any of us know exactly what we are?" Yeah, great, a philosophizing Indian. "Hey," I said, "you got to have a home to be that homely." He just laughed and flipped me the eagle and walked away.

I wander the streets with a regular crew—my teammates, my defenders, my posse. It's Rose of Sharon, Junior, and me. We matter to one another if we don't matter to anybody else. Rose of Sharon is a big woman, about seven feet tall if you're measuring overall effect and about five feet tall if you're only talking about the physical. She's a Yakama Indian of the Wishram variety. Junior is a Colville, but there are about 199 tribes that make up the Colville, so he could be anything. He's good-looking, though, like he just stepped out of some "Don't Litter the Earth" public service advertisement. He's got those great big cheekbones that are like planets, you know, with little moons orbiting them. He gets me jealous, jealous, and jealous. If you put Junior and me next to each other, he's the Before Columbus Arrived Indian and I'm the After Columbus Arrived Indian. I am living proof of the horrible damage that colonialism has done to us Skins. But I'm not going to let you know how scared I sometimes get of history and its ways. I'm a strong man, and I know that silence is the best method of dealing with white folks.

This whole story really started at lunchtime, when Rose of Sharon, Junior, and I were panning the handle down at Pike Place Market. After about two hours of negotiating, we earned five dollars—good enough for a bottle of fortified courage from the most beautiful 7-Eleven in the world. So we headed over that way, feeling like warrior drunks, and we walked past this pawnshop I'd never noticed before. And that was strange, because we Indians have built-in pawnshop radar. But the strangest thing of all was the old powwow-dance regalia I saw hanging in the window.

"That's my grandmother's regalia," I said to Rose of Sharon and Junior.

"How you know for sure?" Junior asked.

I didn't know for sure, because I hadn't seen that regalia in person ever. I'd only seen photographs of my grandmother dancing in it. And those were taken before somebody stole it from her, fifty years ago. But it sure looked like my memory of it, and it had all the same color feathers and beads that my family sewed into our powwow regalia.

"There's only one way to know for sure," I said.

So Rose of Sharon, Junior, and I walked into the pawnshop and greeted the old white man working behind the counter.

"How can I help you?" he asked.

"That's my grandmother's powwow regalia in your window," I

said. "Somebody stole it from her fifty years ago, and my family has been searching for it ever since."

The pawnbroker looked at me like I was a liar. I understood. Pawnshops are filled with liars.

"I'm not lying," I said. "Ask my friends here. They'll tell you."

"He's the most honest Indian I know," Rose of Sharon said.

"All right, honest Indian," the pawnbroker said. "I'll give you the benefit of the doubt. Can you prove it's your grandmother's regalia?"

Because they don't want to be perfect, because only God is perfect, Indian people sew flaws into their powwow regalia. My family always sewed one yellow bead somewhere on our regalia. But we always hid it so that you had to search really hard to find it.

"If it really is my grandmother's," I said, "there will be one yellow bead hidden somewhere on it."

"All right, then," the pawnbroker said. "Let's take a look."

He pulled the regalia out of the window, laid it down on the glass counter, and we searched for that yellow bead and found it hidden beneath the armpit.

"There it is," the pawnbroker said. He didn't sound surprised. "You were right. This is your grandmother's regalia."

"It's been missing for fifty years," Junior said.

"Hey, Junior," I said. "It's my family's story. Let me tell it."

"All right," he said. "I apologize. You go ahead."

"It's been missing for fifty years," I said.

"That's his family's sad story," Rose of Sharon said. "Are you going to give it back to him?"

"That would be the right thing to do," the pawnbroker said. "But I can't afford to do the right thing. I paid a thousand dollars for this. I can't just give away a thousand dollars."

"We could go to the cops and tell them it was stolen," Rose of Sharon said.

"Hey," I said to her. "Don't go threatening people."

The pawnbroker sighed. He was thinking about the possibilities.

"Well, I suppose you could go to the cops," he said. "But I don't think they'd believe a word you said."

He sounded sad about that. As if he was sorry for taking advantage of our disadvantages.

"What's your name?" the pawnbroker asked me.

"Jackson," I said.

"Is that first or last?"

"Both," I said.

"Are you serious?"

"Yes, it's true. My mother and father named me Jackson Jackson. My family nickname is Jackson Squared. My family is funny."

"All right, Jackson Jackson," the pawnbroker said. "You wouldn't happen to have a thousand dollars, would you?"

"We've got five dollars total," I said.

"That's too bad," he said, and thought hard about the possibilities. "I'd sell it to you for a thousand dollars if you had it. Heck, to make it fair, I'd sell it to you for nine hundred and ninety-nine dollars. I'd lose a dollar. That would be the moral thing to do in this case. To lose a dollar would be the right thing."

"We've got five dollars total," I said again.

"That's too bad," he said once more, and thought harder about the possibilities. "How about this? I'll give you twenty-four hours to come up with nine hundred and ninety-nine dollars. You come back here at lunchtime tomorrow with the money and I'll sell it back to you. How does that sound?"

"It sounds all right," I said.

"All right, then," he said. "We have a deal. And I'll get you started. Here's twenty bucks."

He opened up his wallet and pulled out a crisp twenty-dollar bill and gave it to me. And Rose of Sharon, Junior, and I walked out into the daylight to search for nine hundred and seventy-four more dollars.

1 P.M.

Rose of Sharon, Junior, and I carried our twenty-dollar bill and our five dollars in loose change over to the 7-Eleven and bought three bottles of imagination. We needed to figure out how to raise all that money in only one day. Thinking hard, we huddled in an alley beneath the Alaska Way Viaduct and finished off those bottles—one, two, and three.

2 P.M.
Rose of Sharon was gone when I woke up. I heard later that she had hitchhiked back to Toppenish and was living with her sister on the reservation.

Junior had passed out beside me and was covered in his own vomit, or maybe somebody else's vomit, and my head hurt from thinking, so I left him alone and walked down to the water. I love the smell of ocean water. Salt always smells like memory.

When I got to the wharf, I ran into three Aleut cousins, who sat on a wooden bench and stared out at the bay and cried. Most of the homeless Indians in Seattle come from Alaska. One by one, each of them hopped a big working boat in Anchorage or Barrow or Juneau, fished his way south to Seattle, jumped off the boat with a pocketful of cash to party hard at one of the highly sacred and traditional Indian bars, went broke and broker, and has been trying to find his way back to the boat and the frozen north ever since.

These Aleuts smelled like salmon, I thought, and they told me they were going to sit on that wooden bench until their boat came back.

"How long has your boat been gone?" I asked.

"Eleven years," the elder Aleut said.

I cried with them for a while.

"Hey," I said. "Do you guys have any money I can borrow?"

They didn't.

3 P.M.
I walked back to Junior. He was still out cold. I put my face down near his mouth to make sure he was breathing. He was alive, so I dug around in his blue jeans pockets and found half a cigarette. I smoked it all the way down and thought about my grandmother.

Her name was Agnes, and she died of breast cancer when I was fourteen. My father always thought Agnes caught her tumors from the uranium mine on the reservation. But my mother said the disease started when Agnes was walking back from a powwow one night and got run over by a motorcycle. She broke three ribs, and my mother always said those ribs never healed right, and tumors take over when you don't heal right.

Sitting beside Junior, smelling the smoke and the salt and the vomit, I wondered if my grandmother's cancer started when somebody stole her powwow regalia. Maybe the cancer started in her broken heart and then leaked out into her breasts. I know it's crazy, but I wondered whether I could bring my grandmother back to life if I bought back her regalia.

I needed money, big money, so I left Junior and walked over to the Real Change office.

4 P.M.

Real Change is a multifaceted organization that publishes a newspaper, supports cultural projects that empower the poor and the homeless, and mobilizes the public around poverty issues. Real Change's mission is to organize, educate, and build alliances to create solutions to homelessness and poverty. It exists to provide a voice for poor people in our community.

I memorized Real Change's mission statement because I sometimes sell the newspaper on the streets. But you have to stay sober to sell it, and I'm not always good at staying sober. Anybody can sell the paper. You buy each copy for thirty cents and sell it for a dollar, and you keep the profit.

"I need one thousand four hundred and thirty papers," I said to the Big Boss.

"That's a strange number," he said. "And that's a lot of papers."

"I need them."

The Big Boss pulled out his calculator and did the math.

"It will cost you four hundred and twenty-nine dollars for that many," he said.

"If I had that kind of money, I wouldn't need to sell the papers."

"What's going on, Jackson-to-the-Second-Power?" he asked. He is the only person who calls me that. He's a funny and kind man.

I told him about my grandmother's powwow regalia and how much money I needed in order to buy it back.

"We should call the police," he said.

"I don't want to do that," I said. "It's a quest now. I need to win it back by myself."

"I understand," he said. "And, to be honest, I'd give you the papers to sell if I thought it would work. But the record for the most papers sold in one day by one vender is only three hundred and two."

"That would net me about two hundred bucks," I said.

The Big Boss used his calculator. "Two hundred and eleven dollars and forty cents," he said.

"That's not enough," I said.

"And the most money anybody has made in one day is five hundred and twenty-five. And that's because somebody gave Old Blue five hundred dollar bills for some dang reason. The average daily net is about thirty dollars."

"This isn't going to work."

"No."

"Can you lend me some money?"

"I can't do that," he said. "If I lend you money, I have to lend money to everybody."

"What can you do?"

"I'll give you fifty papers for free. But don't tell anybody I did it."

"O.K.," I said.

He gathered up the newspapers and handed them to me. I held them to my chest. He hugged me. I carried the newspapers back toward the water.

5 P.M.

Back on the wharf, I stood near the Bainbridge Island Terminal and tried to sell papers to business commuters boarding the ferry.

I sold five in one hour, dumped the other forty-five in a garbage can, and walked into McDonald's, ordered four cheeseburgers for a dollar each, and slowly ate them.

After eating, I walked outside and vomited on the sidewalk. I hated to lose my food so soon after eating it. As an alcoholic Indian with a busted stomach, I always hope I can keep enough food in me to stay alive.

6 P.M.

With one dollar in my pocket, I walked back to Junior. He was still passed out, and I put my ear to his chest and listened for his heartbeat. He was alive, so I took off his shoes and socks and found one dollar in his left sock and fifty cents in his right sock.

With two dollars and fifty cents in my hand, I sat beside Junior and thought about my grandmother and her stories.

When I was thirteen, my grandmother told me a story about the Second World War. She was a nurse at a military hospital in Sydney, Australia. For two years, she healed and comforted American and Australian soldiers.

One day, she tended to a wounded Maori soldier, who had lost his legs to an artillery attack. He was very dark-skinned. His hair was black and curly and his eyes were black and warm. His face was covered with bright tattoos.

"Are you Maori?" he asked my grandmother.

"No," she said. "I'm Spokane Indian. From the United States."

"Ah, yes," he said. "I have heard of your tribes. But you are the first American Indian I have ever met."

"There's a lot of Indian soldiers fighting for the United States," she said. "I have a brother fighting in Germany, and I lost another brother on Okinawa."

"I am sorry," he said. "I was on Okinawa as well. It was terrible."

"I am sorry about your legs," my grandmother said.

"It's funny, isn't it?" he said.

"What's funny?"

"How we brown people are killing other brown people so white people will remain free."

"I hadn't thought of it that way."

"Well, sometimes I think of it that way. And other times I think of it the way they want me to think of it. I get confused."

She fed him morphine.

"Do you believe in heaven?" he asked.

"Which heaven?" she asked.

"I'm talking about the heaven where my legs are waiting for me."

They laughed.

"Of course," he said, "my legs will probably run away from me when I get to heaven. And how will I ever catch them?"

"You have to get your arms strong," my grandmother said. "So you can run on your hands."

They laughed again.

Sitting beside Junior, I laughed at the memory of my grandmother's story. I put my hand close to Junior's mouth to make sure he was still breathing. Yes, Junior was alive, so I took my two dollars and fifty cents and walked to the Korean grocery store in Pioneer Square.

7 P.M.

At the Korean grocery store, I bought a fifty-cent cigar and two scratch lottery tickets for a dollar each. The maximum cash prize was five hundred dollars a ticket. If I won both, I would have enough money to buy back the regalia.

I loved Mary, the young Korean woman who worked the register. She was the daughter of the owners, and she sang all day.

"I love you," I said when I handed her the money.

"You always say you love me," she said.

"That's because I will always love you."

"You are a sentimental fool."

"I'm a romantic old man."

"Too old for me."

"I know I'm too old for you, but I can dream."

"O.K.," she said. "I agree to be a part of your dreams, but I will only hold your hand in your dreams. No kissing and no sex. Not even in your dreams."

"O.K.," I said. "No sex. Just romance."

"Goodbye, Jackson Jackson, my love. I will see you soon."

I left the store, walked over to Occidental Park, sat on a bench, and smoked my cigar all the way down.

Ten minutes after I finished the cigar, I scratched my first lottery ticket and won nothing. I could win only five hundred dollars now, and that would be only half of what I needed.

Ten minutes after I lost, I scratched the other ticket and won a free ticket—a small consolation and one more chance to win some money.

I walked back to Mary.

"Jackson Jackson," she said. "Have you come back to claim my heart?"

"I won a free ticket," I said.

"Just like a man," she said. "You love money and power more than you love me."

"It's true," I said. "And I'm sorry it's true."

She gave me another scratch ticket, and I took it outside. I like to scratch my tickets in private. Hopeful and sad, I scratched that third ticket and won real money. I carried it back inside to Mary.

"I won a hundred dollars," I said.

She examined the ticket and laughed.

"That's a fortune," she said, and counted out five twenties. Our fingertips touched as she handed me the money. I felt electric and constant.

"Thank you," I said, and gave her one of the bills.

"I can't take that," she said. "It's your money."

"No, it's tribal. It's an Indian thing. When you win, you're supposed to share with your family."

"I'm not your family."

"Yes, you are."

She smiled. She kept the money. With eighty dollars in my pocket, I said goodbye to my dear Mary and walked out into the cold night air.

8 P.M.

I wanted to share the good news with Junior. I walked back to him, but he was gone. I heard later that he had hitchhiked down to Portland, Oregon, and died of exposure in an alley behind the Hilton Hotel.

9 P.M.

Lonesome for Indians, I carried my eighty dollars over to Big Heart's in South Downtown. Big Heart's is an all-Indian bar. Nobody knows how or why Indians migrate to one bar and turn it into an official Indian bar. But Big Heart's has been an Indian bar for twenty-three years. It used to be way up on Aurora Avenue, but a crazy Lummi Indian burned that one down, and the owners moved to the new location, a few blocks south of Safeco Field.

I walked into Big Heart's and counted fifteen Indians—eight men and seven women. I didn't know any of them, but Indians like to belong, so we all pretended to be cousins.

"How much for whiskey shots?" I asked the bartender, a fat white guy.

"You want the bad stuff or the badder stuff?"

"As bad as you got."

"One dollar a shot."

I laid my eighty dollars on the bar top.

"All right," I said. "Me and all my cousins here are going to be drinking eighty shots. How many is that apiece?"

"Counting you," a woman shouted from behind me, "that's five shots for everybody."

I turned to look at her. She was a chubby and pale Indian woman, sitting with a tall and skinny Indian man.

"All right, math genius," I said to her, and then shouted for the whole bar to hear. "Five drinks for everybody!"

All the other Indians rushed the bar, but I sat with the mathematician and her skinny friend. We took our time with our whiskey shots.

"What's your tribe?" I asked.

"I'm Duwamish," she said. "And he's Crow."

"You're a long way from Montana," I said to him.

"I'm Crow," he said. "I flew here."

"What's your name?" I asked them.

"I'm Irene Muse," she said. "And this is Honey Boy."

She shook my hand hard, but he offered his hand as if I was supposed to kiss it. So I did. He giggled and blushed, as much as a dark-skinned Crow can blush.

"You're one of them two-spirits, aren't you?" I asked him.

"I love women," he said. "And I love men."

"Sometimes both at the same time," Irene said.

We laughed.

"Man," I said to Honey Boy. "So you must have about eight or nine spirits going on inside you, enit?"

"Sweetie," he said. "I'll be whatever you want me to be."

"Oh, no," Irene said. "Honey Boy is falling in love."

"It has nothing to do with love," he said.

We laughed.

"Wow," I said. "I'm flattered, Honey Boy, but I don't play on your team."

"Never say never," he said.

"You better be careful," Irene said. "Honey Boy knows all sorts of magic."

"Honey Boy," I said, "you can try to seduce me, but my heart belongs to a woman named Mary."

"Is your Mary a virgin?" Honey Boy asked.

We laughed.

And we drank our whiskey shots until they were gone. But the other Indians bought me more whiskey shots, because I'd been so generous with my money. And Honey Boy pulled out his credit card, and I drank and sailed on that plastic boat.

After a dozen shots, I asked Irene to dance. She refused. But Honey Boy shuffled over to the jukebox, dropped in a quarter, and selected Willie Nelson's "Help Me Make It Through the Night." As Irene and I sat at the table and laughed and drank more whiskey, Honey Boy danced a slow circle around us and sang along with Willie.

"Are you serenading me?" I asked him.

He kept singing and dancing.

"Are you serenading me?" I asked him again.

"He's going to put a spell on you," Irene said.

I leaned over the table, spilling a few drinks, and kissed Irene hard. She kissed me back.

10 P.M.

Irene pushed me into the women's bathroom, into a stall, shut the door behind us, and shoved her hand down my pants. She was short, so I had to lean over to kiss her. I grabbed and squeezed her everywhere I could reach, and she was wonderfully fat, and every part of her body felt like a large, warm, soft breast.

Midnight

Nearly blind with alcohol, I stood alone at the bar and swore I had been standing in the bathroom with Irene only a minute ago.

"One more shot!" I yelled at the bartender.

"You've got no more money!" he yelled back.

"Somebody buy me a drink!" I shouted.

"They've got no more money!"

"Where are Irene and Honey Boy?"

"Long gone!"

2 A.M.

"Closing time!" the bartender shouted at the three or four Indians who were still drinking hard after a long, hard day of drinking. Indian alcoholics are either sprinters or marathoners.

"Where are Irene and Honey Boy?" I asked.

"They've been gone for hours," the bartender said.

"Where'd they do?"

"I told you a hundred times, I don't know."

"What am I supposed to do?"

"It's closing time. I don't care where you go, but you're not staying here."

"You are an ungrateful bastard. I've been good to you."

"You don't leave right now, I'm going to kick your ass."

"Come on, I know how to fight."

He came at me. I don't remember what happened after that.

4 A.M.
I emerged from the blackness and discovered myself walking behind a big warehouse. I didn't know where I was. My face hurt. I felt my nose and decided that it might be broken. Exhausted and cold, I pulled a plastic tarp from a truck bed, wrapped it around me like a faithful lover, and fell asleep in the dirt.

6 A.M.
Somebody kicked me in the ribs. I opened my eyes and looked up at a white cop.

"Jackson," the cop said. "Is that you?"

"Officer Williams," I said. He was a good cop with a sweet tooth. He'd given me hundreds of candy bars over the years. I wonder if he knew I was diabetic.

"What the hell are you doing here?" he asked.

"I was cold and sleepy," I said. "So I lay down."

"You dumb-ass, you passed out on the railroad tracks."

I sat up and looked around. I was lying on the railroad tracks. Dockworkers stared at me. I should have been a railroad-track pizza, a double Indian pepperoni with extra cheese. Sick and scared, I leaned over and puked whiskey.

"What the hell's wrong with you?" Officer Williams asked. "You've never been this stupid."

"It's my grandmother," I said. "She died."

"I'm sorry, man. When did she die?"

"Nineteen seventy-two."

"And you're killing yourself now?"

"I've been killing myself ever since she died."

He shook his head. He was sad for me. Like I said, he was a good cop.

"And somebody beat the hell out of you," he said. "You remember who?"

"Mr. Grief and I went a few rounds."

"It looks like Mr. Grief knocked you out."

"Mr. Grief always wins."

"Come on," he said. "Let's get you out of here."

He helped me up and led me over to his squad car. He put me in the back. "You throw up in there and you're cleaning it up," he said.

"That's fair."

He walked around the car and sat in the driver's seat. "I'm taking you over to detox," he said.

"No, man, that place is awful," I said. "It's full of drunk Indians."

We laughed. He drove away from the docks.

"I don't know how you guys do it," he said.

"What guys?" I asked.

"You Indians. How the hell do you laugh so much? I just picked your ass off the railroad tracks, and you're making jokes. Why the hell do you do that?"

"The two funniest tribes I've ever been around are Indians and Jews, so I guess that says something about the inherent humor of genocide."

We laughed.

"Listen to you, Jackson. You're so smart. Why the hell are you on the street?"

"Give me a thousand dollars and I'll tell you."

"You bet I'd give you a thousand dollars if I knew you'd straighten up your life."

He meant it. He was the second-best cop I'd ever known.

"You're a good cop," I said.

"Come on, Jackson," he said. "Don't blow smoke up my ass."

"No, really, you remind me of my grandfather."

"Yeah, that's what you Indians always tell me."

"No, man, my grandfather was a tribal cop. He was a good cop. He never arrested people. He took care of them. Just like you."

"I've arrested hundreds of scumbags, Jackson. And I've shot a couple in the ass."

"It don't matter. You're not a killer."

"I didn't kill them. I killed their asses. I'm an ass-killer."

We drove through downtown. The missions and shelters had already released their overnighters. Sleepy homeless men and women stood on street corners and stared up at a gray sky. It was the morning after the night of the living dead.

"Do you ever get scared?" I asked Officer Williams.

"What do you mean?"

"I mean, being a cop, is it scary?"

He thought about that for a while. He contemplated it. I liked that about him.

"I guess I try not to think too much about being afraid," he said. "If you think about fear, then you'll be afraid. The job is boring most of the time. Just driving and looking into dark corners, you know, and seeing nothing. But then things get heavy. You're chasing somebody, or fighting them or walking around a dark house, and you just know some crazy guy is hiding around a corner, and hell, yes, it's scary."

"My grandfather was killed in the line of duty," I said.

"I'm sorry. How'd it happen?"

I knew he'd listen closely to my story.

"He worked on the reservation. Everybody knew everybody. It was safe. We aren't like those crazy Sioux or Apache or any of those other warrior tribes. There've only been three murders on my reservation in the last hundred years."

"That is safe."

"Yeah, we Spokane, we're passive, you know. We're mean with words. And we'll cuss out anybody. But we don't shoot people. Or stab them. Not much, anyway."

"So what happened to your grandfather?"

"This man and his girlfriend were fighting down by Little Falls."

"Domestic dispute. Those are the worst."

"Yeah, but this guy was my grandfather's brother. My great-uncle."

"Oh, no."

"Yeah, it was awful. My grandfather just strolled into the house. He'd been there a thousand times. And his brother and his girlfriend were drunk and beating on each other. And my grandfather stepped between them, just as he'd done a hundred times before. And the girlfriend tripped or something. She fell down and hit her head and started crying. And my grandfather kneeled down beside her to make sure she was all right. And for some reason my great-uncle reached down, pulled my grandfather's pistol out of the holster, and shot him in the head."

"That's terrible. I'm sorry."

"Yeah, my great-uncle could never figure out why he did it. He went to prison forever, you know, and he always wrote these long letters. Like fifty pages of tiny little handwriting. And he was always trying to figure out why he did it. He'd write and write and write and try to figure it out. He never did. It's a great big mystery."

"Do you remember your grandfather?"

"A little bit. I remember the funeral. My grandmother wouldn't let them bury him. My father had to drag her away from the grave."

"I don't know what to say."

"I don't, either."

We stopped in front of the detox center.

"We're here," Officer Williams said.

"I can't go in there," I said.

"You have to."

"Please, no. They'll keep me for twenty-four hours. And then it will be too late."

"Too late for what?"

I told him about my grandmother's regalia and the deadline for buying it back.

"If it was stolen, you need to file a report," he said. "I'll investigate it myself. If that thing is really your grandmother's, I'll get it back for you. Legally."

"No," I said. "That's not fair. The pawnbroker didn't know it was stolen. And, besides, I'm on a mission here. I want to be a hero, you know? I want to win it back, like a knight."

"That's romantic crap."

"That may be. But I care about it. It's been a long time since I really cared about something."

Officer Williams turned around in his seat and stared at me. He studied me.

"I'll give you some money," he said. "I don't have much. Only thirty bucks. I'm short until payday. And it's not enough to get back the regalia. But it's something."

"I'll take it," I said.

"I'm giving it to you because I believe in what you believe. I'm hoping, and I don't know why I'm hoping it, but I hope you can turn thirty bucks into a thousand somehow."

"I believe in magic."

"I believe you'll take my money and get drunk on it."

"Then why are you giving it to me?"

"There ain't no such thing as an atheist cop."

"Sure, there is."

"Yeah, well, I'm not an atheist cop."

He let me out of the car, handed me two fivers and a twenty, and shook my hand.

"Take care of yourself, Jackson," he said. "Stay off the railroad tracks."

"I'll try," I said.

He drove away. Carrying my money, I headed back toward the water.

8 A.M.

On the wharf, those three Aleuts still waited on the wooden bench.

"Have you seen your ship?" I asked.

"Seen a lot of ships," the elder Aleut said. "But not our ship."

I sat on the bench with them. We sat in silence for a long time. I wondered if we would fossilize if we sat there long enough.

I thought about my grandmother. I'd never seen her dance in her regalia. And, more than anything, I wished I'd seen her dance at a powwow.

"Do you guys know any songs?" I asked the Aleuts.

"I know all of Hank Williams," the elder Aleut said.

"How about Indian songs?"

"Hank Williams is Indian."

"How about sacred songs?"

"Hank Williams is sacred."

"I'm talking about ceremonial songs. You know, religious ones. The songs you sing back home when you're wishing and hoping."

"What are you wishing and hoping for?"

"I'm wishing my grandmother was still alive."

"Every song I know is about that."

"Well, sing me as many as you can."

The Aleuts sang their strange and beautiful songs. I listened. They sang about my grandmother and about their grandmothers. They were lonesome for the cold and the snow. I was lonesome for everything.

10 A.M.

After the Aleuts finished their last song, we sat in silence for a while. Indians are good at silence.

"Was that the last song?" I asked.

"We sang all the ones we could," the elder Aleut said. "The others are just for our people."

I understood. We Indians have to keep our secrets. And these Aleuts were so secretive they didn't refer to themselves as Indians.

"Are you guys hungry?" I asked.

They looked at one another and communicated without talking.

"We could eat," the elder Aleut said.

11 A.M.

The Aleuts and I walked over to the Big Kitchen, a greasy diner in the International District. I knew they served homeless Indians who'd lucked into money.

"Four for breakfast?" the waitress asked when we stepped inside.

"Yes, we're very hungry," the elder Aleut said.

She took us to a booth near the kitchen. I could smell the food cooking. My stomach growled.

"You guys want separate checks?" the waitress asked.

"No, I'm paying," I said.

"Aren't you the generous one," she said.

"Don't do that," I said.

"Do what?" she asked.

"Don't ask me rhetorical questions. They scare me."

She looked puzzled, and then she laughed.

"O.K., professor," she said. "I'll only ask you real questions from now on."

"Thank you."

"What do you guys want to eat?"

"That's the best question anybody can ask anybody," I said. "What have you got?"

"How much money you got?" she asked.

"Another good question," I said. "I've got twenty-five dollars I can spend. Bring us all the breakfast you can, plus your tip."

She knew the math.

"All right, that's four specials and four coffees and fifteen percent for me."

The Aleuts and I waited in silence. Soon enough, the waitress returned and poured us four coffees, and we sipped at them until she returned again, with four plates of food. Eggs, bacon, toast, hash brown potatoes. It's amazing how much food you can buy for so little money.

Grateful, we feasted.

Noon

I said farewell to the Aleuts and walked toward the pawnshop. I heard later that the Aleuts had waded into the saltwater near Dock 47 and disappeared. Some Indians swore they had walked on the water and headed north. Other Indians saw the Aleuts drown. I don't know what happened to them.

I looked for the pawnshop and couldn't find it. I swear it wasn't in the place where it had been before. I walked twenty or thirty blocks looking for the pawnshop, turned corners and bisected intersections, and looked up its name in the phone books and asked people walking past me if they'd ever heard of it. But that pawnshop seemed to have sailed away like a ghost ship. I wanted to cry. And just when I'd given up, when I turned one last corner and thought I might die if I didn't find that pawnshop, there it was, in a space I swear it hadn't occupied a few minutes ago.

I walked inside and greeted the pawnbroker, who looked a little younger than he had before.

"It's you," he said.

"Yes, it's me," I said.

"Jackson Jackson."
"That is my name."
"Where are your friends?"
"They went traveling. But it's O.K. Indians are everywhere."
"Do you have the money?"
"How much do you need again?" I asked, and hoped the price had changed.
"Nine hundred and ninety-nine dollars."
It was still the same price. Of course, it was the same price. Why would it change?
"I don't have that," I said.
"What do you have?"
"Five dollars."
I set the crumpled Lincoln on the countertop. The pawnbroker studied it.
"Is that the same five dollars from yesterday?"
"No, it's different."
He thought about the possibilities.
"Did you work hard for this money?" he asked.
"Yes," I said.
He closed his eyes and thought harder about the possibilities. Then he stepped into the back room and returned with my grandmother's regalia.
"Take it," he said, and held it out to me.
"I don't have the money."
"I don't want your money."
"But I wanted to win it."
"You did win it. Now take it before I change my mind."
Do you know how many good men live in this world? Too many to count!
I took my grandmother's regalia and walked outside. I knew that solitary yellow bead was part of me. I knew I was that yellow bead in part. Outside, I wrapped myself in my grandmother's regalia and breathed her in. I stepped off the sidewalk and into the intersection. Pedestrians stopped. Cars stopped. The city stopped. They all watched me dance with my grandmother. I was my grandmother, dancing.

2003

James Baldwin

1924–1987

Baldwin first published this story in 1957, in the Partisan Review, *a little magazine with a decidedly left-wing political bent, and it appeared again eight years later in the collection,* Going to Meet the Man. *These years place it in the midst of the modern civil rights movement, which was triggered by the arrest of Rosa Parks in 1955. The story inaugurated Baldwin's own commitment to the civil rights movement, and he became a prominent spokesman for African Americans during the 1960s. The music that figures prominently in this story has a place in this political context. Jazz began in the early twentieth century as a distinctively American form of music that evolved especially in urban, African American communities, like New Orleans. Both its advocates and its detractors thought jazz was modern and edgy and associated it with progressive, even radical lifestyles. But by the 1930s, it had become part of the mainstream of American culture, and many of its producers and consumers were white. After World War II, musicians like Charlie Parker pioneered a new style of music, bebop, that reproduced the original radical character of jazz. Bebop represented an anti-assimilationist African American culture with its roots in the blues of the working class, and thus purposely alienated not only mainstream whites but also many middle-class blacks.*

Sonny's Blues

I read about it in the paper, in the subway, on my way to work. I read it, and I couldn't believe it, and I read it again. Then perhaps I just stared at it, at the newsprint spelling out his name, spelling out the story. I stared at it in the swinging lights of the subway cars and in the faces and bodies of the people, and in my own face, trapped in the darkness which roared outside.

It was not to be believed and I kept telling myself that, as I walked from the subway station to the high school. And at the same time I couldn't doubt it. I was scared, scared for Sonny. He became real to me again. A great block of ice got settled in my belly and kept melting there slowly all day long, while I taught my classes algebra. It was a special kind of ice. It kept melting, sending trickles of ice water all up and down my veins, but it never got less. Sometimes it hardened and seemed to expand until I felt my guts were going to come spilling out or that I was going to choke or scream. This would always be at a moment when I was remembering some specific thing Sonny had once said or done.

When he was about as old as the boys in my classes his face had been bright and open, there was a lot of copper in it; and he'd had wonderfully direct brown eyes, and great gentleness and privacy. I wondered what he looked like now. He had been picked up, the evening before, in a raid on an apartment downtown for peddling and using heroin.

I couldn't believe it: but what I mean by that is that I couldn't find any room for it anywhere inside me. I had kept it outside me for a long time. I hadn't wanted to know. I had had suspicions, but I didn't name them, I kept putting them away. I told myself that Sonny was wild, but he wasn't crazy. And he'd always been a good boy, he hadn't ever turned hard or evil or disrespectful, the way kids can, so quick, so quick, especially in Harlem. I didn't want to believe that I'd ever see my brother going down, coming to nothing, all that light in his face gone out, in the condition I'd already seen so many others. Yet it had happened and here I was, talking about algebra to a lot of boys who might, every one of them for all I knew, be popping off needles every time they went to the head. Maybe it did more for them than algebra could.

I was sure that the first time Sonny had ever had horse, he couldn't have been much older than these boys were now. These boys, now, were living as we'd been living then; they were growing up with a rush and their heads bumped abruptly against the low ceiling of their actual possibilities. They were filled with rage. All they really knew were two darknesses, the darkness of their lives, which was now closing in on them, and the darkness of the movies, which had blinded them to that other darkness, and in which they now, vindictively, dreamed, at once more together than they were at any other time, and more alone.

When the last bell rang, the last class ended, I let out my breath. It seemed I'd been holding it for all that time. My clothes were wet—I may have looked as though I'd been sitting in a steam bath, all dressed up, all afternoon. I sat alone in the classroom a long time. I listened to the boys outside, downstairs, shouting and cursing and laughing. Their laughter struck me for perhaps the first time. It was not the joyous laughter which—God knows why—one associates with children. It was mocking and insular, its intent to denigrate. It was disenchanted, and in this, also, lay the authority of their curses. Perhaps I was listening to them because I was thinking about my brother and in them I heard my brother. And myself.

One boy was whistling a tune, at once very complicated and very simple, it seemed to be pouring out of him as though he were a bird, and it sounded very cool and moving through all that harsh, bright air, only just holding its own through all those other sounds.

I stood up and walked over to the window and looked down into the courtyard. It was the beginning of the spring and the sap was rising in the boys. A teacher passed through them every now and again, quickly, as though he or she couldn't wait to get out of that courtyard, to get those boys out of their sight and off their minds. I started collecting my stuff. I thought I'd better get home and talk to Isabel.

The courtyard was almost deserted by the time I got downstairs. I saw this boy standing in the shadow of a doorway, looking just like Sonny. I almost called his name. Then I saw that it wasn't Sonny, but somebody we used to know, a boy from around our block. He'd been Sonny's friend. He'd never been mine, having been too young for me, and, anyway, I'd never liked him. And now, even though he was a grown-up man, he still hung around that block, still spent hours on the street corners, was always high and raggy. I used to run into him from time to time and he'd often work around to asking me for a quarter or fifty cents. He always had some real good excuse, too, and I always gave it to him, I don't know why.

But now, abruptly, I hated him. I couldn't stand the way he looked at me, partly like a dog, partly like a cunning child. I wanted to ask him what the hell he was doing in the school courtyard.

He sort of shuffled over to me, and he said, "I see you got the papers. So you already know about it."

"You mean about Sonny? Yes, I already knew about it. How come they didn't get you?"

He grinned. It made him repulsive and it also brought to mind what he'd looked like as a kid. "I wasn't there. I stay away from them people."

"Good for you." I offered him a cigarette and I watched him through the smoke. "You come all the way down here just to tell me about Sonny?"

"That's right." He was sort of shaking his head and his eyes looked strange, as though they were about to cross. The bright sun deadened his damp dark brown skin and it made his eyes looks yellow and showed up the dirt in his kinked hair. He smelled funky. I moved a little away from him and I said, "Well, thanks. But I already know about it and I got to get home."

"I'll walk you a little ways," he said. We started walking. There were a couple of kids still loitering in the courtyard and one of them said goodnight to me and looked strangely at the boy beside me.

"What're you going to do?" he asked me. "I mean, about Sonny?"

"Look. I haven't seen Sonny for over a year, I'm not sure I'm going to do anything. Anyway, what the hell *can* I do?"

"That's right," he said quickly, "ain't nothing you can do. Can't much help old Sonny no more, I guess."

It was what I was thinking and so it seemed to me he had no right to say it.

"I'm surprised at Sonny, though," he went on—he had a funny way of talking, he looked straight ahead as though he were talking to himself—"I thought Sonny was a smart boy, I thought he was too smart to get hung."

"I guess he thought so too," I said sharply, "and that's how he got hung. And now about you? You're pretty goddamn smart, I bet."

Then he looked directly at me, just for a minute. "I ain't smart," he said. "If I was smart, I'd have reached for a pistol a long time ago."

"Look. Don't tell *me* your sad story, if it was up to me, I'd give you one." Then I felt guilty—guilty, probably, for never having supposed that the poor bastard *had* a story of his own, much less a sad one, and I asked, quickly, "What's going to happen to him now?"

He didn't answer this. He was off by himself some place. "Funny thing," he said, and from his tone we might have been discussing the quickest way to get to Brooklyn, "when I saw the papers this morning, the first thing I asked myself was if I had anything to do with it. I felt sort of responsible."

I began to listen more carefully. The subway station was on the corner, just before us, and I stopped. He stopped, too. We were in front of a bar and he ducked slightly, peering in, but whoever he was looking for didn't seem to be there. The juke box was blasting away with something black and bouncy and I half watched the barmaid as she danced her way from the juke box to her place behind the bar. And I watched her face as she laughingly responded to something someone said to her, still keeping time to the music. When she smiled one saw the little girl, one sensed the doomed, still-struggling woman beneath the battered face of the semi-whore.

"I never *give* Sonny nothing," the boy said finally, "but a long time ago I come to school high and Sonny asked me how it felt." He paused, I couldn't bear to watch him, I watched the barmaid, and I listened to the music which seemed to be causing the pavement to shake. "I told him it felt great." The music stopped, the barmaid paused and watched the juke box until the music began again. "It did."

All this was carrying me some place I didn't want to go. I certainly didn't want to know how it felt. It filled everything, the people, the houses, the music, the dark, quicksilver barmaid, with menace; and this menace was their reality.

"What's going to happen to him now?" I asked again.

"They'll send him away some place and they'll try to cure him." He shook his head. "Maybe he'll even think he's kicked the habit. Then they'll let him loose"—he gestured, throwing his cigarette into the gutter. "That's all."

"What do you mean, that's *all?*"

But I knew what he meant.

"I *mean*, that's *all.*" He turned his head and looked at me, pulling down the corners of his mouth. "Don't you know what I mean?" he asked, softly.

"How the hell *would* I know what you mean?" I almost whispered it, I don't know why.

"That's right," he said to the air, "how would *he* know what I mean?" He turned toward me again, patient and calm, and yet I somehow felt him shaking, shaking as though he were going to fall apart. I felt that ice in my guts again, the dread I'd felt all afternoon; and again I watched the barmaid, moving about the bar, washing glasses, and singing. "Listen. They'll let him out and then it'll just start all over again. That's what I mean."

"You mean—they'll let him out. And then he'll just start working his way back in again. You mean he'll never kick the habit. Is that what you mean?"

"That's right," he said, cheerfully. "*You* see what I mean."

"Tell me," I said at last, "why does he want to die? He must want to die, he's killing himself, why does he want to die?"

He looked at me in surprise. He licked his lips. "He don't want to die. He wants to live. Don't nobody want to die, ever."

Then I wanted to ask him—too many things. He could not have answered, or if he had, I could not have borne the answers. I started walking. "Well, I guess it's none of my business."

"It's going to be rough on old Sonny," he said. We reached the subway station. "This is your station?" he asked. I nodded. I took one step down. "Damn!" he said, suddenly. I looked up at him. He grinned again. "Damn it if I didn't leave all my money home. You ain't got a dollar on you, have you? Just for a couple of days, is all."

All at once something inside gave and threatened to come pouring out of me. I didn't hate him any more. I felt that in another moment I'd start crying like a child.

"Sure," I said. "Don't sweat." I looked in my wallet and didn't have a dollar, I only had a five. "Here," I said. "That hold you?"

He didn't look at it—he didn't want to look at it. A terrible closed look came over his face, as though he were keeping the number on the bill a secret from him and me. "Thanks," he said, and now he was dying to see me go. "Don't worry about Sonny. Maybe I'll write him or something."

"Sure," I said. "You do that. So long."

"Be seeing you," he said. I went on down the steps.

And I didn't write Sonny or send him anything for a long time. When I finally did, it was just after my little girl died, he wrote me back a letter which made me feel like a bastard.

Here's what he said:

Dear brother,

You don't know how much I needed to hear from you. I wanted to write you many a time but I dug how much I must have hurt you and so I didn't write. But now I feel like a man who's been trying to climb up out of some deep, real deep and funky hole and just saw the sun up there, outside. I got to get outside.

I can't tell you much about how I got here. I mean I don't know how to tell you. I guess I was afraid of something or I was trying to escape from something and you know I have never been very strong in the head (smile). I'm glad Mama and Daddy are dead and can't see what's happened to their son and I swear if I'd known what I was doing I would never have hurt you so, you and a lot of other fine people who were nice to me and who believed in me.

I don't want you to think it had anything to do with me being a musician. It's more than that. Or maybe less than that. I can't get anything straight in my head down here and I try not to think about what's going to happen to me when I get outside again. Sometime I think I'm going to flip and *never* get outside and sometime I think I'll come straight back. I tell you one thing, though, I'd rather blow my brains out than go through this again. But that's what they all say, so they tell me. If I tell you when I'm coming to New York and if you could meet me, I sure would appreciate it. Give my love to Isabel and the kids and I was sure sorry to hear about little Gracie. I wish I could be like Mama and say the Lord's will be done, but I don't know it seems to me that trouble is the one thing that never does get stopped and I don't know what good it does to blame it on the Lord. But maybe it does some good if you believe it.

Your brother,
Sonny

Then I kept in constant touch with him and I sent him whatever I could and I went to meet him when he came back to New York. When I saw him many things I thought I had forgotten came flooding back to me. This was because I had begun, finally, to wonder about Sonny, about the life that Sonny lived inside. This life, whatever it was, had made him older and thinner and it had deepened the distant stillness in which he had always moved. He looked very unlike my baby brother. Yet, when he smiled, when we shook hands, the baby brother I'd never known looked out from the depths of his private life, like an animal waiting to be coaxed into the lights.

"How you been keeping?" he asked me.

"All right. And you?"

"Just fine." He was smiling all over his face. "It's good to see you again."

"It's good to see you!"

The seven years' difference in our ages lay between us like a chasm: I wondered if these years would ever operate between us as a bridge. I was remembering, and it made it hard to catch my breath, that I had been there when he was born; and I had heard the first words he had ever spoken. When he started to walk, he walked from our mother straight to me. I caught him just before he fell when he took the first steps he ever took in this world.

"How's Isabel?"

"Just fine. She's dying to see you."

"And the boys?"

"They're fine, too. They're anxious to see their uncle."

"Oh, come on. You know they don't remember me."

"Are you kidding? Of course they remember you."

He grinned again. We got into a taxi. We had a lot to say to each other, far too much to know how to begin.

As the taxi began to move, I asked, "You still want to go to India?"

He laughed. "You still remember that. Hell, no. This place is Indian enough for me."

"It used to belong to them," I said.

And he laughed again. "They damn sure knew what they were doing when they got rid of it."

Years ago, when he was around fourteen, he'd been all hipped on the idea of going to India. He read books about people sitting on rocks, naked, in all kinds of weather, but mostly bad, naturally, and walking barefoot through hot coals and arriving at wisdom. I used to say that it sounded to me as though they were getting away from wisdom as fast as they could. I think he sort of looked down on me for that.

"Do you mind," he asked, "if we have the driver drive alongside the park? On the west side—I haven't seen the city in so long."

"Of course not," I said. I was afraid that I might sound as though I were humoring him, but I hoped he wouldn't take it that way.

So we drove along, between the green of the park and the stony, lifeless elegance of hotels and apartment buildings, toward the vivid, killing streets of our childhood. These streets hadn't changed, though housing projects jutted up out of them now like rocks in the middle of a boiling sea. Most of the houses in which we had grown up had vanished, as had the stores from which we had stolen, the basements in which we had first tried sex, the rooftops from which we had hurled tin cans and bricks. But houses exactly like the houses of our past yet dominated the landscape, boys exactly like the boys we once had been found themselves smothering in these houses, came down into the streets for light and air, and found themselves encircled by disaster. Some escaped the trap, most didn't. Those who got out always left something of themselves behind, as some animals amputate a leg and leave it in the trap. It might be said, perhaps, that I had escaped, after all, I was a school teacher; or that Sonny had, he hadn't lived in Harlem for years. Yet, as the cab moved uptown through streets which seemed, with a rush, to darken with dark people, and as I covertly studied Sonny's face, it came to me that what we both were seeking through our separate cab windows was that part of ourselves which had been left behind. It's always at the hour of trouble and confrontation that the missing member aches.

We hit 110th Street and started rolling up Lenox Avenue. And I'd known this avenue all my life, but it seemed to me again, as it had seemed on the day I'd first heard about Sonny's trouble, filled with a hidden menace which was its very breath of life.

"We almost there," said Sonny.

"Almost." We were both too nervous to say anything more.

We live in a housing project. It hasn't been up long. A few days after it was up it seemed uninhabitably new, now, of course, it's already rundown. It looks like a parody of the good, clean, faceless life—God knows the people who live in it do their best to make it a parody. The beat-looking grass lying around isn't enough to make their lives green, the hedges will never hold out the streets, and they know it. The big windows fool no one, they aren't big enough to make space out of no space. They don't bother with the windows, they watch the TV screen instead. The playground is most popular with the children who don't play at jacks, or skip rope, or roller skate, or swing, and they can be found in it after dark. We moved in partly because it's not too far from where I teach, and partly for the kids; but it's really just like the houses in which Sonny and I grew up. The same things happen, they'll have the same things to remember. The moment Sonny and I started into the house I had the feeling that I was simply bringing him back into the danger he had almost died trying to escape.

Sonny has never been talkative. So I don't know why I was sure he'd be dying to talk to me when supper was over the first night. Everything went fine, the oldest boy remembered him, and the youngest boy liked him, and Sonny had remembered to bring something for each of them; and Isabel, who is really much nicer than I am, more open and giving, had gone to a lot of trouble about dinner and was genuinely glad to see him. And she's always been able to tease Sonny in a way that I haven't. It was nice to see her face so vivid again and to hear her laugh and watch her make Sonny laugh. She wasn't, or, anyway, she didn't seem to be, at all uneasy or embarrassed. She chatted as though there were no subject which had to be avoided and she got Sonny past his first, faint stiffness. And thank God she was there, for I was filled with that icy dread again. Everything I did seemed awkward to me, and everything I said sounded freighted with hidden meaning. I was trying to remember everything I'd heard about dope addiction and I couldn't help watching Sonny for signs. I wasn't doing it out of malice. I was trying to find out something about my brother. I was dying to hear him tell me he was safe.

"Safe!" my father grunted, whenever Mama suggested trying to move to a neighborhood which might be safer for children. "Safe, hell! Ain't no place safe for kids, nor nobody."

He always went on like this, but he wasn't, ever, really as bad as he sounded, not even on weekends, when he got drunk. As a matter of fact, he was always on the lookout for "something a little better," but he died before he found it. He died suddenly, during a drunken weekend in the middle of the war, when Sonny was fifteen. He and

Sonny hadn't ever got on too well. And this was partly because Sonny was the apple of his father's eye. It was because he loved Sonny so much and was frightened for him, that he was always fighting with him. It doesn't do any good to fight with Sonny. Sonny just moves back, inside himself, where he can't be reached. But the principal reason that they never hit it off is that they were so much alike. Daddy was big and tough and loud-talking, just the opposite of Sonny, but they both had—that same privacy.

Mama tried to tell me something about this, just after Daddy died. I was home on leave from the army.

This was the last time I ever saw my mother alive. Just the same, this picture gets all mixed up in my mind with pictures I had of her when she was younger. The way I always see her is the way she used to be on a Sunday afternoon, say, when the old folks were talking after the big Sunday dinner. I always see her wearing pale blue. She'd be sitting on the sofa. And my father would be sitting in the easy chair, not far from her. And the living room would be full of church folks and relatives. There they sit, in chairs all around the living room, and the night is creeping up outside, but nobody knows it yet. You can see the darkness growing against the windowpanes and you hear the street noises every now and again, or maybe the jangling beat of a tambourine from one of the churches close by, but it's real quiet in the room. For a moment nobody's talking, but every face looks darkening, like the sky outside. And my mother rocks a little from the waist, and my father's eyes are closed. Everyone is looking at something a child can't see. For a minute they've forgotten the children. Maybe a kid is lying on the rug, half asleep. Maybe somebody's got a kid in his lap and is absent-mindedly stroking the kid's head. Maybe there's a kid, quiet and big-eyed, curled up in a big chair in the corner. The silence, the darkness coming, and the darkness in the faces frightens the child obscurely. He hopes that the hand which strokes his forehead will never stop—will never die. He hopes that there will never come a time when the old folks won't be sitting around the living room, talking about where they've come from, and what they've seen, and what's happened to them and their kinfolk.

But something deep and watchful in the child knows that this is bound to end, is already ending. In a moment someone will get up and turn on the light. Then the old folks will remember the children and they won't talk any more that day. And when light fills the room, the child is filled with darkness. He knows that everytime this happens he's moved just a little closer to that darkness outside. The darkness outside is what the old folks have been talking about. It's what they've come from. It's what they endure. The child knows that they won't talk any more because if he knows too much about what's happened to *them*, he'll know too much too soon, about what's going to happen to *him*.

The last time I talked to my mother, I remember I was restless. I wanted to get out and see Isabel. We weren't married then and we had a lot to straighten out between us.

There Mama sat, in black, by the window. She was humming an old church song, *Lord, you brought me from a long ways off.* Sonny was out somewhere. Mama kept watching the streets.

"I don't know," she said, "if I'll ever see you again, after you go off from here. But I hope you'll remember the things I tried to teach you."

"Don't talk like that," I said, and smiled. "You'll be here a long time yet."

She smiled, too, but she said nothing. She was quiet for a long time. And I said, "Mama, don't you worry about nothing. I'll be writing all the time, and you be getting the checks. . . ."

"I want to talk to you about your brother," she said, suddenly. "If anything happens to me he ain't going to have nobody to look out for him."

"Mama," I said, "ain't nothing going to happen to you *or* Sonny. Sonny's all right. He's a good boy and he's got good sense."

"It ain't a question of his being a good boy," Mama said, "nor of his having good sense. It ain't only the bad ones, nor yet the dumb ones that gets sucked under." She stopped, looking at me. "Your Daddy once had a brother," she said, and she smiled in a way that made me feel she was in pain. "You didn't never know that, did you?"

"No," I said, "I never knew that," and I watched her face.

"Oh, yes," she said, "your Daddy had a brother." She looked out of the window again. "I know you never saw your Daddy cry. But *I* did—many a time, through all these years."

I asked her, "What happened to his brother? How come nobody's ever talked about him?"

This was the first time I ever saw my mother look old.

"His brother got killed," she said, "when he was just a little younger than you are now. I knew him. He was a fine boy. He was maybe a little full of the devil, but he didn't mean nobody no harm."

Then she stopped and the room was silent, exactly as it had sometimes been on those Sunday afternoons. Mama kept looking out into the streets.

"He used to have a job in the mill," she said, "and, like all young folks, he just liked to perform on Saturday nights. Saturday nights, him and your father would drift around to different places, go to dances and things like that, or just sit around with people they knew, and your father's brother would sing, he had a fine voice, and play along with himself on his guitar. Well, this particular Saturday night, him and your father was coming home from some place, and they were both a little drunk and there was a moon that night, it was bright like day. Your father's brother was feeling kind of good, and he was whistling to himself, and he had his guitar slung over his shoulder. They was coming down a hill and beneath them was a road that turned off from the highway. Well, your father's brother, being always kind of frisky, decided to run down this hill, and he did, with that guitar banging and clanging behind him, and he ran across the road, and he was making water behind a tree. And your father was sort of amused at him and he was still coming down the hill, kind of slow. Then he heard a car motor and that same minute his brother stepped from behind the tree, into the road, in the moonlight. And he started to cross the road. And your father started to run down the hill, he says he don't know why. This car was full of white men. They was all drunk, and when they seen your father's brother they let out a great whoop and holler and they aimed the car straight at him. They was having fun, they just wanted to scare him, the way they do sometimes, you know. But they was drunk. And I guess the boy, being drunk, too, and scared, kind of lost his head. By the time he jumped it was too late. Your father says he heard his brother scream when the car rolled over him, and he heard the wood of that guitar when it give, and he heard them strings go flying, and he heard them white men shouting, and the car kept on a-going and it ain't stopped till this day. And, time your father got down the hill, his brother weren't nothing but blood and pulp."

Tears were gleaming on my mother's face. There wasn't anything I could say.

"He never mentioned it," she said, "because I never let him mention it before you children. Your Daddy was like a crazy man that night and for many a night thereafter. He says he never in his life seen anything as dark as that road after the lights of that car had gone away. Weren't nothing, weren't nobody on that road, just your Daddy and his brother and that busted guitar. Oh, yes. Your Daddy never did really get right again. Till the day he died he weren't sure but that every white man he saw was the man that killed his brother."

She stopped and took out her handkerchief and dried her eyes and looked at me.

"I ain't telling you all this," she said, "to make you scared or bitter or to make you hate nobody. I'm telling you this because you got a brother. And the world ain't changed."

I guess I didn't want to believe this. I guess she saw this in my face. She turned away from me, toward the window again, searching those streets.

"But I praise my Redeemer," she said at last, "that He called your Daddy home before me. I ain't saying it to throw no flowers at myself, but, I declare, it keeps me from feeling too cast down to know I helped your father get safely through this world. Your father always acted like he was the roughest, strongest man on earth. And everybody took him to be like that. But if he hadn't had *me* there—to see his tears!"

She was crying again. Still, I couldn't move. I said, "Lord, Lord, Mama, I didn't know it was like that."

"Oh, honey," she said, "there's a lot that you don't know. But you are going to find it out." She stood up from the window and came over to me. "You got to hold on to your brother," she said, "and don't let him fall, no matter what it looks like is happening to him and no matter how evil you gets with him. You going to be evil with him many a time. But don't you forget what I told you, you hear?"

"I won't forget," I said. "Don't you worry, I won't forget. I won't let nothing happen to Sonny."

My mother smiled as though she were amused at something she saw in my face. Then, "You may not be able to stop nothing from happening. But you got to let him know you's *there*."

Two days later I was married, and then I was gone. And I had a lot of things on my mind and I pretty well forgot my promise to Mama until I got shipped home on a special furlough for her funeral.

And, after the funeral, with just Sonny and me alone in the empty kitchen, I tried to find out something about him.

"What do you want to do?" I asked him.

"I'm going to be a musician," he said.

For he had graduated, in the time I had been away, from dancing to the juke box to finding out who was playing what, and what they were doing with it, and he had bought himself a set of drums.

"You mean, you want to be a drummer?" I somehow had the feeling that being a drummer might be all right for other people but not for my brother Sonny.

"I don't think," he said, looking at me very gravely, "that I'll ever be a good drummer. But I think I can play a piano."

I frowned. I'd never played the role of the older brother quite so seriously before, had scarcely ever, in fact, *asked* Sonny a damn thing. I sensed myself in the presence of something I didn't really know how to handle, didn't understand. So I made my frown a little deeper as I asked: "What kind of musician do you want to be?"

He grinned. "How many kinds do you think there are?"

"Be *serious*," I said.

He laughed, throwing his head back, and then looked at me. "I *am* serious."

"Well, then, for Christ's sake, stop kidding around and answer a serious question. I mean, do you want to be a concert pianist, you want to play classical music and all that, or—or what?" Long before I finished he was laughing again. "For Christ's *sake*, Sonny!"

He sobered, but with difficulty. "I'm sorry. But you sound so—*scared!*" and he was off again.

"Well, you may think it's funny now, baby, but it's not going to be so funny when you have to make your living at it, let me tell you *that.*" I was furious because I knew he was laughing at me and I didn't know why.

"No," he said, very sober now, and afraid, perhaps that he'd hurt me, "I don't want to be a classical pianist. That isn't what interests me. I mean"—he paused, looking hard at me, as though his eyes would help me to understand, and then gestured helplessly, as though perhaps his hand would help—"I mean, I'll have a lot of studying to do, and I'll have to study *everything*, but, I mean, I want to play *with*—jazz musicians." He stopped. "I want to play jazz," he said.

Well, the word had never before sounded as heavy, as real, as it sounded that afternoon in Sonny's mouth. I just looked at him and I was probably frowning a real frown by this time. I simply couldn't see why on earth he'd want to spend his time hanging around nightclubs, clowning around on bandstands, while people pushed each other around a dance floor. It seemed—beneath him, somehow. I had never thought about it before, had never been forced to, but I suppose I had always put jazz musicians in a class with what Daddy called "good-time people."

"Are you *serious?*"

"Hell, *yes*, I'm serious."

He looked more helpless than ever, and annoyed, and deeply hurt.

I suggested, helpfully. "You mean—like Louis Armstrong?"

His face closed as though I'd struck him. "No. I'm not talking about none of that old-time, down home crap."

"Well, look, Sonny, I'm sorry, don't get mad. I just don't altogether get it, that's all. Name somebody—you know, a jazz musician you admire."

"Bird."

"Who?"

"Bird! Charlie Parker! Don't they teach you nothing in the goddamn army?"

I lit a cigarette. I was surprised and then a little amused to discover that I was trembling. "I've been out of touch," I said. "You'll have to be patient with me. Now. Who's this Parker character?"

"He's just one of the greatest jazz musicians alive," said Sonny, sullenly, his hands in his pockets, his back to me. "Maybe *the* greatest," he added, bitterly, "that's probably why *you* never heard of him."

"All right," I said, "I'm ignorant. I'm sorry. I'll go out and buy all the cat's records right away, all right?"

"It don't," said Sonny, with dignity, "make any difference to me. I don't care what you listen to. Don't do me no favors."

I was beginning to realize that I'd never seen him so upset before. With another part of my mind I was thinking that this would probably turn out to be one of those things kids go through and that I shouldn't make it seem important by pushing it too hard. Still, I didn't think it would do any harm to ask: "Doesn't all this take a lot of time? Can you make a living at it?"

He turned back to me and half leaned, half sat, on the kitchen table. "Everything takes time," he said, "and—well, yes, sure, I can make a living at it. But what I don't seem to be able to make you understand is that it's the only thing I want to do."

"Well, Sonny," I said, gently, "you know people can't always do exactly what they *want* to do—"

"*No*, I don't know that," said Sonny, surprising me. "I think people *ought* to do what they want to do, what else are they alive for?"

"You getting to be a big boy," I said desperately, "it's time you started thinking about your future."

"I'm thinking about my future," said Sonny, grimly. "I think about it all the time."

I gave up. I decided, if he didn't change his mind, that we could always talk about it later. "In the meantime," I said, "you got to finish school." We had already decided that he'd have to move in with Isabel and her folks. I knew this wasn't the ideal arrangement because Isabel's folks are inclined to be dicty and they hadn't especially wanted Isabel to marry me. But I didn't know what else to do. "And we have to get you fixed up at Isabel's."

There was a long silence. He moved from the kitchen table to the window. "That's a terrible idea. You know it yourself."

"Do you have a *better* idea?"

He just walked up and down the kitchen for a minute. He was as tall as I was. He had started to shave. I suddenly had the feeling that I didn't know him at all.

He stopped at the kitchen table and picked up my cigarettes. Looking at me with a kind of mocking, amused defiance, he put one between his lips. "You mind?"

"You smoking already?"

He lit the cigarette and nodded, watching me through the smoke, "I just wanted to see if I'd have the courage to smoke in front of you." He grinned and blew a great cloud of smoke to the ceiling. "It was easy." He looked at my face. "Come on, now. I bet you was smoking at my age, tell the truth."

I didn't say anything but the truth was on my face, and he laughed. But now there was something very strained in his laugh. "Sure. And I bet that ain't all you was doing."

He was frightening me a little. "Cut the crap," I said. "We already decided that you was going to go and live at Isabel's. Now what's got into you all of a sudden?"

"*You* decided it," he pointed out. "*I* didn't decide nothing." He stopped in front of me, leaning against the stove, arms loosely folded. "Look, brother. I don't want to stay in Harlem no more, I really don't." He was very earnest. He looked at me, then over toward the kitchen window. There was something in his eyes I'd never seen before, some thoughtfulness, some worry all his own. He rubbed the muscle of one arm. "It's time I was getting out of here."

"Where do you want to *go*, Sonny?"

"I want to join the army. Or the navy, I don't care. If I say I'm old enough, they'll believe me."

Then I got mad. It was because I was so scared. "You must be crazy. You goddamn fool, what the hell do you want to go and join the *army* for?"

"I just told you. To get out of Harlem."

"Sonny, you haven't even finished *school.* And if you really want to be a musician, how do you expect to study if you're in the *army?*"

He looked at me, trapped, and in anguish. "There's ways. I might be able to work out some kind of deal. Anyway, I'll have the G.I. Bill when I come out."

"*If* you come out." We stared at each other. "Sonny, please. Be reasonable. I know the setup is far from perfect. But we got to do the best we can."

"I ain't learning nothing in school," he said. "Even when I go."

He turned away from me and opened the window and threw his cigarette out into the narrow alley. I watched his back. "At least, I ain't learning nothing you'd want me to learn." He slammed the window so hard I thought the glass would fly out, and turned back to me. "And I'm sick of the stink of these garbage cans!"

"Sonny," I said, "I know how you feel. But if you don't finish school now, you're going to be sorry later that you didn't." I grabbed him by the shoulders. "And you only got another year. It ain't so bad. And I'll come back and I swear I'll help you do *whatever* you want to do. Just try to put up with it till I come back. Will you please do that? For me?"

He didn't answer and he wouldn't look at me.

"Sonny. You hear me?"

He pulled away. "I hear you. But you never hear anything *I* say."

I didn't know what to say to that. He looked out of the window and then back at me. "OK," he said, and sighed. "I'll try."

Then I said, trying to cheer him up a little, "They got a piano at Isabel's. You can practice on it."

And as a matter of fact, it did cheer him up for a minute. "That's right," he said to himself. "I forget that." His face relaxed a little. But the worry, the thoughtfulness, played on it still, the way shadows play on a face which is staring into the fire.

But I thought I'd never hear the end of that piano. At first, Isabel would write me, saying how nice it was that Sonny was so serious about his music and how, as soon as he came in from school, or wherever he had been when he was supposed to be at school, he went straight to that piano and stayed there until suppertime. And, after supper, he went back to that piano and stayed there until everybody went to bed. He was at the piano all day Saturday and all day Sunday. Then he bought a record player and started playing records. He'd play one record over and over again, all day long sometimes, and he'd improvise along with it on the piano. Or he'd play one section of the record, one chord, one change, one progression, then he'd do it on the piano. Then back to the record. Then back to the piano.

Well, I really don't know how they stood it. Isabel finally confessed that it wasn't like living with a person at all, it was like living with sound. And the sound didn't make any sense to her, didn't make any sense to any of them—naturally. They began, in a way, to be afflicted by this presence that was living in their home. It was as though Sonny were some sort of god, or monster. He moved in an atmosphere which wasn't like theirs at all. They fed him and he ate, he washed himself, he walked in and out of their door; he certainly wasn't nasty or unpleasant or rude, Sonny isn't any of those things; but it was as though he were all wrapped up in some cloud, some fire, some vision all his own; and there wasn't any way to reach him.

At the same time, he wasn't really a man yet, he was still a child, and they had to watch out for him in all kinds of ways. They certainly couldn't throw him out. Neither did they dare to make a great scene about that piano because even they dimly sensed, as I sensed, from so many thousand of miles away, that Sonny was at that piano playing for his life.

But he hadn't been going to school. One day a letter came from the school board and Isabel's mother got it—there had, apparently, been other letters but Sonny had torn them up. This day, when Sonny came in, Isabel's mother showed him the letter and asked where he'd been spending his time. And she finally got it out of him that he'd been down in Greenwich Village, with musicians and other characters, in a white girl's apartment. And this scared her and she started to scream at him and what came up, once she began—though she denies it to this day—was what sacrifices they were making to give Sonny a decent home and how little he appreciated it.

Sonny didn't play the piano that day. By evening, Isabel's mother had calmed down but then there was the old man to deal with, and Isabel herself. Isabel says she did her best to be calm but she broke down and started crying. She says she just watched Sonny's face. She could tell, by watching him, what was happening with him. And what was happening was that they penetrated his cloud, they had reached him. Even if their fingers had been a thousand times more gentle than human fingers ever are, he could hardly help feeling that they had stripped him naked and were spitting on that nakedness. For he also had to see that his presence, that music, which was life or death to him, had been torture for them and that they had endured it, not at all for his sake, but only for mine. And

Sonny couldn't take that. He can take it a little better today than he could then but he's still not very good at it and, frankly, I don't know anybody who is.

The silence of the next few days must have been louder than the sound of all the music ever played since time began. One morning, before she went to work, Isabel was in his room for something and she suddenly realized that all of his records were gone. And she knew for certain that he was gone. And he was. He went as far as the navy would carry him. He finally sent me a postcard from some place in Greece and that was the first I knew that Sonny was still alive. I didn't see him any more until we were both back in New York and the war had long been over.

He was a man by then, of course, but I wasn't willing to see it. He came by the house from time to time, but we fought almost every time we met. I didn't like the way he carried himself, loose and dreamlike all the time, and I didn't like his friends, and his music seemed to be merely an excuse for the life he led. It sounded just that weird and disordered.

Then we had a fight, a pretty awful fight, and I didn't see him for months. By and by I looked him up, where he was living, in a furnished room in the Village, and I tried to make it up. But there were lots of people in the room and Sonny just lay on his bed, and he wouldn't come downstairs with me, and he treated these other people as though they were his family and I weren't. So I got mad and then he got mad, and then I told him that he might just as well be dead as live the way he was living. Then he stood up and he told me not to worry about him any more in life, that he *was* dead as far as I was concerned. Then he pushed me to the door and the other people looked on as though nothing were happening, and he slammed the door behind me. I stood in the hallway, staring at the door. I heard somebody laugh in the room and then the tears came to my eyes. I started down the steps, whistling to keep from crying, I kept whistling to myself, *You going to need me, baby, one of these cold, rainy days.*

I read about Sonny's trouble in the spring. Little Grace died in the fall. She was a beautiful little girl. But she only lived a little over two years. She died of polio and she suffered. She had a slight fever for a couple of days, but it didn't seem like anything and we just kept her in bed. And we would certainly have called the doctor, but the fever dropped, she seemed to be all right. So we thought it had just been a cold. Then, one day, she was up, playing, Isabel was in the kitchen fixing lunch for the two boys when they'd come in from school, and she heard Grace fall down in the living room. When you have a lot of children you don't always start running when one of them falls, unless they start screaming or something. And, this time, Grace was quiet. Yet, Isabel says that when she heard that *thump* and then that silence, something happened in her to make her afraid. And she ran to the living room and there was little Grace on the floor, all twisted up, and the reason she hadn't screamed was that she couldn't get her breath. And when she did scream, it was the worst sound, Isabel says, that she'd ever heard in all her life, and she still hears it sometimes in her dreams. Isabel will sometimes wake me up with a low, moaning, strangled sound and I have to be quick to awaken her and hold her to me and where Isabel is weeping against me seems a mortal wound.

I think I may have written Sonny the very day that little Grace was buried. I was sitting in the living room in the dark, by myself, and I suddenly thought of Sonny. My trouble made his real.

One Saturday afternoon, when Sonny had been living with us, or, anyway, been in our house, for nearly two weeks, I found myself wandering aimlessly about the living room, drinking from a can of beer, and trying to work up the courage to search Sonny's room. He was out, he was usually out whenever I was home, and Isabel had taken the children to see their grandparents. Suddenly I was standing still in front of the living room window, watching Seventh Avenue. The idea of searching Sonny's room made me still. I scarcely dared to admit to myself what I'd be searching for, I didn't know what I'd do if I found it. Or if I didn't.

On the sidewalk across from me, near the entrance to a barbecue joint, some people were holding an old-fashioned revival meeting. The barbecue cook, wearing a dirty white apron, his conked hair reddish and metallic in the pale sun, and a cigarette between his lips, stood in the doorway, watching them. Kids and older people paused in their errands and stood there, along with some older men and a couple of very tough-looking women who watched everything that happened on the avenue, as though they owned it, or were maybe owned by it. Well, they were watching this, too. The revival was being carried on by three sisters in black, and a brother. All they had were their voices and their Bibles and a tambourine. The brother was testifying and while he testified two of the sisters stood together, seeming to say, amen, and the third sister walked around with the tambourine outstretched and a couple of people dropped coins into it. Then the brother's testimony ended and the sister who had been taking up the collection dumped the coins into her palm and transferred them to the pocket of her long black robe. Then she raised both hands, striking the tambourine against the air, and then against one hand, and she started to sing. And the two other sisters and the brothers joined in.

It was strange, suddenly, to watch, though I had been seeing these street meetings all my life. So, of course, had everybody else down there. Yet, they paused and watched and listened and I stood still at the window, "*Tis the old ship of Zion,*" they sang, and the sister with the tambourine kept a steady, jangling beat, "*it has rescued many a thousand!*" Not a soul under the sound of their voices was hearing this song for the first time, not one of them had been rescued. Nor had they seen much in the way of rescue work being done around them. Neither did they especially believe in the holiness of the three sisters and the brother, they knew too much about them, knew where they lived, and how. The woman with the tambourine, whose voice dominated the air, whose face was bright with joy, was divided by very little from the woman who stood watching her, a cigarette between her heavy, chapped lips, her hair a cuckoo's nest, her face scarred and swollen from many beatings, and her black eyes glittering like coal. Perhaps they both knew this, which was why, when, as rarely, they addressed each other, they addressed each other as Sister. As the singing filled the air the watching, listening faces underwent a change, the eyes focusing on something within; the music seemed to soothe a poison out of them; and time seemed, nearly, to fall away from the sullen, belligerent, battered faces, as though they were fleeing back to their first condition, while dreaming of their last. The barbecue cook half shook his head and smiled, and dropped his cigarette and disappeared into his joint. A man fumbled in his pockets for change and stood holding it in his hand impatiently, as though he had just remembered a pressing appointment further up the avenue. He looked furious. Then I saw Sonny, standing on the edge of the crowd. He was carrying a wide, flat notebook with a green cover, and it made him look, from where I was standing, almost like a schoolboy. The coppery sun brought out the copper in his skin, he was very faintly smiling, standing very still. Then the singing stopped, the tambourine turned into a collection plate again. The furious man dropped in his coins and vanished, so did a couple of the women, and Sonny dropped some change in the plate, looking directly at the woman with a little smile. He started across the avenue, toward the house. He has a slow, loping walk, something like the way Harlem hipsters walk, only he's imposed on this his own half-beat. I had never really noticed it before.

I stayed at the window, both relieved and apprehensive. As Sonny disappeared from my sight, they began singing again. And they were still singing when his key turned in the lock.

"Hey," he said.

"Hey, yourself. You want some beer?"

"No. Well, maybe." But he came up to the window and stood beside me, looking out. "What a warm voice," he said.

They were singing *If I could only hear my mother pray again!*

"Yes," I said, "and she can sure beat that tambourine."

"But what a terrible song," he said, and laughed. He dropped his notebook on the sofa and disappeared into the kitchen. "Where's Isabel and the kids?"

"I think they went to see their grandparents. You hungry?"

"No." He came back into the living room with his can of beer. "You want to come some place with me tonight?"

I sensed, I don't know how, that I couldn't possibly say no. "Sure. Where?"

He sat down on the sofa and picked up his notebook and started leafing through it. "I'm going to sit in with some fellows in a joint in the Village."

"You mean you're going to play, tonight?"

"That's right." He took a swallow of his beer and moved back to the window. He gave me a sidelong look. "If you can stand it."

"I'll try," I said.

He smiled to himself and we both watched as the meeting across the way broke up. The three sisters and the brother, heads bowed, were singing *God be with you till we meet again.* The faces around them were very quiet. Then the song ended. The small crowd dispersed. We watched the three women and the lone man walk slowly up the avenue.

"When she was singing before," said Sonny, abruptly, "her voice reminded me for a minute of what heroin feels like sometimes—when it's in your veins. It makes you feel sort of warm and cool at the same time. And distant. And—and sure." He sipped his beer, very deliberately not looking at me. I watched his face. "It makes you feel—in control. Sometimes you've got to have that feeling."

"Do you?" I sat down slowly in the easy chair.

"Sometimes." He went to the sofa and picked up his notebook again. "Some people do."

"In order," I asked, "to play?" And my voice was very ugly, full of contempt and anger.

"Well"—he looked at me with great, troubled eyes, as though, in fact, he hoped his eyes would tell me things he could never otherwise say—"they *think* so. And *if* they think so—!"

'And what do *you* think?" I asked.

He sat on the sofa and put his can of beer on the floor. "I don't know," he said, and I couldn't be sure if he were answering my question or pursuing his thoughts. His face didn't tell me. "It's not so much to *play*. It's to *stand* it, to be able to make it at all. On any level." He frowned and smiled: "In order to keep from shaking to pieces."

"But these friends of yours," I said, "they seem to shake themselves to pieces pretty goddamn fast."

"Maybe." He played with the notebook. And something told me that I should curb my tongue, that Sonny was doing his best to talk, that I should listen. "But of course you only know the ones that've gone to pieces. Some don't—or at least they haven't *yet* and that's just about all *any* of us can say." He paused. "And then there are some who just live, really, in hell, and they know it and they see what's happening and they go right on. I don't know." He sighed, dropped the notebook, folded his arms. "Some guys, you can tell from the way they play, they on something *all* the time. And you can see that, well, it makes something real for them. But of course," he picked up his beer from the floor and sipped it and put the can down again, "they *want* to, too, you've got to see that. Even some of them that say they don't—*some*, not all."

"And what about you?" I asked—I couldn't help it. "What about you? Do *you* want to?"

He stood up and walked to the window and remained silent for a long time. Then he sighed. "Me," he said. Then: "While I was downstairs before, on my way here, listening to that woman sing, it struck me all of a sudden how much suffering she must have had to go through—to sing like that. It's *repulsive* to think you have to suffer that much."

I said: "But there's no way not to suffer—is there, Sonny?"

"I believe not," he said and smiled, "but that's never stopped anyone from trying." He looked at me. "Has it?" I realized, with this mocking look, that there stood between us, forever, beyond the power of time or forgiveness, the fact that I had held silence—so long!—when he had needed human speech to help him. He turned back to the window. "No, there's no way not to suffer. But you try all kinds of ways to keep from drowning in it, to keep on top of it, and to make it seem—well, like *you*. Like you did something, all right, and now you're suffering for it. You know?" I said nothing. "Well you know," he said impatiently, "why *do* people suffer? Maybe it's better to do something to give it a reason, *any* reason."

But we just agreed," I said, "that there's no way not to suffer. Isn't it better, then, just to—take it?"

"But nobody just takes it," Sonny cried, "that's what I'm telling you! *Everybody* tries not to. You're just hung up on the *way* some people try—it's not *your* way!"

The hair on my face began to itch, my face felt wet. "That's not true," I said, "That's not true. I don't give a damn what other people do, I don't even care how they suffer. I just care how *you* suffer." And he looked at me. "Please believe me," I said, "I don't want to see you—die—trying not to suffer."

"I won't," he said flatly, "die trying not to suffer. At least, not any faster than anybody else."

"But there's no need," I said, trying to laugh, "is there? in killing yourself."

I wanted to say more, but I couldn't. I wanted to talk about will power and how life could be—well, beautiful. I wanted to say that it was all within; but was it? or, rather, wasn't that exactly the trouble? And I wanted to promise that I would never fail him again. But it would all have sounded—empty words and lies.

So I made the promise to myself and prayed that I would keep it.

"It's terrible sometimes, inside," he said, "that's what's the trouble. You walk these streets, black and funky and cold, and there's not really a living ass to talk to, and there's nothing shaking, and there's no way of getting it out—that storm inside. You can't talk it and you can't make love with it, and when you finally try to get with it and play it, you realize *nobody's* listening. So *you've* got to listen. You got to find a way to listen."

And then he walked away from the window and sat on the sofa again, as though all the wind had suddenly been knocked out of him. "Sometimes you'll do *anything* to play, even cut your mother's throat." He laughed and looked at me. "Or your brother's." Then he sobered. "Or your own." Then: "Don't worry. I'm all right now and I think I'll *be* all right. But I can't forget—where I've been. I don't mean just the physical place I've been, I mean where I've *been*. And *what* I've been."

"What have you been, Sonny?" I asked.

He smiled—but sat sideways on the sofa, his elbow resting on the back, his fingers playing with his mouth and chin, not looking at me. "I've been something I didn't recognize, didn't know I could be. Didn't know anybody could be." He stopped, looking inward, looking helplessly young, looking old. "I'm not talking about it now because I feel *guilty* or anything like that—maybe it would be better if I did, I don't know. Anyway, I can't really talk about it. Not to you, not to anybody," and now he turned and faced me. "Sometimes, you know, and it was actually when I was most *out* of the world, I felt that I was in it, that I was *with* it, really, and I could play or I didn't really have to *play*, it just came out of me, it was there. And I don't know how I played, thinking about it now, but I know I did awful things, those times, sometimes, to people. Or it wasn't that I *did* anything to them—it was that they weren't real." He picked up the beer can; it was empty; he rolled it between his palms. "And other times—well, I needed a fix, I needed to find a place to lean, I needed to clear a space to *listen*—and I couldn't find it, and I—went crazy, I did terrible things to *me*, I was terrible *for* me." He began pressing the beer can between his hands, I watched the metal begin to give. It glittered, as he played with it, like a knife, and I was afraid he would cut himself, but I said nothing. "Oh well. I can never tell you. I was all by myself at the bottom of something, stinking and sweating and crying and shaking, and I smelled it, you know? *my* stink, and I thought I'd die if I couldn't get away from it and yet, all the same, I knew that everything I was doing was just locking me in with it. And I didn't know," he paused, still flattening the beer can, "I didn't know, I still *don't* know, something kept telling me that maybe it was good to smell your own stink, but I didn't think that *that* was what I'd been trying to do—and—who can stand it?" and he abruptly dropped the ruined beer can, looking at me with a small, still smile, and then rose, walking to the window as though it were the lodestone rock. I watched his face, he watched the avenue. "I couldn't tell you when Mama died—but the reason I wanted to leave Harlem so bad was to get away from drugs. And then, when I ran away, that's what I was running from—really. When I came back, nothing had changed. *I* hadn't changed, I was just—older." And he stopped, drumming with his fingers on the windowpane. The sun had vanished, soon darkness would fall. I watched his face. "It can come again, he said, almost as though speaking to himself. Then he turned to me. "It can come again," he repeated. "I just want you to know that."

"All right," I said, at last. "So it can come again, All right."

He smiled, but the smile was sorrowful. "I had to try to tell you," he said.

"Yes," I said. "I understand that."

"You're my brother," he said, looking straight at me, and not smiling at all.

"Yes," I repeated, "yes, I understand that."

He turned back to the window, looking out. "All that hatred down there," he said, "all that hatred and misery and love. It's a wonder it doesn't blow the avenue apart."

We went to the only nightclub on a short, dark street, downtown. We squeezed through the narrow, chattering, jam-packed bar to the entrance of the big room, where the bandstand was. And we stood there for a moment, for the lights were very dim in this room and we couldn't see. Then, "Hello, boy," said a voice and an enormous black man, much older than Sonny or myself, erupted out of all that atmospheric lighting and put an arm around Sonny's shoulder. "I been sitting right here," he said, "waiting for you."

He had a big voice, too, and heads in the darkness turned toward us.

Sonny grinned and pulled a little away, and said, "Creole, this is my brother. I told you about him."

Creole shook my hand. "I'm glad to meet you, son," he said, and it was clear that he was glad to meet me *there*, for Sonny's sake. And he smiled, "You got a real musician in *your* family," and he took his arm from Sonny's shoulder and slapped him, lightly, affectionately, with the back of his hand.

"Well. Now I've heard it all," said a voice behind us. This was another musician, and a friend of Sonny's, a coal-black, cheerful-looking man, built close to the ground. He immediately began confiding to me, at the top of his lungs, the most terrible things about Sonny, his teeth gleaming like a lighthouse and his laugh coming up out of him like the beginning of an earthquake. And it turned out that everyone at the bar knew Sonny, or almost everyone; some were musicians, working there, or nearby, or not working, some were simply hangers-on, and some were there to hear Sonny play. I was introduced to all of them and they were all very polite to me. Yet, it was clear that, for them, I was only Sonny's brother. Here, I was in Sonny's world. Or, rather: his kingdom. Here, it was not even a question that his veins bore royal blood.

They were going to play soon and Creole installed me, by myself, at a table in a dark corner. Then I watched them, Creole, and the little black man, and Sonny, and the others, while they horsed around, standing just below the bandstand. The light from the bandstand spilled just a little short of them and, watching them laughing and gesturing and moving about, I had the feeling that they, nevertheless, were being most careful not to step into that circle of light too suddenly: that if they moved into the light too suddenly, without thinking, they would perish in flame. Then, while I watched, one of them, the small, black man, moved into the light and crossed the bandstand and started fooling around with his drums. Then—being funny and being, also, extremely ceremonious—Creole took Sonny by the arm and led him to the piano. A woman's voice called Sonny's name and a few hands started clapping. And Sonny, also being funny and being ceremonious, and so touched, I think, that he could have cried, but neither hiding it nor showing it, riding it like a man, grinned, and put both hands to his heart and bowed from the waist.

Creole then went to the bass fiddle and a lean, very bright-skinned brown man jumped up on the bandstand and picked up his horn. So there they were, and the atmosphere on the bandstand and in the room began to change and tighten. Someone stepped up to the microphone and announced them. Then there were all kinds of murmurs. Some people at the bar shushed others. The waitress ran around, frantically getting in the last orders, guys and chicks got closer to each other, and the lights on the bandstand, on the quartet, turned to a kind of indigo. Then they all looked different there. Creole looked about him for the last time, as though he were making certain that all his chickens were in the coop, and then he—jumped and struck the fiddle. And there they were.

All I know about music is that not many people ever really hear it. And even then, on the rare occasions when something opens within, and the music enters, what we mainly hear, or hear corroborated, are personal, private, vanishing evocations. But the man who creates the music is hearing something else, is dealing with the roar rising from the void and imposing order on it as it hits the air. What is evoked in him, then, is of another order, more terrible because it has no words, and triumphant, too, for that same reason. And his triumph, when he triumphs, is ours. I just watched Sonny's face. His face was troubled, he was working hard, but he wasn't with it. And I had the feeling that, in a way, everyone on the bandstand was waiting for him, both waiting for him and pushing him along. But as I began to watch Creole, I realized that it was Creole who held them all back. He had them on a short rein. Up there, keeping the beat with his whole body, wailing on the fiddle, with his eyes half closed, he was listening to everything, but he was listening to Sonny. He was having a dialogue with Sonny. He wanted Sonny to leave the shoreline and strike out for the deep water. He was Sonny's witness that deep water and drowning were not the same thing—he had been there, and he knew. And he wanted Sonny to know. He was waiting for Sonny to do the things on the keys which would let Creole know that Sonny was in the water.

And, while Creole listened, Sonny moved, deep within, exactly like someone in torment. I had never before thought of how awful the relationship must be between the musician and his instrument. He has to fill it, this instrument, with the breath of life, his own. He has to make it do what he wants it to do. And a piano is just a piano. It's made out of so much wood and wires and little hammers and big ones, and ivory. While there's only so much you can do with it, the only way to find this out is to try; to try and make it do everything.

And Sonny hadn't been near a piano for over a year. And he wasn't on much better terms with his life, not the life that stretched before him now. He and the piano stammered, started one way, got scared, stopped; started another way, panicked, marked time, started again; then seemed to have found a direction, panicked again, got stuck. And the face I saw on Sonny I'd never seen before. Everything had been burned out of it, and, at the same time, things usually hidden were being burned in, by the fire and fury of the battle which was occurring in him up there.

Yet, watching Creole's face as they neared the end of the first set, I had the feeling that something had happened, something I hadn't heard. Then they finished, there was scattered applause, and then, without an instant's warning, Creole started into something else, it was almost sardonic, it was *Am I Blue.* And, as though he commanded, Sonny began to play. Something began to happen. And Creole let out the reins. The dry, low, black man said something awful on the drums, Creole answered, and the drums talked back. Then the horn insisted, sweet and high, slightly detached perhaps, and Creole listened, commenting now and then, dry, and driving, beautiful and calm and old. Then they all came together again, and Sonny was part of the family again. I could tell this from his face. He seemed to have found, right there beneath his fingers, a damn brand-new piano. It seemed that he couldn't get over it. Then, for awhile, just being happy with Sonny, they seemed to be agreeing with him that brand-new pianos certainly were a gas.

Then Creole stepped forward to remind them that what they

were playing was the blues. He hit something in all of them, he hit something in me, myself, and the music tightened and deepened, apprehension began to beat the air. Creole began to tell us what the blues were all about. They were not about anything very new. He and his boys up there were keeping it new, at the risk of ruin, destruction, madness, and death, in order to find new ways to make us listen. For, while the tale of how we suffer, and how we are delighted, and how we may triumph is never new, it always must be heard. There isn't any other tale to tell, it's the only light we've got in all this darkness.

And this tale, according to that face, that body, those strong hands on those strings, has another aspect in every country, and a new depth in every generation. Listen, Creole seemed to be saying, listen. Now these are Sonny's blues. He made the little black man on the drums know it, and the bright, brown man on the horn. Creole wasn't trying any longer to get Sonny in the water. He was wishing him Godspeed. Then he stepped back, very slowly, filling the air with the immense suggestion that Sonny speak for himself.

Then they all gathered around Sonny and Sonny played. Every now and again one of them seemed to say, amen. Sonny's fingers filled the air with life, his life. But that life contained so many others. And Sonny went all the way back, he really began with the spare, flat statement of the opening phrase of the song. Then he began to make it his. It was very beautiful because it wasn't hurried and it was no longer a lament. I seemed to hear with what burning he had made it his, with what burning we had yet to make it ours, how we could cease lamenting. Freedom lurked around us and I understood, at last, that he could help us to be free if we would listen, that he would never be free until we did. Yet, there was no battle in his face now. I heard what he had gone through, and would continue to go through until he came to rest in earth. He had made it his: that long line, of which we knew only Mama and Daddy. And he was giving it back, as everything must be given back, so that, passing through death, it can live forever. I saw my mother's face again, and felt, for the first time, how the stones of the road she had walked on must have bruised her feet. I saw the moonlit road where my father's brother died. And it brought something else back to me, and carried me past it. I saw my little girl again and felt Isabel's tears again, and I felt my own tears begin to rise. And I was yet aware that this was only a moment, that the world waited outside as hungry as a tiger, and that trouble stretched above us, longer than the sky.

Then it was over. Creole and Sonny let out their breath, both soaking wet, and grinning. There was a lot of applause and some of it was real. In the dark, the girl came by and I asked her to take drinks to the bandstand. There was a long pause, while they talked up there in the indigo light and after awhile I saw the girl put a Scotch and milk on top of the piano for Sonny. He didn't seem to notice it, but just before they started playing again, he sipped from it and looked toward me and nodded. Then he put it back on top of the piano. For me, then, as they began to play again, it glowed and shook above my brother's head like the very cup of trembling.

1957

T. Coraghessan Boyle
b. 1948

Looking back on his career, Boyle has said that among his recurrent themes are "predetermination versus free will" and "sexual war and sexual truce." The title of this story alludes to section 56 of Alfred, Lord Tennyson's "In Memoriam." The speaker in the poem struggles against his doubts about the existence of God, wondering whether there is a life after death. Nature, who is "red in tooth and claw," whose laws oppose themselves to God's "creed," declares that "spirit" means no more than "the breath." Boyle wrote this story around the same time he was working on his 2004 novel, The Inner Circle, *a fictionalized account of Alfred Kinsey, the pioneering sex researcher.*

Tooth and Claw

The weather had absolutely nothing to do with it—though the rain had been falling off and on throughout the day and the way the gutters were dripping made me feel as if despair were the mildest term in the dictionary—because I would have gone down to Daggett's that afternoon even if the sun were shining and all the fronds of the palm trees were gilded with light. The problem was work. Or, more specifically, the lack of it. The boss had called at 6:30 A.M. to tell me not to come in, because the guy I'd been replacing had recovered sufficiently from his wrenched back to feel up to working, and, no, he wasn't firing me, because they'd be on to a new job next week and he could use all the hands he could get. "So take a couple days off and enjoy yourself," he'd rumbled into the phone in his low, hoarse, uneven voice, which always seemed on the verge of morphing into something else altogether—squawks and bleats or maybe just static. "You're young, right? Go out and get yourself some tail. Get drunk. Go to the library. Help old ladies across the street. You know what I mean?"

It had been a long day: breakfast out of a cardboard box while cartoon images flickered and faded and reconstituted themselves on the TV screen, and then some desultory reading, starting with the newspaper and a couple of *National Geographic*s I'd picked up at a yard sale; lunch at the deli, where I had ham and cheese in a tortilla wrap and exchanged exactly eleven words with the girl behind the counter ("Number seven, please, no mayo." "Have a nice day." "You, too"), and a walk to the beach that left my sneakers sodden. And, after all that, it was still only 3:00 in the afternoon and I had to force myself to stay away from the bar till 5:00, 5:00 at least.

I wasn't stupid. And I had no intention of becoming a drunk like all the hard-assed old men in the shopping mall-blighted town I grew up in, silent men with hate in their eyes and complaint eating away at their insides—like my own dead father, for that matter—but I was new here, or relatively new (nine weeks now and counting), and Daggett's was the only place I felt comfortable. And why? Precisely because it was filled with old men drinking themselves into oblivion. It made me think of home. Or feel at home, anyway.

The irony wasn't lost on me. The whole reason I'd moved out to the Coast to live, first with my aunt Kim and her husband, Waverley, and then in my own one-bedroom apartment with kitchenette and a three-by-six-foot balcony with a partially obscured view of the Pacific, half a mile off, was so that I could inject a little excitement into my life and mingle with all the college students in the bars that lined State Street cheek to jowl, but here I was hanging out in an old man's bar that smelled of death and vomit and felt as closed in as a submarine, when just outside the door were all the exotic, sun-struck glories of California. Where it never rained. Except in winter. And it was winter now.

I nodded self-consciously at the six or seven regulars lined up at the bar, then ordered a Jack-and-Coke, the only drink besides beer that I liked the taste of, and I didn't really like the taste of beer. There were sports on the three TVs hanging from the ceiling—this was a sports bar—but the volume was down and the speakers were blaring the same tired hits of the sixties that I could have heard back home. *Ad nauseam.* When the bartender—*he* was young, at least, as were the waitresses—set down my drink, I made a comment about the weather, "Nice day for sunbathing, isn't it?," and the two regulars nearest me glanced up with something like interest in their eyes. "Or maybe bird watching," I added, feeling encouraged, and they swung their heads back to the familiar triangulation of their splayed elbows and cocktail glasses, and that was the end of that.

It must have been seven or so, the rain still coming down and people briefly enlivened by the novelty of it as they came and went in spasms of umbrella furling and unfurling, when a guy about my age—or, no, he must have been thirty, or close to it—came in and took the seat beside me. He was wearing a baseball cap, a jean jacket, and a T-shirt that said OBLIGATORY DEATH, which I took to be the name of a band, though I'd never heard of it. His hair was blond, cut short around the ears, and he had a soul beard that was like a pale stripe painted under his lip by an unsteady hand. We exchanged the standard greeting—*What's up?*—and then he flagged down the bartender and ordered a draft beer, a shot of tomato juice, and two raw eggs.

"Raw eggs?" the bartender echoed, as if he hadn't heard right.

"Yeah. Two raw eggs, in the shell."

The bartender—his name was Chris, or maybe it was Matt—gave a smile and scratched the back of his head. "We can do them over easy or sunny-side up or poached even, but *raw*, I don't know. I mean, nobody's ever requested raw before—"

"Ask the chef, why don't you?"

The bartender shrugged. "Sure," he said, "no problem." He started off in the direction of the kitchen, then pulled up short. "You want toast with that, home fries, or what?"

"Just the eggs."

Everybody was watching now, any little drama worth the price of admission, especially on a night like this, but the bartender—Chris, his name was definitely Chris—just went down to the other end of the bar and communicated the order to the waitress, who made a notation in her pad and disappeared into the kitchen. A moment went by, and then the man turned to me and said in a voice loud enough for everybody to hear, "Jesus, this music sucks. Are we caught in a time warp here, or what?"

The old men—the regulars—glanced up from their drinks and gave him a look, but they were gray-haired and slack in the belly and they knew their limits.

"Yeah," I heard myself say, "it really sucks," and before I knew it I was talking passionately about the bands that meant the most to me even as the new guy poured tomato juice in his beer and sipped the foam off the top, while the music rumbled defiantly on and people with wet shoes and dripping umbrellas crowded in behind us. The eggs, brown-shelled and naked in the middle of a standard dinner plate, were delivered by Daria, a waitress I'd had my eye on, though I hadn't yet worked up the nerve to say more than hello and good-bye to her. "Your order, sir," she said, easing the plate down on the bar. "You need anything with that? Ketchup? Tabasco?"

"No," he said, "that's fine," and everyone was waiting for him to crack the eggs over his beer, but he didn't even look at them. He was looking at Daria, holding her with his eyes. "So, what's your name?" he asked, grinning.

She told him, and she was grinning, too.

"Nice to meet you," he said, taking her hand. "I'm Ludwig."

"Ludwig," she repeated, pronouncing it with a *v*, as he had, though as far as I could tell—from his clothes and accent, which was pure southern California—he wasn't German. Or if he was, he sure had his English down.

"Are you German?" Daria was flirting with him, and the realization of it began to harden me against him in the most rudimentary way.

"No," he said. "I'm from Hermosa Beach, born and raised. It's the name, right?"

"I had this German teacher last year? His name was Ludwig, that's all."

"You're in college?"

She told him she was, which was news to me. Working her way through. Majoring in business. She wanted to own her own restaurant someday.

"It was my mother's idea," he said, as if he'd been mulling it over. "She was listening to the *Eroica* Symphony the night I was born." He shrugged. "It's been my curse ever since."

"I don't know," she said. "I think it's kind of cute. You don't get many Ludwigs, you know?"

"Yeah, tell me about it," he said, sipping his beer.

She lingered, though there were other things she could have been doing. "So, what about the eggs?" she said. "You going to need utensils, or—"

"Or what? Am I going to suck them out of the shell?"

"Yeah," she said, "something like that."

He reached out a hand cluttered with silver to embrace the eggs and gently roll them back and forth across the gleaming expanse of the plate. "No, I'm just going to fondle them," he said, and got the expected response: she laughed. "But does anybody still play dice around here?" he called down the bar as the eyes of the regulars slid in our direction and then away again.

In those days—and this was ten years ago or more—the game of Horse was popular in certain California bars, as were smoking, unprotected sex, and various other adult pleasures that may or may not have been hazardous to your health. There were five dice, shaken in a cup, and you slammed that cup down on the bar, trying for the highest cumulative score, which was thirty. Anything could be bet on, from the next round of drinks to ponying up for the jukebox.

The rain hissed at the door, and it opened briefly to admit a stamping, umbrella-less couple. Ludwig's question hung unanswered on the air. "No? How about you, Daria?"

"I can't—I'm working."

He turned to me. I had no work in the morning or the next morning, either—maybe no work at all. My apartment wasn't what

I'd thought it would be, not without somebody to share it with, and I'd already vowed to myself that I'd rather sleep on the streets than go back to my aunt's, because going back there would represent the worst kind of defeat. *Take good care of my baby, Kim,* my mother had said when she dropped me off. *He's the only one I've got.*

"Sure," I said. "I guess. What're we playing for—for drinks, right?" I began fumbling in my pockets, awkward—I was drunk, I could feel it. "Because I don't have, well, maybe ten bucks—"

"No," he said, "no," already rising from his seat, "you just wait here, just one minute, you'll see," and then he was out the door and into the grip of the rain.

Daria hadn't moved. She was dressed in the standard outfit for Daggett's employees—shorts, white ankle socks, and a T-shirt with the name of the establishement blazoned across the chest, her legs pale and silken in the flickering light of the fake fireplace in the corner. She gave me a sympathetic look, and I shrugged to show her that I was ready for anything, a real man of the world.

There was a noise at the door—a scraping and shifting—and we all looked up to see Ludwig struggling with something there against the backdrop of the rain. His hat had been knocked askew and water dripped from his nose and chin. It took a moment, one shoulder pinning the door open, and then he lifted a cage—a substantial cage, two and a half feet high and maybe four feet long—through the doorway and set it down against the wall. No one moved. No one said a word. There was something in the cage, the apprehension of it as sharp and sudden as the smell it brought with it, something wild and alien and very definitely out of the ordinary on what to this point had been a painfully ordinary night.

Ludwig wiped the moisture from his face with a swipe of his sleeve, straightened out his hat, and came back to the bar, looking jaunty and refreshed. "All right," he said, "don't be shy—go have a look. It won't bite. Or it will, it definitely will, just don't get your fingers near it, that's all."

I saw coiled limbs, claws, yellow eyes. Whatever it was, the thing hadn't moved, not even to blink. I was going to ask what it was when Daria, still at my side, said, "It's a cat, some kind of wildcat, right? A what—a lynx or something?"

"You can't have that thing in here," one of the regulars said, but already he was getting up out of his seat to have a look at it—everyone was getting up now, shoving back chairs and rising from the tables, crowding around.

"It's a serval," Ludwig was saying. "From Africa. Thirty-five pounds of muscle and quicker than a snake."

And where had he got it? He'd won it, in a bar in Arizona, on a roll of the dice.

How long had he had it? Two years.

What was its name? Cat. Just Cat. And, yes, it was a male, and, no, he didn't want to get rid of it but he was moving overseas on a new job and there was just no way he could take it with him, so he felt that it was apropos—that was the word he used, "apropos"—to give it up in the way he'd got it.

He turned to me. "What was your name again?"

"Junior," I said. "James, Jr., Turner, I mean. James Turner, Jr. But everybody calls me Junior." I wanted to add, "Because of my father, so people wouldn't confuse us," but I left it at that, because it got even more complicated considering that my father was six months dead and I could be anybody I wanted.

"O.K., Junior, here's the deal," Ludwig said. "Your ten bucks against the cat, one roll. What do you say?"

I wanted to say that I had no place for the thing, that I didn't want a cat of any kind or even a guinea pig or a fish in a bowl and that the ten dollars was meaningless, but everyone was watching me and I couldn't back out without feeling the shame rise to my face—and there was Daria to consider, because she was watching me, too. "Yeah," I said. "Yeah, O.K., sure."

Sixty seconds later, I was still solvent and richer by one cat and one cage. I'd got lucky—or unlucky, depending on how you want to look at it—and rolled three fives and two fours; Ludwig rolled a combined eleven. He finished his beer in a gulp, took my hand to seal the deal, and then started toward the door. "But what do I feed it?" I called. "I mean, what does it eat?"

"Eggs," he said. "It loves eggs. And meat. Raw. No kibble, forget kibble. This is the real deal, this animal, and you need to treat it right." He was at the door, looking down at the thing with what might have been wistfulness or satisfaction, I couldn't tell which, then he reached down behind the cage to unfasten something there—a gleam of black leather—and toss it to me: it was a glove, or a gauntlet, actually, as long as my arm. "You'll want to wear this when you feed him," he said, and then he was gone.

For a long moment, I stared at the door, trying to work out what had happened, and then I looked at the regulars—at the expressions on their faces—and at the other customers, locals or maybe even tourists, who'd come in for a beer or a burger or the catch of the day and had all this strangeness thrust on them, and finally at the cage. Daria was bent beside it, cooing to the animal inside, Ludwig's eggs cradled in one hand. She was short and compact, conventionally pretty, with the round eyes and symmetrical features of an anime heroine, her running shoes no bigger than a child's, her blond hair pulled back in a ponytail, and I'd noticed all that before, over the course of weeks of study, but now it came to me with the force of revelation. She was beautiful, a beautiful girl propped on one knee, while her shorts rode up in back and her T-shirt bunched beneath her breasts, offering this cat—my cat—the smallest comfort, as if it were a kitten she'd found abandoned on the street.

"Jesus, what are you going to do with the thing?" Chris had come out from behind the bar and he was standing beside me now, looking awed.

I told him that I didn't know. That I hadn't planned on owning a wildcat, hadn't even known they existed—servals, that is—until five minutes ago.

"You live around here?"

"Bayview Apartments."

"They accept pets?"

I'd never really given it much thought, but they did, they must have—the guy next door to me had a pair of yapping little dogs with bows in their hair, and the woman down the hall had a Doberman that was forever scrabbling its nails on the linoleum when she came in and out with it, which she seemed to do about a hundred times a day. But this was something different. This was something that might push at the parameters of the standard lease. "Yeah," I said, "I think so."

There was a single slot where the door of the cage fastened that was big enough to receive an egg without crushing its shell, and

Daria, still cooing, rolled first one egg, then the other, through the aperture. For a moment, nothing happened. Then the cat, hunched against the mesh, shifted position ever so slightly and took the first egg in its mouth—two teeth like hypodermics, a crunch, and then the soft fricative scrape of its tongue.

Daria rose and came to me with a look of wonder. "Don't do a thing till I get off, O.K.?" she said, and in her fervor she took hold of my arm. "I get off at nine, so you wait, O.K.?"

"Yeah," I said. "Sure."

"We can put him in the back of the storage room for now, and then, well, I guess we can use my pickup."

I didn't have the leisure to reflect on how complex things had become all of a sudden, and even if I had I don't think I would have behaved any differently. I just nodded at her, stared into her plenary eyes, and nodded.

"He's going to be all right," she said, and added, "He will," as if I'd been disagreeing with her. "I've got to get back to work, but you wait, O.K.? You wait right here." Chris was watching. The manager was watching. The regulars had all craned their necks and half the dinner customers, too. Daria patted down her apron, smoothed back her hair. "What did you say your name was again?"

So I had a cat. And a girl. We put the thing in the back of her red Toyota pickup, threw a tarp over it to keep the rain off, and drove to Vons, where I watched Daria march up and down the aisles seeking out kitty litter and the biggest cat pan they had (we settled for a dishpan, hard blue plastic that looked all but indestructible), and then it was on to the meat counter. "I've only got ten bucks," I said.

She gave me a withering look. "This animal's got to eat," she informed me, and she reached back to slip the band from her ponytail so that her hair fell glistening across her shoulders, a storm of hair, fluid and loose, the ends trailing down her back like liquid in motion. She tossed her head impatiently. "You do have a credit card, don't you?"

Ten minutes later, I was directing her back to my building, where she parked next to the Mustang I'd inherited when my father died, and then we went up the outside stairs and along the walkway to my apartment, on the second floor. "I'm sorry," I said, swinging open the door and hitting the light switch, "but I'm afraid I'm not much of a housekeeper." I was going to add that I hadn't expected company, either, or I would have straightened up, but Daria just strode right in, cleared a spot on the counter, and set down the groceries. I watched her shoulders as she reached into the depths of one bag after another and extracted the forty-odd dollars' worth of chicken parts and rib-eye steak (marked down for quick sale) that we'd selected in the meat department.

"O.K.," she said, turning to me as soon as she'd made space in the refrigerator for it all, "now where are we going to put the cat, because I don't think we should leave it out there in the truck any longer than we have to, do you? Cats don't like the rain, I know that—I have two of them. Or one's a kitten, really." She was on the other side of the kitchen counter, a clutter of crusted dishes and glasses sprouting colonies of mold between us. "You have a bedroom, right?"

I did. But if I was embarrassed by the state of the kitchen and living room—this was my first venture at living alone, and the need for order hadn't really seemed paramount to me—then the thought of the bedroom, with its funk of dirty clothes and unwashed sheets, the reeking work boots and the duffel bag out of which I'd been living, gave me pause. Here was this beautiful apparition in my kitchen, the only person besides my aunt who'd ever stepped through the door of my apartment, and now she was about to discover the sad, lonely disorder at the heart of my life. "Yeah," I said. "That door there, to the left of the bathroom." But she was already in the room, pushing things aside, a frown of concentration pressed between her eyes.

"You're going to have to clear this out," she said. "The bed, everything. All your clothes."

I was standing in the doorway, watching her. "What do you mean, 'clear it out'?"

She lifted her face. "You don't think that animal can stay caged up like that, do you? There's hardly room for it to turn around. And that's just cruel." She drilled me with that look again, then put her hands on her hips. "I'll help you," she said. "It shouldn't take ten minutes."

Then it was up the stairs with the cat, the two of us fighting the awkwardness of the cage. We kept the tarp knotted tightly in place, both to keep the rain off the cat and to disguise it from any of my neighbors who might happen by, and, though we shifted the angle of the thing coming up the stairs, the animal didn't make a sound. We had a little trouble getting the cage through the doorway—the cat seemed to concentrate its weight as if in silent protest—but we managed, and then we maneuvered it into the bedroom and set it down in the middle of the rug. Daria had already arranged the litter box in the corner, atop several sheets of newspaper, and she'd taken my biggest stew pot, filled it with water, and placed it just inside the door, where I could get to it easily. "O.K.," she said, glancing up at me with a satisfied look, "it's time for the unveiling," and she bent to unfasten the tarp.

The overhead light glared, the tarp slid from the cage and puddled on the floor, and there was the cat, pressed to the mesh in a compression of limbs, its yellow eyes seizing on us. "Nice kitty," Daria cooed. "Does he want out of that awful cage? Hmm? Does he? And meat—does he want meat?"

So far, I'd gone along with everything in a kind of daze, but this was problematic. Who knew what the thing would do, what its habits were, its needs? "How are we going to—" I began, and left the rest unspoken. The light stung my eyes, and the alcohol whispered in my blood. "You remember what that guy said about feeding him, right?" In the back of my head, there was the smallest glimmer of a further complication: once he was out of the cage, how would we—how would I—ever get him back into it?

For the first time, Daria looked doubtful. "We'll have to be quick," she said.

And so we were. Daria stood at the bedroom door, ready to slam it shut, while I leaned forward, my heart pounding, and slipped the bolt on the cage. I was nimble in those days—twenty-three years old and with excellent reflexes despite the four or five Jack-and-Cokes I'd downed in the course of the evening—and I sprang for the door the instant the bolt was released. Exhilaration burned in me. It burned in the cat, too, because at the first click of the bolt it came to life as if it had been hot-wired. A screech tore through the room, the cage flew open, and the thing was an airborne blur slamming against the cheap plywood panel of the bedroom door, even as Daria and I fought to force it shut.

In the morning (she'd slept on the couch, curled up in the fetal position, faintly snoring; I was stretched out on the mattress we'd removed from the bedroom and tucked against the wall under the TV), I was faced with a number of problems. I'd awakened before her, jolted out of a dreamless sleep by a flash of awareness, and for a long while I just lay there watching her. I could have gone on watching her all morning, thrilled by her presence, her hair, the repose of her face, if it weren't for the cat. It hadn't made a sound, and it didn't stink, not yet, but its existence was communicated to me nonetheless—it was there, and I could feel it. I would have to feed it, and after the previous night's episode, that was going to require some thought and preparation, and I would have to offer Daria something, too, if only to hold her here a little longer. Eggs, I could scramble some eggs, but there was no bread for toast, no milk, no sugar for the coffee. And she would want to freshen up in the bathroom—women always freshened up in the morning, I was pretty sure of that. I thought of the neatly folded little matching towels in the guest bathroom at my aunt's and contrasted that image with the corrugated rag wadded up on the floor somewhere in my own bathroom. Maybe I should go out for bagels or muffins or something, I thought—and a new towel. But did they sell towels at 7-Eleven? I didn't have a clue.

We'd stayed up late, sharing the last of the hot cocoa out of the foil packet and talking in a specific way about the cat that had brought us to that moment on the greasy couch in my semi-darkened living room and then more generally about our own lives and thoughts and hopes and ambitions. I'd heard about her mother, her two sisters, the courses she was taking at the university. Heard about Daggett's, the regulars, the tips—or lack of them. And her restaurant fantasy. It was amazingly detailed, right down to the number of tables she was planning on, the dinnerware, the cutlery, and the paintings on the walls, as well as the décor and the clientele—"Late twenties, early thirties, career people, no kids"—and a dozen or more of the dishes she would specialize in. My ambitions were more modest. I'd told her how I'd finished community college without any particular aim or interest, and how I was working setting tile for a friend of my aunt and uncle; beyond that, I was hoping to maybe travel up the coast and see Oregon. I'd heard a lot about Oregon, I told her. Very clean. Very natural up there. Had she ever been to Oregon? No, but she'd like to go. I remembered telling her that she ought to open her restaurant up there, someplace by the water, where people could look out and take in the view. "Yeah," she'd said, "that'd be cool," and then she'd yawned and dropped her head to the pillow.

I was just getting up to see what I could do about the towel in the bathroom, thinking vaguely of splashing some after-shave on it to fight down any offensive odors it might have picked up, when her eyes flashed open. She didn't say my name or wonder where she was or ask for breakfast or where the bathroom was. She just said, "We have to feed that cat."

"Don't you want coffee or anything—breakfast? I can make breakfast."

She threw back the blanket and I saw that her legs were bare. She was wearing the Daggett's T-shirt over a pair of shiny black panties; her running shoes, socks, and shorts were balled up on the rug beneath her. "Sure," she said. "Coffee sounds nice." And she pushed her fingers through her hair on both sides of her head and then let it all fall forward to obscure her face. She sat there a moment before leaning forward to dig a hair clip out of her purse, arch her back, and pull the hair tight in a ponytail. "But I am worried about the cat, in new surroundings and all. The poor thing—we should have fed him last night."

Perhaps so. And I certainly didn't want to contradict her—I wanted to be amicable and charming, wanted to ingratiate myself in any way I could—but we'd both been so terrified of the animal's power in that moment when we'd released it from the cage that neither of us had felt up to the challenge of attempting to feed it. Attempting to feed it would have meant opening that door again, and that was going to take some thought and commitment. "Yeah," I said. "We should have. And we will, we will, but coffee, coffee first—you want a cup? I can make you a cup?"

So we drank coffee and ate the strawberry Pop-Tarts I found in the cupboard above the sink and made small talk as if we'd awakened together a hundred mornings running, and it was so tranquil and so domestic and so right I never wanted it to end. We were talking about work and about what time she had to be in that afternoon, when her brow furrowed and her eyes sharpened and she said, "I wish I could see it. When we feed it, I mean. Couldn't you, like, cut a peephole in the door or something?"

I was glad for the distraction, damage deposit notwithstanding. And the idea appealed to me: now we could see what the thing—my pet—was up to, and if we could see it, then it wouldn't seem so unapproachable and mysterious. I'd have to get to know it eventually, have to name it and tame it, maybe even walk it on a leash. I had a brief vision of myself sauntering down the sidewalk, this id with claws at my side, turning heads and cowing the weightlifters with their Dobermans and Rottweilers, and then I fished my power drill out from under the sink and cut a neat hole, half an inch in diameter, in the bedroom door. As soon as it was finished, Daria put her eye to it.

"Well?"

"The poor thing. He's pacing back and forth like an animal in a zoo."

She moved to the side and took my arm as I pressed my eye to the hole. The cat flowed like molten ore from one corner of the room to the other, its yellow eyes fixed on the door, the dun, faintly spotted skin stretched like spandex over its seething muscles. I saw that the kitty litter had been upended and the hard blue plastic pan reduced to chewed-over pellets, and wondered about that, about where the thing would do its business if not in the pan. "It turned over the kitty pan," I said.

She was still holding my arm. "I know."

"It chewed it to shreds."

"Metal. We'll have to get a metal one, like a trough or something."

I took my eye from the peephole and turned to her. "But how am I going to change it—don't you have to change it?"

Her eyes were shining. "Oh, it'll settle down. It's just a big kitty, that's all"—and then for the cat, in a syrupy coo—"Isn't that right, kittums?" Next, she went to the refrigerator and extracted one of the steaks, a good pound and a half of meat. "Put on the glove," she said, "and I'll hold onto the doorknob while you feed him."

"What about the blood—won't the blood get on the carpet?"

The gauntlet smelled of saddle soap and it was gouged and pitted down the length of it; it fit me as if it had been custom-made.

"I'll press the blood out with a paper towel—here, look," she said, dabbing at the meat in the bottom of the sink and then lifting it on the end of a fork. I took the fork from her and together we went to the bedroom door.

I don't know if the cat smelled the blood or if it heard us at the door, but the instant I turned the knob it was there. I counted three, then jerked the door back just enough to get my arm and the dangle of meat into the room even as the cat exploded against the doorframe and the meat vanished. We pushed the door to—Daria's face was flushed and she seemed to be giggling or gasping for air—and then we took turns watching the thing drag the steak back and forth across the rug as if it still needed killing. By the time the cat was done, there was blood everywhere, even on the ceiling.

After Daria left for work, I didn't know what to do with myself. The cat was ominously silent and when I pressed my eye to the peephole I saw that it had dragged its cage into the far corner and was slumped behind it, apparently asleep. I flicked on the TV and sat through the usual idiocy, which was briefly enlivened by a nature show on the Serengeti that gave a cursory glimpse of a cat like mine—"The serval lives in rocky kopjes, where it keeps a wary eye on its enemies, the lion and the hyena, feeding principally on small prey, rabbits, birds, even snakes and lizards," the narrator informed me in a hushed voice—and then I went to the sandwich shop and ordered the No. 7 special, no mayo, and took it down to the beach. It was a clear day, all the haze and particulate matter washed out of the air by the previous day's deluge, and I sat there with the sun on my face and watched the waves ride in on top of one another while I ate and considered the altered condition of my life. Daria's face had got serious as she stood at the door, her T-shirt rumpled, her hair pulled back so tightly from her scalp I could make out each individual strand. "Take care of our cat now, O.K.?" she said. "I'll be back as soon as I get off." I shrugged in a helpless, submissive way, the pain of her leaving as acute as anything I'd ever felt. "Sure," I said, and then she reached for my shoulders and pulled me to her for a kiss—on the lips. "You're sweet," she said.

So I was sweet. No one had ever called me sweet before, not since childhood, anyway, and I have to admit the designation thrilled me, bloomed inside me like the promise of things to come. I began to see her as a prime mover in my life, her naked legs stretched out on the couch, the hair falling across her shoulders at the kitchen table, her lips locked on mine. But as I sat there eating my ham-and-cheese wrap a conflicting thought came to me: there had to be someone in her life already, a girl that beautiful, working in a bar, and I was deluding myself to think I had a chance with her. She had to have a boyfriend—she could even be engaged, for all I knew. I tried to focus on the previous night, on her hands and fingers—had she been wearing a ring? And, if she had, then where was the fiancé, the boyfriend, whoever he was? I hated him already, and I didn't even know if he existed.

The upshot of all this was that I found myself in the cool subterranean glow of Daggett's at 3:30 in the afternoon, nursing a Jack-and-Coke like one of the regulars while Daria, the ring finger of her left hand as unencumbered as mine, cleared up after the lunch crowd and set the tables for the dinner rush. Chris came on at 5:00, and he called me by my name and refreshed my drink before he even glanced at the regulars, and for the next hour or so, during the lulls, we conversed about any number of things, beginning with the most obvious—the cat—but veering into sports, music, books, and films, and I found myself expanding into a new place altogether. At one point, Daria stopped by to ask if the cat was settling in—was he still pacing around neurotically or what?—and I could tell her with some assurance that he was asleep. "He's probably nocturnal," I said, "or something like that." And then, with Chris looking on, I couldn't help adding, "You're still coming over, right? After work? To help me feed him, I mean."

She looked to Chris, then let her gaze wander out over the room. "Oh, yeah," she said, "yeah," and there was a catch of hesitation in her voice. "I'll be there."

I let that hang a moment, but I was insecure and the alcohol was having its effect and I couldn't leave it alone. "We can drive over together," I said, "because I didn't bring my car."

She was looking tired by the end of her shift, the bounce gone out of her step, her hair a shade duller under the drab lights, and even as I switched to coffee I noticed Chris slipping her a shot of something down at the end of the bar. I'd had a sandwich around 6:00, and then, so as not to seem overanxious, I'd taken a walk, which brought me into another bar down the street, where I had a Jack-and-Coke and didn't say a word to anyone, and then I'd returned at 8:00 to drink coffee and hold her to her promise.

We didn't say much on the way over to my place. It was only a five-minute drive, and there was a song on that we both liked. Plus, it seemed to me that when you were comfortable with someone you could respect the silences. I'd gone to the cash machine earlier and in a hopeful mood stocked up on breakfast things—eggs, English muffins, a quart each of no-fat and two-percent milk, an expensive Chinese tea that came in individual foil packets—and I'd picked up two bottles of a local Chardonnay that was supposed to be really superior, or at least that was what the guy in the liquor department had told me, as well as a bag of corn chips and a jar of salsa. There were two new bathroom towels hanging on the rack beside the medicine cabinet, and I'd given the whole place a good vacuuming and left the dishes to soak in a sink of scalding water and the last few molecules of dish soap left in the plastic container I'd brought with me from my aunt's. The final touch was a pair of clean sheets and a light blanket folded suggestively over the arm of the couch.

Daria didn't seem to notice—she went straight to the bedroom door and affixed her eye to the peephole. "I can't see anything," she said, leaning into the door, the muscles of her calves flexing as she went up on her toes. "It's too bad we didn't think of a nightlight or something."

I was watching her out of the corner of my eye—admiring her, amazed all over again at her presence—while working the corkscrew in the bottle. I asked her if she'd like a glass of wine. "Chardonnay," I said. "It's a local one, really superior."

"I'd love a glass," she said, turning away from the door and crossing the room to me. I didn't have wineglasses, so we made do with the milky-looking water glasses my aunt had dug out of a box in her basement. "I wonder if you could maybe slip your arm in the door and turn on the light in there," she said. "I'm worried about him. And, plus, we've got to feed him again, right?"

"Sure," I said, "yeah, no problem," but I was in no hurry. I refilled our glasses and broke out the chips and salsa, which she seemed happy enough to see. For a long while, we stood at the kitchen counter, dipping chips and savoring the wine, and then she went to the refrigerator, extracted a slab of meat, and began patting it down with paper towels. I took her cue, donned the gauntlet, braced myself, and jerked the bedroom door open just enough to get my hand in and flick on the light. The cat, which of course had sterling night vision, nearly tore the glove from my arm, and yet the suddenness of the light seemed to confuse it just long enough for me to salvage the situation. The door slammed on a puzzled yowl.

Daria immediately put her eye to the peephole. "Oh my God," she murmured.

"What's he doing?"

"Pacing. But here, you have a look."

The carpeting—every last strip of it—had been torn out of the floor, leaving an expanse of dirty plywood studded with nails, and there seemed to be a hole in the plasterboard just to the left of the window. A substantial hole. Even through the closed door I could smell the reek of cat piss or spray or whatever it was. "There goes my deposit," I said.

She was right there beside me, her hand on my shoulder. "He'll settle down," she assured me, "once he gets used to the place. All cats are like that—they have to establish their territory is all."

"You don't think he can get inside the walls, do you?"

"No," she said, "no way. He's too big."

The only thing I could think to do, especially after an entire day of drinking, was to pour more wine, which I did. Then we repeated the ritual of the morning's feeding—the steak on the fork, the blur of the cat, the savage thump at the door—and took turns watching it eat. After a while, bored with the spectacle—or perhaps *sated* is a better word—we found ourselves on the couch and there was a movie on TV and we finished the wine and the chips and we never stopped talking, a comment on this movie leading to a discussion of movies in general, a reflection on the wine dredging up our mutual experiences of wine tastings and the horrors of Cribari red and Boone's Farm and all the rest. It was midnight before we knew it and she was yawning and stretching.

"I've really got to get home," she said, but she didn't move. "I'm wiped. Just wiped."

"You're welcome to stay over," I said, "I mean, if you don't want to drive, after the wine and all—"

A moment drifted by, neither of us speaking, and then she made a sort of humming noise—"Mmm"—and held out her arms to me even as she sank down into the couch.

I was up before her in the morning, careful not to wake her as I eased myself from the mattress where we'd wound up sleeping because the couch was too narrow for the two of us. My head ached—I wasn't used to so much alcohol—and the effigy of the cat lurked somewhere behind that ache, but I felt buoyant and optimistic. Daria was asleep on the mattress, the cat was hunkered down in his room, and all was right with the world. I brewed coffee, toasted muffins, and fried eggs, and when she woke I was there to feed her. "What do you say to breakfast in bed?" I murmured, easing down beside her with a plate of eggs over easy and a mug of coffee.

I was so intent on watching her eat that I barely touched my own food. After a while, I got up and turned on the radio and there was that song again, the one we'd heard coming home the night before, and we both listened to it all the way through without saying a word. When the DJ came on with his gasping juvenile voice and lame jokes, she got up and went to the bathroom, passing right by the bedroom door without a thought for the cat. She was in the bathroom a long while, running water, flushing, showering, and I felt lost without her. I wanted to tell her that I loved her, wanted to extend a whole list of invitations to her: she could move in with me, stay here indefinitely, bring her cats with her, no problem, and we could both look after the big cat together, see to its needs, tame it, and make it happy in its new home—no more cages, and meat, plenty of meat. I was scrubbing the frying pan when she emerged, her hair wrapped in one of the new towels. She was wearing makeup and she was dressed in her Daggett's outfit. "Hey," I said.

She didn't answer. She was bent over the couch now, stuffing things into her purse.

"You look terrific," I said.

There was a sound from the bedroom then, a low moan that might have been the expiring gasp of the cat's prey, and I wondered if it had found something in there, a rat, a stray bird attracted to the window, an escaped hamster or lizard. "Listen, Junior," she said, ignoring the moaning, which grew higher and more attenuated now, "you're a nice guy, you really are."

I was behind the Formica counter. My hands were in the dishwater. Something pounded in my head, and I knew what was coming, heard it in her voice, saw it in the way she ducked her head and averted her eyes.

"I can't—I have to tell you something, O.K.? Because you're sweet, you are, and I want to be honest with you."

She raised her face to me all of a sudden, let her eyes stab at mine and then dodge away again. "I have a boyfriend. He's away at school. And I don't know why . . . I mean, I just don't want to give you the wrong impression. It was nice. It was."

The moaning cut off abruptly on a rising note. I didn't know what to say—I was new at this, new and useless. Suddenly I was desperate, looking for anything, any strategem, the magic words that would make it all right again. "The cat," I said. "What about the cat?"

Her voice was soft. "He'll be all right. Just feed him. Be nice to him." She was at the door, the purse slung over one shoulder. "Patience," she said, "that's all it takes. A little patience."

"Wait," I said. "Wait."

"I've got to go."

"Will I see you later?"

"No," she said. "No, I don't think so."

As soon as her pickup pulled out of the lot, I called my boss. He answered on the first ring, raising his voice to be heard over the ambient noise. I could hear the tile saw going in the background, the irregular banging of a hammer, the radio tuned to some jittery right-wing propagandist. "I want to come in," I said.

"Who is this?"

"Junior."

"Monday, Monday at the earliest."

I told him I was going crazy cooped up in my apartment, but he didn't seem to hear me. "What is it?" he said. "Money? Because I'll advance you on next week if you really need it, though it'll mean a trip to the bank I wasn't planning on. Which is a pain in the ass. But I'll do it. Just say the word."

"No, it's not the money, it's just—"

He cut me off. "Don't you ever listen to anything I say? Didn't I tell you to go out and get yourself laid? That's what you're supposed to be doing at your age. It's what I'd be doing."

"Can't I just, I don't know, help out?"

"Monday," he said.

I was angry suddenly and I slammed the phone down. My eyes went to the hole cut in the bedroom door and then to the breakfast plates, egg yolk congealing there in bright yellow stripes, the muffin, Daria's muffin, untouched but for a single neat bite cut out of the round. It was Friday. I hated my life. How could I have been so stupid?

There was no sound from the bedroom, and as I laced my sneakers I fought down the urge to go to the peephole and see what the cat had accomplished in the night—I just didn't want to think about it. Whether it had vanished like a bad dream or chewed through the wall and devoured the neighbor's yapping little dogs or broken loose and smuggled itself onto a boat back to Africa, it was all the same to me. The only thing I did know was that there was no way I was going to attempt to feed that thing on my own, not without Daria there. It could starve, for all I cared, starve and rot.

Eventually, I fished a jean jacket out of a pile of clothes on the floor and went down to the beach. The day was overcast and a cold wind out of the east scoured the sand. I must have walked for hours and then, for lack of anything better to do, I went to a movie, after which I had a sandwich at a new place downtown where college students were rumored to hang out. There were no students there as far as I could see, just old men who looked exactly like the regulars at Daggett's, except that they had their square-shouldered old wives with them and their squalling unhappy children. By 4:00 I'd hit my first bar, and by 6:00 I was drunk.

I tried to stay away from Daggett's—*Give her a day or two,* I told myself. *Don't nag, don't be a burden*—but at quarter of 9:00 I found myself at the bar, ordering a Jack-and-Coke from Chris. Chris gave me a look, and everything had changed since yesterday. "You sure?" he said.

I asked him what he meant.

"You look like you've had enough, buddy."

I craned my neck to look for Daria, but all I saw were the regulars, hunched over their drinks. "Just pour," I said.

The music was there like a persistent annoyance, dead music, ancient, appreciated by no one, not even the regulars. It droned on. Chris set down my drink and I lifted it to my lips. "Where's Daria?" I asked.

"She got off early. Said she was tired. Slow night, you know?"

I felt a stab of disappointment, jealousy, hate. "You have a number for her?"

Chris gave me a wary look, as if he knew something I didn't. "You mean she didn't give you her number?"

"No," I said. "We never—well, she was at my house . . ."

"We can't give out personal information."

"To me? I said she was at my house. Last night. I need to talk to her, and it's urgent—about the cat. She's really into the cat, you know?"

"Sorry."

I threw it back at him. "You're sorry? Well, fuck you—I'm sorry, too."

"You know what, buddy—"

"Junior, the name's Junior."

He leaned into the bar, both arms propped before him, and in a very soft voice he said, "I think you'd better leave now."

It had begun to rain again, a soft patter in the leaves that grew steadier and harder as I walked home. Cars went by on the boulevard with the sound of paper tearing, and they dragged whole worlds behind them. The streetlights were dim. There was nobody out. When I came up the hill to my apartment, I saw the Mustang standing there under the carport, and though I'd always been averse to drinking and driving—a lesson I'd learned from my father's hapless example—I got behind the wheel and drove up to the job site with a crystalline clarity that would have scared me in any other state of mind. There was an aluminum ladder there, and I focused on that—the picture of it lying against the building—until I arrived and hauled it out of the mud and tied it to the roof of the car, without a thought for the paint job or anything else.

When I got back, I fumbled in the rain with my overzealous knots until I got the ladder free and then I hauled it around back of the apartment building. I was drunk, yes, but cautious, too—if anyone had seen me, in the dark, propping a ladder against the wall of an apartment building, even my own apartment building, things could have got difficult in a hurry. I couldn't very well claim to be painting, could I? Not at night. Not in the rain. Luckily, though, no one was around. I made my way up the ladder, and when I got to the level of the bedroom the odor hit me, a rank fecal wind sifting out of the dark slit of the window. The cat. The cat was in there, watching me. I was sure of it. I must have waited in the rain for fifteen minutes or more before I got up the nerve to fling the window open, and then I ducked my head and crouched reflexively against the wall. Nothing happened. After a moment, I made my way down the ladder.

I didn't want to go into the apartment, didn't want to think about it, didn't know if a cat that size could climb down the rungs of a ladder or leap twenty feet into the air or unfurl its hidden wings and fly. I stood and watched the dense black hole of the window for a long while and then I went back to the car and sat listening to the radio in the dark until I fell asleep.

In the morning—there were no heraldic rays of sunshine, nothing like that, just more rain—I let myself into the apartment and crept across the room as stealthily as if I'd come to burgle it. When I reached the bedroom door, I put my eye to the peephole and saw a mound of carpet propped up against an empty cage—a den, a makeshift den—and only then did I begin to feel something for the cat, for its bewilderment, its fear and distrust of an alien environment: this was no rocky kopje, this was my bedroom on the second floor of a run-down apartment building in a seaside town a whole continent and a fathomless ocean away from its home. Nothing moved inside. Surely it must have gone by now, one great leap and then the bounding limbs, grass beneath its feet, solid earth. It was gone. Sure it was. I steeled myself, pulled open the door, and slipped inside. And then—and I don't know why—I pulled the door shut behind me.

2003

Raymond Carver
1938–1988

Carver is famous for his minimalist style of prose, which he often described as stripped down to not just the bone but the marrow. His characters are also typically pessimistic and unhappy. But in the context of Carver's life's work, "Cathedral" marks a turn toward a fuller prose style and more congenial (if not entirely happy) characters. Carver himself recognized that "Cathedral" is "more generous and maybe more affirmative" than the "smallness of vision and execution" of his previous work. In one interview he commented on the building of cathedrals to emphasize the collaborative and anonymous character of art.

Cathedral

This blind man, an old friend of my wife's, he was on his way to spend the night. His wife had died. So he was visiting the dead wife's relatives in Connecticut. He called my wife from his in-laws'. Arrangements were made. He would come by train, a five-hour trip, and my wife would meet him at the station. She hadn't seen him since she worked for him one summer in Seattle ten years ago. But she and the blind man had kept in touch. They made tapes and mailed them back and forth. I wasn't enthusiastic about his visit. He was no one I knew. And his being blind bothered me. My idea of blindness came from the movies. In the movies, the blind moved slowly and never laughed. Sometimes they were led by seeing-eye dogs. A blind man in my house was not something I looked forward to.

That summer in Seattle she had needed a job. She didn't have any money. The man she was going to marry at the end of the summer was in officers' training school. He didn't have any money, either. But she was in love with the guy, and he was in love with her, etc. She'd seen something in the paper: HELP WANTED—*Reading to Blind Man,* and a telephone number. She phoned and went over, was hired on the spot. She'd worked with this blind man all summer. She read stuff to him, case studies, reports, that sort of thing. She helped him organize his little office in the county social-service department. They'd become good friends, my wife and the blind man. How do I know these things? She told me. And she told me something else. On her last day in the office, the blind man asked if he could touch her face. She agreed to this. She told me he touched his fingers to every part of her face, her nose—even her neck! She never forgot it. She even tried to write a poem about it. She was always trying to write a poem. She wrote a poem or two every year, usually after something really important had happened to her.

When we first started going out together, she showed me the poem. In the poem, she recalled his fingers and the way they had moved around over her face. In the poem, she talked about what she had felt at the time, about what went through her mind when the blind man touched her nose and lips. I can remember I didn't think much of the poem. Of course, I didn't tell her that. Maybe I just don't understand poetry. I admit it's not the first thing I reach for when I pick up something to read.

Anyway, this man who'd first enjoyed her favors, the officer-to-be, he'd been her childhood sweetheart. So okay. I'm saying that at the end of the summer she let the blind man run his hands over her face, said goodbye to him, married her childhood etc., who was now a commissioned officer, and she moved away from Seattle. But they'd kept in touch, she and the blind man. She made the first contact after a year or so. She called him up one night from an Air Force base in Alabama. She wanted to talk. They talked. He asked her to send him a tape and tell him about her life. She did this. She sent the tape. On the tape, she told the blind man about her husband and about their life together in the military. She told the blind man she loved her husband but she didn't like it where they lived and she didn't like it that he was a part of the military-industrial thing. She told the blind man she'd written a poem about what it was like to be an Air Force officer's wife. The poem wasn't finished yet. She was still writing it. The blind man made a tape. He sent her the tape. She made a tape. This went on for years. My wife's officer was posted to one base and then another. She sent tapes from Moody AFB, McGuire, McConnell, and finally Travis, near Sacramento, where one night she got to feeling lonely and cut off from people she kept losing in that moving-around life. She got to feeling she couldn't go it another step. She went in and swallowed all the pills and capsules in the medicine chest and washed them down with a bottle of gin. Then she got into a hot bath and passed out.

But instead of dying, she got sick. She threw up. Her officer—why should he have a name? he was the childhood sweetheart, and what more does he want?—came home from somewhere, found her, and called the ambulance. In time, she put it all on a tape and sent the tape to the blind man. Over the years, she put all kinds of stuff on tapes and sent the tapes off lickety-split. Next to writing a poem every year, I think it was her chief means of recreation. On one tape, she told the blind man she'd decided to live away from her officer for a time. On another tape, she told him about her divorce. She and I began going out, and of course she told her blind man about it. She told him everything, or so it seemed to me. Once she asked me if I'd like to hear the latest tape from the blind man. This was a year ago. I was on the tape, she said. So I said okay, I'd listen to it. I got us drinks and we settled down in the living room. We made ready to listen. First she inserted the tape into the player and adjusted a couple of dials. Then she pushed a lever. The tape squeaked and someone began to talk in this loud voice. She lowered the volume. After a few minutes of harmless chitchat, I heard my own name in the mouth of this stranger, this blind man I didn't even know! And then this: "From all you've said about him, I can only conclude—" But we were interrupted, a knock at the door, something, and we didn't ever get back to the tape. Maybe it was just as well. I'd heard all I wanted to.

Now this same blind man was coming to sleep in my house.

"Maybe I could take him bowling," I said to my wife. She was at the draining board doing scalloped potatoes. She put down the knife she was using and turned around.

"If you love me," she said, "you can do this for me. If you don't love me, okay. But if you had a friend, any friend, and the friend came to visit, I'd make him feel comfortable." She wiped her hands with the dish towel.

"I don't have any blind friends," I said.

"You don't have *any* friends," she said. "Period. Besides," she said, "goddamn it, his wife's just died! Don't you understand that? The man's lost his wife!"

I didn't answer. She'd told me a little about the blind man's wife.

Her name was Beulah. Beulah! That's a name for a colored woman.

"Was his wife a Negro?" I asked.

"Are you crazy?" my wife said. "Have you just flipped or something?" She picked up a potato. I saw it hit the floor, then roll under the stove. "What's wrong with you?" she said. "Are you drunk?"

"I'm just asking," I said.

Right then my wife filled me in with more detail than I cared to know. I made a drink and sat at the kitchen table to listen. Pieces of the story began to fall into place.

Beulah had gone to work for the blind man the summer after my wife had stopped working for him. Pretty soon Beulah and the blind man had themselves a church wedding. It was a little wedding—who'd want to go to such a wedding in the first place?—just the two of them, plus the minister and the minister's wife. But it was a church wedding just the same. It was what Beulah had wanted, he'd said. But even then Beulah must have been carrying the cancer in her glands. After they had been inseparable for eight years—my wife's word, *inseparable*—Beulah's health went into a rapid decline. She died in a Seattle hospital room, the blind man sitting beside the bed and holding on to her hand. They'd married, lived and worked together, slept together—had sex, sure—and then the blind man had to bury her. All this without his having ever seen what the goddamned woman looked like. It was beyond my understanding. Hearing this, I felt sorry for the blind man for a little bit. And then I found myself thinking what a pitiful life this woman must have led. Imagine a woman who could never see herself as she was seen in the eyes of her loved one. A woman who could go on day after day and never receive the smallest compliment from her beloved. A woman whose husband could never read the expression on her face, be it misery or something better. Someone who could wear makeup or not—what difference to him? She could, if she wanted, wear green eye-shadow around one eye, a straight pin in her nostril, yellow slacks and purple shoes, no matter. And then to slip off into death, the blind man's hand on her hand, his blind eyes streaming tears—I'm imagining now—her last thought maybe this: that he never even knew what she looked like, and she on an express to the grave. Robert was left with a small insurance policy and half of a twenty-peso Mexican coin. The other half of the coin went into the box with her. Pathetic.

So when the time rolled around, my wife went to the depot to pick him up. With nothing to do but wait—sure, I blamed him for that—I was having a drink and watching the TV when I heard the car pull into the drive. I got up from the sofa with my drink and went to the window to have a look.

I saw my wife laughing as she parked the car. I saw her get out of the car and shut the door. She was still wearing a smile. Just amazing. She went around to the other side of the car to where the blind man was already starting to get out. This blind man, feature this, he was wearing a full beard! A beard on a blind man! Too much, I say. The blind man reached into the back seat and dragged out a suitcase. My wife took his arm, shut the car door, and, talking all the way, moved him down the drive and then up the steps to the front porch. I turned off the TV. I finished my drink, rinsed the glass, dried my hands. Then I went to the door.

My wife said, "I want you to meet Robert. Robert, this is my husband. I've told you all about him." She was beaming. She had this blind man by his coat sleeve.

The blind man let go of his suitcase and up came his hand.

I took it. He squeezed hard, held my hand, and then he let it go.

"I feel like we've already met," he boomed.

"Likewise," I said. I didn't know what else to say. Then I said, "Welcome. I've heard a lot about you." We began to move then, a little group, from the porch into the living room, my wife guiding him by the arm. The blind man was carrying his suitcase in his other hand. My wife said things like, "To your left here, Robert. That's right. Now watch it, there's a chair. That's it. Sit down right here. This is the sofa. We just bought this sofa two weeks ago."

I started to say something about the old sofa. I'd liked that old sofa. But I didn't say anything. Then I wanted to say something else, small-talk, about the scenic ride along the Hudson. How going *to* New York, you should sit on the right-hand side of the train, and coming *from* New York, the left-hand side.

"Did you have a good train ride?" I said. "Which side of the train did you sit on, by the way?"

"What a question, which side!" my wife said. "What's it matter which side?" she said.

"I just asked," I said.

"Right side," the blind man said. "I hadn't been on a train in nearly forty years. Not since I was a kid. With my folks. That's been a long time. I'd nearly forgotten the sensation. I have winter in my beard now," he said. "So I've been told, anyway. Do I look distinguished, my dear?" the blind man said to my wife.

"You look distinguished, Robert," she said. "Robert," she said. "Robert, it's just so good to see you."

My wife finally took her eyes off the blind man and looked at me. I had the feeling she didn't like what she saw. I shrugged.

I've never met, or personally known, anyone who was blind. This blind man was late forties, a heavy-set, balding man with stooped shoulders, as if he carried a great weight there. He wore brown slacks, brown shoes, a light-brown shirt, a tie, a sports coat. Spiffy. He also had this full beard. But he didn't use a cane and he didn't wear dark glasses. I'd always thought dark glasses were a must for the blind. Fact was, I wished he had a pair. At first glance, his eyes looked like anyone else's eyes. But if you looked close, there was something different about them. Too much white in the iris, for one thing, and the pupils seemed to move around in the sockets without his knowing it or being able to stop it. Creepy. As I stared at his face, I saw the left pupil turn in toward his nose while the other made an effort to keep in one place. But it was only an effort, for that eye was on the roam without his knowing it or wanting it to be.

I said, "Let me get you a drink. What's your pleasure? We have a little of everything. It's one of our pastimes."

"Bub, I'm a Scotch man myself," he said fast enough in this big voice.

"Right," I said. Bub! "Sure you are. I knew it."

He let his fingers touch his suitcase, which was sitting alongside the sofa. He was taking his bearings. I didn't blame him for that.

"I'll move that up to your room," my wife said.

"No, that's fine," the blind man said loudly. "It can go up when I go up."

"A little water with the Scotch?" I said.

"Very little," he said.

"I knew it," I said.

He said, "Just a tad. The Irish actor, Barry Fitzgerald? I'm like that fellow. When I drink water, Fitzgerald said, I drink water.

When I drink whiskey, I drink whiskey." My wife laughed. The blind man brought his hand up under his beard. He lifted his beard slowly and let it drop.

I did the drinks, three big glasses of Scotch with a splash of water in each. Then we made ourselves comfortable and talked about Robert's travels. First the long flight from the West Coast to Connecticut, we covered that. Then from Connecticut up here by train. We had another drink concerning that leg of the trip.

I remembered having read somewhere that the blind didn't smoke because, as speculation had it, they couldn't see the smoke they exhaled. I thought I knew that much and that much only about blind people. But this blind man smoked his cigarette down to the nubbin and then lit another one. This blind man filled his ashtray and my wife emptied it.

When we sat down at the table for dinner, we had another drink. My wife heaped Robert's plate with cube steak, scalloped potatoes, green beans. I buttered him up two slices of bread. I said, "Here's bread and butter for you." I swallowed some of my drink. "Now let us pray," I said, and the blind man lowered his head. My wife looked at me, her mouth agape. "Pray the phone won't ring and the food doesn't get cold," I said.

We dug in. We ate everything there was to eat on the table. We ate like there was no tomorrow. We didn't talk. We ate. We scarfed. We grazed that table. We were into serious eating. The blind man had right away located his foods, he knew just where everything was on his plate. I watched with admiration as he used his knife and fork on the meat. He'd cut two pieces of meat, fork the meat into his mouth, and then go all out for the scalloped potatoes, the beans next, and then he'd tear off a hunk of buttered bread and eat that. He'd follow this up with a big drink of milk. It didn't seem to bother him to use his fingers once in a while, either.

We finished everything, including half a strawberry pie. For a few moments, we sat as if stunned. Sweat beaded on our faces. Finally, we got up from the table and left the dirty plates. We didn't look back. We took ourselves into the living room and sank into our places again. Robert and my wife sat on the sofa. I took the big chair. We had us two or three more drinks while they talked about the major things that had come to pass for them in the past ten years. For the most part, I just listened. Now and then I joined in. I didn't want him to think I'd left the room, and I didn't want her to think I was feeling left out. They talked of things that had happened to them—to them!—these past ten years. I waited in vain to hear my name on my wife's sweet lips: "And then my dear husband came into my life"—something like that. But I heard nothing of the sort. More talk of Robert. Robert had done a little of everything, it seemed, a regular blind jack-of-all-trades. But most recently he and his wife had had an Amway distributorship, from which, I gathered, they'd earned their living, such as it was. The blind man was also a ham radio operator. He talked in his loud voice about conversations he'd had with fellow operators in Guam, in the Philippines, in Alaska, and even in Tahiti. He said he'd have a lot of friends there if he ever wanted to go visit those places. From time to time, he'd turn his blind face toward me, put his hand under his beard, ask me something. How long had I been in my present position? (Three years.) Did I like my work? (I didn't.) Was I going to stay with it? (What were the options?) Finally, when I thought he was beginning to run down, I got up and turned on the TV.

My wife looked at me with irritation. She was heading toward a boil. Then she looked at the blind man and said, "Robert, do you have a TV?"

The blind man said, "My dear, I have two TVs. I have a color set and a black-and-white thing, an old relic. It's funny, but if I turn the TV on, and I'm always turning it on, I turn on the color set. It's funny, don't you think?"

I didn't know what to say to that. I had absolutely nothing to say to that. No opinion. So I watched the news program and tried to listen to what the announcer was saying.

"This is a color TV," the blind man said. "Don't ask me how, but I can tell."

"We traded up a while ago," I said.

The blind man had another taste of his drink. He lifted his beard, sniffed it, and let it fall. He leaned forward on the sofa. He positioned his ashtray on the coffee table, then put the lighter to his cigarette. He leaned back on the sofa and crossed his legs at the ankles.

My wife covered her mouth, and then she yawned. She stretched. She said, "I think I'll go upstairs and put on my robe. I think I'll change into something else. Robert, you make yourself comfortable," she said.

"I'm comfortable," the blind man said.

"I want you to feel comfortable in this house," she said.

"I am comfortable," the blind man said.

After she'd left the room, he and I listened to the weather report and then to the sports roundup. By that time, she'd been gone so long I didn't know if she was going to come back. I thought she might have gone to bed. I wished she'd come back downstairs. I didn't want to be left alone with a blind man. I asked him if he wanted to smoke some dope with me. I said I'd just rolled a number. I hadn't, but I planned to do so in about two shakes.

"I'll try some with you," he said.

"Damn right," I said. "That's the stuff."

I got our drinks and sat down on the sofa with him. Then I rolled us two fat numbers. I lit one and passed it. I brought it to his fingers. He took it and inhaled.

"Hold it as long as you can," I said. I could tell he didn't know the first thing.

My wife came back downstairs wearing her pink robe and her pink slippers.

"What do I smell?" she said.

"We thought we'd have us some cannabis," I said.

My wife gave me a savage look. Then she looked at the blind man and said, "Robert, I didn't know you smoked."

He said, "I do now, my dear. There's a first time for everything. But I don't feel anything yet."

"This stuff is pretty mellow," I said. "This stuff is mild. It's dope you can reason with," I said. "It doesn't mess you up."

"Not much it doesn't, bub," he said, and laughed.

My wife sat on the sofa between the blind man and me. I passed her the number. She took it and toked and then passed it back to me. "Which way is this going?" she said. Then she said, "I shouldn't be smoking this. I can hardly keep my eyes open as it is. That dinner did me in. I shouldn't have eaten so much."

"It was the strawberry pie," the blind man said. "That's what did it," he said, and he laughed his big laugh. Then he shook his head.

"There's more strawberry pie," I said.

"Do you want some more, Robert?" my wife said.

"Maybe in a little while," he said.

We gave our attention to the TV. My wife yawned again. She said, "Your bed is made up when you feel like going to bed, Robert. I know you must have had a long day. When you're ready to go to bed, say so." She pulled his arm. "Robert?"

He came to and said, "I've had a real nice time. This beats tapes, doesn't it?"

I said, "Coming at you," and I put the number between his fingers. He inhaled, held the smoke, and then let it go. It was like he'd been doing it since he was nine years old.

"Thanks, bub," he said. "But I think this is all for me. I think I'm beginning to feel it," he said. He held the burning roach out for my wife.

"Same here," she said. "Ditto. Me, too." She took the roach and passed it to me. "I may just sit here for a while between you two guys with my eyes closed. But don't let me bother you, okay? Either one of you. If it bothers you, say so. Otherwise, I may just sit here with my eyes closed until you're ready to go to bed," she said. "Your bed's made up, Robert, when you're ready. It's right next to our room at the top of the stairs. We'll show you up when you're ready. You wake me up now, you guys, if I fall asleep." She said that and then she closed her eyes and went to sleep.

The news program ended. I got up and changed the channel. I sat back down on the sofa. I wished my wife hadn't pooped out. Her head lay across the back of the sofa, her mouth open. She'd turned so that her robe had slipped away from her legs, exposing a juicy thigh. I reached to draw her robe back over her, and it was then that I glanced at the blind man. What the hell! I flipped the robe open again.

"You say when you want some strawberry pie," I said.

"I will," he said.

I said, "Are you tired? Do you want me to take you up to your bed? Are you ready to hit the hay?"

"Not yet," he said. "No, I'll stay up with you, bub. If that's all right. I'll stay up until you're ready to turn in. We haven't had a chance to talk. Know what I mean? I feel like me and her monopolized the evening." He lifted his beard and he let it fall. He picked up his cigarettes and lighter.

"That's all right," I said. Then I said, "I'm glad for the company."

And I guess I was. Every night I smoked dope and stayed up as long as I could before I fell asleep. My wife and I hardly ever went to bed at the same time. When I did go to sleep, I had these dreams. Sometimes I'd wake up from one of them, my heart going crazy.

Something about the church and the Middle Ages was on the TV. Not your run-of-the-mill TV fare. I wanted to watch something else. I turned to the other channels. But there was nothing on them, either. So I turned back to the first channel and apologized.

"Bub, it's all right," the blind man said. "It's fine with me. Whatever you want to watch is okay. I'm always learning something. Learning never ends. It won't hurt me to learn something tonight. I got ears," he said.

We didn't say anything for a time. He was leaning forward with his head turned at me, his right ear aimed in the direction of the set. Very disconcerting. Now and then his eyelids dropped and then they snapped open again. Now and then he put his fingers into his beard and tugged, like he was thinking about something he was hearing on the television.

On the screen, a group of men wearing cowls was being set upon and tormented by men dressed in skeleton costumes and men dressed as devils. The men dressed as devils wore devil masks, horns, and long tails. This pageant was part of a procession. The Englishman who was narrating the thing said it took place in Spain once a year. I tried to explain to the blind man what was happening.

"Skeletons," he said. "I know about skeletons," he said, and he nodded.

The TV showed this one cathedral. Then there was a long, slow look at another one. Finally, the picture switched to the famous one in Paris,[1] with its flying buttresses and its spires reaching up to the clouds. The camera pulled away to show the whole of the cathedral rising above the skyline.

1. Notre Dame.

There were times when the Englishman who was telling the thing would shut up, would simply let the camera move around over the cathedrals. Or else the camera would tour the countryside, men in fields walking behind oxen. I waited as long as I could. Then I felt I had to say something. I said, "They're showing the outside of this cathedral now. Gargoyles. Little statues carved to look like monsters. Now I guess they're in Italy. Yeah, they're in Italy. There's paintings on the walls of this one church."

"Are those fresco paintings, bub?" he asked, and he sipped from his drink.

I reached for my glass. But it was empty. I tried to remember what I could remember. "You're asking me are those frescoes?" I said. "That's a good question. I don't know."

The camera moved to a cathedral outside Lisbon. The differences in the Portuguese cathedral compared with the French and Italian were not that great. But they were there. Mostly the interior stuff. Then something occurred to me, and I said, "Something has occurred to me. Do you have any idea what a cathedral is? What they look like, that is? Do you follow me? If somebody says cathedral to you, do you have any notion what they're talking about? Do you know the difference between that and a Baptist church, say?"

He let the smoke dribble from his mouth. "I know they took hundreds of workers fifty or a hundred years to build," he said. "I just heard the man say that, of course. I know generations of the same families worked on a cathedral. I heard him say that, too. The men who began their life's work on them, they never lived to see the completion of their work. In that wise, bub, they're no different from the rest of us, right?" He laughed. Then his eyelids drooped again. His head nodded. He seemed to be snoozing. Maybe he was imagining himself in Portugal. The TV was showing another cathedral now. This one was in Germany. The Englishman's voice droned on. "Cathedrals," the blind man said. He sat up and rolled his head back and forth. "If you want the truth, bub, that's about all I know. What I just said. What I heard him say. But maybe you could describe one to me? I wish you'd do it. I'd like that. If you want to know, I really don't have a good idea."

I stared hard at the shot of the cathedral on the TV. How could I even begin to describe it? But say my life depended on it. Say my life was being threatened by an insane guy who said I had to do it or else.

I stared some more at the cathedral before the picture flipped off into the countryside. There was no use. I turned to the blind man and said, "To begin with, they're very tall." I was looking around the room for clues. "They reach way up. Up and up. Toward the sky. They're so big, some of them, they have to have these supports. To help hold them up, so to speak. These supports are called buttresses. They remind me of viaducts, for some reason. But maybe you don't know viaducts, either? Sometimes the cathedrals have devils and such carved into the front. Sometimes lords and ladies. Don't ask me why this is," I said.

He was nodding. The whole upper part of his body seemed to be moving back and forth.

"I'm not doing so good, am I?" I said.

He stopped nodding and leaned forward on the edge of the sofa. As he listened to me, he was running his fingers through his beard. I wasn't getting through to him, I could see that. But he waited for me to go on just the same. He nodded, like he was trying to encourage me. I tried to think what else to say. "They're really big," I said. "They're massive. They're built of stone. Marble, too, sometimes. In those olden days, when they built cathedrals, men wanted to be close to God. In those olden days, God was an important part of everyone's life. You could tell this from their cathedral-building. I'm sorry," I said, "but it looks like that's the best I can do for you. I'm just no good at it."

"That's all right, bub," the blind man said. "Hey, listen. I hope you don't mind my asking you. Can I ask you something? Let me ask you a simple question, yes or no. I'm just curious and there's no offense. You're my host. But let me ask if you are in any way religious? You don't mind my asking?"

I shook my head. He couldn't see that, though. A wink is the same as a nod to a blind man. "I guess I don't believe in it. In anything. Sometimes it's hard. You know what I'm saying?"

"Sure, I do," he said.

"Right," I said.

The Englishman was still holding forth. My wife sighed in her sleep. She drew a long breath and went on with her sleeping.

"You'll have to forgive me," I said. "But I can't tell you what a cathedral looks like. It just isn't in me to do it. I can't do any more than I've done."

The blind man sat very still, his head down as he listened to me.

I said, "The truth is, cathedrals don't mean anything special to me. Nothing. Cathedrals. They're something to look at on late-night TV. That's all they are."

It was then that the blind man cleared his throat. He brought something up. He took a handkerchief from his back pocket. Then he said, "I get it, bub. It's okay. It happens. Don't worry about it," he said. "Hey, listen to me. Will you do me a favor? I got an idea. Why don't you find us some heavy paper? And a pen. We'll do something. We'll draw one together. Get us a pen and some heavy paper. Go on, bub, get the stuff," he said.

So I went upstairs. My legs felt like they didn't have any strength in them. They felt like they did after I'd done some running. In my wife's room, I looked around. I found some ballpoints in a little basket on her table. And then I tried to think where to look for the kind of paper he was talking about.

Downstairs, in the kitchen, I found a shopping bag with onion skins at the bottom of the bag. I emptied the bag and shook it. I brought it into the living room and sat down with it near his legs. I moved some things, smoothed the wrinkles from the bag, spread it out on the coffee table.

The blind man got down from the sofa and sat next to me on the carpet.

He ran his fingers over the paper. He went up and down the sides of the paper. The edges, even the edges. He fingered the corners.

"All right," he said. "All right, let's do her."

He found my hand, the hand with the pen. He closed his hand over my hand. "Go ahead, bub, draw," he said. "Draw. You'll see. I'll follow along with you. It'll be okay. Just begin now like I'm telling you. You'll see. Draw," the blind man said.

So I began. First I drew a box that looked like a house. It could have been the house I lived in. Then I put a roof on it. At either end of the roof, I drew spires. Crazy.

"Swell," he said. "Terrific. You're doing fine," he said. "Never thought anything like this could happen in your lifetime, did you, bub? Well, it's a strange life, we all know that. Go on now. Keep it up."

I put in windows with arches. I drew flying buttresses. I hung great doors. I couldn't stop. The TV station went off the air. I put down the pen and closed and opened my fingers. The blind man felt around over the paper. He moved the tips of his fingers over the paper, all over what I had drawn, and he nodded.

"Doing fine," the blind man said.

I took up the pen again, and he found my hand. I kept at it. I'm no artist. But I kept drawing just the same.

My wife opened up her eyes and gazed at us. She sat up on the sofa, her robe hanging open. She said, "What are you doing? Tell me, I want to know."

I didn't answer her.

The blind man said, "We're drawing a cathedral. Me and him are working on it. Press hard," he said to me. "That's right. That's good," he said. "Sure. You got it, bub. I can tell. You didn't think you could. But you can, can't you? You're cooking with gas now. You know what I'm saying? We're going to really have us something here in a minute. How's the old arm?" he said. "Put some people in there now. What's a cathedral without people?"

My wife said, "What's going on? Robert, what are you doing? What's going on?"

"It's all right," he said to her. "Close your eyes now," the blind man said to me.

I did it. I closed them just like he said.

"Are they closed?" he said. "Don't fudge."

"They're closed," I said.

"Keep them that way," he said. He said, "Don't stop now. Draw."

So we kept on with it. His fingers rode my fingers as my hand went over the paper. It was like nothing else in my life up to now.

Then he said, "I think that's it. I think you got it," he said. "Take a look. What do you think?"

But I had my eyes closed. I thought I'd keep them that way for a little longer. I thought it was something I ought to do.

"Well?" he said. "Are you looking?"

My eyes were still closed. I was in my house. I knew that. But I didn't feel like I was inside anything.

"It's really something," I said.

1981

John Cheever
1912–1982

Many of Cheever's stories deal with American suburbia's promise of heaven on earth, and quite a few use the strange mix of realism and fantasy that we find in "The Swimmer." Cheever wrote this story for The New Yorker, *so we might think of his primary audience as that magazine's upper-middle-class clientele, in New York but also throughout the country. Many readers have struggled to figure out exactly what* happens *in this story. Cheever himself was a bit disdainful whenever he was asked about "The Swimmer." Tongue in cheek, he suggested that Neddy was a latter-day Narcissus pursuing the reflection of his own face and pursuing death. Cheever also pointed out how the story was popular in communist Russia, presumably for its portrayal of capitalists. The incongruous details, Cheever insisted, "ought to be taken at face value."*

The Swimmer

It was one of those midsummer Sundays when everyone sits around saying, "I *drank* too much last night." You might have heard it whispered by the parishioners leaving church, heard it from the lips of the priest himself, struggling with his cassock in the *vestiarium*,[1] heard it from the golf links and the tennis courts, heard it from the wildlife preserve where the leader of the Audubon group was suffering from a terrible hangover. "I *drank* too much," said Donald Westerhazy. "We all *drank* too much," said Lucinda Merrill. "It must have been the wine," said Helen Westerhazy. "I *drank* too much of that claret."

This was at the edge of the Westerhazys' pool. The pool, fed by an artesian well with a high iron content, was a pale shade of green. It was a fine day. In the west there was a massive stand of cumulus cloud so like a city seen from a distance—from the bow of an approaching ship—that it might have had a name. Lisbon. Hackensack. The sun was hot. Neddy Merrill sat by the green water, one hand in it, one around a glass of gin. He was a slender man—he

1. Vestry, a room attached to the church where the clergy put on their vestments.

seemed to have the especial slenderness of youth—and while he was far from young he had slid down his banister that morning and given the bronze backside of Aphrodite on the hall table a smack, as he jogged toward the smell of coffee in his dining room. He might have been compared to a summer's day, particularly the last hours of one, and while he lacked a tennis racket or a sail bag the impression was definitely one of youth, sport, and clement weather. He had been swimming and now he was breathing deeply, stertorously as if he could gulp into his lungs the components of that moment, the heat of the sun, the intenseness of his pleasure. It all seemed to flow into his chest. His own house stood in Bullet Park, eight miles to the south, where his four beautiful daughters would have had their lunch and might be playing tennis. Then it occurred to him that by taking a dogleg to the southwest he could reach his home by water.

His life was not confining and the delight he took in this observation could not be explained by its suggestion of escape. He seemed to see, with a cartographer's eye, that string of swimming pools, that quasi-subterranean stream that curved across the county. He had made a discovery, a contribution to modern geography; he would name the stream Lucinda after his wife. He was not a practical joker nor was he a fool but he was determinedly original and had a vague and modest idea of himself as a legendary figure. The day was beautiful and it seemed to him that a long swim might enlarge and celebrate its beauty.

He took off a sweater that was hung over his shoulders and dove in. He had an inexplicable contempt for men who did not hurl themselves into pools. He swam a choppy crawl, breathing either with every stroke or every fourth stroke and counting somewhere well in the back of his mind the one-two one-two of a flutter kick. It was not a serviceable stroke for long distances but the domestication of swimming had saddled the sport with some customs and in his part of the world a crawl was customary. To be embraced and sustained by the light green water was less a pleasure, it seemed, than the resumption of a natural condition, and he would have liked to swim without trunks, but this was not possible, considering his project. He hoisted himself up on the far curb—he never used the ladder—and started across the lawn. When Lucinda asked where he was going he said he was going to swim home.

The only maps and charts he had to go by were remembered or imaginary but these were clear enough. First there were the Grahams, the Hammers, the Lears, the Howlands, and the Crosscups. He would cross Ditmar Street to the Bunkers and come, after a short portage, to the Levys, the Welchers, and the public pool in Lancaster. Then there were the Hallorans, the Sachses, the Biswangers, Shirley Adams, the Gilmartins, and the Clydes. The day was lovely, and that he lived in a world so generously supplied with water seemed like a clemency, a beneficence. His heart was high and he ran across the grass. Making his way home by an uncommon route gave him the feeling that he was a pilgrim, an explorer, a man with a destiny, and he knew that he would find friends all along the way; friends would line the banks of the Lucinda River.

He went through a hedge that separated the Westerhazys' land from the Grahams', walked under some flowering apple trees, passed the shed that housed their pump and filter, and came out at the Grahams' pool. "Why, Neddy," Mrs. Graham said, "what a marvelous surprise. I've been trying to get you on the phone all morning. Here, let me get you a drink." He saw then, like any explorer, that the hospitable customs and traditions of the natives would have to be handled with diplomacy if he was ever going to reach his destination. He did not want to mystify or seem rude to the Grahams nor did he have the time to linger there. He swam the length of their pool and joined them in the sun and was rescued, a few minutes later, by the arrival of two carloads of friends from Connecticut. During the uproarious reunions he was able to slip away. He went down by the front of the Grahams' house, stepped over a thorny hedge, and crossed a vacant lot to the Hammers'. Mrs. Hammer, looking up from her roses, saw him swim by although she wasn't quite sure who it was. The Lears heard him splashing past the open windows of their living room. The Howlands and the Crosscups were away. After leaving the Howlands' he crossed Ditmar Street and started for the Bunkers', where he could hear, even at that distance, the noise of a party.

The water refracted the sound of voices and laughter and seemed to suspend it in midair. The Bunkers' pool was on a rise and he climbed some stairs to a terrace where twenty-five or thirty men and women were drinking. The only person in the water was Rusty

Towers, who floated there on a rubber raft. Oh, how bonny and lush were the banks of the Lucinda River! Prosperous men and women gathered by the sapphire-colored waters while caterer's men in white coats passed them cold gin. Overhead a red de Haviland trainer was circling around and around and around in the sky with something like the glee of a child in a swing. Ned felt a passing affection for the scene, a tenderness for the gathering, as if it was something he might touch. In the distance he heard thunder. As soon as Enid Bunker saw him she began to scream: "Oh, look who's here! What a marvelous surprise! When Lucinda said that you couldn't come I thought I'd *die*." She made her way to him through the crowd, and when they had finished kissing she led him to the bar, a progress that was slowed by the fact that he stopped to kiss eight or ten other women and shake the hands of as many men. A smiling bartender he had seen at a hundred parties gave him a gin and tonic and he stood by the bar for a moment, anxious not to get stuck in any conversation that would delay his voyage. When he seemed about to be surrounded he dove in and swam close to the side to avoid colliding with Rusty's raft. At the far end of the pool he bypassed the Tomlinsons with a broad smile and jogged up the garden path. The gravel cut his feet but this was the only unpleasantness. The party was confined to the pool, and as he went toward the house he heard the brilliant, watery sound of voices fade, heard the noise of a radio from the Bunkers' kitchen, where someone was listening to a ball game. Sunday afternoon. He made his way through the parked cars and down the grassy border of their driveway to Alewives Lane. He did not want to be seen on the road in his bathing trunks but there was no traffic and he made the short distance to the Levys' driveway, marked with a PRIVATE PROPERTY sign and a green tube for *The New York Times*. All the doors and windows of the big house were open but there were no signs of life; not even a dog barked. He went around the side of the house to the pool and saw that the Levys had only recently left. Glasses and bottles and dishes of nuts were on a table at the deep end, where there was a bathhouse or gazebo, hung with Japanese lanterns. After swimming the pool he got himself a glass and poured a drink. It was his fourth or fifth drink and he had swum nearly half the length of the Lucinda River. He felt tired, clean, and pleased at that moment to be alone; pleased with everything.

It would storm. The stand of cumulus cloud—that city—had risen and darkened, and while he sat there he heard the percussiveness of thunder again. The de Haviland trainer was still circling overhead and it seemed to Ned that he could almost hear the pilot laugh with pleasure in the afternoon; but when there was another peal of thunder he took off for home. A train whistle blew and he wondered what time it had gotten to be. Four? Five? He thought of the provincial station at that hour, where a waiter, his tuxedo concealed by a raincoat, a dwarf with some flowers wrapped in newspaper, and a woman who had been crying would be waiting for the local. It was suddenly growing dark; it was that moment when the pinheaded birds seemed to organize their song into some acute and knowledgeable recognition of the storm's approach. Then there was a fine noise of rushing water from the crown of an oak at his back, as if a spigot there had been turned. Then the noise of fountains came from the crowns of all the tall trees. Why did he love storms, what was the meaning of his excitement when the door sprang open and the rain wind fled rudely up the stairs, why had the simple task of shutting the windows of an old house seemed fitting and urgent, why did the first watery notes of a storm wind have for him the unmistakable sound of good news, cheer, glad tidings? Then there was an explosion, a smell of cordite, and rain lashed the Japanese lanterns that Mrs. Levy had bought in Kyoto the year before last, or was it the year before that?

He stayed in the Levys' gazebo until the storm had passed. The rain had cooled the air and he shivered. The force of the wind had stripped a maple of its red and yellow leaves and scattered them over the grass and the water. Since it was midsummer the tree must be blighted, and yet he felt a peculiar sadness at this sign of autumn. He braced his shoulders, emptied his glass, and started for the Welchers' pool. This meant crossing the Lindleys' riding ring and he was surprised to find it overgrown with grass and all the jumps dismantled. He wondered if the Lindleys had sold their horses or gone away for the summer and put them out to board. He seemed to remember having heard something about the Lindleys and their horses but the memory was unclear. On he went, barefoot through the wet grass, to the Welchers', where he found their pool was dry.

This breach in his chain of water disappointed him absurdly, and he felt like some explorer who seeks a torrential headwater and finds a dead stream. He was disappointed and mystified. It was common enough to go away for the summer but no one ever drained his pool. The Welchers had definitely gone away. The pool furniture was folded, stacked, and covered with a tarpaulin. The bathhouse was locked. All the windows of the house were shut, and when he went around to the driveway, in front he saw a FOR SALE sign nailed to a tree. When had he last heard from the Welchers—when, that is, had he and Lucinda last regretted an invitation to dine with them? It seemed only a week or so ago. Was his memory failing or had he so disciplined it in the repression of unpleasant facts that he had damaged his sense of the truth? Then in the distance he heard the sound of a tennis game. This cheered him, cleared away all his apprehensions and let him regard the overcast sky and the cold air with indifference. This was the day that Neddy Merrill swam across the county. That was the day! He started off then for his most difficult portage.

Had you gone for a Sunday afternoon ride that day you might have seen him, close to naked, standing on the shoulders of Route 424, waiting for a chance to cross. You might have wondered if he was the victim of foul play, had his car broken down, or was he merely a fool. Standing barefoot in the deposits of the highway—beer cans, rags, and blowout patches—exposed to all kinds of ridicule, he seemed pitiful. He had known when he started that this was a part of his journey—it had been on his maps—but confronted with the lines of traffic, worming through the summery light, he found himself unprepared. He was laughed at, jeered at, a beer can was thrown at him, and he had no dignity or humor to bring to the situation. He could have gone back, back to the Westerhazys', where Lucinda would still be sitting in the sun. He had signed nothing, vowed nothing, pledged nothing, not even to himself. Why, believing as he did, that all human obduracy was susceptible to common sense, was he unable to turn back? Why was he determined to complete his journey even if it meant putting his life in danger? At what point had this prank, this joke, this piece of horseplay become serious? He could not go back, he could not even recall with any clearness the green water at the Westerhazys', the sense of inhaling the day's components, the friendly and relaxed voices saying that they had *drunk* too much. In the space of an hour, more or less, he had covered a distance that made his return impossible.

An old man, tooling down the highway at fifteen miles an hour, let him get to the middle of the road, where there was a grass divider. Here he was exposed to the ridicule of the northbound traffic, but after ten or fifteen minutes he was able to cross. From here he had only a short walk to the Recreation Center at the edge of the village of Lancaster, where there were some handball courts and a public pool.

The effect of the water on voices, the illusion of brilliance and suspense, was the same here as it had been at the Bunkers' but the sounds here were louder, harsher, and more shrill, and as soon as he entered the crowded enclosure he was confronted with regimentation. "ALL SWIMMERS MUST TAKE A SHOWER BEFORE USING THE POOL. ALL SWIMMERS MUST USE THE FOOTBATH. ALL SWIMMERS MUST WEAR THEIR IDENTIFICATION DISKS." He took a shower, washed his feet in a cloudy and bitter solution, and made his way to the edge of the water. It stank of chlorine and looked to him like a sink. A pair of lifeguards in a pair of towers blew police whistles at what seemed to be regular intervals and abused the swimmers through a public address system. Neddy remembered the sapphire water at the Bunkers' with longing and thought that he might contaminate himself—damage his own prosperousness and charm—by swimming in this murk, but he reminded himself that he was an explorer, a pilgrim, and that this was merely a stagnant bend in the Lucinda River. He dove, scowling with distaste, into the chlorine and had to swim with his head above water to avoid collisions, but even so he was bumped into, splashed, and jostled. When he got to the shallow end both lifeguards were shouting at him: "Hey, you, you without the identification disk, get outa the water." He did, but they had no way of pursuing him and he went through the reek of suntan oil and chlorine out through the hurricane fence and passed the handball courts. By crossing the road he entered the wooded part of the Halloran estate. The woods were not cleared and the footing was treacherous and difficult until he reached the lawn and the clipped beech hedge that encircled their pool.

The Hallorans were friends, an elderly couple of enormous wealth who seemed to bask in the suspicion that they might be Communists. They were zealous reformers but they were not Communists, and yet when they were accused, as they sometimes were, of subversion, it seemed to gratify and excite them. Their beech hedge was yellow and he guessed this had been blighted like the Levys' maple. He called hullo, hullo, to warn the Hallorans of his approach, to palliate his invasion of their privacy. The Hallorans, for reasons that had never been explained to him, did not wear bathing suits. No explanations were in order, really. Their nakedness was a detail in their uncompromising zeal for reform and he stepped politely out of his trunks before he went through the opening in the hedge.

Mrs. Halloran, a stout woman with white hair and a serene face, was reading the *Times*. Mr. Halloran was taking beech leaves out of the water with a scoop. They seemed not surprised or displeased to see him. Their pool was perhaps the oldest in the country, a fieldstone rectangle, fed by a brook. It had no filter or pump and its waters were the opaque gold of the stream.

"I'm swimming across the county," Ned said.

"Why, I didn't know one could," exclaimed Mrs. Halloran.

"Well, I've made it from the Westerhazys'," Ned said. "That must be about four miles."

He left his trunks at the deep end, walked to the shallow end, and swam this stretch. As he was pulling himself out of the water he heard Mrs. Halloran say, "We've been *terribly* sorry to hear about all your misfortunes, Neddy."

"My misfortunes?" Ned asked. "I don't know what you mean."

"Why, we heard that you'd sold the house and that your poor children . . ."

"I don't recall having sold the house," Ned said, "and the girls are at home."

"Yes," Mrs. Halloran sighed. "Yes . . ." Her voice filled the air with an unseasonable melancholy and Ned spoke briskly. "Thank you for the swim."

"Well, have a nice trip," said Mrs. Halloran.

Beyond the hedge he pulled on his trunks and fastened them. They were loose and he wondered if, during the space of an afternoon, he could have lost some weight. He was cold and he was tired and the naked Hallorans and their dark water had depressed him. The swim was too much for his strength but how could he have guessed this, sliding down the banister that morning and sitting in the Westerhazys' sun? His arms were lame. His legs felt rubbery and ached at the joints. The worst of it was the cold in his bones and the feeling that he might never be warm again. Leaves were falling down around him and he smelled wood smoke on the wind. Who would be burning wood at this time of year?

He needed a drink. Whiskey would warm him, pick him up, carry him through the last of his journey, refresh his feeling that it was original and valorous to swim across the county. Channel swimmers took brandy. He needed a stimulant. He crossed the lawn in front of the Hallorans' house and went down a little path to where they had built a house for their only daughter, Helen, and her husband, Eric Sachs. The Sachses' pool was small and he found Helen and her husband there.

"Oh, *Neddy,*" Helen said. "Did you lunch at Mother's?"

"Not *really,*" Ned said. "I *did* stop to see your parents." This seemed to be explanation enough. "I'm terribly sorry to break in on you like this but I've taken a chill and I wonder if you'd give me a drink."

"Why, I'd *love* to," Helen said, "but there hasn't been anything in this house to drink since Eric's operation. That was three years ago."

Was he losing his memory, had his gift for concealing painful facts let him forget that he had sold his house, that his children were in trouble, and that his friend had been ill? His eyes slipped from Eric's face to his abdomen, where he saw three pale, sutured scars, two of them at least a foot long. Gone was his navel, and what, Neddy thought, would the roving hand, bed-checking one's gifts at 3 A.M., make of a belly with no navel, no link to birth, this breach in the succession?

"I'm sure you can get a drink at the Biswangers'," Helen said. "They're having an enormous do. You can hear it from here. Listen!"

She raised her head and from across the road, the lawns, the gardens, the woods, the fields, he heard again the brilliant noise of voices over water. "Well, I'll get wet," he said, still feeling that he had no freedom of choice about his means of travel. He dove into the Sachses' cold water and, gasping, close to drowning, made his way from one end of the pool to the other. "Lucinda and I want *terribly* to see you," he said over his shoulder, his face set toward the Biswangers'. "We're sorry it's been so long and we'll call you *very* soon."

He crossed some fields to the Biswangers' and the sounds of revelry there. They would be honored to give him a drink, they would be happy to give him a drink. The Biswangers invited him and Lucinda for dinner four times a year, six weeks in advance. They were always rebuffed and yet they continued to send out their invitations, unwilling to comprehend the rigid and undemocratic realities of their society. They were the sort of people who discussed the price of things at cocktails, exchanged market tips during dinner, and after dinner told dirty stories to mixed company. They did not belong to Neddy's set—they were not even on Lucinda's Christmas card list. He went toward their pool with feelings of indifference, charity, and some unease, since it seemed to be getting dark and these were the longest days of the year. The party when he joined it was noisy and large. Grace Biswanger was the kind of hostess who asked the optometrist, the veterinarian, the real-estate dealer, and the dentist. No one was swimming and the twilight, reflected on the water of the pool, had a wintry gleam. There was a bar and he started for this. When Grace Biswanger saw him she came toward him, not affectionately as he had every right to expect, but bellicosely.

"Why, this party has everything," she said loudly, "including a gate crasher."

She could not deal him a social blow—there was no question about this and he did not flinch. "As a gate crasher," he asked politely, "do I rate a drink?"

"Suit yourself," she said. "You don't seem to pay much attention to invitations."

She turned her back on him and joined some guests, and he went to the bar and ordered a whiskey. The bartender served him but he served him rudely. His was a world in which the caterer's men kept the social score, and to be rebuffed by a part-time barkeep meant that he had suffered some loss of social esteem. Or perhaps the man was new and uninformed. Then he heard Grace at his back say:

"They went for broke overnight—nothing but income—and he showed up drunk one Sunday and asked us to loan him five thousand dollars. . . ." She was always talking about money. It was worse than eating your peas off a knife. He dove into the pool, swam its length and went away.

The next pool on his list, the last but two, belonged to his old mistress, Shirley Adams. If he had suffered any injuries at the Biswangers' they would be cured here. Love—sexual roughhouse in fact—was the supreme elixir, the pain killer, the brightly colored pill that would put the spring back into his step, the joy of life in his heart. They had had an affair last week, last month, last year. He couldn't remember. It was he who had broken it off, his was the upper hand, and he stepped through the gate of the wall that surrounded her pool with nothing so considered as self-confidence. It seemed in a way to be his pool, as the lover, particularly the illicit lover, enjoys the possessions of his mistress with an authority unknown to holy matrimony. She was there, her hair the color of brass, but her figure, at the edge of the lighted, cerulean water, excited in him no profound memories. It had been, he thought, a lighthearted affair, although she had wept when he broke it off. She seemed confused to see him and he wondered if she was still wounded. Would she, God forbid, weep again?

"What do you want?" she asked.

"I'm swimming across the county."

"Good Christ. Will you ever grow up?"

"What's the matter?"

"If you've come here for money," she said, "I won't give you another cent."

"You could give me a drink."

"I could but I won't. I'm not alone."

"Well, I'm on my way."

He dove in and swam the pool, but when he tried to haul himself up onto the curb he found that the strength in his arms and shoulders had gone, and he paddled to the ladder and climbed out. Looking over his shoulder he saw, in the lighted bathhouse, a young man. Going out onto the dark lawn he smelled chrysanthemums or marigolds—some stubborn autumnal fragrance—on the night air, strong as gas. Looking overhead he saw that the stars had come out, but why should he seem to see Andromeda, Cepheus, and Cassiopeia? What had become of the constellations of midsummer? He began to cry.

It was probably the first time in his adult life that he had ever cried, certainly the first time in his life that he had ever felt so miserable, cold, tired, and bewildered. He could not understand the rudeness of the caterer's barkeep or the rudeness of a mistress who had come to him on her knees and showered his trousers with tears. He had swum too long, he had been immersed too long, and his nose and his throat were sore from the water. What he needed then was a drink, some company, and some clean, dry clothes, and while he could have cut directly across the road to his home he went on to the Gilmartins' pool. Here, for the first time in his life, he did not dive but went down the steps into the icy water and swam a hobbled sidestroke that he might have learned as a youth. He staggered with fatigue on his way to the Clydes' and paddled the length of their pool, stopping again and again with his hand on the curb to rest. He climbed up the ladder and wondered if he had the strength to get home. He had done what he wanted, he had swum the county, but he was so stupefied with exhaustion that his triumph seemed vague. Stooped, holding on to the gateposts for support, he turned up the driveway of his own house.

The place was dark. Was it so late that they had all gone to bed? Had Lucinda stayed at the Westerhazys' for supper? Had the girls joined her there or gone someplace else? Hadn't they agreed, as they usually did on Sunday, to regret all their invitations and stay at home? He tried the garage doors to see what cars were in but the doors were locked and rust came off the handles onto his hands. Going toward the house, he saw that the force of the thunderstorm had knocked one of the rain gutters loose. It hung down over the front door like an umbrella rib, but it could be fixed in the morning. The house was locked, and he thought that the stupid cook or the stupid maid must have locked the place up until he remembered that it had been some time since they had employed a maid or a cook. He shouted, pounded on the door, tried to force it with his shoulder, and then, looking in at the windows, saw that the place was empty.

1964

Anton Chekhov
1860–1904

At the age of thirty, already the most famous writer in Russia with the exception of Tolstoy and suffering from tuberculosis, Chekhov decided to attempt the arduous three-month journey across Siberia to visit the penal colony on Sakhalin Island in the North Pacific. Chekhov was a doctor as well as a writer, and he went to inspect the conditions of the convicts and to report the information back to Moscow. "In Exile" is one of two stories inspired by the experience. The story came out in 1892, just after Chekhov, who was known for his political quietude, started publishing in liberal, reformist newspapers. Though the choice facing the Tartar in the story might symbolize Chekhov's view of the human condition, it is also disturbingly realistic.

In Exile[1]

Old Semyon, whose nickname was Preacher, and a young Tartar, whose name no one knew, were sitting by a campfire on the bank of the river; the other three ferrymen were inside the hut. Semyon, a gaunt, toothless old man of sixty, broad-shouldered and still healthy-looking, was drunk; he would have gone to bed long ago, but he had a bottle in his pocket and was afraid his comrades in the hut would ask him for a drink of vodka. The Tartar was worn out and ill, and, wrapping himself in his rags, he talked about how good it was in the province of Simbirsk,[2] and what a beautiful and clever wife he had left at home. He was not more than twenty-five, and in the firelight his pale, sickly face and woebegone expression made him seem like a boy.

"Well, this is no paradise, of course," said Preacher. "You can see for yourself: water, bare banks, nothing but clay wherever you look. . . . It's long past Easter and there's still ice on the river . . . and this morning there was snow."

"Bad! Bad!" said the Tartar, surveying the landscape with dismay.

A few yards away the dark, cold river flowed, growling and sluic-

1. Translated by Ann Dunnigan.
2. In southeast central Russia, along the Volga River.

ing against the pitted clay banks as it sped on to the distant sea. At the edge of the bank loomed a capacious barge, which ferrymen call a *karbas*. Far away on the opposite bank crawling snakes of fire were dying down then reappearing—last year's grass being burned. Beyond the snakes there was darkness again. Little blocks of ice could be heard knocking against the barge. It was cold and damp. . . .

The Tartar glanced at the sky. There were as many stars as there were at home, the same blackness, but something was lacking. At home, in the province of Simbirsk, the stars and the sky seemed altogether different.

"Bad! Bad!" he repeated.

"You'll get used to it!" said Preacher with a laugh. "You're still young and foolish—the milk's hardly dry on your lips—and in your foolishness you think there's no one more unfortunate than you, but the time will come when you'll say to yourself: may God give everyone such a life. Just look at me. In a week's time the floods will be over and we'll launch the ferry; you'll all go gadding about Siberia, while I stay here, going back and forth, from one bank to the other. For twenty-two years now that's what I've been doing. Day and night. The pike and the salmon under the water and me on it. That's all I want. God give everyone such a life."

The Tartar threw some brushwood onto the fire, lay down closer to it, and said, "My father is sick man. When he dies, my mother, my wife, will come here. Have promised."

"And what do you want a mother and a wife for?" asked Preacher. "Just foolishness, brother. It's the devil stirring you up, blast his soul! Don't listen to him, the Evil One! Don't give in to him. When he goes on about women, spite him: I don't want them! When he talks to you about freedom, you stand up to him: I don't want it! I want nothing! No father, no mother, no wife, no freedom, no house nor home! I want nothing, damn their souls!"

Preacher took a swig at the bottle and went on, "I'm no simple peasant, brother; I don't come from the servile class; I'm a deacon's son, and when I was free I lived in Kursk,[3] and used to go around in a frock coat; but now I've brought myself to such a point that I can sleep naked on the ground and eat grass. And God give everyone

3. City in Russia, south of Moscow.

such a life. I don't want anything, I'm not afraid of anyone, and the way I see it, there's no man richer or freer than I am. When they sent me here from Russia, from the very first day I jibbed: I want nothing! The devil was at me about my wife, about my kin, about freedom, but I told him: I want nothing! And I stuck to it; and here, you see, I live well, I don't complain. But if anyone humors the devil and listens to him even once, he's lost, no salvation for him. He'll be stuck fast in the bog, up to his ears, and he'll never get out.

"It's not only the likes of you, foolish peasants, that are lost, but even the well-born and educated. Fifteen years ago they sent a gentleman here from Russia. He forged a will or something—wouldn't share with his brothers. It was said he was a prince or a baron, but maybe he was only an official, who knows? Well, the gentleman came here, and the first thing, he bought himself a house and land in Mukhortinskoe.[4] 'I want to live by my own labor,' says he, 'in the sweat of my brow, because I'm no longer a gentleman, but an exile.' . . . 'Well,' says I, 'may God help you, that's the right thing.' He was a young man then, a hustler, always on the move; he used to do the mowing himself, catch fish, ride sixty versts on horseback. But here was the trouble: from the very first year he began riding to Gyrino to the post office. He used to stand on my ferry and sigh, 'Ah, Semyon, for a long time now they haven't sent me any money from home.' . . . 'You don't need money, Vasily Sergeich. What good is it? Throw off the past, forget it as if it had never happened, as if it was only a dream, and start life afresh. Don't listen to the devil,' I tell him, 'he'll bring you to no good; he'll tighten the noose. Now you want money,' says I, 'and in a little while, before you know it, you'll want something else, and then more and more. But,' says I, 'if you want to be happy, the very first thing is not to want anything.' Yes. . . . 'And if fate has cruelly wronged you and me,' says I, 'it's no good going down on your knees to her and asking her favor; you have to spurn her and laugh at her, otherwise she'll laugh at you.' That's what I said to him. . . .

"Two years later I ferried him over to this side, and he was rubbing his hands together and laughing. 'I'm going to Gyrino,' says

4. A town in the Krasnodo region of Siberia.

he, 'to meet my wife. She has taken pity on me and come here. She's so kind and good!' He was panting with joy. Next day he comes with his wife. A young, beautiful lady in a hat, carrying a baby girl in her arms. And plenty of baggage of all sorts. My Vasily Sergeich was spinning around her; couldn't take his eyes off her; couldn't praise her enough. 'Yes, brother Semyon, even in Siberia people can live!' . . . 'Well,' thinks I, 'just you wait; better not rejoice too soon.' . . . And from that time on, almost every week he went to Gyrino to find out if money had been sent from Russia. As for money—it took plenty! 'It's for my sake that her youth and beauty are going to ruin here in Siberia,' he says, 'sharing with me my bitter fate, and for this,' he says, 'I ought to provide her with every diversion.' To make it more cheerful for his lady he took up with the officials and with all sorts of riffraff. And there had to be food and drink for this crowd, of course, and they must have a piano, and a fuzzy little lap dog on the sofa—may it croak! . . . Luxury, in short, indulgence. The lady did not stay with him long. How could she? Clay, water, cold, no vegetables for you, no fruit; uneducated and drunken people all around, no manners at all, and she a pampered lady from the capital. . . . Naturally, she grew tired of it. Besides, her husband, say what you like, was no longer a gentleman, but an exile—not exactly an honor.

"Three years later, I remember, on the eve of the Assumption,[5] someone shouted from the other side. I went over in the ferry, and what do I see but the lady—all muffled up, and with her a young gentleman, an official. There was a troika. . . . And after I ferried them across, they got in it and vanished into thin air! That was the last that was seen of them. Toward morning Vasily Sergeich galloped up to the ferry. 'Didn't my wife pass this way, Semyon, with a gentleman in spectacles?' . . . 'She did,' says I. 'Seek the wind in the fields!' He galloped off in pursuit of them, and didn't stop for five days and five nights. Afterwards, when I took him over to the other side, he threw himself down on the ferry, beat his head against the planks, and howled. 'So that's how it is,' says I. . . . I laughed and recalled to him: 'Even in Siberia people can live!' And he beat his head all the more.

5. August 15, observed in commemoration of the Assumption of the Virgin Mary (that is, the taking of Mary up to heaven).

"After that he began to long for freedom. His wife had slipped away to Russia, so, naturally, he was drawn there, both to see her and to rescue her from her lover. And, my friend, he took to galloping off every day, either to the post office or the authorities; he kept sending in petitions, and presenting them personally, asking to be pardoned so he could go back home; and he used to tell how he had spent some two hundred rubles on telegrams alone. He sold his land, and mortgaged his house to the Jews. He grew gray, stooped, and yellow in the face, as if he was consumptive. He'd talk to you and go: khe-khe-khe . . . and there would be tears in his eyes. He struggled with those petitions for eight years, but now he has recovered his spirits and is more cheerful: he's thought up a new indulgence. His daughter, you see, has grown up. He keeps an eye on her, dotes on her. And, to tell the truth, she's all right, a pretty little thing, black-browed, and with a lively disposition. Every Sunday he goes to church with her in Gyrino. Side by side they stand on the ferry, she laughing and he not taking his eyes off her. 'Yes, Semyon,' says he, 'even in Siberia people can live. Even in Siberia there is happiness. Look,' says he, 'see what a daughter I've got! I suppose you wouldn't find another like her if you went a thousand versts.' . . . 'Your daughter,' says I, 'is a fine young lady, that's true, certainly. . . .' But I think to myself: Wait a while. . . . The girl is young, her blood is dancing, she wants to live, and what life is there here? And, my friend, she did begin to fret. . . . She withered and withered, wasted away, fell ill; and now she's completely worn out. Consumption.

"That's your Siberian happiness for you, the pestilence take it! That's how people can live in Siberia! . . . He's taken to running after doctors and taking them home with him. As soon as he hears that there's a doctor or quack two or three hundred versts away, he goes to fetch him. A terrible lot of money has been spent on doctors; to my way of thinking, it would have been better to spend it on drink. . . . She'll die anyway. She's certain to die, and then he'll be completely lost. He'll hang himself from grief, or run away to Russia—that's sure. He'll run away, they'll catch him, there'll be a trial, and then hard labor; they'll give him a taste of the lash. . . ."

"Good, good," muttered the Tartar, shivering with cold.

"What's good?" asked Preacher.

"Wife and daughter. . . . Let hard labor, let suffer; he saw his wife and daughter. . . . You say: want nothing. But nothing is bad! Wife was with him three years—God gave him that. Nothing is bad; three years is good. How you not understand?"

Shivering and stuttering, straining to pick out the Russian words, of which he knew so few, the Tartar said God forbid one should fall sick and die in a strange land, and be buried in the cold, sodden earth; that if his wife came to him even for one day, even for one hour, he would be willing to accept any torture whatsoever, and thank God for it. Better one day of happiness than nothing.

After that he again described the beautiful and clever wife he had left at home; then, clutching his head with both hands, he began crying and assuring Semyon that he was innocent and had been falsely accused. His two brothers and his uncle stole some horses from a peasant, and beat the old man till he was half dead, and the commune had not judged fairly, but had contrived a sentence by which all three brothers were sent to Siberia, while the uncle, a rich man, remained at home.

"You'll get u-u-used to it!" said Semyon.

The Tartar relapsed into silence and fixed his tearful eyes on the fire; his face expressed bewilderment and fright, as though he still did not understand why he was here in the dark, in the damp, among strangers, instead of in the province of Simbirsk. Preacher lay down near the fire, chuckled at something, and began singing in an undertone.

"What joy has she with her father?" he said a little later. "He loves her, she's a consolation to him, it's true; but you have to mind your p's and q's with him, brother: he's a strict old man, a severe old man. And strictness is not what young girls want. . . . They want petting and ha-ha-ha and ho-ho-ho, scents and pomades! Yes. . . . Ekh, life, life!" sighed Semyon, getting up with difficulty. "The vodka's all gone, so it's time to sleep. Eh? I'm going, my boy."

Left alone, the Tartar put more brushwood onto the fire, lay down, and, looking into the blaze, began thinking of his native village, and of his wife: if she would come only for a month, even for a day, then, if she liked, she might go back again. Better a month or even a day than nothing. But if she kept her promise and came, how could he provide for her? Where could she live?

"If not something to eat, how you live?" the Tartar asked aloud.

He was paid only ten kopecks for working at the oars a day and a night; the passengers gave him tips, it was true, but the ferrymen shared everything among themselves, giving nothing to the Tartar, but only making fun of him. And he was hungry, cold, and frightened from want. . . . Now, when his whole body was shivering and aching, he ought to go into the hut and lie down to sleep, but he had nothing there to cover himself with, and it was colder there than on the river bank; here, too, he had nothing to put over him, but at least he could make a fire. . . .

In another week, when the floods had subsided and the ferry could sail, none of the ferrymen except Semyon would be needed, and the Tartar would begin going from village to village, looking for work and begging alms. His wife was only seventeen years old; beautiful, pampered, shy—could she possibly go from village to village, her face unveiled, begging? No, even to think of it was dreadful. . . .

It was already growing light; the barge, the bushes of rose-willow, and the ripples on the water were clearly distinguishable, and looking back there was the steep clay precipice, below it the little hut thatched with brown straw, and above clung the huts of the villagers. The cocks were already crowing in the village.

The red clay precipice, the barge, the river, the strange, unkind people, hunger, cold, illness—perhaps all this did not exist in reality. Probably it was all a dream, thought the Tartar. He felt that he was asleep, and hearing his own snoring. . . . Of course, he was at home in the province of Simbirsk, and he had only to call his wife by name for her to answer, and in the next room his mother. . . . However, what awful dreams there are! Why? The Tartar smiled and opened his eyes. What river was this? The Volga?

"Bo-o-at!" someone shouted from the other side. "Karba-a-s!"

The Tartar woke up and went to wake his comrades, to row over to the other side. Putting on their torn sheepskins as they came, the ferrymen appeared on the bank, swearing in hoarse, sleepy voices, and shivering from the cold. After their sleep, the river, from which there came a piercing gust of cold air, evidently struck them as revolting and sinister. They were not quick to jump into the barge. The Tartar and the three ferrymen took up the long, broad-bladed oars, which looked like crabs' claws in the darkness. Semyon leaned his belly against the long tiller. The shouting from the other side continued, and two shots were fired from a revolver; the man probably thought that the ferrymen were asleep or had gone off to the village tavern.

"All right, plenty of time!" said Preacher in the tone of a man who is convinced that there is no need to hurry in this world—that it makes no difference, really, and nothing will come of it.

The heavy, clumsy barge drew away from the bank and floated between the rose-willows; and only because the willows slowly receded was it possible to see that the barge was not standing still but moving. The ferrymen plied the oars evenly, in unison; Preacher hung over the tiller on his belly, and, describing an arc in the air, flew from one side of the boat to the other. In the darkness it looked as if the men were sitting on some antideluvian animal with long paws, and sailing to a cold, bleak land, the very one of which we sometimes dream in nightmares.

They passed beyond the willows and floated out into the open. The rhythmic thump and splash of the oars were now audible on the further shore, and someone shouted, "Hurry! Hurry!" Another ten minutes passed and the barge bumped heavily against the landing stage.

"And it keeps coming down, and coming down!" muttered Semyon, wiping the snow from his face. "Where it comes from, God only knows!"

On the other side stood a thin old man of medium height wearing a jacket lined with fox fur and a white lambskin cap. He was standing at a little distance from his horses and not moving; he had a concentrated, morose expression, as if, trying to remember something, he had grown angry with his unyielding memory. When Semyon went up to him with a smile and took off his cap, he said, "I'm hastening to Anastasyevka. My daughter is worse again, and they say there's a new doctor at Anastasyevka."

They dragged the tarantass[6] onto the barge and rowed back. The man, whom Semyon called Vasily Sergeich, stood motionless all the way back, his thick lips tightly compressed, his eyes fixed on one spot; when the coachman asked permission to smoke in his pres-

6. A type of carriage used in Russia in the 1800s.

ence, he made no reply, as if he had not heard. And Semyon, hanging over the tiller on his belly, glanced mockingly at him and said, "Even in Siberia people can live. Li-i-ve!"

There was a triumphant expression on Preacher's face, as if he had proved something and was rejoicing that it had turned out exactly as he had surmised. The helpless, unhappy look of the man in the fox-lined jacket evidently afforded him great satisfaction.

"It's muddy driving now, Vasily Sergeich," he said when the horses were harnessed on the bank. "You'd better have waited a week or two till it gets drier. . . . Or else not have gone at all. . . . If there were any sense in going, but, as you yourself know, people have been driving about for ever and ever, by day and by night, and there's never any sense in it. That's the truth!"

Vasily Sergeich tipped him without a word, got into the tarantass, and drove off.

"See there, he's gone galloping off for a doctor!" said Semyon, shrinking with cold. "Yes, looking for a real doctor is like chasing the wind in the fields, or catching the devil by the tail, damn your soul! What freaks! Lord forgive me, a sinner!"

The Tartar went up to Preacher and, looking at him with hatred and abhorrence, trembling, mixing Tartar words with his broken Russian, said, "He is good—good. You bad! You bad! Gentleman is good soul, excellent, and you beast, you bad! Gentleman alive and you dead. . . . God created man to be live, be joyful, be sad and sorrow, but you want nothing. . . . You not live, you stone, clay! Stone want nothing and you want nothing. . . . You stone—and God not love you, love gentleman!"

Everyone laughed; the Tartar frowned scornfully and, with a gesture of despair, wrapped himself in his rags and went to the fire. Semyon and the ferrymen trailed off to the hut.

"It's cold," said one of the ferrymen hoarsely as he stretched out on the straw that covered the damp floor.

"Well, it's not warm!" one of the others agreed. "It's a hard life!"

They all lay down. The door was blown open by the wind, and snow drifted into the hut. No one felt like getting up and closing the door; it was cold and they were lazy.

"I'm all right!" said Semyon, falling asleep. "God give everyone such a life."

"You're a hard case, we know that. Even the devils won't take you!"

From outside there came sounds like the howling of a dog.

"What's that? Who's there?"

"It's the Tartar crying."

"He'll get u-u-used to it!" said Semyon, and instantly fell asleep.

Soon the others fell asleep too. And the door remained unclosed.

1892

Kate Chopin

1851–1904

Chopin wrote "The Story of an Hour" in the spring of 1894, but it was rejected by many magazine editors, at least once for being "unethical." Finally, Vogue *published it in December, paying Chopin ten dollars and also the compliment of presenting her to the public as a daring writer. Like the writing of Charlotte Perkins Gilman, Chopin's work helped energize feminists in her own day and continues to do so today. The theme of this story is autobiographical, though the details are not. Chopin, the mother of six, was widowed at the age of thirty-two. A month after finishing this story, she wrote in her diary that if her husband had lived, she "would have to forget the past ten years of my growth—my real growth." Nevertheless, she does not dismiss marriage as merely a prison for women. A sentence later she admits that she would have given up her ten years of growth in "the spirit of perfect acquiescence."*

The Story of an Hour

Knowing that Mrs. Mallard was afflicted with a heart trouble, great care was taken to break to her as gently as possible the news of her husband's death.

It was her sister Josephine who told her, in broken sentences; veiled hints that revealed in half concealing. Her husband's friend Richards was there, too, near her. It was he who had been in the newspaper office when intelligence of the railroad disaster was received, with Brently Mallard's name leading the list of "killed." He had only taken the time to assure himself of its truth by a second telegram, and had hastened to forestall any less careful, less tender friend in bearing the sad message.

She did not hear the story as many women have heard the same, with a paralyzed inability to accept its significance. She wept at once, with sudden, wild abandonment, in her sister's arms. When the storm of grief had spent itself she went away to her room alone. She would have no one follow her.

There stood, facing the open window, a comfortable, roomy armchair. Into this she sank, pressed down by a physical exhaustion that haunted her body and seemed to reach into her soul.

She could see in the open square before her house the tops of trees that were all aquiver with the new spring life. The delicious breath of rain was in the air. In the street below a peddler was crying his wares. The notes of a distant song which some one was singing reached her faintly, and countless sparrows were twittering in the eaves.

There were patches of blue sky showing here and there through the clouds that had met and piled one above the other in the west facing her window.

She sat with her head thrown back upon the cushion of the chair, quite motionless, except when a sob came up into her throat and shook her, as a child who has cried itself to sleep continues to sob in its dreams.

She was young, with a fair, calm face, whose lines bespoke repression and even a certain strength. But now there was a dull stare in her eyes, whose gaze was fixed away off yonder on one of those patches of blue sky. It was not a glance of reflection, but rather indicated a suspension of intelligent thought.

There was something coming to her and she was waiting for it, fearfully. What was it? She did not know; it was too subtle and elusive to name. But she felt it, creeping out of the sky, reaching toward her through the sounds, the scents, the color that filled the air.

Now her bosom rose and fell tumultuously. She was beginning to recognize this thing that was approaching to possess her, and she was striving to beat it back with her will—as powerless as her two white slender hands would have been.

When she abandoned herself a little whispered word escaped her slightly parted lips. She said it over and over under her breath: "free, free, free!" The vacant stare and the look of terror that had followed it went from her eyes. They stayed keen and bright. Her pulses beat fast, and the coursing blood warmed and relaxed every inch of her body.

She did not stop to ask if it were or were not a monstrous joy that held her. A clear and exalted perception enabled her to dismiss the suggestion as trivial.

She knew that she would weep again when she saw the kind, tender hands folded in death; the face that had never looked save with love upon her, fixed and gray and dead. But she saw beyond that bitter moment a long procession of years to come that would belong to her absolutely. And she opened and spread her arms out to them in welcome.

There would be no one to live for her during those coming years; she would live for herself. There would be no powerful will bending hers in that blind persistence with which men and women believe they have a right to impose a private will upon a fellow-creature. A kind intention or a cruel intention made the act seem no less a crime as she looked upon it in that brief moment of illumination.

And yet she had loved him—sometimes. Often she had not. What did it matter! What could love, the unsolved mystery, count for in face of this possession of self-assertion which she suddenly recognized as the strongest impulse of her being!

"Free! Body and soul free!" she kept whispering.

Josephine was kneeling before the closed door with her lips to the keyhold, imploring for admission. "Louise, open the door! I beg; open the door—you will make yourself ill. What are you doing, Louise? For heaven's sake open the door."

"Go away. I am not making myself ill." No; she was drinking in a very elixir of life through that open window.

Her fancy was running riot along those days ahead of her. Spring days, and summer days, and all sorts of days that would be her own. She breathed a quick prayer that life might be long. It was only yesterday she had thought with a shudder that life might be long.

She arose at length and opened the door to her sister's importunities. There was a feverish triumph in her eyes, and she carried herself unwittingly like a goddess of Victory. She clasped her sister's waist, and together they descended the stairs. Richards stood waiting for them at the bottom.

Some one was opening the front door with a latchkey. It was Brently Mallard who entered, a little travel-stained, composedly carrying his grip-sack and umbrella. He had been far from the scene of accident, and did not even know there had been one. He stood amazed at Josephine's piercing cry; at Richards' quick motion to screen him from the view of his wife.

But Richards was too late.

When the doctors came they said she had died of heart disease—of joy that kills.

1894

Stephen Crane

1871–1900

In 1897, Crane was working as a reporter when he boarded the Commodore, *a gunrunning freighter supplying Cuban rebels out of Jacksonville, Florida. After running aground twice, the ship finally made it out to sea, where it began to slowly sink. Most of the crew and the Cuban fighters were evacuated on three big lifeboats, but Crane waited to the very end and escaped in a ten-foot dinghy with the ship's captain, an oiler named William Higgins, and the cook. One of the lifeboats foundered, and the men in the dinghy watched seven others drown. After thirty hours at sea, the four finally came ashore at Daytona. Crane wrote a newspaper dispatch right away. Six months later he wrote "The Open Boat," which covered the ordeal on the sea. Contemporary readers did not think of it as fiction, and neither did Crane (consider the story's subtitle). "The Open Boat" is considered one of the finest examples of American naturalism: an irreligious philosophy that views the universe as indifferent to the existence and struggles of humans.*

The Open Boat

A Tale Intended to Be after the Fact: Being the Experience of Four Men from the Sunk Steamer COMMODORE

I

None of them knew the color of the sky. Their eyes glanced level and were fastened upon the waves that swept toward them. These waves were of the hue of slate, save for the tops, which were of foaming white, and all of the men knew the colors of the sea. The horizon narrowed and widened, and dipped and rose, and at all times its edge was jagged with waves that seemed thrust up in points like rocks.

Many a man ought to have a bathtub larger than the boat which here rode upon the sea. These waves were most wrongfully and barbarously abrupt and tall, and each froth-top was a problem in small-boat navigation.

The cook squatted in the bottom, and looked with both eyes at the six inches of gunwale which separated him from the ocean. His sleeves were rolled over his fat forearms, and the two flaps of his unbuttoned vest dangled as he bent to bail out the boat. Often he said, "Gawd! that was a narrow clip." As he remarked it he invariably gazed eastward over the broken sea.

The oiler, steering with one of the two oars in the boat, sometimes raised himself suddenly to keep clear of water that swirled in over the stern. It was a thin little oar, and it seemed often ready to snap.

The correspondent, pulling at the other oar, watched the waves and wondered why he was there.

The injured captain, lying in the bow, was at this time buried in that profound dejection and indifference which comes, temporarily at least, to even the bravest and most enduring when, willy-nilly, the firm fails, the army loses, the ship goes down. The mind of the master of a vessel is rooted deep in the timbers of her, though he command for a day or a decade; and this captain had on him the stern impression of a scene in the grays of dawn of seven turned faces, and later a stump of a topmast with a white ball on it that slashed to and fro at the waves, went low and lower, and down. Thereafter there was something strange in his voice. Although steady, it was deep with mourning, and of a quality beyond oration or tears.

"Keep'er a little more south, Billie," said he.

"A little more south, sir," said the oiler in the stern.

A seat in his boat was not unlike a seat upon a bucking broncho, and by the same token a broncho is not much smaller. The craft pranced and reared and plunged like an animal. As each wave came, and she rose for it, she seemed like a horse making at a fence outrageously high. The manner of her scramble over these walls of water is a mystic thing, and, moreover, at the top of them were ordinarily these problems in white water, the foam racing down from the summit of each wave requiring a new leap, and a leap from the air. Then, after scornfully bumping a crest, she would slide and race and splash down a long incline, and arrive bobbing and nodding in front of the next menace.

A singular disadvantage of the sea lies in the fact that after successfully surmounting one wave you discover that there is another behind it just as important and just as nervously anxious to do something effective in the way of swamping boats. In a ten-foot dinghy one can get an idea of the resources of the sea in the line of waves that is not probable to the average experience, which is never at sea in a dinghy. As each slaty wall of water approached, it shut all else from the view of the men in the boat, and it was not difficult to imagine that this particular wave was the final outburst of the ocean, the last effort of the grim water. There was a terrible grace in the move of the waves, and they came in silence, save for the snarling of the crests.

In the wan light the faces of the men must have been gray. Their eyes must have glinted in strange ways as they gazed steadily astern. Viewed from a balcony, the whole thing would, doubtless, have been weirdly picturesque. But the men in the boat had not time to see it, and if they had had leisure, there were other things to occupy their minds. The sun swung steadily up the sky, and they knew it was broad day because the color of the sea changed from slate to emerald green streaked with amber lights, and the foam was like tumbling snow. The process of the breaking day was unknown to them. They were aware only of this effect upon the color of the waves that rolled toward them.

In disjointed sentences the cook and the correspondent argued as to the difference between a life-saving station and a house of refuge. The cook had said: "There's a house of refuge just north of the Mosquito Inlet Light, and as soon as they see us they'll come off in their boat and pick us up."

"As soon as who see us?" said the correspondent.

"The crew," said the cook.

"Houses of refuge don't have crews," said the correspondent. "As I understand them, they are only places where clothes and grub are stored for the benefit of shipwrecked people. They don't carry crews."

"Oh, yes, they do," said the cook.

"No, they don't," said the correspondent.

"Well, we're not there yet, anyhow," said the oiler in the stern.

"Well," said the cook, "perhaps it's not a house of refuge that I'm thinking of as being near Mosquito Inlet Light; perhaps it's a life-saving station."

"We're not there yet," said the oiler in the stern.

II

As the boat bounced from the top of each wave the wind tore through the hair of the hatless men, and as the craft plopped her stern down again the spray slashed past them. The crest of each of these waves was a hill, from the top of which the men surveyed for a moment a broad tumultuous expanse, shining and wind-riven. It was probably splendid, it was probably glorious, this play of the free sea, wild with lights of emerald and white and amber.

"Bully good thing it's an on-shore wind, said the cook. "If not, where would we be? Wouldn't have a show."

"That's right," said the correspondent.

The busy oiler nodded his assent.

Then the captain, in the bow, chuckled in a way that expressed humor, contempt, tragedy, all in one. "Do you think we've got much of a show now, boys?" said he.

Whereupon the three were silent, save for a trifle of hemming and hawing. To express any particular optimism at this time they felt to be childish and stupid, but they all doubtless possessed this sense of the situation in their minds. A young man thinks doggedly at such times. On the other hand, the ethics of their condition was decidedly against any open suggestion of hopelessness. So they were silent.

"Oh, well," said the captain, soothing his children, "we'll get ashore all right."

But there was that in his tone which made them think; so the oiler quoth, "Yes! if this wind holds."

The cook was bailing. "Yes! if we don't catch hell in the surf."

Canton-flannel gulls flew near and far. Sometimes they sat down on the sea, near patches of brown seaweed that rolled over the waves with a movement like carpets on a line in a gale. The birds sat comfortably in groups, and they were envied by some in the dinghy, for the wrath of the sea was no more to them than it was to a covey of prairie chickens a thousand miles inland. Often they came very close and stared at the men with black beadlike eyes. At these times they were uncanny and sinister in their unblinking scrutiny, and the men hooted angrily at them, telling them to be gone. One came, and evidently decided to alight on the top of the captain's head. The bird flew parallel to the boat and did not circle, but made short sidelong jumps in the air in chicken fashion. His black eyes were wistfully fixed upon the captain's head. "Ugly brute," said the oiler to the bird. "You look as if you were made with a jackknife." The cook and the correspondent swore darkly at the creature. The captain naturally wished to knock it away with the end of the heavy painter, but he did not dare do it, because anything resembling an emphatic gesture would have capsized this freighted boat; and so, with his open hand, the captain gently and carefully waved the gull away. After it had been discouraged from the pursuit the captain breathed easier on account of his hair, and others breathed easier because the bird struck their minds at this time as being somehow gruesome and ominous.

In the meantime the oiler and the correspondent rowed; and also they rowed. They sat together in the same seat, and each rowed an oar. Then the oiler took both oars; then the correspondent took both oars, then the oiler; then the correspondent. They rowed and they rowed. The very ticklish part of the business was when the time came for the reclining one in the stern to take his turn at the oars. By the very last star of truth, it is easier to steal eggs from under a hen than it was to change seats in the dinghy. First the man in the stern slid his hand along the thwart and moved with care, as if he were of Sèvres.[1] Then the man in the rowing-seat slid his hand along the other thwart. It was all done with the most extraordinary care. As the two sidled past each other, the whole party kept watchful eyes on the coming wave, and the captain cried: "Look out, now! Steady, there!"

The brown mats of seaweed that appeared from time to time were like islands, bits of earth. They were travelling, apparently, neither one way nor the other. They were, to all intents, stationary. They informed the men in the boat that it was making progress slowly toward the land.

The captain, rearing cautiously in the bow after the dinghy soared on a great swell, said that he had seen the lighthouse at Mosquito Inlet. Presently the cook remarked that he had seen it. The correspondent was at the oars then, and for some reason he too wished to look at the lighthouse; but his back was toward the far shore, and the waves were important, and for some time he could not seize an opportunity to turn his head. But at last there came a wave more gentle than the others, and when at the crest of it he swiftly scoured the western horizon.

"See it?" said the captain.

"No," said the correspondent, slowly; "I didn't see anything."

"Look again," said the captain. He pointed. "It's exactly in that direction."

At the top of another wave the correspondent did as he was bid, and this time his eyes chanced on a small, still thing on the edge of the swaying horizon. It was precisely like the point of a pin. It took an anxious eye to find a lighthouse so tiny.

"Think we'll make it, Captain?"

"If this wind holds and the boat don't swamp, we can't do much else," said the captain.

1. I.e., as if he were made of china.

The little boat, lifted by each towering sea and splashed viciously by the crests, made progress that in the absence of seaweed was not apparent to those in her. She seemed just a wee thing wallowing, miraculously top up, at the mercy of five oceans. Occasionally a great spread of water, like white flames, swarmed into her.

"Bail her, cook," said the captain, serenely.

"All right, Captain," said the cheerful cook.

III

It would be difficult to describe the subtle brotherhood of men that was here established on the seas. No one said that it was so. No one mentioned it. But it dwelt in the boat, and each man felt it warm him. They were a captain, an oiler, a cook, and a correspondent, and they were friends—friends in a more curiously iron-bound degree than may be common. The hurt captain, lying against the water jar in the bow, spoke always in a low voice and calmly; but he could never command a more ready and swiftly obedient crew than the motley three of the dinghy. It was more than a mere recognition of what was best for the common safety. There was surely in it a quality that was personal and heartfelt. And after this devotion to the commander of the boat, there was this comradeship, that the correspondent, for instance, who had been taught to be cynical of men, knew even at the time was the best experience of his life. But no one said that it was so. No one mentioned it.

"I wish we had a sail," remarked the captain. "We might try my overcoat on the end of an oar, and give you two boys a chance to rest." So the cook and the correspondent held the mast and spread wide the overcoat; the oiler steered; and the little boat made good way with her new rig. Sometimes the oiler had to scull sharply to keep a sea from breaking into the boat, but otherwise sailing was a success.

Meanwhile the lighthouse had been growing slowly larger. It had now almost assumed color, and appeared like a little gray shadow on the sky. The man at the oars could not be prevented from turning his head rather often to try for a glimpse of this little gray shadow.

At last, from the top of each wave, the men in the tossing boat could see land. Even as the lighthouse was an upright shadow on the sky, this land seemed but a long black shadow on the sea. It certainly was thinner than paper. "We must be about opposite New Smyrna,"[2] said the cook, who had coasted this shore often in schooners. "Captain, by the way, I believe they abandoned that life-saving station there about a year ago."

"Did they?" said the captain.

The wind slowly died away. The cook and the correspondent were not now obliged to slave in order to hold high the oar. But the waves continued their old impetuous swooping at the dinghy, and the little craft, no longer underway, struggled woundily over them. The oiler or the correspondent took the oars again.

Shipwrecks are *apropos* of nothing. If men could only train for them and have them occur when the men had reached pink condition, there would be less drowning at sea. Of the four in the dinghy none had slept any time worth mentioning for two days and two nights previous to embarking in the dinghy, and in the excitement of clambering about the deck of a foundering ship they had also forgotten to eat heartily.

For these reasons, and for others, neither the oiler nor the correspondent was fond of rowing at this time. The correspondent wondered ingenuously how in the name of all that was sane could there be people who thought it amusing to row a boat. It was not an amusement; it was a diabolical punishment, and even a genius of mental aberrations could never conclude that it was anything but a horror to the muscles and a crime against the back. He mentioned to the boat in general how the amusement of rowing struck him, and the weary-faced oiler smiled in full sympathy. Previously to the foundering, by the way, the oiler had worked a double watch in the engine-room of the ship.

"Take her easy, now, boys," said the captain. "Don't spend yourselves. If we have to run a surf you'll need all your strength, because we'll sure have to swim for it. Take your time."

Slowly the land arose from the sea. From a black line it became a line of black and a line of white—trees and sand. Finally the captain said that he could make out a house on the shore. "That's the house

2. A town about eighty miles south of Jacksonville, Florida.

of refuge, sure," said the cook. "They'll see us before long, and come out after us."

The distant lighthouse reared high. "The keeper ought to be able to make us out now, if he's looking through a glass," said the captain. "He'll notify the life-saving people."

"None of those other boats could have got ashore to give word of the wreck," said the oiler, in a low voice, "else the life-boat would be out hunting us."

Slowly and beautifully the land loomed out of the sea. The wind came again. It had veered from the northeast to the southeast. Finally a new sound struck the ears of the men in the boat. It was the low thunder of the surf on the shore. "We'll never be able to make the lighthouse now," said the captain. "Swing her head a little more north, Billie."

"A little more north, sir," said the oiler.

Whereupon the little boat turned her nose once more down the wind, and all but the oarsman watched the shore grow. Under the influence of this expansion doubt and direful apprehension were leaving the minds of the men. The management of the boat was still most absorbing, but it could not prevent a quiet cheerfulness. In an hour, perhaps, they would be ashore.

Their backbones had become thoroughly used to balancing in the boat, and they now rode this wild colt of a dinghy like circus men. The correspondent thought that he had been drenched to the skin, but happening to feel in the top pocket of his coat, he found therein eight cigars. Four of them were soaked with sea-water, four were perfectly scatheless. After a search, somebody produced three dry matches; and thereupon the four waifs rode impudently in their little boat and, with an assurance of an impending rescue shining in their eyes, puffed at the big cigars, and judged well and ill of all men. Everybody took a drink of water.

IV

"Cook," remarked the captain, "there don't seem to be any signs of life about your house of refuge."

"No," replied the cook. "Funny they don't see us!"

A broad stretch of lowly coast lay before the eyes of the men. It was of low dunes topped with dark vegetation. The roar of the surf was plain, and sometimes they could see the white lip of a wave as it spun up the beach. A tiny house was blocked out black upon the sky. Southward, the slim lighthouse lifted its little gray length.

Tide, wind, and waves were swinging the dinghy northward. "Funny they don't see us," said the men.

The surf's roar was here dulled, but its tone was nevertheless thunderous and mighty. As the boat swam over the great rollers the men sat listening to this roar. "We'll swamp sure," said everybody.

It is fair to say here that there was not a life-saving station within twenty miles in either direction; but the men did not know this fact, and in consequence they made dark and opprobrious remarks concerning the eyesight of the nation's life-savers. Four scowling men sat in the dinghy and surpassed records in the invention of epithets.

"Funny they don't see us."

The lightheartedness of a former time had completely faded. To their sharpened minds it was easy to conjure pictures of all kinds of incompetency and blindness and, indeed, cowardice. There was the shore of the populous land, and it was bitter and bitter to them that from it came no sign.

"Well," said the captain, ultimately, "I suppose we'll have to make a try for ourselves. If we stay out here too long, we'll none of us have strength left to swim after the boat swamps."

And so the oiler, who was at the oars, turned the boat straight for the shore. There was a sudden tightening of muscles. There was some thinking.

"If we don't all get ashore," said the captain—"if we don't all get ashore, I suppose you fellows know where to send news of my finish?"

They then briefly exchanged some addresses and admonitions. As for the reflections of the men, there was a great deal of rage in them. Perchance they might be formulated thus: "If I am going to be drowned—if I am going to be drowned—if I am going to be drowned, why in the name of the seven mad gods who rule the sea, was I allowed to come thus far and contemplate sand and trees? Was I brought here merely to have my nose dragged away as I was about to nibble the sacred cheese of life? It is preposterous. If this old ninny-woman, Fate, cannot do better than this, she should be deprived of the management of men's fortunes. She is an old hen who knows not her intention. If she has decided to drown me, why did she not do it in the beginning and save me all this trouble? The whole affair is absurd. . . . But no; she cannot mean to drown me. She dare not drown me. She cannot drown me. Not after all this work." Afterward the man might have had an impulse to shake his fist at the clouds. "Just you drown me, now, and then hear what I call you!"

The billows that came at this time were more formidable. They seemed always just about to break and roll over the little boat in a turmoil of foam. There was a preparatory and long growl in the speech of them. No mind unused to the sea would have concluded that the dinghy could ascend these sheer heights in time. The shore was still afar. The oiler was a wily surfman. "Boys," he said, swiftly, "she won't live three minutes more, and we're too far out to swim. Shall I take her to sea again, Captain?"

"Yes; go ahead!" said the captain.

This oiler, by a series of quick miracles and fast and steady oarsmanship, turned the boat in the middle of the surf and took her safely to sea again.

There was a considerable silence as the boat bumped over the furrowed sea to deeper water. Then somebody in gloom spoke: "Well, anyhow, they must have seen us from the shore by now."

The gulls went in slanting flight up the wind toward the gray, desolate east. A squall, marked by dingy clouds and clouds brick-red, like smoke from a burning building, appeared from the south-east.

"What do you think of those life-saving people? Ain't they peaches?"

"Funny they haven't seen us."

"Maybe they think we're out here for sport! Maybe they think we're fishin'. Maybe they think we're damned fools."

It was a long afternoon. A changed tide tried to force them southward, but wind and wave said northward. Far ahead, where coastline, sea, and sky formed their mighty angle, there were little dots which seemed to indicate a city on the shore.

"St. Augustine?"

The captain shook his head. "Too near Mosquito Inlet."

And the oiler rowed, and then the correspondent rowed; then the oiler rowed. It was a weary business. The human back can become the seat of more aches and pains than are registered in books for the composite anatomy of a regiment. It is a limited area, but it can become the theatre of innumerable muscular conflicts, tangles, wrenches, knots, and other comforts.

"Did you ever like to row, Billie?" asked the correspondent.

"No," said the oiler, "hang it!"

When one exchanged the rowing-seat for a place in the bottom of the boat, he suffered a bodily depression that caused him to be careless of everything save an obligation to wiggle one finger. There was cold sea-water swashing to and from in the boat, and he lay in it. His head, pillowed on a thwart, was within an inch of the swirl of a wave-crest, and sometimes a particularly obstreperous sea came inboard and drenched him once more. But these matters did not annoy him. It is almost certain that if the boat had capsized he would have tumbled comfortably out upon the ocean as if he felt sure that it was a great soft mattress.

"Look! There's a man on the shore!"

"Where?"

"There? See 'im? See 'im?"

"Yes, sure! He's walking along."

"Now he's stopped. Look! He's facing us!"

"He's waving at us!"

"So he is! By thunder!"

"Ah, now we're all right! Now we're all right! There'll be a boat out here for us in half an hour."

"He's going on. He's running. He's going up to that house, there."

The remote beach seemed lower than the sea, and it required a searching glance to discern the little black figure. The captain saw a floating stick, and they rowed to it. A bath towel was by some weird chance in the boat, and, tying this on the stick, the captain waved it. The oarsman did not dare turn his head, so he was obliged to ask questions.

"What's he doing now?"

"He's standing still again. He's looking, I think. . . . There he goes again—toward the house. . . . Now he's stopped again."

"Is he waving at us?"

"No, not now; he was, though."

"Look! There comes another man!"

"He's running."

"Look at him go, would you!"

"Why, he's on a bicycle. Now he's met the other man. They're both waving at us. Look!"

"There comes something up the beach."

"What the devil is that thing?"

"Why, it looks like a boat."

"Why, certainly, it's a boat."

"No; it's on wheels."

"Yes, so it is. Well, that must be the life-boat. They drag them along shore on a wagon."

"That's the life-boat, sure."

"No, by God, it's—it's an omnibus."

"I tell you it's a life-boat."

"It is not! It's an omnibus. I can see it plain. See? One of these big hotel omnibuses."

"By thunder, you're right. It's an omnibus, sure as fate. What do you suppose they are doing with an omnibus? Maybe they are going around collecting the life-crew, hey?"

"That's it, likely. Look! There's a fellow waving a little black flag. He's standing on the steps of the omnibus. There come those other two fellows. Now they're all talking together. Look at the fellow with the flag. Maybe he ain't waving it!"

"That ain't a flag, is it? That's his coat. Why, certainly, that's his coat."

"So it is; it's his coat. He's taken it off and is waving it around his head. But would you look at him swing it!"

"Oh, say, there isn't any life-saving station there. That's just a winter-resort hotel omnibus that has brought over some of the boarders to see us drown."

"What's that idiot with the coat mean? What's he signaling, anyhow?"

"It looks as if he were trying to tell us to go north. There must be a life-saving station up there."

"No; he thinks we're fishing. Just giving us a merry hand. See? Ah, there, Willie!"

"Well, I wish I could make something out of those signals. What do you suppose he means?"

"He don't mean anything; he's just playing."

"Well, if he'd just signal us to try the surf again, or to go to sea and wait, or go north, or go south, or go to hell, there would be some reason in it. But look at him! He just stands there and keeps his coat revolving like a wheel. The ass!"

"There come more people."

"Now there's quite a mob. Look! Isn't that a boat?"

"Where? Oh, I see where you mean. No, that's no boat."

"That fellow is still waving his coat."

"He must think we like to see him do that. Why don't he quit it? It don't mean anything."

"I don't know. I think he is trying to make us go north. It must be that there's a life-saving station there somewhere."

"Say, he ain't tired yet. Look at 'im wave!"

"Wonder how long he can keep that up. He's been revolving his coat ever since he caught sight of us. He's an idiot. Why aren't they getting men to bring a boat out? A fishing boat—one of those big yawls—could come out here all right. Why don't he do something?"

"Oh, it's all right now."

"They'll have a boat out here for us in less than no time, now that they've seen us."

A faint yellow tone came into the sky over the low land. The shadows on the sea slowly deepened. The wind bore coldness with it, and the men began to shiver.

"Holy smoke!" said one, allowing his voice to express his impious mood, "if we keep on monkeying out here! If we've got to flounder out here all night!"

"Oh, we'll never have to stay here all night! Don't you worry. They've seen us now, and it won't be long before they'll come chasing out after us."

The shore grew dusky. The man waving a coat blended gradually into this gloom, and it swallowed in the same manner the omnibus and the group of people. The spray, when it dashed uproariously over the side, made the voyagers shrink and swear like men who were being branded.

"I'd like to catch the chump who waved the coat. I feel like socking him one, just for luck."

"Why? What did he do?"

"Oh, nothing, but then he seemed so damned cheerful."

In the meantime the oiler rowed, and then the correspondent rowed, and then the oiler rowed. Gray-faced and bowed forward, they mechanically, turn by turn, plied the leaden oars. The form of the lighthouse had vanished from the southern horizon, but finally a pale star appeared, just lifting from the sea. The streaked saffron in the west passed before the all-merging darkness, and the sea to the east was black. The land had vanished, and was expressed only by the low and drear thunder of the surf.

"If I am going to be drowned—if I am going to be drowned—if I am going to be drowned, why, in the name of the seven mad gods who rule the sea, was I allowed to come thus far and contemplate sand and trees? Was I brought here merely to have my nose dragged away as I was about to nibble the sacred cheese of life?"

The patient captain, drooped over the water-jar, was sometimes obliged to speak to the oarsman.

"Keep her head up! Keep her head up!"

"Keep her head up, sir." The voices were weary and low.

This was surely a quiet evening. All save the oarsman lay heavily and listlessly in the boat's bottom. As for him, his eyes were just capable of noting the tall black waves that swept forward in a most sinister silence, save for an occasional subdued growl of a crest.

The cook's head was on a thwart, and he looked without interest at the water under his nose. He was deep in other scenes. Finally he spoke. "Billie," he murmured, dreamfully, "what kind of pie do you like best?"

V

"Pie!" said the oiler and the correspondent, agitatedly. "Don't talk about those things, blast you!"

"Well," said the cook, "I was just thinking about ham sandwiches, and—"

A night on the sea in an open boat is a long night. As darkness settled finally, the shine of the light, lifting from the sea in the south, changed to full gold. On the northern horizon a new light appeared, a small bluish gleam on the edge of the waters. These two lights were the furniture of the world. Otherwise there was nothing but waves.

Two men huddled in the stern, and distances were so magnificent in the dinghy that the rower was enabled to keep his feet partly warm by thrusting them under his companions. Their legs indeed extended far under the rowing-seat until they touched the feet of the captain forward. Sometimes, despite the efforts of the tired oarsman, a wave came piling into the boat, an icy wave of the night, and the chilling water soaked them anew. They would twist their bodies for a moment and groan, and sleep the dead sleep once more, while the water in the boat gurgled about them as the craft rocked.

The plan of the oiler and the correspondent was for one to row until he lost the ability, and then arouse the other from his sea-water couch in the bottom of the boat.

The oiler plied the oars until his head drooped forward and the overpowering sleep blinded him; and he rowed yet afterward. Then he touched a man in the bottom of the boat, and called his name. "Will you spell me for a little while?" he said meekly.

"Sure, Billie," said the correspondent, awaking and dragging himself to a sitting position. They exchanged places carefully, and the oiler, cuddling down in the sea-water at the cook's side, seemed to go to sleep instantly.

The particular violence of the sea had ceased. The waves came without snarling. The obligation of the man at the oars was to keep the boat headed so that the tilt of the rollers would not capsize her, and to preserve her from filling when the crests rushed past. The black waves were silent and hard to be seen in the darkness. Often one was almost upon the boat before the oarsman was aware.

In a low voice the correspondent addressed the captain. He was not sure that the captain was awake, although this iron man seemed to be always awake. "Captain, shall I keep her making for that light north, sir?"

The same steady voice answered him. "Yes. Keep it about two points off the port bow."

The cook had tied a life-belt around himself in order to get even the warmth which this clumsy cork contrivance could donate, and he seemed almost stove like when a rower, whose teeth invariably chattered wildly as soon as he ceased his labor, dropped down to sleep.

The correspondent, as he rowed, looked down at the two men sleeping underfoot. The cook's arm was around the oiler's shoulders and, with their fragmentary clothing and haggard faces, they were the babes of the sea—a grotesque rendering of the old babes in the wood.[3]

Later he must have grown stupid at his work, for suddenly there was a growling of water, and a crest came with a roar and a swash into the boat, and it was a wonder that it did not set the cook afloat in his life-belt. The cook continued to sleep, but the oiler sat up, blinking his eyes and shaking with the new cold.

"Oh, I'm awful sorry, Billie," said the correspondent, contritely.

"That's all right, old boy," said the oiler, and lay down again and was asleep.

Presently it seemed that even the captain dozed, and the correspondent thought that he was the one man afloat on all the ocean. The wind had a voice as it came over the waves, and it was sadder than the end.

There was a long, loud swishing astern of the boat, and a gleaming trail of phosphorescence, like blue flame, was furrowed on the black waters. It might have been made by a monstrous knife.

Then there came a stillness, while the correspondent breathed with open mouth and looked at the sea.

Suddenly there was another swish and another long flash of bluish light, and this time it was alongside the boat, and might almost have been reached with an oar. The correspondent saw an enormous fin speed like a shadow through the water, hurling the crystalline spray and leaving the long glowing trail.

3. "Babes in the Wood" is the name of an old nursery rhyme about two orphans who are abandoned in the woods. Crane might be referring to the image evoked by the lines: "In one another's armes they dyed, / As babes wanting relief."

The correspondent looked over his shoulder at the captain. His face was hidden, and he seemed to be asleep. He looked at the babes of the sea. They certainly were asleep. So, being bereft of sympathy, he leaned a little way to one side and swore softly into the sea.

But the thing did not then leave the vicinity of the boat. Ahead or astern, on one side or the other, at intervals long or short, fled the long sparkling streak, and there was to be heard the *whirroo* of the dark fin. The speed and power of the thing was greatly to be admired. It cut the water like a gigantic and keen projectile.

The presence of this biding thing did not affect the man with the same horror that it would if he had been a picnicker. He simply looked at the sea dully and swore in an undertone.

Nevertheless, it is true that he did not wish to be alone with the thing. He wished one of his companions to awake by chance and keep him company with it. But the captain hung motionless over the water-jar and the oiler and the cook in the bottom of the boat were plunged in slumber.

VI

"If I am going to be drowned—if I am going to be drowned—if I am going to be drowned, why in the name of the seven mad gods who rule the sea, was I allowed to come thus far and contemplate sand and trees?"

During this dismal night, it may be remarked that a man would conclude that it was really the intention of the seven mad gods to drown him, despite the abominable injustice of it. For it was certainly an abominable injustice to drown a man who had worked so hard, so hard. The man felt it would be a crime most unnatural. Other people had drowned at sea since galleys swarmed with painted sails, but still——

When it occurs to a man that nature does not regard him as important and that she feels she would not maim the universe by disposing of him, he at first wishes to throw bricks at the temple, and he hates deeply the fact that there are no bricks and no temples. Any visible expression of nature would surely be pelleted with his jeers.

Then, if there be no tangible thing to hoot, he feels, perhaps, the desire to confront a personification and indulge in pleas, bowed to one knee, and with hands supplicant, saying, "Yes, but I love myself."

A high cold star on a winter's night is the word he feels that she says to him. Thereafter he knows the pathos of his situation.

The men in the dinghy had not discussed these matters, but each had, no doubt, reflected upon them in silence and according to his mind. There was seldom any expression upon their faces save the general one of complete weariness. Speech was devoted to the business of the boat.

To chime the notes of his emotions, a verse mysteriously entered the correspondent's head. He had even forgotten that he had forgotten this verse, but it suddenly was in his mind.

A soldier of the Legion lay dying in Algiers;
There was lack of woman's nursing,
there was dearth of woman's tears;
But a comrade stood beside him,
and he took the comrade's hand,
And he said, "I never more shall see
my own, my native land."[4]

In his childhood the correspondent had been made acquainted with the fact that a soldier of the Legion lay dying in Algiers, but he had never regarded it as important. Myriads of his schoolfellows had informed him of the soldier's plight, but the dinning had naturally ended by making him perfectly indifferent. He had never considered it his affair that a soldier of the Legion lay dying in Algiers, nor had it appeared to him as a matter for sorrow. It was less to him than the breaking of a pencil's point.

Now, however, it quaintly came to him as a human, living thing. It was no longer merely a picture of a few throes in the breast of a poet, meanwhile drinking tea and warming his feet at the grate; it was an actuality—stern, mournful, and fine.

The correspondent plainly saw the soldier. He lay on the sand with his feet out straight and still. While his pale left hand was

4. From "Bingen on the Rhine," a popular poem by the English poet and feminist Caroline Norton (1808–1877).

upon his chest in an attempt to thwart the going of his life, the blood came between his fingers. In the far Algerian distance, a city of low square forms was set against a sky that was faint with the last sunset hues. The correspondent, plying the oars and dreaming of the slow and slower movements of the lips of the soldier, was moved by a profound and perfectly impersonal comprehension. He was sorry for the soldier of the Legion who lay dying in Algiers.

The thing which had followed the boat and waited had evidently grown bored at the delay. There was no longer to be heard the slash of the cutwater, and there was no longer the flame of the long trail. The light in the north still glimmered, but it was apparently no nearer to the boat. Sometimes the boom of the surf rang in the correspondent's ears, and he turned the craft seaward then and rowed harder. Southward, some one had evidently built a watchfire on the beach. It was too low and too far to be seen, but it made a shimmering, roseate reflection upon the bluff in back of it, and this could be discerned from the boat. The wind came stronger, and sometimes a wave suddenly raged out like a mountain-cat, and there was to be seen the sheen and sparkle of a broken crest.

The captain, in the bow, moved on his water-jar and sat erect. "Pretty long night," he observed to the correspondent. He looked at the shore. "Those life-saving people take their time."

"Did you see that shark playing around?"

"Yes, I saw him. He was a big fellow, all right."

"Wish I had known you were awake."

Later the correspondent spoke into the bottom of the boat. "Billie!" There was a slow and gradual disentanglement. "Billie, will you spell me?"

"Sure," said the oiler.

As soon as the correspondent touched the cold, comfortable seawater in the bottom of the boat and had huddled close to the cook's life-belt he was deep in sleep, despite the fact that his teeth played all the popular airs. This sleep was so good to him that it was but a moment before he heard a voice call his name in a tone that demonstrated the last stages of exhaustion. "Will you spell me?"

"Sure, Billie."

The light in the north had mysteriously vanished, but the correspondent took his course from the wide-awake captain.

Later in the night they took the boat farther out to sea, and the captain directed the cook to take one oar at the stern and keep the boat facing the seas. He was to call out if he should hear the thunder of the surf. This plan enabled the oiler and the correspondent to get respite together. "We'll give those boys a chance to get into shape again," said the captain. They curled down and, after a few preliminary chatterings and trembles, slept once more the dead sleep. Neither knew they had bequeathed to the cook the company of another shark, or perhaps the same shark.

As the boat caroused on the waves, spray occasionally bumped over the side and gave them a fresh soaking, but this had no power to break their repose. The ominous slash of the wind and the water affected them as it would have affected mummies.

"Boys," said the cook, with the notes of every reluctance in his voice, "she's drifted in pretty close. I guess one of you had better take her to sea again." The correspondent, aroused, heard the crash of the toppled crests.

As he was rowing, the captain gave him some whiskey-and-water, and this steadied the chills out of him. "If I ever get ashore and anybody shows me even a photograph of an oar——"

At last there was a short conversation.

"Billie! . . . Billie, will you spell me?"

"Sure," said the oiler.

VII

When the correspondent again opened his eyes, the sea and the sky were each of the gray hue of the dawning. Later, carmine and gold was painted upon the waters. The morning appeared finally, in its splendor, with a sky of pure blue, and the sunlight flamed on the tips of the waves.

On the distant dunes were set many little black cottages, and a tall white windmill reared above them. No man, nor dog, nor bicycle appeared on the beach. The cottages might have formed a deserted village.

The voyagers scanned the shore. A conference was held in the boat. "Well," said the captain, "if no help is coming, we might better try a run through the surf right away. If we stay out here much longer we will be too weak to do anything for ourselves at all." The others silently acquiesced in this reasoning. The boat was headed for the beach. The correspondent wondered if none ever ascended the tall wind-tower, and if then they never looked seaward. This tower was a giant, standing with its back to the plight of the ants. It represented in a degree, to the correspondent, the serenity of nature amid the struggles of the individual—nature in the wind, and nature in the vision of men. She did not seem cruel to him then, nor beneficent, nor treacherous, nor wise. But she was indifferent, flatly indifferent. It is, perhaps, plausible that a man in this situation, impressed with the unconcern of the universe, should see the innumerable flaws of his life, and have them taste wickedly in his mind, and wish for another chance. A distinction between right and wrong seems absurdly clear to him, then, in this new ignorance of the grave-edge, and he understands that if he were given another opportunity he would mend his conduct and his words, and be better and brighter during an introduction or at a tea.

"Now, boys," said the captain, "she is going to swamp sure. All we can do is to work her in as far as possible, and then when she swamps, pile out and scramble for the beach. Keep cool now, and don't jump until she swamps sure."

The oiler took the oars. Over his shoulders he scanned the surf. "Captain," he said, "I think I'd better bring her about and keep her head-on to the seas and back her in."

"All right, Billie," said the captain. "Back her in." The oiler swung the boat then, and, seated in the stern, the cook and the correspondent were obliged to look over their shoulders to contemplate the lonely and indifferent shore.

The monstrous inshore rollers heaved the boat high until the men were again enabled to see the white sheets of water scudding up the slanted beach. "We won't get in very close," said the captain. Each time a man could wrest his attention from the rollers, he turned his glance toward the shore, and in the expression of the eyes during this contemplation there was a singular quality. The correspondent, observing the others, knew that they were not afraid, but the full meaning of their glances was shrouded.

As for himself, he was too tired to grapple fundamentally with the fact. He tried to coerce his mind into thinking of it, but the mind was dominated at this time by the muscles, and the muscles said they did not care. It merely occurred to him that if he should drown it would be a shame.

There were no hurried words, no pallor, no plain agitation. The men simply looked at the shore. "Now, remember to get well clear of the boat when you jump," said the captain.

Seaward the crest of a roller suddenly fell with a thunderous crash, and the long white comber came roaring down upon the boat.

"Steady now," said the captain. The men were silent. They turned their eyes from the shore to the comber and waited. The boat slid up the incline, leaped at the furious top, bounced over it, and swung down the long back of the wave. Some water had been shipped, and the cook bailed it out.

But the next crest crashed also. The tumbling, boiling flood of white water caught the boat and whirled it almost perpendicular. Water swarmed in from all sides. The correspondent had his hands on the gunwale at this time, and when the water entered at that place he swiftly withdrew his fingers, as if he objected to wetting them.

The little boat, drunken with this weight of water, reeled and snuggled deeper into the sea.

"Bail her out, cook! Bail her out!" said the captain.

"All right, Captain," said the cook.

"Now, boys, the next one will do for us sure," said the oiler. "Mind to jump clear of the boat."

The third wave moved forward, huge, furious, implacable. It fairly swallowed the dinghy, and almost simultaneously the men tumbled into the sea. A piece of life-belt had lain in the bottom of the boat, and as the correspondent went overboard he held this to his chest with his left hand.

The January water was icy, and he reflected immediately that it was colder than he had expected to find it off the coast of Florida. This appeared to his dazed mind as a fact important enough to be noted at the time. The coldness of the water was sad; it was tragic. This fact was somehow mixed and confused with his opinion of his own situation, so that it seemed almost a proper reason for tears. The water was cold.

When he came to the surface he was conscious of little but the noisy water. Afterward he saw his companions in the sea. The oiler was ahead in the race. He was swimming strongly and rapidly. Off to the correspondent's left, the cook's great white and corked back bulged out of the water, and in the rear the captain was hanging with his one good hand to the keel of the overturned dinghy.

There is a certain immovable quality to a shore, and the correspondent wondered at it amid the confusion of the sea.

It seemed also very attractive; but the correspondent knew that it was a long journey, and he paddled leisurely. The piece of life-preserver lay under him, and sometimes he whirled down the incline of a wave as if he were on a hand-sled.

But finally he arrived at a place in the sea where travel was beset with difficulty. He did not pause swimming to inquire what manner of current had caught him, but there his progress ceased. The shore was set before him like a bit of scenery on a stage, and he looked at it and understood with his eyes each detail of it.

As the cook passed, much farther to the left, the captain was calling to him, "Turn over on your back, cook! Turn over on your back and use the oar."

"All right, sir." The cook turned on his back, and, paddling with an oar, went ahead as if he were a canoe.

Presently the boat also passed to the left of the correspondent, with the captain clinging with one hand to the keel. He would have appeared like a man raising himself to look over a board fence if it were not for the extraordinary gymnastics of the boat. The correspondent marvelled that the captain could still hold to it.

They passed on nearer to shore—the oiler, the cook, the captain—and following them went the water-jar, bouncing gaily over the seas.

The correspondent remained in the grip of this strange new enemy, a current. The shore, with its white slope of sand and its green bluff topped with little silent cottages, was spread like a picture before him. It was very near to him then, but he was impressed as one who, in a gallery, looks at a scene from Brittany or Algiers.

He thought: "I am going to drown? Can it be possible? Can it be possible? Can it be possible?" Perhaps an individual must consider his own death to be the final phenomenon of nature.

But later a wave perhaps whirled him out of this small deadly current, for he found suddenly that he could again make progress toward the shore. Later still he was aware that the captain, clinging with one hand to the keel of the dinghy, had his face turned away from the shore and toward him, and was calling his name. "Come to the boat! Come to the boat!"

In his struggle to reach the captain and the boat, he reflected that when one gets properly wearied drowning must really be a comfortable arrangement—a cessation of hostilities accompanied by a large degree of relief; and he was glad of it, for the main thing in his mind for some moments had been horror of the temporary agony; he did not wish to be hurt.

Presently he saw a man running along the shore. He was undressing with most remarkable speed. Coat, trousers, shirt, everything flew magically off him.

"Come to the boat!" called the captain.

"All right, Captain." As the correspondent paddled, he saw the captain let himself down to bottom and leave the boat. Then the correspondent performed his one little marvel of the voyage. A large wave caught him and flung him with ease and supreme speed completely over the boat and far beyond it. It struck him even then as an event in gymnastics, and a true miracle of the sea. An overturned boat in the surf is not a plaything to a swimming man.

The correspondent arrived in water that reached only to his waist, but his condition did not enable him to stand for more than a moment. Each wave knocked him into a heap, and the undertow pulled at him.

Then he saw the man who had been running and undressing and undressing and running, come bounding into the water. He dragged ashore the cook, and then waded toward the captain; but the captain waved him away and sent him to the correspondent. He was naked—naked as a tree in winter; but a halo was about his head, and he shone like a saint. He gave a strong pull, and a long drag, and a bully heave at the correspondent's hand. The correspondent, schooled in the minor formulae, said, "Thanks, old man." But suddenly the man cried, "What's that?" He pointed a swift finger. The correspondent said, "Go."

In the shallows, face downward, lay the oiler. His forehead touched sand that was periodically, between each wave, clear of the sea.

The correspondent did not know all that transpired afterward. When he achieved safe ground he fell, striking the sand with each particular part of his body. It was as if he had dropped from a roof, but the thud was grateful to him.

It seems that instantly the beach was populated with men with blankets, clothes, and flasks, and women with coffee-pots and all the remedies sacred to their minds. The welcome of the land to the men from the sea was warm and generous; but a still and dripping shape was carried slowly up the beach, and the land's welcome for it could only be the different and sinister hospitality of the grave.

When it came night, the white waves paced to and fro in the moonlight, and the wind brought the sound of the great sea's voice to the men on the shore, and they felt that they could then be interpreters.

1897

Louise Erdrich
b. 1954

Most of Erdrich's fiction treats the lives of Native Americans—characters appear and reappear in her various novels and short stories, creating a rich fictional history of three families living around Argus, North Dakota. Part Chippewa herself, also a Catholic, Erdrich often melds Native American traditions with European traditions in her fiction. In this story, for example, the narrator's adventure parallels the quest motif of chivalric literature.

I'm a Mad Dog Biting Myself for Sympathy

Who I am is just the habit of what I always was, and who I'll be is the result. This comes clear to me at the wrong time. I am standing in a line, almost rehabilitated. Walgreens is the store in downtown Fargo. I have my purchase in my arms, and I am listening to canned carols on the loudspeaker. I plan to buy this huge stuffed parrot with purple wings and a yellow beak. Really, it is a toucan, I get told this later in the tank.

You think you know everything about yourself—how much money it would take, for instance, to make you take it. How you would react when caught. But then you find yourself walking out the door with a stuffed toucan, just to see if shit happens, if do-do occurs. And it does, though no one stops me right at first.

My motive is my girlfriend's Christmas present. And it is strange because I do have the money to pay for a present, though nothing very big or elaborate. I think of Dawn the minute I see the bird, and wish I'd won it for her at a county fair, though we never went to a fair. I see myself throwing a half-dozen softballs and hitting every wooden milk jug, or maybe tossing rings. But those things are weighted or loaded wrong and that's another reason I never could have won this toucan for Dawn, because the whole thing's a cheat in general. So what the hell, I think, and lift the bird.

Outside in the street it is one of my favorite kind of days, right there in the drag middle of winter when the snow is a few hard gray clumps and a dusty grass shows on the boulevards. I like the smell in the air, the dry dirt, the patches of water shrinking and the threat of snow, too, in the gloom of the sky.

The usual rubber-neck turns to look at me. This bird is really huge and furry, with green underneath its floppy wings and fat stuffed orange feet. I don't know why they'd have a strange thing like this in Walgreens. Maybe a big promotion, maybe some kind of come-on for the holiday season. And then the manager yells at me from the door. I am halfway down the street when I hear him. "Come back here!" Probably pointing at me, too, though there is no reason, as I stick out plenty and still more when I run.

First I put the bird underneath my arm. But it throws off my balance. So I clutch it to my chest; that is no better. Thinking back now I should have ditched it, and slipped off through the alleys and disappeared. Of course, I didn't—otherwise none of all that happened would have happened. I sit the bird on my shoulders and hold the lumpy feet under my chin and then I bear down, like going for the distance or the gold, let my legs churn beneath me. I leap curbs, dodge among old men in long gray coats and babies in strollers, shoot up and over car hoods until I come to the railroad depot and, like it is some sort of destination, though it isn't, I slip in the door and look out the window.

A gathering crowd follows with the manager. There is a police-woman, a few local mall-sitters, passersby. They are stumbling and talking together and making big circles of their arms, to illustrate the toucan, and closing in.

That's when my stroke of luck, good or bad is no telling, occurs. The car drives into the parking lot, a solid plastic luggage rack strapped on its roof. A man and a woman jump out, late for a connection, and they leave the car running in neutral. I walk out of the depot and stand before the car. At that moment, it seems as though events are taking me somewhere. I open up the hinges on the plastic rack, stuff in the bird. No one seems to notice me. Encouraged, I get in. I put my hands on the wheel. I take the car out of neutral and we start to roll, back out of the lot. I change gears, then turn at the crossroads, and look both ways.

I don't know what you'd do in this situation. I'll ask you. There you are in a car. It isn't yours but for the time being that doesn't matter. You look up the street one way. It's clear. You look down the other, and a clump of people still are arguing and trying to describe you with their hands. Either way, the road will take you straight out of town. The clear way is north, where you don't know anyone. South, what's there?

I let the car idle.

My parents. It's not like I hate them or anything. I just can't see them. I can close my eyes and form my sister's face behind my eyelids, but not my parents' faces. Where their eyes should meet mine, nothing. That's all. I shouldn't show up at the farm, not with the toucan. Much less the car. I think a few seconds longer. The bird on the roof. It is for Dawn. You could say she got me into this, so Dawn should get me out. But she doesn't live in Fargo anymore, she lives south. She lives in Colorado, which complicates everything later for it means crossing state lines and all just to bring her that bird, and then another complexity, although at the time I don't realize, occurs when the woman at the depot, the one who has left the car, appears very suddenly in the rearview mirror.

I have just started moving south when I hear a thump from behind. It is so surprising. Just imagine. She is there on the trunk, hanging on as though by magnetics. She reaches up and grabs the hitches on the roof-top luggage rack, gets a better grip, and sprawls across the back window. She is a little woman. Through the side-view, I see her blue heels in the air, the edge of a black coat. I hear her shrieking in an inhuman desperate way that horrifies me so much I floor the gas.

We must go by everyone fast, but the effect is dreamlike, so slow. I see the faces of the clump of people, their mouths falling open, arms stretching and grasping as I turn the corner and the woman rolls over and over like a seal in water. Then she flies off the trunk and bowls them before in her rush so they heap on the ground. She is in their arms. They put her down as though she is a live torpedo and keep running after me.

"Scandinavians," I think, because my grandmother's one, "they don't give up the ghost." I just want to yell out, tell them. "OK, so it's stolen. It's gone! It's a cheap stuffed bird anyhow and I will *park* the car. I promise."

I start talking to myself. "I'll check the oil in Sioux Falls. No sweat." Then the worst thing comes about, and all of a sudden I understand the woman with her eyes rearing back in her skull, her little heels pointed in the air. I understand the faces of the people in the group, their blurting voices, "b . . . b . . . baby".

As from the back seat, it wails.

I have my first reaction, disbelief. I have taken the scenic route at a fast clip, but I know the view anyway. I am down near the river and have decided from there I will take 30 and avoid the Interstate, always so well patrolled. I park and turn around in a frantic whirl. I revolve twice in my seat. And I still can't see the baby. I am behind on the new equipment. He sits in something round and firm, shaped like a big football, strapped down the chest and over the waist, held tight by a padded cushion. Above his face there is a little diamond attachment made of plastic, a bunch of keys and plastic balls that dangle out of reach.

I have never seen a child this little before, so small that it is not a child yet. Its face is tiny and dark, almost reddish, or copper, and its fingers, splayed out against its cheeks, are the feet of a sparrow. There is a bottle of milk in a bag beside it. I put the end in its mouth and it sucks. But it will not hold the bottle. I keep putting the end in its hand, and it won't grasp.

"Oh screw it," I finally say, and gun right out of there. Its cry begins again and I wish I knew how to stop it. I have to slow down to get through some traffic. Sirens rush ahead on their way to the Interstate, passing in a squeal which surprises me. This car, this pack on top, I am so obvious. I think I'll maybe park at the old King Leo's, get out, and run. But then I pass it. I think it will be better if I get down south around the South Dakota border, or in the sandhills, where I can hide out in cow shelters. So I do go south. Over me the sky is bearing down and bearing down, so I think now maybe snow will fall. A White Christmas like the music in the drugstore. I know how to drive in snow and this car has decent tires, I can feel them. They never lose grip or plane above the road. They just keep rolling, humming, below me, all four in this unified direction, so dull that after some time it all seems right again.

The baby drops off, stops crying. It shouldn't have been there, should it. I have to realize the situation. There is no use in thinking back, in saying to myself, well you shouldn't have stole the damn bird in the first place, because I did do that and then, well as you see, it is like I went along with the arrangement of things as they happened.

Of course, around halfway down there is a smokey waiting, which I knew would happen, but not whether it would be before or behind me. So now my answer comes. The officer's car turns off a dirt road and starts flashing, starts coming at me from the rear. I take it up to eighty and we move, *move*, so the frozen water standing in the fields flashes by like scarves and the silver snow whirls out of nowhere, to either side of us, and what rushes up before us is a heat of road and earth.

I am not all that afraid. I never am and that's my problem. I feel sure they will not use their weapons. I keep driving and then, as we take a turn, as we come to a railroad crossing, I hear the plastic roof rack snap open. I look through the rearview by reflex, and see the bird as it dives out of the sky, big and plush, a purple blur that plunges its yellow beak through the windshield and throws the state police off course so that they skid, roll over once, come back with such force the car righted itself. They sit there in shock.

I keep on going. The pack blows off and I reason that now the car is less obvious. I should have thought about that in the first place, but then the bird would not have hatched out and demolished the police car. Just about this time, however, being as the toucan is gone, I begin to feel perhaps there is no reason to go on traveling this way. I begin to think I will just stop at the nearest farm, leave the car and the baby, and keep hitching south. I begin to think if I show up at Dawn's, even with nothing, on a Christmas Eve, she will not throw me out. She will have to take me, let me stay there, on the couch. She lives with someone now, a guy ten years older than me, five years older than her. By now he has probably taken her places, shown her restaurants and zoos, gone camping in the wilderness, skied. She will know things and I will still be the same person that I was the year before. And I am glad about the toucan, then, which would have made me look ridiculous. Showing up there like a kid in junior high school with a stuffed animal, when her tastes have broadened. I should have sent her chocolates, a little red and green box. I was wishing I had. And then I look past the road in front of me and realize it is snowing.

It isn't just like ordinary snow even from the first. It is like that rhyme or story in the second grade, the sky falling and let's go and tell the king. It comes down. I think to myself, *well, let it come down.* And I keep driving. I know you'll say it, you'll wonder, you'll think what about the child in back of him, that baby, only three weeks old, little Mason Joseph Andrews? Because he does have a name and all, but what could I know of that?

I talk to it. I am good at driving in the snow but I need to talk while I'm driving. I'll tell this now, it doesn't matter. I say, "You little bastard you, what are you doing here!" It is my state of mind. I put the window open. Snow whites out the windshield and I can't see the road in front of us. I watch the margin, try to follow the yellow line which is obscured by a twisting blanket. I am good at this though I need my concentration, which vanishes when he bawled. My ears are full. He roars and I hear the sound as wind, as sounds that came out of its mother. I hit the plastic egg and feel the straps give, feel the car give on the road. I swerve into another car's ruts, weave along the dotted yellow, and then under me is snow and still I keep going at a steady pace although the ground feels all hollow and uncertain. The tracks narrow into one, and then widen, so I suddenly realize this: I have followed a snowmobile trail and now I am somewhere off the road. Immediately, just like in a cartoon, like Dumbo flying and he realizes that he isn't supposed to be up in the air, I panic and get stuck.

So now I am in awful shape, out there in a field, in a storm that could go on for three more minutes or three more days. I sit there thinking until the baby gets discouraged and falls asleep. And get this. It is a white car. Harder to see than ever. And not a bit of this did I ever think or plan for. I can't remember what they say in the papers every fall, the advice about what to do when a blizzard hits. Whether to stay on the road, with the car, or set out walking for help. There is the baby. It is helpless, but does not seem so helpless. I know now that I should have left the car run, the heater, but at the time I don't think. Except I do rip that dangle of toys off its seat and tie it on the aerial when I go out, and I do leave its blankets in there, never take any. I just wrap my arms around my chest and start walking south.

By not stopping for a minute I live through the storm, though I am easy to catch after it lets up, and I freeze an ear. All right, you know that baby wasn't hurt anyway. You heard. Cold, yes, but it lived. They ask me in court why I didn't take it along with me, bundled in my jacket, and I say, well it lived, didn't it? Proving I did right. But I know better sometimes, now that I've spent time alone here in Mandan, more time running than I knew I had available.

I think about that boy. He'll grow up, but already I am more to him than his own father because I taught him what I know about the cold. It sinks in, there to stay, doesn't it? And people. They will leave you, no matter what you say there's no return. There's just the emptiness all around, and you in it, like singing up from the bottom of a well, like nothing else, until you harm yourself, until you are a mad dog just biting yourself for sympathy, because there is no relenting, and there is no hand that falls, and there is no woman to come home to take you in her arms.

I know I taught that boy something in those hours I was walking south. I know I'll always be inside him, cold and black, about the size of a coin, maybe, something he touches against and skids. And he'll say, *what is this,* and the thing is he won't know it is a piece of thin ice I have put there, the same as I have in me.

1990

William Faulkner
1897–1962

"A Rose for Emily" was Faulkner's first published story. It combines two real-life events from Faulkner's home in Mississippi. One story was of a local woman who refused to release her dead son's body to the undertaker, and the other was of a romance between a Southern belle and a Northerner who came South to pave streets. Nearly all critics think Emily symbolizes the decay of the old order, the dissolution of the Southern aristocracy. Faulkner himself disowned symbolic readings and described the story as the tragedy of "a young girl that just wanted to be loved and to love and to have a husband and a family" but was "kept down by her father, a selfish man, who didn't want her to leave home because he wanted a housekeeper." According to Faulkner, her impulses drove her to do things that she knew were wrong. Note that the narrator in this story is first person plural, *which is uncommon.*

A Rose for Emily

I

When Miss Emily Grierson died, our whole town went to her funeral: the men through a sort of respectful affection for a fallen monument, the women mostly out of curiosity to see the inside of her house, which no one save an old manservant—a combined gardener and cook—had seen in at least ten years.

It was a big, squarish frame house that had once been white, decorated with cupolas and spires and scrolled balconies in the heavily lightsome style of the seventies, set on what had once been our most select street. But garages and cotton gins had encroached and obliterated even the august names of that neighborhood; only Miss Emily's house was left, lifting its stubborn and coquettish decay above the cotton wagons and the gasoline pumps—an eyesore among eyesores. And now Miss Emily had gone to join the representatives of those august names where they lay in the cedar-bemused cemetery among the ranked and anonymous graves of Union and Confederate soldiers who fell at the battle of Jefferson.

Alive, Miss Emily had been a tradition, a duty, and a care; a sort of hereditary obligation upon the town, dating from that day in 1894 when Colonel Sartoris, the mayor—he who fathered the edict that no Negro woman should appear on the streets without an apron—remitted her taxes, the dispensation dating from the death of her father on into perpetuity. Not that Miss Emily would have accepted charity. Colonel Sartoris invented an involved tale to the effect that Miss Emily's father had loaned money to the town, which the town, as a matter of business, preferred this way of repaying. Only a man of Colonel Sartoris' generation and thought could have invented it, and only a woman could have believed it.

When the next generation, with its more modern ideas, became mayors and aldermen, this arrangement created some little dissatisfaction. On the first of the year they mailed her a tax notice. February came, and there was no reply. They wrote her a formal letter, asking her to call at the sheriff's office at her convenience. A week later the mayor wrote her himself, offering to call or to send his car for her, and received in reply a note on paper of an archaic shape, in a thin, flowing calligraphy in faded ink, to the effect that she no longer went out at all. The tax notice was also enclosed, without comment.

They called a special meeting of the Board of Aldermen. A deputation waited upon her, knocked at the door through which no visitor had passed since she ceased giving china-painting lessons eight or ten years earlier. They were admitted by the old Negro into a dim hall from which a stairway mounted into still more shadow. It smelled of dust and disuse—a close, dank smell. The Negro led them into the parlor. It was furnished in heavy, leather-covered furniture. When the Negro opened the blinds of one window, they could see that the leather was cracked; and when they sat down, a faint dust rose sluggishly about their thighs, spinning with slow motes in the single sun-ray. On a tarnished gilt easel before the fireplace stood a crayon portrait of Miss Emily's father.

They rose when she entered—a small, fat woman in black, with a thin gold chain descending to her waist and vanishing into her belt, leaning on an ebony cane with a tarnished gold head. Her skeleton was small and spare; perhaps that was why what would have been merely plumpness in another was obesity in her. She looked bloated, like a body long submerged in motionless water, and of that pallid hue. Her eyes, lost in the fatty ridges of her face, looked like two small pieces of coal pressed into a lump of dough as they moved from one face to another while the visitors stated their errand.

She did not ask them to sit. She just stood in the door and listened quietly until the spokesman came to a stumbling halt. Then they could hear the invisible watch ticking at the end of the gold chain.

Her voice was dry and cold. "I have no taxes in Jefferson. Colonel Sartoris explained it to me. Perhaps one of you can gain access to the city records and satisfy yourselves."

"But we have. We are the city authorities, Miss Emily. Didn't you get a notice from the sheriff, signed by him?"

"I received a paper, yes," Miss Emily said. "Perhaps he considers himself the sheriff. . . . I have no taxes in Jefferson."

"But there is nothing on the books to show that, you see. We must go by the—"

"See Colonel Sartoris. I have no taxes in Jefferson."

"But, Miss Emily—"

"See Colonel Sartoris." (Colonel Sartoris had been dead almost ten years.) "I have no taxes in Jefferson. Tobe!" The Negro appeared. "Show these gentlemen out."

II

So she vanquished them, horse and foot,[1] just as she had vanquished their fathers thirty years before about the smell. That was two years after her father's death and a short time after her sweetheart—the one we believed would marry her—had deserted her. After her father's death she went out very little; after her sweetheart went away, people hardly saw her at all. A few of the ladies had the temerity to call, but were not received, and the only sign of life about the place was the Negro man—a young man then—going in and out with a market basket.

1. I.e., she vanquished them thoroughly. "Horse and foot" is a nineteenth-century phrase meaning, roughly, "the whole army, both cavalry and infantry."

"Just as if a man—any man—could keep a kitchen properly," the ladies said; so they were not surprised when the smell developed. It was another link between the gross, teeming world and the high and mighty Griersons.

A neighbor, a woman, complained to the mayor, Judge Stevens, eighty years old.

"But what will you have me do about it, madam?" he said.

"Why, send her word to stop it," the woman said. "Isn't there a law?"

"I'm sure that won't be necessary," Judge Stevens said. "It's probably just a snake or a rat that nigger of hers killed in the yard. I'll speak to him about it."

The next day he received two more complaints, one from a man who came in diffident deprecation. "We really must do something about it, Judge. I'd be the last one in the world to bother Miss Emily, but we've got to do something." That night the Board of Aldermen met—three graybeards and one younger man, a member of the rising generation.

"It's simple enough," he said. "Send her word to have her place cleaned up. Give her a certain time to do it in, and if she don't . . ."

"Dammit, sir," Judge Stevens said, "will you accuse a lady to her face of smelling bad?"

So the next night, after midnight, four men crossed Miss Emily's lawn and slunk about the house like burglars, sniffing along the base of the brickwork and at the cellar openings while one of them performed a regular sowing motion with his hand out of a sack slung from his shoulder. They broke open the cellar door and sprinkled lime there, and in all the outbuildings. As they recrossed the lawn, a window that had been dark was lighted and Miss Emily sat in it, the light behind her, and her upright torso motionless as that of an idol. They crept quietly across the lawn and into the shadow of the locusts that lined the street. After a week or two the smell went away.

That was when people had begun to feel really sorry for her. People in our town, remembering how old lady Wyatt, her great-aunt, had gone completely crazy at last, believed that the Griersons held themselves a little too high for what they really were. None of the young men were quite good enough for Miss Emily and such. We had long thought of them as a tableau, Miss Emily a slender figure in white in the background, her father a spraddled silhouette in the foreground, his back to her and clutching a horsewhip, the two of them framed by the back-flung front door. So when she got to be thirty and was still single, we were not pleased exactly, but vindicated; even with insanity in the family she wouldn't have turned down all of her chances if they had really materialized.

When her father died, it got about that the house was all that was left to her; and in a way, people were glad. At last they could pity Miss Emily. Being left alone, and a pauper, she had become humanized. Now she too would know the old thrill and the old despair of a penny more or less.

The day after his death all the ladies prepared to call at the house and offer condolence and aid, as is our custom. Miss Emily met them at the door, dressed as usual and with no trace of grief on her face. She told them that her father was not dead. She did that for three days, with the ministers calling on her, and the doctors, trying to persuade her to let them dispose of the body. Just as they were about to resort to law and force, she broke down, and they buried her father quickly.

We did not say she was crazy then. We believed she had to do that. We remembered all the young men her father had driven away, and we knew that with nothing left, she would have to cling to that which had robbed her, as people will.

III

She was sick for a long time. When we saw her again, her hair was cut short, making her look like a girl, with a vague resemblance to those angels in colored church windows—sort of tragic and serene.

The town had just let the contracts for paving the sidewalks, and in the summer after her father's death they began the work. The construction company came with niggers and mules and machinery, and a foreman named Homer Barron, a Yankee—a big, dark, ready man, with a big voice and eyes lighter than his face. The little boys would follow in groups to hear him cuss the niggers, and the niggers singing in time to the rise and fall of picks. Pretty soon he knew everybody in town. Whenever you heard a lot of laughing anywhere about the square, Homer Barron would be in the center of the group. Presently we began to see him and Miss Emily on Sunday afternoons driving in the yellow-wheeled buggy and the matched team of bays from the livery stable.

At first we were glad that Miss Emily would have an interest, because the ladies all said, "Of course a Grierson would not think seriously of a Northerner, a day laborer." But there were still others, older people, who said that even grief could not cause a real lady to forget *noblesse oblige*—without calling it *noblesse oblige*.[2] They just said, "Poor Emily. Her kinsfolk should come to her." She had some kin in Alabama; but years ago her father had fallen out with them over the estate of old lady Wyatt, the crazy woman, and there was no communication between the two families. They had not even been represented at the funeral.

And as soon as the old people said, "Poor Emily," the whispering began. "Do you suppose it's really so?" they said to one another. "Of course it is. What else could . . ." This behind their hands; rustling of craned silk and satin behind jalousies closed upon the sun of Sunday afternoon as the thin, swift clop-clop-clop of the matched team passed: "Poor Emily."

She carried her head high enough—even when we believed that she was fallen. It was as if she demanded more than ever the recognition of her dignity as the last Grierson; as if it had wanted that touch of earthiness to reaffirm her imperviousness. Like when she bought the rat poison, the arsenic. That was over a year after they had begun to say "Poor Emily," and while the two female cousins were visiting her.

"I want some poison," she said to the druggist. She was over thirty then, still a slight woman, though thinner than usual, with cold, haughty black eyes in a face the flesh of which was strained across the temples and about the eye sockets as you imagine a lighthouse-keeper's face ought to look. "I want some poison," she said.

"Yes, Miss Emily. What kind? For rats and such? I'd recom—"

"I want the best you have. I don't care what kind."

2. The responsibility to behave honorably associated with people of higher birth; literally, "nobility obligates" (French).

The druggist named several. "They'll kill anything up to an elephant. But what you want is—"

"Arsenic," Miss Emily said. "Is that a good one?"

"Is . . . arsenic? Yes, ma'am. But what you want—"

"I want arsenic."

The druggist looked down at her. She looked back at him, erect, her face like a strained flag. "Why, of course," the druggist said. "If that's what you want. But the law requires you to tell what you are going to use it for."

Miss Emily just stared at him, her head tilted back in order to look him eye for eye, until he looked away and went and got the arsenic and wrapped it up. The Negro delivery boy brought her the package; the druggist didn't come back. When she opened the package at home there was written on the box, under the skull and bones: "For rats."

IV

So the next day we all said, "She will kill herself"; and we said it would be the best thing. When she had first begun to be seen with Homer Barron, we had said, "She will marry him." Then we said, "She will persuade him yet," because Homer himself had remarked—he liked men, and it was known that he drank with the younger men in the Elks' Club that he was not a marrying man. Later we said, "Poor Emily" behind the jalousies as they passed on Sunday afternoon in the glittering buggy, Miss Emily with her head high and Homer Barron with his hat cocked and a cigar in his teeth, reins and whip in a yellow glove.

Then some of the ladies began to say that it was a disgrace to the town and a bad example to the young people. The men did not want to interfere, but at last the ladies forced the Baptist minister—Miss Emily's people were Episcopal—to call upon her. He would never divulge what happened during that interview, but he refused to go back again. The next Sunday they again drove about the streets, and the following day the minister's wife wrote to Miss Emily's relations in Alabama.

So she had blood-kin under her roof again and we sat back to watch developments. At first nothing happened. Then we were sure that they were to be married. We learned that Miss Emily had been to the jeweler's and ordered a man's toilet set in silver, with the letters H. B. on each piece. Two days later we learned that she had bought a complete outfit of men's clothing, including a nightshirt, and we said, "They are married." We were really glad. We were glad because the two female cousins were even more Grierson than Miss Emily had ever been.

So we were not surprised when Homer Barron—the streets had been finished some time since—was gone. We were a little disappointed that there was not a public blowing-off, but we believed that he had gone on to prepare for Miss Emily's coming, or to give her a chance to get rid of the cousins. (By that time it was a cabal, and we were all Miss Emily's allies to help circumvent the cousins.) Sure enough, after another week they departed. And, as we had expected all along, within three days Homer Barron was back in town. A neighbor saw the Negro man admit him at the kitchen door at dusk one evening.

And that was the last we saw of Homer Barron. And of Miss Emily for some time. The Negro man went in and out with the market basket, but the front door remained closed. Now and then we would see her at a window for a moment, as the men did that night when they sprinkled the lime, but for almost six months she did not appear on the streets. Then we knew that this was to be expected too; as if that quality of her father which had thwarted her woman's life so many times had been too virulent and too furious to die.

When we next saw Miss Emily, she had grown fat and her hair was turning gray. During the next few years it grew grayer and grayer until it attained an even pepper-and-salt iron-gray, when it ceased turning. Up to the day of her death at seventy-four it was still that vigorous iron-gray, like the hair of an active man.

From that time on her front door remained closed, save for a period of six or seven years, when she was about forty, during which she gave lessons in china-painting. She fitted up a studio in one of the downstairs rooms, where the daughters and granddaughters of Colonel Sartoris' contemporaries were sent to her with the same regularity and in the same spirit that they were sent to church on Sundays with a twenty-five-cent piece for the collection plate. Meanwhile her taxes had been remitted.

Then the newer generation became the backbone and the spirit of the town, and the painting pupils grew up and fell away and did not send their children to her with boxes of color and tedious brushes and pictures cut from the ladies' magazines. The front door closed upon the last one and remained closed for good. When the town got free postal delivery, Miss Emily alone refused to let them fasten the metal numbers above her door and attach a mailbox to it. She would not listen to them.

Daily, monthly, yearly we watched the Negro grow grayer and more stooped, going in and out with the market basket. Each December we sent her a tax notice, which would be returned by the post office a week later, unclaimed. Now and then we would see her in one of the downstairs windows—she had evidently shut up the top floor of the house—like the carven torso of an idol in a niche, looking or not looking at us, we could never tell which. Thus she passed from generation to generation—dear, inescapable, impervious, tranquil, and perverse.

And so she died. Fell ill in the house filled with dust and shadows, with only a doddering Negro man to wait on her. We did not even know she was sick; we had long since given up trying to get any information from the Negro. He talked to no one, probably not even to her, for his voice had grown harsh and rusty, as if from disuse.

She died in one of the downstairs rooms, in a heavy walnut bed with a curtain, her gray head propped on a pillow yellow and moldy with age and lack of sunlight.

V

The Negro met the first of the ladies at the front door and let them in, with their hushed, sibilant voices and their quick, curious glances, and then he disappeared. He walked right through the house and out the back and was not seen again.

The two female cousins came at once. They held the funeral on the second day, with the town coming to look at Miss Emily beneath a mass of bought flowers, with the crayon face of her father musing profoundly above the bier and the ladies sibilant and macabre; and the very old men—some in their brushed Confederate uniforms—on the porch and the lawn, talking of Miss Emily as if she had been a contemporary of theirs, believing that they had danced with her and courted her perhaps, confusing time with its mathematical progression, as the old do, to whom all the past is not a diminishing road but, instead, a huge meadow which no winter ever quite touches, divided from them now by the narrow bottleneck of the most recent decade of years.

Already we knew that there was one room in that region above stairs which no one had seen in forty years, and which would have to be forced. They waited until Miss Emily was decently in the ground before they opened it.

The violence of breaking down the door seemed to fill this room with pervading dust. A thin, acrid pall as of the tomb seemed to lie everywhere upon this room decked and furnished as for a bridal: upon the valance curtains of faded rose color, upon the rose-shaded lights, upon the dressing table, upon the delicate array of crystal and the man's toilet things backed with tarnished silver, silver so tarnished that the monogram was obscured. Among them lay a collar and tie, as if they had just been removed, which, lifted, left upon the surface a pale crescent in the dust. Upon a chair hung the suit, carefully folded; beneath it the two mute shoes and the discarded socks.

The man himself lay in the bed.

For a long while we just stood there, looking down at the profound and fleshless grin. The body had apparently once lain in the attitude of an embrace, but now the long sleep that outlasts love, that conquers even the grimace of love, had cuckolded him. What was left of him, rotted beneath what was left of the nightshirt, had become inextricable from the bed in which he lay; and upon him and upon the pillow beside him lay that even coating of the patient and biding dust.

Then we noticed that in the second pillow was the indentation of a head. One of us lifted something from it, and leaning forward, that faint and invisible dust dry and acrid in the nostrils, we saw a long strand of iron-gray hair.

1930

Gabriel García Márquez
b. 1928

Garciá Márquez was a central figure in the 1960s Latin American literary movement called "The Boom." The writers of this movement were cosmopolitan and wrote for an international Spanish-speaking audience. A few, like García Márquez, were also conscious of writing for audiences who would only read their work in translation. Even so, García Márquez typically grounds his stories in fairly isolated rural villages where myth and fantasy mix on equal terms with "reality." His technique has been dubbed magical realism, *and you can devise a pretty good definition of that term by analyzing "A Very Old Man with Enormous Wings." We could regard the story as an allegory, perhaps, but magical realism extends its effect beyond allegory. Of equal importance to the story line—who the protagonist is, what the conflict and resolution are—is the effect of García Márquez's style.*

A Very Old Man with Enormous Wings[1]

A Tale for Children

On the third day of rain they had killed so many crabs inside the house that Pelayo had to cross his drenched courtyard and throw them into the sea, because the newborn child had a temperature all night and they thought it was due to the stench. The world had been sad since Tuesday. Sea and sky were a single ash-gray thing and the sands of the beach, which on March nights glimmered like powdered light, had become a stew of mud and rotten shellfish. The light was so weak at noon that when Pelayo was coming back to the house after throwing away the crabs, it was hard for him to see what it was that was moving and groaning in the rear of the courtyard. He had to go very close to see that it was an old man, a very old man, lying face down in the mud, who, in spite of his tremendous efforts, couldn't get up, impeded by his enormous wings.

1. Translated by Gregory Rabassa.

Frightened by that nightmare, Pelayo ran to get Elisenda, his wife, who was putting compresses on the sick child, and he took her to the rear of the courtyard. They both looked at the fallen body with mute stupor. He was dressed like a ragpicker. There were only a few faded hairs left on his bald skull and very few teeth in his mouth, and his pitiful condition of a drenched great-grandfather had taken away any sense of grandeur he might have had. His huge buzzard wings, dirty and half-plucked, were forever entangled in the mud. They looked at him so long and so closely that Pelayo and Elisenda very soon overcame their surprise and in the end found him familiar. Then they dared speak to him, and he answered in an incomprehensible dialect with a strong sailor's voice. That was how they skipped over the inconvenience of the wings and quite intelligently concluded that he was a lonely castaway from some foreign ship wrecked by the storm. And yet, they called in a neighbor woman who knew everything about life and death to see him, and all she needed was one look to show them their mistake.

"He's an angel," she told them. "He must have been coming for the child, but the poor fellow is so old that the rain knocked him down."

On the following day everyone knew that a flesh-and-blood angel was held captive in Pelayo's house. Against the judgment of the wise neighbor woman, for whom angels in those times were the fugitive survivors of a celestial conspiracy, they did not have the heart to club him to death. Pelayo watched over him all afternoon from the kitchen, armed with his bailiff's club, and before going to bed he dragged him out of the mud and locked him up with the hens in the wire chicken coop. In the middle of the night, when the rain stopped, Pelayo and Elisenda were still killing crabs. A short time afterward the child woke up without a fever and with a desire to eat. Then they felt magnanimous and decided to put the angel on a raft with fresh water and provisions for three days and leave him to his fate on the high seas. But when they went out into the courtyard with the first light of dawn, they found the whole neighborhood in front of the chicken coop having fun with the angel, without the slightest reverence, tossing him things to eat through the openings in the wire as if he weren't a supernatural creature but a circus animal.

Father Gonzaga arrived before seven o'clock, alarmed at the strange news. By that time onlookers less frivolous than those at dawn had already arrived and they were making all kinds of conjectures concerning the captive's future. The simplest among them thought that he should be named mayor of the world. Others of sterner mind felt that he should be promoted to the rank of five-star general in order to win all wars. Some visionaries hoped that he could be put to stud in order to implant on earth a race of winged wise men who could take charge of the universe. But Father Gonzaga, before becoming a priest, had been a robust woodcutter. Standing by the wire, he reviewed his catechism in an instant and asked them to open the door so that he could take a close look at that pitiful man who looked more like a huge decrepit hen among the fascinated chickens. He was lying in a corner drying his open wings in the sunlight among the fruit peels and breakfast leftovers that the early risers had thrown him. Alien to the impertinences of the world, he only lifted his antiquarian eyes and murmured something in his dialect when Father Gonzaga went into the chicken coop and said good morning to him in Latin. The parish priest had his first suspicion of an imposter when he saw that he did not understand the language of God or know how to greet His ministers. Then he noticed that seen close up he was much too human: he had an unbearable smell of the outdoors, the back side of his wings was strewn with parasites and his main feathers had been mistreated by terrestial winds, and nothing about him measured up to the proud dignity of angels. Then he came out of the chicken coop and in a brief sermon warned the curious against the risks of being ingenuous. He reminded them that the devil had the bad habit of making use of carnival tricks in order to confuse the unwary. He argued that if wings were not the essential element in determining the difference between a hawk and an airplane, they were even less so in the recognition of angels. Nevertheless, he promised to write a letter to his bishop so that the latter would write to his primate so that the latter would write to the Supreme Pontiff in order to get the final verdict from the highest courts.

His prudence fell on sterile hearts. The news of the captive angel spread with such rapidity that after a few hours the courtyard had the bustle of a marketplace and they had to call in troops with fixed bayonets to disperse the mob that was about to knock the house down. Elisenda, her spine all twisted from sweeping up so much marketplace trash, then got the idea of fencing in the yard and charging five cents admission to see the angel.

The curious came from far away. A traveling carnival arrived with a flying acrobat who buzzed over the crowd several times, but no one paid any attention to him because his wings were not those of an angel but, rather, those of a sidereal bat. The most unfortunate invalids on earth came in search of health: a poor woman who since childhood had been counting her heartbeats and had run out of numbers; a Portuguese man who couldn't sleep because the noise of the stars disturbed him; a sleepwalker who got up at night to undo the things he had done while awake; and many others with less serious ailments. In the midst of that shipwreck disorder that made the earth tremble, Pelayo and Elisenda were happy with fatigue, for in less than a week they had crammed their rooms with money and the line of pilgrims waiting their turn to enter still reached beyond the horizon.

The angel was the only one who took no part in his own act. He spent his time trying to get comfortable in his borrowed nest, befuddled by the hellish heat of the oil lamps and sacramental candles that had been placed along the wire. At first they tried to make him eat some mothballs, which, according to the wisdom of the wise neighbor woman, were the food prescribed for angels. But he turned them down, just as he turned down the papal lunches[2] that the penitents brought him, and they never found out whether it was because he was an angel or because he was an old man that in the end he ate nothing but eggplant mush. His only supernatural virtue seemed to be patience. Especially during the first days, when the hens pecked at him, searching for the stellar parasites that proliferated in his wings, and the cripples pulled out feathers to touch their defective parts with, and even the most merciful threw stones at him, trying to get him to rise so they could see him standing. The only time they succeeded in arousing him was when they burned his side with an iron for branding steers, for he had been motionless for so many hours that they thought he was dead. He awoke with a start, ranting in his

2. Expensive meals.

hermetic language and with tears in his eyes, and he flapped his wings a couple of times, which brought on a whirlwind of chicken dung and lunar dust and a gale of panic that did not seem to be of this world. Although many thought that his reaction had been one not of rage but of pain, from then on they were careful not to annoy him, because the majority understood that his passivity was not that of a hero taking his ease but that of a cataclysm in repose.

Father Gonzaga held back the crowd's frivolity with formulas of maidservant inspiration while awaiting the arrival of a final judgment on the nature of the captive. But the mail from Rome showed no sense of urgency. They spent their time finding out if the prisoner had a navel, if his dialect had any connection with Aramaic, how many times he could fit on the head of a pin, or whether he wasn't just a Norwegian with wings. Those meager letters might have come and gone until the end of time if a providential event had not put an end to the priest's tribulations.

It so happened that during those days, among so many other carnival attractions, there arrived in town the traveling show of the woman who had been changed into a spider for having disobeyed her parents. The admission to see her was not only less than the admission to see the angel, but people were permitted to ask her all manner of questions about her absurd state and to examine her up and down so that no one would ever doubt the truth of her horror. She was a frightful tarantula the size of a ram and with the head of a sad maiden. What was most heartrending, however, was not her outlandish shape but the sincere affliction with which she recounted the details of her misfortune. While still practically a child she had sneaked out of her parents' house to go to a dance, and while she was coming back through the woods after having danced all night without permission, a fearful thunderclap rent the sky in two and through the crack came the lightning bolt of brimstone that changed her into a spider. Her only nourishment came from the meatballs that charitable souls chose to toss into her mouth. A spectacle like that, full of so much human truth and with such a fearful lesson, was bound to defeat without even trying that of a haughty angel who scarcely deigned to look at mortals. Besides, the few miracles attributed to the angel showed a certain mental disorder, like the blind man who didn't recover his sight but grew three new teeth, or the paralytic who didn't get to walk but almost won the lottery, and the leper whose sores sprouted sunflowers. Those consolation miracles, which were more like mocking fun, had already ruined the angel's reputation when the woman who had been changed into a spider finally crushed him completely. That was how Father Gonzaga was cured forever of his insomnia and Pelayo's courtyard went back to being as empty as during the time it had rained for three days and crabs walked through the bedrooms.

The owners of the house had no reason to lament. With the money they saved they built a two-story mansion with balconies and gardens and high netting so that crabs wouldn't get in during the winter, and with iron bars on the windows so that angels wouldn't get in. Pelayo also set up a rabbit warren close to town and gave up his job as bailiff for good, and Elisenda bought some satin pumps with high heels and many dresses of iridescent silk, the kind worn on Sunday by the most desirable women in those times. The chicken coop was the only thing that didn't receive any attention. If they washed it down with creolin[3] and burned tears of myrrh inside it every so often, it was not in homage to the angel but to drive away the dungheap stench that still hung everywhere like a ghost and was turning the new house into an old one. At first, when the child learned to walk, they were careful that he not get too close to the chicken coop. But then they began to lose their fears and got used to the smell, and before the child got his second teeth he'd gone inside the chicken coop to play, where the wires were falling apart. The angel was no less standoffish with him than with other mortals, but he tolerated the most ingenious infamies with the patience of a dog who had no illusions. They both came down with chicken pox at the same time. The doctor who took care of the child couldn't resist the temptation to listen to the angel's heart, and he found so much whistling in the heart and so many sounds in his kidneys that it seemed impossible for him to be alive. What surprised him most, however, was the logic of his wings. They seemed so natural on that completely human organism that he couldn't understand why other men didn't have them too.

When the child began school it had been some time since the sun

3. A disinfectant.

and rain had caused the collapse of the chicken coop. The angel went dragging himself about here and there like a stray dying man. They would drive him out of the bedroom with a broom and a moment later find him in the kitchen. He seemed to be in so many places at the same time that they grew to think that he'd been duplicated, that he was reproducing himself all through the house, and the exasperated and unhinged Elisenda shouted that it was awful living in that hell full of angels. He could scarcely eat and his antiquarian eyes had also become so foggy that he went about bumping into posts. All he had left were the bare cannulae[4] of his last feathers. Pelayo threw a blanket over him and extended him the charity of letting him sleep in the shed, and only then did they notice that he had a temperature at night, and was delirious with the tongue twisters of an old Norwegian. That was one of the few times they became alarmed, for they thought he was going to die and not even the wise neighbor woman had been able to tell them what to do with dead angels.

And yet he not only survived his worst winter, but seemed improved with the first sunny days. He remained motionless for several days in the farthest corner of the courtyard, where no one would see him, and at the beginning of December some large, stiff feathers began to grow on his wings, the feathers of a scarecrow, which looked more like another misfortune of decrepitude. But he must have known the reason for those changes, for he was quite careful that no one should notice them, that no one should hear the sea chanteys[5] that he sometimes sang under the stars. One morning Elisenda was cutting some bunches of onions for lunch when a wind that seemed to come from the high seas blew into the kitchen. Then she went to the window and caught the angel in his first attempts at flight. They were so clumsy that his fingernails opened a furrow in the vegetable patch and he was on the point of knocking the shed down with the ungainly flapping that slipped on the light and couldn't get a grip on the air. But he did manage to gain altitude. Elisenda let out a sigh of relief, for herself and for him, when she saw him pass over the last houses, holding himself up in some way with the risky flapping of a senile vulture. She kept watching

4. The tubes that attach feathers to the body.
5. Songs sung by sailors to the rhythm of their work.

him even when she was through cutting the onions and she kept on watching until it was no longer possible for her to see him, because then he was no longer an annoyance in her life but an imaginary dot on the horizon of the sea.

1968

Charlotte Perkins Gilman

1860–1935

Gilman's "The Yellow Wallpaper" was closely based on her own experience. She married at the age of twenty-four and immediately got pregnant, had a child, and fell into depression. An eminent doctor, S. Weir Mitchell, treated her with his now notorious "rest cure," which was identical to Jane's treatment in the story. The "inevitable result," as Gilman wrote in her autobiography, was "progressive insanity." She said that her own treatment drove her "as far as one could go [toward insanity] and get back." After leaving her husband and moving to California, she regained her mental and physical health. When she published the story in 1892, doctors praised the accuracy of its psychological depiction, and apparently, Mitchell subsequently abandoned the rest cure. This was Gilman's avowed purpose: to "convince [Mitchell] of the error of his ways." Though Gilman had this narrow intention, the story has much to say about the general condition of women in late-nineteenth-century American society..

The Yellow Wallpaper

It is very seldom that mere ordinary people like John and myself secure ancestral halls for the summer.

A colonial mansion, a hereditary estate, I would say a haunted house and reach the height of romantic felicity—but that would be asking too much of fate!

Still I will proudly declare that there is something queer about it.

Else, why should it be let so cheaply? And why have stood so long untenanted?

John laughs at me, of course, but one expects that.

John is practical in the extreme. He has no patience with faith, an intense horror of superstition, and he scoffs openly at any talk of things not to be felt and seen and put down in figures.

John is a physician, and *perhaps*—(I would not say it to a living soul, of course, but this is dead paper and a great relief to my mind)—*perhaps* that is one reason I do not get well faster.

You see, he does not believe I am sick! And what can one do?

If a physician of high standing, and one's own husband, assures friends and relatives that there is really nothing the matter with one but temporary nervous depression—a slight hysterical tendency[1]—what is one to do?

My brother is also a physician, and also of high standing, and he says the same thing.

So I take phosphates or phosphites—whichever it is, and tonics, and journeys, and air, and exercise, and am absolutely forbidden to "work" until I am well again.

Personally, I disagree with their ideas.

Personally, I believe that congenial work, with excitement and change, would do me good.

But what is one to do?

I did write for a while in spite of them; but it *does* exhaust me a good deal—having to be so sly about it, or else meet with heavy opposition.

I sometimes fancy that in my condition if I had less opposition and more society and stimulus—but John says the very worst thing I can do is to think about my condition, and I confess it always makes me feel bad.

So I will let it alone and talk about the house.

The most beautiful place! It is quite alone, standing well back from the road, quite three miles from the village. It makes me think of English places that you read about, for there are hedges and walls and gates that lock, and lots of separate little houses for the gardeners and people.

1. In the nineteenth century, the term *hysteria* was used to describe a host of symptoms indicating emotional disturbance or dysfunction thought to be especially prevalent among women and often considered to be either a manifestation of repressed sexual urges or an attempt by affected women to avoid their duties as wives and mothers.

There is a *delicious* garden! I never saw such a garden—large and shady, full of box-bordered paths, and lined with long grape-covered arbors with seats under them.

There were greenhouses, too, but they are all broken now.

There was some legal trouble, I believe, something about the heirs and co-heirs; anyhow, the place has been empty for years.

That spoils my ghostliness, I am afraid, but I don't care—there is something strange about the house—I can feel it.

I even said so to John one moonlight evening, but he said what I felt was a *draught,* and shut the window.

I get unreasonably angry with John sometimes. I'm sure I never used to be so sensitive. I think it is due to this nervous condition.

But John says if I feel so, I shall neglect proper self-control; so I take pains to control myself—before him, at least, and that makes me very tired.

I don't like our room a bit. I wanted one downstairs that opened on the piazza and had roses all over the window, and such pretty old-fashioned chintz hangings! but John would not hear of it.

He said there was only one window and not room for two beds, and no near room for him if he took another.

He is very careful and loving, and hardly lets me stir without special direction.

I have a schedule prescription for each hour in the day; he takes all care from me, and so I feel basely ungrateful not to value it more.

He said we came here solely on my account, that I was to have perfect rest and all the air I could get. "Your exercise depends on your strength, my dear," said he, "and your food somewhat on your appetite; but air you can absorb all the time." So we took the nursery at the top of the house.

It is a big, airy room, the whole floor nearly, with windows that look all ways, and air and sunshine galore. It was nursery first and then playroom and gymnasium, I should judge; for the windows are barred for little children, and there are rings and things in the walls.

The paint and paper look as if a boys' school had used it. It is stripped off—the paper—in great patches all around the head of my bed, about as far as I can reach, and in a great place on the other side of the room low down. I never saw a worse paper in my life. One of those sprawling flamboyant patterns committing every artistic sin.

It is dull enough to confuse the eye in following, pronounced enough to constantly irritate and provoke study, and when you follow the lame uncertain curves for a little distance they suddenly commit suicide—plunge off at outrageous angles, destroy themselves in unheard-of contradictions.

The color is repellant, almost revolting; a smouldering unclean yellow, strangely faded by the slow-turning sunlight. It is a dull yet lurid orange in some places, a sickly sulphur tint in others.

No wonder the children hated it! I should hate it myself if I had to live in this room long.

There comes John, and I must put this away—he hates to have me write a word.

We have been here two weeks, and I haven't felt like writing before, since that first day.

I am sitting by the window now, up in this atrocious nursery, and there is nothing to hinder my writing as much as I please, save lack of strength.

John is away all day, and even some nights when his cases are serious.

I am glad my case is not serious!

But these nervous troubles are dreadfully depressing.

John does not know how much I really suffer. He knows there is no reason to suffer, and that satisfies him.

Of course it is only nervousness. It does weigh on me so not to do my duty in any way!

I mean to be such a help to John, such a real rest and comfort, and here I am a comparative burden already!

Nobody would believe what an effort it is to do what little I am able—to dress and entertain, and order things.

It is fortunate Mary is so good with the baby. Such a dear baby!

And yet I *cannot* be with him, it makes me so nervous.

I suppose John never was nervous in his life. He laughs at me so about this wallpaper!

At first he meant to repaper the room, but afterwards he said that I was letting it get the better of me, and that nothing was worse for a nervous patient than to give way to such fancies.

He said that after the wallpaper was changed it would be the heavy bedstead, and then the barred windows, and then that gate at the head of the stairs, and so on.

"You know the place is doing you good," he said, "and really, dear, I don't care to renovate the house just for a three months' rental."

"Then do let us go downstairs," I said. "There are such pretty rooms there."

Then he took me in his arms and called me a blessed little goose, and said he would go down cellar, if I wished, and have it whitewashed into the bargain.

But he is right enough about the beds and windows and things.

It is as airy and comfortable a room as anyone need wish, and, of course, I would not be so silly as to make him uncomfortable just for a whim.

I'm really getting quite fond of the big room, all but that horrid paper.

Out of one window I can see the garden—those mysterious deep-shaded arbors, the riotous old-fashioned flowers, and bushes and gnarly trees.

Out of another I get a lovely view of the bay and a little private wharf belonging to the estate. There is a beautiful shaded lane that runs down there from the house. I always fancy I see people walking in these numerous paths and arbors, but John has cautioned me not to give way to fancy in the least. He says that with my imaginative power and habit of story-making, a nervous weakness like mine is sure to lead to all manner of excited fancies, and that I ought to use my will and good sense to check the tendency. So I try.

I think sometimes that if I were only well enough to write a little it would relieve the press of ideas and rest me.

But I find I get pretty tired when I try.

It is so discouraging not to have any advice and companionship about my work. When I get really well, John says we will ask Cousin Henry and Julia down for a long visit; but he says he would as soon put fireworks in my pillowcase as to let me have those stimulating people about now.

I wish I could get well faster.

But I must not think about that. This paper looks to me as if it *knew* what a vicious influence it had!

There is a recurrent spot where the pattern lolls like a broken neck and two bulbous eyes stare at you upside down.

I get positively angry with the impertinence of it and the everlastingness. Up and down and sideways they crawl, and those absurd unblinking eyes are everywhere. There is one place where two breadths didn't match, and the eyes go all up and down the line, one a little higher than the other.

I never saw so much expression in an inanimate thing before, and we all know how much expression they have! I used to lie awake as a child and get more entertainment and terror out of blank walls and plain furniture than most children could find in a toy-store.

I remember what a kindly wink the knobs of our big old bureau used to have, and there was one chair that always seemed like a strong friend.

I used to feel that if any of the other things looked too fierce I could always hop into that chair and be safe.

The furniture in this room is no worse than inharmonious, however, for we had to bring it all from downstairs. I suppose when this was used as a playroom they had to take the nursery things out, and no wonder! I never saw such ravages as the children have made here.

The wallpaper, as I said before, is torn off in spots, and it sticketh closer than a brother—they must have had perseverance as well as hatred.

Then the floor is scratched and gouged and splintered, the plaster itself is dug out here and there, and this great heavy bed which is all we found in the room, looks as if it had been through the wars.

But I don't mind it a bit—only the paper.

There comes John's sister. Such a dear girl as she is, and so careful of me! I must not let her find me writing.

She is a perfect and enthusiastic housekeeper, and hopes for no better profession. I verily believe she thinks it is the writing which made me sick!

But I can write when she is out, and see her a long way off from these windows.

There is one that commands the road, a lovely shaded winding road, and one that just looks off over the country. A lovely country too, full of great elms and velvet meadows.

This wallpaper has a kind of sub-pattern in a different shade, a particularly irritating one, for you can only see it in certain lights, and not clearly then.

But in the places where it isn't faded and where the sun is just so—I can see a strange, provoking, formless sort of figure that seems to skulk about behind that silly and conspicuous front design.

There's sister on the stairs!

Well, the Fourth of July is over! The people are all gone, and I am tired out. John thought it might do me good to see a little company, so we just had Mother and Nellie and the children down for a week.

Of course I didn't do a thing. Jennie sees to everything now.

But it tired me all the same.

John says if I don't pick up faster he shall send me to Weir Mitchell in the fall.

But I don't want to go there at all. I had a friend who was in his hands once, and she says he is just like John and my brother, only more so!

Besides, it is such an undertaking to go so far.

I don't feel as if it was worthwhile to turn my hand over for anything, and I'm getting dreadfully fretful and querulous.

I cry at nothing, and cry most of the time.

Of course I don't when John is here, or anybody else, but when I am alone.

And I am alone a good deal just now. John is kept in town very often by serious cases, and Jennie is good and lets me alone when I want her to.

So I walk a little in the garden or down that lovely lane, sit on the porch under the roses, and lie down up here a good deal.

I'm getting really fond of the room in spite of the wallpaper. Perhaps *because* of the wallpaper.

It dwells in my mind so!

I lie here on this great immovable bed—it is nailed down, I believe—and follow that pattern about by the hour. It is as good as gymnastics, I assure you. I start, we'll say, at the bottom, down in the corner over there where it has not been touched, and I determine for the thousandth time that I *will* follow that pointless pattern to some sort of conclusion.

I know a little of the principle of design, and I know this thing was not arranged on any laws of radiation, or alternation, or repetition, or symmetry, or anything else that I ever heard of.

It is repeated, of course, by the breadths, but not otherwise.

Looked at in one way, each breadth stands alone; the bloated curves and flourishes—a kind of "debased Romanesque" with delirium tremens[2]—go waddling up and down in isolated columns of fatuity.

But, on the other hand, they connect diagonally, and the sprawling outlines run off in great slanting waves of optic horror, like a lot of wallowing sea weeds in full chase.

The whole thing goes horizontally, too, at least it seems so, and I exhaust myself trying to distinguish the order of its going in that direction.

They have used a horizontal breadth for a frieze,[3] and that adds wonderfully to the confusion.

There is one end of the room where it is almost intact, and there, when the crosslights fade and the low sun shines directly upon it, I can almost fancy radiation after all—the interminable grotesque seems to form around a common center and rush off in headlong plunges of equal distraction.

It makes me tired to follow it. I will take a nap, I guess.

I don't know why I should write this.

I don't want to.

2. A mental and nervous disorder, often associated with alcoholism, accompanied by violent trembling and hallucinations. "Romanesque" refers to a profuse ornamental style.

3. An ornamental band running along the top of a wall.

I don't feel able.

And I know John would think it absurd. But I *must* say what I feel and think in some way—it is such a relief!

But the effort is getting to be greater than the relief.

Half the time now I am awfully lazy, and lie down ever so much.

John says I mustn't lose my strength, and has me take cod liver oil and lots of tonics and things, to say nothing of ale and wine and rare meat.

Dear John! He loves me very dearly, and hates to have me sick. I tried to have a real earnest reasonable talk with him the other day, and tell him how I wish he would let me go and make a visit to Cousin Henry and Julia.

But he said I wasn't able to go, nor able to stand it after I got there; and I did not make out a very good case for myself, for I was crying before I had finished.

It is getting to be a great effort for me to think straight. Just this nervous weakness, I suppose.

And dear John gathered me up in his arms, and just carried me upstairs and laid me on the bed, and sat by me and read to me till it tired my head.

He said I was his darling and his comfort and all he had, and that I must take care of myself for his sake, and keep well.

He says no one but myself can help me out of it, that I must use my will and self-control and not let any silly fancies run away with me.

There's one comfort—the baby is well and happy, and does not have to occupy this nursery with the horrid wallpaper.

If we had not used it, that blessed child would have! What a fortunate escape! Why, I wouldn't have a child of mine, an impressionable little thing, live in such a room for worlds.

I never thought of it before, but it is lucky that John kept me here after all, I can stand it so much easier than a baby, you see.

Of course I never mention it to them any more—I am too wise—but I keep watch for it all the same.

There are things in that paper that nobody knows about but me, or ever will.

Behind that outside pattern the dim shapes get clearer every day.

It is always the same shape, only very numerous.

And it is like a woman stooping down and creeping about behind that pattern. I don't like it a bit. I wonder—I begin to think—I wish John would take me away from here!

It is so hard to talk with John about my case, because he is so wise, and because he loves me so.

But I tried it last night.

It was moonlight. The moon shines in all around just as the sun does.

I hate to see it sometimes, it creeps so slowly, and always comes in by one window or another.

John was asleep and I hated to waken him, so I kept still and watched the moonlight on that undulating wallpaper till I felt creepy.

The faint figure behind seemed to shake the pattern, just as if she wanted to get out.

I got up softly and went to feel and see if the paper *did* move, and when I came back John was awake.

"What is it, little girl?" he said. "Don't go walking about like that—you'll get cold."

I thought it was a good time to talk, so I told him that I really was not gaining here, and that I wished he would take me away.

"Why darling!" said he. "Our lease will be up in three weeks, and I can't see how to leave before.

"The repairs are not done at home, and I cannot possibly leave town just now. Of course if you were in any danger, I could and would, but you really are better, dear, whether you can see it or not. I am a doctor, dear, and I know. You are gaining flesh and color, your appetite is better, I feel really much easier about you."

"I don't weigh a bit more," said I, "nor as much; and my appetite may be better in the evening when you are here but it is worse in the morning when you are away!"

"Bless her little heart!" said he with a big hug. "She shall be as sick as she pleases! But now let's improve the shining hours by going to sleep, and talk about it in the morning!"

"And you won't go away?" I asked gloomily.

"Why, how can I, dear? It is only three weeks more and then we will take a nice little trip of a few days while Jennie is getting the house ready. Really, dear, you are better!"

"Better in body perhaps—" I began, and stopped short, for he sat up straight and looked at me with such a stern, reproachful look that I could not say another word.

"My darling," said he, "I beg of you, for my sake and for our child's sake, as well as for your own, that you will never for one instant let that idea enter your mind! There is nothing so dangerous, so fascinating, to a temperament like yours. It is a false and foolish fancy. Can you not trust me as a physician when I tell you so?"

So of course I said no more on that score, and we went to sleep before long. He thought I was asleep first; but I wasn't, and lay there for hours trying to decide whether that front pattern and the back pattern really did move together or separately.

On a pattern like this, by daylight, there is a lack of sequence, a defiance of law, that is a constant irritant to a normal mind.

The color is hideous enough, and unreliable enough, and infuriating enough, but the pattern is torturing.

You think you have mastered it, but just as you get well under way in following, it turns a back somersault and there you are. It slaps you in the face, knocks you down, and tramples upon you. It is like a bad dream.

The outside pattern is a florid arabesque, reminding one of a fungus. If you can imagine a toadstool in joints; an interminable string of toadstools, budding and sprouting in endless convolutions—why, that is something like it.

That is, sometimes!

There is one marked peculiarity about this paper, a thing nobody seems to notice but myself, and that is that it changes as the light changes.

When the sun shoots in through the east window—I always watch for that first long, straight ray—it changes so quickly that I never can quite believe it.

That is why I watch it always.

By moonlight—the moon shines in all night when there is a moon—I wouldn't know it was the same paper.

At night in any kind of light, in twilight, candlelight, lamplight, and worst of all by moonlight, it becomes bars! The outside pattern, I mean, and the woman behind it is as plain as can be.

I didn't realize for a long time what the thing was that showed behind that dim sub pattern, but now I am quite sure it is a woman.

By daylight she is subdued, quiet. I fancy it is the pattern that keeps her so still. It is so puzzling. It keeps me quiet by the hour.

I lie down ever so much now. John says it is good for me, and to sleep all I can.

Indeed he started the habit by making me lie down for an hour after each meal.

It is a very bad habit I am convinced, for you see, I don't sleep.

And that cultivates deceit, for I don't tell them I'm awake—O no!

The fact is I am getting a little afraid of John.

He seems very queer sometimes, and even Jennie has an inexplicable look.

It strikes me occasionally, just as a scientific hypothesis, that perhaps it is the paper!

I have watched John when he did not know I was looking, and come into the room suddenly on the most innocent excuses, and I've caught him several times *looking at the paper!* And Jennie too. I caught Jennie with her hand on it once.

She didn't know I was in the room, and when I asked her in a quiet, a very quiet voice, with the most restrained manner possible, what she was doing with the paper—she turned around as if she had been caught stealing, and looked quite angry—asked me why I should frighten her so!

Then she said that the paper stained everything it touched, that she had found yellow smooches[4] on all my clothes and John's, and she wished we would be more careful!

Did not that sound innocent? But I know she was studying that pattern, and I am determined that nobody shall find it out but myself!

Life is very much more exciting now than it used to be. You see I have something more to expect, to look forward to, to watch. I really do eat better, and am more quiet than I was.

John is so pleased to see me improve! He laughed a little

4. Smudges, smears.

the other day, and said I seemed to be flourishing in spite of my wallpaper.

I turned it off with a laugh. I had no intention of telling him it was *because* of the wallpaper—he would make fun of me. He might even want to take me away.

I don't want to leave now until I have found it out. There is a week more, and I think that will be enough.

I'm feeling so much better!

I don't sleep much at night, for it is so interesting to watch developments; but I sleep a good deal during the daytime.

In the daytime it is tiresome and perplexing.

There are always new shoots on the fungus, and new shades of yellow all over it. I cannot keep count of them, though I have tried conscientiously.

It is the strangest yellow, that wallpaper! It makes me think of all the yellow things I ever saw—not beautiful ones like buttercups, but old, foul, bad yellow things.

But there is something else about that paper—the smell! I noticed it the moment we came into the room, but with so much air and sun it was not bad. Now we have had a week of fog and rain, and whether the windows are open or not, the smell is here.

It creeps all over the house.

I find it hovering in the dining-room, skulking in the parlor, hiding in the hall, lying in wait for me on the stairs.

It gets into my hair.

Even when I go to ride, if I turn my head suddenly and surprise it—there is that smell!

Such a peculiar odor, too! I have spent hours in trying to analyze it, to find what it smelled like.

It is not bad—at first—and very gentle, but quite the subtlest, most enduring odor I ever met.

In this damp weather it is awful, I wake up in the night and find it hanging over me.

It used to disturb me at first. I thought seriously of burning the house—to reach the smell.

But now I am used to it. The only thing I can think of that it is like is the *color* of the paper! A yellow smell.

There is a very funny mark on this wall, low, down, near the mopboard.[5] A streak that runs round the room. It goes behind every piece of furniture, except the bed, a long straight, even *smooch*, as if it had been rubbed over and over.

I wonder how it was done and who did it, and what they did it for. Round and round and round—round and round and round—it makes me dizzy!

I really have discovered something at last.

Through watching so much at night, when it changes so, I have finally found out.

The front pattern *does* move—and no wonder! The woman behind shakes it!

Sometimes I think there are a great many women behind, and sometimes only one, and she crawls around fast, and her crawling shakes it all over.

Then in the very bright spots she keeps still, and in the very shady spots she just takes hold of the bars and shakes them hard.

And she is all the time trying to climb through. But nobody could climb through that pattern—it strangles so; I think that is why it has so many heads.

They get through, and then the pattern strangles them off and turns them upside down, and makes their eyes white!

If those heads were covered or taken off it would not be half so bad.

I think that woman gets out in the daytime!

And I'll tell you why—privately—I've seen her!

I can see her out of every one of my windows!

It is the same woman, I know, for she is always creeping, and most women do not creep by daylight.

I see her in that long shaded lane, creeping up and down. I see her in those dark grape arbors, creeping all around the garden.

5. Baseboard.

I see her on that long road under the trees, creeping along, and when a carriage comes she hides under the blackberry vines.

I don't blame her a bit. It must be very humiliating to be caught creeping by daylight!

I always lock the door when I creep by daylight. I can't do it at night, for I know John would suspect something at once.

And John is so queer now that I don't want to irritate him. I wish he would take another room! Besides, I don't want anybody to get that woman out at night but myself.

I often wonder if I could see her out of all the windows at once.

But, turn as fast as I can, I can only see out of one at one time.

And though I always see her, she *may* be able to creep faster than I can turn! I have watched her sometimes away off in the open country, creeping as fast as a cloud shadow in a wind.

If only that top pattern could be gotten off from the under one! I mean to try it, little by little.

I have found out another funny thing, but I shan't tell it this time! It does not do to trust people too much.

There are only two more days to get this paper off, and I believe John is beginning to notice. I don't like the look in his eyes.

And I heard him ask Jennie a lot of professional questions about me. She had a very good report to give.

She said I slept a good deal in the daytime.

John knows I don't sleep very well at night, for all I'm so quiet!

He asked me all sorts of questions, too, and pretended to be very loving and kind.

As if I couldn't see through him!

Still, I don't wonder he acts so, sleeping under this paper for three months.

It only interests me, but I feel sure John and Jennie are affected by it.

Hurrah! This is the last day, but it is enough. John is to stay in town over night, and won't be out until this evening.

Jennie wanted to sleep with me—the sly thing, but I told her I should undoubtedly rest better for a night all alone.

That was clever, for really I wasn't alone a bit! As soon as it was moonlight and that poor thing began to crawl and shake the pattern, I got up and ran to help her.

I pulled and she shook, I shook and she pulled, and before morning we had peeled off yards of that paper.

A strip about as high as my head and half around the room.

And then when the sun came and that awful pattern began to laugh at me, I declared I would finish it today!

We go away tomorrow, and they are moving all my furniture down again to leave things as they were before.

Jennie looked at the wall in amazement, but I told her merrily that I did it out of pure spite at the vicious thing.

She laughed and said she wouldn't mind doing it herself, but I must not get tired.

How she betrayed herself that time!

But I am here, and no person touches this paper but Me—not *alive!*

She tried to get me out of the room—it was too patent! But I said it was so quiet and empty and clean now that I believed I would lie down again and sleep all I could; and not to wake me even for dinner—I would call when I woke.

So now she is gone, and the servants are gone, and the things are gone, and there is nothing left but that great bedstead nailed down, with the canvas mattress we found on it.

We shall sleep downstairs tonight, and take the boat home tomorrow.

I quite enjoy the room, now it is bare again.

How those children did tear about here!

This bedstead is fairly gnawed!

But I must get to work.

I have locked the door and thrown the key down into the front path.

I don't want to go out, and I don't want to have anybody come in, till John comes.

I want to astonish him.

I've got a rope up here that even Jennie did not find. If that woman does get out, and tries to get away, I can tie her!

But I forgot I could not reach far without anything to stand on!

This bed will *not* move!

I tried to lift and push it until I was lame, and then I got so angry I bit off a little piece at one corner—but it hurt my teeth.

Then I peeled off all the paper I could reach standing on the floor. It sticks horribly and the pattern just enjoys it! All those strangled heads and bulbous eyes and waddling fungus growths just shriek with derision!

I am getting angry enough to do something desperate. To jump out of the window would be admirable exercise, but the bars are too strong even to try.

Besides I wouldn't do it. Of course not. I know well enough that a step like that is improper and might be misconstrued.

I don't like to *look* out of the windows even—there are so many of those creeping women, and they creep so fast.

I wonder if they all come out of that wallpaper as I did?

But I am securely fastened now by my well-hidden rope—you don't get *me* out in the road there!

I suppose I shall have to get back behind the pattern when it comes night, and that is hard!

It is so pleasant to be out in this great room and creep around as I please!

I don't want to go outside. I won't, even if Jennie asks me to.

For outside you have to creep on the ground, and everything is green instead of yellow.

But here I can creep smoothly on the floor, and my shoulder just fits in that long smooch around the wall, so I cannot lose my way.

Why there's John at the door!

It is no use, young man, you can't open it!

How he does call and pound!

Now he's crying to Jennie for an axe.

It would be a shame to break down that beautiful door!

"John dear!" said I in the gentlest voice. "The key is down by the front steps, under a plantain leaf!"

That silenced him for a few moments.

Then he said—very quietly indeed, "Open the door, my darling!"

"I can't," said I. "The key is down by the front door under a plantain leaf!"

And then I said it again, several times, very gently and slowly, and said it so often that he had to go and see, and he got it of course, and came in. He stopped short by the door.

"What is the matter?" he cried. "For God's sake, what are you doing!"

I kept on creeping just the same, but I looked at him over my shoulder.

"I've got out at last," said I, "in spite of you and Jane! And I've pulled off most of the paper, so you can't put me back!"

Now why should that man have fainted? But he did, and right across my path by the wall, so that I had to creep over him every time!

1892

Nathaniel Hawthorne

1804–1864

"Young Goodman Brown" was not especially admired until the twentieth century, when it came to be recognized as one of America's best short stories. Its allegorical treatment of innocence and sin seems to anticipate Freud's descriptions of the psyche's repressed sexual impulses. The devil's proclamation, "This night it shall be granted you to know their secret deeds," perhaps also has a political dimension: its reference to the unacknowledged truths of our own history. Three of the women in the story were modeled after women actually accused of witchcraft in Salem, two of whom were executed in 1692. Goodman Brown's father and grandfather are based on Hawthorne's own ancestors: his great-great-grandfather had a Quaker woman stripped half-naked and roped to a cart that pulled her through the streets while a constable followed behind whipping her; another kinsmen burned an Indian village and, as magistrate, actually presided over some witch trials.

Young Goodman Brown

Young Goodman Brown came forth at sunset into the street of Salem village,[1] but put his head back, after crossing the threshold, to exchange a parting kiss with his young wife. And Faith, as the wife was aptly named, thrust her own pretty head into the street, letting the wind play with the pink ribbons of her cap while she called to Goodman Brown.

"Dearest heart," whispered she, softly and rather sadly, when her lips were close to his ear, "prithee put off your journey until sunrise and sleep in your own bed to-night. A lone woman is troubled with such dreams and such thoughts that she's afeard of herself sometimes. Pray tarry with me this night, dear husband, of all nights in the year!"

"My love and my Faith," replied young Goodman Brown, "of all nights in the year, this one night must I tarry away from thee. My journey, as thou callest it, forth and back again, must needs be done 'twixt now and sunrise. What, my sweet, pretty wife, dost thou doubt me already, and we but three months married?"

"Then God bless you!" said Faith, with the pink ribbons; "and may you find all well when you come back."

"Amen!" cried Goodman Brown. "Say thy prayers, dear Faith, and go to bed at dusk, and no harm will come to thee."

So they parted; and the young man pursued his way until, being about to turn the corner by the meeting-house, he looked back and saw the head of Faith still peeping after him with a melancholy air, in spite of her pink ribbons.

"Poor little Faith!" thought he, for his heart smote him. "What a wretch am I to leave her on such an errand! She talks of dreams, too. Methought as she spoke there was trouble in her face, as if a dream had warned her what work is to be done to-night. But no, no; 't would kill her to think it. Well, she's a blessed angel on earth; and after this one night I'll cling to her skirts and follow her to heaven."

With this excellent resolve for the future, Goodman Brown felt

1. Salem, Massachusetts, where the famous witch trials of 1692 took place. Goodman: title of respect for a man below the rank of gentleman.

himself justified in making more haste on his present evil purpose. He had taken a dreary road, darkened by all the gloomiest trees of the forest, which barely stood aside to let the narrow path creep through, and closed immediately behind. It was all as lonely as could be; and there is this peculiarity in such a solitude, that the traveller knows not who may be concealed by the innumerable trunks and the thick boughs overhead; so that with lonely footsteps he may yet be passing through an unseen multitude.

"There may be a devilish Indian behind every tree," said Goodman Brown to himself; and he glanced fearfully behind him as he added, "What if the devil himself should be at my very elbow!"

His head being turned back, he passed a crook of the road, and, looking forward again, beheld the figure of a man, in grave and decent attire, seated at the foot of an old tree. He arose at Goodman Brown's approach and walked onward side by side with him.

"You are late, Goodman Brown," said he. "The clock of the Old South was striking as I came through Boston; and that is full fifteen minutes agone."[2]

"Faith kept me back a while," replied the young man, with a tremor in his voice, caused by the sudden appearance of his companion, though not wholly unexpected.

It was now deep dusk in the forest, and deepest in that part of it where these two were journeying. As nearly as could be discerned, the second traveller was about fifty years old, apparently in the same rank of life as Goodman Brown, and bearing a considerable resemblance to him, though perhaps more in expression than features. Still they might have been taken for father and son. And yet, though the elder person was as simply clad as the younger, and as simple in manner too, he had an indescribable air of one who knew the world, and would not have felt abashed at the governor's dinner table or in King William's[3] court, were it possible that his affairs should call him thither. But the only thing about him that could be fixed upon as remarkable was his staff, which bore the likeness of a great black snake, so curiously wrought that it might almost be seen

2. Boston is some fifteen miles from Salem. This might indicate the supernatural speed of the speaker's travel.

3. King William III of England (ruled 1689–1702).

to twist and wriggle itself like a living serpent. This, of course, must have been an ocular deception, assisted by the uncertain light.

"Come, Goodman Brown!" cried his fellow-traveller, "this is a dull pace for the beginning of a journey. Take my staff, if you are so soon weary."

"Friend," said the other, exchanging his slow pace for a full stop, "having kept covenant by meeting thee here it is my purpose now to return whence I came. I have scruples touching the matter thou wot'st[4] of."

"Sayest thou so?" replied he of the serpent, smiling apart. "Let us walk on, nevertheless, reasoning as we go; and if I convince thee not thou shalt turn back. We are but a little way in the forest yet."

"Too far, too far!" exclaimed the goodman, unconsciously resuming his walk. "My father never went into the woods on such an errand, nor his father before him. We have been a race of honest men and good Christians since the days of the martyrs; and shall I be the first of the name of Brown that ever took this path and kept—"

"Such company, thou wouldst say," observed the elder person, interpreting his pause. "Well said, Goodman Brown! I have been as well acquainted with your family as with ever a one among the Puritans; and that's no trifle to say. I helped your grandfather, the constable, when he lashed the Quaker woman so smartly through the streets of Salem; and it was I that brought your father a pitch-pine knot, kindled at my own hearth, to set fire to an Indian village, in King Philip's war.[5] They were my good friends, both, and many a pleasant walk have we had along this path, and returned merrily after midnight. I would fain be friends with you for their sake."

"If it be as thou sayest," replied Goodman Brown, "I marvel they never spoke of these matters; or, verily, I marvel not, seeing that the least rumor of the sort would have driven them from New England. We are a people of prayer, and good works to boot, and abide no such wickedness."

"Wickedness or not," said the traveller with the twisted staff, "I have a very general acquaintance here in New England. The deacons of many a church have drunk the communion wine with me; the

4. Know.
5. War between Native Americans and white settlers (1675–76).

selectmen of divers towns make me their chairman; and a majority of the Great and General Court are firm supporters of my interest. The governor and I, too—But these are state secrets."

"Can this be so?" cried Goodman Brown, with a stare of amazement at his undisturbed companion. "Howbeit, I have nothing to do with the governor and council; they have their own ways, and are no rule for a simple husbandman like me. But, were I to go on with thee, how should I meet the eye of that good old man, our minister, at Salem village? Oh, his voice would make me tremble both Sabbath day and lecture day."

Thus far the elder traveller had listened with due gravity; but now burst into a fit of irrepressible mirth, shaking himself so violently that his snakelike staff actually seemed to wriggle in sympathy.

"Ha! ha! ha!" shouted he again and again; then composing himself, "Well, go on, Goodman Brown, go on; but, prithee, don't kill me with laughing."

"Well, then, to end the matter at once," said Goodman Brown, considerably nettled, "there is my wife, Faith. It would break her dear little heart; and I'd rather break my own."

"Nay, if that be the case," answered the other, "e'en go thy ways, Goodman Brown. I would not for twenty old women like the one hobbling before us that Faith should come to any harm."

As he spoke he pointed his staff at a female figure on the path, in whom Goodman Brown recognized a very pious and exemplary dame, who had taught him his catechism in youth, and was still his moral and spiritual adviser, jointly with the minister and Deacon Gookin.

"A marvel, truly, that Goody[6] Cloyse should be so far in the wilderness at nightfall," said he. "But with your leave, friend, I shall take a cut through the woods until we have left this Christian woman behind. Being a stranger to you, she might ask whom I was consorting with and whither I was going."

"Be it so," said his fellow-traveller. "Betake you to the woods, and let me keep the path."

Accordingly the young man turned aside, but took care to watch his companion, who advanced softly along the road until he had

6. Short for "goodwife," a title of respect for a married woman below the rank of lady.

come within a staff's length of the old dame. She, meanwhile was making the best of her way, with singular speed for so aged a woman, and mumbling some indistinct words—a prayer, doubtless—as she went. The traveller put forth his staff and touched her withered neck with what seemed the serpent's tail.

"The devil!" screamed the pious old lady.

"Then Goody Cloyse knows her old friend?" observed the traveller, confronting her and leaning on his writhing stick.

"Ah, forsooth, and is it your worship indeed?" cried the good dame. "Yea, truly is it, and in the very image of my old gossip,[7] Goodman Brown, the grandfather of the silly fellow that now is. But—would your worship believe it?—my broomstick hath strangely disappeared, stolen, as I suspect, by that unhanged witch, Goody Cory, and that, too when I was all anointed with the juice of smallage, and cinquefoil, and wolf's-bane—"[8]

"Mingled with fine wheat and the fat of a newborn babe," said the shape of old Goodman Brown.

"Ah, your worship knows the recipe," cried the old lady, cackling aloud. "So, as I was saying, being all ready for the meeting, and no horse to ride on, I made up my mind to foot it; for they tell me there is a nice young man to be taken into communion tonight. But now your good worship will lend me your arm, and we shall be there in a twinkling."

"That can hardly be," answered her friend. "I may not spare you my arm, Goody Cloyse; but here is my staff, if you will."

So saying, he threw it down at her feet, where, perhaps, it assumed life, being one of the rods which its owner had formerly lent to the Egyptian magi.[9] Of this fact, however, Goodman Brown could not take cognizance. He had cast up his eyes in astonishment, and, looking down again, beheld neither Goody Cloyse nor the serpentine staff, but this fellow-traveller alone, who waited for him as calmly as if nothing had happened.

7. Friend.

8. Plants sometimes associated with witchcraft.

9. Reference to Exodus 7.8–12, in which God instructs Aaron to show Pharaoh a miracle by casting a rod before him, whereupon it will become a serpent. Pharaoh, in order to show that this is sorcery and not a miracle, has his magicians replicate the transformation. Hawthorne's line suggests that the rods used by the Egyptian magicians (magi) were lent to them by the devil.

"That old woman taught me my catechism," said the young man; and there was a world of meaning in this simple comment.

They continued to walk onward, while the elder traveller exhorted his companion to make good speed and persevere in the path, discoursing so aptly that his arguments seemed rather to spring up in the bosom of his auditor than to be suggested by himself. As they went he plucked a branch of maple, to serve for a walking stick, and began to strip it of the twigs and little boughs, which were wet with evening dew. The moment his fingers touched them they became strangely withered and dried up as with a week's sunshine. Thus the pair proceeded, at a good free pace, until suddenly, in a gloomy hollow of the road, Goodman Brown sat himself down on the stump of a tree and refused to go any farther.

"Friend," said he, stubbornly, "my mind is made up. Not another step will I budge on this errand. What if a wretched old woman do choose to go to the devil when I thought she was going to heaven: is that any reason why I should quit my dear Faith and go after her?"

"You will think better of this by and by," said his acquaintance, composedly. "Sit here and rest yourself a while; and when you feel like moving again, there is my staff to help you along."

Without more words, he threw his companion the maple stick, and was as speedily out of sight as if he had vanished into the deepening gloom. The young man sat a few moments by the roadside, applauding himself greatly, and thinking with how clear a conscience he should meet the minister in his morning walk, nor shrink from the eye of good old Deacon Gookin. And what calm sleep would be his that very night, which was to have been spent so wickedly, but so purely and sweetly now, in the arms of Faith! Amidst these pleasant and praiseworthy meditations, Goodman Brown heard the tramp of horses along the road, and deemed it advisable to conceal himself within the verge of the forest, conscious of the guilty purpose that had brought him thither, though now so happily turned from it.

On came the hoof tramps and the voices of the riders, two grave old voices, conversing soberly as they drew near. These mingled sounds appeared to pass along the road, within a few yards of the young man's hiding-place; but, owing doubtless to the depth of the gloom at that particular spot, neither the travellers nor their steeds were visible. Though their figures brushed the small boughs by the wayside, it could not be seen that they intercepted, even for a moment, the faint gleam from the strip of bright sky athwart which they must have passed. Goodman Brown alternately crouched and stood on tiptoe, pulling aside the branches and thrusting forth his head as far as he durst without discerning so much as a shadow. It vexed him the more, because he could have sworn, were such a thing possible, that he recognized the voices of the minister and Deacon Gookin, jogging along quietly, as they were wont to do, when bound to some ordination or ecclesiastical council. While yet within hearing, one of the riders stopped to pluck a switch.

"Of the two, reverend sir," said the voice like the deacon's, "I had rather miss an ordination dinner than to-night's meeting. They tell me that some of our community are to be here from Falmouth and beyond, and others from Connecticut and Rhode Island, besides several of the Indian powwows, who, after their fashion, know almost as much deviltry as the best of us. Moreover, there is a goodly young woman to be taken into communion."

"Mighty well, Deacon Gookin!" replied the solemn old tones of the minister. "Spur up, or we shall be late. Nothing can be done, you know, until I get on the ground."

The hoofs clattered again; and the voices, talking so strangely in the empty air, passed on through the forest, where no church had ever been gathered or solitary Christian prayed. Whither, then, could these holy men be journeying so deep into the heathen wilderness? Young Goodman Brown caught hold of a tree for support, being ready to sink down on the ground, faint and overburdened with the heavy sickness of his heart. He looked up to the sky, doubting whether there really was a heaven above him. Yet there was the blue arch, and the stars brightening in it.

"With heaven above and Faith below, I will yet stand firm against the devil!" cried Goodman Brown.

While he still gazed upward into the deep arch of the firmament and had lifted his hands to pray, a cloud, though no wind was stirring, hurried across the zenith and hid the brightening stars. The blue sky was still visible, except directly overhead, where this black mass of cloud was sweeping swiftly northward. Aloft in the air, as if from the depths of the cloud, came a confused and doubtful sound of voices. Once the listener fancied that he could distinguish the accents of towns-people of his own, men and women, both pious and ungodly, many of whom he had met at the communion table, and had seen others rioting at the tavern. The next moment, so indistinct were the sounds, he doubted whether he had heard aught but the murmur of the old forest, whispering without a wind. Then came a stronger swell of those familiar tones, heard daily in the sunshine at Salem village, but never until now from a cloud of night. There was one voice, of a young woman, uttering lamentations, yet with an uncertain sorrow, and entreating for some favor, which, perhaps, it would grieve her to obtain; and all the unseen multitude, both saints and sinners, seemed to encourage her onward.

"Faith!" shouted Goodman Brown, in a voice of agony and desperation; and the echoes of the forest mocked him, crying, "Faith! Faith!" as if bewildered wretches were seeking her all through the wilderness.

The cry of grief, rage, and terror was yet piercing the night, when the unhappy husband held his breath for a response. There was a scream, drowned immediately in a louder murmur of voices, fading into far-off laughter, as the dark cloud swept away, leaving the clear and silent sky above Goodman Brown. But something fluttered lightly down through the air and caught on the branch of a tree. The young man seized it, and beheld a pink ribbon.

"My Faith is gone!" cried he, after one stupefied moment. "There is no good on earth; and sin is but a name. Come, devil; for to thee is this world given."

And, maddened with despair, so that he laughed loud and long, did Goodman Brown grasp his staff and set forth again, at such a rate that he seemed to fly along the forest path rather than to walk or run. The road grew wilder and drearier and more faintly traced, and vanished at length, leaving him in the heart of the dark wilderness, still rushing onward with the instinct that guides mortal man to evil. The whole forest was peopled with frightful sounds—the creaking of the trees, the howling of wild beasts, and the yell of Indians; while sometimes the wind tolled like a distant church bell, and sometimes gave a broad roar around the traveller, as if all Nature were laughing him to scorn. But he was himself the chief horror of the scene, and shrank not from its other horrors.

"Ha! ha! ha!" roared Goodman Brown when the wind laughed at him. "Let us hear which will laugh loudest. Think not to frighten me with your deviltry. Come witch, come wizard, come Indian powwow, come devil himself, and here comes Goodman Brown. You may as well fear him as he fear you."

In truth, all through the haunted forest, there could be nothing more frightful than the figure of Goodman Brown. On he flew among the black pines, brandishing his staff with frenzied gestures, now giving vent to an inspiration of horrid blasphemy, and now shouting forth such laughter as set all the echoes of the forest laughing like demons around him. The fiend in his own shape is less hideous than when he rages in the breast of man. Thus sped the demoniac on his course, until, quivering among the trees, he saw a red light before him, as when the felled trunks and branches of a clearing have been set on fire, and throw up their lurid blaze against the sky, at the hour of midnight. He paused, in a lull of the tempest that had driven him onward, and heard the swell of what seemed a hymn, rolling solemnly from a distance with the weight of many voices. He knew the tune; it was a familiar one in the choir of the village meeting-house. The verse died heavily away, and was lengthened by a chorus, not of human voices, but of all the sounds of the benighted wilderness pealing in awful harmony together. Goodman Brown cried out, and his cry was lost to his own ear, by its unison with the cry of the desert.

In the interval of silence he stole forward until the light glared full upon his eyes. At one extremity of an open space, hemmed in by the dark wall of the forest, arose a rock, bearing some rude, natural resemblance either to an altar or a pulpit, and surrounded by four blazing pines, their tops aflame, their stems untouched, like candles at an evening meeting. The mass of foliage that had overgrown the summit of the rock was all on fire, blazing high into the night and fitfully illuminating the whole field. Each pendent twig and leafy festoon was in a blaze. As the red light arose and fell, a numerous congregation alternately shone forth, then disappeared in shadow, and again grew, as it were, out of the darkness, peopling the heart of the solitary woods at once.

"A grave and dark-clad company," quoth Goodman Brown.

In truth they were such. Among them, quivering to and fro between gloom and splendor, appeared faces that would be seen next day at the council board of the province, and others which, Sabbath after Sabbath, looked devoutly heavenward, and benignantly over the crowded pews, from the holiest pulpits in the land. Some affirm that the lady of the governor was there. At least there were high dames well known to her, and wives of honored husbands, and widows, a great multitude, and ancient maidens, all of excellent repute, and fair young girls, who trembled lest their mothers should espy them. Either the sudden gleams of light flashing over the obscure field bedazzled Goodman Brown, or he recognized a score of the church members of Salem village famous for their especial sanctity. Good old Deacon Gookin had arrived, and waited at the skirts of that venerable saint, his revered pastor. But, irreverently consorting with these grave, reputable, and pious people, these elders of the church, these chaste dames and dewy virgins, there were men of dissolute lives and women of spotted fame, wretches given over to all mean and filthy vice, and suspected even of horrid crimes. It was strange to see that the good shrank not from the wicked, nor were the sinners abashed by the saints. Scattered also among their pale-faced enemies were the Indian priests, or powwows, who had often scared their native forest with more hideous incantations than any known to English witchcraft.

"But where is Faith?" thought Goodman Brown; and, as hope came into his heart, he trembled.

Another verse of the hymn arose, a slow and mournful strain, such as the pious love, but joined to words which expressed all that our nature can conceive of sin, and darkly hinted at far more. Unfathomable to mere mortals is the lore of fiends. Verse after verse was sung, and still the chorus of the desert swelled between like the deepest tone of a mighty organ; and with the final peal of that dreadful anthem there came a sound, as if the roaring wind, the rushing streams, the howling beasts, and every other voice of the unconverted wilderness were mingling and according with the voice of guilty man in homage to the prince of all. The four blazing pines threw up a loftier flame, and obscurely discovered shapes and visages of horror on the smoke wreaths above the impious assembly. At the same moment the fire on the rock shot redly forth and formed a glowing arch above its base, where now appeared a figure. With reverence be it spoken, the apparition bore no slight similitude, both in garb and manner, to some grave divine of the New England churches.

"Bring forth the converts!" cried a voice that echoed through the field and rolled into the forest.

At the word, Goodman Brown stepped forth from the shadow of the trees and approached the congregation, with whom he felt a loathful brotherhood by the sympathy of all that was wicked in his heart. He could have well-nigh sworn that the shape of his own dead father beckoned him to advance, looking downward from a smoke wreath, while a woman, with dim features of despair, threw out her hand to warn him back. Was it his mother? But he had no power to retreat one step, nor to resist, even in thought, when the minister and good old Deacon Gookin seized his arms and led him to the blazing rock. Thither came also the slender form of a veiled female, led between Goody Cloyse, that pious teacher of the catechism, and Martha Carrier, who had received the devil's promise to be queen of hell. A rampant hag was she. And there stood the proselytes beneath the canopy of fire.

"Welcome, my children," said the dark figure, "to the communion of your race. Ye have found thus young your nature and your destiny. My children, look behind you!"

They turned; and flashing forth, as it were, in a sheet of flame, the fiend worshippers were seen; the smile of welcome gleamed darkly on every visage.

"There," resumed the sable form, "are all whom ye have reverenced from youth. Ye deemed them holier than yourselves, and shrank from your own sin, contrasting it with their lives of righteousness and prayerful aspirations heavenward. Yet here are they all in my worshipping assembly. This night it shall be granted you to know their secret deeds: how hoary-bearded elders of the church have whispered wanton words to the young maids of their households; how many a woman, eager for widows' weeds, has given her husband a drink at bedtime and let him sleep his last sleep in her bosom; how beardless youths have made haste to inherit their fathers' wealth; and how fair damsels—blush not, sweet ones—have dug little graves in the garden, and bidden me, the sole guest, to an infant's funeral. By the sympathy of your human hearts for sin ye shall scent out all the places—whether in church, bed-chamber, street, field, or forest—where crime has been committed, and shall exult to behold the whole earth one stain of guilt, one mighty blood spot. Far more than this. It shall be yours to penetrate, in every bosom, the deep mystery of sin, the fountain of all wicked arts, and which inexhaustibly supplies more evil impulses than human power—than my power at its utmost—can make manifest in deeds. And now, my children, look upon each other."

They did so; and, by the blaze of the hell-kindled torches, the wretched man beheld his Faith, and the wife her husband, trembling before that unhallowed altar.

"Lo, there ye stand, my children," said the figure, in a deep and solemn tone, almost sad with its despairing awfulness, as if his once angelic nature could yet mourn for our miserable race. "Depending upon one another's hearts, ye had still hoped that virtue were not all a dream. Now are ye undeceived. Evil is the nature of mankind. Evil must be your only happiness. Welcome again, my children, to the communion of your race."

"Welcome," repeated the fiend worshippers, in one cry of despair and triumph.

And there they stood, the only poor, as it seemed, who were yet hesitating on the verge of wickedness in this dark world. A basin was hollowed, naturally, in the rock. Did it contain water, reddened by the lurid light? or was it blood? or, perchance, a liquid flame? Herein did the shape of evil dip his hand and prepare to lay the mark of baptism upon their foreheads, that they might be partakers of the mystery of sin, more conscious of the secret guilt of others, both in deed and thought, than they could now be of their own. The husband cast one look at his pale wife, and Faith at him. What polluted wretches would the next glance show them to each other, shuddering alike at what they disclosed and what they saw!

"Faith! Faith!" cried the husband, "look up to Heaven, and resist the wicked one."

Whether Faith obeyed he knew not. Hardly had he spoken when he found himself amid calm night and solitude, listening to a roar of the wind which died heavily away through the forest. He staggered against the rock and felt it chill and damp, while a hanging twig, that had been all on fire, besprinkled his cheek with the coldest dew.

The next morning young Goodman Brown came slowly into the street of Salem village, staring around him like a bewildered man. The good old minister was taking a walk along the graveyard, to get an appetite for breakfast and meditate his sermon, and bestowed a blessing, as he passed, on Goodman Brown. He shrank from the venerable saint as if to avoid an anathema. Old Deacon Gookin was at domestic worship, and the holy words of his prayer were heard through the open window. "What God doth the wizard pray to?" quoth Goodman Brown. Goody Cloyse, that excellent old Christian, stood in the early sunshine, at her own lattice, catechizing a little girl who had brought her a pint of morning's milk. Goodman Brown snatched away the child as from the grasp of the fiend himself. Turning the corner by the meeting-house, he spied the head of Faith, with the pink ribbons, gazing anxiously forth, and bursting into such joy at sight of him that she skipped along the street and almost kissed her husband before the whole village. But Goodman Brown looked sternly and sadly into her face, and passed on without a greeting.

Had Goodman Brown fallen asleep in the forest, and only dreamed a wild dream of a witch-meeting?

Be it so if you will; but, alas! it was a dream of evil omen for young Goodman Brown. A stern, a sad, a darkly meditative, a distrustful, if not a desperate man did he become from the night of that fearful dream. On the Sabbath day, when the congregation were singing a holy psalm, he could not listen because an anthem of sin rushed loudly upon his ear and drowned all the blessed strain. When the minister spoke from the pulpit with power and fervid eloquence, and, with his hand on the open Bible, of the sacred truths of our religion, and of saint-like lives and triumphant deaths, and of future bliss or misery unutterable, then did Goodman Brown turn pale, dreading lest the roof should thunder down upon the gray blasphemer and his hearers. Often, awaking suddenly at midnight, he shrank from the bosom of Faith; and at morning or eventide, when the family knelt down at prayer, he scowled and muttered to himself, and gazed sternly at his wife, and turned away. And when he had lived long, and was borne to his grave a hoary corpse, followed by Faith, an aged woman, and children and grandchildren, a goodly procession, besides neighbors not a few, they carved no hopeful verse upon his tombstone, for his dying hour was gloom.

1835

Ernest Hemingway

1899–1961

Hemingway finished writing "Hills Like White Elephants" while on his honeymoon in France in May 1927. His second wife was Catholic, and Hemingway also considered himself to be Catholic at the time, which could be significant, given the subject matter of this story. Perhaps that's why he set the story in Spain, one of the most traditional and Catholic countries in Europe in the 1920s. Hemingway explained, "I met a girl in Prunier where I'd gone to eat oysters before lunch. I knew she'd had an abortion. I went over and we talked, not about that, but on the way home I thought of the story, skipped lunch, and spent that afternoon writing it." This anecdote exemplifies Hemingway's writing technique: what is said merely hints at and suggests the wealth of what is not said.

Hills Like White Elephants

The hills across the valley of the Ebro[1] were long and white. On this side there was no shade and no trees and the station was between two lines of rails in the sun. Close against the side of the station there was the warm shadow of the building and a curtain, made of strings of bamboo beads, hung across the open door into the bar, to keep out flies. The American and the girl with him sat at a table in the shade, outside the building. It was very hot and the express from Barcelona would come in forty minutes. It stopped at this junction for two minutes and went on to Madrid.

"What should we drink?" the girl asked. She had taken off her hat and put it on the table.

"It's pretty hot," the man said.

1. River in northern Spain.

"Let's drink beer."

"Dos cervezas," the man said into the curtain.

"Big ones?" a woman asked from the doorway.

"Yes. Two big ones."

The woman brought two glasses of beer and two felt pads. She put the felt pads and the beer glasses on the table and looked at the man and the girl. The girl was looking off at the line of hills. They were white in the sun and the country was brown and dry.

"They look like white elephants," she said.

"I've never seen one," the man drank his beer.

"No, you wouldn't have."

"I might have," the man said. "Just because you say I wouldn't have doesn't prove anything."

The girl looked at the bead curtain. "They've painted something on it," she said. "What does it say?"

"Anis del Toro. It's a drink."

"Could we try it?"

The man called "Listen" through the curtain. The woman came out from the bar.

"Four reales."[2]

"We want two Anis del Toro."

"With water?"

"Do you want it with water?"

"I don't know," the girl said. "Is it good with water?"

"It's all right."

"You want them with water?" asked the woman.

"Yes, with water."

"It tastes like licorice," the girl said and put the glass down.

"That's the way with everything."

"Yes," said the girl. "Everything tastes of licorice. Especially all the things you've waited so long for, like absinthe."[3]

"Oh, cut it out."

"You started it," the girl said. "I was being amused. I was having a fine time."

2. Spanish coins.

3. A liquor, flavored with anise, made by distilling wormwood. Reportedly a dangerous hallucinogen, it was banned in the United States in 1912 and in France in 1915. Miscarriage is one of its reported effects.

"Well, let's try and have a fine time."

"All right, I was trying. I said the mountains looked like white elephants. Wasn't that bright?"

"That was bright."

"I wanted to try this new drink. That's all we do, isn't it—look at things and try new drinks?"

"I guess so."

The girl looked across at the hills.

"They're lovely hills," she said. "They don't really look like white elephants. I just meant the coloring of their skin through the trees."

"Should we have another drink?"

"All right."

The warm wind blew the bead curtain against the table.

"The beer's nice and cool," the man said.

"It's lovely," the girl said.

"It's really an awfully simple operation, Jig," the man said. "It's not really an operation at all."

The girl looked at the ground the table legs rested on.

"I know you wouldn't mind it, Jig. It's really not anything. It's just to let the air in."

The girl did not say anything.

"I'll go with you and I'll stay with you all the time. They just let the air in and then it's all perfectly natural."

"Then what will we do afterward?"

"We'll be fine afterward. Just like we were before."

"What makes you think so?"

"That's the only thing that bothers us. It's the only thing that's made us unhappy."

The girl looked at the bead curtain, put her hand out and took hold of two of the strings of beads.

"And you think then we'll be all right and be happy."

"I know we will. You don't have to be afraid. I've known lots of people that have done it."

"So have I," said the girl. "And afterward they were all so happy."

"Well," the man said, "if you don't want to you don't have to. I wouldn't have you do it if you didn't want to. But I know it's perfectly simple."

"And you really want to?"

"I think it's the best thing to do. But I don't want you to do it if you don't really want to."

"And if I do it you'll be happy and things will be like they were and you'll love me?"

"I love you now. You know I love you."

"I know. But if I do it, then it will be nice again if I say things are like white elephants, and you'll like it?"

"I'll love it. I love it now but I just can't think about it. You know how I get when I worry."

"If I do it you won't ever worry?"

"I won't worry about that because it's perfectly simple."

"Then I'll do it. Because I don't care about me."

"What do you mean?"

"I don't care about me."

"Well, I care about you."

"Oh, yes. But I don't care about me. And I'll do it and then everything will be fine."

"I don't want you to do it if you feel that way."

The girl stood up and walked to the end of the station. Across, on the other side, were fields of grain and trees along the banks of the Ebro. Far away, beyond the river, were mountains. The shadow of a cloud moved across the field of grain and she saw the river through the trees.

"And we could have all this," she said. "And we could have everything and every day we make it more impossible."

"What did you say?"

"I said we could have everything."

"We can have everything."

"No, we can't."

"We can have the whole world."

"No, we can't."

"We can go everywhere."

"No, we can't. It isn't ours any more."

"It's ours."

"No, it isn't. And once they take it away, you never get it back."

"But they haven't taken it away."

"We'll wait and see."

"Come on back in the shade," he said. "You mustn't feel that way."

"I don't feel any way," the girl said. "I just know things."

"I don't want you to do anything that you don't want to do—"

"Nor that isn't good for me," she said. "I know. Could we have another beer?"

"All right. But you've got to realize—"

"I realize," the girl said. "Can't we maybe stop talking?"

They sat down at the table and the girl looked across at the hills on the dry side of the valley and the man looked at her and at the table.

"You've got to realize," he said, "that I don't want you to do it if you don't want to. I'm perfectly willing to go through with it if it means anything to you."

"Doesn't it mean anything to you? We could get along."

"Of course it does. But I don't want anybody but you. I don't want any one else. And I know it's perfectly simple."

"Yes, you know it's perfectly simple."

"It's all right for you to say that, but I do know it."

"Would you do something for me now?"

"I'd do anything for you."

"Would you please please please please please please please stop talking?"

He did not say anything but looked at the bags against the wall of the station. There were labels on them from all the hotels where they had spent nights.

"But I don't want you to," he said, "I don't care anything about it."

"I'll scream," the girl said.

The woman came out through the curtains with two glasses of beer and put them down on the damp felt pads. "The train comes in five minutes," she said.

"What did she say?" asked the girl.

"That the train is coming in five minutes."

The girl smiled brightly at the woman, to thank her.

"I'd better take the bags over to the other side of the station," the man said. She smiled at him.

"All right. Then come back and we'll finish the beer."

He picked up the two heavy bags and carried them around the station to the other tracks. He looked up the tracks but could not see the train. Coming back, he walked through the barroom, where people waiting for the train were drinking. He drank an Anis at the bar and looked at the people. They were all waiting reasonably for the train. He went out through the bead curtain. She was sitting at the table and smiled at him.

"Do you feel better?" he asked.

"I feel fine," she said. "There's nothing wrong with me. I feel fine."

1927

O. Henry

1862–1910

O. Henry (born William Sidney Porter) wrote most of his stories for newspapers. Because his stories were so popular with common readers, newspapers competed to get his work, and so he always wrote under the pressure of deadlines. Sometimes he even paid friends for plots that he could then flesh out. He wrote "The Furnished Room" for a newspaper, the World, *and he republished it in his 1906 collection,* Four Million. *A short preface explained the title: a socialite had remarked "that there were only 'Four Hundred' people in New York City who were really worth noticing." But O. Henry used "the census taker" to come up with a "larger estimate of human interest." Four million people lived in New York in 1900; each lived a story worthy of notice. As the preface advertised, O. Henry relished his reputation for ennobling the life of the unheralded and lowly.*

The Furnished Room

Restless, shifting, fugacious as time itself is a certain vast bulk of the population of the red brick district of the lower West Side. Homeless, they have a hundred homes. They flit from furnished room to furnished room, transients forever—transients in abode, transients in heart and mind. They sing "Home, Sweet Home" in ragtime; they carry their *lares et penates*[1] in a bandbox; their vine is entwined about a picture hat; a rubber plant is their fig tree.

Hence the houses of this district, having had a thousand dwellers, should have a thousand tales to tell, mostly dull ones, no doubt; but it would be strange if there could not be found a ghost or two in the wake of all these vagrant guests.

One evening after dark a young man prowled among these crumbling red mansions, ringing their bells. At the twelfth he rested his lean hand-baggage upon the step and wiped the dust from his hatband and forehead. The bell sounded faint and far away in some remote, hollow depths.

To the door of this, the twelfth house whose bell he had rung, came a housekeeper who made him think of an unwholesome, surfeited worm that had eaten its nut to a hollow shell and now sought to fill the vacancy with edible lodgers.

He asked if there was a room to let.

"Come in," said the housekeeper. Her voice came from her throat; her throat seemed lined with fur. "I have the third-floor back, vacant since a week back. Should you wish to look at it?"

The young man followed her up the stairs. A faint light from no particular source mitigated the shadows of the halls. They trod noiselessly upon a stair carpet that its own loom would have forsworn. It seemed to have become vegetable; to have degenerated in that rank, sunless air to lush lichen or spreading moss that grew in patches to the stair-case and was viscid under the foot like organic matter. At each turn of the stairs were vacant niches in the wall. Perhaps plants had once been set within them. If so they had died in that foul and tainted air. It may be that statues of the saints had stood there, but it was not difficult to conceive that imps and devils had dragged them forth in the darkness and down to the unholy depths of some furnished pit below.

"This is the room," said the housekeeper, from her furry throat. "It's a nice room. It ain't often vacant. I had some most elegant people in it last summer—no trouble at all, and paid in advance to the minute. The water's at the end of the hall. Sprowls and Mooney

1. Cherished possessions of a family or household. Lares and Penates were household gods in ancient Rome.

kept it three months. They done a vaudeville sketch. Miss B'retta Sprowls—you may have heard of her—Oh, that was just the stage names—right there over the dresser is where the marriage certificate hung, framed. The gas is here, and you see there is plenty of closet room. It's a room everybody likes. It never stays idle long."

"Do you have many theatrical people rooming here?" asked the young man.

"They comes and goes. A good proportion of my lodgers is connected with the theatres. Yes, sir, this is the theatrical district. Actor people never stays long anywhere. I get my share. Yes, they comes and they goes."

He engaged the room, paying for a week in advance. He was tired, he said, and would take possession at once. He counted out the money. The room had been made ready, she said, even to towels and water. As the housekeeper moved away he put, for the thousandth time, the question that he carried at the end of his tongue.

"A young girl—Miss Vashner—Miss Eloise Vashner—do you remember such a one among your lodgers? She would be singing on the stage, most likely. A fair girl, of medium height and slender, with reddish, gold hair and dark mole near her left eyebrow."

"No, I don't remember the name. Them stage people has names they change as often as their rooms. They comes and they goes. No, I don't call that one to mind."

No. Always no. Five months of ceaseless interrogation and the inevitable negative. So much time spent by day in questioning managers, agents, schools and choruses; by night among the audiences of theatres from all-star casts down to music halls so low that he dreaded to find what he most hoped for. He who had loved her best had tried to find her. He was sure that since her disappearance from home this great, water-girt city held her somewhere, but it was like a monstrous quicksand, shifting its particles constantly, with no foundation, its upper granules of today buried tomorrow in ooze and slime.

The furnished room received its latest guest with a first glow of pseudo-hospitality, a hectic, haggard, perfunctory welcome like the specious smile of a demirep.[2] The sophistical comfort came in reflected gleams from the decayed furniture, the ragged brocade up-

2. A woman of doubtful or compromised reputation, often a prostitute.

holstery of a couch and two chairs, a foot-wide cheap pier-glass between the two windows, from one or two gilt picture frames and a brass bedstead in a corner.

The guest reclined, inert, upon a chair, while the room, confused in speech as though it were an apartment in Babel,[3] tried to discourse to him of its divers tenantry.

A polychromatic rug like some brilliant-flowered, rectangular, tropical islet lay surrounded by a billowy sea of soiled matting. Upon the gay-papered wall were those pictures that pursue the homeless one from house to house—The Huguenot Lovers, The First Quarrel, The Wedding Breakfast, Psyche at the Fountain. The mantel's chastely severe outline was ingloriously veiled behind some pert drapery drawn rakishly askew like the sashes of the Amazonian ballet. Upon it was some desolate flotsam cast aside by the room's marooned when a lucky sail had borne them to a fresh port—a trifling vase or two, pictures of actresses, a medicine bottle, some stray cards out of a deck.

One by one, as the characters of a cryptograph became explicit, the little signs left by the furnished room's procession of guests developed a significance. The threadbare space in the rug in front of the dresser told that lovely women had marched in the throng. The tiny fingerprints on the wall spoke of little prisoners trying to feel their way to sun and air. A splattered stain, raying like the shadow of a bursting bomb, witnessed where a hurled glass or bottle had splintered with its contents against the wall. Across the pier-glass had been scrawled with a diamond in staggering letters the name "Marie." It seemed that the succession of dwellers in the furnished room had turned in fury—perhaps tempted beyond forbearance by its garish coldness—and wreaked upon it their passions. The furniture was chipped and bruised; the couch, distorted by bursting springs, seemed a horrible monster that had been slain during the stress of some grotesque convulsion. Some more potent upheaval had cloven a great slice from the marble mantel. Each plank in the floor owned its particular cant and shriek as from a separate and in-

3. The biblical Tower of Babel was built to reach heaven. God punished its builders by changing the one language of the world into several different languages so people would not understand one another (Genesis 11.1–9).

dividual agony. It seemed incredible that all this malice and injury had been wrought upon the room by those who had called it for a time their home; and yet it may have been the cheated home instinct surviving blindly, the resentful rage at false household gods that had kindled their wrath. A hut that is our own we can sweep and adorn and cherish.

The young tenant in the chair allowed these thoughts to file, soft-shod, through his mind, while there drifted into the room furnished sounds and furnished scents. He heard in one room a tittering and incontinent, slack laughter; in others the monologue of a scold, the rattling of dice, a lullaby, and one crying dully; above him a banjo tinkled with spirit. Doors banged somewhere; the elevated trains roared intermittently; a cat yowled miserably upon a back fence. And he breathed the breath of the house—a dank savor rather than a smell—a cold, musty effluvium as from underground vaults mingled with the reeking exhalations of linoleum and mildewed and rotten woodwork.

Then suddenly, as he rested there, the room was filled with the strong, sweet odor of mignonette.[4] It came as upon a single buffet of wind with such sureness and fragrance and emphasis that it almost seemed a living visitant. And the man cried aloud: "What, dear?" as if he had been called, and sprang up and faced about. The rich odor clung to him and wrapped him around. He reached out his arms for it, all his senses for the time confused and commingled. How could one be peremptorily called by an odor? Surely it must have been a sound. But, was it not the sound that had touched, that had caressed him?

"She has been in this room," he cried, and he sprang to wrest from it a token, for he knew he would recognize the smallest thing that had belonged to her or that she had touched. This enveloping scent of mignonette, the odor that she had loved and made her own—whence came it?

The room had been but carelessly set in order. Scattered upon the flimsy dresser scarf were half a dozen hairpins—those discreet, indistinguishable friends of womankind, feminine of gender, infi-

4. A perfume sold by Sears Roebuck at the turn of the twentieth century; the fragrance was meant to resemble that of the greenish flower of the same name.

nite of mood and uncommunicative of tense. These he ignored, conscious of their triumphant lack of identity. Ransacking the drawers of the dresser he came upon a discarded, tiny, ragged handkerchief. He pressed it to his face. It was racy and insolent with heliotrope;[5] he hurled it to the floor. In another drawer he found odd buttons, a theatre programme, a pawnbroker's card, two lost marshmallows, a book on the divination of dreams. In the last was a woman's black satin hair bow, which halted him, poised between ice and fire. But the black satin hair bow also is femininity's demure, impersonal common ornament and tells no tales.

And then he traversed the room like a hound on the scent, skimming the walls, considering the corners of the bulging matting on his hands and knees, rummaging mantel and tables, the curtains and hangings, the drunken cabinet in the corner, for a visible sign, unable to perceive that she was there beside, around, against, within, above him, clinging to him, wooing him, calling him so poignantly through the finer senses that even his grosser ones became cognizant of the call. Once again he answered loudly: "Yes, dear!" and turned, wild-eyed, to gaze on vacancy, for he could not yet discern form and color and love and outstretched arms in the odor of mignonette. Oh, God! whence that odor, and since when have odors had a voice to call? Thus he groped.

He burrowed in crevices and corners, and found corks and cigarettes. These he passed in passive contempt. But once he found in a fold of the matting a half-smoked cigar, and this he ground beneath his heel with a green and trenchant oath. He sifted the room from end to end. He found dreary and ignoble small records of many a peripatetic tenant; but of her whom he sought, and who may have lodged there, and whose spirit seemed to hover there, he found no trace.

And then he thought of the housekeeper.

He ran from the haunted room downstairs and to a door that showed a crack of light. She came out to his knock. He smothered his excitement as best he could.

"Will you tell me, madam," he besought her, "who occupied the room I have before I came?"

"Yes, sir. I can tell you again. 'Twas Sprowls and Mooney, as I

5. A fragrance meant to imitate the scent of the purplish flowers of the same name.

said. Miss B'retta Sprowls it was in the theatres, but Missis Mooney she was. My house is well known for respectability. The marriage certificate hung, framed, on a nail over—"

"What kind of a lady was Miss Sprowls—in looks, I mean?"

"Why, black-haired, sir, short, and stout, with a comical face. They left a week ago Tuesday."

"And before they occupied it?"

"Why, there was a single gentleman connected with the draying[6] business. He left owing me a week. Before him was Missis Crowder and her two children, that stayed four months; and back of them was old Mr. Doyle, whose sons paid for him. He kept the room six months. That goes back a year, sir, and further I do not remember."

He thanked her and crept back to his room. The room was dead. The essence that had vivified it was gone. The perfume of mignonette had departed. In its place was the old, stale odor of mouldy house furniture, of atmosphere in storage.

The ebbing of his hope drained his faith. He sat staring at the yellow, singing gaslight. Soon he walked to the bed and began to tear the sheets into strips. With the blade of his knife he drove them tightly into every crevice around windows and door. When all was snug and taut he turned out the light, turned the gas full on again and laid himself gratefully upon the bed.

It was Mrs. McCool's night to go with the can for beer. So she fetched it and sat with Mrs. Purdy in one of those subterranean retreats where housekeepers foregather and the worm dieth seldom.

"I rented out my third-floor-back this evening," said Mrs. Purdy, across a fine circle of foam. "A young man took it. He went up to bed two hours ago."

"Now, did ye, Mrs. Purdy, ma'am?" said Mrs. McCool, with intense admiration. "You do be a wonder for rentin' rooms of that kind. And did ye tell him, then?" she concluded in a husky whisper laden with mystery.

"Rooms," said Mrs. Purdy, in her furriest tones, "are furnished for to rent. I did not tell him, Mrs. McCool."

" 'Tis right ye are, ma'am; 'tis by renting rooms we kape alive. Ye

6. Hauling.

have the rale sense for business, ma'am. There be many people will rayjict the rentin' of a room if they be tould a suicide has been after dyin' in the bed of it."

"As you say, we has our living to be making," remarked Mrs. Purdy.

"Yis, ma'am; 'tis true. 'Tis just one wake ago this day I helped ye lay out the third-floor-back. A pretty slip of a colleen she was to be killin' herself wid the gas—a swate little face she had, Mrs. Purdy, ma'am."

"She'd a-been called handsome, as you say," said Mrs. Purdy, assenting but critical, "but for that mole she had a-growin' by her left eyebrow. Do fill up your glass again, Mrs. McCool."

1904

James Joyce
1882–1941

Joyce wrote "Araby" in September 1905 while living in Trieste. That year he had left Ireland to find a less restrictive atmosphere on the Continent. Ireland, he felt, was paralyzed by a combination of Catholic ideology and British imperial capitalism, and he wrote this story and the fourteen others that make up Dubliners *in order to give his Irish readers "one good look at themselves in my nicely polished looking-glass." By comparing his stories to a mirror, Joyce put them in the category of realism—literature that tries to faithfully mirror reality, often to expose to readers some defect in themselves or society. But critics often point to the highly literary character of "Araby," which compares the narrator's trip to the bazaar to a romantic quest. The narrator's experience at the conclusion is a fine example of an* epiphany, *a literary term Joyce invented. An epiphany, according to Joyce, is "a sudden spiritual manifestation" revealed usually in some mundane or seemingly trivial gesture or phrase.*

Araby

North Richmond Street, being blind,[1] was a quiet street except at the hour when the Christian Brothers'[2] School set the boys free. An uninhabited house of two storeys stood at the blind end, detached from its neighbours in a square ground. The other houses of the street, conscious of decent lives within them, gazed at one another with brown imperturbable faces.

The former tenant of our house, a priest, had died in the back drawing-room. Air, musty from having been long enclosed, hung in all the rooms, and the waste room behind the kitchen was littered with old useless papers. Among these I found a few paper-covered books, the pages of which were curled and damp: *The Abbot*, by Walter Scott, *The Devout Communicant* and *The Memoirs of Vidocq*. I liked the last best because its leaves were yellow. The wild garden behind the house contained a central apple-tree and a few straggling bushes under one of which I found the late tenant's rusty bicycle-pump. He had been a very charitable priest; in his will he had left all his money to institutions and the furniture of his house to his sister.

When the short days of winter came dusk fell before we had well eaten our dinners. When we met in the street the houses had grown sombre. The space of sky above us was the colour of ever-changing violet and towards it the lamps of the street lifted their feeble lanterns. The cold air stung us and we played till our bodies glowed. Our shouts echoed in the silent street. The career of our play brought us through the dark muddy lanes behind the houses where we ran the gantlet of the rough tribes from the cottages, to the back doors of the dark dripping gardens where odours arose from the ash-pits, to the dark odorous stables where a coachman smoothed and combed the horse or shook music from the buckled harness. When we returned to the street light from the kitchen windows had filled the areas. If my uncle was seen turning the corner we hid in the shadow until we had seen him safely housed. Or if Mangan's sister

1. A dead end.
2. A Roman Catholic order that catered to the poor.

came out on the doorstep to call her brother in to his tea we watched her from our shadow peer up and down the street. We waited to see whether she would remain or go in and, if she remained, we left our shadow and walked up to Mangan's steps resignedly. She was waiting for us, her figure defined by the light from the half-opened door. Her brother always teased her before he obeyed and I stood by the railings looking at her. Her dress swung as she moved her body and the soft rope of her hair tossed from side to side.

Every morning I lay on the floor in the front parlour watching her door. The blind was pulled down to within an inch of the sash so that I could not be seen. When she came out on the doorstep my heart leaped, I ran to the hall, seized my books and followed her. I kept her brown figure always in my eye and, when we came near the point at which our ways diverged, I quickened my pace and passed her. This happened morning after morning. I had never spoken to her, except for a few casual words, and yet her name was like a summons to all my foolish blood.

Her image accompanied me even in places the most hostile to romance. On Saturday evenings when my aunt went marketing I had to go to carry some of the parcels. We walked through the flaring streets, jostled by drunken men and bargaining women, amid the curses of labourers, the shrill litanies of shop-boys who stood on guard by the barrels of pigs' cheeks, the nasal chanting of street-singers, who sang a *come-all-you* about O'Donovan Rossa,[3] or a ballad about the troubles in our native land. These noises converged in a single sensation of life for me: I imagined that I bore my chalice safely through a throng of foes. Her name sprang to my lips at moments in strange prayers and praises which I myself did not understand. My eyes were often full of tears (I could not tell why) and at times a flood from my heart seemed to pour itself out into my bosom. I thought little of the future. I did not know whether I would ever speak to her or not or, if I spoke to her, how I could tell her of my confused adoration. But my body was like a harp and her words and gestures were like fingers running upon the wires.

3. Jeremiah O'Donovan Rossa (1831–1915) was a member of the Fenians, who were precursors to the present-day Irish Republican Army. O'Donovan Rossa was banished from Ireland, but a number of nationalist ballads (which often began with the words "Come all you . . .") kept his anti-English exploits in the popular imagination.

One evening I went into the back drawing-room in which the priest had died. It was a dark rainy evening and there was no sound in the house. Through one of the broken panes I heard the rain impinge upon the earth, the fine incessant needles of water playing in the sodden beds. Some distant lamp or lighted window gleamed below me. I was thankful that I could see so little. All my senses seemed to desire to veil themselves and, feeling that I was about to slip from them, I pressed the palms of my hands together until they trembled, murmuring: *O love! O love!* many times.

At last she spoke to me. When she addressed the first words to me I was so confused that I did not know what to answer. She asked me was I going to *Araby*.[4] I forget whether I answered yes or no. It would be a splendid bazaar, she said; she would love to go.

—And why can't you? I asked.

While she spoke she turned a silver bracelet round and round her wrist. She could not go, she said, because there would be a retreat[5] that week in her convent. Her brother and two other boys were fighting for their caps and I was alone at the railings. She held one of the spikes, bowing her head towards me. The light from the lamp opposite our door caught the white curve of her neck, lit up her hair that rested there and, falling, lit up the hand upon the railing. It fell over one side of her dress and caught the white border of a petticoat, just visible as she stood at ease.

—It's well for you, she said.

—If I go, I said, I will bring you something.

What innumerable follies laid waste my waking and sleeping thoughts after that evening! I wished to annihilate the tedious intervening days. I chafed against the work of school. At night in my bedroom and by day in the classroom her image came between me and the page I strove to read. The syllables of the word *Araby* were called to me through the silence in which my soul luxuriated and cast an Eastern enchantment over me. I asked for leave to go to the bazaar on Saturday night. My aunt was surprised and hoped it

4. When Joyce was a boy, a charity bazaar called "Araby" did visit Dublin. Admission was one shilling.

5. A special gathering for prayer and moral instruction. The "convent" is a Catholic school.

was not some Freemason affair.[6] I answered few questions in class. I watched my master's face pass from amiability to sternness; he hoped I was not beginning to idle. I could not call my wandering thoughts together. I had hardly any patience with the serious work of life which, now that it stood between me and my desire, seemed to me child's play, ugly monotonous child's play.

On Saturday morning I reminded my uncle that I wished to go to the bazaar in the evening. He was fussing at the hallstand, looking for the hat-brush, and answered me curtly:

—Yes, boy, I know.

As he was in the hall I could not go into the front parlour and lie at the window. I left the house in bad humour and walked slowly towards the school. The air was pitilessly raw and already my heart misgave me.

When I came home to dinner my uncle had not yet been home. Still it was early. I sat staring at the clock for some time and, when its ticking began to irritate me, I left the room. I mounted the staircase and gained the upper part of the house. The high cold empty gloomy rooms liberated me and I went from room to room singing. From the front window I saw my companions playing below in the street. Their cries reached me weakened and indistinct and, leaning my forehead against the cool glass, I looked over at the dark house where she lived. I may have stood there for an hour, seeing nothing but the brown-clad figure cast by my imagination, touched discreetly by the lamplight at the curved neck, at the hand upon the railings and at the border below the dress.

When I came downstairs again I found Mrs. Mercer sitting at the fire. She was an old garrulous woman, a pawnbroker's widow, who collected used stamps for some pious purpose. I had to endure the gossip of the tea-table. The meal was prolonged beyond an hour and still my uncle did not come. Mrs. Mercer stood up to go: she was sorry she couldn't wait any longer, but it was after eight o'clock and she did not like to be out late, as the night air was bad for her. When she had gone I began to walk up and down the room, clenching my fists. My aunt said:

6. The Masons were a quasi-religious, semi-secret society devoted to, among other things, the demise of Roman Catholicism.

—I'm afraid you may put off your bazaar for this night of Our Lord.

At nine o'clock I heard my uncle's latchkey in the halldoor. I heard him talking to himself and heard the hallstand rocking when it had received the weight of his overcoat. I could interpret these signs. When he was midway through his dinner I asked him to give me the money to go to the bazaar. He had forgotten.

—The people are in bed and after their first sleep now, he said.

I did not smile. My aunt said to him energetically:

—Can't you give him the money and let him go? You've kept him late enough as it is.

My uncle said he was very sorry he had forgotten. He said he believed in the old saying: *All work and no play makes Jack a dull boy.* He asked me where I was going and, when I had told him a second time he asked me did I know *The Arab's Farewell to his Steed.*[7] When I left the kitchen he was about to recite the opening lines of the piece to my aunt.

I held a florin[8] tightly in my hand as I strode down Buckingham Street towards the station. The sight of the streets thronged with buyers and glaring with gas recalled to me the purpose of my journey. I took my seat in a third-class carriage of a deserted train. After an intolerable delay the train moved out of the station slowly. It crept onward among ruinous houses and over the twinkling river. At Westland Row Station a crowd of people pressed to the carriage doors; but the porters moved them back, saying that it was a special train for the bazaar. I remained alone in the bare carriage. In a few minutes the train drew up beside an improvised wooden platform. I passed out on to the road and saw by the lighted dial of a clock that it was ten minutes to ten. In front of me was a large building which displayed the magical name.

I could not find any sixpenny entrance and, fearing that the bazaar would be closed, I passed in quickly through a turnstile, handing a shilling to a weary-looking man. I found myself in a big hall girdled at half its height by a gallery. Nearly all the stalls were

7. Sentimental poem by Caroline Norton (1808–1877), in which an Arab boy sells his horse, but as the horse is being led away, changes his mind and runs after the man he sold it to in order to return the money and reclaim his love.

8. British coin worth two shillings.

closed and the greater part of the hall was in darkness. I recognised a silence like that which pervades a church after a service. I walked into the centre of the bazaar timidly. A few people were gathered about the stalls which were still open. Before a curtain, over which the words *Café Chantant*[9] were written in coloured lamps, two men were counting money on a salver. I listened to the fall of the coins.

Remembering with difficulty why I had come I went over to one of the stalls and examined porcelain vases and flowered tea-sets. At the door of the stall a young lady was talking and laughing with two young gentlemen. I remarked their English accents and listened vaguely to their conversation.

—O, I never said such a thing!

—O, but you did!

—O, but I didn't!

—Didn't she say that?

—Yes. I heard her.

—O, there's a . . . fib!

Observing me the young lady came over and asked me did I wish to buy anything. The tone of her voice was not encouraging; she seemed to have spoken to me out of a sense of duty. I looked humbly at the great jars that stood like eastern guards at either side of the dark entrance to the stall and murmured:

—No, thank you.

The young lady changed the position of one of the vases and went back to the two young men. They began to talk of the same subject. Once or twice the young lady glanced at me over her shoulder.

I lingered before her stall, though I knew my stay was useless, to make my interest in her wares seem the more real. Then I turned away slowly and walked down the middle of the bazaar. I allowed the two pennies to fall against the sixpence in my pocket. I heard a voice call from one end of the gallery that the light was out. The upper part of the hall was now completely dark.

Gazing up into the darkness I saw myself as a creature driven and derided by vanity; and my eyes burned with anguish and anger.

1904

9. Singing Café (French), a café offering musical entertainment.

Franz Kafka
1883–1924

Kafka wrote this story in February 1922, when he was suffering from tuberculosis and a depression that manifested itself in insomnia and extreme fatigue. But the physical deterioration of the central figure in this story goes well beyond Kafka's own physical condition. In fact, you have to suspend disbelief to enjoy Kafka's stories, which tend toward allegory. Many critics believe that the hunger artist stands for artists in general and that the story depicts Kafka's relation to his own audiences. Kafka was what we would today call a "modernist." Modernism produced a refined and intellectual style that often alienated the artist from general readers by pursuing as its goal art for art's sake, rather than art that edifies society. At the same time, modernists criticized the banality of European life after World War I—especially the life of the middle class—and made artists the heroes of their fiction, at least in so much as their alienated, self-sacrificing, doomed protagonists can be called "heroes."

A Hunger Artist[1]

During these last decades the interest in professional fasting has markedly diminished. It used to pay very well to stage such great performances under one's own management, but today that is quite impossible. We live in a different world now. At one time the whole town took a lively interest in the hunger artist; from day to day of his fast the excitement mounted; everybody wanted to see him at least once a day; there were people who bought season tickets for the last few days and sat from morning till night in front of his small barred cage; even in the nighttime there were visiting hours, when the whole effect was heightened by torch flares; on fine days the cage was set out in the open air, and then it was the children's special treat to see the hunger artist; for their elders he was often just a joke that happened to be in fashion, but the children stood open-mouthed, holding each other's hands for

1. Translated by Edwin and Willa Muir.

greater security, marveling at him as he sat there pallid in black tights, with his ribs sticking out so prominently, not even on a seat but down among straw on the ground, sometimes giving a courteous nod, answering questions with a constrained smile, or perhaps stretching an arm through the bars so that one might feel how thin it was, and then again withdrawing deep into himself, paying no attention to anyone or anything, not even to the all-important striking of the clock that was the only piece of furniture in his cage, but merely staring into vacancy with half shut eyes, now and then taking a sip from a tiny glass of water to moisten his lips.

Besides casual onlookers there were also relays of permanent watchers selected by the public, usually butchers, strangely enough, and it was their task to watch the hunger artist day and night, three of them at a time, in case he should have some secret recourse to nourishment. This was nothing but a formality, instituted to reassure the masses, for the initiates knew well enough that during his fast the artist would never in any circumstances, not even under forcible compulsion, swallow the smallest morsel of food: the honor of his profession forbade it. Not every watcher, of course, was capable of understanding this, there were often groups of night watchers who were very lax in carrying out their duties and deliberately huddled together in a retired corner to play cards with great absorption, obviously intending to give the hunger artist the chance of a little refreshment, which they supposed he could draw from some private hoard. Nothing annoyed the artist more than such watchers; they made him miserable; they made his fast seem unendurable; sometimes he mastered his feebleness sufficiently to sing during their watch for as long as he could keep going, to show them how unjust their suspicions were. But that was of little use; they only wondered at his cleverness in being able to fill his mouth even while singing. Much more to his taste were the watchers who sat close up to the bars, who were not content with the dim night lighting of the hall but focused him in the full glare of the electric pocket torch given them by the impresario.[2] The harsh light did not trouble him at all, in any case he could never sleep properly, and he could always drowse a little, whatever the light, at any hour, even when the hall

2. Promoter and manager of an entertainment.

was thronged with noisy onlookers. He was quite happy at the prospect of spending a sleepless night with such watchers; he was ready to exchange jokes with them, to tell them stories out of his nomadic life, anything at all to keep them awake and demonstrate to them again that he had no eatables in his cage and that he was fasting as not one of them could fast. But his happiest moment was when the morning came and an enormous breakfast was brought them, at his expense, on which they flung themselves with the keen appetite of healthy men after a weary night of wakefulness. Of course there were people who argued that this breakfast was an unfair attempt to bribe the watchers, but that was going rather too far, and when they were invited to take on a night's vigil without a breakfast, merely for the sake of the cause, they made themselves scarce, although they stuck stubbornly to their suspicions.

Such suspicions, anyhow, were a necessary accompaniment to the profession of fasting. No one could possibly watch the hunger artist continuously, day and night, and so no one could produce first-hand evidence that the fast had really been rigorous and continuous; only the artist himself could know that, he was therefore bound to be the sole completely satisfied spectator of his own fast. Yet for other reasons he was never satisfied; it was not perhaps mere fasting that had brought him to such skeleton thinness that many people had regretfully to keep away from his exhibitions, because the sight of him was too much for them, perhaps it was dissatisfaction with himself that had worn him down. For he alone knew, what no other initiate knew, how easy it was to fast. It was the easiest thing in the world. He made no secret of this, yet people did not believe him, at the best they set him down as modest, most of them, however, thought he was out for publicity or else was some kind of cheat who found it easy to fast because he had discovered a way of making it easy, and then had the impudence to admit the fact, more or less. He had to put up with all that, and in the course of time had got used to it, but his inner dissatisfaction always rankled, and never yet, after any term of fasting—this must be granted to his credit—had he left the cage of his own free will. The longest period of fasting was fixed by his impresario at forty days, beyond that term he was not allowed to go, not even in great cities, and there was good reason for it, too. Experience had proved that for about forty days the interest of the public could be stimulated by a steadily increasing pressure of advertisement, but after that the town began to lose interest, sympathetic support began notably to fall off; there were of course local variations as between one town and another or one country and another, but as a general rule forty days marked the limit. So on the fortieth day the flower-bedecked cage was opened, enthusiastic spectators filled the hall, a military band played, two doctors entered the cage to measure the results of the fast, which were announced through a megaphone, and finally two young ladies appeared, blissful at having been selected for the honor, to help the hunger artist down the few steps leading to a small table on which was spread a carefully chosen invalid repast. And at this very moment the artist always turned stubborn. True, he would entrust his bony arms to the outstretched helping hands of the ladies bending over him, but stand up he would not. Why stop fasting at this particular moment, after forty days of it? He had held out for a long time, an illimitably long time; why stop now, when he was in his best fasting form, or rather, not yet quite in his best fasting form? Why should he be cheated of the fame he would get for fasting longer, for being not only the record hunger artist of all time, which presumably he was already, but for beating his own record by a performance beyond human imagination, since he felt that there were no limits to his capacity for fasting? His public pretended to admire him so much, why should it have so little patience with him; if he could endure fasting longer, why shouldn't the public endure it? Besides, he was tired, he was comfortable sitting in the straw, and now he was supposed to lift himself to his full height and go down to a meal the very thought of which gave him a nausea that only the presence of the ladies kept him from betraying, and even that with an effort. And he looked up into the eyes of the ladies who were apparently so friendly and in reality so cruel, and shook his head, which felt too heavy on its strengthless neck. But then there happened yet again what always happened. The impresario came forward, without a word—for the band made speech impossible—lifted his arms in the air above the artist, as if inviting Heaven to look down upon its creature here in the straw, this suffering martyr, which indeed he was, although in quite another sense; grasped him round the emaciated waist, with exaggerated caution, so that the frail condition he was in might be appreciated; and committed him to the care of the blenching[3] ladies, not without secretly giving him a shaking so that his legs and body tottered and swayed. The artist now submitted completely; his head lolled on his breast as if it had landed there by chance; his body was hollowed out; his legs in a spasm of self-preservation clung close to each other at the knees, yet scraped on the ground as if it were not really solid ground, as if they were only trying to find solid ground; and the whole weight of his body, a feather-weight after all, relapsed onto one of the ladies, who, looking round for help and panting a little—this post of honor was not at all what she had expected it to be—first stretched her neck as far as she could to keep her face at least free from contact with the artist, when finding this impossible, and her more fortunate companion not coming to her aid but merely holding extended on her own trembling hand the little bunch of knucklebones that was the artist's, to the great delight of the spectators burst into tears and had to be replaced by an attendant who had long been stationed in readiness. Then came the food, a little of which the impresario managed to get between the artist's lips, while he sat in a kind of half-fainting trance, to the accompaniment of cheerful patter designed to distract the public's attention from the artist's condition; after that, a toast was drunk to the public, supposedly prompted by a whisper from the artist in the impresario's ear; the band confirmed it with a mighty flourish, the spectators melted away, and no one had any cause to be dissatisfied with the proceedings, no one except the hunger artist himself, he only, as always.

So he lived for many years, with small regular intervals of recuperation, in visible glory, honored by the world, yet in spite of that troubled in spirit, and all the more troubled because no one would take his trouble seriously. What comfort could he possibly need? What more could he possibly wish for? And if some good-natured person, feeling sorry for him, tried to console him by pointing out that his melancholy was probably caused by fasting, it could happen, especially when he had been fasting for some time, that he reacted with an outburst of fury and to the general alarm began to shake the bars of his cage like a wild animal. Yet the impresario had

3. Flinching, shrinking back.

a way of punishing these outbreaks which he rather enjoyed putting into operation. He would apologize publicly for the artist's behavior, which was only to be excused, he admitted, because of the irritability caused by fasting; a condition hardly to be understood by well-fed people; then by natural transition he went on to mention the artist's equally incomprehensible boast that he could fast for much longer than he was doing; he praised the high ambition, the good will, the great self-denial undoubtedly implicit in such a statement; and then quite simply countered it by bringing out photographs, which were also on sale to the public, showing the artist on the fortieth day of a fast lying in bed almost dead from exhaustion. This perversion of the truth, familiar to the artist though it was, always unnerved him afresh and proved too much for him. What was a consequence of the premature ending of his fast was here presented as the cause of it! To fight against this lack of understanding, against a whole world of non-understanding, was impossible. Time and again in good faith he stood by the bars listening to the impresario, but as soon as the photographs appeared he always let go and sank with a groan back on to his straw, and the reassured public could once more come close and gaze at him.

A few years later when the witnesses of such scenes called them to mind, they often failed to understand themselves at all. For meanwhile the aforementioned change in public interest had set in; it seemed to happen almost overnight; there may have been profound causes for it, but who was going to bother about that; at any rate the pampered hunger artist suddenly found himself deserted one fine day by the amusement seekers, who went streaming past him to other more favored attractions. For the last time the impresario hurried him over half Europe to discover whether the old interest might still survive here and there; all in vain; everywhere, as if by secret agreement, a positive revulsion from professional fasting was in evidence. Of course it could not really have sprung up so suddenly as all that, and many premonitory symptoms which had not been sufficiently remarked or suppressed during the rush and glitter of success now came retrospectively to mind, but it was now too late to take any countermeasures. Fasting would surely come into fashion again at some future date, yet that was no comfort for those living in the present. What, then, was the hunger artist to do?

He had been applauded by thousands in his time and could hardly come down to showing himself in a street booth at village fairs, and as for adopting another profession, he was not only too old for that but too fanatically devoted to fasting. So he took leave of the impresario, his partner in an unparalleled career, and hired himself to a large circus; in order to spare his own feelings he avoided reading the conditions of his contract.

A large circus with its enormous traffic in replacing and recruiting men, animals and apparatus can always find a use for people at any time, even for a hunger artist, provided of course that he does not ask too much, and in this particular case anyhow it was not only the artist who was taken on but his famous and long-known name as well, indeed considering the peculiar nature of his performance, which was not impaired by advancing age, it could not be objected that here was an artist past his prime, no longer at the height of his professional skill, seeking a refuge in some quiet corner of a circus; on the contrary, the hunger artist averred that he could fast as well as ever, which was entirely credible, he even alleged that if he were allowed to fast as he liked, and this was at once promised him without more ado, he could astound the world by establishing a record never yet achieved, a statement which certainly provoked a smile among the other professionals, since it left out of account the change in public opinion, which the hunger artist in his zeal conveniently forgot.

He had not, however, actually lost his sense of the real situation and took it as a matter of course that he and his cage should be stationed, not in the middle of the ring as a main attraction, but outside, near the animal cages, on a site that was after all easily accessible. Large and gaily painted placards made a frame for the cage and announced what was to be seen inside it. When the public came thronging out in the intervals to see the animals, they could hardly avoid passing the hunger artist's cage and stopping there for a moment, perhaps they might even have stayed longer had not those pressing behind them in the narrow gangway, who did not understand why they should be held up on their way toward the excitements of the menagerie, made it impossible for anyone to stand gazing quietly for any length of time. And that was the reason why the hunger artist, who had of course been looking forward to these visiting hours as the main achievement of his life, began instead to shrink from them. At first he could hardly wait for the intervals; it was exhilarating to watch the crowds come streaming his way, until only too soon—not even the most obstinate self-deception, clung to almost consciously, could hold out against the fact—the conviction was borne in upon him that these people, most of them, to judge from their actions, again and again, without exception, were all on their way to the menagerie. And the first sight of them from the distance remained the best. For when they reached his cage he was at once deafened by the storm of shouting and abuse that arose from the two contending factions, which renewed themselves continuously, of those who wanted to stop and stare at him—he soon began to dislike them more than the others—not out of real interest but only out of obstinate self-assertiveness, and those who wanted to go straight on to the animals. When the first great rush was past, the stragglers came along, and these, whom nothing could have prevented from stopping to look at him as long as they had breath, raced past with long strides, hardly even glancing at him, in their haste to get to the menagerie in time. And all too rarely did it happen that he had a stroke of luck, when some father of a family fetched up before him with his children, pointed a finger at the hunger artist and explained at length what the phenomenon meant, telling stories of earlier years when he himself had watched similar but much more thrilling performances, and the children, still rather uncomprehending, since neither inside nor outside school had they been sufficiently prepared for this lesson—what did they care about fasting?—yet showed by the brightness of their intent eyes that new and better times might be coming. Perhaps, said the hunger artist to himself many a time, things would be a little better if his cage were set not quite so near the menagerie. That made it too easy for people to make their choice, to say nothing of what he suffered from the stench of the menagerie, the animals' restlessness by night, the carrying past of raw lumps of flesh for the beasts of prey, the roaring at feeding times, which depressed him continually. But he did not dare to lodge a complaint with the management; after all, he had the animals to thank for the troops of people who passed his cage, among whom there might always be one here and there to take an interest in him, and who could tell where they might seclude him if he called attention to his existence and thereby to the fact that, strictly speaking, he was only an impediment on the way to the menagerie.

A small impediment, to be sure, one that grew steadily less. People grew familiar with the strange idea that they could be expected, in times like these, to take an interest in a hunger artist, and with this familiarity the verdict went out against him. He might fast as much as he could, and he did so; but nothing could save him now, people passed him by. Just try to explain to anyone the art of fasting! Anyone who has no feeling for it cannot be made to understand it. The fine placards grew dirty and illegible, they were torn down; the little notice board telling the number of fast days achieved, which at first was changed carefully every day, had long stayed at the same figure, for after the first few weeks even this small task seemed pointless to the staff; and so the artist simply fasted on and on, as he had once dreamed of doing, and it was no trouble to him, just as he had always foretold, but no one counted the days, no one, not even the artist himself, knew what records he was already breaking, and his heart grew heavy. And when once in a time some leisurely passer-by stopped, made merry over the old figure on the board and spoke of swindling, that was in its way the stupidest lie ever invented by indifference and inborn malice, since it was not the hunger artist who was cheating; he was working honestly, but the world was cheating him of his reward.

Many more days went by, however, and that too came to an end. An overseer's eye fell on the cage one day and he asked the attendants why this perfectly good cage should be left standing there unused with dirty straw inside it; nobody knew, until one man, helped out by the notice board, remembered about the hunger artist. They poked into the straw with sticks and found him in it. "Are you still fasting?" asked the overseer. "When on earth do you mean to stop?" "Forgive me, everybody," whispered the hunger artist; only the overseer, who had his ear to the bars, understood him. "Of course," said the overseer, and tapped his forehead with a finger to let the attendants know what state the man was in, "we forgive you." "I always wanted you to admire my fasting," said the hunger artist. "We do admire it," said the overseer, affably. "But you shouldn't admire it," said the hunger artist.

"Well, then we don't admire it," said the overseer, "but why shouldn't we admire it?" "Because I have to fast, I can't help it," said the hunger artist. "What a fellow you are," said the overseer, "and why can't you help it?" "Because," said the hunger artist, lifting his head a little and speaking, with his lips pursed, as if for a kiss, right into the overseer's ear, so that no syllable might be lost, "because I couldn't find the food I liked. If I had found it, believe me, I should have made no fuss and stuffed myself like you or anyone else." These were his last words, but in his dimming eyes remained the firm though no longer proud persuasion that he was still continuing to fast.

"Well, clear this out now!" said the overseer, and they buried the hunger artist, straw and all. Into the cage they put a young panther. Even the most insensitive felt it refreshing to see this wild creature leaping around the cage that had so long been dreary. The panther was all right. The food he liked was brought him without hesitation by the attendants; he seemed not even to miss his freedom; his noble body, furnished almost to the bursting point with all that it needed, seemed to carry freedom around with it too; somewhere in his jaws it seemed to lurk; and the joy of life streamed with such ardent passion from his throat that for the onlookers it was not easy to stand the shock of it. But they braced themselves, crowded round the cage, and did not want ever to move away.

1924

Jamaica Kincaid

b. 1949

"Girl" is a short short story, a sub-genre that sometimes defies the conventions of story, especially of plot. All of Kincaid's work is noted for its highly lyrical quality, and it might make sense to read "Girl" the way you read a poem or listen to a song. "Girl" was the story that launched Kincaid's career. First published in The New Yorker *in 1978, it was the first story in her first book,* At the Bottom of the River. *Most of the stories in that book develop the mother/daughter theme introduced here. Much of Kincaid's fiction, like this story, has the flavor of her West Indian culture.*

Girl

Wash the white clothes on Monday and put them on the stone heap; wash the color clothes on Tuesday and put them on the clothesline to dry; don't walk barehead in the hot sun; cook pumpkin fritters in very hot sweet oil; soak your little clothes right after you take them off; when buying cotton to make yourself a nice blouse, be sure that it doesn't have gum on it, because that way it won't hold up well after a wash; soak salt fish overnight before you cook it; is it true that you sing benna[1] in Sunday school?; always eat your food in such a way that it won't turn someone else's stomach; on Sundays try to walk like a lady and not like the slut you are so bent on becoming; don't sing benna in Sunday school; you mustn't speak to wharf-rat boys, not even to give directions; don't eat fruits on the street—flies will follow you; *but I don't sing benna on Sundays at all and never in Sunday school*; this is how to sew on a button; this is how to make a buttonhole for the button you have just sewed on; this is how to hem a dress when you see the hem coming down and so to prevent yourself from looking like the slut I know you are so bent on becoming; this is how you iron your father's khaki shirt so that it doesn't have a crease; this is how you iron your father's khaki pants so that they don't have a crease; this is how you grow okra—far from the house, because okra tree harbors red ants; when you are growing dasheen, make sure it gets plenty of water or else it makes your throat itch when you are eating it; this is how you sweep a corner; this is how you sweep a whole house; this is how you sweep a yard; this is how you smile to someone you don't like too much; this is how you smile to someone you don't like at all; this is how you smile to someone you like completely; this is how you set a table for tea; this is how you set a table for dinner; this is how you set a table for dinner with an important guest; this is how you set a table for lunch; this is how you set a table for breakfast; this is how to behave in the presence of men who don't know you very well, and this way they won't recognize immediately the slut I have warned you against becoming; be sure

1. A percussive style of song and dance first associated with *carnival.*

to wash every day, even if it is with your own spit; don't squat down to play marbles—you are not a boy, you know; don't pick people's flowers—you might catch something; don't throw stones at black birds, because it might not be a blackbird at all; this is how to make a bread pudding; this is how to make doukona; this is how to make pepper pot;[2] this is how to make a good medicine for a cold; this is how to make a good medicine to throw away a child before it even becomes a child; this is how to catch a fish; this is how to throw back a fish you don't like, and that way something bad won't fall on you; this is how to bully a man; this is how a man bullies you; this is how to love a man, and if this doesn't work there are other ways, and if they don't work don't feel too bad about giving up; this is how to spit up in the air if you feel like it, and this is how to move quick so that it doesn't fall on you; this is how to make ends meet; always squeeze bread to make sure it's fresh; *but what if the baker won't let me feel the bread?*; you mean to say that after all you are really going to be the kind of woman who the baker won't let near the bread?

1978

D. H. Lawrence

1885–1930

Lawrence wrote the first draft of "The Horse Dealer's Daughter" in 1915 while living in what he considered the wild, Celtic, pre-Christian environment of Cornwall, on the extreme coast of southwest England. His novel The Rainbow *had just been suppressed because of its sexual explicitness, and its sequel,* Women in Love, *would be rejected by publishers for the same reason. After World War I, he wandered from Italy to Australia to the American Southwest to Mexico, finding these places more congenial to his beliefs. The setting of the story is based on his hometown, a coal town in central England, and he prided himself on capturing the language and manners of the poor. Peasants and other poor country folk, like the native peoples of the places to which he traveled, represented to*

2. Pepper pot and doukona are both traditional Antiguan dishes.

Lawrence and to many intellectuals of the 1920s an antidote to the stupefying and corrupting influences of European civilization.

The Horse Dealer's Daughter

"Well, Mabel, and what are you going to do with yourself?" asked Joe, with foolish flippancy. He felt quite safe himself. Without listening for an answer, he turned aside, worked a grain of tobacco to the tip of his tongue, and spat it out. He did not care about anything, since he felt safe himself.

The three brothers and the sister sat round the desolate breakfast-table, attempting some sort of desultory consultation. The morning's post had given the final tap to the family fortunes, and all was over. The dreary dining-room itself, with its heavy mahogany furniture, looked as if it were waiting to be done away with.

But the consultation amounted to nothing. There was a strange air of ineffectuality about the three men, as they sprawled at table, smoking and reflecting vaguely on their own condition. The girl was alone, a rather short, sullen-looking young woman of twenty-seven. She did not share the same life as her brothers. She would have been good-looking, save for the impressive fixity of her face, "bull-dog," as her brothers called it.

There was a confused tramping of horses' feet outside. The three men all sprawled round in their chairs to watch. Beyond the dark holly bushes that separated the strip of lawn from the high-road, they could see a cavalcade of shire horses[1] swinging out of their own yard, being taken for exercise. This was the last time. These were the last horses that would go through their hands. The young men watched with critical, callous look. They were all frightened at the collapse of their lives, and the sense of disaster in which they were involved left them no inner freedom.

Yet they were three fine, well-set fellows enough. Joe, the eldest, was a man of thirty-three, broad and handsome in a hot, flushed way. His face was red, he twisted his black moustache over a thick finger, his eyes were shallow and restless. He had a sensual way of

1. Breed of draft horse.

uncovering his teeth when he laughed, and his bearing was stupid. Now he watched the horses with a glazed look of helplessness in his eyes, a certain stupor of downfall.

The great draught-horses swung past. They were tied head to tail, four of them, and they heaved along to where a lane branched off from the high-road, planting their great hoofs floutingly in the fine black mud, swinging their great rounded haunches sumptuously, and trotting a few sudden steps as they were led into the lane, round the corner. Every movement showed a massive, slumbrous strength, and a stupidity which held them in subjection. The groom at the head looked back, jerking the leading rope. And the cavalcade moved out of sight up the lane, the tail of the last horse, bobbed up tight and stiff, held out taut from the swinging great haunches as they rocked behind the hedges in a motion-like sleep.

Joe watched with glazed hopeless eyes. The horses were almost like his own body to him. He felt he was done for now. Luckily he was engaged to a woman as old as himself, and therefore her father, who was steward of a neighbouring estate, would provide him with a job. He would marry and go into harness. His life was over, he would be a subject animal now.

He turned uneasily aside, the retreating steps of the horses echoing in his ears. Then, with foolish restlessness, he reached for the scraps of bacon-rind from the plates, and making a faint whistling sound, flung them to the terrier that lay against the fender.[2] He watched the dog swallow them, and waited till the creature looked into his eyes. Then a faint grin came on his face, and in a high, foolish voice he said:

"You won't get much more bacon, shall you, you little b——?"

The dog faintly and dismally wagged its tail, then lowered its haunches, circled round, and lay down again.

There was another helpless silence at the table. Joe sprawled uneasily in his seat, not willing to go till the family conclave was dissolved. Fred Henry, the second brother, was erect, clean-limbed, alert. He had watched the passing of the horses with more *sang-froid*.[3] If he was an animal, like Joe, he was an animal which con-

2. Low metal screen before a fireplace.
3. Coolness (French).

trols, not one which is controlled. He was master of any horse, and he carried himself with a well-tempered air of mastery. But he was not master of the situations of life. He pushed his coarse brown moustache upwards, off his lip, and glanced irritably at his sister, who sat impassive and inscrutable.

"You'll go and stop with Lucy for a bit, shan't you?" he asked. The girl did not answer.

"I don't see what else you can do," persisted Fred Henry.

"Go as a skivvy,"[4] Joe interpolated laconically.

The girl did not move a muscle.

"If I was her, I should go in for training for a nurse," said Malcolm, the youngest of them all. He was the baby of the family, a young man of twenty-two with a fresh, jaunty *museau.*[5]

But Mabel did not take any notice of him. They had talked at her and round her for so many years, that she hardly heard them at all.

The marble clock on the mantelpiece softly chimed the half-hour, the dog rose uneasily from the hearth rug and looked at the party at the breakfast table. But still they sat in an ineffectual conclave.

"Oh, all right," said Joe suddenly, apropos of nothing. "I'll get a move on."

He pushed back his chair, straddled his knees with a downward jerk, to get them free, in horsey fashion, and went to the fire. Still he did not go out of the room; he was curious to know what the others would do or say. He began to charge his pipe, looking down at the dog and saying in a high, affected voice:

"Going wi' me? Going wi' me are ter? Tha'rt goin' further than tha counts on just now, dost hear?"

The dog faintly wagged his tail, the man stuck out his jaw and covered his pipe with his hands, and puffed intently, losing himself in the tobacco, looking down all the while at the dog with an absent brown eye. The dog looked up at him in mournful distrust. Joe stood with his knees stuck out, in real horsey fashion.

"Have you had a letter from Lucy?" Fred Henry asked of his sister.

4. Female domestic servant.

5. Face; literally, "muzzle" (French).

"Last week," came the neutral reply.

"And what does she say?"

There was no answer.

"Does she *ask* you to go and stop there?" persisted Fred Henry.

"She says I can if I like."

"Well, then, you'd better. Tell her you'll come on Monday."

This was received in silence.

"That's what you'll do then, is it?" said Fred Henry, in some exasperation.

But she made no answer. There was a silence of futility and irritation in the room. Malcolm grinned fatuously.

"You'll have to make up your mind between now and next Wednesday," said Joe loudly, "or else find yourself lodgings on the kerbstone."

The face of the young woman darkened, but she sat on immutable.

"Here's Jack Ferguson!" exclaimed Malcolm, who was looking aimlessly out of the window.

"Where?" exclaimed Joe loudly.

"Just gone past."

"Coming in?"

Malcolm craned his neck to see the gate.

"Yes," he said.

There was a silence. Mabel sat on like one condemned, at the head of the table. Then a whistle was heard from the kitchen. The dog got up and barked sharply. Joe opened the door and shouted:

"Come on."

After a moment a young man entered. He was muffled up in overcoat and a purple woollen scarf, and his tweed cap, which he did not remove, was pulled down on his head. He was of medium height, his face was rather long and pale, his eyes looked tired.

"Hello, Jack! Well, Jack!" exclaimed Malcolm and Joe. Fred Henry merely said: "Jack."

"What's doing?" asked the newcomer, evidently addressing Fred Henry.

"Same. We've got to be out by Wednesday. Got a cold?"

"I have—got it bad, too."

"Why don't you stop in?"

"*Me* stop in? When I can't stand on my legs, perhaps I shall have a chance." The young man spoke huskily. He had a slight Scotch accent.

"It's a knock-out, isn't it," said Joe, boisterously, "if a doctor goes round croaking with a cold. Looks bad for the patients, doesn't it?"

The young doctor looked at him slowly.

"Anything the matter with *you*, then?" he asked sarcastically.

"Not as I know of. Damn your eyes, I hope not. Why?"

"I thought you were very concerned about the patients, wondered if you might be one yourself."

"Damn it, no, I've never been patient to no flaming doctor, and hope I never shall be," returned Joe.

At this point Mabel rose from the table, and they all seemed to become aware of her existence. She began putting the dishes together. The young doctor looked at her, but did not address her. He had not greeted her. She went out of the room with the tray, her face impassive and unchanged.

"When are you off then, all of you?" asked the doctor.

"I'm catching the eleven-forty," replied Malcolm. "Are you goin' down wi' th' trap, Joe?"

"Yes, I've told you I'm going down wi' th' trap, haven't I?"

"We'd better be getting her in then. So long Jack, if I don't see you before I go," said Malcolm, shaking hands.

He went out, followed by Joe, who seemed to have his tail between his legs.

"Well, this is the devil's own," exclaimed the doctor, when he was left alone with Fred Henry. "Going before Wednesday, are you?"

"That's the orders," replied the other.

"Where, to Northampton?"

"That's it."

"The devil!" exclaimed Ferguson, with quiet chagrin.

And there was silence between the two.

"All settled up, are you?" asked Ferguson.

"About."

There was another pause.

"Well, I shall miss yer, Freddy, boy," said the young doctor.

"And I shall miss thee, Jack," returned the other.

"Miss you like hell," mused the doctor.

Fred Henry turned aside. There was nothing to say. Mabel came in again, to finish clearing the table.

"What are *you* going to do, then, Miss Pervin?" asked Ferguson. "Going to your sister's, are you?"

Mabel looked at him with her steady, dangerous eyes, that always made him uncomfortable, unsettling his superficial ease.

"No," she said.

"Well, what in the name of fortune *are* you going to do? Say what you mean to do," cried Fred Henry, with futile intensity.

But she only averted her head, and continued her work. She folded the white table-cloth, and put on the chenille cloth.

"The sulkiest bitch that ever trod!" muttered her brother.

But she finished her task with perfectly impassive face, the young doctor watching her interestedly all the while. Then she went out.

Fred Henry stared after her, clenching his lips, his blue eyes fixing in sharp antagonism, as he made a grimace of sour exasperation.

"You could bray[6] her into bits, and that's all you'd get out of her," he said, in a small, narrowed tone.

The doctor smiled faintly.

"What's she *going* to do, then?" he asked.

"Strike me if *I* know!" returned the other.

There was a pause. Then the doctor stirred.

"I'll be seeing you tonight, shall I?" he said to his friend.

"Ay—where's it to be? Are we going over to Jessdale?"

"I don't know. I've got such a cold on me. I'll come round to the 'Moon and Stars', anyway."

"Let Lizzie and May miss their night for once, eh?"

"That's it—if I feel as I do now."

"All's one——"

The two young men went through the passage and down to the back door together. The house was large, but it was servantless now, and desolate. At the back was a small brick house-yard and beyond that a big square, graveled fine and red, and having stables on two sides. Sloping, dank, winter-dark fields stretched away on the open sides.

6. Crush or grind.

But the stables were empty. Joseph Pervin, the father of the family, had been a man of no education, who had become a fairly large horse dealer. The stables had been full of horses, there was a great turmoil and come-and-go of horses and of dealers and grooms. Then the kitchen was full of servants. But of late things had declined. The old man had married a second time, to retrieve his fortunes. Now he was dead and everything was gone to the dogs, there was nothing but debt and threatening.

For months, Mabel had been servantless in the big house, keeping the home together in penury for her ineffectual brothers. She had kept house for ten years. But previously it was with unstinted means. Then, however brutal and coarse everything was, the sense of money had kept her proud, confident. The men might be foul-mouthed, the women in the kitchen might have bad reputations, her brothers might have illegitimate children. But so long as there was money, the girl felt herself established, and brutally proud, reserved.

No company came to the house, save dealers and coarse men. Mabel had no associates of her own sex, after her sister went away. But she did not mind. She went regularly to church, she attended to her father. And she lived in the memory of her mother, who had died when she was fourteen, and whom she had loved. She had loved her father, too, in a different way, depending upon him, and feeling secure in him, until at the age of fifty-four he married again. And then she had set hard against him. Now he had died and left them all hopelessly in debt.

She had suffered badly during the period of poverty. Nothing, however, could shake the curious, sullen, animal pride that dominated each member of the family. Now, for Mabel, the end had come. Still she would not cast about her. She would follow her own way just the same. She would always hold the keys of her own situation. Mindless and persistent, she endured from day to day. Why should she think? Why should she answer anybody? It was enough that this was the end, and there was no way out. She need not pass any more darkly along the main street of the small town, avoiding every eye. She need not demean herself any more, going into the shops and buying the cheapest food. This was at an end. She thought of nobody, not even of herself. Mindless and persistent, she seemed in a sort of ecstasy to be coming nearer to her fulfillment, her own glorification, approaching her dead mother, who was glorified.

In the afternoon, she took a little bag, with shears and sponge and a small scrubbing brush, and went out. It was a grey, wintry day, with saddened, dark green fields and an atmosphere blackened by the smoke of foundries not far off. She went quickly, darkly along the causeway, heeding nobody, through the town to the churchyard.

There she always felt secure, as if no one could see her, although as a matter of fact she was exposed to the stare of everyone who passed along under the churchyard wall. Nevertheless, once under the shadow of the great looming church, among the graves, she felt immune from the world, reserved within the thick churchyard wall as in another country.

Carefully she clipped the grass from the grave, and arranged the pinky white, small chrysanthemums in the tin cross. When this was done, she took an empty jar from a neighbouring grave, brought water, and carefully, most scrupulously sponged the marble headstone and the coping-stone.

It gave her sincere satisfaction to do this. She felt in immediate contact with the world of her mother. She took minute pains, went through the park in a state bordering on pure happiness, as if in performing this task she came into a subtle, intimate connection with her mother. For the life she followed here in the world was far less real than the world of death she inherited from her mother.

The doctor's house was just by the church. Ferguson, being a mere hired assistant, was slave to the country-side. As he hurried now to attend to the out-patients in the surgery, glancing across the graveyard with his quick eye, he saw the girl at her task at the grave. She seemed so intent and remote, it was like looking into another world. Some mystical element was touched in him. He slowed down as he walked, watching her as if spellbound.

She lifted her eyes, feeling him looking. Their eyes met. And each looked away again at once, each feeling, in some way, found out by the other. He lifted his cap and passed on down the road. There remained distinct in his consciousness, like a vision, the memory of her face, lifted from the tombstone in the churchyard, and looking at him with slow, large, portentous eyes. It *was* portentous, her face. It seemed to mesmerize him. There was a heavy power in her eyes which laid hold of his whole being, as if he had drunk some powerful drug. He had been feeling weak and done before. Now the life came back into him, he felt delivered from his own fretted, daily self.

He finished his duties at the surgery as quickly as might be, hastily filling up the bottles of the waiting people with cheap drugs. Then, in perpetual haste, he set off again to visit several cases in another part of his round, before tea-time. At all times he preferred to walk if he could, but particularly when he was not well. He fancied the motion restored him.

The afternoon was falling. It was grey, deadened, and wintry, with a slow, moist, heavy coldness sinking in and deadening all the faculties. But why should he think or notice? He hastily climbed the hill and turned across the dark green fields, following the black cinder-track. In the distance, across a shallow dip in the country, the small town was clustered like smouldering ash, a tower, a spire, a heap of low, raw, extinct houses. And on the nearest fringe of the town, sloping into the dip, was Oldmeadow, the Pervins' house. He could see the stables and the outbuildings distinctly, as they lay towards him on the slope. Well, he would not go there many more times! Another resource would be lost to him, another place gone: the only company he cared for in the alien, ugly little town he was losing. Nothing but work, drudgery, constant hastening from dwelling to dwelling among the colliers and the iron-workers. It wore him out, but at the same time he had a craving for it. It was a stimulant to him to be in the homes of the working people, moving, as it were, through the innermost body of their life. His nerves were excited and gratified. He could come so near, into the very lives of the rough, inarticulate, powerfully emotional men and women. He grumbled, he said he hated the hellish hole. But as a matter of fact it excited him, the contact with the rough, strongly feeling people was a stimultant applied direct to his nerves.

Below Oldmeadow, in the green, shallow, soddened hollow of fields, lay a square, deep pond. Roving across the landscape, the doctor's quick eye detected a figure in black passing through the gate of the field, down towards the pond. He looked again. It would be Mabel Pervin. His mind suddenly became alive and attentive.

Why was she going down there? He pulled up on the path on the slope above, and stood staring. He could just make sure of the small black figure moving in the hollow of the failing day. He seemed to see her in the midst of such obscurity, that he was like a clairvoyant, seeing rather with the mind's eye than with ordinary sight. Yet he could see her positively enough, whilst he kept his eye attentive. He felt, if he looked away from her, in the thick, ugly falling dusk, he would lose her altogether.

He followed her minutely as she moved, direct and intent, like something transmitted rather than stirring in voluntary activity, straight down the field towards the pond. There she stood on the bank for a moment. She never raised her head. Then she waded slowly into the water.

He stood motionless as the small black figure walked slowly and deliberately towards the center of the pond, very slowly, gradually moving deeper into the motionless water, and still moving forward as the water got up to her breast. Then he could see her no more in the dusk of the dead afternoon.

"There!" he exclaimed. "Would you believe it?"

And he hastened straight down, running over the wet, soddened fields, pushing through the hedges, down into the depression of callous wintry obscurity. It took him several minutes to come to the pond. He stood on the bank, breathing heavily. He could see nothing. His eyes seemed to penetrate the dead water. Yes, perhaps that was the dark shadow of her black clothing beneath the surface of the water.

He slowly ventured into the pond. The bottom was deep, soft clay, he sank in, and the water clasped dead cold round his legs. As he stirred he could smell the cold, rotten clay that fouled up into the water. It was objectionable in his lungs. Still, repelled and yet not heeding, he moved deeper into the pond. The cold water rose over his thighs, over his loins, upon his abdomen. The lower part of his body was all sunk in the hideous cold element. And the bottom was so deeply soft and uncertain, he was afraid of pitching with his mouth underneath. He could not swim, and was afraid.

He crouched a little, spreading his hands under the water and moving them round trying to feel for her. The dead cold pond swayed upon his chest. He moved again, a little deeper, and again, with his hands underneath, he felt all around under the water. And he touched her clothing. But it evaded his fingers. He made a desperate effort to grasp it.

And so doing he lost his balance and went under, horribly, suffocating in the foul earthy water, struggling madly for a few moments. At last, after what seemed an eternity, he got his footing, rose again into the air and looked around. He gasped, and knew he was in the world. Then he looked at the water. She had risen near him. He grasped her clothing, and drawing her nearer, turned to take his way to land again.

He went very slowly, carefully, absorbed in the slow progress. He rose higher, climbing out of the pond. The water was now only about his legs; he was thankful, full of relief to be out of the clutches of the pond. He lifted her and staggered onto the bank, out of the horror of wet, grey clay.

He laid her down on the bank. She was quite unconscious and running with water. He made the water come from her mouth, he worked to restore her. He did not have to work very long before he could feel the breathing begin again in her; she was breathing naturally. He worked a little longer. He could feel her live beneath his hands; she was coming back. He wiped her face, wrapped her in his overcoat, looked round into the dim, dark grey world, then lifted her and staggered down the bank and across the fields.

It seemed an unthinkably long way, and his burden so heavy he felt he would never get to the house. But at last he was in the stable-yard, and then in the house-yard. He opened the door and went into the house. In the kitchen he laid her down on the hearth-rug and called. The house was empty. But the fire was burning in the grate.

Then again he kneeled to attend to her. She was breathing regularly, her eyes were wide open and as if conscious, but there seemed something missing in her look. She was conscious in herself, but unconscious of her surroundings.

He ran upstairs, took blankets from a bed, and put them before the fire to warm. Then he removed her saturated, earthy-smelling clothing, rubbed her dry with a towel, and wrapped her naked in the blankets. Then he went into the dining-room, to look for spirits. There was a little whisky. He drank a gulp himself, and put some into her mouth.

The effect was instantaneous. She looked full into his face, as if she had been seeing him for some time, and yet had only just become conscious of him.

"Dr. Ferguson?" she said.

"What?" he answered.

He was divesting himself of his coat, intending to find some dry clothing upstairs. He could not bear the smell of the dead, clayey water, and he was mortally afraid for his own health.

"What did I do?" she asked.

"Walked into the pond," he replied. He had begun to shudder like one sick, and could hardly attend to her. Her eyes remained full on him, he seemed to be going dark in his mind, looking back at her helplessly. The shuddering became quieter in him, his life came back to him, dark and unknowing, but strong again.

"Was I out of my mind?" she asked, while her eyes were fixed on him all the time.

"Maybe, for the moment," he replied. He felt quiet, because his strength had come back. The strange fretful strain had left him.

"Am I out of my mind now?" she asked.

"Are you?" he reflected a moment. "No," he answered truthfully. "I don't see that you are." He turned his face aside. He was afraid now, because he felt dazed, and felt dimly that her power was stronger than his, in this issue. And she continued to look at him fixedly all the time. "Can you tell me where I shall find some dry things to put on?" he asked.

"Did you dive into the pond for me?" she asked.

"No," he answered. "I walked in. But I went in over head as well."

There was silence for a moment. He hesitated. He very much wanted to go upstairs to get into dry clothing. But there was another desire in him. And she seemed to hold him. His will seemed to have gone to sleep, and left him, standing there slack before her. But he felt warm inside himself. He did not shudder at all, though his clothes were sodden on him.

"Why did you?" she asked.

"Because I didn't want you to do such a foolish thing," he said.

"It wasn't foolish," she said, still gazing at him as she lay on the floor, with a sofa cushion under her head. "It was the right thing to do. *I* knew best, then."

"I'll go and shift these wet things," he said. But still he had not the power to move out of her presence, until she sent him. It was as if she had the life of his body in her hands, and he could not extricate himself. Or perhaps he did not want to.

Suddenly she sat up. Then she became aware of her own immediate condition. She felt the blankets about her, she knew her own limbs. For a moment it seemed as if her reason were going. She looked round, with wild eye, as if seeking something. He stood still with fear. She saw her clothing lying scattered.

"Who undressed me?" she asked, her eyes resting full and inevitable on his face.

"I did," he replied, "to bring you round."

For some moments she sat and gazed at him awfully, her lips parted.

"Do you love me, then?" she asked.

He only stood and stared at her, fascinated. His soul seemed to melt.

She shuffled forward on her knees, and put her arms round him, round his legs, as he stood there, pressing her breasts against his knees and thighs, clutching him with strange, convulsive certainty, pressing his thighs against her, drawing him to her face, her throat, as she looked up at him with flaring, humble eyes of transfiguration, triumphant in first possession.

"You love me," she murmured, in strange transport, yearning and triumphant and confident. "You love me. I know you love me, I know."

And she was passionately kissing his knees, through the wet clothing, passionately and indiscriminately kissing his knees, his legs, as if unaware of everything.

He looked down at the tangled wet hair, the wild, bare, animal shoulders. He was amazed, bewildered, and afraid. He had never thought of loving her. He had never wanted to love her. When he rescued her and restored her, he was a doctor, and she was a patient. He had had no single personal thought of her. Nay, this introduction of the personal element was very distasteful to him, a violation of his professional honour. It was horrible to have her there embracing his knees. It was horrible. He revolted from it, violently. And yet—and yet—he had not the power to break away.

She looked at him again, with the same supplication of powerful love, and that same transcendent, frightening light of triumph. In view of the delicate flame which seemed to come from her face like a light, he was powerless. And yet he had never intended to love her. He had never intended. And something stubborn in him could not give way.

"You love me," she repeated, in a murmur of deep, rhapsodic assurance. "You love me."

Her hands were drawing him, drawing him down to her. He was afraid, even a little horrified. For he had, really, no intention of loving her. Yet her hands were drawing him towards her. He put out his hand quickly to steady himself, and grasped her bare shoulder. A flame seemed to burn the hand that grasped her soft shoulder. He had no intention of loving her: his whole will was against his yielding. It was horrible. And yet wonderful was the touch of her shoulders, beautiful the shining of her face. Was she perhaps mad? He had a horror of yielding to her. Yet something in him ached also.

He had been staring away at the door, away from her. But his hand remained on her shoulder. She had gone suddenly very still. He looked down at her. Her eyes were now wide with fear, with doubt, the light was dying from her face, a shadow of terrible greyness was returning. He could not bear the touch of her eyes' question upon him, and the look of death behind the question.

With an inward groan he gave way, and let his heart yield towards her. A sudden gentle smile came on his face. And her eyes, which never left his face, slowly, slowly filled with tears. He watched the strange water rise in her eyes, like some slow fountain coming up. And his heart seemed to burn and melt away in his breast.

He could not bear to look at her any more. He dropped on his knees and caught her head with his arms and pressed her face against his throat. She was very still. His heart, which seemed to have broken, was burning with a kind of agony in his breast. And he felt her slow, hot tears wetting his throat. But he could not move.

He felt the hot tears wet his neck and the hollows of his neck, and he remained motionless, suspended through one of man's eternities. Only now it had become indispensable to him to have her face pressed close to him; he could never let her go again. He could never let her head go away from the close clutch of his arm. He wanted to remain like that for ever, with his heart hurting him in a pain that was also life to him. Without knowing, he was looking down on her damp, soft brown hair.

Then, as it were suddenly, he smelt the horrid stagnant smell of that water. And at the same moment she drew away from him and looked at him. Her eyes were wistful and unfathomable. He was afraid of them, and he fell to kissing her, not knowing what he was doing. He wanted her eyes not to have that terrible, wistful, unfathomable look.

When she turned her face to him again, a faint delicate flush was glowing, and there was again dawning that terrible shining of joy in her eyes, which really terrified him, and yet which he now wanted to see, because he feared the look of doubt still more.

"You love me?" she said, rather faltering.

"Yes." The word cost him a painful effort. Not because it wasn't true. But because it was too newly true, the *saying* seemed to tear open again his newly-torn heart. And he hardly wanted it to be true, even now.

She lifted her face to him, and he bent forward and kissed her on the mouth, gently, with the one kiss that is an eternal pledge. And as he kissed her his heart strained again in his breast. He never intended to love her. But now it was over. He had crossed over the gulf to her, and all that he had left behind had shrivelled and become void.

After the kiss, her eyes again slowly filled with tears. She sat still, away from him, with her face drooped aside, and her hands folded in her lap. The tears fell very slowly. There was complete silence. He too sat there motionless and silent on the hearth rug. The strange pain of his heart that was broken seemed to consume him. That he should love her? That this was love! That he should be ripped open in this way! Him, a doctor! How they would all jeer if they knew! It was agony to him to think they might know.

In the curious naked pain of the thought he looked again to her. She was sitting there drooped into a muse. He saw a tear fall, and his heart flared hot. He saw for the first time that one of her shoulders was quite uncovered, one arm bare, he could see one of her small breasts; dimly, because it had become almost dark in the room.

"Why are you crying?" he asked, in an altered voice.

She looked up at him, and behind her tears the consciousness of her situation for the first time brought a dark look of shame to her eyes.

"I'm not crying, really," she said, watching him, half frightened.

He reached his hand, and softly closed it on her bare arm.

"I love you! I love you!" he said in a soft, low vibrating voice, unlike himself.

She shrank, and dropped her head. The soft, penetrating grip of his hand on her arm distressed her. She looked up at him.

"I want to go," she said. "I want to go and get you some dry things."

"Why?" he said. "I'm all right."

"But I want to go," she said. "And I want you to change your things."

He released her arm, and she wrapped herself in the blanket, looking at him rather frightened. And still she did not rise.

"Kiss me," she said wistfully.

He kissed her, but briefly, half in anger.

Then, after a second, she rose nervously, all mixed up in the blanket. He watched her in her confusion as she tried to extricate herself and wrap herself up so that she could walk. He watched her relentlessly, as she knew. And as she went, the blanket trailing, and as he saw a glimpse of her feet and her white leg, he tried to remember her as she was when he had wrapped her in the blanket. But then he didn't want to remember, because she had been nothing to him then, and his nature revolted from remembering her as she was when she was nothing to him.

A tumbling, muffled noise from within the dark house startled him. Then he heard her voice: "There are clothes." He rose and went to the foot of the stairs, and gathered up the garments she had thrown down. Then he came back to the fire, to rub himself down and dress. He grinned at his own appearance when he had finished.

The fire was sinking, so he put on coal. The house was now quite dark, save for the light of a street-lamp that shone in faintly from beyond the holly trees. He lit the gas with matches he found on the mantelpiece. Then he emptied the pockets of his own clothes, and threw all his wet things in a heap into the scullery. After which he gathered up her sodden clothes, gently, and put them in a separate heap on the copper-top in the scullery.

It was six o'clock on the clock. His own watch had stopped. He ought to go back to the surgery. He waited, and still she did not come down. So he went to the foot of the stairs and called:

"I shall have to go."

Almost immediately he heard her coming down. She had on her best dress of black voile, and her hair was tidy, but still damp. She looked at him—and in spite of herself, smiled.

"I don't like you in those clothes," she said.

"Do I look a sight?" he answered:

They were shy of one another.

"I'll make you some tea," she said.

"No, I must go."

"Must you?" And she looked at him again with the wide, strained, doubtful eyes. And again, from the pain of his breast, he knew how he loved her. He went and bent to kiss her, gently, passionately, with his heart's painful kiss.

"And my hair smells so horrible," she murmured in distraction. "And I'm so awful, I'm so awful! Oh no, I'm too awful." And she broke into bitter, heartbroken sobbing. "You can't want to love me, I'm horrible."

"Don't be silly, don't be silly," he said, trying to comfort her, kissing her, holding her in his arms. "I want you, I want to marry you, we're going to be married, quickly, quickly—to-morrow if I can."

But she only sobbed terribly, and cried:

"I feel awful. I feel awful. I feel I'm horrible to you."

"No, I want you, I want you," was all he answered, blindly, with that terrible intonation which frightened her almost more than her horror lest he should *not* want her.

1922

Beth Lordan
b. 1948

Lordan has said that she wants to give readers a strong sense of the importance of the untold stories in our lives. Of "Digging," she said, "we can see that there is another story within the one being told. That's what literature does: it gives us privileged glimpses into the lives of the characters, who may or may not know the whole story." This story was first published in the The Atlantic Monthly, *and later in* But Come Ye Back, *a collection of stories about a couple's ("Lyle" and "Mary") marriage. The title alludes to a poem of the same name by Seamus Heaney, a contemporary Irish poet. Bogs figure in many of Heaney's poems, and, as in this story, they function as repositories of the past.*

Digging

So one day a farmer—his name was Seamus Sullivan, and this was in County Mayo, not far from Knock, where, when Seamus was fifteen, the Virgin had appeared—says to the wife, "I'm off up the field, then," and he goes off in his boots in the early afternoon with the dog at his heel and a shovel in his hand. His only idea is to be out there, as far from the house as he can go without leaving his own bit of land, digging; what he wants is the heft and smell and slide of his own earth at his command. He doesn't wonder whether a man can own something like land; he owns this field and the dirt within it, and the field goes straight down to the center of the earth.

So he goes after the roots of a furze bush. It's the first edge of spring, and thin lips of yellow show here and there on the bush. This digging is hard work, starting away from the thorny bush to make sure he's beyond the spread of the roots, but it's a long day ahead with nothing else he need do, and he dedicates himself to it. He's forty-five, still strong enough to spend the whole day driving the shovel in and piling the good dirt out. But the furze is a shallow weed, and after only an hour the excuse work is mostly done, the thorny bush as root-exposed as if he were planting it instead of casting it out. So he pulls it to the center of the field and sets it afire.

Then he goes back to crouch beside his dug pit and roll a cigarette with his dog lolling beside him while the bush burns. It's a pitch-filled thing, a furze bush, so it burns hot and fast. As he tosses the damp end bit of tobacco and paper away, he sees the wife standing down by their house, shading her eyes to watch the last of the flames. Bridget is just a girl still after two years of being married to him, who's older than her husband ought to be. That's enough; he stands and takes up his shovel again.

Maybe the sun comes out for a few minutes, and he feels so good, digging in the thin sunlight in his field, that he wonders why he doesn't do this once a week. His muscles are limber, the rhythm steady, and then his shovel hits something not dirt. Even that, even the challenge of going now into the next layer of his land, where rocks will complicate the digging—even that feels good. He moves the shovel back a few inches and drives it in again and lifts up the dirt and sees there, mud-encrusted and bent, a chalice, the gold pale and shining where his shovel has struck it.

So there stands Seamus, rubbing the dirt from the cup with his broad, callused fingers for a few seconds before he looks guiltily down the slope to see if Bridget is still watching him. She isn't, so he has a chance to decide: Will he keep digging and see if he can find more? Will he take just this one thing? Will he have a good look and then, tenderly, tuck it back where it came from and replace the dirt and pray for the grass to grow over it all?

In this same midafternoon, in Cork instead of Mayo, Mary Alice O'Driscoll comes hurrying along the road into Clonakilty, tears in her pretty eyes. She's nineteen and a strapping girl, tall and strong, and she has dreams. This is a difficult situation, being a strapping girl with dreams, because nobody believes the combination is natural.

Her sister Rosie is the beauty, and people assume she has dreams, Mary Alice is sturdy, and her mother, a practical woman, sees no reason for Mary Alice not to marry Jimmy Curtin, who owns his own boat and has the hope of a house when his father passes on. He's a hard worker and a decent man, and if Mary Alice would just be reasonable, she'd see that decency is quite a bit to get in a husband, and Jimmy's not that old, not forty yet, and he fancies the girl.

Mary Alice *is* reasonable, so she has already abandoned any number of dreams without ever having mentioned them to anyone—gracefulness, for example, and a piano, a quick wit in conversation, a holiday in Switzerland, and a wedding in Saint Colman's Cathedral, in Queenstown, the most beautiful thing she has ever seen and as far from Rosscarbery as she's ever been—but now her mother says she can't go to the dance on Saturday in Glandore. Missing the dance shouldn't matter, given all those other things she knows she'll never have, but it does matter. Mary Alice believes her heart is breaking. So she's on her way down the road to complain to her aunt Margaret, who was the strapping sister herself and knows where you end up if you don't hold on to some dream—where she is, housekeeper to the priest.

So here's Mary Alice, her head up so that the tears won't spill, tapping at the kitchen door of the priest's house, tapping and tapping, and not until Father Moran himself, a book in his hand, pulls open the door does she realize that she has come into town with her apron still on and her hair still in last night's plait. Not that Father Moran is tidy, standing there in his stockinged feet and his hair mussed as if he has just waked up and here it is almost time for his tea.

"Oh, Father," she says, "I'm sorry to bother you. I was looking for Aunt Margaret."

"You were, of course," he says, but because he has indeed only just waked from a doze in his chair, his voice is much curter than he intended, and Mary Alice loses her hold on her tears, and they fall from her pretty eyes in two silver lines down her face.

She has no idea how lovely she looks to Father Moran, who isn't a young man but also isn't old enough to be her father.

Father Moran himself hardly has any idea of how lovely she looks to him, at this dusky moment in the kitchen when her aunt Margaret isn't there and he's barely awake and can't tell exactly who he is, priest or man, but he manages to say, "Here, now, what's this all about?"

Mary Alice can't say what it's all about, not to him, not in his stockinged feet, and so she sobs four times, trying to think of an appropriate thing to say to a priest, and says, "I was thinking of Saint Colman's Cathedral."

Father Moran has seen Saint Colman's Cathedral, so he almost understands why this girl—he has known her name at some moment, though it escapes him now—weeps so hopelessly, and he's touched by it, and moved to transfer his book from his left hand to his right, and to reach his left hand out to touch and comfort her. He means to pat her shoulder in a fatherly, priestly gesture, but his hand takes itself instead to her cheek, where the tears are cool against her firm, warm skin.

As soon as she has spoken, Mary Alice begins actually to think of Saint Colman's, its soaring beauty, and how she'll never be a bride there, never have a life that includes a piano or quick wit or holidays, all because her mother won't allow her to go to the dance in Glandore this Saturday night, where some young man might magically appear who would love her, and when the priest's gentle hand touches her tears, she has no choice in the matter; she covers his hand with her own and presses it to her face, and before either of them is quite certain why or how such a thing could happen, his book is on the floor and their mouths are sweet together with salt tears on all their lips.

By now Seamus has come in for his tea, with his chest full of his secret. Bridget sees that he has got something going on, something that makes him feel big this evening, and she wonders about it as she cuts the bread. He's been nowhere, just up the field the whole afternoon, digging. She has her doubts about whether potatoes will grow there in the second field, the sun's so poor below the hill, but the potatoes are his business. What is hers is this house, this empty house, with no child in it.

"Come up," he says behind her, and she hears the dog clip from the corner and into his lap.

So, Bridget thinks. *So*. And she cuts the bread thicker. When she has finished, she cooks him a buttered egg and brings out the last jar of her sister's blackberry jam. Her sister has the five boys and two girls. "Is it Christmas?" he asks when he comes to the table, but he's gentle about it, and she smiles just a bit, pouring the tea. "The field's ready, is it?" she says, and he says it is, nearly.

After the meal he goes out with the dog and smokes again, looking up at the field where the cup and four gold bracelets lie hidden in the dirt, though he can feel their presence still behind his ribs. He has dug them a deeper hiding place up there, and will leave them for now. He has nowhere to sell them, and no idea how to explain where the money came from if he did. Besides, he thinks the gold isn't that kind of treasure. It's something else, and he has spent the afternoon trying to get it figured out—how the gold stands for something ancient and splendid and connected to him. He has decided that when he's got it straight in his head, the time will come and he'll go to the priest and tell him what he's found, and ask him to write to the proper people so they can come and get it and take it to the museum. They'll make a card for it, he thinks, saying SEAMUS SULLIVAN, COUNTY MAYO. All day the idea of that card has been growing in him, a weighted restlessness in his chest, as he's been digging. He'll plant potatoes there when the time comes. It's no sin, he's sure, to take his pleasure privately now, thinking of himself as a man with gold in his field. No sin either to turn to his wife in bed tonight and take that pleasure as well; and when the time comes, when the washing up is done and the fire's banked and the two of them sigh into their rest, he does so, and she answers him gladly, a rare easy sweetness between them. As he falls asleep, his last thought is of the shimmering power of gold hidden in a field; hers is that these moments may get them a child.

Before that happens, back in the kitchen in Clonakilty, Mary Alice, weak in the knees, and Father Moran, utterly without a thought in his head, linger through the long moment of their kiss as if dependent for balance on their joined mouths, as if suspended from each other's lips, or from their hands on her cheek. And then, of course, they hear a sound from somewhere, a reminder that Aunt Margaret hasn't vanished from the earth, that priests and girls with pretty eyes aren't free to kiss in kitchens in this world, and they lurch apart. For a single second they stare at each other, blankly, and then the horror gathers. She turns and flies out of the house and down the narrow street of the town, eyes dry now and nearly blind. As soon as she's free of the houses, she turns off the road and sets out across the fields for home.

A mile or so along, as she's walking more slowly but still not daring to think of anything, she sees below her the ring of standing stones that people call the Druid's Altar. The light is failing fast, and the stones take on the look of giant shawled women, some standing, some kneeling. She takes herself down from the little ridge to them, between them, into the center of the circle.

"I've kissed a priest," she says aloud.

Maybe she sways with the enormity of what she has done, and it's just an illusion that the stone women stir, but Mary Alice O'Driscoll doesn't wait to see whether the women are welcoming her or casting her out. She takes to her heels, down across the fields in the twilight, and rushes into the kitchen, where her mother is getting the tea with a scowl on her face. Breathless, she says, "I'll marry him, Mother—I'll marry Jimmy if you say." What else could she do, a girl who would tempt a priest and bring stones to life by confessing it? If she didn't marry as quick as that, who knows what shame she might bring on them all?

So, say that was a Tuesday, in March of 1910. By Sunday, when the banns are read for Mary Alice O'Driscoll and James Patrick Curtin, Seamus Sullivan has been laid to rest (that weight in his chest was his heart failing, and he never knew, dreaming of his neighbors thumping his back in congratulation when the gold came pouring out of his land, and he may be dreaming it still, if heaven is as it should be), and Bridget's brother Pat has walked the three fields and found them poor, Seamus's plan for potatoes in the second field foolishness. He'll let it go back to grass and put his own sheep on it. He does that, and takes Bridget to keep house for him half a mile away, and when her son is born, in the winter, he'll be the one who insists the child be named Kevin, for their father, instead of Seamus, for his own. By that time, down in Cork, Mary Alice will be amazed to find herself a little in love with Jimmy Curtin, whose awkward chatter covers a thousand apt generosities, and when their first child is born, the next year, his name, without question, is James. Nor does the family hesitate when the chance comes for them (three more of them now, all strapping children), through the death of one cousin and the emigration of three others, to move to a small house in Galway. And of course the boys will follow their father and become fishermen. In fact, the only question that ever disturbs Mary Alice arises when her James comes to her at the age of fifteen and says, "Mother, I've a calling to be a priest." "You have not," she says, but he scowls and says, "Why not? I've the marks, and Father Kennedy says—" And what can she say but "I don't care what Father Kennedy says, you'll be no priest"? That's as close as she'll ever come to allowing herself to remember the forbidden salty kiss in the kitchen, and that's a story she'll never tell to a soul.

Seamus's story of finding the gold never gets told either, and the gold is never found, so when Bridget dies, with Kevin only eleven, his uncle Pat sees no reason not to take him off to America, where things will have to be better than they are at home with all the mess there is now. It's 1922, and who knows how things will turn out? So off they go, leaving the two houses to fall down around themselves, and if South Boston doesn't vault Pat into the prosperity he expected, it does vault young Kevin into a world of streetcorners and movies and—once he leaves school, at just fifteen—pubs and nicknames and fistfights. He's one of a gang of fellows on the corner of E Street and Bowen; they all live at home, work here and there on the docks and in the factories, fight about anything, spend their money foolishly, and try to impress girls. When Kevin's twenty, he falls mad in love with a girl five years older, and before he knows what he's about, he's going to be a father. It's 1931 now, and he sees no way to avoid taking his bride back to the cramped flat over the barbershop and Uncle Pat's vicious hospitality. He's twenty-one when his son, Lyle, is born, and twenty-two on Christmas Eve when, far gone in drink, he decides to swim the icy Charles River to sober up before going home to the wife and kid.

This same Christmas Eve, 1932, back in Galway City, James Curtin, who has put away his wish to be a priest as his mother once put away her wish to go to Switzerland, proposes marriage to Norah Silke, who turns him down. Two months later he marries her sister Maeve. They have a daughter, Róisín, and then another daughter, Mary, and then sons; before the sons are old enough to go out on the boat, which James has always hated, he sells the boat and buys a poor bit of land. But he has no talent as a farmer, and when his children offer to leave—Mary for America, one son to be a priest, another for Australia—he's glad to have them go. He's a harsh man, and real poverty makes him more so; but he's no worse than other fathers, better than some, which Maeve tells the children so often that even she believes it.

So when Lyle Sullivan and Mary Curtin meet at last, in 1960, at a huge company picnic on Cape Cod, they could have a load of stories to tell each other, but they don't. Mary doesn't work for the company; she has come with a girlfriend who does, and the girlfriend insists that Mary's perfectly welcome. Her whole life—she's twenty-four—Mary has worried about being where she doesn't belong, and she has never quite figured out where she does belong. When she knew she was going to America, she was terrified and excited; once she got there, she was so homesick that she'd have gone back if she'd had the money, and if the ones at home hadn't needed the money she sent. She can't imagine living her whole life so far from home, but now that she's been here a year, she can't imagine what life she'd be living if she were still there. So even here, at a picnic, she doesn't dare go very far from her friend and doesn't join in conversations. That's where she is when Lyle first sees her.

He doesn't know that she looks a lot like his grandmother Bridget, who wore her long, dark, curling hair much the way Mary wears hers, in a soft bun high on her head, and whose mouth had a similar sweet patience. He doesn't know what Bridget looked like because he has never seen the one photograph of her, which his mother hoards, along with the eight other things that belonged to his father, Kevin, in a locked metal box in the back of her closet. He won't even find that box until after his mother's death, three years later; when Mary comes back from Ireland to marry him, she'll have cut her hair and taken to setting it on brush rollers for the bouffant effect that is the American style in 1963. This day on Cape Cod all he knows is that she looks good to him. He doesn't even think of her as pretty, although she is, and it's a good thing he doesn't. Long ago he developed the unconscious habit of avoiding anything that might distract him from his duty to his mother, so he never speaks to girls he thinks of as pretty. This isn't his mother's fault: she's not old in her mid-fifties, not bitter or pitiful. True, she has always tried to impress upon Lyle the dangers of drink and wild friends—but hasn't she good reason for that, since drink and wild friends killed her young husband and left her with a son to raise and no skills beyond laundry work, which she couldn't do anymore after she hurt her back, when Lyle was only seventeen? Not exactly her fault, or his, but it has come to this: Lyle lives the life of a middle-aged husband, although he's only twenty-eight. He's good at his office job with a hardware company, frugal, responsible. He likes some television programs, and he likes to drink a beer or, more rarely, a little whiskey and play a game or two of hearts in the evening with his mother in the oddly comforting cloud of her cigarette smoke. He's not unhappy, and he's not particularly eager to marry, but still, this pretty day on Cape Cod, the girl in the dark skirt and soft blouse looks good to him, and he keeps an eye on her, the way she's shy but cheery, and when he passes almost accidentally near enough to hear her talking with her friend, he hears that she's Irish, and he's a goner.

He doesn't recognize that he's a goner though. He has never been a goner before. As a teenager, back in Vermont, he kissed a few girls and longed in a shameful way for others, and once, after he brought his mother back to Boston to live, he dated one woman three times. But he hasn't been a goner. He thinks he feels sorry for this girl, so far from home, and that in itself is so unusual for him that it's almost dusk, almost time for the fireworks, before he finds a way to meet her.

She's alone at last—her friend has gone to get them some more lemonade. She's alone, crouching to spread the blanket where she and her friend will sit to watch the fireworks, and dusk is coming on, and the ocean is stirring, and she hasn't the least hint how appealing she looks to Lyle. He sees the domesticity of her task, and remembers the quick, dancing, foreign murmur of her voice. He isn't given to imagining (Mary's friend, who works in his department, calls him rude and bossy), but he imagines that she might be lonely, and that's what he means to ask her when he comes up beside her—he means to say something like "You're far from home," in the sort of joking tone he assumes men use with women they haven't met yet. Instead he says, "Hello—I'm Lyle Sullivan, from Production Control," just as if it were a staff meeting. Mary gives a little leap, she's so startled.

She has been thinking not of home but of underwear, actually—

about the difference between Irish underwear and American underwear in her admittedly limited experience. Her job is minding the children of the Cunninghams, in Brookline, who lent her the fare to come over. The oldest of the Cunningham children is a girl, twelve, rather pretty, who has been teasing her mother for pettipants; for days now Mary has been wondering in odd moments just what pettipants might be, whether they're something she ought to buy. In April she finished paying her debt to the Cunninghams. She now sends half her small salary back to Róisín each month and saves most of the rest, but she has a bit she keeps out for pleasure, and she's wondering if the cost of pettipants (whatever they are) would match the pleasure of them. That's what she's wondering when this fellow comes up and startles her.

She blushes, because of the underwear and because he's the fellow she noticed earlier and asked her friend about and because he has recognized, as she knew someone would, that she has no right to be at the picnic.

He blushes, because he didn't mean to startle her and didn't mean to say such a stupid thing, but there they are.

Mary straightens up and puts out her hand. "I'm Mary Curtin, from Galway," she says, and she smiles, because she's relieved at last of the dread of discovery that has tagged behind her all day. "I don't work for the company," she says.

He's handsomer than she thought, though she thought him handsome enough in the sunshine and from a distance.

She's lovely, looking up at him with that smile, and the quick, cooing way she says *doon't* and *company*; he nearly forgets to shake her hand.

Maybe the first of the rockets goes up then and burst in gold and silver in the sky. Or maybe Lyle gathers his wits and asks where Galway is, or where she does work, and they talk a little more before her friend comes back and Lyle takes his leave. They won't turn out to be the sort of couple that reminisces about their first meeting; years from now, when their younger son, Jimmy, asks her bitterly, "How did you end up with him, anyway?" she'll just say, "I met him at a picnic." If in saying that she remembers any of this—the fireworks, and how the crowd around her made a full, reverent chorus of their pleasure while she hugged to herself the thrilling certainty that shy, handsome Lyle Sullivan from Production Control fancied her—she won't say so.

It'll be their older son, Kevin, when he's about ten and curious, who asks his father, "Did Mom used to be pretty?" Maybe the question lurches Lyle back to this moment, standing in the dark beneath the brilliant, slow explosions of light, studying how straight her back is; then she turns and bends toward her friend and something in the tilting of her body wallops him with a desire so harsh he makes a sound. Maybe that's why his answer to his son is so harsh—"What difference does that make?" He can't answer his son directly, can he? Or tell how he was utterly certain, talking to her, that if he put out his hand and touched the spun darkness of the hair at her temple, her smile would only deepen?

So. No stories get told this night, and the story of this night will never be told, even between them, but it goes on for all that. Lyle goes home a goner, Mary goes home just as bad, and then the waiting part begins, because this is still 1960, long before young ladies began telephoning young men, and this is still Lyle, who hasn't stopped being cautious and mostly content just because of the way a girl he met says "It's grand, so," and makes him imagine touching her hair. When he can't get her voice out of his head but begins to be afraid that he doesn't remember it quite right, he still has to work his way around to finding out where she is, and that involves her friend in his department, and with one thing and another it's well into September before he telephones her and asks her to a movie. She says yes, and says yes when he calls her again, although it's October by then; this is the pattern of almost involuntary patience she'll never quite lose and he'll never quite recognize as patience, which will make him even more impatient with everyone else in his life, including his sons, who don't practice it in his behalf. But by the time he calls her again, to invite her to Thanksgiving dinner to meet his mother (things have gone that well, or that inevitably), she's gone.

Years later she'll tell stories of her childhood, of Irish people and Irish adventures, funny stories and inspiring stories and now and then a sad story, but she'll never tell the story of how she answered the doorbell and took the telegram that was addressed to Mary Curtin and stared at it as if it weren't her own name. She'll never explain how distant her own horror at herself seemed when she read the words MOTHER DYING and heard herself thinking *I'd be too late.* She'll never admit that she doesn't know what she'd have done next if her employer hadn't come into the corridor then and asked what was wrong.

But she doesn't have to know that, because Mrs. Cunningham does come into the corridor, so Mary does the right things. She explains, she apologizes; she has the price of the ticket back in her savings; she must go; she doesn't know if she'll come back. She does it all with dignity and calm, the telephoning, the packing, the leaving itself, and not until she's on the plane and night has fallen does the terrible thick guilt of it begin to squeeze her across the chest.

She lands at Shannon, takes the Galway bus, and gets out in the still early morning in Oranmore. A man happens to come up the footpath and sees her, and he says, "You'd be the Curtin girl, come back from America," and when she says, "Yes," he says, "Sorry for your trouble," so she knows, as she walks the last three miles, that she's too late, and she doesn't need the black ribbon on the door of the house to choke her with grief and regret, and she doesn't need Róisín's bitterness to make her feel the tug of the halter of shame at the nape of her neck, but she gets it anyway.

Róisín opens the door to her and turns back into the house without a word. It's left to Mrs. Joyce, who has come to help, to ask, "Would you see her?" So Mary steps unwelcomed and unembraced into the front room, still in her coat, and touches her mother's hand for the last time. She knows what her mother would say, what a load Róisín has carried alone this past year. As she stands there in the cold, Mary accepts Róisín's bitterness as just, and bearable. She believes that before spring she'll be back in America; if the Cunninghams don't want to sponsor her again, Father Martin may find her someone else. Or she can get some kind of work here and save.

But when she leaves that room, meaning to put her suitcase in a corner and take up some task in preparation for the wake, her father has come in the house, and Róisín dries her hands to embrace her. "I was taken strange," Róisín says, "seeing you there so American in your coat. You're welcome, Mary," she says, "you're welcome home again. The tea is on."

Mary's mortally tired; she hasn't slept for thirty hours. She kisses her sister and turns to kiss her father, who stands beside the fire. "It's good you've come," he says, "with Róisín off in Galway City now."

"Off?" Mary says.

"Oh," Róisín says, with the breath of a laugh, "I didn't write it to you, but Michael Joyce and I are being married. In Christmas week."

Mary stares, Róisín grins, Da folds his arms and snorts. "Did you think you were away?" he says.

For just that one moment Mary believes they have killed her, but in the next moment she is simply lost, unhappy, and at home.

Right then, without a cup of tea or a bit of rest, she accepts their tribal, intimate revenge, begins her penance for the sins of abandonment, hope, desire.

She takes on her mother's work and then her sister's, and protects her heart with prayer and exhaustion. She doesn't recognize the slow creep of hopelessness, doesn't know she's sinking, settling into the suffocating bog of it, until Lyle's letter arrives in mid-January and she finds herself unable to breathe.

It's only a letter, and rather short, though she reads it a dozen times. He writes about the weather, which is bad in Boston this winter, and says he's being promoted at work. He doesn't mention that his mother has had a stroke and that he spends his evenings now, after the nurse has gone, trying to pretend she isn't drooling, trying to pretend he doesn't understand her demands for cigarettes he'll have to hold for her. He never does tell Mary about that first year, or the guilt that stains his relief when he finally puts his mother into a nursing home and lives alone but still not free of her in the apartment they shared for so long. In the same way, Mary never tells him about Da's growing strangeness—the way he has taken to shouting up the chimney and hiding food and sometimes staring at her as if he suspects her of something—or Róisín's small, breezy cruelties. She writes instead of the weather and farming in Oranmore, he tells her about Irish politics, and she tells him droll bits about Irish people; she wonders about movies, and he tells her she's missing little. After the first year she asks him about world affairs, and he mentions his mother's illness; he writes vaguely of hoping to travel, and she mentions her sister's babies and her youngest brother's departure for work in England; she asks about his work, and he explains why buying a house is more sensible than renting. The courtship is odd and awkward, but it sustains their hearts through a long dark time.

And then one day in the third year, a week to the day after his mother's death, Lyle drives to a travel agency. His only idea is to be going somewhere, away from the empty apartment and the closet full of his mother's things, to be making arrangements, putting large and permanent things in motion and order. He writes a check; in four days he'll be on an airplane for Dublin, where he'll get a train to Galway and a bus to Oranmore. He figures he can take a taxi from there, or rent a bicycle, or walk if he has to. He doesn't question the propriety of paying an unannounced transatlantic call on a woman he has met only three times; he wants to see her, and she has always said yes, and he has nowhere else to go.

At the same moment—though it's late afternoon there on the small farm in County Galway—Mary is sitting on her bed dabbing a wet rag on the cut on her cheekbone Da's punch opened. She's panting, but not as badly as she was, and although she keeps a wary eye on her door, she isn't really afraid. Still, something will have to be done: she'll clean herself up and walk to Galway and speak with Róisín. She can't talk him past these sudden rages anymore, and with nobody left at home except her, he'll eventually knock down somebody who doesn't love him.

Five days later, as two elderly gardai lean smoking against their car with her suddenly cooperative father, Mary searches under his bed for the shoes he says he's got to have if he is to go with the lads to Saint Bridget's Hospital. She finds a plate of moldy potatoes, two copies of *Key of Heaven*, three knives, and a sock stuffed full of one- and five-pound notes. And the shoes. She runs to the car with the shoes, her heart pounding, and says, "Da," and he meets her eyes with his sly ones and winks. For an instant there in the thin sunshine he's the father of her best childhood mornings.

"Your mother made me them stockings," he says.

"Did she," she says.

"She did," he says, yawning. "Fine heavy stockings. I'm off, so," he says, and throws the cigarette away.

She watches the car down the yard, and she's crying, of course, but she'd hardly be human if some corner of her heart weren't preparing to wake into something new, if some corner of her mind weren't calculating how much money a sock could hold. So when she imagines that the fellow wobbling along the road now on a bicycle looks like Lyle Sullivan, she tells herself, *I'd not be human if I didn't think of him now*, but in penance for that humanity she stands a minute longer, waiting for him to pass by and prove her foolishness.

2001

Bobbie Ann Mason
b. 1940

Mason's distinctive style is often called "minimalist" in the tradition of Ernest Hemingway and Raymond Carver—a stripped-down, unadorned, almost consciously unliterary style. Her particular brand of minimalism is sometimes called "Kmart realism," because she writes about and uses language that seems perfectly natural to those middle- and lower-middle-class, rural, and small-city Americans who shop there. The style and subject matter of her stories is purposely democratic—highly accessible, often resistant to literary criticism, the attention to physical detail often defying those who want to extract a paraphraseable meaning.

Shiloh

Leroy Moffitt's wife, Norma Jean, is working on her pectorals. She lifts three-pound dumbbells to warm up, then progresses to a twenty-pound barbell. Standing with her legs apart, she reminds Leroy of Wonder Woman.

"I'd give anything if I could just get these muscles to where they're real hard," says Norma Jean. "Feel this arm. It's not as hard as the other one."

"That's 'cause you're right-handed," says Leroy, dodging as she swings the barbell in an arc.

"Do you think so?"

"Sure."

Leroy is a truckdriver. He injured his leg in a highway accident four months ago, and his physical therapy, which involves weights and a pulley, prompted Norma Jean to try building herself up. Now she is attending a body-building class. Leroy has been collecting temporary disability since his tractor-trailer jackknifed in Missouri, badly twisting his left leg in its socket. He has a steel pin in his hip. He will probably not be able to drive his rig again. It sits in the backyard, like a gigantic bird that has flown home to roost. Leroy has been home in Kentucky for three months, and his leg is almost healed, but the accident frightened him and he does not want to drive any more long hauls. He is not sure what to do next. In the meantime, he makes things from craft kits. He started by building a miniature log cabin from notched Popsicle sticks. He varnished it and placed it on the TV set, where it remains. It reminds him of a rustic Nativity scene. Then he tried string art (sailing ships on black velvet), a macramé owl kit, a snap-together B-17 Flying Fortress, and a lamp made out of a model truck, with a light fixture screwed in the top of the cab. At first the kits were diversions, something to kill time, but now he is thinking about building a full-scale log house from a kit. It would be considerably cheaper than building a regular house, and besides, Leroy has grown to appreciate how things are put together. He has begun to realize that in all the years he was on the road he never took time to examine anything. He was always flying past scenery.

"They won't let you build a log cabin in any of the new subdivisions," Norma Jean tells him.

"They will if I tell them it's for you," he says, teasing her. Ever since they were married, he has promised Norma Jean he would build her a new home one day. They have always rented, and the house they live in is small and nondescript. It does not even feel like a home, Leroy realizes now.

Norma Jean works at the Rexall drugstore, and she has acquired an amazing amount of information about cosmetics. When she explains to Leroy the three stages of complexion care, involving creams, toners, and moisturizers, he thinks happily of other petroleum products—axle grease, diesel fuel. This is a connection between him and Norma Jean. Since he has been home, he has felt unusually tender about his wife and guilty over his long absences. But he can't tell what she feels about him. Norma Jean has never complained about his traveling; she has never made hurt remarks, like calling his truck a "widow-maker." He is reasonably certain she has been faithful to him, but he wishes she would celebrate his permanent homecoming more happily. Norma Jean is often startled to find Leroy at home, and he thinks she seems a little disappointed about it. Perhaps he reminds her too much of the early days of their marriage, before he went on the road. They had a child who died as an infant, years ago. They never speak about their memories of Randy, which have almost faded, but now that Leroy is home all the time, they sometimes feel awkward around each other, and Leroy wonders if one of them should mention the child. He has the feeling that they are waking up out of a dream together—that they must create a new marriage, start afresh. They are lucky they are still married. Leroy has read that for most people losing a child destroys the marriage—or else he heard this on *Donahue*. He can't always remember where he learns things anymore.

At Christmas, Leroy bought an electric organ for Norma Jean. She used to play the piano when she was in high school. "It don't leave you," she told him once. "It's like riding a bicycle."

The new instrument had so many keys and buttons that she was bewildered by it at first. She touched the keys tentatively, pushed some buttons, then pecked out "Chopsticks." It came out in an amplified fox-trot rhythm, with marimba sounds.

"It's an orchestra!" she cried.

The organ had a pecan-look finish and eighteen preset chords, with optional flute, violin, trumpet, clarinet, and banjo accompaniments. Norma Jean mastered the organ almost immediately. At first she played Christmas songs. Then she bought *The Sixties Songbook* and learned every tune in it, adding variations to each with the rows of brightly colored buttons.

"I didn't like these old songs back then," she said. "But I have this crazy feeling I missed something."

"You didn't miss a thing," said Leroy.

Leroy likes to lie on the couch and smoke a joint and listen to Norma Jean play "Can't Take My Eyes Off You" and "I'll Be Back." He is back again. After fifteen years on the road, he is finally settling down with the woman he loves. She is still pretty. Her skin is flawless. Her frosted curls resemble pencil trimmings.

Now that Leroy has come home to stay, he notices how much the town has changed. Subdivisions are spreading across western Kentucky like an oil slick. The sign at the edge of town says "Pop: 11,500"—only seven hundred more than it said twenty years before. Leroy can't figure out who is living in all the new houses. The farmers who used to gather around the courthouse square on Saturday afternoons to play checkers and spit tobacco juice have gone. It has been years since Leroy has thought about the farmers, and they have disappeared without his noticing.

Leroy meets a kid named Stevie Hamilton in the parking lot at the new shopping center. While they pretend to be strangers meeting over a stalled car, Stevie tosses an ounce of marijuana under the front seat of Leroy's car. Stevie is wearing orange jogging shoes and a T-shirt that says CHATTAHOOCHEE SUPER-RAT. His father is a prominent doctor who lives in one of the expensive subdivisions in a new white-columned brick house that looks like a funeral parlor. In the phone book under his name there is a separate number, with the listing "Teenagers."

"Where do you get this stuff?" asks Leroy. "From your pappy?"

"That's for me to know and you to find out," Stevie says. He is slit-eyed and skinny.

"What else you got?"

"What you interested in?"

"Nothing special. Just wondered."

Leroy used to take speed on the road. Now he has to go slowly. He needs to be mellow. He leans back against the car and says, "I'm aiming to build me a log house, soon as I get time. My wife, though, I don't think she likes the idea."

"Well, let me know when you want me again," Stevie says. He has a cigarette in his cupped palm, as though sheltering it from the wind. He takes a long drag, then stomps it on the asphalt and slouches away.

Stevie's father was two years ahead of Leroy in high school. Leroy is thirty-four. He married Norma Jean when they were both eighteen, and their child Randy was born a few months later, but he died at the age of four months and three days. He would be about Stevie's age now. Norma Jean and Leroy were at the drive-in, watching a double feature (*Dr. Strangelove* and *Lover Come Back*), and the baby was sleeping in the back seat. When the first movie ended, the baby was dead. It was the sudden infant death syndrome. Leroy remembers handing Randy to a nurse at the emergency room, as though he were offering her a large doll as a present. A dead baby feels like a sack of flour. "It just happens sometimes," said the doctor, in what Leroy always recalls as a nonchalant tone. Leroy can hardly remember the child anymore, but he still sees vividly a scene from *Dr. Strangelove* in which the President of the United States was talking in a folksy voice on the hot line to the Soviet premier about the bomber accidentally headed toward Russia. He was in the War Room, and the world map was lit up. Leroy remembers Norma Jean standing catatonically beside him in the hospital and himself thinking: Who is this strange girl? He had forgotten who she was. Now scientists are saying that crib death is caused by a virus. Nobody knows anything, Leroy thinks. The answers are always changing.

When Leroy gets home from the shopping center, Norma Jean's mother, Mabel Beasley, is there. Until this year, Leroy has not realized how much time she spends with Norma Jean. When she visits, she inspects the closets and then the plants, informing Norma Jean when a plant is droopy or yellow. Mabel calls the plants "flowers," although there are never any blooms. She always notices if Norma Jean's laundry is piling up. Mabel is a short, overweight woman whose tight, brown-dyed curls look more like a wig than the actual wig she sometimes wears. Today she has brought Norma Jean an off-white dust ruffle she made for the bed; Mabel works in a custom-upholstery shop.

"This is the tenth one I made this year," Mabel says. "I got started and couldn't stop."

"It's real pretty," says Norma Jean.

"Now we can hide things under the bed," says Leroy, who gets along with his mother-in-law primarily by joking with her. Mabel has never really forgiven him for disgracing her by getting Norma Jean pregnant. When the baby died, she said that fate was mocking her.

"What's that thing?" Mabel says to Leroy in a loud voice, pointing to a tangle of yarn on a piece of canvas.

Leroy holds it up for Mabel to see. "It's my needlepoint," he explains. "This is a *Star Trek* pillow cover."

"That's what a woman would do," says Mabel. "Great day in the morning!"

"All the big football players on TV do it," he says.

"Why, Leroy, you're always trying to fool me. I don't believe you for one minute. You don't know what to do with yourself—that's the whole trouble. Sewing!"

"I'm aiming to build us a log house," says Leroy. "Soon as my plans come."

"Like *heck* you are," says Norma Jean. She takes Leroy's needlepoint and shoves it into a drawer. "You have to find a job first. Nobody can afford to build now anyway."

Mabel straightens her girdle and says, "I still think before you get tied down y'all ought to take a little run to Shiloh."

"One of these days, Mama," Norma Jean says impatiently.

Mabel is talking about Shiloh, Tennessee. For the past few years, she has been urging Leroy and Norma Jean to visit the Civil War battleground there. Mabel went there on her honeymoon—the only real trip she ever took. Her husband died of a perforated ulcer when Norma Jean was ten, but Mabel, who was accepted into the United Daughters of the Confederacy in 1975, is still preoccupied with going back to Shiloh.

"I've been to kingdom come and back in that truck out yonder," Leroy says to Mabel, "but we never yet set foot in that battleground. Ain't that something? How did I miss it?"

"It's not even that far," Mabel says.

After Mabel leaves, Norma Jean reads to Leroy from a list she has made. "Things you could do," she announces. "You could get a job as a guard at Union Carbide, where they'd let you set on a stool. You could get on at the lumberyard. You could do a little carpenter work, if you want to build so bad. You could—"

"I can't do something where I'd have to stand up all day."

"You ought to try standing up all day behind a cosmetics counter. It's amazing that I have strong feet, coming from two parents that never had strong feet at all." At the moment Norma Jean is holding on to the kitchen counter, raising her knees one at a time as she talks. She is wearing two-pound ankle weights.

"Don't worry," says Leroy. "I'll do something."

"You could truck calves to slaughter for somebody. You wouldn't have to drive any big old truck for that."

"I'm going to build you this house," says Leroy. "I want to make you a real home."

"I don't want to live in any log cabin."

"It's not a cabin. It's a house."

"I don't care. It looks like a cabin."

"You and me together could lift those logs. It's just like lifting weights."

Norma Jean doesn't answer. Under her breath, she is counting. Now she is marching through the kitchen. She is doing goose steps.

Before his accident, when Leroy came home he used to stay in the house with Norma Jean, watching TV in bed and playing cards. She would cook fried chicken, picnic ham, chocolate pie—all his favorites. Now he is home alone much of the time. In the mornings, Norma Jean disappears, leaving a cooling place in the bed. She eats a cereal called Body Buddies, and she leaves the bowl on the table, with the soggy tan balls floating in a milk puddle. He sees things about Norma Jean that he never realized before. When she chops onions, she stares off into a corner, as if she can't bear to look. She puts on her house slippers almost precisely at nine o'clock every evening and nudges her jogging shoes under the couch. She saves bread heels for the birds. Leroy watches the birds at the feeder. He notices the peculiar way goldfinches fly past the window. They close their wings, then fall, then spread their wings to catch and lift themselves. He wonders if they close their eyes when they fall. Norma Jean closes her eyes when they are in bed. She wants the lights turned out. Even then, he is sure she closes her eyes.

He goes for long drives around town. He tends to drive a car rather carelessly. Power steering and an automatic shift make a car feel so small and inconsequential that his body is hardly involved in the driving process. His injured leg stretches out comfortably. Once or twice he has almost hit something, but even the prospect of an accident seems minor in a car. He cruises the new subdivisions, feeling like a criminal rehearsing for a robbery. Norma Jean is probably right about a log house being inappropriate here in the new subdivisions. All the houses look grand and complicated. They depress him.

One day when Leroy comes home from a drive he finds Norma Jean in tears. She is in the kitchen making a potato and mushroom-soup casserole, with grated-cheese topping. She is crying because her mother caught her smoking.

"I didn't hear her coming. I was standing here puffing away pretty as you please," Norma Jean says, wiping her eyes.

"I knew it would happen sooner or later," says Leroy, putting his arm around her.

"She don't know the meaning of the word 'knock,' " says Norma Jean. "It's a wonder she hadn't caught me years ago."

"Think of it this way," Leroy says. "What if she caught me with a joint?"

"You better not let her!" Norma Jean shrieks. "I'm warning you, Leroy Moffitt!"

"I'm just kidding. Here, play me a tune. That'll help you relax."

Norma Jean puts the casserole in the oven and sets the timer. Then she plays a ragtime tune, with horns and banjo, as Leroy lights up a joint and lies on the couch, laughing to himself about Mabel's catching him at it. He thinks of Stevie Hamilton—a doctor's son pushing grass. Everything is funny. The whole town seems crazy and small. He is reminded of Virgil Mathis, a boastful policeman Leroy used to shoot pool with. Virgil recently led a drug bust in a back room at a bowling alley, where he seized ten thousand dollars' worth of marijuana. The newspaper had a picture of him holding up the bags of grass and grinning widely. Right now, Leroy can imagine Virgil breaking down the door and arresting him with a lungful of smoke. Virgil would probably have been alerted to the scene because of all the racket Norma Jean is making. Now she sounds like a hard-rock band. Norma Jean is terrific. When she switches to a Latin-rhythm version of "Sunshine Superman," Leroy hums along. Norma Jean's foot goes up and down, up and down.

"Well, what do you think?" Leroy says, when Norma Jean pauses to search through her music.

"What do I think about what?"

His mind has gone blank. Then he says, "I'll sell my rig and build us a house." That wasn't what he wanted to say. He wanted to know what she thought—what she *really* thought—about them.

"Don't start in on that again," says Norma Jean. She begins playing "Who'll Be the Next in Line?"

Leroy used to tell hitchhikers his whole life story—about his travels, his hometown, the baby. He would end with a question: "Well, what do you think?" It was just a rhetorical question. In time, he had the feeling that he'd been telling the same story over and over to the same hitchhikers. He quit talking to hitchhikers when he realized how his voice sounded—whining and self-pitying, like some teenage-tragedy song. Now Leroy has the sudden impulse to tell Norma Jean about himself, as if he had just met her. They have known each other so long they have forgotten a lot about each other. They could become reacquainted. But when the oven timer goes off and she runs to the kitchen, he forgets why he wants to do this.

The next day, Mabel drops by. It is Saturday and Norma Jean is cleaning. Leroy is studying the plans of his log house, which have finally come in the mail. He has them spread out on the table—big sheets of stiff blue paper, with diagrams and numbers printed in white. While Norma Jean runs the vacuum, Mabel drinks coffee. She sets her coffee cup on a blueprint.

"I'm just waiting for time to pass," she says to Leroy, drumming her fingers on the table.

As soon as Norma Jean switches off the vacuum, Mabel says in a loud voice, "Did you hear about the datsun dog that killed the baby?"

Norma Jean says, "The word is 'dachshund.' "

"They put the dog on trial. It chewed the baby's legs off. The mother was in the next room all the time." She raises her voice. "They thought it was neglect."

Norma Jean is holding her ears. Leroy manages to open the refrigerator and get some Diet Pepsi to offer Mabel. Mabel still has some coffee and she waves away the Pepsi.

"Datsuns are like that," Mabel says. "They're jealous dogs. They'll tear a place to pieces if you don't keep an eye on them."

"You better watch out what you're saying, Mabel," says Leroy.

"Well, facts is facts."

Leroy looks out the window at his rig. It is like a huge piece of furniture gathering dust in the backyard. Pretty soon it will be an antique. He hears the vacuum cleaner. Norma Jean seems to be cleaning the living room rug again.

Later, she says to Leroy, "She just said that about the baby because she caught me smoking. She's trying to pay me back."

"What are you talking about?" Leroy says, nervously shuffling blueprints.

"You know good and well," Norma Jean says. She is sitting in a kitchen chair with her feet up and her arms wrapped around her knees. She looks small and helpless. She says, "The very idea, her bringing up a subject like that! Saying it was neglect."

"She didn't mean that," Leroy says.

"She might not have *thought* she meant it. She always says things like that. You don't know how she goes on."

"But she didn't really mean it. She was just talking."

Leroy opens a king-sized bottle of beer and pours it into two glasses, dividing it carefully. He hands a glass to Norma Jean and she takes it from him mechanically. For a long time, they sit by the kitchen window watching the birds at the feeder.

Something is happening. Norma Jean is going to night school. She has graduated from her six-week body-building course and now she is taking an adult-education course in composition at Paducah Community College. She spends her evenings outlining paragraphs.

"First you have a topic sentence," she explains to Leroy. "Then you divide it up. Your secondary topic has to be connected to your primary topic."

To Leroy, this sounds intimidating. "I never was any good in English," he says.

"It makes a lot of sense."

"What are you doing this for, anyhow?"

She shrugs. "It's something to do." She stands up and lifts her dumbbells a few times.

"Driving a rig, nobody cared about my English."

"I'm not criticizing your English."

Norma Jean used to say, "If I lose ten minutes' sleep, I just drag all day." Now she stays up late, writing compositions. She got a B on her first paper—a how-to theme on soup-based casseroles. Recently Norma Jean has been cooking unusual foods—tacos, lasagna, Bombay chicken. She doesn't play the organ anymore, though her second paper was called "Why Music Is Important to Me." She sits at the kitchen table, concentrating on her outlines, while Leroy plays with his log house plans, practicing with a set of Lincoln Logs. The thought of getting a truckload of notched, numbered logs scares him, and he wants to be prepared. As he and Norma Jean work together at the kitchen table, Leroy has the hopeful thought that they are sharing something, but he knows he is a fool to think this. Norma Jean is miles away. He knows he is going to lose her. Like Mabel, he is just waiting for time to pass.

One day, Mabel is there before Norma Jean gets home from work, and Leroy finds himself confiding in her. Mabel, he realizes, must know Norma Jean better than he does.

"I don't know what's got into that girl," Mabel says. "She used to go to bed with the chickens. Now you say she's up all hours. Plus her a-smoking. I like to died."

"I want to make her this beautiful home," Leroy says, indicating the Lincoln Logs. "I don't think she even wants it. Maybe she was happier with me gone."

"She don't know what to make of you, coming home like this."

"Is that it?"

Mabel takes the roof off his Lincoln Log cabin. "You couldn't get *me* in a log cabin," she says. "I was raised in one. It's no picnic, let me tell you."

"They're different now," says Leroy.

"I tell you what," Mabel says, smiling oddly at Leroy.

"What?"

"Take her on down to Shiloh. Y'all need to get out together, stir a little. Her brain's all balled up over them books."

Leroy can see traces of Norma Jean's features in her mother's face. Mabel's worn face has the texture of crinkled cotton, but suddenly she looks pretty. It occurs to Leroy that Mabel has been hinting all along that she wants them to take her with them to Shiloh.

"Let's all go to Shiloh," he says. "You and me and her. Come Sunday."

Mabel throws up her hands in protest. "Oh, no, not me. Young folks want to be by theirselves."

When Norma Jean comes in with groceries, Leroy says excitedly, "Your mama here's been dying to go to Shiloh for thirty-five years. It's about time we went, don't you think?"

"I'm not going to butt in on anybody's second honeymoon," Mabel says.

"Who's going on a honeymoon, for Christ's sake?" Norma Jean says loudly.

"I never raised no daughter of mine to talk that-a-way," Mabel says.

"You ain't seen nothing yet," says Norma Jean. She starts putting away boxes and cans, slamming cabinet doors.

"There's a log cabin at Shiloh," Mabel says. "It was there during the battle. There's bullet holes in it."

"When are you going to *shut up* about Shiloh, Mama?" asks Norma Jean.

"I always thought Shiloh was the prettiest place, so full of history," Mabel goes on. "I just hoped y'all could see it once before I die, so you could tell me about it." Later, she whispers to Leroy, "You do what I said. A little change is what she needs."

"Your name means 'the king,' " Norma Jean says to Leroy that evening. He is trying to get her to go to Shiloh, and she is reading a book about another century.

"Well, I reckon I ought to be right proud."

"I guess so."

"Am I still king around here?"

Norma Jean flexes her biceps and feels them for hardness. "I'm not fooling around with anybody, if that's what you mean," she says.

"Would you tell me if you were?"

"I don't know."

"What does *your* name mean?"

"It was Marilyn Monroe's real name."

"No kidding!"

"Norma comes from the Normans. They were invaders," she says. She closes her book and looks hard at Leroy. "I'll go to Shiloh with you if you'll stop staring at me."

On Sunday, Norma Jean packs a picnic and they go to Shiloh. To Leroy's relief, Mabel says she does not want to come with them. Norma Jean drives, and Leroy, sitting beside her, feels like some boring hitchhiker she has picked up. He tries some conversation, but she answers him in monosyllables. At Shiloh, she drives aimlessly through the park, past bluffs and trails and steep ravines. Shiloh is an immense place, and Leroy cannot see it as a battleground. It is not what he expected. He thought it would look like a golf course. Monuments are everywhere, showing through the thick clusters of trees. Norma Jean passes the log cabin Mabel mentioned. It is surrounded by tourists looking for bullet holes.

"That's not the kind of log house I've got in mind," says Leroy apologetically.

"I know *that*."

"This is a pretty place. Your mama was right."

"It's O.K.," says Norma Jean. "Well, we've seen it. I hope she's satisfied."

They burst out laughing together.

At the park museum, a movie on Shiloh is shown every half hour, but they decide that they don't want to see it. They buy a souvenir Confederate flag for Mabel, and then they find a picnic spot near the cemetery. Norma Jean has brought a picnic cooler, with pimiento sandwiches, soft drinks, and Yodels. Leroy eats a sandwich and then smokes a joint, hiding it behind the picnic cooler. Norma Jean has quit smoking altogether. She is picking cake crumbs from the cellophane wrapper, like a fussy bird.

Leroy says, "So the boys in gray ended up in Corinth. The Union soldiers zapped 'em finally. April 7, 1862."

They both know that he doesn't know any history. He is just talking about some of the historical plaques they have read. He feels awkward, like a boy on a date with an older girl. They are still just making conversation.

"Corinth is where Mama eloped to," says Norma Jean.

They sit in silence and stare at the cemetery for the Union dead and, beyond, at a tall cluster of trees. Campers are parked nearby, bumper to bumper, and small children in bright clothing are cavorting and squealing. Norma Jean wads up the cake wrapper and squeezes it tightly in her hand. Without looking at Leroy, she says, "I want to leave you."

Leroy takes a bottle of Coke out of the cooler and flips off the cap. He holds the bottle poised near his mouth but cannot remember to take a drink. Finally he says, "No, you don't."

"Yes, I do."

"I won't let you."

"You can't stop me."

"Don't do me that way."

Leroy knows Norma Jean will have her own way. "Didn't I promise to be home from now on?" he says.

"In some ways, a woman prefers a man who wanders," says Norma Jean. "That sounds crazy, I know."

"You're not crazy."

Leroy remembers to drink from his Coke. Then he says, "Yes, you *are* crazy. You and me could start all over again. Right back at the beginning."

"We *have* started all over again," says Norma Jean. "And this is how it turned out."

"What did I do wrong?"

"Nothing."

"Is this one of those women's lib things?" Leroy asks.

"Don't be funny."

The cemetery, a green slope dotted with white markers, looks like a subdivision site. Leroy is trying to comprehend that his marriage is breaking up, but for some reason he is wondering about white slabs in a graveyard.

"Everything was fine till Mama caught me smoking," says Norma Jean, standing up. "That set something off."

"What are you talking about?"

"She won't leave me alone—*you* won't leave me alone." Norma Jean seems to be crying, but she is looking away from him. "I feel eighteen again. I can't face that all over again." She starts walking away. "No, it *wasn't* fine. I don't know what I'm saying. Forget it."

Leroy takes a lungful of smoke and closes his eyes as Norma Jean's words sink in. He tries to focus on the fact that thirty-five hundred soldiers died on the grounds around him. He can only think of that war as a board game with plastic soldiers. Leroy almost smiles, as he compares the Confederates' daring attack on the Union camps and Virgil Mathis's raid on the bowling alley. General Grant, drunk and furious, shoved the Southerners back to Corinth, where Mabel and Jet Beasley were married years later, when Mabel was still thin and good-looking. The next day, Mabel and Jet visited the battleground, and then Norma Jean was born, and then she married Leroy and they had a baby, which they lost, and now Leroy and Norma Jean are here at the same battleground. Leroy knows he is leaving out a lot. He is leaving out the insides of history. History was always just names and dates to him. It occurs to him that building a house out of logs is similarly empty—too simple. And the real inner workings of a marriage, like most of history, have escaped him. Now he sees that building a log house is the dumbest idea he could have had. It was clumsy of him to think Norma Jean would want a log house. It was a crazy idea. He'll have to think of something else, quickly. He will wad the blueprints into tight balls and fling them into the lake. Then he'll get moving again. He opens his eyes. Norma Jean has moved away and is walking through the cemetery, following a serpentine brick path.

Leroy gets up to follow his wife, but his good leg is asleep and his bad leg still hurts him. Norma Jean is far away, walking rapidly toward the bluff by the river, and he tries to hobble toward her. Some children run past him, screaming noisily Norma Jean has reached the bluff, and she is looking out over the Tennessee River. Now she turns toward Leroy and waves her arms. Is she beckoning to him? She seems to be doing an exercise for her chest muscles. The sky is unusually pale—the color of the dust ruffle Mabel made for their bed.

1982

James Alan McPherson
b. 1943

"A Loaf of Bread" is as ambiguous a story as any in this collection. The meaning of Mr. Reed's gesture at the end, though apparently perfectly understood by Mr. Green, is a matter of interpretation. McPherson's story is unusual among twentieth-century fiction for its frankly political subject matter. Though it's difficult to say exactly what McPherson's own position is, his direct exploration of social issues puts him in the company of earlier writers, like Charles Dickens and Upton Sinclair. We would do the writer a disservice if, in addition to undertaking the usual literary analysis, we did not let the story challenge our view of our social institutions, such as the marketplace in a capitalist economy.

A Loaf of Bread

It was one of those obscene situations, pedestrian to most people, but invested with meaning for a few poor folk whose lives are usually spent outside the imaginations of their fellow citizens. A grocer named Harold Green was caught red-handed selling to one group of people the very same goods he sold at lower prices at similar outlets in better neighborhoods. He had been doing this for many years, and at first he could not understand the outrage heaped upon him. He acted only from habit, he insisted, and had nothing personal against the people whom he served. They were his neighbors. Many of them he had carried on the cuff during hard times. Yet, through some mysterious access to a television station, the poor folk were now empowered to make grand denunciations of the grocer. Green's children now saw their father's business being picketed on the Monday evening news.

No one could question the fact that the grocer had been overcharging the people. On the news even the reporter grimaced distastefully while reading the statistics. His expression said, "It is my job to report the news, but sometimes even I must disassociate myself from it to protect my honor." This, at least, was the impression the grocer's children seemed to bring away from the television.

Their father's name had not been mentioned, but there was a close-up of his store with angry black people, and a few outraged whites, marching in groups of three in front of it. There was also a close-up of his name. After seeing this, they were in no mood to watch cartoons. At the dinner table, disturbed by his children's silence, Harold Green felt compelled to say, "I am not a dishonest man." Then he felt ashamed. The children, a boy and his older sister, immediately left the table, leaving Green alone with his wife. "Ruth, I am not dishonest," he repeated to her.

Ruth Green did not say anything. She knew, and her husband did not, that the outraged people had also picketed the school attended by their children. They had threatened to return each day until Green lowered his prices. When they called her at home to report this, she had promised she would talk with him. Since she could not tell him this, she waited for an opening. She looked at her husband across the table.

"I did not make the world," Green began, recognizing at once the seriousness in her stare. "My father came to this country with nothing but his shirt. He was exploited for as long as he couldn't help himself. He did not protest or picket. He put himself in a position to play by the rules he had learned." He waited for his wife to answer, and when she did not, he tried again. "I did not make this world," he repeated. "I only make my way in it. Such people as these, they do not know enough to not be exploited. If not me, there would be a Greek, a Chinaman, maybe an Arab or a smart one of their own kind. Believe me, I deal with them. There is something in their style that lacks the patience to run a concern such as mine. If I closed down, take my word on it, someone else would do what has to be done."

But Ruth Green was not thinking of his leaving. Her mind was on other matters. Her children had cried when they came home early from school. She had no special feeling for the people who picketed, but she did not like to see her children cry. She had kissed them generously, then sworn them to silence. "One day this week," she told her husband, "you will give free, for eight hours, anything your customers come in to buy. There will be no publicity, except what they spread by word of mouth. No matter what they say to you, no matter what they take, you will remain silent." She stared deeply into him for what she knew was there. "If you refuse, you have seen the last of your children and myself."

Her husband grunted. Then he leaned toward her. "I will not knuckle under," he said. "I will *not* give!"

"We shall see," his wife told him.

The black pickets, for the most part, had at first been frightened by the audacity of their undertaking. They were peasants whose minds had long before become resigned to their fate as victims. None of them, before now, had thought to challenge this. But now, when they watched themselves on television, they hardly recognized the faces they saw beneath the hoisted banners and placards. Instead of reflecting the meekness they all felt, the faces looked angry. The close-ups looked especially intimidating. Several of the first pickets, maids who worked in the suburbs, reported that their employers, seeing the activity on the afternoon news, had begun treating them with new respect. One woman, midway through the weather report, called around the neighborhood to disclose that her employer had that very day given her a new china plate for her meals. The paper plates, on which all previous meals had been served, had been thrown into the wastebasket. One recipient of this call, a middle-aged woman known for her bashfulness and humility, rejoined that her husband, a sheet-metal worker, had only a few hours before been called "Mister" by his supervisor, a white man with a passionate hatred of color. She added the tale of a neighbor down the street, a widow-woman named Murphy, who had at first been reluctant to join the picket; this woman now was insisting it should be made a daily event. Such talk as this circulated among the people who had been instrumental in raising the issue. As news of their victory leaked into the ears of others who had not participated, they received all through the night calls from strangers requesting verification, offering advice, and vowing support. Such strangers listened, and then volunteered stories about indignities inflicted on them by city officials, policemen, other grocers. In this way, over a period of hours, the community became even more incensed and restless than it had been at the time of the initial picket.

Soon, the man who had set events in motion found himself a hero. His name was Nelson Reed, and all his adult life he had been employed as an assembly-line worker. He was a steady husband, the father of three children, and a deacon in the Baptist church. All his life he had trusted in God and gotten along. But now something in him capitulated to the reality that came suddenly into focus. "I was wrong," he told people who called him. "The onliest thing that matters in this world is *money*. And when was the last time you seen a picture of Jesus on a dollar bill?" This line, which he repeated over and over, caused a few callers to laugh nervously, but not without some affirmation that this was indeed the way things were. Many said they had known it all along. Others argued that although it was certainly true, it was one thing to live without money and quite another to live without faith. But still most callers laughed and said, "You right. You *know* I know you right. Ain't it the truth, though?" Only a few people, among them Nelson Reed's wife, said nothing and looked very sad.

Why they looked sad, however, they would not communicate. And anyone observing their troubled faces would have to trust his own intuition. It is known that Reed's wife, Betty, measured all events against the fullness of her own experience. She was skeptical of everything. Brought to the church after a number of years of living openly with a jazz musician, she had embraced religion when she married Nelson Reed. But though she no longer believed completely in the world, she nonetheless had not fully embraced God. There was something in the nature of Christ's swift rise that had always bothered her, and something in the blood and vengeance of the Old Testament that was mellowing and refreshing. But she had never communicated these thoughts to anyone, especially her husband. Instead, she smiled vacantly while others professed leaps of faith, remained silent when friends spoke fiercely of their convictions. The presence of this vacuum in her contributed to her personal mystery; people said she was beautiful, although she was not outwardly so. Perhaps it was because she wished to protect this inner beauty that she did not smile now, and looked extremely sad, listening to her husband on the telephone.

Nelson Reed had no reason to be sad. He seemed to grow more

energized and talkative as the days passed. He was invited by an alderman, on the Tuesday after the initial picket, to tell his story on a local television talk show. He sweated heavily under the hot white lights and attempted to be philosophical. "I notice," the host said to him, "that you are not angry at this exploitative treatment. What, Mr. Reed, is the source of your calm?" The assembly-line worker looked unabashedly into the camera and said, "I have always believed in *Justice* with a capital *J*. I was raised up from a baby believin' that God ain't gonna let nobody go *too* far. See, in *my* mind God is in charge of *all* the capital letters in the alphabet of this world. It say in the Scripture He is Alpha and Omega, the first and the last. He is just about the *onliest* capitalizer they is." Both Reed and the alderman laughed. "Now, when *men* start to capitalize, they gets *greedy*. They put a little *j* in *joy* and a littler one in *justice*. They raise up a big *G* in *Greed* and a big *E* in *Evil*. Well, soon as they commence to put a little *g* in *god*, you can expect some kind of reaction. The Savior will just raise up the *H* in *Hell* and go on from there. And that's just what I'm doin', giving these sharpies *HELL* with a big *H*." The talk show host laughed along with Nelson Reed and the alderman. After the taping they drank coffee in the back room of the studio and talked about the sad shape of the world.

Three days before he was to comply with his wife's request, Green, the grocer, saw this talk show on television while at home. The words of Nelson Reed sent a chill through him. Though Reed had attempted to be philosophical, Green did not perceive the statement in this light. Instead, he saw a vindictive-looking black man seated between an ambitious alderman and a smug talk-show host. He saw them chatting comfortably about the nature of evil. The cameraman had shot mostly close-ups, and Green could see the set in Nelson Reed's jaw. The color of Reed's face was maddening. When his children came into the den, the grocer was in a sweat. Before he could think, he had shouted at them and struck the button turning off the set. The two children rushed from the room screaming. Ruth Green ran in from the kitchen. She knew why he was upset because she had received a call about the show; but she said nothing and pretended ignorance. Her children's school had been picketed that day, as it had the day before. But both children were still forbidden to speak of this to their father.

"Where do they get so much power?" Green said to his wife. "Two days ago, nobody would have cared. Now, everywhere, even in my home, I am condemned as a rascal. And what do I own? An airline? A multinational? Half of South America? *No!* I own three stores, one of which happens to be in a certain neighborhood inhabited by people who cost me money to run it." He sighed and sat upright on the sofa, his chubby legs spread wide. "A cab driver has a meter that clicks as he goes along. I pay extra for insurance, iron bars, pilfering by customers and employees. Nothing clicks. But when I add a little overhead to my prices, suddenly everything clicks. But for someone else. When was there last such a world?" He pressed the palms of both hands to his temples, suggesting a bombardment of brain-stinging sounds.

This gesture evoked no response from Ruth Green. She remained standing by the door, looking steadily at him. She said, "To protect yourself, I would not stock any more fresh cuts of meat in the store until after the giveaway on Saturday. Also, I would not tell it to the employees until after the first customer of the day has begun to check out. But I would urge you to hire several security guards to close the door promptly at seven-thirty, as is usual." She wanted to say much more than this, but did not. Instead she watched him. He was looking at the blank gray television screen, his palms still pressed against his ears. "In case you need to hear again," she continued in a weighty tone of voice, "I said two days ago, and I say again now, that if you fail to do this you will not see your children again for many years."

He twisted his head and looked up at her. "What is the color of these people?" he asked.

"Black," his wife said.

"And what is the name of my children?"

"Green."

The grocer smiled. "There is your answer," he told his wife. "Green is the only color I am interested in."

His wife did not smile. "Insufficient," she said.

"The world is mad!" he moaned. "But it is a point of sanity with me to not bend. I will not bend." He crossed his legs and pressed one hand firmly atop his knee. "*I will not bend,*" he said.

"We will see," his wife said.

Nelson Reed, after the television interview, became the acknowledged leader of the disgruntled neighbors. At first a number of them met in the kitchen at his house; then, as space was lacking for curious newcomers, a mass meeting was held on Thursday in an abandoned theater. His wife and three children sat in the front row. Behind them sat the widow Murphy, Lloyd Dukes, Tyrone Brown, Les Jones—those who had joined him on the first picket line. Behind these sat people who bought occasionally at the store, people who lived on the fringes of the neighborhood, people from other neighborhoods come to investigate the problem, and the merely curious. The middle rows were occupied by a few people from the suburbs, those who had seen the talk show and whose outrage at the grocer proved much more powerful than their fear of black people. In the rear of the theater crowded aging, old-style leftists, somber students, cynical young black men with angry grudges to explain with inarticulate gestures. Leaning against the walls, huddled near the doors at the rear, tape-recorder-bearing social scientists looked as detached and serene as bookies at the track. Here and there, in this diverse crowd, a politician stationed himself, pumping hands vigorously and pressing his palms gently against the shoulders of elderly people. Other visitors passed out leaflets, buttons, glossy color prints of men who promoted causes, the familiar and obscure. There was a hubbub of voices, a blend of the strident and the playful, the outraged and the reverent, lending an undercurrent of ominous energy to the assembly.

Nelson Reed spoke from a platform on the stage, standing before a yellowed, shredded screen that had once reflected the images of matinee idols. "I don't mind sayin' that I have always been a sucker," he told the crowd. "All my life I have been a sucker for the words of Jesus. Being a natural-born fool, I just ain't never had the *sense* to learn no better. Even right today, while the whole world is sayin' wrong is right and up is down, I'm so dumb I'm *still* steady believin' what is wrote in the Good Book . . ."

From the audience, especially the front rows, came a chorus singing, "Preach!"

"I have no doubt," he continued in a low baritone, "that it's true what is writ in the Good Book: 'The last shall be first and the first shall be last.' I don't know about y'all, but I have *always* been the last. I never wanted to be the first, but sometimes it look like the world get so bad that them that's holdin' onto the tree of life is the onliest ones left when God commence to blowin' dead leafs off the branches."

"Now you preaching," someone called.

In the rear of the theater a white student shouted an awkward "Amen."

Nelson Reed began walking across the stage to occupy the major part of his nervous energy. But to those in the audience, who now hung on his every word, it looked as though he strutted. "All my life," he said, "I have claimed to be a man without earnin' the right to call myself that. You know, the *average* man ain't really a man. The average man is a *boot-licker*. In fact, the *average* man would *run away* if he found hisself standing alone facin' down a adversary. I have done that *too many a time* in my life! But *not no more*. Better to be *once* was than *never* was a man. I will tell you tonight, there is somethin' *wrong* in being average. *I intend to stand up!* Now, if your average man that ain't really a man stand up, two things gonna happen: *One*, he g'on bust through all the weights that been place on his head, and, *two*, he g'on feel a lot of pain. But that same hurt is what make things fall in place. That, and gettin' your hands on one of these slick four-flushers tight enough so's you can squeeze him and say, '*No more!*' You do that, you g'on hurt some, but *you won't be average no more . . .*"

"No *more!*" a few people in the front rows repeated.

"I say *no more!*" Nelson Reed shouted.

"*No more! No more! No more!*" The chant rustled through the crowd like the rhythm of an autumn wind against a shedding tree.

Then people laughed and chattered in celebration.

As for the grocer, from the evening of the television interview he had begun to make plans. Unknown to his wife, he cloistered himself several times with his brother-in-law, an insurance salesman, and plotted a course. He had no intention of tossing steaks to the crowd. "And why should I, Tommy?" he asked his wife's brother, a lean, bald-headed man named Thomas. "I don't cheat anyone. I have never cheated anyone. The businesses I run are always on the up-and-up. So why should I pay?"

"Quite so," the brother-in-law said, chewing an unlit cigarillo. "The world has gone crazy. Next they will say that people in my business are responsible for prolonging life. I have found that people who refuse to believe in death refuse also to believe in the harshness of life. I sell well by saying that death is a long happiness. I show people the realities of life and compare this to a funeral with dignity, *and* the promise of a bundle for every loved one salted away. When they look around hard at life, they usually buy."

"So?" asked Green. Thomas was a college graduate with a penchant for philosophy.

"So," Thomas answered. "You must fight to show these people the reality of both your situation and theirs. How would it be if you visited one of their meetings and chalked out, on a blackboard, the dollars and cents of your operation? Explain your overhead, your security fees, all the additional expenses. If you treat them with respect, they might understand."

Green frowned. "That I would never do," he said. "It would be admission of a certain guilt."

The brother-in-law smiled, but only with one corner of his mouth. "Then you have something to feel guilty about?" he asked.

The grocer frowned at him. "*Nothing!*" he said with great emphasis.

"So?" Thomas said.

This first meeting between the grocer and his brother-in-law took place on Thursday, in a crowded barroom.

At the second meeting, in a luncheonette, it was agreed that the grocer should speak privately with the leader of the group, Nelson Reed. The meeting at which this was agreed took place on Friday afternoon. After accepting this advice from Thomas, the grocer resigned himself to explain to Reed, in as finite detail as possible, the economic structure of his operation. He vowed to suppress no information. He would explain everything: inventories, markups, sale items, inflation, balance sheets, specialty items, overhead, and that mysterious item called profit. This last item, promising to be the most difficult to explain, Green and his brother-in-law debated over for several hours. They agreed first of all that a man should not work for free, then they agreed that it was unethical to ruthlessly exploit. From these parameters, they staked out an area between fifteen and forty percent, and agreed that someplace between these two borders lay an amount of return that could be called fair. This was easy, but then Thomas introduced the factor of circumstance. He questioned whether the fact that one serviced a risky area justified the earning of profits, closer to the forty-percent edge of the scale. Green was unsure. Thomas smiled. "Here is a case that will point out an analogy," he said, licking a cigarillo. "I read in the papers that a family wants to sell an electric stove. I call the home and the man says fifty dollars. I ask to come out and inspect the merchandise. When I arrive I see they are poor, have already bought a new stove that is connected, and are selling the old one for fifty dollars because they want it out of the place. The electric stove is in good condition, worth much more than fifty. But because I see what I see I offer forty-five."

Green, for some reason, wrote down this figure on the back of the sales slip for the coffee they were drinking.

The brother-in-law smiled. He chewed his cigarillo. "The man agrees to take forty-five dollars, saying he has had no other calls. I look at the stove again and see a spot of rust. I say I will give him forty dollars. He agrees to this, on condition that I myself haul it away. I say I will haul it away if he comes down to thirty. You, of course, see where I am going."

The grocer nodded. "The circumstances of his situation, his need to get rid of the stove quickly, placed him in a position where he has little room to bargain?"

"Yes," Thomas answered. "So? Is it ethical, Harry?"

Harold Green frowned. He had never liked his brother-in-law, and now he thought the insurance agent was being crafty. "But," he answered, "this man does not *have* to sell! It is his choice whether to wait for other calls. It is not the fault of the buyer that the seller is in a hurry. It is the right of the buyer to get what he wants at the lowest price possible. That is the rule. That has *always* been the rule. And the reverse of it applies to the seller as well."

"Yes," Thomas said, sipping coffee from the Styrofoam cup. "But suppose that in addition to his hurry to sell, the owner was also of a weak soul. There are, after all, many such people." He smiled. "Suppose he placed no value on the money?"

"Then," Green answered, "your example is academic. Here we are not talking about real life. One man lives by the code, one man does not. Who is there free enough to make a judgment?" He laughed. "Now you see," he told his brother-in-law. "Much more than a few dollars are at stake. If this one buyer is to be condemned, then so are most people in the history of the world. An examination of history provides the only answer to your question. This code will be here tomorrow, long after the ones who do not honor it are not."

They argued fiercely late into the afternoon, the brother-in-law leaning heavily on his readings. When they parted, a little before 5:00 P.M., nothing had been resolved.

Neither was much resolved during the meeting between Green and Nelson Reed. Reached at home by the grocer in the early evening, the leader of the group spoke coldly at first, but consented finally to meet his adversary at a nearby drugstore for coffee and a talk. They met at the lunch counter, shook hands awkwardly, and sat for a few minutes discussing the weather. Then the grocer pulled two gray ledgers from his briefcase. "You have for years come into my place," he told the man. "In my memory I have always treated you well. Now our relationship has come to this." He slid the books along the counter until they touched Nelson Reed's arm.

Reed opened the top book and flipped the thick green pages with his thumb. He did not examine the figures. "All I know," he said, "is over at your place a can of soup cost me fifty-five cents, and two miles away at your other store for white folks you chargin' thirty-nine cents." He said this with the calm authority of an outraged soul. A quality of condescension tinged with pity crept into his gaze.

The grocer drummed his fingers on the counter top. He twisted his head and looked away, toward shelves containing cosmetics, laxatives, toothpaste. His eyes lingered on a poster of a woman's apple red lips and milk white teeth. The rest of the face was missing.

"Ain't no use to hide," Nelson Reed said, as to a child. "*I* know you wrong, *you* know you wrong, and before I finish, *everybody in this city* g'on know you wrong. God don't *like* ugly." He closed his eyes and gripped the cup of coffee. Then he swung his head suddenly and faced the grocer again. "Man, why you want to *do* people that way?" he asked. "We human, same as you."

"Before *God!*" Green exclaimed, looking squarely into the face of Nelson Reed. "Before God!" he said again. "*I am not an evil man!*" These last words sounded more like a moan as he tightened the muscles in his throat to lower the sound of his voice. He tossed his left shoulder as if adjusting the sleeve of his coat, or as if throwing off some unwanted weight. Then he peered along the counter top. No one was watching. At the end of the counter the waitress was scrubbing the coffee urn. "Look at these figures, please," he said to Reed.

The man did not drop his gaze. His eyes remained fixed on the grocer's face.

"All right," Green said. "Don't look. I'll tell you what is in these books, believe me if you want. I work twelve hours a day, one day off per week, running my business in three stores. I am not a wealthy person. In one place, in the area you call white, I get by barely by smiling lustily at old ladies, stocking gourmet stuff on the chance I will build a reputation as a quality store. The two clerks there cheat me; there is nothing I can do. In this business you must be friendly with everybody. The second place is on the other side of town, in a neighborhood as poor as this one. I get out there seldom. The profits are not worth the gas. I use the loss there as a write-off against some other properties." He paused. "Do you understand write-off?" he asked Nelson Reed.

"Naw," the man said.

Harold Green laughed. "What does it matter?" he said in a tone of voice intended for himself alone. "In this area I will admit I make a profit, but it is not so much as you think. But I do not make a profit here because the people are black. I make a profit because a profit is here to be made. I invest more here in window bars, theft losses, insurance, spoilage; I deserve to make more here than at the other places." He looked, almost imploringly, at the man seated next to him. "You don't accept this as the right of a man in business?"

Reed grunted. "Did the bear shit in the woods?" he said.

Again Green laughed. He gulped his coffee awkwardly, as if eager to go. Yet his motions slowed once he had set his coffee cup down on the blue plastic saucer. "Place yourself in *my* situation," he said, his voice high and tentative. "If *you* were running my store in this neighborhood, what would be *your* position? Say on a profit scale of fifteen to forty percent, at what point in between would you draw the line?"

Nelson Reed thought. He sipped his coffee and seemed to chew the liquid. "Fifteen to forty?" he repeated.

"Yes."

"I'm a churchgoin' man," he said. "Closer to fifteen than to forty."

"How close?"

Nelson Reed thought. "In church you tithe ten percent."

"In restaurants you tip fifteen," the grocer said quickly.

"All right," Reed said. "Over fifteen."

"How much over?"

Nelson Reed thought.

"Twenty, thirty, thirty-five?" Green chanted, leaning closer to Reed.

Still the man thought.

"Forty? Maybe even forty-five or fifty?" the grocer breathed in Reed's ear. "In the supermarkets, you know, they have more subtle ways of accomplishing such feats."

Reed slapped his coffee cup with the back of his right hand. The brown liquid swirled across the counter top, wetting the books. "*Damn this!*" he shouted.

Startled, Green rose from his stool.

Nelson Reed was trembling. "I ain't *you*," he said in a deep baritone. "I ain't the *supermarket* neither. All I is is a poor man that works *too* hard to see his pay slip through his fingers like rainwater. All I know is you done *cheat* me, you done *cheat* everybody in the neighborhood, and we organized now to get some of it *back!*" Then he stood and faced the grocer. "My daddy sharecropped down in Mississippi and bought in the company store. He owed them twenty-three years when he died. I paid off five of them years and then run away to up here. Now, I'm a deacon in the Baptist church. I raised my kids the way my daddy raise me and don't bother nobody. Now come to find out, after all my runnin', they done lift that *same company store* up out of Mississippi and slip it down on us here! Well, my daddy was a *fighter*, and if he hadn't owed all them years he would of raise him some hell. Me, I'm steady my daddy's child, plus I got seniority in my union. I'm a free man. Buddy, don't you know *I'm gonna raise me some hell!*"

Harold Green reached for a paper napkin to sop the coffee soaking into his books.

Nelson Reed threw a dollar on top of the books and walked away.

"I *will not* do it!" Harold Green said to his wife that same evening. They were in the bathroom of their home. Bending over the face bowl, she was washing her hair with a towel draped around her neck. The grocer stood by the door, looking in at her. "I will not bankrupt myself tomorrow," he said.

"I've been thinking about it, too," Ruth Green said, shaking her wet hair. "You'll do it, Harry."

"Why should I?" he asked. "You won't leave. You know it was a bluff. I've waited this long for you to calm down. Tomorrow is Saturday. This week has been a hard one. Tonight let's be realistic."

"Of course you'll do it," Ruth Green said. She said it the way she would say "Have some toast." She said, "You'll do it because you want to see your children grow up."

"And for what other reason?" he asked.

She pulled the towel tighter around her neck. "Because you are at heart a moral man."

He grinned painfully. "If I am, why should I have to prove it to *them*?"

"Not them," Ruth Green said, freezing her movements and looking in the mirror. "Certainly not them. By no means them. They have absolutely nothing to do with this."

"Who, then?" he asked, moving from the door into the room. "Who else should I prove something to?"

His wife was crying. But her entire face was wet. The tears moved secretly down her face.

"Who else?" Harold Green asked.

It was almost 11:00 P.M. and the children were in bed. They had also cried when they came home from school. Ruth Green said, "For yourself, Harry. For the love that lives inside your heart."

All night the grocer thought about this.

Nelson Reed also slept little that Friday night. When he returned home from the drugstore, he reported to his wife as much of the conversation as he could remember. At first he had joked about the exchange between himself and the grocer, but as more details returned to his conscious mind he grew solemn and then bitter. "He ask me to put myself in *his* place," Reed told his wife. "Can you imagine that kind of gumption? I never cheated nobody in my life. All my life I have lived on Bible principles. I am a deacon in the church. I have work all my life for other folks and I don't even own the house I live in." He paced up and down the kitchen, his big arms flapping loosely at his sides. Betty Reed sat at the table, watching. "This here's a low-down, ass-kicking world," he said. "I swear to God it is! All my life I have lived on principle and I ain't got a dime in the bank. Betty," he turned suddenly toward her, "don't you think I'm a fool?"

"Mr. Reed," she said. "Let's go on to bed."

But he would not go to bed. Instead, he took the fifth of bourbon from the cabinet under the sink and poured himself a shot. His wife refused to join him. Reed drained the glass of whiskey, and then another, while he resumed pacing the kitchen floor. He slapped his hands against his sides. "*I* think I'm a fool," he said. "Ain't got a dime in the bank, ain't got a pot to *pee* in or a wall to pitch it over, and that there *cheat* ask me to put myself inside *his* shoes. Hell, I can't even *afford* the kind of shoes he wears." He stopped pacing and looked at his wife.

"Mr. Reed," she whispered, "tomorrow ain't a work day. Let's go to bed."

Nelson Reed laughed, the bitterness in his voice rattling his wife. "The *hell* I will!" he said.

He strode to the yellow telephone on the wall beside the sink and began to dial. The first call was to Lloyd Dukes, a neighbor two blocks away and a lieutenant in the organization. Dukes was not at home. The second call was to McElroy's Bar on the corner of 65th and Carroll, where Stanley Harper, another of the lieutenants, worked as a bartender. It was Harper who spread the word, among those men at the bar, that the organization would picket the grocer's store the following morning. And all through the night, in the bedroom of their house, Betty Reed was awakened by telephone calls coming from Lester Jones, Nat Lucas, Mrs. Tyrone Brown, the widow-woman named Murphy, all coordinating the time when they would march in a group against the store owned by Harold Green. Betty Reed's heart beat loudly beneath the covers as she listened to the bitterness and rage in her husband's voice. On several occasions, hearing him declare himself a fool, she pressed the pillow against her eyes and cried.

The grocer opened later than usual this Saturday morning, but still it was early enough to make him one of the first walkers in the neighborhood. He parked his car one block from the store and strolled to work. There were no birds singing. The sky in this area was not blue. It was smog-smutted and gray, seeming on the verge of a light rain. The street, as always, was littered with cans, papers, bits of broken glass. As always the garbage cans overflowed. The morning breeze plastered a sheet of newspaper playfully around the sides of a rusted garbage can. For some reason, using his right foot, he loosened the paper and stood watching it slide into the street and down the block. The movement made him feel good. He whistled while unlocking the bars shielding the windows and door of his store. When he had unlocked the main door he stepped in quickly and threw a switch to the right of the jamb, before the shrill sound of the alarm could shatter his mood. Then he switched on the lights. Everything was as it had been the night before. He had already telephoned his two employees and given them the day off. He busied himself doing the usual things—hauling milk and vegetables from the cooler, putting cash in the till—not thinking about the silence of his wife, or the look in her eyes, only an hour before when he left home. He had determined, at some point while driving through the city, that today it would be business as usual. But he expected very few customers.

The first customer of the day was Mrs. Nelson Reed. She came in around 9:30 A.M. and wandered about the store. He watched her from the checkout counter. She seemed uncertain of what she wanted to buy. She kept glancing at him down the center aisle. His suspicions aroused, he said finally, "Yes, may I help you, Mrs. Reed?" His words caused her to jerk, as if some devious thought had been perceived going through her mind. She reached over quickly and lifted a loaf of whole wheat bread from the rack and walked with it to the counter. She looked at him and smiled. The smile was a broad, shy one, that rare kind of smile one sees on virgin girls when they first confess love to themselves. Betty Reed was a woman of about forty-five. For some reason he could not comprehend, this gesture touched him. When she pulled a dollar from her purse and laid it on the counter, an impulse, from no place he could locate with his mind, seized control of his tongue. "Free," he told Betty Reed. She paused, then pushed the dollar toward him with a firm and determined thrust of her arm. "Free," he heard himself saying strongly, his right palm spread and meeting her thrust with absolute force. She clutched the loaf of bread and walked out of his store.

The next customer, a little girl, arriving well after 10:30 A.M., selected a candy bar from the rack beside the counter. "Free," Green said cheerfully. The little girl left the candy on the counter and ran out of the store.

At 11:15 A.M. a wino came in looking desperate enough to sell his soul. The grocer watched him only for an instant. Then he went to the wine counter and selected a half-gallon of medium-grade red wine. He shoved the jug into the belly of the wino, the man's sour breath bathing his face. "Free," the grocer said. "But you must not drink it in here."

He felt good about the entire world, watching the wino through the window gulping the wine and looking guiltily around.

At 11:25 A.M. the pickets arrived.

Two dozen people, men and women, young and old, crowded the pavement in front of his store. Their signs, placards, and voices denounced him as a parasite. The grocer laughed inside himself. He felt lighthearted and wild, like a man drugged. He rushed to the meat counter and pulled a long roll of brown wrapping paper from the rack, tearing it neatly with a quick shift of his body resembling a dance step practiced fervently in his youth. He laid the paper on the chopping block and with the black-inked, felt-tipped marker scrawled, in giant letters, the word FREE. This he took to the window and pasted in place with many strands of Scotch tape. He was laughing wildly. "Free!" he shouted from behind the brown paper. "Free! Free! Free! Free! Free! Free!" He rushed to the door, pushed his head out, and screamed to the confused crowd, "*Free!*" Then he ran back to the counter and stood behind it, like a soldier at attention.

They came in slowly.

Nelson Reed entered first, working his right foot across the dirty tile as if tracking a squiggling worm. The others followed: Lloyd Dukes dragging a placard, Mr. and Mrs. Tyrone Brown, Stanley Harper walking with his fists clenched, Lester Jones with three of his children, Nat Lucas looking sheepish and detached, a clutch of winos, several bashful nuns, ironic-smiling teenagers and a few students. Bringing up the rear was a bearded social scientist holding a tape recorder to his chest. "Free!" the grocer screamed. He threw up his arms in a gesture that embraced, or dismissed, the entire store. "*All free!*" he shouted. He was grinning with the grace of a madman.

The winos began grabbing first. They stripped the shelf of wine in a matter of seconds. Then they fled, dropping bottles on the tile in their wake. The others, stepping quickly through this liquid, soon congealed it into a sticky, bloodlike consistency. The young men went for the cigarettes and luncheon meats and beer. One of them had the prescience to grab a sack from the counter, while the others loaded their arms swiftly, hugging cartons and packages of cold cuts like long-lost friends. The students joined them, less for greed than for the thrill of the experience. The two nuns backed toward the door. As for the older people, men and women, they stood at first as if stuck to the wine-smeared floor. Then Stanley Harper, the bartender, shouted, "The man said *free*, y'all heard him." He paused. "Didn't you say *free* now?" he called to the grocer.

"I said free," Harold Green answered, his temples pounding.

A cheer went up. The older people began grabbing, as if the secret lusts of a lifetime had suddenly seized command of their arms and eyes. They grabbed toilet tissue, cold cuts, pickles, sardines, boxes of raisins, boxes of starch, cans of soup, tins of tuna fish and salmon, bottles of spices, cans of boned chicken, slippery cans of olive oil. Here a man, Lester Jones, burdened himself with several heads of lettuce, while his wife, in another aisle, shouted for him to drop those small items and concentrate on the gourmet section. She herself took imported sardines, wheat crackers, bottles of candied pickles, herring, anchovies, imported olives, French wafers, an ancient, half-rusted can of pâté, stocked, by mistake, from the inventory of another store. Others packed their arms with detergents, hams, chocolate-coated cereal, whole chickens with hanging asses, wedges of bologna and salami like squashed footballs, chunks of cheeses, yellow and white, shriveled onions, and green peppers. Mrs. Tyrone Brown hung a curve of pepperoni around her neck and seemed to take on instant dignity, much like a person of noble birth in possession now of a long sought-after gem. Another woman, the widow Murphy, stuffed tomatoes into her bosom, holding a half-chewed lemon in her mouth. The more enterprising fought desperately over the three rusted shopping carts, and the victors wheeled these along the narrow aisles, sweeping into them bulk items—beer in six-packs, sacks of sugar, flour, glass bottles of syrup, toilet cleanser, sugar cookies, prune, apple and tomato juices—while others endeavored to snatch the carts from them. There were several fistfights and much cursing. The grocer, standing behind the counter, hummed and rang his cash register like a madman.

Nelson Reed, the first into the store, followed the nuns out, empty-handed.

In less than half an hour the others had stripped the store and vanished in many directions up and down the block. But still more people came, those late in hearing the news. And when they saw the shelves were bare, they cursed soberly and chased those few stragglers still bearing away goods. Soon only the grocer and the social scientist remained, the latter stationed at the door with his tape recorder sucking in leftover sounds. Then he too slipped away up the block.

By 12:10 P.M. the grocer was leaning against the counter, trying to make his mind slow down. Not a man given to drink during work hours, he nonetheless took a swallow from a bottle of wine, a dusty bottle from beneath the wine shelf, somehow overlooked by the winos. Somewhat recovered, he was preparing to remember what he should do next when he glanced toward a figure at the door. Nelson Reed was standing there, watching him.

"All gone," Harold Green said. "My friend, Mr. Reed, there is no more." Still the man stood in the doorway, peering into the store.

The grocer waved his arms about the empty room. Not a display case had a single item standing. "All gone," he said again, as if addressing a stupid child. "There is nothing left to get. You, my friend, have come back too late for a second load. I am cleaned out."

Nelson Reed stepped into the store and strode toward the counter. He moved through wine-stained flour, lettuce leaves, red, green, and blue labels, bits and pieces of broken glass. He walked toward the counter.

"All day," the grocer laughed, not quite hysterically now, "all day long I have not made a single cent of profit. The entire day was a loss. This store, like the others, is *bleeding* me." He waved his arms about the room in a magnificent gesture of uncaring loss. "Now do you understand?" he said. "Now will you put yourself in my shoes? I have nothing here. Come, now, Mr. Reed, would it not be so bad a thing to walk in my shoes?"

"Mr. Green," Nelson Reed said coldly. "My wife bought a loaf of bread in here this mornin'. She forgot to pay you. I, myself, have come here to pay you your money."

"Oh," the grocer said.

"I think it was brown bread. Don't that cost more than white?"

The two men looked away from each other, but not at anything in the store.

"In my store, yes," Harold Green said. He rang the register with the most casual movement of his finger. The register read fifty-five cents.

Nelson Reed held out a dollar.

"And two cents tax," the grocer said.

The man held out the dollar.

"After all," Harold Green said. "We are all, after all, Mr. Reed, in debt to the government."

He rang the register again. It read fifty-seven cents.

Nelson Reed held out a dollar.

1977

Herman Melville
1819–1891

"Bartleby the Scrivener" appeared in the 1853 volume, The Piazza Tales, *just two years after Melville's novel,* Moby-Dick, *was published. Today that book is recognized as an American classic, but it was largely ignored in Melville's lifetime, as was most of his writing. Some critics read this story at least partially as a biographical allegory, in which Bartleby figures as the misunderstood artist for whom modern society has no use. Within a few years of inventing this character, Melville himself withdrew from public life and literature, and spent his final decades in obscurity. Melville is one of the earliest writers to examine the new type of society that was expanding in the mid-nineteenth century (it expanded even more dramatically in the next decade as a consequence of the Civil War), the world so familiar to us as "corporate" America.*

Bartleby, the Scrivener
A Story of Wall-Street

I am a rather elderly man. The nature of my avocations for the last thirty years has brought me into more than ordinary contact with what would seem an interesting and somewhat singular set of men, of whom as yet nothing that I know of has ever been written:—I mean the law-copyists or scriveners. I have known very many of them, professionally and privately, and if I pleased, could relate divers histories, at which good-natured gentlemen might smile, and sentimental souls might weep. But I waive the biographies of all other scriveners for a few passages in the life of Bartleby, who was a scrivener the strangest I ever saw or heard of. While of other law-copyists I might write the complete life, of Bartleby nothing of that sort can be done. I believe that no materials exist for a full and satisfactory biography of this man. It is an irreparable loss to literature. Bartleby was one of those beings of whom nothing is ascertainable, except from the original sources, and in his case those are very small. What my own astonished eyes saw of Bartleby, *that* is all I know of him, except, indeed, one vague report which will appear in the sequel.

Ere introducing the scrivener, as he first appeared to me, it is fit I make some mention of myself, my *employés*, my business, my chambers, and general surroundings; because some such description is indispensable to an adequate understanding of the chief character about to be presented.

Imprimis: I am a man who, from his youth upwards, has been filled with a profound conviction that the easiest way of life is the best. Hence, though I belong to a profession proverbially energetic and nervous, even to turbulence, at times, yet nothing of that sort have I ever suffered to invade my peace. I am one of those unambitious lawyers who never addresses a jury, or in any way draws down public applause; but in the cool tranquillity of a snug retreat, do a snug business among rich men's bonds and mortgages and title-deeds. All who know me, consider me an eminently *safe* man. The late John Jacob Astor, a personage little given to poetic enthusiasm, had no hesitation in pronouncing my first grand point to be prudence; my next, method. I do not speak it in vanity, but simply record the fact, that I was not unemployed in my profession by the late John Jacob Astor; a name which, I admit, I love to repeat, for it hath a rounded and orbicular sound to it, and rings like unto bullion. I will freely add, that I was not insensible to the late John Jacob Astor's good opinion.

Some time prior to the period at which this little history begins, my avocations had been largely increased. The good old office, now extinct in the State of New York, of a Master in Chancery, had been conferred upon me. It was not a very arduous office, but very pleasantly remunerative. I seldom lose my temper; much more seldom indulge in dangerous indignation at wrongs and outrages; but I must be permitted to be rash here and declare, that I consider the sudden and violent abrogation of the office of Master in Chancery, by the new Constitution, as a—premature act; inasmuch as I had counted upon a life-lease of the profits, whereas I only received those of a few short years. But this is by the way.

My chambers were up stairs at No. — Wall-street. At one end they looked upon the white wall of the interior of a spacious sky-light shaft, penetrating the building from top to bottom. This view might have been considered rather tame than otherwise, deficient in what landscape painters call "life." But if so, the view from the other end of my chambers offered, at least, a contrast, if nothing more. In that direction my windows commanded an unobstructed view of a lofty brick wall, black by age and everlasting shade; which wall required no spy-glass to bring out its lurking beauties, but for the benefit of all nearsighted spectators, was pushed up to within ten feet of my window panes. Owing to the great height of the surrounding buildings, and my chambers being on the second floor, the interval between this wall and mine not a little resembled a huge square cistern.

At the period just preceding the advent of Bartleby, I had two persons as copyists in my employment, and a promising lad as an office-boy. First, Turkey; second, Nippers; third, Ginger Nut. These may seem names, the like of which are not usually found in the Directory. In truth they were nicknames, mutually conferred upon each other by my three clerks, and were deemed expressive of their respective persons or characters. Turkey was a short, pursy Englishman of about my own age, that is, somewhere not far from sixty. In the morning, one might say, his face was of a fine florid hue, but after twelve o'clock, meridian—his dinner hour—it blazed like a grate full of Christmas coals; and continued blazing—but, as it were, with a gradual wane—till 6 o'clock, P.M. or thereabouts, after which I saw no more of the proprietor of the face, which gaining its meridian with the sun, seemed to set with it, to rise, culminate, and decline the following day, with the like regularity and undiminished glory. There are many singular coincidences I have known in the course of my life, not the least among which was the fact, that exactly when Turkey displayed his fullest beams from his red and radiant countenance, just then, too, at that critical moment, began the daily period when I considered his business capacities as seriously disturbed for the remainder of the twenty-four hours. Not that he was absolutely idle, or averse to business then; far from it. The difficulty was, he was apt to be altogether too energetic. There was a strange, inflamed, flurried, flighty recklessness of activity about him. He would be incautious in dipping his pen into his inkstand. All his blots upon my documents, were dropped there after twelve o'clock, meridian. Indeed, not only would he be reckless and sadly given to making blots in the afternoon, but some days he went further, and was rather noisy. At such times, too, his face flamed with augmented blazonry, as if cannel coal had been heaped on anthracite. He made an unpleasant racket with his chair; spilled his sandbox; in mending his pens, impatiently split them all to pieces, and threw them on the floor in a sudden passion; stood up and leaned over his table, boxing his papers about in a most indecorous manner, very sad to behold in an elderly man like him. Nevertheless, as he was in many ways a most valuable person to me, and all the time before twelve o'clock, meridian, was the quickest, steadiest creature too, accomplishing a great deal of work in a style not easy to be matched—for these reasons, I was willing to overlook his eccentricities, though indeed, occasionally, I remonstrated with him. I did this very gently, however, because, though the civilest, nay, the blandest and most reverential of men in the morning, yet in the afternoon he was disposed, upon provocation, to be slightly rash with his tongue, in fact, insolent. Now, valuing his morning services as I did, and resolved not to lose them; yet, at the same time made uncomfortable by his inflamed ways after twelve o'clock; and being a man of peace, unwilling by my admonitions to call forth unseemly retorts from him; I took upon me, one Saturday noon (he was always worse on Saturdays), to hint to him, very kindly, that perhaps now that he was growing old, it might be well to abridge his labors; in short, he need not come to my chambers after twelve o'clock, but, dinner over, had best go home to his lodgings and rest himself till tea-time. But no; he insisted upon his afternoon devotions. His countenance became intolerably fervid, as he oratorically assured me—gesticulating with a long ruler at the other end of the room—that if his services in the morning were useful, how indispensable, then, in the afternoon?

"With submission, sir," said Turkey on this occasion, "I consider myself your right-hand man. In the morning I but marshal and deploy my columns; but in the afternoon I put myself at their head, and gallantly charge the foe, thus!"—and he made a violent thrust with the ruler.

"But the blots, Turkey," intimated I.

"True—but, with submission, sir, behold these hairs! I am getting old. Surely, sir, a blot or two of a warm afternoon is not to be severely urged against gray hairs. Old age—even if it blot the page—is honorable. With submission, sir, we *both* are getting old."

This appeal to my fellow-feeling was hardly to be resisted. At all events, I saw that go he would not. So I made up my mind to let him stay, resolving, nevertheless, to see to it, that during the afternoon he had to do with my less important papers.

Nippers, the second on my list, was a whiskered, sallow, and, upon the whole, rather piratical-looking young man of about five and twenty. I always deemed him the victim of two evil powers—ambition and indigestion. The ambition was evinced by a certain impatience of the duties of a mere copyist, an unwarrantable usurpation of strictly professional affairs, such as the original drawing up of legal documents. The indigestion seemed betokened in an occasional nervous testiness and grinning irritability, causing the teeth to audibly grind together over mistakes committed in copying; unnecessary maledictions, hissed, rather than spoken, in the heat of business; and especially by a continual discontent with the height of the table where he worked. Though of a very ingenious mechanical turn, Nippers could never get this table to suit him. He put chips under it, blocks of various sorts, bits of pasteboard, and at last went so far as to attempt an exquisite adjustment by final pieces of folded blotting-paper. But no invention would answer. If, for the sake of easing his back, he brought the table lid at a sharp angle well up towards his chin, and wrote there like a man using the steep roof of a Dutch house for his desk—then he declared that it stopped the circulation in his arms. If now he lowered the table to his waistbands, and stooped over it in writing, then there was a sore aching in his back. In short, the truth of the matter was Nippers knew not what he wanted. Or, if he wanted any thing, it was to be rid of a scrivener's table altogether. Among the manifestations of his diseased ambition was a fondness he had for receiving visits from certain ambiguous-looking fellows in seedy coats, whom he called his clients. Indeed I was aware that not only was he, at times, considerable of a ward-politician, but he occasionally did a little business at the Justices' courts, and was not unknown on the steps of the Tombs. I have good reason to believe, however, that one individual who called upon him at my chambers, and who, with a grand air, he insisted was his client, was no other than a dun, and the alleged title-deed, a bill. But with all his failings, and the annoyances he caused me, Nippers, like his compatriot Turkey, was a very useful man to me; wrote a neat, swift hand; and, when he chose, was not deficient in a gentlemanly sort of deportment. Added to this, he always dressed in a gentlemanly sort of way; and so, incidentally, reflected credit upon my chambers. Whereas with respect to Turkey, I had much ado to keep him from being a reproach to me. His clothes were apt to look oily and smell of eating-houses. He wore his pantaloons very loose and baggy in summer. His coats were execrable; his hat not to be handled. But while the hat was a thing of indifference to me, inasmuch as his natural civility and deference, as a dependent Englishman, always led him to doff it the moment he entered the room, yet his coat was another matter. Concerning his coats, I reasoned with him; but with no effect. The truth was, I suppose, that a man with so small an income, could not afford to sport such a lustrous face and a lustrous coat at one and the same time. As Nippers once observed, Turkey's money went chiefly for red ink. One winter day I presented Turkey with a highly-respectable looking coat of my own, a padded gray coat, of a most comfortable warmth, and which buttoned straight up from the knee to the neck. I thought Turkey would appreciate the favor, and abate his rashness and obstreperousness of afternoons. But no. I verily believe that buttoning himself up in so downy and blanket-like a coat had a pernicious effect upon him; upon the same principle that too much oats are bad for horses. In fact, precisely as a rash, restive horse is said to feel his oats, so Turkey felt his coat. It made him insolent. He was a man whom prosperity harmed.

Though concerning the self-indulgent habits of Turkey I had my own private surmises, yet touching Nippers I was well persuaded that whatever might be his faults in other respects, he was, at least, a temperate young man. But indeed, nature herself seemed to have been his vintner, and at his birth charged him so thoroughly with an irritable, brandy-like disposition, that all subsequent potations were needless. When I consider how, amid the stillness of my chambers, Nippers would sometimes impatiently rise from his seat, and stooping over his table, spread his arms wide apart, seize the whole desk, and move it, and jerk it, with a grim, grinding motion on the floor, as if the table were a perverse voluntary agent, intent on thwarting and vexing him; I plainly perceive that for Nippers, brandy and water were altogether superfluous.

It was fortunate for me that, owing to its peculiar cause—indigestion—the irritability and consequent nervousness of Nippers, were mainly observable in the morning, while in the afternoon he was comparatively mild. So that Turkey's paroxysms only coming on about twelve o'clock, I never had to do with their eccentricities at one time. Their fits relieved each other like guards. When Nippers' was on, Turkey's was off; and *vice versa*. This was a good natural arrangement under the circumstances.

Ginger Nut, the third on my list, was a lad some twelve years old. His father was a carman, ambitious of seeing his son on the bench instead of a cart, before he died. So he sent him to my office as student at law, errand boy, and cleaner and sweeper, at the rate of one dollar a week. He had a little desk to himself, but he did not use it much. Upon inspection, the drawer exhibited a great array of the shells of various sorts of nuts. Indeed, to this quick-witted youth the whole noble science of the law was contained in a nut-shell. Not the least among the employments of Ginger Nut, as well as one which he discharged with the most alacrity, was his duty as cake and apple purveyor for Turkey and Nippers. Copying law papers being proverbially a dry, husky sort of business, my two scriveners were fain to moisten their mouths very often with Spitzenbergs to be had at the numerous stalls nigh the Custom House and Post Office. Also, they sent Ginger Nut very frequently for that peculiar cake—small, flat, round, and very spicy—after which he had been named by them. Of a cold morning when business was but dull, Turkey would gobble up scores of these cakes, as if they were mere wafers—indeed they sell them at the rate of six or eight for a penny—the scrape of his pen blending with the crunching of the crisp particles in his mouth. Of all the fiery afternoon blunders and flurried rashnesses of Turkey, was his once moistening a ginger-cake between his lips, and clapping it on to a mortgage for a seal. I came within an ace of dismissing him then. But he mollified me by making an oriental bow, and saying—"With submission, sir, it was generous of me to find you in stationery on my own account."

Now my original business—that of a conveyancer and title hunter, and drawer-up of recondite documents of all sorts—was considerably increased by receiving the master's office. There was now great work for scriveners. Not only must I push the clerks already with me, but I must have additional help. In answer to my advertisement, a motionless young man one morning, stood upon my office threshold, the door being open, for it was summer. I can see that figure now—pallidly neat, pitiably respectable, incurably forlorn! It was Bartleby.

After a few words touching his qualifications, I engaged him, glad to have among my corps of copyists a man of so singularly sedate an aspect, which I thought might operate beneficially upon the flighty temper of Turkey, and the fiery one of Nippers.

I should have stated before that ground glass folding-doors divided my premises into two parts, one of which was occupied by my scriveners, the other by myself. According to my humor I threw open these doors, or closed them. I resolved to assign Bartleby a corner by the folding-doors, but on my side of them, so as to have this quiet man within easy call, in case any trifling thing was to be done. I placed his desk close up to a small side-window in that part of the room, a window which originally had afforded a lateral view of certain grimy backyards and bricks, but which, owing to subsequent erections, commanded at present no view at all, though it gave some light. Within three feet of the panes was a wall, and the light came down from far above, between two lofty buildings, as from a very small opening in a dome. Still further to a satisfactory arrangement, I procured a high green folding screen, which might entirely isolate Bartleby from my sight, though not remove him from my voice. And thus, in a manner, privacy and society were conjoined.

At first Bartleby did an extraordinary quantity of writing. As if long famishing for something to copy, he seemed to gorge himself on my documents. There was no pause for digestion. He ran a day and night line, copying by sun-light and by candle-light. I should have been quite lelighted with his application, had he been cheerfully industrious. But he wrote on silently, palely, mechanically.

It is, of course, an indispensable part of a scrivener's business to verify the accuracy of his copy, word by word. Where there are two or more scriveners in an office, they assist each other in this examination, one reading from the copy, the other holding the original. It is a very dull, wearisome, and lethargic affair. I can readily imagine that to some sanguine temperaments it would be altogether intolerable. For example, I cannot credit that the mettlesome poet Byron would have contentedly sat down with Bartleby to examine a law document of, say five hundred pages, closely written in a crimpy hand.

Now and then, in the haste of business, it had been my habit to assist in comparing some brief document myself, calling Turkey or Nippers for this purpose. One object I had in placing Bartleby so handy to me behind the screen, was to avail myself of his services on such trivial occasions. It was on the third day, I think, of his being with me, and before any necessity had arisen for having his own writing examined, that, being much hurried to complete a small affair I had in hand, I abruptly called to Bartleby. In my haste and natural expectancy of instant compliance, I sat with my head bent over the original on my desk, and my right hand sideways, and somewhat nervously extended with the copy, so that immediately upon emerging from his retreat, Bartleby might snatch it and proceed to business without the least delay.

In this very attitude did I sit when I called to him, rapidly stating what it was I wanted him to do—namely, to examine a small paper with me. Imagine my surprise, nay, my consternation, when without moving from his privacy, Bartleby in a singularly mild, firm voice, replied, "I would prefer not to."

I sat awhile in perfect silence, rallying my stunned faculties. Immediately it occurred to me that my ears had deceived me, or Bartleby had entirely misunderstood my meaning. I repeated my request in the clearest tone I could assume. But in quite as clear a one came the previous reply, "I would prefer not to."

"Prefer not to," echoed I, rising in high excitement, and crossing the room with a stride. "What do you mean? Are you moon-struck? I want you to help me compare this sheet here—take it," and I thrust it towards him.

"I would prefer not to," said he.

I looked at him steadfastly. His face was leanly composed; his gray eye dimly calm. Not a wrinkle of agitation rippled him. Had there been the least uneasiness, anger, impatience or impertinence in his manner; in other words, had there been any thing ordinarily human about him, doubtless I should have violently dismissed him from the premises. But as it was, I should have as soon thought of turning my pale plaster-of-paris bust of Cicero out of doors. I stood gazing at him awhile, as he went on with his own writing, and then reseated myself at my desk. This is very strange, thought I. What had one best do? But my business hurried me. I concluded to forget the matter for the present, reserving it for my future leisure. So calling Nippers from the other room, the paper was speedily examined.

A few days after this, Bartleby concluded four lengthy documents, being quadruplicates of a week's testimony taken before me in my High Court of Chancery. It became necessary to examine them. It was an important suit, and great accuracy was imperative. Having all things arranged I called Turkey, Nippers and Ginger Nut from the next room, meaning to place the four copies in the hands of my four clerks, while I should read from the original. Accordingly Turkey, Nippers and Ginger Nut had taken their seats in a row, each with his document in hand, when I called to Bartleby to join this interesting group.

"Bartleby! quick, I am waiting."

I heard a slow scrape of his chair legs on the uncarpeted floor, and soon he appeared standing at the entrance of his hermitage.

"What is wanted?" said he mildly.

"The copies, the copies," said I hurriedly. "We are going to examine them. There"—and I held towards him the fourth quadruplicate.

"I would prefer not to," he said, and gently disappeared behind the screen.

For a few moments I was turned into a pillar of salt, standing at the head of my seated column of clerks. Recovering myself, I advanced towards the screen, and demanded the reason for such extraordinary conduct.

"*Why* do you refuse?"

"I would prefer not to."

With any other man I should have flown outright into a dreadful passion, scorned all further words, and thrust him ignominiously from my presence. But there was something about Bartleby that not only strangely disarmed me, but in a wonderful manner touched and disconcerted me. I began to reason with him.

"These are your own copies we are about to examine. It is labor saving to you, because one examination will answer for your four papers. It is common usage. Every copyist is bound to help examine his copy. Is it not so? Will you not speak? Answer!"

"I prefer not to," he replied in a flute-like tone. It seemed to me that while I had been addressing him, he carefully revolved every statement that I made; fully comprehended the meaning; could not gainsay the irresistible conclusion; but, at the same time, some paramount consideration prevailed with him to reply as he did.

"You are decided, then, not to comply with my request—a request made according to common usage and common sense?"

He briefly gave me to understand that on that point my judgment was sound. Yes: his decision was irreversible.

It is not seldom the case that when a man is browbeaten in some unprecedented and violently unreasonable way, he begins to stagger in his own plainest faith. He begins, as it were, vaguely to surmise that, wonderful as it may be, all the justice and all the reason is on the other side. Accordingly, if any disinterested persons are present, he turns to them for some reinforcement for his own faltering mind.

"Turkey," said I, "what do you think of this? Am I not right?"

"With submission, sir," said Turkey, with his blandest tone, "I think that you are."

"Nippers," said I, "what do *you* think of it?"

"I think I should kick him out of the office."

(The reader of nice perceptions will here perceive that, it being morning, Turkey's answer is couched in polite and tranquil terms, but Nippers replies in ill-tempered ones. Or, to repeat a previous sentence, Nippers's ugly mood was on duty, and Turkey's off.)

"Ginger Nut," said I, willing to enlist the smallest suffrage in my behalf, "what do *you* think of it?"

"I think, sir, he's a little *luny*," replied Ginger Nut, with a grin.

"You hear what they say," said I, turning towards the screen, "come forth and do your duty."

But he vouchsafed no reply. I pondered a moment in sore perplexity. But once more business hurried me. I determined again to postpone the consideration of this dilemma to my future leisure. With a little trouble we made out to examine the papers without Bartleby, though at every page or two, Turkey deferentially dropped his opinion that this proceeding was quite out of the common;

while Nippers, twitching in his chair with a dyspeptic nervousness, ground out between his set teeth occasional hissing maledictions against the stubborn oaf behind the screen. And for his (Nippers's) part, this was the first and the last time he would do another man's business without pay.

Meanwhile Bartleby sat in his hermitage, oblivious to every thing but his own peculiar business there.

Some days passed, the scrivener being employed upon another lengthy work. His late remarkable conduct led me to regard his ways narrowly. I observed that he never went to dinner; indeed that he never went any where. As yet I had never of my personal knowledge known him to be outside of my office. He was a perpetual sentry in the corner. At about eleven o'clock though, in the morning, I noticed that Ginger Nut would advance towards the opening in Bartleby's screen, as if silently beckoned thither by a gesture invisible to me where I sat. The boy would then leave the office jingling a few pence, and reappear with a handful of ginger-nuts which he delivered in the hermitage, receiving two of the cakes for his trouble.

He lives, then, on ginger-nuts, thought I; never eats a dinner, properly speaking; he must be a vegetarian then; but no; he never eats even vegetables, he eats nothing but ginger-nuts. My mind then ran on in reveries concerning the probable effects upon the human constitution of living entirely on ginger-nuts. Ginger-nuts are so called because they contain ginger as one of their peculiar constituents, and the final flavoring one. Now what was ginger? A hot, spicy thing. Was Bartleby hot and spicy? Not at all. Ginger, then, had no effect upon Bartleby. Probably he preferred it should have none.

Nothing so aggravates an earnest person as a passive resistance. If the individual so resisted be of a not inhumane temper, and the resisting one perfectly harmless in his passivity; then, in the better moods of the former, he will endeavor charitably to construe to his imagination what proves impossible to be solved by his judgment. Even so, for the most part, I regarded Bartleby and his ways. Poor fellow! thought I, he means no mischief; it is plain he intends no insolence; his aspect sufficiently evinces that his eccentricities are involuntary. He is useful to me. I can get along with him. If I turn him away, the chances are he will fall in with some less indulgent employer, and then he will be rudely treated, and perhaps driven forth miserably to starve. Yes. Here I can cheaply purchase a delicious self-approval. To befriend Bartleby; to humor him in his strange wilfulness, will cost me little or nothing, while I lay up in my Soul what will eventually prove a sweet morsel for my conscience. But his mood was not invariable with me. The passiveness of Bartleby sometimes irritated me. I felt strangely goaded on to encounter him in new opposition, to elicit some angry spark from him answerable to my own. But indeed I might as well have essayed to strike fire with my knuckles against a bit of Windsor soap. But one afternoon the evil impulse in me mastered me, and the following little scene ensued:

"Bartleby," said I, "when those papers are all copied, I will compare them with you."

"I would prefer not to."

"How? Surely you do not mean to persist in that mulish vagary?"

No answer.

I threw open the folding-doors near by, and turning upon Turkey and Nippers, exclaimed:

"Bartleby a second time says, he won't examine his papers. What do you think of it, Turkey?"

It was afternoon, be it remembered. Turkey sat glowing like a brass boiler, his bald head steaming, his hands reeling among his blotted papers.

"Think of it?" roared Turkey; "I think I'll just step behind his screen, and black his eyes for him!"

So saying, Turkey rose to his feet and threw his arms into a pugilistic position. He was hurrying away to make good his promise, when I detained him, alarmed at the effect of incautiously rousing Turkey's combativeness after dinner.

"Sit down, Turkey," said I, "and hear what Nippers has to say. What do you think of it, Nippers? Would I not be justified in immediately dismissing Bartleby?"

"Excuse me, that is for you to decide, sir. I think his conduct quite unusual, and indeed unjust, as regards Turkey and myself. But it may only be a passing whim."

"Ah," exclaimed I, "you have strangely changed your mind then—you speak very gently of him now."

"All beer," cried Turkey; "gentleness is effects of beer—Nippers and I dined together to-day. You see how gentle *I* am, sir. Shall I go and black his eyes?"

"You refer to Bartleby, I suppose. No, not to-day, Turkey," I replied; "pray, put up your fists."

I closed the doors, and again advanced towards Bartleby. I felt additional incentives tempting me to my fate. I burned to be rebelled against again. I remembered that Bartleby never left the office.

"Bartleby," said I, "Ginger Nut is away; just step round to the Post Office, won't you? (it was but a three minutes walk,) and see if there is any thing for me."

"I would prefer not to."

"You *will* not?"

"I *prefer* not."

I staggered to my desk, and sat there in a deep study. My blind inveteracy returned. Was there any other thing in which I could procure myself to be ignominiously repulsed by this lean, penniless wight?—my hired clerk? What added thing is there, perfectly reasonable, that he will be sure to refuse to do?

"Bartleby!"

No answer.

"Bartleby," in a louder tone.

No answer.

"Bartleby," I roared.

Like a very ghost, agreeably to the laws of magical invocation, at the third summons, he appeared at the entrance of his hermitage.

"Go to the next room, and tell Nippers to come to me."

"I prefer not to," he respectfully and slowly said, and mildly disappeared.

"Very good, Bartleby," said I, in a quiet sort of serenely severe self-possessed tone, intimating the unalterable purpose of some terrible retribution very close at hand. At the moment I half intended something of the kind. But upon the whole, as it was drawing towards my dinner-hour, I thought it best to put on my hat and walk home for the day, suffering much from perplexity and distress of mind.

Shall I acknowledge it? The conclusion of this whole business was, that it soon became a fixed fact of my chambers, that a pale young scrivener, by the name of Bartleby, had a desk there; that he copied for me at the usual rate of four cents a folio (one hundred words); but he was permanently exempt from examining the work done by him, that duty being transferred to Turkey and Nippers, out of compliment doubtless to their superior acuteness; moreover, said Bartleby was never on any account to be dispatched on the most trivial errand of any sort; and that even if entreated to take upon him such a matter, it was generally understood that he would prefer not to—in other words, that he would refuse point-blank.

As days passed on, I became considerably reconciled to Bartleby. His steadiness, his freedom from all dissipation, his incessant industry (except when he chose to throw himself into a standing revery behind his screen), his great stillness, his unalterableness of demeanor under all circumstances, made him a valuable acquisition. One prime thing was this,—*he was always there;*—first in the morning, continually through the day, and the last at night. I had a singular confidence in his honesty. I felt my most precious papers perfectly safe in his hands. Sometimes to be sure I could not, for the very soul of me, avoid falling into sudden spasmodic passions with him. For it was exceeding difficult to bear in mind all the time those strange peculiarities, privileges, and unheard of exemptions, forming the tacit stipulations on Bartleby's part under which he remained in my office. Now and then, in the eagerness of dispatching pressing business, I would inadvertently summon Bartleby, in a short, rapid tone, to put his finger, say, on the incipient tie of a bit of red tape with which I was about compressing some papers. Of course, from behind the screen the usual answer, "I prefer not to," was sure to come; and then, how could a human creature with the common infirmities of our nature, refrain from bitterly exclaiming upon such perverseness—such unreasonableness. However, every added repulse of this sort which I received only tended to lessen the probability of my repeating the inadvertence.

Here it must be said, that according to the custom of most legal gentlemen occupying chambers in densely-populated law buildings, there were several keys to my door. One was kept by a woman residing in the attic, which person weekly scrubbed and daily swept and dusted my apartments. Another was kept by Turkey for convenience sake. The third I sometimes carried in my own pocket. The fourth I knew not who had.

Now, one Sunday morning I happened to go to Trinity Church, to hear a celebrated preacher, and finding myself rather early on the ground, I thought I would walk round to my chambers for a while. Luckily I had my key with me; but upon applying it to the lock, I found it resisted by something inserted from the inside. Quite surprised, I called out; when to my consternation a key was turned from within; and thrusting his lean visage at me, and holding the door ajar, the apparition of Bartleby appeared, in his shirt sleeves, and otherwise in a strangely tattered dishabille, saying quietly that he was sorry, but he was deeply engaged just then, and—preferred not admitting me at present. In a brief word or two, he moreover added, that perhaps I had better walk round the block two or three times, and by that time he would probably have concluded his affairs.

Now, the utterly unsurmised appearance of Bartleby, tenanting my law-chambers of a Sunday morning, with his cadaverously gentlemanly *nonchalance*, yet withal firm and self-possessed, had such a strange effect upon me, that incontinently I slunk away from my own door, and did as desired. But not without sundry twinges of impotent rebellion against the mild effrontery of this unaccountable scrivener. Indeed, it was his wonderful mildness chiefly, which not only disarmed me, but unmanned me, as it were. For I consider that one, for the time, is a sort of unmanned when he tranquilly permits his hired clerk to dictate to him, and order him away from his own premises. Furthermore, I was full of uneasiness as to what Bartleby could possibly be doing in my office in his shirt sleeves, and in an otherwise dismantled condition of a Sunday morning. Was any thing amiss going on? Nay, that was out of the question. It was not to be thought of for a moment that Bartleby was an immoral person. But what could he be doing there?—copying? Nay again, whatever might be his eccentricities, Bartleby was an eminently decorous person. He would be the last man to sit down to his desk in any state approaching to nudity. Besides, it was Sunday; and there was something about Bartleby that forbade the supposition that he would by any secular occupation violate the proprieties of the day.

Nevertheless, my mind was not pacified; and full of a restless curiosity, at last I returned to the door. Without hindrance I inserted my key, opened it, and entered. Bartleby was not to be seen. I looked round anxiously, peeped behind his screen; but it was very plain that he was gone. Upon more closely examining the place, I surmised that for an indefinite period Bartleby must have ate, dressed, and slept in my office, and that too without plate, mirror, or bed. The cushioned seat of a ricketty old sofa in one corner bore the faint impress of a lean, reclining form. Rolled away under his desk, I found a blanket; under the empty grate, a blacking box and brush; on a chair, a tin basin, with soap and a ragged towel; in a newspaper a few crumbs of ginger-nuts and a morsel of cheese. Yes, thought I, it is evident enough that Bartleby has been making his home here, keeping bachelor's hall all by himself. Immediately then the thought came sweeping across me, What miserable friendlessness and loneliness are here revealed! His poverty is great; but his solitude, how horrible! Think of it. Of a Sunday, Wall-street is deserted as Petra; and every night of every day it is an emptiness. This building too, which of week-days hums with industry and life, at nightfall echoes with sheer vacancy, and all through Sunday is forlorn. And here Bartleby makes his home; sole spectator of a solitude which he has seen all populous—a sort of innocent and transformed Marius brooding among the ruins of Carthage!

For the first time in my life a feeling of overpowering stinging melancholy seized me. Before, I had never experienced aught but a not-unpleasing sadness. The bond of a common humanity now drew me irresistibly to gloom. A fraternal melancholy! For both I and Bartleby were sons of Adam. I remembered the bright silks and sparkling faces I had seen that day, in gala trim, swan-like sailing down the Mississippi of Broadway; and I contrasted them with the pallid copyist, and thought to myself, Ah, happiness courts the light, so we deem the world is gay; but misery hides aloof, so we deem that misery there is none. These sad fancyings—chimeras, doubtless, of a sick and silly brain—led on to other and more special thoughts, concerning the eccentricities of Bartleby. Presentiments of strange discoveries hovered round me. The scrivener's pale form appeared to me laid out, among uncaring strangers, in its shivering winding sheet.

Suddenly I was attracted by Bartleby's closed desk, the key in open sight left in the lock.

I mean no mischief, seek the gratification of no heartless curiosity, thought I; besides, the desk is mine, and its contents too, so I will make bold to look within. Every thing was methodically arranged, the papers smoothly placed. The pigeon holes were deep, and removing the files of documents, I groped into their recesses. Presently I felt something there, and dragged it out. It was an old bandanna handkerchief, heavy and knotted. I opened it, and saw it was a savings' bank.

I now recalled all the quiet mysteries which I had noted in the man. I remembered that he never spoke but to answer; that though at intervals he had considerable time to himself, yet I had never seen him reading—no, not even a newspaper; that for long periods he would stand looking out, at his pale window behind the screen, upon the dead brick wall; I was quite sure he never visited any refectory or eating house; while his pale face clearly indicated that he never drank beer like Turkey, or tea and coffee even, like other men; that he never went any where in particular that I could learn; never went out for a walk, unless indeed that was the case at present; that he had declined telling who he was, or whence he came, or whether he had any relatives in the world; that though so thin and pale, he never complained of ill health. And more than all, I remembered a certain unconscious air of pallid—how shall I call it?—of pallid haughtiness, say, or rather an austere reserve about him, which had positively awed me into my tame compliance with his eccentricities, when I had feared to ask him to do the slightest incidental thing for me, even though I might know, from his long-continued motionlessness, that behind his screen he must be standing in one of those dead-wall reveries of his.

Revolving all these things, and coupling them with the recently discovered fact that he made my office his constant abiding place and home, and not forgetful of his morbid moodiness; revolving all these things, a prudential feeling began to steal over me. My first emotions had been those of pure melancholy and sincerest pity; but just in proportion as the forlornness of Bartleby grew and grew to my imagination, did that same melancholy merge into fear, that pity into repulsion. So true it is, and so terrible too, that up to a certain point the thought or sight of misery enlists our best affections; but, in certain special cases, beyond that point it does not. They err who would assert that invariably this is owing to the inherent selfishness of the human heart. It rather proceeds from a certain hopelessness of remedying excessive and organic ill. To a sensitive being, pity is not seldom pain. And when at last it is perceived that such pity cannot lead to effectual succor, common sense bids the soul be rid of it. What I saw that morning persuaded me that the scrivener was the victim of innate and incurable disorder. I might give alms to his body; but his body did not pain him; it was his soul that suffered, and his soul I could not reach.

I did not accomplish the purpose of going to Trinity Church that morning. Somehow, the things I had seen disqualified me for the time from church-going. I walked homeward, thinking what I would do with Bartleby. Finally, I resolved upon this;—I would put certain calm questions to him the next morning, touching his history, &c., and if he declined to answer them openly and unreservedly (and I supposed he would prefer not), then to give him a twenty dollar bill over and above whatever I might owe him, and tell him his services were no longer required; but that if in any other way I could assist him, I would be happy to do so, especially if he desired to return to his native place, wherever that might be, I would willingly help to defray the expenses. Moreover, if, after reaching home, he found himself at any time in want of aid, a letter from him would be sure of a reply.

The next morning came.

"Bartleby," said I, gently calling to him behind his screen.

No reply.

"Bartleby," said I, in a still gentler tone, "come here; I am not going to ask you to do any thing you would prefer not to do—I simply wish to speak to you."

Upon this he noiselessly slid into view.

"Will you tell me, Bartleby, where you were born?"

"I would prefer not to."

"Will you tell me *any thing* about yourself?"

"I would prefer not to."

"But what reasonable objection can you have to speak to me? I feel friendly towards you."

He did not look at me while I spoke, but kept his glance fixed upon my bust of Cicero, which as I then sat, was directly behind me, some six inches above my head.

"What is your answer, Bartleby?" said I, after waiting a considerable time for a reply, during which his countenance remained immovable, only there was the faintest conceivable tremor of the white attenuated mouth.

"At present I prefer to give no answer," he said, and retired into his hermitage.

It was rather weak in me I confess, but his manner on this occasion nettled me. Not only did there seem to lurk in it a certain calm disdain, but his perverseness seemed ungrateful, considering the undeniable good usage and indulgence he had received from me.

Again I sat ruminating what I should do. Mortified as I was at his behavior, and resolved as I had been to dismiss him when I entered my office, nevertheless I strangely felt something superstitious knocking at my heart, and forbidding me to carry out my purpose, and denouncing me for a villain if I dared to breathe one bitter word against this forlornest of mankind. At last, familiarly drawing my chair behind his screen, I sat down and said: "Bartleby, never mind then about revealing your history; but let me entreat you, as a friend, to comply as far as may be with the usages of this office. Say now you will help to examine papers tomorrow or next day: in short, say now that in a day or two you will begin to be a little reasonable:—say so, Bartleby."

"At present I would prefer not to be a little reasonable," was his mildly cadaverous reply.

Just then the folding-doors opened, and Nippers approached. He seemed suffering from an unusually bad night's rest, induced by severer indigestion than common. He overheard those final words of Bartleby.

"*Prefer not*, eh?" gritted Nippers—"I'd *prefer* him, if I were you, sir," addressing me—"I'd *prefer* him; I'd give him preferences, the stubborn mule! What is it, sir, pray, that he *prefers* not to do now?"

Bartleby moved not a limb.

"Mr. Nippers," said I, "I'd prefer that you would withdraw for the present."

Somehow, of late I had got into the way of involuntarily using this word "prefer" upon all sorts of not exactly suitable occasions. And I trembled to think that my contact with the scrivener had already and seriously affected me in a mental way. And what further and deeper aberration might it not yet produce? This apprehension had not been without efficacy in determining me to summary measures.

As Nippers, looking very sour and sulky, was departing, Turkey blandly and deferentially approached.

"With submission, sir," said he, "yesterday I was thinking about Bartleby here, and I think that if he would but prefer to take a quart of good ale every day, it would do much towards mending him, and enabling him to assist in examining his papers."

"So you have got the word too," said I, slightly excited.

"With submission, what word, sir," asked Turkey, respectfully crowding himself into the contracted space behind the screen, and by so doing, making me jostle the scrivener. "What word, sir?"

"I would prefer to be left alone here," said Bartleby, as if offended at being mobbed in his privacy.

"*That's* the word, Turkey," said I—"*that's* it."

"Oh, *prefer*? oh yes—queer word. I never use it myself. But, sir, as I was saying, if he would but prefer—"

"Turkey," interrupted I, "you will please withdraw."

"Oh certainly, sir, if you prefer that I should."

As he opened the folding-doors to retire, Nippers at his desk caught a glimpse of me, and asked whether I would prefer to have a certain paper copied on blue paper or white. He did not in the least roguishly accent the word *prefer*. It was plain that it involuntarily rolled from his tongue. I thought to myself, surely I must get rid of a demented man, who already has in some degree turned the tongues, if not the heads of myself and clerks. But I thought it prudent not to break the dismission at once.

The next day I noticed that Bartleby did nothing but stand at his window in his dead-wall revery. Upon asking him why he did not write, he said that he had decided upon doing no more writing.

"Why, how now? what next?" exclaimed I, "do no more writing?"

"No more."

"And what is the reason?"

"Do you not see the reason for yourself," he indifferently replied.

I looked steadfastly at him, and perceived that his eyes looked dull and glazed. Instantly it occurred to me, that his unexampled diligence in copying by his dim window for the first few weeks of his stay with me might have temporarily impaired his vision.

I was touched. I said something in condolence with him. I hinted that of course he did wisely in abstaining from writing for a while; and urged him to embrace that opportunity of taking wholesome exercise in the open air. This, however, he did not do. A few days after this, my other clerks being absent, and being in a great hurry to dispatch certain letters by the mail, I thought that, having nothing else earthly to do, Bartleby would surely be less inflexible than usual, and carry these letters to the post-office. But he blankly declined. So, much to my inconvenience, I went myself.

Still added days went by. Whether Bartleby's eyes improved or not, I could not say. To all appearance, I thought they did. But when I asked him if they did, he vouchsafed no answer. At all events, he would do no copying. At last, in reply to my urgings, he informed me that he had permanently given up copying.

"What!" exclaimed I; "suppose your eyes should get entirely well—better than ever before—would you not copy then?"

"I have given up copying," he answered, and slid aside.

He remained as ever, a fixture in my chamber. Nay—if that were possible—he became still more of a fixture than before. What was to be done? He would do nothing in the office: why should he stay there? In plain fact, he had now become a millstone to me, not only useless as a necklace, but afflictive to bear. Yet I was sorry for him. I speak less than truth when I say that, on his own account, he occasioned me uneasiness. If he would but have named a single relative or friend, I would instantly have written, and urged their taking the poor fellow away to some convenient retreat. But he seemed alone, absolutely alone in the universe. A bit of wreck in the mid Atlantic. At length, necessities connected with my business tyrannized over all other considerations. Decently as I could, I told Bartleby that in six days' time he must unconditionally leave the office. I warned him to take measures, in the interval, for procuring some other abode. I offered to assist him in this endeavor, if he himself would but take the first step towards a removal. "And when you finally quit me, Bartleby," added I, "I shall see that you go not away entirely unprovided. Six days from this hour, remember."

At the expiration of that period, I peeped behind the screen, and lo! Bartleby was there.

I buttoned up my coat, balanced myself; advanced slowly towards him, touched his shoulder, and said, "The time has come; you must quit this place; I am sorry for you; here is money; but you must go."

"I would prefer not," he replied, with his back still towards me.

"You *must*."

He remained silent.

Now I had an unbounded confidence in this man's common honesty. He had frequently restored to me sixpences and shillings carelessly dropped upon the floor, for I am apt to be very reckless in such shirt-button affairs. The proceeding then which followed will not be deemed extraordinary.

"Bartleby," said I, "I owe you twelve dollars on account; here are thirty-two; the odd twenty are yours.—Will you take it?" and I handed the bills towards him.

But he made no motion.

"I will leave them here then," putting them under a weight on the table. Then taking my hat and cane and going to the door I tranquilly turned and added—"After you have removed your things from these offices, Bartleby, you will of course lock the door—since every one is now gone for the day but you—and if you please, slip your key underneath the mat, so that I may have it in the morning. I shall not see you again; so good-bye to you. If hereafter in your new place of abode I can be of any service to you, do not fail to advise me by letter. Good-bye, Bartleby, and fare you well."

But he answered not a word; like the last column of some ruined temple, he remained standing mute and solitary in the middle of the otherwise deserted room.

As I walked home in a pensive mood, my vanity got the better of my pity. I could not but highly plume myself on my masterly management in getting rid of Bartleby. Masterly I call it, and such it must appear to any dispassionate thinker. The beauty of my procedure seemed to consist in its perfect quietness. There was no vulgar bullying, no bravado of any sort, no choleric hectoring, and striding to and fro across the apartment jerking out vehement commands for Bartleby to bundle himself off with his beggarly traps. Nothing of the kind. Without loudly bidding Bartleby depart—as an inferior genius might have done—I *assumed* the ground that depart he must; and upon that assumption built all I had to say. The more I thought over my procedure, the more I was charmed with it. Nevertheless, next morning, upon awakening, I had my doubts,—I had somehow slept off the fumes of vanity. One of the coolest and wisest hours a man has, is just after he awakes in the morning. My procedure seemed as sagacious as ever,—but only in theory. How it would prove in practice—there was the rub. It was truly a beautiful thought to have assumed Bartleby's departure; but, after all, that assumption was simply my own, and none of Bartleby's. The great point was, not whether I had assumed that he would quit me, but whether he would prefer so to do. He was more a man of preferences than assumptions.

After breakfast, I walked down town, arguing the probabilities *pro* and *con*. One moment I thought it would prove a miserable failure, and Bartleby would be found all alive at my office as usual; the next moment it seemed certain that I should find his chair empty. And so I kept veering about. At the corner of Broadway and Canal-street, I saw quite an excited group of people standing in earnest conversation.

"I'll take odds he doesn't," said a voice as I passed.

"Doesn't go?—done!" said I, "put up your money."

I was instinctively putting my hand in my pocket to produce my own, when I remembered that this was an election day. The words I had overheard bore no reference to Bartleby, but to the success or non-success of some candidate for the mayoralty. In my intent frame of mind, I had, as it were, imagined that all Broadway shared in my excitement, and were debating the same question with me. I passed on, very thankful that the uproar of the street screened my momentary absent-mindedness.

As I had intended, I was earlier than usual at my office door. I stood listening for a moment. All was still. He must be gone. I tried the knob. The door was locked. Yes, my procedure had worked to a charm; he indeed must be vanished. Yet a certain melancholy mixed with this; I was almost sorry for my brilliant success. I was fumbling under the door mat for the key, which Bartleby was to have left there for me, when accidentally my knee knocked against a panel, producing a summoning sound, and in response a voice came to me from within—"Not yet; I am occupied."

It was Bartleby.

I was thunderstruck. For an instant I stood like the man who, pipe in mouth, was killed one cloudless afternoon long ago in Virginia, by summer lightning; at his own warm open window he was killed, and remained leaning out there upon the dreamy afternoon, till some one touched him, when he fell.

"Not gone!" I murmured at last. But again obeying that wondrous ascendancy which the inscrutable scrivener had over me, and from which ascendancy, for all my chafing, I could not completely escape, I slowly went down stairs and out into the street, and while walking round the block, considered what I should next do in this unheard-of perplexity. Turn the man out by an actual thrusting I could not; to drive him away by calling him hard names would not do; calling in the police was an unpleasant idea; and yet, permit him to enjoy his cadaverous triumph over me,—this too I could not think of. What was to be done? or, if nothing could be done, was there any thing further that I could *assume* in the matter? Yes, as before I had prospectively assumed that Bartleby would depart, so now I might retrospectively assume that departed he was. In the legitimate carrying out of this assumption, I might enter my office in a great hurry, and pretending not to see Bartleby at all, walk straight against him as if he were air. Such a proceeding would in a singular degree have the appearance of a home-thrust. It was hardly possible that Bartleby could withstand such an application of the doctrine of assumptions. But upon second thoughts the success of the plan seemed rather dubious. I resolved to argue the matter over with him again.

"Bartleby," said I, entering the office, with a quietly severe expression, "I am seriously displeased. I am pained, Bartleby. I had thought better of you. I had imagined you of such a gentlemanly organization, that in any delicate dilemma a slight hint would suffice—in short, an assumption. But it appears I am deceived. Why,"

I added, unaffectedly starting, "you have not even touched that money yet," pointing to it, just where I had left it the evening previous.

He answered nothing.

"Will you, or will you not, quit me?" I now demanded in a sudden passion, advancing close to him.

"I would prefer *not* to quit you," he replied, gently emphasizing the *not.*

"What earthly right have you to stay here? Do you pay any rent? Do you pay my taxes? Or is this property yours?"

He answered nothing.

"Are you ready to go on and write now? Are your eyes recovered? Could you copy a small paper for me this morning? or help examine a few lines? or step round to the post-office? In a word, will you do any thing at all, to give a coloring to your refusal to depart the premises?"

He silently retired into his hermitage.

I was now in such a state of nervous resentment that I thought it but prudent to check myself at present from further demonstrations. Bartleby and I were alone. I remembered the tragedy of the unfortunate Adams and the still more unfortunate Colt in the solitary office of the latter; and how poor Colt, being dreadfully incensed by Adams, and imprudently permitting himself to get wildly excited, was at unawares hurried into his fatal act—an act which certainly no man could possibly deplore more than the actor himself. Often it had occurred to me in my ponderings upon the subject, that had that altercation taken place in the public street, or at a private residence, it would not have terminated as it did. It was the circumstance of being alone in a solitary office, up stairs, of a building entirely unhallowed by humanizing domestic associations—an uncarpeted office, doubtless, of a dusty, haggard sort of appearance;—this it must have been, which greatly helped to enhance the irritable desperation of the hapless Colt.

But when this old Adam of resentment rose in me and tempted me concerning Bartleby, I grappled him and threw him. How? Why, simply by recalling the divine injunction: "A new commandment give I unto you, that ye love one another." Yes, this it was that saved me. Aside from higher considerations, charity often operates as a vastly wise and prudent principle—a great safeguard to its possessor. Men have committed murder for jealousy's sake, and anger's sake, and hatred's sake, and selfishness' sake, and spiritual pride's sake; but no man that ever I heard of, ever committed a diabolical murder for sweet charity's sake. Mere self-interest, then, if no better motive can be enlisted, should, especially with high-tempered men, prompt all beings to charity and philanthropy. At any rate, upon the occasion in question, I strove to drown my exasperated feelings towards the scrivener by benevolently construing his conduct. Poor fellow, poor fellow! thought I, he don't mean any thing; and besides, he has seen hard times, and ought to be indulged.

I endeavored also immediately to occupy myself, and at the same time to comfort my despondency. I tried to fancy that in the course of the morning, at such time as might prove agreeable to him, Bartleby, of his own free accord, would emerge from his hermitage, and take up some decided line of march in the direction of the door. But no. Half-past twelve o'clock came; Turkey began to glow in the face, overturn his inkstand, and become generally obstreperous; Nippers abated down into quietude and courtesy; Ginger Nut munched his noon apple; and Bartleby remained standing at his window in one of his profoundest dead-wall reveries. Will it be credited? Ought I to acknowledge it? That afternoon I left the office without saying one further word to him.

Some days now passed, during which, at leisure intervals I looked a little into "Edwards on the Will," and "Priestley on Necessity." Under the circumstances, those books induced a salutary feeling. Gradually I slid into the persuasion that these troubles of mine touching the scrivener, had been all predestinated from eternity, and Bartleby was billeted upon me for some mysterious purpose of an all-wise Providence, which it was not for a mere mortal like me to fathom. Yes, Bartleby, stay there behind your screen, thought I; I shall persecute you no more; you are harmless and noiseless as any of these old chairs; in short, I never feel so private as when I know you are here. At last I see it, I feel it; I penetrate to the predestinated purpose of my life. I am content. Others may have loftier parts to enact; but my mission in this world, Bartleby, is to furnish you with office-room for such period as you may see fit to remain.

I believe that this wise and blessed frame of mind would have continued with me, had it not been for the unsolicited and uncharitable remarks obtruded upon me by my professional friends who visited the rooms. But thus it often is, that the constant friction of illiberal minds wears out at last the best resolves of the more generous. Though to be sure, when I reflected upon it, it was not strange that people entering my office should be struck by the peculiar aspect of the unaccountable Bartleby, and so be tempted to throw out some sinister observations concerning him. Sometimes an attorney having business with me, and calling at my office, and finding no one but the scrivener there, would undertake to obtain some sort of precise information from him touching my whereabouts; but without heeding his idle talk, Bartleby would remain standing immovable in the middle of the room. So after contemplating him in that position for a time, the attorney would depart, no wiser than he came.

Also, when a Reference was going on, and the room full of lawyers and witnesses and business was driving fast; some deeply occupied legal gentleman present, seeing Bartleby wholly unemployed, would request him to run round to his (the legal gentleman's) office and fetch some papers for him. Thereupon, Bartleby would tranquilly decline, and yet remain idle as before. Then the lawyer would give a great stare, and turn to me. And what could I say? At last I was made aware that all through the circle of my professional acquaintance, a whisper of wonder was running round, having reference to the strange creature I kept at my office. This worried me very much. And as the idea came upon me of his possibly turning out a long-lived man, and keep occupying my chambers, and denying my authority; and perplexing my visitors; and scandalizing my professional reputation; and casting a general gloom over the premises; keeping soul and body together to the last upon his savings (for doubtless he spent but a half a dime a day), and in the end perhaps outlive me, and claim possession of my office by right of his perpetual occupancy: as all these dark anticipations crowded upon me more and more, and my friends continually intruded their relentless remarks upon the apparition in my room; a great change was wrought in me. I resolved to gather all my faculties together, and for ever rid me of this intolerable incubus.

Ere revolving any complicated project, however, adapted to this end, I first simply suggested to Bartleby the propriety of his permanent departure. In a calm and serious tone, I commended the idea to his careful and mature consideration. But having taken three days to meditate upon it, he apprised me that his original determination remained the same; in short, that he still preferred to abide with me.

What shall I do? I now said to myself, buttoning up my coat to the last button. What shall I do? what ought I to do? what does conscience say I *should* do with this man, or rather ghost? Rid myself of him, I must, go, he shall. But how? You will not thrust him, the poor, pale, passive mortal,—you will not thrust such a helpless creature out of your door? you will not dishonor yourself by such cruelty? No, I will not, I cannot do that. Rather would I let him live and die here, and then mason up his remains in the wall. What then will you do? For all your coaxing, he will not budge. Bribes he leaves under your own paper-weight on your table; in short, it is quite plain that he prefers to cling to you.

Then something severe, something unusual must be done. What! surely you will not have him collared by a constable, and commit his innocent pallor to the common jail? And upon what ground could you procure such a thing to be done?—a vagrant, is he? What! he a vagrant, a wanderer, who refuses to budge? It is because he will *not* be a vagrant, then, that you seek to count him *as* a vagrant. That is too absurd. No visible means of support: there I have him. Wrong again: for indubitably he *does* support himself, and that is the only unanswerable proof that any man can show of his possessing the means so to do. No more then. Since he will not quit me, I must quit him. I will change my offices; I will move elsewhere; and give him fair notice, that if I find him on my new premises I will then proceed against him as a common trespasser.

Acting accordingly, next day I thus addressed him: "I find these chambers too far from the City Hall; the air is unwholesome. In a word, I propose to remove my offices next week, and shall no longer require your services. I tell you this now, in order that you may seek another place."

He made no reply, and nothing more was said.

On the appointed day I engaged carts and men, proceeded to my chambers, and having but little furniture, every thing was removed in a few hours. Throughout, the scrivener remained standing behind the screen, which I directed to be removed the last thing. It was withdrawn; and being folded up like a huge folio, left him the motionless occupant of a naked room. I stood in the entry watching him a moment, while something from within me upbraided me.

I re-entered, with my hand in my pocket—and—and my heart in my mouth.

"Good-bye, Bartleby; I am going—good-bye, and God some way bless you; and take that," slipping something in his hand. But it dropped upon the floor, and then,—strange to say—I tore myself from him whom I had so longed to be rid of.

Established in my new quarters, for a day or two I kept the door locked, and started at every footfall in the passages. When I returned to my rooms after any little absence, I would pause at the threshold for an instant, and attentively listen, ere applying my key. But these fears were needless. Bartleby never came nigh me.

I thought all was going well, when a perturbed looking stranger visited me, inquiring whether I was the person who had recently occupied rooms at No. — Wall-street.

Full of forebodings, I replied that I was.

"Then sir," said the stranger, who proved a lawyer, "you are responsible for the man you left there. He refuses to do any copying; he refuses to do any thing; he says he prefers not to; and he refuses to quit the premises."

"I am very sorry, sir," said I, with assumed tranquillity, but an inward tremor, "but, really, the man you allude to is nothing to me—he is no relation or apprentice of mine, that you should hold me responsible for him."

"In mercy's name, who is he?"

"I certainly cannot inform you. I know nothing about him. Formerly I employed him as a copyist; but he has done nothing for me now for some time past."

"I shall settle him then,—good morning, sir."

Several days passed, and I heard nothing more; and though I often felt a charitable prompting to call at the place and see poor Bartleby, yet a certain squeamishness of I know not what withheld me.

All is over with him, by this time, thought I at last, when through another week no further intelligence reached me. But coming to my room the day after, I found several persons waiting at my door in a high state of nervous excitement.

"That's the man—here he comes," cried the foremost one, whom I recognized as the lawyer who had previously called upon me alone.

"You must take him away, sir, at once," cried a portly person among them, advancing upon me, and whom I knew to be the landlord of No. — Wall-street. "These gentlemen, my tenants, cannot stand it any longer; Mr. B——" pointing to the lawyer, "has turned him out of his room, and he now persists in haunting the building generally, sitting upon the banisters of the stairs by day, and sleeping in the entry by night. Every body is concerned; clients are leaving the offices; some fears are entertained of a mob; something you must do, and that without delay."

Aghast at this torrent, I fell back before it, and would fain have locked myself in my new quarters. In vain I persisted that Bartleby was nothing to me—no more than to any one else. In vain:—I was the last person known to have any thing to do with him, and they held me to the terrible account. Fearful then of being exposed in the papers (as one person present obscurely threatened) I considered the matter, and at length said, that if the lawyer would give me a confidential interview with the scrivener, in his (the lawyer's) own room, I would that afternoon strive my best to rid them of the nuisance they complained of.

Going up stairs to my old haunt, there was Bartleby silently sitting upon the banister at the landing.

"What are you doing here, Bartleby?" said I.

"Sitting upon the banister," he mildly replied.

I motioned him into the lawyer's room, who then left us.

"Bartleby," said I, "are you aware that you are the cause of great tribulation to me, by persisting in occupying the entry after being dismissed from the office?"

No answer.

"Now one of two things must take place. Either you must do something, or something must be done to you. Now what sort of business would you like to engage in? Would you like to re-engage in copying for some one?"

"No; I would prefer not to make any change."

"Would you like a clerkship in a dry-goods store?"

"There is too much confinement about that. No, I would not like a clerkship; but I am not particular."

"Too much confinement," I cried, "why you keep yourself confined all the time!"

"I would prefer not to take a clerkship," he rejoined, as if to settle that little item at once.

"How would a bar-tender's business suit you? There is no trying of the eyesight in that."

"I would not like it at all; though, as I said before, I am not particular."

His unwonted wordiness inspirited me. I returned to the charge.

"Well then, would you like to travel through the country collecting bills for the merchants? That would improve your health."

"No, I would prefer to be doing something else."

"How then would going as a companion to Europe, to entertain some young gentleman with your conversation,—how would that suit you?"

"Not at all. It does not strike me that there is any thing definite about that. I like to be stationary. But I am not particular."

"Stationary you shall be then," I cried, now losing all patience, and for the first time in all my exasperating connection with him fairly flying into a passion. "If you do not go away from these premises before night, I shall feel bound—indeed I *am* bound—to—to—to quit the premises myself!" I rather absurdly concluded, knowing not with what possible threat to try to frighten his immobility into compliance. Despairing of all further efforts, I was precipitately leaving him, when a final thought occurred to me—one which had not been wholly unindulged before.

"Bartleby," said I, in the kindest tone I could assume under such exciting circumstances, "will you go home with me now—not to my office, but my dwelling—and remain there till we can conclude upon some convenient arrangement for you at our leisure? Come, let us start now, right away."

"No: at present I would prefer not to make any change at all."

I answered nothing; but effectually dodging every one by the suddenness and rapidity of my flight, rushed from the building, ran up Wall-street towards Broadway, and jumping into the first omnibus was soon removed from pursuit. As soon as tranquillity returned I distinctly perceived that I had now done all that I possibly could, both in respect to the demands of the landlord and his tenants, and with regard to my own desire and sense of duty, to benefit Bartleby, and shield him from rude persecution. I now strove to be entirely care-free and quiescent; and my conscience justified me in the attempt; though indeed it was not so successful as I could have wished. So fearful was I of being again hunted out by the incensed landlord and his exasperated tenants, that, surrendering my business to Nippers, for a few days I drove about the upper part of the town and through the suburbs, in my rockaway; crossed over to Jersey City and Hoboken, and paid fugitive visits to Manhattanville and Astoria. In fact I almost lived in my rockaway for the time.

When again I entered my office, lo, a note from the landlord lay upon the desk. I opened it with trembling hands. It informed me that the writer had sent to the police, and had Bartleby removed to the Tombs as a vagrant. Moreover, since I knew more about him than any one else, he wished me to appear at that place, and make a suitable statement of the facts. These tidings had a conflicting effect upon me. At first I was indignant; but at last almost approved. The landlord's energetic, summary disposition, had led him to adopt a procedure which I do not think I would have decided upon myself; and yet as a last resort, under such peculiar circumstances, it seemed the only plan.

As I afterwards learned, the poor scrivener, when told that he must be conducted to the Tombs, offered not the slightest obstacle, but in his pale unmoving way, silently acquiesced.

Some of the compassionate and curious bystanders joined the party; and headed by one of the constables arm in arm with Bartleby, the silent procession filed its way through all the noise, and heat, and joy of the roaring thoroughfares at noon.

The same day I received the note I went to the Tombs, or to speak more properly, the Halls of Justice. Seeking the right officer, I stated the purpose of my call, and was informed that the individual I described was indeed within. I then assured the functionary that Bartleby was a perfectly honest man, and greatly to be compassionated, however unaccountably eccentric. I narrated all I knew, and closed by suggesting the idea of letting him remain in as indulgent confinement as possible till something less harsh might be done—though indeed I hardly knew what. At all events, if nothing else could be decided upon, the alms-house must receive him. I then begged to have an interview.

Being under no disgraceful charge, and quite serene and harmless in all his ways, they had permitted him freely to wander about the prison, and especially in the inclosed grass-platted yards thereof. And so I found him there, standing all alone in the quietest of the yards, his face towards a high wall, while all around, from the narrow slits of the jail windows, I thought I saw peering out upon him the eyes of murderers and thieves.

"Bartleby!"

"I know you," he said, without looking round,—"and I want nothing to say to you."

"It was not I that brought you here, Bartleby," said I, keenly pained at his implied suspicion. "And to you, this should not be so vile a place. Nothing reproachful attaches to you by being here. And see, it is not so sad a place as one might think. Look, there is the sky, and here is the grass."

"I know where I am," he replied, but would say nothing more, and so I left him.

As I entered the corridor again, a broad meat-like man, in an apron, accosted me, and jerking his thumb over his shoulder said—"Is that your friend?"

"Yes."

"Does he want to starve? If he does, let him live on the prison fare, that's all."

"Who are you?" asked I, not knowing what to make of such an unofficially speaking person in such a place.

"I am the grub-man. Such gentlemen as have friends here, hire me to provide them with something good to eat."

"Is this so?" said I, turning to the turnkey.

He said it was.

"Well then," said I, slipping some silver into the grub-man's hands (for so they called him). "I want you to give particular attention to my friend there; let him have the best dinner you can get. And you must be as polite to him as possible."

"Introduce me, will you?" said the grub-man, looking at me with an expression which seemed to say he was all impatience for an opportunity to give a specimen of his breeding.

Thinking it would prove of benefit to the scrivener, I acquiesced; and asking the grub-man his name, went up with him to Bartleby.

"Bartleby, this is Mr. Cutlets; you will find him very useful to you."

"Your sarvant, sir, your sarvant," said the grub-man, making a low salutation behind his apron. "Hope you find it pleasant here, sir; nice grounds—cool apartments, sir—hope you'll stay with us some time—try to make it agreeable. May Mrs. Cutlets and I have the pleasure of your company to dinner, sir, in Mrs. Cutlets' private room?"

"I prefer not to dine to-day," said Bartleby, turning away. "It would disagree with me; I am unused to dinners." So saying he slowly moved to the other side of the inclosure, and took up a position fronting the dead-wall.

"How's this?" said the grub-man, addressing me with a stare of astonishment. "He's odd, aint he?"

"I think he is a little deranged," said I, sadly.

"Deranged? deranged is it? Well now, upon my word, I thought that friend of yourn was a gentleman forger; they are always pale and genteel-like, them forgers. I can't help pity 'em—can't help it, sir. Did you know Monroe Edwards?" he added touchingly, and paused. Then, laying his hand pityingly on my shoulder, sighed, "he died of consumption at Sing-Sing. So you weren't acquainted with Monroe?"

"No, I was never socially acquainted with any forgers. But I cannot stop longer. Look to my friend yonder. You will not lose by it. I will see you again."

Some few days after this, I again obtained admission to the Tombs, and went through the corridors in quest of Bartleby; but without finding him.

"I saw him coming from his cell not long ago," said a turnkey, "may be he's gone to loiter in the yards."

So I went in that direction.

"Are you looking for the silent man?" said another turnkey passing me. "Yonder he lies—sleeping in the yard there. 'Tis not twenty minutes since I saw him lie down."

The yard was entirely quiet. It was not accessible to the common prisoners. The surrounding walls, of amazing thickness, kept off all sounds behind them. The Egyptian character of the masonry weighed upon me with its gloom. But a soft imprisoned turf grew under foot. The heart of the eternal pyramids, it seemed, wherein, by some strange magic, through the clefts, grass-seed, dropped by birds, had sprung.

Strangely huddled at the base of the wall, his knees drawn up, and lying on his side, his head touching the cold stones, I saw the wasted Bartleby. But nothing stirred. I paused; then went close up to him; stooped over, and saw that his dim eyes were open; otherwise he seemed profoundly sleeping. Something prompted me to touch him. I felt his hand, when a tingling shiver ran up my arm and down my spine to my feet.

The round face of the grub-man peered upon me now. "His dinner is ready. Won't he dine to-day, either? Or does he live without dining?"

"Lives without dining," said I, and closed the eyes.

"Eh!—He's asleep, aint he?"

"With kings and counsellors," murmured I.

There would seem little need for proceeding further in this history. Imagination will readily supply the meagre recital of poor Bartleby's interment. But ere parting with the reader, let me say, that if this little narrative has sufficiently interested him, to awaken curiosity as to who Bartleby was, and what manner of life he led prior to the present narrator's making his acquaintance, I can only reply, that in such curiosity I fully share, but am wholly unable to gratify it. Yet here I hardly know whether I should divulge one little item of rumor, which came to my ear a few months after the scrivener's decease. Upon what basis it rested, I could never ascertain; and hence, how true it is I cannot now tell. But inasmuch as this vague report has not been without a certain strange suggestive interest to me, however sad, it may prove the same with some others; and so I will briefly mention it. The report was this: that Bartleby had been a subordinate clerk in the Dead Letter Office at Washington, from which he had been suddenly removed by a change in the administration. When I think over this rumor, hardly can I express the emotions which seize me. Dead letters! does it not sound like dead men? Conceive a man by nature and misfortune prone to a pallid hopelessness, can any business seem more fitted to heighten it than that of continually handling these dead letters, and assorting them for the flames? For by the cart-load they are annually burned. Sometimes from out the folded paper the pale clerk takes a ring:—the finger it was meant for, perhaps, moulders in the grave; a bank-note sent in swiftest charity:—he whom it would relieve, nor eats nor hungers any more; pardon for those who died despairing; hope for those who died unhoping; good tidings for those who died stifled by unrelieved calamities. On errands of life, these letters speed to death.

Ah Bartleby! Ah humanity!

1853

Joyce Carol Oates

b. 1938

One of Oates's inspirations for this story was a Life *magazine feature on the "Pied Piper of Tucson," a serial killer who seduced and murdered teenaged girls. What attracted Oates to the story was that a group of teenagers knew about the man, but the killer's inexplicable charm prevented them from telling anyone. She described her first draft of the story—which she called "Death and the Maiden—as "realistic allegory." In revision, Oates eliminated any "suggestion that 'Arnold Friend' has seduced and murdered other young girls, or even that he necessarily intends to murder Connie." Also gone was her original attraction to the story: a group of teenagers who knew what Friend was up to. What is left is a "shallow, vain, silly, hopeful, doomed" young girl who is capable, nonetheless, "of an unexpected gesture of heroism at the story's end. . . . We don't know the nature of her sacrifice," Oates says, "only that she is generous enough to make it."*

Where Are You Going, Where Have You Been?

for Bob Dylan[1]

Her name was Connie. She was fifteen and she had a quick, nervous giggling habit of craning her neck to glance into mirrors or checking other people's faces to make sure her own was all right. Her mother, who noticed everything and knew everything and who hadn't much reason any longer to look at her own face, always scolded Connie about it. "Stop gawking at yourself. Who are you? You think you're so pretty?" she would say. Connie would raise her eyebrows at these familiar old complaints and look right through her mother, into a shadowy vision of herself as she was right at that moment: she knew she was pretty and that was everything. Her mother had been pretty once too, if you could believe those old snapshots in the album, but now her looks were gone and that was why she was always after Connie.

"Why don't you keep your room clean like your sister? How've you got your hair fixed—what the hell stinks? Hair spray? You don't see your sister using that junk."

Her sister June was twenty-four and still lived at home. She was a secretary in the high school Connie attended, and if that wasn't bad enough—with her in the same building—she was so plain and chunky and steady that Connie had to hear her praised all the time by her mother and her mother's sisters. June did this, June did that, she saved money and helped clean the house and cooked and Connie couldn't do a thing, her mind was all filled with trashy daydreams. Their father was away at work most of the time and when he came home he wanted supper and he read the newspaper at supper and after supper he went to bed. He didn't bother talking much to them, but around his bent head Connie's mother kept picking at her until Connie wished her mother was dead and she herself was dead and it was all over. "She makes me want to throw up sometimes," she complained to her friends. She had a high, breathless,

1. Folk and rock singer and songwriter (1941–). Oates has said that the idea for this story came to her after listening to his song "It's All Over Now, Baby Blue."

amused voice that made everything she said sound a little forced, whether it was sincere or not.

There was one good thing: June went places with girl friends of hers, girls who were just as plain and steady as she, and so when Connie wanted to do that her mother had no objections. The father of Connie's best girl friend drove the girls the three miles to town and left them at a shopping plaza so they could walk through the stores or go to a movie, and when he came to pick them up again at eleven he never bothered to ask what they had done.

They must have been familiar sights, walking around the shopping plaza in their shorts and flat ballerina slippers that always scuffed the sidewalk, with charm bracelets jingling on their thin wrists; they would lean together to whisper and laugh secretly if someone passed who amused or interested them. Connie had long dark blond hair that drew anyone's eye to it, and she wore part of it pulled up on her head and puffed out and the rest of it she let fall down her back. She wore a pull-over jersey blouse that looked one way when she was at home and another way when she was away from home. Everything about her had two sides to it, one for home and one for anywhere that was not home: her walk, which could be childlike and bobbing, or languid enough to make anyone think she was hearing music in her head; her mouth, which was pale and smirking most of the time, but bright and pink on these evenings out; her laugh, which was cynical and drawling at home—"Ha, ha, very funny,"—but high-pitched and nervous anywhere else, like the jingling of the charms on her bracelet.

Sometimes they did go shopping or to a movie, but sometimes they went across the highway, ducking fast across the busy road, to a drive-in restaurant where older kids hung out. The restaurant was shaped like a big bottle, though squatter than a real bottle, and on its cap was a revolving figure of a grinning boy holding a hamburger aloft. One night in midsummer they ran across, breathless with daring, and right away someone leaned out a car window and invited them over, but it was just a boy from high school they didn't like. It made them feel good to be able to ignore him. They went up through the maze of parked and cruising cars to the bright-lit, fly-infested restaurant, their faces pleased and expectant as if they were entering a sacred building that loomed up out of the night to give them what haven and blessing they yearned for. They sat at the counter and crossed their legs at the ankles, their thin shoulders rigid with excitement, and listened to the music that made everything so good: the music was always in the background, like music at a church service; it was something to depend upon.

A boy named Eddie came in to talk with them. He sat backwards on his stool, turning himself jerkily around in semicircles and then stopping and turning back again, and after a while he asked Connie if she would like something to eat. She said she would and so she tapped her friend's arm on her way out—her friend pulled her face up into a brave, droll look—and Connie said she would meet her at eleven, across the way. "I just hate to leave her like that," Connie said earnestly, but the boy said that she wouldn't be alone for long. So they went out to his car, and on the way Connie couldn't help but let her eyes wander over the windshields and faces all around her, her face gleaming with a joy that had nothing to do with Eddie or even this place; it might have been the music. She drew her shoulders up and sucked in her breath with the pure pleasure of being alive, and just at that moment she happened to glance at a face just a few feet from hers. It was a boy with shaggy black hair, in a convertible jalopy painted gold. He stared at her and then his lips widened into a grin. Connie slit her eyes at him and turned away, but she couldn't help glancing back and there he was, still watching her. He wagged a finger and laughed and said, "Gonna get you, baby," and Connie turned away again without Eddie noticing anything.

She spent three hours with him, at the restaurant where they ate hamburgers and drank Cokes in wax cups that were always sweating, and then down an alley a mile or so away, and when he left her off at five to eleven only the movie house was still open at the plaza. Her girl friend was there, talking with a boy. When Connie came up, the two girls smiled at each other and Connie said, "How was the movie?" and the girl said, "*You* should know." They rode off with the girl's father, sleepy and pleased, and Connie couldn't help but look back at the darkened shopping plaza with its big empty parking lot and its signs that were faded and ghostly now, and over at the drive-in restaurant where cars were still circling tirelessly. She couldn't hear the music at this distance.

Next morning June asked her how the movie was and Connie said, "So-so."

She and that girl and occasionally another girl went out several times a week, and the rest of the time Connie spent around the house—it was summer vacation—getting in her mother's way and thinking, dreaming about the boys she met. But all the boys fell back and dissolved into a single face that was not even a face but an idea, a feeling, mixed up with the urgent insistent pounding of the music and the humid night air of July. Connie's mother kept dragging her back to the daylight by finding things for her to do or saying suddenly, "What's this about the Pettinger girl?"

And Connie would say nervously, "Oh, her. That dope." She always drew thick clear lines between herself and such girls, and her mother was simple and kind enough to believe it. Her mother was so simple, Connie thought, that it was maybe cruel to fool her so much. Her mother went scuffling around the house in old bedroom slippers and complained over the telephone to one sister about the other, then the other called up and the two of them complained about the third one. If June's name was mentioned her mother's tone was approving, and if Connie's name was mentioned it was disapproving. This did not really mean she disliked Connie, and actually Connie thought that her mother preferred her to June just because she was prettier, but the two of them kept up a pretense of exasperation, a sense that they were tugging and struggling over something of little value to either of them. Sometimes, over coffee, they were almost friends, but something would come up—some vexation that was like a fly buzzing suddenly around their heads—and their faces went hard with contempt.

One Sunday Connie got up at eleven—none of them bothered with church—and washed her hair so that it could dry all day long in the sun. Her parents and sister were going to a barbecue at an aunt's house and Connie said no, she wasn't interested, rolling her eyes to let her mother know just what she thought of it. "Stay home alone then," her mother said sharply. Connie sat out back in a lawn chair and watched them drive away, her father quiet and bald, hunched around so that he could back the car out, her mother with a look that was still angry and not at all softened through the windshield, and in the back seat poor old June, all dressed up as if she didn't know what a barbecue was, with all the running yelling kids and the flies. Connie sat with her eyes closed in the sun, dreaming and dazed with the warmth about her as if this were a kind of love, the caresses of love, and her mind slipped over onto thoughts of the boy she had been with the night before and how nice he had been, how sweet it always was, not the way someone like June would suppose but sweet, gentle, the way it was in movies and promised in songs; and when she opened her eyes she hardly knew where she was, the back yard ran off into weeds and a fence-like line of trees and behind it the sky was perfectly blue and still. The asbestos "ranch house" that was now three years old startled her—it looked small. She shook her head as if to get awake.

It was too hot. She went inside the house and turned on the radio to drown out the quiet. She sat on the edge of her bed, barefoot, and listened for an hour and a half to a program called XYZ Sunday Jamboree, record after record of hard, fast, shrieking songs she sang along with, interspersed by exclamations from "Bobby King": "An' look here, you girls at Napoleon's—Son and Charley want you to pay real close attention to this song coming up!"

And Connie paid close attention herself, bathed in a glow of slow-pulsed joy that seemed to rise mysteriously out of the music itself and lay languidly about the airless little room, breathed in and breathed out with each gentle rise and fall of her chest.

After a while she heard a car coming up the drive. She sat up at once, startled, because it couldn't be her father so soon. The gravel kept crunching all the way in from the road—the driveway was long—and Connie ran to the window. It was a car she didn't know. It was an open jalopy, painted a bright gold that caught the sunlight opaquely. Her heart began to pound and her fingers snatched at her hair, checking it, and she whispered, "Christ. Christ," wondering how bad she looked. The car came to a stop at the side door and the horn sounded four short taps, as if this were a signal Connie knew.

She went into the kitchen and approached the door slowly, then hung out the screen door, her bare toes curling down off the step. There were two boys in the car and now she recognized the driver: he had shaggy, shabby black hair that looked crazy as a wig and he was grinning at her.

"I ain't late, am I?" he said.

"Who the hell do you think you are?" Connie said.

"Toldja I'd be out, didn't I?"

"I don't even know who you are."

She spoke sullenly, careful to show no interest or pleasure, and he spoke in a fast, bright monotone. Connie looked past him to the other boy, taking her time. He had fair brown hair, with a lock that fell onto his forehead. His sideburns gave him a fierce, embarrassed look, but so far he hadn't even bothered to glance at her. Both boys wore sunglasses. The driver's glasses were metallic and mirrored everything in miniature.

"You wanta come for a ride?" he said.

Connie smirked and let her hair fall loose over one shoulder.

"Don'tcha like my car? New paint job," he said. "Hey."

"What?"

"You're cute."

She pretended to fidget, chasing flies away from the door.

"Don'tcha believe me, or what?" he said.

"Look, I don't even know who you are," Connie said in disgust.

"Hey, Ellie's got a radio, see. Mine broke down." He lifted his friend's arm and showed her the little transistor radio the boy was holding, and now Connie began to hear the music. It was the same program that was playing inside the house.

"Bobby King?" she said.

"I listen to him all the time. I think he's great."

"He's kind of great," Connie said reluctantly.

"Listen, that guy's *great*. He knows where the action is."

Connie blushed a little, because the glasses made it impossible for her to see just what this boy was looking at. She couldn't decide if she liked him or if he was just a jerk, and so she dawdled in the doorway and wouldn't come down or go back inside. She said, "What's all that stuff painted on your car?"

"Can'tcha read it?" He opened the door very carefully, as if he were afraid it might fall off. He slid out just as carefully, planting his feet firmly on the ground, the tiny metallic world in his glasses slowing down like gelatine hardening, and in the midst of it Connie's bright green blouse. "This here is my name, to begin with," he said. ARNOLD FRIEND was written in tarlike black letters on the side, with a drawing of a round, grinning face that reminded Connie of a pumpkin, except it wore sunglasses. "I wanta introduce myself, I'm Arnold Friend and that's my real name and I'm gonna be your friend, honey, and inside the car's Ellie Oscar, he's kinda shy." Ellie brought his transistor radio up to his shoulder and balanced it there. "Now, these numbers are a secret code, honey," Arnold Friend explained. He read off the numbers 33, 19, 17 and raised his eyebrows at her to see what she thought of that, but she didn't think much of it. The left rear fender had been smashed and around it was written, on the gleaming gold background: DONE BY CRAZY WOMAN DRIVER. Connie had to laugh at that. Arnold Friend was pleased at her laughter and looked up at her. "Around the other side's a lot more—you wanta come and see them?"

"No."

"Why not?"

"Why should I?"

"Don'tcha wanta see what's on the car? Don'tcha wanta go for a ride?"

"I don't know."

"Why not?"

"I got things to do."

"Like what?"

"Things."

He laughed as if she had said something funny. He slapped his thighs. He was standing in a strange way, leaning back against the car as if he were balancing himself. He wasn't tall, only an inch or so taller than she would be if she came down to him. Connie liked the way he was dressed, which was the way all of them dressed: tight faded jeans stuffed into black, scuffed boots, a belt that pulled his waist in and showed how lean he was, and a white pull-over shirt that was a little soiled and showed the hard small muscles of his arms and shoulders. He looked as if he probably did hard work, lifting and carrying things. Even his neck looked muscular. And his face was a familiar face, somehow: the jaw and chin and cheeks slightly darkened because he hadn't shaved for a day or two, and the nose long and hawklike, sniffing as if she were a treat he was going to gobble up and it was all a joke.

"Connie, you ain't telling the truth. This is your day set aside for a ride with me and you know it," he said, still laughing. The way he straightened and recovered from his fit of laughing showed that it had been all fake.

"How do you know what my name is?" she said suspiciously.

"It's Connie."

"Maybe and maybe not."

"I know my Connie," he said, wagging his finger. Now she remembered him even better, back at the restaurant, and her cheeks warmed at the thought of how she had sucked in her breath just at the moment she passed him—how she must have looked to him. And he had remembered her. "Ellie and I come out here especially for you," he said. "Ellie can sit in back. How about it?"

"Where?"

"Where what?"

"Where're we going?"

He looked at her. He took off the sunglasses and she saw how pale the skin around his eyes was, like holes that were not in shadow but instead in light. His eyes were like chips of broken glass that catch the light in an amiable way. He smiled. It was as if the idea of going for a ride somewhere, to someplace, was a new idea to him.

"Just for a ride, Connie sweetheart."

"I never said my name was Connie," she said.

"But I know what it is. I know your name and all about you, lots of things," Arnold Friend said. He had not moved yet but stood still leaning back against the side of his jalopy. "I took a special interest in you, such a pretty girl, and found out all about you—like I know your parents and sister are gone somewheres and I know where and how long they're going to be gone, and I know who you were with last night, and your best girl friend's name is Betty. Right?"

He spoke in a simple lilting voice, exactly as if he were reciting the words to a song. His smile assured her that everything was fine. In the car Ellie turned up the volume on his radio and did not bother to look around at them.

"Ellie can sit in the back seat," Arnold Friend said. He indicated his friend with a casual jerk of his chin, as if Ellie did not count and she should not bother with him.

"How'd you find out all that stuff?" Connie said.

"Listen: Betty Schultz and Tony Fitch and Jimmy Pettinger and

Nancy Pettinger," he said in a chant. "Raymond Stanley and Bob Hutter—"

"Do you know all those kids?"

"I know everybody."

"Look, you're kidding. You're not from around here."

"Sure."

"But—how come we never saw you before?"

"Sure you saw me before," he said. He looked down at his boots, as if he were a little offended. "You just don't remember."

"I guess I'd remember you," Connie said.

"Yeah?" He looked up at this, beaming. He was pleased. He began to mark time with the music from Ellie's radio, tapping his fists lightly together. Connie looked away from his smile to the car, which was painted so bright it almost hurt her eyes to look at it. She looked at that name, ARNOLD FRIEND. And up at the front fender was an expression that was familiar—MAN THE FLYING SAUCERS. It was an expression kids had used the year before but didn't use this year. She looked at it for a while as if the words meant something to her that she did not yet know.

"What're you thinking about? Huh?" Arnold Friend demanded. "Not worried about your hair blowing around in the car, are you?"

"No."

"Think I maybe can't drive good?"

"How do I know?"

"You're a hard girl to handle. How come?" he said. "Don't you know I'm your friend? Didn't you see me put my sign in the air when you walked by?"

"What sign?"

"My sign." And he drew an X in the air, leaning out toward her. They were maybe ten feet apart. After his hand fell back to his side the X was still in the air, almost visible. Connie let the screen door close and stood perfectly still inside it, listening to the music from her radio and the boy's blend together. She stared at Arnold Friend. He stood there so stiffly relaxed, pretending to be relaxed, with one hand idly on the door handle as if he were keeping himself up that way and had no intention of ever moving again. She recognized most things about him, the tight jeans that showed his thighs and buttocks and the greasy leather boots and the tight shirt, and even that slippery friendly smile of his, that sleepy dreamy smile that all the boys used to get across ideas they didn't want to put into words. She recognized all this and also the singsong way he talked, slightly mocking, kidding, but serious and a little melancholy, and she recognized the way he tapped one fist against the other in homage to the perpetual music behind him. But all these things did not come together.

She said suddenly, "Hey, how old are you?"

His smiled faded. She could see then that he wasn't a kid, he was much older—thirty, maybe more. At this knowledge her heart began to pound faster.

"That's a crazy thing to ask. Can'tcha see I'm your own age?"

"Like hell you are."

"Or maybe a coupla years older. I'm eighteen."

"Eighteen?" she said doubtfully.

He grinned to reassure her and lines appeared at the corners of his mouth. His teeth were big and white. He grinned so broadly his eyes became slits and she saw how thick the lashes were, thick and black as if painted with a black tarlike material. Then, abruptly, he seemed to become embarrassed and looked over his shoulder at Ellie. "*Him*, he's crazy," he said. "Ain't he a riot? He's a nut, a real character." Ellie was still listening to the music. His sunglasses told nothing about what he was thinking. He wore a bright orange shirt unbuttoned halfway to show his chest, which was a pale, bluish chest and not muscular like Arnold Friend's. His shirt collar was turned up all around and the very tips of the collar pointed out past his chin as if they were protecting him. He was pressing the transistor radio up against his ear and sat there in a kind of daze, right in the sun.

"He's kinda strange," Connie said.

"Hey, she says you're kinda strange! Kinda strange!" Arnold Friend cried. He pounded on the car to get Ellie's attention. Ellie turned for the first time and Connie saw with shock that he wasn't a kid either—he had a fair, hairless face, cheeks reddened slightly as if the veins grew too close to the surface of his skin, the face of a forty-year-old baby. Connie felt a wave of dizziness rise in her at this sight and she stared at him as if waiting for something to change the shock of the moment, make it all right again. Ellie's lips kept shaping words, mumbling along with the words blasting in his ear.

"Maybe you two better go away," Connie said faintly.

"What? How come?" Arnold Friend cried. "We come out here to take you for a ride. It's Sunday." He had the voice of the man on the radio now. It was the same voice, Connie thought. "Don'tcha know it's Sunday all day? And honey, no matter who you were with last night, today you're with Arnold Friend and don't you forget it! Maybe you better step out here," he said, and this last was in a different voice. It was a little flatter, as if the heat was finally getting to him.

"No. I got things to do."

"Hey."

"You two better leave."

"We ain't leaving until you come with us."

"Like hell I am—"

"Connie, don't fool around with me. I mean—I mean, don't fool *around*," he said, shaking his head. He laughed incredulously. He placed his sunglasses on top of his head, carefully, as if he were indeed wearing a wig, and brought the stems down behind his ears. Connie stared at him, another wave of dizziness and fear rising in her so that for a moment he wasn't even in focus but was just a blur standing there against his gold car, and she had the idea that he had driven up the driveway all right but had come from nowhere before that and belonged nowhere and that everything about him and even about the music that was so familiar to her was only half real.

"If my father comes and sees you—"

"He ain't coming. He's at a barbecue."

"How do you know that?"

"Aunt Tillie's. Right now they're—uh—they're drinking. Sitting around," he said vaguely, squinting as if he were staring all the way to town and over to Aunt Tillie's back yard. Then the vision seemed to get clear and he nodded energetically. "Yeah. Sitting around. There's your sister in a blue dress, huh? And high heels, the poor sad bitch—nothing like you, sweetheart! And your mother's helping some fat woman with the corn, they're cleaning the corn—husking the corn—"

"What fat woman?" Connie cried.

"How do I know what fat woman, I don't know every goddamn fat woman in the world!" Arnold Friend laughed.

"Oh, that's Mrs. Hornsby. . . . Who invited her?" Connie said. She felt a little lightheaded. Her breath was coming quickly.

"She's too fat. I don't like them fat. I like them the way you are, honey," he said, smiling sleepily at her. They stared at each other for a while through the screen door. He said softly, "Now, what you're going to do is this: you're going to come out that door. You're going to sit up front with me and Ellie's going to sit in the back, the hell with Ellie, right? This isn't Ellie's date. You're my date. I'm your lover, honey."

"What? You're crazy—"

"Yes, I'm your lover. You don't know what that is but you will," he said. "I know that too. I know all about you. But look: it's real nice and you couldn't ask for nobody better than me, or more polite. I always keep my word. I'll tell you how it is, I'm always nice at first, the first time. I'll hold you so tight you won't think you have to try to get away or pretend anything because you'll know you can't. And I'll come inside you where it's all secret and you'll give in to me and you'll love me—"

"Shut up! You're crazy!" Connie said. She backed away from the door. She put her hands up against her ears as if she'd heard something terrible, something not meant for her. "People don't talk like that, you're crazy," she muttered. Her heart was almost too big now for her chest and its pumping made sweat break out all over her. She looked out to see Arnold Friend pause and then take a step toward the porch, lurching. He almost fell. But, like a clever drunken man, he managed to catch his balance. He wobbled in his high boots and grabbed hold of one of the porch posts.

"Honey?" he said. "You still listening?"

"Get the hell out of here!"

"Be nice, honey. Listen."

"I'm going to call the police—"

He wobbled again and out of the side of his mouth came a fast spat curse, an aside not meant for her to hear. But even this "Christ!" sounded forced. Then he began to smile again. She watched this smile come, awkward as if he were smiling from inside a mask. His whole face was a mask, she thought wildly, tanned down to his throat but then running out as if he had plastered make-up on his face but had forgotten about his throat.

"Honey—? Listen, here's how it is. I always tell the truth and I promise you this: I ain't coming in that house after you."

"You better not! I'm going to call the police if you—if you don't—"

"Honey," he said, talking right through her voice, "honey, I'm not coming in there but you are coming out here. You know why?"

She was panting. The kitchen looked like a place she had never seen before, some room she had run inside but that wasn't good enough, wasn't going to help her. The kitchen window had never had a curtain, after three years, and there were dishes in the sink for her to do—probably—and if you ran your hand across the table you'd probably feel something sticky there.

"You listening, honey? Hey?"

"—going to call the police—"

"Soon as you touch the phone I don't need to keep my promise and can come inside. You won't want that."

She rushed forward and tried to lock the door. Her fingers were shaking. "But why lock it," Arnold Friend said gently, talking right into her face. "It's just a screen door. It's just nothing." One of his boots was at a strange angle, as if his foot wasn't in it. It pointed out to the left, bent at the ankle. "I mean, anybody can break through a screen door and glass and wood and iron or anything else if he needs to, anybody at all, and specially Arnold Friend. If the place got lit up with a fire, honey, you'd come runnin' out into my arms, right into my arms an' safe at home—like you knew I was your lover and'd stopped fooling around. I don't mind a nice shy girl but I don't like no fooling around." Part of those words were spoken with a slight rhythmic lilt, and Connie somehow recognized them—the echo of a song from last year, about a girl rushing into her boy friend's arms and coming home again—

Connie stood barefoot on the linoleum floor, staring at him. "What do you want?" she whispered.

"I want you," he said.

"What?"

"Seen you that night and thought, that's the one, yes sir. I never needed to look anymore."

"But my father's coming back. He's coming to get me. I had to wash my hair first—" She spoke in a dry, rapid voice, hardly raising it for him to hear.

"No, your daddy is not coming and yes, you had to wash your hair and you washed it for me. It's nice and shining and all for me. I thank you sweetheart," he said with a mock bow, but again he almost lost his balance. He had to bend and adjust his boots. Evidently his feet did not go all the way down; the boots must have been stuffed with something so that he would seem taller. Connie stared out at him and behind him at Ellie in the car, who seemed to be looking off toward Connie's right, into nothing. This Ellie said, pulling the words out of the air one after another as if he were just discovering them, "You want me to pull out the phone?"

"Shut your mouth and keep it shut," Arnold Friend said, his face red from bending over or maybe from embarrassment because Connie had seen his boots. "This ain't none of your business."

"What—what are you doing? What do you want?" Connie said. "If I call the police they'll get you, they'll arrest you—"

"Promise was not to come in unless you touch that phone, and I'll keep that promise," he said. He resumed his erect position and tried to force his shoulders back. He sounded like a hero in a movie, declaring something important. But he spoke too loudly and it was as if he were speaking to someone behind Connie. "I ain't made plans for coming in that house where I don't belong but just for you to come out to me, the way you should. Don't you know who I am?"

"You're crazy," she whispered. She backed away from the door but did not want to go into another part of the house, as if this would give him permission to come through the door. "What do you . . . you're crazy, you. . . ."

"Huh? What're you saying, honey?"

Her eyes darted everywhere in the kitchen. She could not remember what it was, this room.

"This is how it is, honey: you come out and we'll drive away, have a nice ride. But if you don't come out we're gonna wait till your people come home and then they're all going to get it."

"You want that telephone pulled out?" Ellie said. He held the radio away from his ear and grimaced, as if without the radio the air was too much for him.

"I toldja shut up, Ellie," Arnold Friend said, "you're deaf, get a hearing aid, right? Fix yourself up. This little girl's no trouble and's gonna be nice to me, so Ellie keep to yourself, this ain't your date—right? Don't hem in on me, don't hog, don't crush, don't bird dog, don't trail me," he said in a rapid, meaningless voice, as if he were running through all the expressions he'd learned but was no longer sure which of them was in style, then rushing on to new ones, making them up with his eyes closed. "Don't crawl under my fence, don't squeeze in my chipmunk hole, don't sniff my glue, suck my Popsicle, keep your own greasy fingers on yourself!" He shaded his eyes and peered in at Connie, who was backed against the kitchen table. "Don't mind him, honey, he's just a creep. He's a dope. Right? I'm the boy for you and like I said, you come out here nice like a lady and give me your hand, and nobody else gets hurt, I mean, your nice old bald-headed daddy and your mummy and your sister in her high heels. Because listen: why bring them in this?"

"Leave me alone," Connie whispered.

"Hey, you know that old woman down the road, the one with the chickens and stuff—you know her?"

"She's dead!"

"Dead? What? You know her?" Arnold Friend said.

"She's dead—"

"Don't you like her?"

"She's dead—she's—she isn't here any more—"

"But don't you like her, I mean, you got something against her? Some grudge or something?" Then his voice dipped as if he were conscious of a rudeness. He touched the sunglasses perched up on top of his head as if to make sure they were still there. "Now, you be a good girl."

"What are you going to do?"

"Just two things, or maybe three," Arnold Friend said. "But I promise it won't last long and you'll like me the way you get to like people you're close to. You will. It's all over for you here, so come on out. You don't want your people in any trouble, do you?"

She turned and bumped against a chair or something, hurting

her leg, but she ran into the back room and picked up the telephone. Something roared in her ear, a tiny roaring, and she was so sick with fear that she could do nothing but listen to it—the telephone was clammy and very heavy and her fingers groped down to the dial but were too weak to touch it. She began to scream into the phone, into the roaring. She cried out, she cried for her mother, she felt her breath start jerking back and forth in her lungs as if it were something Arnold Friend was stabbing her with again and again with no tenderness. A noisy sorrowful wailing rose all about her and she was locked inside it the way she was locked inside this house.

After a while she could hear again. She was sitting on the floor with her wet back against the wall.

Arnold Friend was saying from the door, "That's a good girl. Put the phone back."

She kicked the phone away from her.

"No, honey. Pick it up. Put it back right."

She picked it up and put it back. The dial tone stopped.

"That's a good girl. Now, you come outside."

She was hollow with what had been fear but what was now just an emptiness. All that screaming had blasted it out of her. She sat, one leg cramped under her, and deep inside her brain was something like a pinpoint of light that kept going and would not let her relax. She thought, I'm not going to see my mother again. She thought, I'm not going to sleep in my bed again. Her bright green blouse was all wet.

Arnold Friend said, in a gentle-loud voice that was like a stage voice, "The place where you came from ain't there any more, and where you had in mind to go is cancelled out. This place you are now—inside your daddy's house—is nothing but a cardboard box I can knock down any time. You know that and always did know it. You hear me?"

She thought, I have got to think. I have got to know what to do.

"We'll go out to a nice field, out in the country here where it smells so nice and it's sunny," Arnold Friend said. "I'll have my arms tight around you so you won't need to try to get away and I'll show you what love is like, what it does. The hell with this house! It looks solid all right," he said. He ran a fingernail down the screen and the noise did not make Connie shiver, as it would have the day before.

"Now, put your hand on your heart, honey. Feel that? That feels solid too but we know better. Be nice to me, be sweet like you can because what else is there for a girl like you but to be sweet and pretty and give in?—and get away before her people come back?"

She felt her pounding heart. Her hand seemed to enclose it. She thought for the first time in her life that it was nothing that was hers, that belonged to her, but just a pounding, living thing inside this body that wasn't really hers either.

"You don't want them to get hurt," Arnold Friend went on. "Now, get up, honey. Get up all by yourself."

She stood.

"Now, turn this way. That's right. Come over here to me.—Ellie, put that away, didn't I tell you? You dope. You miserable creepy dope," Arnold Friend said. His words were not angry but only part of an incantation. The incantation was kindly. "Now, come out through the kitchen to me, honey, and let's see a smile, try it, you're a brave, sweet little girl and now they're eating corn and hot dogs cooked to bursting over an outdoor fire, and they don't know one thing about you and never did and honey, you're better than them because not a one of them would have done this for you."

Connie felt the linoleum under her feet; it was cool. She brushed her hair back out of her eyes. Arnold Friend let go of the post tentatively and opened his arms for her, his elbows pointing in toward each other and his wrists limp, to show that this was an embarrassed embrace and a little mocking, he didn't want to make her self-conscious.

She put out her hand against the screen. She watched herself push the door slowly open as if she were back safe somewhere in the other doorway, watching this body and this head of long hair moving out into the sunlight where Arnold Friend waited.

"My sweet little blue-eyed girl," he said in a half-sung sigh that had nothing to do with her brown eyes but was taken up just the same by the vast sunlit reaches of the land behind him and on all sides of him—so much land that Connie had never seen before and did not recognize except to know that she was going to it.

1966

Tim O'Brien
b. 1946

O'Brien fought in Vietnam as part of a unit like the one depicted in this story. Though O'Brien first published "The Things They Carried" as a short story in Esquire *magazine, he eventually made it the first chapter in his 1990 novel bearing the same title, in which the lives of the characters in this story continue in the subsequent chapters. Perhaps its style is the most striking feature of "The Things They Carried." Jimmy Cross's story is embedded within emotionless recitations of the weights of each item the soldiers carried into the field. Many readers might not consider this information important, but O'Brien's including it was surely purposeful.*

The Things They Carried

First Lieutenant Jimmy Cross carried letters from a girl named Martha, a junior at Mount Sebastian College in New Jersey. They were not love letters, but Lieutenant Cross was hoping, so he kept them folded in plastic at the bottom of his rucksack. In the late afternoon, after a day's march, he would dig his foxhole, wash his hands under a canteen, unwrap the letters, hold them with the tips of his fingers, and spend the last hour of light pretending. He would imagine romantic camping trips into the White Mountains in New Hampshire. He would sometimes taste the envelope flaps, knowing her tongue had been there. More than anything, he wanted Martha to love him as he loved her, but the letters were mostly chatty, elusive on the matter of love. She was a virgin, he was almost sure. She was an English major at Mount Sebastian, and she wrote beautifully about her professors and roommates and midterm exams, about her respect for Chaucer and her great affection for Virginia Woolf. She often quoted lines of poetry; she never mentioned the war, except to say, Jimmy, take care of yourself. The letters weighed ten ounces. They were signed "Love, Martha," but Lieutenant Cross understood that "Love" was only a way of signing and did not mean what he sometimes pretended it meant. At dusk, he would carefully return the letters to his rucksack. Slowly, a bit distracted, he would get up and move among his men, checking the perimeter, then at full dark he would return to his hole and watch the night and wonder if Martha was a virgin.

The things they carried were largely determined by necessity. Among the necessities or near necessities were P-38 can openers, pocket knives, heat tabs, wrist watches, dog tags, mosquito repellent, chewing gum, candy, cigarettes, salt tablets, packets of Kool-Aid, lighters, matches, sewing kits, Military Payment Certificates, C rations, and two or three canteens of water. Together, these items weighed between fifteen and twenty pounds, depending upon a man's habits or rate of metabolism. Henry Dobbins, who was a big man, carried extra rations; he was especially fond of canned peaches in heavy syrup over pound cake. Dave Jensen, who practiced field hygiene, carried a toothbrush, dental floss, and several hotel-size bars of soap he'd stolen on R&R[1] in Sydney, Australia. Ted Lavender, who was scared, carried tranquilizers until he was shot in the head outside the village of Than Khe in mid-April. By necessity, and because it was SOP,[2] they all carried steel helmets that weighed five pounds including the liner and camouflage cover. They carried the standard fatigue jackets and trousers. Very few carried underwear. On their feet they carried jungle boots—2.1 pounds—and Dave Jensen carried three pairs of socks and a can of Dr. Scholl's foot powder as a precaution against trench foot. Until he was shot, Ted Lavender carried six or seven ounces of premium dope, which for him was a necessity. Mitchell Sanders, the RTO,[3] carried condoms. Norman Bowker carried a diary. Rat Kiley carried comic books. Kiowa, a devout Baptist, carried an illustrated New Testament that had been presented to him by his father, who taught Sunday school in Oklahoma City, Oklahoma. As a hedge against bad times, however, Kiowa also carried his grandmother's distrust of the white man, his grandfather's old hunting hatchet. Necessity dictated. Because the land was mined and booby-trapped, it was SOP for each man to carry a steel-centered, nylon-covered flak jacket, which weighed 6.7 pounds, but which on hot days seemed much heavier. Because you could die so quickly, each man carried at least one large compress bandage, usually in the helmet band for easy access. Because the nights were cold, and because

1. Rest and recreation leave.
2. Standard operating procedure.
3. Radio and telephone operator.

the monsoons were wet, each carried a green plastic poncho that could be used as a raincoat or ground sheet or makeshift tent. With its quilted liner, the poncho weighed almost two pounds, but it was worth every ounce. In April, for instance, when Ted Lavender was shot, they used his poncho to wrap him up then to carry him across the paddy, then to lift him into the chopper that took him away.

They were called legs or grunts.

To carry something was to "hump" it, as when Lieutenant Jimmy Cross humped his love for Martha up the hills and through the swamps. In its intransitive form, "to hump" meant "to walk," or "to march," but it implied burdens far beyond the intransitive.

Almost everyone humped photographs. In his wallet, Lieutenant Cross carried two photographs of Martha. The first was a Kodachrome snapshot signed "Love," though he knew better. She stood against a brick wall. Her eyes were gray and neutral, her lips slightly open as she stared straight-on at the camera. At night, sometimes, Lieutenant Cross wondered who had taken the picture, because he knew she had boyfriends, because he loved her so much, and because he could see the shadow of the picture taker spreading out against the brick wall. The second photograph had been clipped from the 1968 Mount Sebastian yearbook. It was an action shot—women's volleyball—and Martha was bent horizontal to the floor, reaching, the palms of her hands in sharp focus, the tongue taut, the expression frank and competitive. There was no visible sweat. She wore white gym shorts. Her legs, he thought, were almost certainly the legs of a virgin, dry and without hair, the left knee cocked and carrying her entire weight, which was just over one hundred pounds. Lieutenant Cross remembered touching that left knee. A dark theater, he remembered, and the movie was *Bonnie and Clyde*, and Martha wore a tweed skirt, and during the final scene, when he touched her knee, she turned and looked at him in a sad, sober way that made him pull his hand back, but he would always remember the feel of the tweed skirt and the knee beneath it and the sound of the gunfire that killed Bonnie and Clyde, how embarrassing it was, how slow and oppressive. He remembered kissing her good night at the dorm door. Right then, he thought, he should've done something brave. He should've carried her up the stairs to her room and tied her to the bed and touched that left knee all night long. He should've risked it. Whenever he looked at the photographs, he thought of new things he should've done.

What they carried was partly a function of rank, partly of field specialty.

As a first lieutenant and platoon leader, Jimmy Cross carried a compass, maps, code books, binoculars, and a .45-caliber pistol that weighed 2.9 pounds fully loaded. He carried a strobe light and the responsibility for the lives of his men.

As an RTO, Mitchell Sanders carried the PRC-25 radio, a killer, twenty-six pounds with its battery.

As a medic, Rat Kiley carried a canvas satchel filled with morphine and plasma and malaria tablets and surgical tape and comic books and all the things a medic must carry, including M&M's for especially bad wounds, for a total weight of nearly twenty pounds.

As a big man, therefore a machine gunner, Henry Dobbins carried the M-60, which weighed twenty-three pounds unloaded, but which was almost always loaded. In addition, Dobbins carried between ten and fifteen pounds of ammunition draped in belts across his chest and shoulders.

As PFCs or Spec 4s,[4] most of them were common grunts and carried the standard M-16 gas-operated assault rifle. The weapon weighed 7.5 pounds unloaded, 8.2 pounds with its full twenty-round magazine. Depending on numerous factors, such as topography and psychology, the riflemen carried anywhere from twelve to twenty magazines, usually in cloth bandoliers, adding on another 8.4 pounds at minimum, fourteen pounds at maximum. When it was available, they also carried M-16 maintenance gear—rods and steel brushes and swabs and tubes of LSA oil[5]—all of which weighed about a pound. Among the grunts, some carried the M-79 grenade launcher, 5.9 pounds unloaded, a reasonably light weapon except for the ammunition, which was heavy. A single round weighed ten ounces. The typical load was twenty-five rounds. But Ted Lavender, who was scared, carried thirty-four rounds when he was shot and killed outside

4. PFC: Private First Class. Spec 4: Specialist Fourth Class, an army rank immediately above Private First Class.

5. Small arms lubricant.

Than Khe, and he went down under an exceptional burden, more than twenty pounds of ammunition, plus the flak jacket and helmet and rations and water and toilet paper and tranquilizers and all the rest, plus the unweighed fear. He was dead weight. There was no twitching or flopping. Kiowa, who saw it happen, said it was like watching a rock fall, or a big sandbag or something—just boom, then down—not like the movies where the dead guy rolls around and does fancy spins and goes ass over teakettle—not like that, Kiowa said, the poor bastard just flat-fuck fell. Boom. Down. Nothing else. It was a bright morning in mid-April. Lieutenant Cross felt the pain. He blamed himself. They stripped off Lavender's canteens and ammo, all the heavy things, and Rat Kiley said the obvious, the guy's dead, and Mitchell Sanders used his radio to report one U.S. KIA[6] and to request a chopper. Then they wrapped Lavender in his poncho. They carried him out to a dry paddy, established security, and sat smoking the dead man's dope until the chopper came. Lieutenant Cross kept to himself. He pictured Martha's smooth young face, thinking he loved her more than anything, more than his men, and now Ted Lavender was dead because he loved her so much and could not stop thinking about her. When the dust-off[7] arrived, they carried Lavender aboard. Afterward they burned Than Khe. They marched until dusk, then dug their holes, and that night Kiowa kept explaining how you had to be there, how fast it was, how the poor guy just dropped like so much concrete. Boom-down, he said. Like cement.

In addition to the three standard weapons—the M-60, M-16, and M-79—they carried whatever presented itself, or whatever seemed appropriate as a means of killing or staying alive. They carried catch-as-catch-can. At various times, in various situations, they carried M-14s and CAR-15s and Swedish Ks and grease guns and captured AK-47s and Chi-Coms and RPGs and Simonov carbines and black-market Uzis and .38-caliber Smith & Wesson handguns and 66 mm LAWs and shotguns and silencers and blackjacks and bayonets and C-4 plastic explosives. Lee Strunk carried a slingshot; a

6. Killed in action.
7. Helicopter.

weapon of last resort, he called it. Mitchell Sanders carried brass knuckles. Kiowa carried his grandfather's feathered hatchet. Every third or fourth man carried a Claymore antipersonnel mine—3.5 pounds with its firing device. They all carried fragmentation grenades—fourteen ounces each. They all carried at least one M-18 colored smoke grenade—twenty-four ounces. Some carried CS or tear-gas grenades. Some carried white-phosphorus grenades. They carried all they could bear, and then some, including a silent awe for the terrible power of the things they carried.

In the first week of April, before Lavender died, Lieutenant Jimmy Cross received a good-luck charm from Martha. It was a simple pebble, an ounce at most. Smooth to the touch, it was a milky-white color with flecks of orange and violet, oval-shaped, like a miniature egg. In the accompanying letter, Martha wrote that she had found the pebble on the Jersey shoreline, precisely where the land touched water at high tide, where things came together but also separated. It was this separate-but-together quality, she wrote, that had inspired her to pick up the pebble and to carry it in her breast pocket for several days, where it seemed weightless, and then to send it through the mail, by air, as a token of her truest feelings for him. Lieutenant Cross found this romantic. But he wondered what her truest feelings were, exactly, and what she meant by separate-but-together. He wondered how the tides and waves had come into play on that afternoon along the Jersey shoreline when Martha saw the pebble and bent down to rescue it from geology. He imagined bare feet. Martha was a poet, with the poet's sensibilities, and her feet would be brown and bare, the toenails unpainted, the eyes chilly and somber like the ocean in March, and though it was painful, he wondered who had been with her that afternoon. He imagined a pair of shadows moving along the strip of sand where things came together but also separated. It was phantom jealousy, he knew, but he couldn't help himself. He loved her so much. On the march, through the hot days of early April, he carried the pebble in his mouth, turning it with his tongue, tasting sea salts and moisture. His mind wandered. He had difficulty keeping his attention on the war. On occasion he would yell at his men to spread out the column, to keep their eyes open, but then he would slip away into daydreams, just pretending, walking barefoot along the Jersey shore, with Martha, carrying nothing. He would feel himself rising. Sun and waves and gentle winds, all love and lightness.

What they carried varied by mission.

When a mission took them to the mountains, they carried mosquito netting, machetes, canvas tarps, and extra bug juice.

If a mission seemed especially hazardous, or if it involved a place they knew to be bad, they carried everything they could. In certain heavily mined AOs,[8] where the land was dense with Toe Poppers and Bouncing Betties, they took turns humping a twenty-eight-pound mine detector. With its headphones and big sensing plate, the equipment was a stress on the lower back and shoulders, awkward to handle, often useless because of the shrapnel in the earth, but they carried it anyway, partly for safety, partly for the illusion of safety.

On ambush, or other night missions, they carried peculiar little odds and ends. Kiowa always took along his New Testament and a pair of moccasins for silence. Dave Jensen carried night-sight vitamins high in carotin. Lee Strunk carried his slingshot; ammo, he claimed, would never be a problem. Rat Kiley carried brandy and M&M's. Until he was shot, Ted Lavender carried the starlight scope, which weighed 6.3 pounds with its aluminum carrying case. Henry Dobbins carried his girlfriend's pantyhose wrapped around his neck as a comforter. They all carried ghosts. When dark came, they would move out single file across the meadows and paddies to their ambush coordinates, where they would quietly set up the Claymores and lie down and spend the night waiting.

Other missions were more complicated and required special equipment. In mid-April it was their mission to search out and destroy the elaborate tunnel complexes in the Than Khe area south of Chu Lai. To blow the tunnels, they carried one-pound blocks of pentrite high explosives, four blocks to a man, sixty-eight pounds in all. They carried wiring, detonators, and battery-powered clackers. Dave Jensen carried earplugs. Most often, before blowing the tunnels, they were ordered by higher command to search them, which was consid-

8. Areas of operations.

ered bad news, but by and large they just shrugged and carried out orders. Because he was a big man, Henry Dobbins was excused from tunnel duty. The others would draw numbers. Before Lavender died there were seventeen men in the platoon, and whoever drew the number seventeen would strip off his gear and crawl in head first with a flashlight and Lieutenant Cross's .45-caliber pistol. The rest of them would fan out as security. They would sit down or kneel, not facing the hole, listening to the ground beneath them, imagining cobwebs and ghosts, whatever was down there—the tunnel walls squeezing in—how the flashlight seemed impossibly heavy in the hand and how it was tunnel vision in the very strictest sense, compression in all ways, even time, and how you had to wiggle in—ass and elbows—a swallowed-up feeling—and how you found yourself worrying about odd things—will your flashlight go dead? Do rats carry rabies? If you screamed, how far would the sound carry? Would your buddies hear it? Would they have the courage to drag you out? In some respects, though not many, the waiting was worse than the tunnel itself. Imagination was a killer.

On April 16, when Lee Strunk drew the number seventeen, he laughed and muttered something and went down quickly. The morning was hot and very still. Not good, Kiowa said. He looked at the tunnel opening, then out across a dry paddy toward the village of Than Khe. Nothing moved. No clouds or birds or people. As they waited, the men smoked and drank Kool-Aid, not talking much, feeling sympathy for Lee Strunk but also feeling the luck of the draw. You win some, you lose some, said Mitchell Sanders, and sometimes you settle for a rain check. It was a tired line and no one laughed.

Henry Dobbins ate a tropical chocolate bar. Ted Lavender popped a tranquilizer and went off to pee.

After five minutes, Lieutenant Jimmy Cross moved to the tunnel, leaned down, and examined the darkness. Trouble, he thought—a cave-in maybe. And then suddenly, without willing it, he was thinking about Martha. The stresses and fractures, the quick collapse, the two of them buried alive under all that weight. Dense, crushing love. Kneeling, watching the hole, he tried to concentrate on Lee Strunk and the war, all the dangers, but his love was too much for him, he felt paralyzed, he wanted to sleep inside her lungs and breathe her blood and be smothered. He wanted her to be a virgin and not a virgin, all at once. He wanted to know her. Intimate secrets—why poetry? Why so sad? Why that grayness in her eyes? Why so alone? Not lonely just alone—riding her bike across campus or sitting off by herself in the cafeteria. Even dancing, she danced alone—and it was the aloneness that filled him with love. He remembered telling her that one evening. How she nodded and looked away. And how, later, when he kissed her, she received the kiss without returning it, her eyes wide open, not afraid, not a virgin's eyes, just flat and uninvolved.

Lieutenant Cross gazed at the tunnel. But he was not there. He was buried with Martha under the white sand at the Jersey shore. They were pressed together, and the pebble in his mouth was her tongue. He was smiling. Vaguely, he was aware of how quiet the day was, the sullen paddies, yet he could not bring himself to worry about matters of security. He was beyond that. He was just a kid at war, in love. He was twenty-two years old. He couldn't help it.

A few moments later Lee Strunk crawled out of the tunnel. He came up grinning, filthy but alive. Lieutenant Cross nodded and closed his eyes while the others clapped Strunk on the back and made jokes about rising from the dead.

Worms, Rat Kiley said. Right out of the grave. Fuckin' zombie.

The men laughed. They all felt great relief.

Spook City, said Mitchell Sanders.

Lee Strunk made a funny ghost sound, a kind of moaning, yet very happy, and right then, when Strunk made that high happy moaning sound, when he went *Ahhooooo*, right then Ted Lavender was shot in the head on his way back from peeing. He lay with his mouth open. The teeth were broken. There was a swollen black bruise under his left eye. The cheekbone was gone. Oh shit, Rat Kiley said, the guy's dead. The guy's dead, he kept saying, which seemed profound—the guy's dead. I mean really.

The things they carried were determined to some extent by superstition. Lieutenant Cross carried his good-luck pebble. Dave Jensen carried a rabbit's foot. Norman Bowker, otherwise a very gentle person, carried a thumb that had been presented to him as a gift by Mitchell Sanders. The thumb was dark brown, rubbery to the touch, and weighed four ounces at most. It had been cut from a

VC[9] corpse, a boy of fifteen or sixteen. They'd found him at the bottom of an irrigation ditch, badly burned, flies in his mouth and eyes. The boy wore black shorts and sandals. At the time of his death he had been carrying a pouch of rice, rifle, and three magazines of ammunition.

You want my opinion, Mitchell Sanders said, there's a definite moral here.

He put his hand on the dead boy's wrist. He was quiet for a time, as if counting a pulse, then he patted the stomach, almost affectionately, and used Kiowa's hunting hatchet to remove the thumb.

Henry Dobbins asked what the moral was.

Moral?

You know. *Moral.*

Sanders wrapped the thumb in toilet paper and handed it across to Norman Bowker. There was no blood. Smiling, he kicked the boy's head, watched the flies scatter, and said, It's like with that old TV show—Paladin. Have gun, will travel.

Henry Dobbins thought about it.

Yeah, well, he finally said. I don't see no moral.

There it *is*, man.

Fuck off.

They carried USO[10] stationery and pencils and pens. They carried Sterno,[11] safety pins, trip flares, signal flares, spools of wire, razor blades, chewing tobacco, liberated joss sticks and statuettes of the smiling Buddha, candles, grease pencils, *The Stars and Stripes,* fingernail clippers, Psy Ops[12] leaflets, bush hats, bolos, and much more. Twice a week, when the resupply choppers came in, they carried hot chow in green Mermite cans and large canvas bags filled with iced beer and soda pop. They carried plastic water containers, each with a two-gallon capacity. Mitchell Sanders carried a set of starched tiger fatigues for special occasions. Henry Dobbins carried Black Flag insecticide. Dave Jensen carried empty sandbags that could be filled at night for added protection. Lee Strunk carried tan-

9. Vietcong.
10. United Service Organization, which provided entertainment to the troops.
11. Canned fuel for a portable stove.
12. Psychological Operations.

ning lotion. Some things they carried in common. Taking turns, they carried the big PRC-77 scrambler radio, which weighed thirty pounds with its battery. They shared the weight of memory. They took up what others could no longer bear. Often, they carried each other, the wounded or weak. They carried infections. They carried chess sets, basketballs, Vietnamese-English dictionaries, insignia of rank, Bronze Stars and Purple Hearts, plastic cards imprinted with the Code of Conduct. They carried diseases, among them malaria and dysentery. They carried lice and ringworm and leeches and paddy algae and various rots and molds. They carried the land itself—Vietnam, the place, the soil—a powdery orange-red dust that covered their boots and fatigues and faces. They carried the sky. The whole atmosphere, they carried it, the humidity, the monsoons, the stink of fungus and decay, all of it, they carried gravity. They moved like mules. By daylight they took sniper fire, at night they were mortared, but it was not battle, it was just the endless march, village to village, without purpose, nothing won or lost. They marched for the sake of the march. They plodded along slowly, dumbly, leaning forward against the heat, unthinking, all blood and bone, simple grunts, soldiering with their legs, toiling up the hills and down into the paddies and across the rivers and up again and down just humping, one step and then the next and then another, but no volition, no will, because it was automatic, it was anatomy, and the war was entirely a matter of posture and carriage, the hump was everything, a kind of inertia, a kind of emptiness, a dullness of desire and intellect and conscience and hope and human sensibility. Their principles were in their feet. Their calculations were biological. They had no sense of strategy or mission. They searched the villages without knowing what to look for, not caring, kicking over jars of rice, frisking children and old men, blowing tunnels, sometimes setting fires and sometimes not, then forming up and moving on to the next village, then other villages, where it would always be the same. They carried their own lives. The pressures were enormous. In the heat of early afternoon, they would remove their helmets and flak jackets, walking bare, which was dangerous but which helped ease the strain. They would often discard things along the route of march. Purely for comfort, they would throw away rations, blow their Claymores and grenades, no matter, because by nightfall the resupply choppers would arrive with more of the same, then a day or two later still more, fresh watermelons and crates of ammunition and sunglasses and woolen sweaters—the resources were stunning—sparklers for the Fourth of July, colored eggs for Easter. It was the great American war chest the fruits of science, the smokestacks, the canneries, the arsenals at Hartford, the Minnesota forests, the machine shops, the vast fields of corn and wheat—they carried like freight trains; they carried it on their backs and shoulders—and for all the ambiguities of Vietnam, all the mysteries and unknowns, there was at least the single abiding certainty that they would never be at a loss for things to carry.

After the chopper took Lavender away, Lieutenant Jimmy Cross led his men into the village of Than Khe. They burned everything. They shot chickens and dogs, they trashed the village well, they called in artillery and watched the wreckage, then they marched for several hours through the hot afternoon, and then at dusk, while Kiowa explained how Lavender died, Lieutenant Cross found himself trembling.

He tried not to cry. With his entrenching tool, which weighed five pounds, he began digging a hole in the earth.

He felt shame. He hated himself. He had loved Martha more than his men, and as a consequence Lavender was now dead, and this was something he would have to carry like a stone in his stomach for the rest of the war.

All he could do was dig. He used his entrenching tool like an ax, slashing, feeling both love and hate, and then later, when it was full dark, he sat at the bottom of his foxhole and wept. It went on for a long while. In part, he was grieving for Ted Lavender, but mostly it was for Martha, and for himself, because she belonged to another world, which was not quite real, and because she was a junior at Mount Sebastian College in New Jersey, a poet and a virgin and uninvolved, and because he realized she did not love him and never would.

Like cement, Kiowa whispered in the dark. I swear to God—boom-down. Not a word.

I've heard this, said Norman Bowker.

A pisser, you know? Still zipping himself up. Zapped while zipping.

All right, fine. That's enough.

Yeah, but you had to see it, the guy just—

I *heard*, man. Cement. So why not shut the fuck *up*?

Kiowa shook his head sadly and glanced over at the hole where Lieutenant Jimmy Cross sat watching the night. The air was thick and wet. A warm, dense fog had settled over the paddies and there was the stillness that precedes rain.

After a time Kiowa sighed.

One thing for sure, he said. The Lieutenant's in some deep hurt. I mean that crying jag—the way he was carrying on—it wasn't fake or anything, it was real heavy-duty hurt. The man cares.

Sure, Norman Bowker said.

Say what you want, the man does care.

We all got problems.

Not Lavender.

No, I guess not. Bowker said. Do me a favor, though.

Shut up?

That's a smart Indian. Shut up.

Shrugging, Kiowa pulled off his boots. He wanted to say more, just to lighten up his sleep, but instead he opened his New Testament and arranged it beneath his head as a pillow. The fog made things seem hollow and unattached. He tried not to think about Ted Lavender, but then he was thinking how fast it was, no drama, down and dead, and how it was hard to feel anything except surprise. It seemed un-Christian. He wished he could find some great sadness, or even anger, but the emotion wasn't there and he couldn't make it happen. Mostly he felt pleased to be alive. He liked the smell of the New Testament under his cheek, the leather and ink and paper and glue, whatever the chemicals were. He liked hearing the sounds of night. Even his fatigue, it felt fine, the stiff muscles and the prickly awareness of his own body, a floating feeling. He enjoyed not being dead. Lying there, Kiowa admired Lieutenant Jimmy Cross's capacity for grief. He wanted to share the man's pain, he wanted to care as Jimmy Cross cared. And yet when he closed his eyes, all he could think was Boom-down, and all he could feel was the pleasure of having his boots off and the fog curling in around him and the damp soil and the Bible smells and the plush comfort of night.

After a moment Norman Bowker sat up in the dark.

What the hell, he said. You want to talk, *talk*. Tell it to me.

Forget it.

No, man, go on. One thing I hate, it's a silent Indian.

For the most part they carried themselves with poise, a kind of dignity. Now and then, however, there were times of panic, when they squealed or wanted to squeal but couldn't, when they twitched and made moaning sounds and covered their heads and said Dear Jesus and flopped around on the earth and fired their weapons blindly and cringed and sobbed and begged for the noise to stop and went wild and made stupid promises to themselves and to God and to their mothers and fathers, hoping not to die. In different ways, it happened to all of them. Afterward, when the firing ended, they would blink and peek up. They would touch their bodies, feeling shame, then quickly hiding it. They would force themselves to stand. As if in slow motion, frame by frame, the world would take on the old logic—absolute silence, then the wind, then sunlight, then voices. It was the burden of being alive. Awkwardly, the men would reassemble themselves, first in private, then in groups, becoming soldiers again. They would repair the leaks in their eyes. They would check for casualties, call in dust-offs, light cigarettes, try to smile, clear their throats and spit and begin cleaning their weapons. After a time someone would shake his head and say, No lie, I almost shit my pants, and someone else would laugh, which meant it was bad, yes, but the guy had obviously not shit his pants, it wasn't that bad, and in any case nobody would ever do such a thing and then go ahead and talk about it. They would squint into the dense, oppressive sunlight. For a few moments, perhaps, they would fall silent, lighting a joint and tracking its passage from man to man, inhaling, holding in the humiliation. Scary stuff, one of them might say. But then someone else would grin or flick his eyebrows and say, Roger-dodger, almost cut me a new asshole, *almost*.

There were numerous such poses. Some carried themselves with a sort of wistful resignation, others with pride or stiff soldierly discipline or good humor or macho zeal. They were afraid of dying but they were even more afraid to show it.

They found jokes to tell.

They used a hard vocabulary to contain the terrible softness. *Greased*, they'd say. *Offed, lit up, zapped while zipping.* It wasn't cruelty, just stage presence. They were actors and the war came at them in 3-D. When someone died, it wasn't quite dying, because in a curious way it seemed scripted, and because they had their lines mostly memorized, irony mixed with tragedy, and because they called it by other names, as if to encyst and destroy the reality of death itself. They kicked corpses. They cut off thumbs. They talked grunt lingo. They told stories about Ted Lavender's supply of tranquilizers, how the poor guy didn't feel a thing, how incredibly tranquil he was.

There's a moral here, said Mitchell Sanders.

They were waiting for Lavender's chopper, smoking the dead man's dope.

The moral's pretty obvious, Sanders said, and winked. Stay away from drugs. No joke, they'll ruin your day every time.

Cute, said Henry Dobbins.

Mind-blower, get it? Talk about wiggy—nothing left, just blood and brains.

They made themselves laugh.

There it is, they'd say, over and over, as if the repetition itself were an act of poise, a balance between crazy and almost crazy, knowing without going. There it is, which meant be cool, let it ride, because oh yeah man, you can't change what can't be changed, there it is, there it absolutely and positively and fucking well *is*.

They were tough.

They carried all the emotional baggage of men who might die. Grief, terror, love, longing—these were intangibles, but the intangibles had their own mass and specific gravity, they had tangible weight. They carried shameful memories. They carried the common secret of cowardice barely restrained, the instinct to run or freeze or hide, and in many respects this was the heaviest burden of all, for it could never be put down, it required perfect balance and perfect posture. They carried their reputations. They carried the soldier's greatest fear, which was the fear of blushing. Men killed, and died, because they were embarrassed not to. It was what had brought them to the war in the first place, nothing positive, no dreams of glory or honor, just to avoid the blush of dishonor. They died so as not to die of embarrassment. They crawled into tunnels and walked point and advanced under fire. Each morning, despite the unknowns, they made their legs move. They endured. They kept humping. They did not submit to the obvious alternative, which was simply to close the eyes and fall. So easy, really. Go limp and tumble to the ground and let the muscles unwind and not speak and not budge until your buddies picked you up and lifted you into the chopper that would roar and dip its nose and carry you off to the world. A mere matter of falling, yet no one ever fell. It was not courage, exactly; the object was not valor. Rather, they were too frightened to be cowards.

By and large they carried these things inside, maintaining the masks of composure. They sneered at sick call. They spoke bitterly about guys who had found release by shooting off their own toes or fingers. Pussies, they'd say. Candyasses. It was fierce, mocking talk, with only a trace of envy or awe, but even so, the image played itself out behind their eyes.

They imagined the muzzle against flesh. They imagined the quick, sweet pain, then the evacuation to Japan, then a hospital with warm beds and cute geisha[13] nurses.

They dreamed of freedom birds.

At night, on guard, staring into the dark, they were carried away by jumbo jets. They felt the rush of takeoff. *Gone!* they yelled. And then velocity, wings and engines, a smiling stewardess—but it was more than a plane, it was a real bird, a big sleek silver bird with feathers and talons and high screeching. They were flying. The weights fell off, there was nothing to bear. They laughed and held on tight, feeling the cold slap of wind and altitude, soaring, thinking *It's over, I'm gone!*—they were naked, they were light and free—it was all lightness, bright and fast and buoyant, light as light, a helium buzz in the brain, a giddy bubbling in the lungs as they were taken up over the clouds

13. Japanese girls and women trained to be professional entertainers and companions for men.

and the war, beyond duty, beyond gravity and mortification and global entanglements—*Sin loi!*[14] they yelled, *I'm sorry, motherfuckers, but I'm out of it, I'm goofed, I'm on a space cruise, I'm gone!*—and it was a restful, disencumbered sensation, just riding the light waves, sailing that big silver freedom bird over the mountains and oceans, over America, over the farms and great sleeping cities and cemeteries and highways and the golden arches of McDonald's. It was flight, a kind of fleeing, a kind of falling, falling higher and higher, spinning off the edge of the earth and beyond the sun and through the vast, silent vacuum where there were no burdens and where everything weighed exactly nothing. *Gone!* they screamed, *I'm sorry but I'm gone!* And so at night, not quite dreaming, they gave themselves over to lightness, they were carried, they were purely borne.

On the morning after Ted Lavender died, First Lieutenant Jimmy Cross crouched at the bottom of his foxhole and burned Martha's letters. Then he burned the two photographs. There was a steady rain falling, which made it difficult, but he used heat tabs and Sterno to build a small fire, screening it with his body, holding the photographs over the tight blue flame with the tips of his fingers.

He realized it was only a gesture. Stupid, he thought. Sentimental, too, but mostly just stupid.

Lavender was dead. You couldn't burn the blame.

Besides, the letters were in his head. And even now, without photographs, Lieutenant Cross could see Martha playing volleyball in her white gym shorts and yellow T-shirt. He could see her moving in the rain.

When the fire died out, Lieutenant Cross pulled his poncho over his shoulders and ate breakfast from a can.

There was no great mystery, he decided.

In those burned letters Martha had never mentioned the war, except to say, Jimmy, take care of yourself. She wasn't involved. She signed the letters "Love," but it wasn't love, and all the fine lines and technicalities did not matter.

The morning came up wet and blurry. Everything seemed part of everything else, the fog and Martha and the deepening rain.

14. Sorry about that (Vietnamese).

It was a war, after all.

Half smiling, Lieutenant Jimmy Cross took out his maps. He shook his head hard, as if to clear it, then bent forward and began planning the day's march. In ten minutes, or maybe twenty, he would rouse the men and they would pack up and head west, where the maps showed the country to be green and inviting. They would do what they had always done. The rain might add some weight, but otherwise it would be one more day layered upon all the other days.

He was realistic about it. There was that new hardness in his stomach.

No more fantasies, he told himself.

Henceforth, when he thought about Martha, it would be only to think that she belonged elsewhere. He would shut down the daydreams. This was not Mount Sebastian, it was another world, where there were no pretty poems or midterm exams, a place where men died because of carelessness and gross stupidity. Kiowa was right. Boom down, and you were dead, never partly dead.

Briefly, in the rain, Lieutenant Cross saw Martha's gray eyes gazing back at him.

He understood.

It was very sad, he thought. The things men carried inside. The things men did or felt they had to do.

He almost nodded at her, but didn't.

Instead he went back to his maps. He was now determined to perform his duties firmly and without negligence. It wouldn't help Lavender, he knew that, but from this point on he would comport himself as a soldier. He would dispose of his good-luck pebble. Swallow it, maybe, or use Lee Strunk's slingshot, or just drop it along the trail. On the march he would impose strict field discipline. He would be careful to send out flank security, to prevent straggling or bunching up, to keep his troops moving at the proper pace and at the proper interval. He would insist on clean weapons. He would confiscate the remainder of Lavender's dope. Later in the day, perhaps, he would call the men together and speak to them plainly. He would accept the blame for what had happened to Ted Lavender. He would be a man about it. He would look them in the eyes, keeping his chin level, and he would issue the new SOPs in a calm, impersonal tone of voice, an officer's voice, leaving no room for argument or discussion. Commencing immediately, he'd tell them, they would no longer abandon equipment along the route of march. They would police up their acts. They would get their shit together, and keep it together, and maintain it neatly and in good working order.

He would not tolerate laxity. He would show strength, distancing himself.

Among the men there would be grumbling, of course, and maybe worse, because their days would seem longer and their loads heavier, but Lieutenant Cross reminded himself that his obligation was not to be loved but to lead. He would dispense with love; it was not now a factor. And if anyone quarreled or complained, he would simply tighten his lips and arrange his shoulders in the correct command posture. He might give a curt little nod. Or he might not. He might just shrug and say Carry on, then they would saddle up and form into a column and move out toward the villages of Than Khe.

1986

Flannery O'Connor

1925–1964

O'Connor, a Catholic from Georgia, always insisted that her faith informed her fiction, despite her stories' being filled with grotesques and violence. "A Good Man Is Hard to Find," she explained, is grotesque the way a child's drawing is. The child "doesn't intend to distort but to set down exactly what he sees." O'Connor advised readers to be on the lookout not for dead bodies but for "the action of grace," which as O'Connor explained, "can and does use as its medium the imperfect, purely human, and even hypocritical." The choice facing the characters in this story, as for the characters in most of O'Connor's stories, is to accept or cut oneself off from grace.

A Good Man Is Hard to Find

The grandmother didn't want to go to Florida. She wanted to visit some of her connections in east Tennessee and she was seizing every chance to change Bailey's mind. Bailey was the son she lived with, her only boy. He was sitting on the edge of his chair at the table, bent over the orange sports section of the *Journal*. "Now look here, Bailey," she said, "see here, read this," and she stood with one hand on her thin hip and the other rattling the newspaper at his bald head. "Here this fellow that calls himself The Misfit is aloose from the Federal Pen and headed toward Florida and you read here what it says he did to these people. Just you read it. I wouldn't take my children in any direction with a criminal like that aloose in it. I couldn't answer to my conscience if I did."

Bailey didn't look up from his reading so she wheeled around then and faced the children's mother; a young woman in slacks, whose face was as broad and innocent as a cabbage and was tied around with a green headkerchief that had two points on the top like rabbit's ears. She was sitting on the sofa, feeding the baby his apricots out of a jar. "The children have been to Florida before," the old lady said. "You all ought to take them somewhere else for a change so they would see different parts of the world and be broad. They never have been to east Tennessee."

The children's mother didn't seem to hear her, but the eight-year-old boy, John Wesley, a stocky child with glasses, said, "If you don't want to go to Florida, why dontcha stay at home?" He and the little girl, June Star, were reading the funny papers on the floor.

"She wouldn't stay at home to be queen for a day," June Star said without raising her yellow head.

"Yes, and what would you do if this fellow, The Misfit, caught you?" the grandmother asked.

"I'd smack his face," John Wesley said.

"She wouldn't stay at home for a million bucks," June Star said. "Afraid she'd miss something. She has to go everywhere we go."

"All right, Miss," the grandmother said. "Just remember that the next time you want me to curl your hair."

June Star said her hair was naturally curly.

The next morning the grandmother was the first one in the car, ready to go. She had her big black valise that looked like the head of a hippopotamus in one corner, and underneath it she was hiding a basket with Pitty Sing,[1] the cat, in it. She didn't intend for the cat to be left alone in the house for three days because he would miss her too much and she was afraid he might brush against one of the gas burners and accidentally asphyxiate himself. Her son, Bailey, didn't like to arrive at a motel with a cat.

She sat in the middle of the back seat with John Wesley and June Star on either side of her. Bailey and the children's mother and the baby sat in the front and they left Atlanta at eight forty-five with the mileage on the car at 55890. The grandmother wrote this down because she thought it would be interesting to say how many miles they had been when they got back. It took them twenty minutes to reach the outskirts of the city.

The old lady settled herself comfortably, removing her white cotton gloves and putting them up with her purse on the shelf in front of the back window. The children's mother still had on slacks and still had her head tied up in a green kerchief, but the grandmother had on a navy blue straw sailor hat with a bunch of white violets on the brim and a navy blue dress with a small white dot in the print. Her collar and cuffs were white organdy trimmed with lace and at her neckline she had pinned a purple spray of cloth violets containing a sachet. In case of an accident, anyone seeing her dead on the highway would know at once that she was a lady.

She said she thought it was going to be a good day for driving, neither too hot nor too cold, and she cautioned Bailey that the speed limit was fifty-five miles an hour and that the patrolmen hid themselves behind billboards and small clumps of trees and sped out after you before you had a chance to slow down. She pointed out interesting details of the scenery: Stone Mountain; the blue granite that in some places came up to both sides of the highway; the brilliant red clay banks slightly streaked with purple; and the various crops that made rows of green lace-work on the ground. The trees were full of silver-white sunlights and the meanest of

1. Pitti-Sing is a character in Gilbert and Sullivan's comic opera *The Mikado* (1885).

them sparkled. The children were reading comic magazines and their mother had gone back to sleep.

"Let's go through Georgia fast so we won't have to look at it much," John Wesley said.

"If I were a little boy," said the grandmother, "I wouldn't talk about my native state that way. Tennessee has the mountains and Georgia has the hills."

"Tennessee is just a hillbilly dumping ground," John Wesley said, "and Georgia is a lousy state too."

"You said it," June Star said.

"In my time," said the grandmother, folding her thin veined fingers, "children were more respectful of their native states and their parents and everything else. People did right then. Oh look at the cute little pickaninny!" she said and pointed to a Negro child standing in the door of a shack. "Wouldn't that make a picture, now?" she asked and they all turned and looked at the little Negro out of the back window. He waved.

"He didn't have any britches on," June Star said.

"He probably didn't have any," the grandmother explained. "Little niggers in the country don't have things like we do. If I could paint, I'd paint that picture," she said.

The children exchanged comic books.

The grandmother offered to hold the baby and the children's mother passed him over the front seat to her. She set him on her knee and bounced him and told him about the things they were passing. She rolled her eyes and screwed up her mouth and stuck her leathery thin face into his smooth bland one. Occasionally he gave her a faraway smile. They passed a large cotton field with five or six graves fenced in the middle of it, like a small island. "Look at the graveyard!" the grandmother said, pointing it out. "That was the old family burying ground. That belonged to the plantation."

"Where's the plantation?" John Wesley asked.

"Gone With the Wind,"[2] said the grandmother. "Ha. Ha."

When the children finished all the comic books they had

2. Title of the best-selling novel (1936) by Margaret Mitchell about the passing of the old South.

brought, they opened the lunch and ate it. The grandmother ate a peanut butter sandwich and an olive and would not let the children throw the box and the paper napkins out the window. When there was nothing else to do they played a game by choosing a cloud and making the other two guess what shape it suggested. John Wesley took one the shape of a cow and June Star guessed a cow and John Wesley said, no, an automobile, and June Star said he didn't play fair, and they began to slap each other over the grandmother.

The grandmother said she would tell them a story if they would keep quiet. When she told a story, she rolled her eyes and waved her head and was very dramatic. She said once when she was a maiden lady she had been courted by a Mr. Edgar Atkins Teagarden from Jasper, Georgia. She said he was a very good-looking man and a gentleman and that he brought her a watermelon every Saturday afternoon with his initials cut in it, E.A.T. Well, one Saturday, she said, Mr. Teagarden brought the watermelon and there was nobody at home and he left it on the front porch and returned in his buggy to Jasper, but she never got the watermelon, she said, because a nigger boy ate it when he saw the initials, E.A.T.! This story tickled John Wesley's funny bone and he giggled and giggled but June Star didn't think it was any good. She said she wouldn't marry a man that just brought her a watermelon on Saturday. The grandmother said she would have done well to marry Mr. Teagarden because he was a gentleman and had bought Coca-Cola stock when it first came out and that he had died only a few years ago, a very wealthy man.

They stopped at The Tower for barbecued sandwiches. The Tower was a part-stucco and part-wood filling station and dance hall set in a clearing outside of Timothy. A fat man named Red Sammy Butts ran it and there were signs stuck here and there on the building and for miles up and down the highway saying, TRY RED SAMMY'S FAMOUS BARBECUE. NONE LIKE FAMOUS RED SAMMY'S! RED SAM! THE FAT BOY WITH THE HAPPY LAUGH. A VETERAN! RED SAMMY'S YOUR MAN!

Red Sammy was lying on the bare ground outside The Tower with his head under a truck while a gray monkey about a foot high, chained to a small chinaberry tree, chattered nearby. The monkey sprang back into the tree and got on the highest limb as soon as he saw the children jump out of the car and run toward him.

Inside, The Tower was a long dark room with a counter at one end and tables at the other and dancing space in the middle. They all sat down at a broad table next to the nickelodeon[3] and Red Sam's wife, a tall burnt-brown woman with hair and eyes lighter than her skin, came and took their order. The children's mother put a dime in the machine and played "The Tennessee Waltz," and the grandmother said that tune always made her want to dance. She asked Bailey if he would like to dance but he only glared at her. He didn't have a naturally sunny disposition like she did and trips made him nervous. The grandmother's brown eyes were very bright. She swayed her head from side to side and pretended she was dancing in her chair. June Star said play something she could tap to so the children's mother put in another dime and played a fast number and June Star stepped out onto the dance floor and did her tap routine.

"Ain't she cute?" Red Sam's wife said, leaning over the counter. "Would you like to come be my little girl?"

"No, I certainly wouldn't," June Star said. "I wouldn't live in a broken-down place like this for a million bucks!" and she ran back to the table.

"Ain't she cute?" the woman repeated, stretching her mouth politely.

"Aren't you ashamed?" hissed the grandmother.

Red Sam came in and told his wife to quit lounging on the counter and hurry up with these people's order. His khaki trousers reached just to his hip bones and his stomach hung over them like a sack of meal swaying under his shirt. He came over and sat down at a table nearby and let out a combination sigh and yodel. "You can't win," he said. "You can't win," and he wiped his sweating red face off with a gray handkerchief. "These days you don't know who to trust," he said. "Ain't that the truth?"

"People are certainly not nice like they used to be," said the grandmother.

"Two fellers come in here last week," Red Sammy said, "driving a Chrysler. It was an old beat-up car but it was a good one and these boys looked all right to me. Said they worked at the mill and you

3. Jukebox.

know I let them fellers charge the gas they bought? Now why did I do that?"

"Because you're a good man!" the grandmother said at once.

"Yes'm, I suppose so," Red Sam said as if he were struck with this answer.

His wife brought the orders, carrying the five plates all at once without a tray, two in each hand and one balanced on her arm. "It isn't a soul in this green world of God's that you can trust," she said. "And I don't count nobody out of that, not nobody," she repeated, looking at Red Sammy.

"Did you read about that criminal, The Misfit, that's escaped?" asked the grandmother.

"I wouldn't be a bit surprised if he didn't attack this place right here," said the woman. "If he hears about it being here, I wouldn't be none surprised to see him. If he hears it's two cent in the cash register, I wouldn't be a tall surprised if he . . ."

"That'll do," Red Sam said. "Go bring these people their Co'-Colas," and the woman went off to get the rest of the order.

"A good man is hard to find," Red Sammy said. "Everything is getting terrible. I remember the day you could go off and leave your screen door unlatched. Not no more."

He and the grandmother discussed better times. The old lady said that in her opinion Europe was entirely to blame for the way things were now. She said the way Europe acted you would think we were made of money and Red Sam said it was no use talking about it, she was exactly right. The children ran outside into the white sunlight and looked at the monkey in the lacy chinaberry tree. He was busy catching fleas on himself and biting each one carefully between his teeth as if it were a delicacy.

They drove off again into the hot afternoon. The grandmother took cat naps and woke up every few minutes with her own snoring. Outside of Toombsboro she woke up and recalled an old plantation that she had visited in this neighborhood once when she was a young lady. She said the house had six white columns across the front and that there was an avenue of oaks leading up to it and two little wooden trellis arbors on either side in front where you sat down with your suitor after a stroll in the garden. She recalled exactly which road to turn off to get to it. She knew that Bailey would not be willing to lose any time looking at an old house, but the more she talked about it, the more she wanted to see it once again and find out if the little twin arbors were still standing. "There was a secret panel in this house," she said craftily, not telling the truth but wishing that she were, "and the story went that all the family silver was hidden in it when Sherman[4] came through but it was never found . . ."

"Hey!" John Wesley said. "Let's go see it! We'll find it! We'll poke all the woodwork and find it! Who lives there? Where do you turn off at? Hey Pop, can't we turn off there?"

"We never have seen a house with a secret panel!" June Star shrieked. "Let's go to the house with the secret panel! Hey, Pop, can't we go see the house with the secret panel!"

"It's not far from here, I know," the grandmother said. "It wouldn't take over twenty minutes."

Bailey was looking straight ahead. His jaw was as rigid as a horseshoe. "No," he said.

The children began to yell and scream that they wanted to see the house with the secret panel. John Wesley kicked the back of the front seat and June Star hung over her mother's shoulder and whined desperately into her ear that they never had any fun even on their vacation, that they could never do what THEY wanted to do. The baby began to scream and John Wesley kicked the back of the seat so hard that his father could feel the blows in his kidney.

"All right!" he shouted and drew the car to a stop at the side of the road. "Will you all shut up? Will you all just shut up for one second? If you don't shut up, we won't go anywhere."

"It would be very educational for them," the grandmother murmured.

"All right," Bailey said, "but get this. This is the only time we're going to stop for anything like this. This is the one and only time."

"The dirt road that you have to turn down is about a mile back," the grandmother directed. "I marked it when we passed."

"A dirt road," Bailey groaned.

After they had turned around and were headed toward the dirt

4. In 1864 the Union general William Tecumseh Sherman and his army marched from Atlanta to Savannah, burning many civilian farms and houses along the way.

road, the grandmother recalled other points about the house, the beautiful glass over the front doorway and the candle lamp in the hall. John Wesley said that the secret panel was probably in the fireplace.

"You can't go inside this house," Bailey said. "You don't know who lives there."

"While you all talk to the people in front, I'll run around behind and get in a window," John Wesley suggested.

"We'll all stay in the car," his mother said.

They turned onto the dirt road and the car raced roughly along in a swirl of pink dust. The grandmother recalled the times when there were no paved roads and thirty miles was a day's journey. The dirt road was hilly and there were sudden washes in it and sharp curves on dangerous embankments. All at once they would be on a hill, looking down over the blue tops of trees for miles around, then the next minute, they would be in a red depression with the dust-coated trees looking down on them.

"This place had better turn up in a minute," Bailey said, "or I'm going to turn around."

The road looked as if no one had traveled on it in months.

"It's not much farther," the grandmother said and just as she said it, a horrible thought came to her. The thought was so embarrassing that she turned red in the face and her eyes dilated and her feet jumped up, upsetting her valise in the corner. The instant the valise moved, the newspaper top she had over the basket under it rose with a snarl and Pitty Sing, the cat, sprang onto Bailey's shoulder.

The children were thrown to the floor and their mother, clutching the baby, was thrown out the door onto the ground; the old lady was thrown into the front seat. The car turned over once and landed right-side-up in a gulch on the side of the road. Bailey remained in the driver's seat with the cat—gray-striped with a broad white face and an orange nose—clinging to his neck like a caterpillar.

As soon as the children saw they could move their arms and legs, they scrambled out of the car, shouting, "We've had an ACCIDENT!" The grandmother was curled up under the dashboard, hoping she was injured so that Bailey's wrath would not come down on her all at once. The horrible thought she had had before the accident was that the house she had remembered so vividly was not in Georgia but in Tennessee.

Bailey removed the cat from his neck with both hands and flung it out the window against the side of a pine tree. Then he got out of the car and started looking for the children's mother. She was sitting against the side of the red gutted ditch, holding the screaming baby, but she only had a cut down her face and a broken shoulder. "We've had an ACCIDENT!" the children screamed in a frenzy of delight.

"But nobody's killed," June Star said with disappointment as the grandmother limped out of the car, her hat still pinned to her head but the broken front brim standing up at a jaunty angle and the violet spray hanging off the side. They all sat down in the ditch, except the children, to recover from the shock. They were all shaking.

"Maybe a car will come along," said the children's mother hoarsely.

"I believe I have injured an organ," said the grandmother, pressing her side, but no one answered her. Bailey's teeth were clattering. He had on a yellow sport shirt with bright blue parrots designed in it and his face was as yellow as the shirt. The grandmother decided that she would not mention that the house was in Tennessee.

The road was about ten feet above and they could see only the tops of the trees on the other side of it. Behind the ditch they were sitting in there were more woods, tall and dark and deep. In a few minutes they saw a car some distance away on top of a hill, coming slowly as if the occupants were watching them. The grandmother stood up and waved both arms dramatically to attract their attention. The car continued to come on slowly, disappeared around a bend and appeared again, moving even slower, on top of the hill they had gone over. It was a big black battered hearselike automobile. There were three men in it.

It came to a stop over them and for some minutes, the driver looked down with a steady expressionless gaze to where they were sitting, and didn't speak. Then he turned his head and muttered something to the other two and they got out. One was a fat boy in black trousers and a red sweat shirt with a silver stallion embossed on the front of it. He moved around on the right side of them and stood staring, his mouth partly open in a kind of loose grin. The other had on khaki pants and a blue striped coat and a gray hat pulled down very low, hiding most of his face. He came around slowly on the left side. Neither spoke.

The driver got out of the car and stood by the side of it, looking down at them. He was an older man than the other two. His hair was just beginning to gray and he wore silver-rimmed spectacles that gave him a scholarly look. He had a long creased face and didn't have on any shirt or undershirt. He had on blue jeans that were too tight for him and was holding a black hat and a gun. The two boys also had guns.

"We've had an ACCIDENT!" the children screamed.

The grandmother had the peculiar feeling that the bespectacled man was someone she knew. His face was as familiar to her as if she had known him all her life but she could not recall who he was. He moved away from the car and began to come down the embankment, placing his feet carefully so that he wouldn't slip. He had on tan and white shoes and no socks, and his ankles were red and thin. "Good afternoon," he said. "I see you all had you a little spill."

"We turned over twice!" said the grandmother.

"Oncet," he corrected. "We seen it happen. Try their car and see will it run, Hiram," he said quietly to the boy with the gray hat.

"What you got that gun for?" John Wesley asked. "Whatcha gonna do with that gun?"

"Lady," the man said to the children's mother, "would you mind calling them children to sit down by you? Children make me nervous. I want all you all to sit down right together there where you're at."

"What are you telling us what to do for?" June Star asked.

Behind them the line of woods gaped like a dark open mouth. "Come here," said their mother.

"Look here now," Bailey began suddenly, "we're in a predicament! We're in . . ."

The grandmother shrieked. She scrambled to her feet and stood staring.

"You're The Misfit!" she said. "I recognized you at once!"

"Yes'm," the man said, smiling slightly as if he were pleased in spite of himself to be known, "but it would have been better for all of you, lady, if you hadn't of reckernized me."

Bailey turned his head sharply and said something to his mother that shocked even the children. The old lady began to cry and The Misfit reddened.

"Lady," he said, "don't you get upset. Sometimes a man says things he don't mean. I don't reckon he meant to talk to you thataway."

"You wouldn't shoot a lady, would you?" the grandmother said and removed a clean handkerchief from her cuff and began to slap at her eyes with it.

The Misfit pointed the toe of his shoe into the ground and made a little hole and then covered it up again. "I would hate to have to," he said.

"Listen," the grandmother almost screamed, "I know you're a good man. You don't look a bit like you have common blood. I know you must come from nice people!"

"Yes mam," he said, "finest people in the world." When he smiled he showed a row of strong white teeth. "God never made a finer woman than my mother and my daddy's heart was pure gold," he said. The boy with the red sweat shirt had come around behind them and was standing with his gun at his hip. The Misfit squatted down on the ground. "Watch them children, Bobby Lee," he said. "You know they make me nervous." He looked at the six of them huddled together in front of him and he seemed to be embarrassed as if he couldn't think of anything to say. "Ain't a cloud in the sky," he remarked, looking up at it. "Don't see no sun but don't see no cloud neither."

"Yes, it's a beautiful day," said the grandmother. "Listen," she said, "you shouldn't call yourself The Misfit because I know you're a good man at heart. I can just look at you and tell."

"Hush!" Bailey yelled. "Hush! Everybody shut up and let me handle this!" He was squatting in the position of a runner about to spring forward but he didn't move.

"I pre-chate that, lady," The Misfit said and drew a little circle in the ground with the butt of his gun.

"It'll take a half a hour to fix this here car," Hiram called, looking over the raised hood of it.

"Well, first you and Bobby Lee get him and that little boy to step over yonder with you," The Misfit said, pointing to Bailey and John Wesley. "The boys want to ask you something," he said to

Bailey. "Would you mind stepping back in them woods there with them?"

"Listen," Bailey began, "we're in a terrible predicament! Nobody realizes what this is," and his voice cracked. His eyes were as blue and intense as the parrots in his shirt and he remained perfectly still.

The grandmother reached up to adjust her hat brim as if she were going to the woods with him but it came off in her hand. She stood staring at it and after a second she let it fall on the ground. Hiram pulled Bailey up by the arm as if he were assisting an old man. John Wesley caught hold of his father's hand and Bobby Lee followed. They went off toward the woods and just as they reached the dark edge, Bailey turned and supporting himself against a gray naked pine trunk, he shouted, "I'll be back in a minute, Mamma, wait on me!"

"Come back this instant!" his mother shrilled but they all disappeared into the woods.

"Bailey Boy!" the grandmother called in a tragic voice but she found she was looking at The Misfit squatting on the ground in front of her. "I just know you're a good man," she said desperately. "You're not a bit common!"

"Nome, I ain't a good man," The Misfit said after a second as if he had considered her statement carefully, "but I ain't the worst in the world neither. My daddy said I was a different breed of dog from my brothers and sisters. 'You know,' Daddy said, 'it's some that can live their whole life out without asking about it and it's others has to know why it is, and this boy is one of the latters. He's going to be into everything!' " He put on his black hat and looked up suddenly and then away deep into the woods as if he were embarrassed again. "I'm sorry I don't have on a shirt before you ladies," he said, hunching his shoulders slightly. "We buried our clothes that we had on when we escaped and we're just making do until we can get better. We borrowed these from some folks we met," he explained.

"That's perfectly all right," the grandmother said. "Maybe Bailey has an extra shirt in his suitcase."

"I'll look and see terrectly," The Misfit said.

"Where are they taking him?" the children's mother screamed.

"Daddy was a card himself," The Misfit said. "You couldn't put anything over on him. He never got in trouble with the Authorities though. Just had the knack of handling them."

"You could be honest too if you'd only try," said the grandmother. "Think how wonderful it would be to settle down and live a comfortable life and not have to think about somebody chasing you all the time."

The Misfit kept scratching in the ground with the butt of his gun as if he were thinking about it. "Yes'm, somebody is always after you," he murmured.

The grandmother noticed how thin his shoulder blades were just behind his hat because she was standing up looking down on him. "Do you ever pray?" she asked.

He shook his head. All she saw was the black hat wiggle between his shoulder blades. "Nome," he said.

There was a pistol shot from the woods, followed closely by another. Then silence. The old lady's head jerked around. She could hear the wind move through the tree tops like a long satisfied insuck of breath. "Bailey Boy!" she called.

"I was a gospel singer for a while," The Misfit said. "I been most everything. Been in the arm service, both land and sea, at home and abroad, been twict married, been an undertaker, been with the railroads, plowed Mother Earth, been in a tornado, seen a man burnt alive oncet," and he looked up at the children's mother and the little girl who were sitting close together, their faces white and their eyes glassy; "I even seen a woman flogged," he said.

"Pray, pray," the grandmother began, "pray, pray . . ."

"I never was a bad boy that I remember of," The Misfit said in an almost dreamy voice, "but somewheres along the line I done something wrong and got sent to the penitentiary. I was buried alive," and he looked up and held her attention to him by a steady stare.

"That's when you should have started to pray," she said. "What did you do to get sent to the penitentiary that first time?"

"Turn to the right, it was a wall," The Misfit said, looking up again at the cloudless sky. "Turn to the left, it was a wall. Look up it was a ceiling, look down it was a floor. I forget what I done, lady. I set there and set there, trying to remember what it was I done and I ain't recalled it to this day. Oncet in a while, I would think it was coming to me, but it never come."

"Maybe they put you in by mistake," the old lady said vaguely.

"Nome," he said. "It wasn't no mistake. They had the papers on me."

"You must have stolen something," she said.

The Misfit sneered slightly. "Nobody had nothing I wanted," he said. "It was a head-doctor at the penitentiary said what I had done was kill my daddy but I known that for a lie. My daddy died in nineteen ought nineteen of the epidemic flu[5] and I never had a thing to do with it. He was buried in the Mount Hopewell Baptist churchyard and you can go there and see for yourself."

"If you would pray," the old lady said, "Jesus would help you."

"That's right," The Misfit said.

"Well then, why don't you pray?" she asked trembling with delight suddenly.

"I don't want no hep," he said. "I'm doing all right by myself."

Bobby Lee and Hiram came ambling back from the woods. Bobby Lee was dragging a yellow shirt with bright blue parrots in it.

"Throw me that shirt, Bobby Lee," The Misfit said. The shirt came flying at him and landed on his shoulder and he put it on. The grandmother couldn't name what the shirt reminded her of. "No, lady," The Misfit said while he was buttoning up, "I found out the crime don't matter. You can do one thing or you can do another, kill a man or take a tire off his car, because sooner or later you're going to forget what it was you done and just be punished for it."

The children's mother had begun to make heaving noises as if she couldn't get her breath. "Lady," he asked, "would you and that little girl like to step off yonder with Bobby Lee and Hiram and join your husband?"

"Yes, thank you," the mother said faintly. Her left arm dangled helplessly and she was holding the baby, who had gone to sleep, in the other. "Hep that lady up, Hiram," The Misfit said as she struggled to climb out of the ditch, "and Bobby Lee, you hold onto that little girl's hand."

"I don't want to hold hands with him," June Star said. "He reminds me of a pig."

5. A deadly influenza spread through much of the world in 1918–19.

The fat boy blushed and laughed and caught her by the arm and pulled her off into the woods after Hiram and her mother.

Alone with The Misfit, the grandmother found that she had lost her voice. There was not a cloud in the sky nor any sun. There was nothing around her but woods. She wanted to tell him that he must pray. She opened and closed her mouth several times before anything came out. Finally she found herself saying, "Jesus, Jesus," meaning, Jesus will help you, but the way she was saying it, it sounded as if she might be cursing.

"Yes'm," The Misfit said as if he agreed. "Jesus thrown everything off balance. It was the same case with Him as with me except He hadn't committed any crime and they could prove I had committed one because they had the papers on me. Of course," he said, "they never shown me my papers. That's why I sign myself now. I said long ago, you get you a signature and sign everything you do and keep a copy of it. Then you'll know what you done and you can hold up the crime to the punishment and see do they match and in the end you'll have something to prove you ain't been treated right. I call myself The Misfit," he said, "because I can't make what all I done wrong fit what all I gone through in punishment."

There was a piercing scream from the woods, followed closely by a pistol report. "Does it seem right to you, lady, that one is punished a heap and another ain't punished at all?"

"Jesus!" the old lady cried. "You've got good blood! I know you wouldn't shoot a lady! I know you come from nice people! Pray! Jesus, you ought not to shoot a lady. I'll give you all the money I've got!"

"Lady," The Misfit said, looking beyond her far into the woods, "there never was a body that give the undertaker a tip."

There were two more pistol reports and the grandmother raised her head like a parched old turkey hen crying for water and called, "Bailey Boy, Bailey Boy!" as if her heart would break.

"Jesus was the only One that ever raised the dead," The Misfit continued, "and He shouldn't have done it. He thrown everything off balance. If He did what He said, then it's nothing for you to do but throw away everything and follow Him, and if He didn't then it's nothing for you to do but enjoy the few minutes you got left the best way you can—by killing somebody or burning down his house or doing some other meanness to him. No pleasure but meanness," he said and his voice had become almost a snarl.

"Maybe He didn't raise the dead," the old lady mumbled, not knowing what she was saying and feeling so dizzy that she sank down in the ditch with her legs twisted under her.

"I wasn't there so I can't say He didn't," The Misfit said, "I wisht I had of been there," he said, hitting the ground with his fist. "It ain't right I wasn't there because if I had of been there I would of known. Listen lady," he said in a high voice, "if I had of been there I would of known and I wouldn't be like I am now." His voice seemed about to crack and the grandmother's head cleared for an instant. She saw the man's face twisted close to her own as if he were going to cry and she murmured, "Why, you're one of my babies. You're one of my own children!" She reached out and touched him on the shoulder. The Misfit sprang back as if a snake had bitten him and shot her three times through the chest. Then he put his gun down on the ground and took off his glasses and began to clean them.

Hiram and Bobby Lee returned from the woods and stood over the ditch, looking down at the grandmother who half sat and half lay in a puddle of blood with her legs crossed under her like a child's and her face smiling up at the cloudless sky.

Without his glasses, The Misfit's eyes were red-rimmed and pale and defenseless-looking. "Take her off and throw her where you thrown the others," he said, picking up the cat that was rubbing itself against his leg.

"She was a talker, wasn't she?" Bobby Lee said, sliding down the ditch with a yodel.

"She would of been a good woman," The Misfit said, "if it had been somebody there to shoot her every minute of her life."

"Some fun!" Bobby Lee said.

"Shut up, Bobby Lee," The Misfit said. "It's no real pleasure in life."

1953

Frank O'Connor
1903–1966

O'Connor (born Michael O'Donovan) became active in the Irish Volunteers when he was fifteen. The Volunteers were a nationalist militia dedicated to freeing Ireland from English rule. After a treaty was concluded, he enlisted with the Irish Republican Army, which fought a civil war against the new native government rather than accept the exclusion of six northern counties from the Irish nation. At the age of nineteen, O'Connor resisted orders to shoot unarmed government soldiers. That incident probably inspired "Guests of the Nation," though the soldiers who were Irish in reality are English in the story. O'Connor was a careful theorist of the short story as a genre. He distinguished it from novels on the basis of its ideology rather than its form. Novels, he wrote in The Lonely Voice, *adhere to a belief that humans are living in a community, that society works or can work. The short story depicts people as romantics, as intransigent, individuals remote from a society that does not and cannot work.*

Guests of the Nation

I

At dusk the big Englishman, Belcher, would shift his long legs out of the ashes and say "Well, chums, what about it?" and Noble or me would say "All right, chum" (for we had picked up some of their curious expressions), and the little Englishman, Hawkins, would light the lamp and bring out the cards. Sometimes Jeremiah Donovan would come up and supervise the game and get excited over Hawkins's cards, which he always played badly, and shout at him as if he was one of our own "Ah, you divil, you, why didn't you play the tray?"

But ordinarily Jeremiah was a sober and contented poor devil like the big Englishman, Belcher, and was looked up to only because he was a fair hand at documents, though he was slow enough even with them. He wore a small cloth hat and big gaiters over his long pants; and you seldom saw him with his hands out of his pockets. He reddened when you talked to him, tilting from toe to heel and back, and looking down all the time at his big farmer's feet. Noble and me used to make fun of his broad accent, because we were from the town.

I couldn't at the time see the point of me and Noble guarding Belcher and Hawkins at all, for it was my belief that you could have planted that pair down anywhere from this to Claregalway and they'd have taken root there like a native weed. I never in my short experience seen two men to take to the country as they did.

They were handed on to us by the Second Battalion when the search[1] for them became too hot, and Noble and myself, being young, took over with a natural feeling of responsibility, but Hawkins made us look like fools when he showed that he knew the country better than we did.

"You're the bloke they calls Bonaparte," he says to me. "Mary Brigid O'Connell told me to ask you what you done with the pair of her brother's socks you borrowed."

For it seemed, as they explained it, that the Second used to have little evenings, and some of the girls of the neighbourhood turned in, and, seeing they were such decent chaps, our fellows couldn't leave the two Englishmen out of them. Hawkins learned to dance "The Walls of Limerick," "The Siege of Ennis," and "The Waves of Tory"[2] as well as any of them, though naturally, he couldn't return the compliment, because our lads at that time did not dance foreign dances on principle.

So whatever privileges Belcher and Hawkins had with the Second they just naturally took with us, and after the first day or two we gave up all pretence of keeping a close eye on them. Not that they could have got far, for they had accents you could cut with a knife and wore khaki tunics and overcoats with civilian pants and boots. But it's my belief that they never had any idea of escaping and were quite content to be where they were.

It was a treat to see how Belcher got off with the old woman of

1. Belcher and Hawkins are British soldiers captured by Irish irregulars during the 1921 Anglo-Irish War.

2. These are Irish dances that, because they are nationalist, are implicitly anti-English.

the house where we were staying. She was a great warrant to scold, and cranky even with us, but before ever she had a chance to giving our guests, as I may call them, a lick of her tongue, Belcher had made her his friend for life. She was breaking sticks, and Belcher, who hadn't been more than ten minutes in the house, jumped up from his seat and went over to her.

"Allow me, madam," he says, smiling his queer little smile, "please allow me"; and he takes the bloody hatchet. She was struck too paralytic to speak, and after that, Belcher would be at her heels, carrying a bucket, a basket, or a load of turf, as the case might be. As Noble said, he got into looking before she leapt, and hot water, or any little thing she wanted, Belcher would have it ready for her. For such a huge man (and though I am five foot ten myself I had to look up at him) he had an uncommon shortness—or should I say lack?—of speech. It took us some time to get used to him, walking in and out, like a ghost, without a word. Especially because Hawkins talked enough for a platoon, it was strange to hear big Belcher with his toes in the ashes come out with a solitary "Excuse me, chum," or "That's right, chum." His one and only passion was cards, and I will say for him that he was a good card-player. He could have fleeced myself and Noble, but whatever we lost to him Hawkins lost to us, and Hawkins played with the money Belcher gave him.

Hawkins lost to us because he had too much old gab, and we probably lost to Belcher for the same reason. Hawkins and Noble would spit at one another about religion into the early hours of the morning, and Hawkins worried the soul out of Noble, whose brother was a priest, with a string of questions that would puzzle a cardinal. To make it worse even in treating of holy subjects, Hawkins had a deplorable tongue. I never in all my career met a man who could mix such a variety of cursing and bad language into an argument. He was a terrible man, and a fright to argue. He never did a stroke of work, and when he had no one else to talk to, he got stuck in the old woman.

He met his match in her, for one day when he tried to get her to complain profanely of the drought, she gave him a great comedown by blaming it entirely on Jupiter Pluvius (a deity neither Hawkins nor I had ever heard of, though Noble said that among the pagans it was believed that he had something to do with the rain).[3] Another day he was swearing at the capitalists for starting the German war[4] when the old lady laid down her iron, puckered up her little crab's mouth, and said: "Mr. Hawkins, you can say what you like about the war, and think you'll deceive me because I'm only a simple poor countrywoman, but I know what started the war. It was the Italian Count that stole the heathen divinity out of the temple in Japan. Believe me, Mr. Hawkins, nothing but sorrow and want can follow the people that disturb the hidden powers."

A queer old girl, all right.

II

We had our tea one evening, and Hawkins lit the lamp and we all sat into cards. Jeremiah Donovan came in too, and sat down and watched us for a while, and it suddenly struck me that he had no great love for the two Englishmen. It came as a great surprise to me, because I hadn't noticed anything about him before.

Late in the evening a really terrible argument blew up between Hawkins and Noble, about capitalists and priests and love of your country.

"The capitalists," says Hawkins with an angry gulp, "pays the priests to tell you about the next world so as you won't notice what the bastards are up to in this."

"Nonsense, man!" says Noble, losing his temper. "Before ever a capitalist was thought of, people believed in the next world."

Hawkins stood up as though he was preaching a sermon.

"Oh, they did, did they?" he says with a sneer. "They believed all the things you believe, isn't that what you mean? And you believe that God created Adam, and Adam created Shem, and Shem created Jehoshophat.[5] You believe all that silly old fairytale about Eve and Eden and the apple. Well, listen to me, chum. If you're entitled

3. Jupiter Pluvius is the rainmaker in Roman mythology.

4. World War I, in which England was at war with Germany.

5. A condensation of Old Testament genealogy; though Adam, Shem, and Jehoshophat appear in the Bible in that order, they lived many generations apart.

to hold a silly belief like that, I'm entitled to hold my silly belief—which is that the first thing your God created was a bleeding capitalist, with morality and Rolls-Royce complete. Am I right, chum?" he says to Belcher.

"You're right, chum," says Belcher with his amused smile, and got up from the table to stretch his long legs into the fire and stroke his moustache. So, seeing that Jeremiah Donovan was going, and that there was no knowing when the argument about religion would be over, I went out with him. We strolled down to the village together, and then he stopped and started blushing and mumbling and saying I ought to be behind, keeping guard on the prisoners. I didn't like the tone he took with me, and anyway I was bored with life in the cottage, so I replied by asking him what the hell we wanted guarding them at all for. I told him I'd talked it over with Noble, and that we'd both rather be out with a fighting column.

"What use are those fellows to us?" says I.

He looked at me in surprise and said: "I thought you knew we were keeping them as hostages."

"Hostages?" I said.

"The enemy have prisoners belonging to us," he says, "and now they're talking of shooting them. If they shoot our prisoners, we'll shoot theirs."

"Shoot them?" I said.

"What else did you think we were keeping them for?" he says.

"Wasn't it very unforeseen of you not to warn Noble and myself of that in the beginning?" I said.

"How was it?" says he. "You might have known it."

"We couldn't know it, Jeremiah Donovan," says I. "How could we when they were on our hands so long?"

"The enemy have our prisoners as long and longer," says he.

"That's not the same thing at all," says I.

"What difference is there?" says he.

I couldn't tell him, because I knew he wouldn't understand. If it was only an old dog that was going to the vet's, you'd try and not get too fond of him, but Jeremiah Donovan wasn't a man that would ever be in danger of that.

"And when is this thing going to be decided?" says I.

"We might hear tonight," he says. "Or tomorrow or the next day at latest. So if it's only hanging round here that's a trouble to you, you'll be free soon enough."

It wasn't the hanging round that was a trouble to me at all by this time. I had worse things to worry about. When I got back to the cottage the argument was still on. Hawkins was holding forth in his best style, maintaining that there was no next world, and Noble was maintaining that there was; but I could see that Hawkins had had the best of it.

"Do you know what, chum?" he was saying with a saucy smile. "I think you're just as big a bleeding unbeliever as I am. You say you believe in the next world, and you know just as much about the next world as I do, which is sweet damn-all. What's heaven? You don't know. Where's heaven? You don't know. You know sweet damn-all! I ask you again, do they wear wings?"

"Very well, then," says Noble, "they do. Is that enough for you? They do wear wings."

"Where do they get them, then? Who makes them? Have they a factory for wings? Have they a sort of store where you hands in your chit and takes your bleeding wings?"

"You're an impossible man to argue with," says Noble. "Now, listen to me—" And they were off again.

It was long after midnight when we locked up and went to bed. As I blew out the candle I told Noble what Jeremiah Donovan was after telling me. Noble took it very quietly. When we'd been in bed about an hour he asked me did I think we ought to tell the Englishmen. I didn't think we should, because it was more than likely that the English wouldn't shoot our men, and even if they did, the brigade officers, who were always up and down with the Second Battalion and knew the Englishmen well, wouldn't be likely to want them plugged. "I think so too," says Noble. "It would be great cruelty to put the wind to them now."

"It was very unforeseen of Jeremiah Donovan anyhow," says I.

It was next morning that we found it so hard to face Belcher and Hawkins. We went about the house all day scarcely saying a word. Belcher didn't seem to notice; he was stretched into the ashes as usual, with his look unusual of waiting in quietness for something unforeseen to happen, but Hawkins noticed and put it down to Noble's being beaten in the argument of the night before.

"Why can't you take a discussion in the proper spirit?" he says severely. "You and your Adam and Eve! I'm a Communist, that's what I am. Communist or anarchist, it all comes to much the same thing." And for hours he went round the house, muttering when the fit took him. "Adam and Eve! Adam and Eve! Nothing better to do with their time than picking bleeding apples!"

III

I don't know how we got through that day, but I was very glad when it was over, the tea things were cleared away, and Belcher said in his peaceable way: "Well, chums, what about it?" We sat round the table and Hawkins took out the cards, and just then I heard Jeremiah Donovan's footstep on the path and a dark presentiment crossed my mind. I rose from the table and caught him before he reached the door.

"What do you want?" I asked.

"I want those two soldier friends of yours," he says, getting red.

"Is that the way, Jeremiah Donovan?" I asked.

"That's the way. There were four of our lads shot this morning, one of them a boy of sixteen."

"That's bad," I said.

At that moment Noble followed me out, and the three of us walked down the path together, talking in whispers. Feeney, the local intelligence officer was standing by the gate.

"What are you going to do about it?" I asked Jeremiah Donovan.

"I want you and Noble to get them out; tell them they're being shifted again; that'll be the quietest way."

"Leave me out of that," says Noble under his breath.

Jeremiah Donovan looks at him hard.

"All right," he says. "You and Feeney get a few tools from the shed and dig a hole by the far end of the bog. Bonaparte and myself will be after you. Don't let anyone see you with the tools. I wouldn't like it to go beyond ourselves."

We saw Feeney and Noble go round to the shed and went in ourselves. I left Jeremiah Donovan to do the explanations. He told them that he had orders to send them back to the Second Battalion.

Hawkins let out a mouthful of curses, and you could see that though Belcher didn't say anything, he was a bit upset too. The old woman was for having them stay in spite of us, and she didn't stop advising them until Jeremiah Donovan lost his temper and turned on her. He had a nasty temper, I noticed. It was pitch-dark in the cottage by this time, but no one thought of lighting the lamp, and in the darkness the two Englishmen fetched their topcoats and said good-bye to the old woman.

"Just as a man makes a home of a bleeding place, some bastard at headquarters thinks you're too cushy and shunts you off," says Hawkins, shaking her hand.

"A thousand thanks, madam," says Belcher. "A thousand thanks for everything"—as though he'd made it up.

We went round to the back of the house and down towards the bog. It was only then that Jeremiah Donovan told them. He was shaking with excitement.

"There were four of our fellows shot in Cork this morning and now you're to be shot as a reprisal."

"What are you talking about?" snaps Hawkins. "It's bad enough being mucked about as we are without having to put up with your funny jokes."

"It isn't a joke," says Donovan. "I'm sorry, Hawkins, but it's true," and begins on the usual rigmarole about duty and how unpleasant it is.

I never noticed that people who talk a lot about duty find it much of a trouble to them.

"Oh, cut it out!" says Hawkins.

"Ask Bonaparte," says Donovan, seeing that Hawkins isn't taking him seriously. "Isn't it true, Bonaparte?"

"It is," I say, and Hawkins stops.

"Ah, for Christ's sake, chum!"

"You don't sound as if you meant it."

"If he doesn't mean it, I do," says Donovan, working himself up.

"What have you against me, Jeremiah Donovan?"

"I never said I had anything against you. But why did your people take out four of our prisoners and shoot them in cold blood?"

He took Hawkins by the arm and dragged him on, but it was impossible to make him understand that we were in earnest. I had the

Smith and Wesson[6] in my pocket and I kept fingering it and wondering what I'd do if they put up a fight for it or ran, and wishing to God they'd do one or the other. I knew if they did run for it, that I'd never fire on them. Hawkins wanted to know was Noble in it, and when we said yes, he asked us why Noble wanted to plug him. Why did any of us want to plug him? What had he done to us? Weren't we all chums? Didn't we understand him and didn't he understand us? Did we imagine for an instant that he'd shoot us for all the so-and-so officers in the so-and-so British Army?

By this time we'd reached the bog, and I was so sick I couldn't even answer him. We walked along the edge of it in the darkness, and every now and then Hawkins would call a halt and begin all over again, as if he was wound up, about our being chums, and I knew that nothing but the sight of the grave would convince him that we had to do it. And all the time I was hoping that something would happen; that they'd run for it or that Noble would take over the responsibility from me. I had the feeling that it was worse on Noble than on me.

IV

At last we saw the lantern in the distance and made towards it. Noble was carrying it, and Feeney was standing somewhere in the darkness behind him, and the picture of them so still and silent in the bogland brought it home to me that we were in earnest, and banished the last bit of hope I had.

Belcher, on recognizing Noble, said: "Hallo, chum," in his quiet way, but Hawkins flew at him at once, and the argument began all over again, only this time Noble had nothing to say for himself and stood with his head down, holding the lantern between his legs.

It was Jeremiah Donovan who did the answering. For the twentieth time, as though it was haunting his mind, Hawkins asked if anybody thought he'd shoot Noble.

"Yes, you would," says Jeremiah Donovan.

"No, I wouldn't, damn you!"

6. A revolver, as is the Webley, further on in the story.

"You would, because you'd know you'd be shot for not doing it."

"I wouldn't, not if I was to be shot twenty times over. I wouldn't shoot a pal. And Belcher wouldn't—isn't that right, Belcher?"

"That's right, chum," Belcher said, but more by way of answering the question than of joining in the argument. Belcher sounded as though whatever unforeseen thing he'd always been waiting for had come at last.

"Anyway, who says Noble would be shot if I wasn't? What do you think I'd do if I was in his place, out in the middle of a blasted bog?"

"What would you do?" asks Donovan.

"I'd go with him wherever he was going, of course. Share my last bob[7] with him and stick by him through thick and thin. No one can ever say of me that I let down a pal."

"We had enough of this," says Jeremiah Donovan, cocking his revolver. "Is there any message you want to send?"

"No, there isn't."

"Do you want to say your prayers?"

Hawkins came out with a cold-blooded remark that even shocked me and turned on Noble again.

"Listen to me, Noble," he says. "You and me are chums. You can't come over to my side, so I'll come over to your side. That show you I mean what I say? Give me a rifle and I'll go along with you and the other lads."

Nobody answered him. We knew that was no way out.

"Hear what I'm saying?" he says. "I'm through with it. I'm a deserter or anything else you like. I don't believe in your stuff, but it's no worse than mine. That satisfy you?"

Noble raised his head, but Donovan began to speak and he lowered it again without replying.

"For the last time, have you any messages to send?" says Donovan in a cold excited sort of voice.

"Shut up, Donovan! You don't understand me, but these lads do. They're not the sort to make a pal and kill a pal. They're not the tools of any capitalist."

7. Shilling (British slang).

I alone of the crowd saw Donovan raise his Webley to the back of Hawkins's neck, and as he did so I shut my eyes and tried to pray. Hawkins had begun to say something else when Donovan fired, and as I opened my eyes at the bang, I saw Hawkins stagger at the knees and lie out flat at Noble's feet, slowly and as quiet as a kid falling asleep, with the lantern-light on his lean legs and bright farmer's boots. We all stood very still, watching him settle out in the last agony.

Then Belcher took out a handkerchief and began to tie it about his own eyes (in our excitement we'd forgotten to do the same for Hawkins), and, seeing it wasn't big enough, turned and asked for the loan of mine. I gave it to him and he knotted the two together and pointed with his foot at Hawkins.

"He's not quite dead," he says. "Better give him another."

Sure enough, Hawkins's left knee is beginning to rise. I bend down and put my gun to his head; then, recollecting myself, I get up again. Belcher understands what's in my mind.

"Give him his first," he says. "I don't mind. Poor bastard, we don't know what's happening to him now."

I knelt and fired. By this time I didn't seem to know what I was doing. Belcher, who was fumbling a bit awkwardly with the handkerchiefs, came out with a laugh as he heard the shot. It was the first time I heard him laugh and it sent a shudder down my back; it sounded so unnatural.

"Poor bugger!" he said quietly. "And last night he was so curious about it all. It's very queer, chums, I always think. Now he knows as much about it as they'll ever let him know, and last night he was all in the dark."

Donovan helped him to tie the handkerchiefs about his eyes. "Thanks, chum," he said. Donovan asked if there were any messages he wanted sent.

"No, chum," he says. "Not for me. If any of you would like to write to Hawkins's mother, you'll find a letter from her in his pocket. He and his mother were great chums. But my missus left me eight years ago. Went away with another fellow and took the kid with her. I like the feeling of a home, as you may have noticed, but I couldn't start again after that."

It was an extraordinary thing, but in those few minutes Belcher said more than in all the weeks before. It was just as if the sound of the shot had started a flood of talk in him and he could go on the whole night like that, quite happily, talking about himself. We stood round like fools now that he couldn't see us any longer. Donovan looked at Noble, and Noble shook his head. Then Donovan raised his Webley, and at that moment Belcher gives his queer laugh again. He may have thought we were talking about him, or perhaps he noticed the same thing I'd noticed and couldn't understand it.

"Excuse me, chums," he says. "I feel I'm talking the hell of a lot, and so silly, about my being so handy about a house and things like that. But this thing came on me suddenly. You'll forgive me, I'm sure."

"You don't want to say a prayer?" asks Donovan.

"No, chum," he says. "I don't think it would help. I'm ready, and you boys want to get it over."

"You understand that we're only doing our duty?" says Donovan.

Belcher's head was raised like a blind man's so that you could only see his chin and the tip of his nose in the lantern-light.

"I never could make out what duty was myself," he said. "I think you're all good lads, if that's what you mean. I'm not complaining."

Noble, just as if he couldn't bear any more of it, raised his fist at Donovan, and in a flash Donovan raised his gun and fired. The big man went over like a sack of meal, and this time there was no need for a second shot.

I don't remember much about the burying, but that it was worse than all the rest because we had to carry them to the grave. It was all mad lonely with nothing but a patch of lantern light between ourselves and the dark, and birds hooting and screeching all round, disturbed by the guns. Noble went through Hawkins's belongings to find the letter from his mother, and then joined his hands together. He did the same with Belcher. Then, when we'd filled in the grave, we separated from Jeremiah Donovan and Feeney and took our tools back to the shed. All the way we didn't speak a word. The kitchen was dark and cold as we'd left it, and the old woman was sitting over the hearth, saying her beads. We walked past her into the room, and Noble struck a match to light the lamp. She rose quietly and came to the doorway with all her cantankerousness gone.

"What did ye do with them?" she asked in a whisper, and Noble started so that the match went out in his hand.

"What's that?" he asked without turning round.

"I heard ye," she said.

"What did you hear?" asked Noble.

"I heard ye. Do ye think I didn't hear ye, putting the spade back in the houseen?"[8]

Noble struck another match and this time the lamp lit for him.

"Was that what ye did to them?" she asked.

Then, by God, in the very doorway, she fell on her knees and began praying, and after looking at her for a minute or two Noble did the same by the fireplace. I pushed my way out past her and left them at it. I stood at the door, watching the stars and listening to the shrieking of the birds dying out over the bogs. It is so strange what you feel at times like that that you can't describe it. Noble says he saw everything ten times the size, as though there were nothing in the whole world but that little patch of bog with the two Englishmen stiffening into it, but with me it was as if the patch of bog where the Englishmen were was a million miles away, and even Noble and the old woman, mumbling behind me, and the birds and the bloody stars were all far away, and I was somehow very small and very lost and lonely like a child astray in the snow. And anything that happened to me afterwards, I never felt the same about again.

1930

Tillie Olsen

1913–2007

The form of Olsen's stories, she said, "is dependent on . . . my personal situation, . . . both material and personal: that is, the writing time available to me; what is happening in my work and family life, and in the larger environment, in society." She wrote and rewrote "I Stand Here Ironing" on an ironing board, late at night, and the "back and forth movement as the iron moves" is reflected in the story

8. "Een" is an Irish suffix meaning "little," hence "little house," or in this case, "shed."

itself. Her original impulse to write this story came from the situation of a friend, whose teenage son had been arrested for drinking beer in a car. The friend was summoned to court to prove she was a fit mother; because she had a boyfriend who often slept over, the court considered her immoral. During this crisis, Olsen said that she "gagged at the difference between the way you're judged from the outside and the true reality" of a single mother's life. She wrote the story to instruct "the kind of people who had the power to take away one's child." But in the writing, Olsen's own life took over the story: it is largely autobiographical. Olsen complained that many of the anthologies that include her story direct students to consider the narrator's feelings of guilt. "One is guilty," she wrote, "only for what one oneself is responsible." Instead, the reader should focus on "society and its institutions" that force the narrator to suffer anguish.

I Stand Here Ironing

I stand here ironing, and what you asked me moves tormented back and forth with the iron.

"I wish you would manage the time to come in and talk with me about your daughter. I'm sure you can help me understand her. She's a youngster who needs help and whom I'm deeply interested in helping."

"Who needs help." . . . Even if I came, what good would it do? You think because I am her mother I have a key, or that in some way you could use me as a key? She has lived for nineteen years. There is all that life that has happened outside of me, beyond me.

And when is there time to remember, to sift, to weigh, to estimate, to total? I will start and there will be an interruption and I will have to gather it all together again. Or I will become engulfed with all I did or did not do, with what should have been and what cannot be helped.

She was a beautiful baby. The first and only one of our five that was beautiful at birth. You do not guess how new and uneasy her tenancy in her now-loveliness. You did not know her all those years she was thought homely, or see her poring over her baby pictures, making me tell her over and over how beautiful she had been—and would be, I would tell her—and was now, to the seeing eye. But the seeing eyes were few or non-existent. Including mine.

I nursed her. They feel that's important nowadays. I nursed all the children, but with her, with all the fierce rigidity of first motherhood, I did like the books then said. Though her cries battered me to trembling and my breasts ached with swollenness, I waited till the clock decreed.

Why do I put that first? I do not even know if it matters, or if it explains anything.

She was a beautiful baby. She blew shining bubbles of sound. She loved motion, loved light, loved color and music and textures. She would lie on the floor in her blue overalls patting the surface so hard in ecstasy her hands and feet would blur. She was a miracle to me, but when she was eight months old I had to leave her daytimes with the woman downstairs to whom she was no miracle at all, for I worked or looked for work and for Emily's father, who "could no longer endure" (he wrote in his good-bye note) "sharing want with us."

I was nineteen. It was the pre-relief, pre-WPA[1] world of the depression. I would start running as soon as I got off the streetcar, running up the stairs, the place smelling sour, and awake or asleep to startle awake, when she saw me she would break into a clogged weeping that could not be comforted, a weeping I can hear yet.

After a while I found a job hashing at night so I could be with her days, and it was better. But it came to where I had to bring her to his family and leave her.

It took a long time to raise the money for her fare back. Then she got chicken pox and I had to wait longer. When she finally came, I hardly knew her, walking quick and nervous like her father, looking like her father, thin, and dressed in a shoddy red that yellowed her skin and glared at the pockmarks. All the baby loveliness gone.

She was two. Old enough for nursery school they said, and I did not know then what I know now—the fatigue of the long day, and the lacerations of group life in the kinds of nurseries that are only parking places for children.

Except that it would have made no difference if I had known. It

1. Works Progress Administration, a U.S. government agency established in 1935 to provide jobs, especially in public works; it was abolished in 1943.

was the only place there was. It was the only way we could be together, the only way I could hold a job.

And even without knowing, I knew. I knew the teacher that was evil because all these years it has curdled into my memory, the little boy hunched in the corner, her rasp, "why aren't you outside, because Alvin hits you? that's no reason, go out, scaredy." I knew Emily hated it even if she did not clutch and implore "don't go Mommy" like the other children, mornings.

She always had a reason why we should stay home. Momma, you look sick, Momma. I feel sick. Momma, the teachers aren't there today, they're sick. Momma, we can't go, there was a fire there last night. Momma, it's a holiday today, no school, they told me.

But never a direct protest, never rebellion. I think of our others in their three-, four-year-oldness—the explosions, the tempers, the denunciations, the demands—and I feel suddenly ill. I put the iron down. What in me demanded that goodness in her? And what was the cost, the cost to her of such goodness?

The old man living in the back once said in his gentle way: "You should smile at Emily more when you look at her." What *was* in my face when I looked at her? I loved her. There were all the acts of love.

It was only with the others I remembered what he said, and it was the face of joy, and not of care or tightness or worry I turned to them—too late for Emily. She does not smile easily, let alone almost always as her brothers and sisters do. Her face is closed and sombre, but when she wants, how fluid. You must have seen it in her pantomimes, you spoke of her rare gift for comedy on the stage that rouses a laughter out of the audience so dear they applaud and applaud and do not want to let her go.

Where does it come from, that comedy? There was none of it in her when she came back to me that second time, after I had had to send her away again. She had a new daddy now to learn to love, and I think perhaps it was a better time.

Except when we left her alone nights, telling ourselves she was old enough.

"Can't you go some other time, Mommy, like tomorrow?" she would ask. "Will it be just a little while you'll be gone? Do you promise?"

The time we came back, the front door open, the clock on the floor in the hall. She rigid awake. "It wasn't just a little while. I didn't cry. Three times I called you, just three times, and then I ran downstairs to open the door so you could come faster. The clock talked loud. I threw it away, it scared me what it talked."

She said the clock talked loud again that night I went to the hospital to have Susan. She was delirious with the fever that comes before red measles, but she was fully conscious all the week I was gone and the week after we were home when she could not come near the new baby or me.

She did not get well. She stayed skeleton thin, not wanting to eat, and night after night she had nightmares. She would call for me, and I would rouse from exhaustion to sleepily call back: "You're all right, darling, go to sleep, it's just a dream," and if she still called, in a sterner voice, "now go to sleep, Emily, there's nothing to hurt you." Twice, only twice, when I had to get up for Susan anyhow, I went in to sit with her.

Now when it is too late (as if she would let me hold and comfort her like I do the others) I get up and go to her at once at her moan or restless stirring. "Are you awake, Emily? Can I get you something?" And the answer is always the same: "No, I'm all right, go back to sleep, Mother."

They persuaded me at the clinic to send her away to a convalescent home in the country where "she can have the kind of food and care you can't manage for her, and you'll be free to concentrate on the new baby." They still send children to that place. I see pictures on the society page of sleek young women planning affairs to raise money for it, or dancing at the affairs, or decorating Easter eggs or filling Christmas stockings for the children.

They never have a picture of the children so I do not know if the girls still wear those gigantic red bows and the ravaged looks on the every other Sunday when parents can come to visit "unless otherwise notified"—as we were notified the first six weeks.

Oh it is a handsome place, green lawns and tall trees and fluted flower beds. High up on the balconies of each cottage the children stand, the girls in their red bows and white dresses, the boys in white suits and giant red ties. The parents stand below shrieking up to be heard and the children shriek down to be heard, and between them the invisible wall "Not To Be Contaminated by Parental Germs or Physical Affection."

There was a tiny girl who always stood hand in hand with Emily. Her parents never came. One visit she was gone. "They moved her to Rose Cottage" Emily shouted in explanation. "They don't like you to love anybody here."

She wrote once a week, the labored writing of a seven-year-old. "I am fine. How is the baby. If I write my leter nicly I will have a star. Love." There never was a star. We wrote every other day, letters she could never hold or keep but only hear read—once. "We simply do not have room for children to keep any personal possessions," they patiently explained when we pieced one Sunday's shrieking together to plead how much it would mean to Emily, who loved so to keep things, to be allowed to keep her letters and cards.

Each visit she looked frailer. "She isn't eating," they told us.

(They had runny eggs for breakfast or mush with lumps, Emily said later, I'd hold it in my mouth and not swallow. Nothing ever tasted good, just when they had chicken.)

It took us eight months to get her released home, and only the fact that she gained back so little of her seven lost pounds convinced the social worker.

I used to try to hold and love her after she came back, but her body would stay stiff, and after a while she'd push away. She ate little. Food sickened her, and I think much of life too. Oh she had physical lightness and brightness, twinkling by on skates, bouncing like a ball up and down up and down over the jump rope, skimming over the hill; but these were momentary.

She fretted about her appearance, thin and dark and foreign-looking at a time when every little girl was supposed to look or thought she should look a chubby blonde replica of Shirley Temple. The doorbell sometimes rang for her, but no one seemed to come and play in the house or be a best friend. Maybe because we moved so much.

There was a boy she loved painfully through two school semesters. Months later she told me how she had taken pennies from my purse to buy him candy. "Licorice was his favorite and I brought him some every day, but he still liked Jennifer better'n me. Why, Mommy?" The kind of question for which there is no answer.

School was a worry to her. She was not glib or quick in a world where glibness and quickness were easily confused with ability to learn. To her overworked and exasperated teachers she was an over-conscientious "slow learner" who kept trying to catch up and was absent entirely too often.

I let her be absent, though sometimes the illness was imaginary. How different from my now-strictness about attendance with the others. I wasn't working. We had a new baby, I was home anyhow. Sometimes, after Susan grew old enough, I would keep her home from school, too, to have them all together.

Mostly Emily had asthma, and her breathing, harsh and labored, would fill the house with a curiously tranquil sound. I would bring the two old dresser mirrors and her boxes of collections to her bed. She would select beads and single earrings, bottle tops and shells, dried flowers and pebbles, old postcards and scraps, all sorts of oddments; then she and Susan would play Kingdom, setting up landscapes and furniture, peopling them with action.

Those were the only times of peaceful companionship between her and Susan. I have edged away from it, that poisonous feeling between them, that terrible balancing of hurts and needs I had to do between the two, and did so badly, those earlier years.

Oh there are conflicts between the others too, each one human, needing, demanding, hurting, taking—but only between Emily and Susan, no, Emily toward Susan that corroding resentment. It seems so obvious on the surface, yet it is not obvious. Susan, the second child, Susan, golden- and curly-haired and chubby, quick and articulate and assured, everything in appearance and manner Emily was not; Susan, not able to resist Emily's precious things, losing or sometimes clumsily breaking them; Susan telling jokes and riddles to company for applause while Emily sat silent (to say to me later: that was *my* riddle, Mother, I told it to Susan); Susan, who for all the five years' difference in age was just a year behind Emily in developing physically.

I am glad for that slow physical development that widened the difference between her and her contemporaries, though she suffered over it. She was too vulnerable for that terrible world of youthful competition, of preening and parading, of constant measuring of yourself against every other, of envy, "If I had that copper hair," "If

I had that skin. . . .” She tormented herself enough about not looking like the others, there was enough of the unsureness, the having to be conscious of words before you speak, the constant caring—what are they thinking of me? without having it all magnified by the merciless physical drives.

Ronnie is calling. He is wet and I change him. It is rare there is such a cry now. That time of motherhood is almost behind me when the ear is not one's own but must always be racked and listening for the child cry, the child call. We sit for a while and I hold him, looking out over the city spread in charcoal with its soft aisles of light. *“Shoogily,”* he breathes and curls closer. I carry him back to bed, asleep. *Shoogily.* A funny word, a family word, inherited from Emily, invented by her to say: *comfort.*

In this and other ways she leaves her seal, I say aloud. And startle at my saying it. What do I mean? What did I start to gather together, to try and make coherent? I was at the terrible, growing years. War years. I do not remember them well. I was working, there were four smaller ones now, there was not time for her. She had to help be a mother, and housekeeper, and shopper. She had to set her seal. Mornings of crisis and near hysteria trying to get lunches packed, hair combed, coats and shoes found, everyone to school or Child Care on time, the baby ready for transportation. And always the paper scribbled on by a smaller one, the book looked at by Susan then mislaid, the homework not done. Running out to that huge school where she was one, she was lost, she was a drop; suffering over the unpreparedness, stammering and unsure in her classes.

There was so little time left at night after the kids were bedded down. She would struggle over books, always eating (it was in those years she developed her enormous appetite that is legendary in our family) and I would be ironing, or preparing food for the next day, or writing V-mail[2] to Bill, or tending the baby. Sometimes, to make me laugh, or out of her despair, she would imitate happenings or types at school.

I think I said once: “Why don't you do something like this in the school amateur show?” One morning she phoned me at work,

2. Overseas mail service for the U.S. armed forces during World War II. Short for Victory Mail.

hardly understandable through the weeping: "Mother, I did it. I won, I won; they gave me first prize; they clapped and clapped and wouldn't let me go."

Now suddenly she was Somebody, and as imprisoned in her difference as she had been in anonymity.

She began to be asked to perform at other high schools, even in colleges, then at city and statewide affairs. The first one we went to, I only recognized her that first moment when thin, shy, she almost drowned herself into the curtains. Then: Was this Emily? The control, the command, the convulsing and deadly clowning, the spell, then the roaring, stamping audience, unwilling to let this rare and precious laughter out of their lives.

Afterwards: You ought to do something about her with a gift like that—but without money or knowing how, what does one do? We have left it all to her, and the gift has as often eddied inside, clogged and clotted, as been used and growing.

She is coming. She runs up the stairs two at a time with her light graceful step, and I know she is happy tonight. Whatever it was that occasioned your call did not happen today.

"Aren't you ever going to finish the ironing, Mother? Whistler painted his mother in a rocker.[3] I'd have to paint mine standing over an ironing board." This is one of her communicative nights and she tells me everything and nothing as she fixes herself a plate of food out of the icebox.

She is so lovely. Why did you want me to come in at all? Why were you concerned? She will find her way.

She starts up the stairs to bed. "Don't get me up with the rest in the morning." "But I thought you were having midterms." "Oh, those," she comes back in, kisses me, and says quite lightly, "in a couple of years when we'll all be atom-dead they won't matter a bit."

She has said it before. She *believes* it. But because I have been dredging the past, and all that compounds a human being is so heavy and meaningful in me, I cannot endure it tonight.

I will never total it all. I will never come in to say: She was a child seldom smiled at. Her father left me before she was a year old. I had

3. *Arrangement in Grey and Black* (1872), by the American painter James Whistler (1834–1903).

to work her first six years when there was work, or I sent her home and to his relatives. There were years she had care she hated. She was dark and thin and foreign-looking in a world where the prestige went to blondeness and curly hair and dimples, she was slow where glibness was prized. She was a child of anxious, not proud, love. We were poor and could not afford for her the soil of easy growth. I was a young mother, I was a distracted mother. There were the other children pushing up, demanding. Her younger sister seemed all that she was not. There were years she did not want me to touch her. She kept too much in herself, her life was such she had to keep too much in herself. My wisdom came too late. She has much to her and probably little will come of it. She is a child of her age, of depression, of war, of fear.

Let her be. So all that is in her will not bloom—but in how many does it? There is still enough left to live by. Only help her to know—help make it so there is cause for her to know—that she is more than this dress on the ironing board, helpless before the iron.

1960

Edgar Allan Poe

1809–1849

Poe wrote "The Cask of Amontillado" relatively late in his career, in 1846. Though made famous the year before by his long poem "The Raven," Poe envied the successes of lesser writers and entangled himself in bitter battles with these rivals, which led to his banishment from the New York and New England literary circles. His ostracism and poverty may have inspired this tale of revenge, which, like Poe's other stories, is justly remembered for its weird grotesques. But Poe's stories continue to fascinate us because of their psychological complexities—the individual, unique psyche of his characters. "The Cask of Amontillado" reaches this level of complexity when the reader remembers that it is told from Montresor's point of view. To sound the depths of the story, we must question everything he tells us, even about Fortunato's supposed offense. You might also consider to whom and why Montresor confesses this story.

The Cask of Amontillado

The thousand injuries of Fortunato I had borne as I best could; but when he ventured upon insult, I vowed revenge. You, who so well know the nature of my soul, will not suppose, however, that I gave utterance to a threat. *At length* I would be avenged; this was a point definitively settled—but the very definitiveness with which it was resolved, precluded the idea of risk. I must not only punish, but punish with impunity. A wrong is unredressed when retribution overtakes its redresser. It is equally unredressed when the avenger fails to make himself felt as such to him who has done the wrong.

It must be understood, that neither by word nor deed had I given Fortunato cause to doubt my good-will. I continued, as was my wont, to smile in his face, and he did not perceive that my smile *now* was at the thought of his immolation.

He had a weak point—this Fortunato—although in other regards he was a man to be respected and even feared. He prided himself on his connoisseurship in wine. Few Italians have the true virtuoso spirit. For the most part their enthusiasm is adopted to suit the time and opportunity—to practise imposture upon the British and Austrian *millionnaires*. In painting and gemmary[1] Fortunato, like his countrymen, was a quack—but in the matter of old wines he was sincere. In this respect I did not differ from him materially: I was skilful in the Italian vintages myself, and bought largely whenever I could.

It was about dusk, one evening during the supreme madness of the carnival season,[2] that I encountered my friend. He accosted me with excessive warmth, for he had been drinking much. The man wore motley.[3] He had on a tight-fitting parti-striped dress, and his head was surmounted by the conical cap and bells. I was so pleased to see him, that I thought I should never have done wringing his hand.

1. Gems as objects of connoisseurship.

2. Time of feast and merrymaking just before Lent.

3. A suit of different colors, typically worn by old-time fools and jesters.

I said to him: "My dear Fortunato, you are luckily met. How remarkably well you are looking to-day! But I have received a pipe of what passes for Amontillado,[4] and I have my doubts."

"How?" said he. "Amontillado? A pipe? Impossible! And in the middle of the carnival!"

"I have my doubts," I replied; "and I was silly enough to pay the full Amontillado price without consulting you in the matter. You were not to be found, and I was fearful of losing a bargain."

"Amontillado!"

"I have my doubts."

"Amontillado!"

"And I must satisfy them."

"Amontillado!"

"As you are engaged, I am on my way to Luchesi. If any one has a critical turn, it is he. He will tell me—"

"Luchesi cannot tell Amontillado from Sherry."

"And yet some fools will have it that his taste is a match for your own."

"Come, let us go."

"Whither?"

"To your vaults."

"My friend, no; I will not impose upon your good nature. I perceive you have an engagement. Luchesi—"

"I have no engagement;—come."

"My friend, no. It is not the engagement, but the severe cold with which I perceive you are afflicted. The vaults are insufferably damp. They are encrusted with nitre."[5]

"Let us go, nevertheless. The cold is merely nothing. Amontillado! You have been imposed upon. And as for Luchesi, he cannot distinguish Sherry from Amontillado."

Thus speaking, Fortunato possessed himself of my arm. Putting on a mask of black silk, and drawing a *roquelaire*[6] closely about my person, I suffered him to hurry me to my palazzo.

There were no attendants at home; they had absconded to make merry in honor of the time. I had told them that I should not re-

4. A type of Spanish sherry. A pipe is a large cask used to hold wine.

5. Naturally occurring sodium nitrate, often found in soil and encrusted on rock.

6. Cloak (French).

turn until the morning, and had given them explicit orders not to stir from the house. These orders were sufficient, I well knew, to insure their immediate disappearance, one and all, as soon as my back was turned.

I took from their sconces two flambeaux, and giving one to Fortunato, bowed him through several suites of rooms to the archway that led into the vaults. I passed down a long and winding staircase, requesting him to be cautious as he followed. We came at length to the foot of the descent, and stood together on the damp ground of the catacombs of the Montresors.

The gait of my friend was unsteady, and the bells upon his cap jingled as he strode.

"The pipe?" said he.

"It is farther on," said I; "but observe the white web-work which gleams from these cavern walls."

He turned toward me, and looked into my eyes with two filmy orbs that distilled the rheum of intoxication.

"Nitre?" he asked, at length.

"Nitre," I replied. "How long have you had that cough?"

"Ugh! ugh! ugh!—ugh! ugh! ugh!—ugh! ugh! ugh!—ugh! ugh! ugh!—ugh! ugh! ugh!"

My poor friend found it impossible to reply for many minutes.

"It is nothing," he said, at last.

"Come," I said, with decision, "we will go back; your health is precious. You are rich, respected, admired, beloved; you are happy, as once I was. You are a man to be missed. For me it is no matter. We will go back; you will be ill, and I cannot be responsible. Besides, there is Luchesi—"

"Enough," he said; "the cough is a mere nothing; it will not kill me. I shall not die of a cough."

"True—true," I replied; "and, indeed, I had no intention of alarming you unnecessarily; but you should use all proper caution. A draught of this Medoc[7] will defend us from the damps."

Here I knocked off the neck of a bottle which I drew from a long row of its fellows that lay upon the mould.

"Drink," I said, presenting him the wine.

7. A red Bordeaux wine.

He raised it to his lips with a leer. He paused and nodded to me familiarly, while his bells jingled.

"I drink," he said, "to the buried that repose around us."

"And I to your long life."

He again took my arm, and we proceeded.

"These vaults," he said, "are extensive."

"The Montresors," I replied, "were a great and numerous family."

"I forget your arms."

"A huge human foot d'or,[8] in a field azure; the foot crushes a serpent rampant whose fangs are imbedded in the heel."

"And the motto?"

"Nemo me impune lacessit."[9]

"Good!" he said.

The wine sparkled in his eyes and the bells jingled. My own fancy grew warm with the Medoc. We had passed through walls of piled bones, with casks and puncheons[10] intermingling, into the inmost recesses of the catacombs. I paused again, and this time I made bold to seize Fortunato by an arm above the elbow.

"The nitre!" I said; "see, it increases. It hangs like moss upon the vaults. We are below the river's bed. The drops of moisture trickle among the bones. Come, we will go back ere it is too late. Your cough—"

"It is nothing," he said; "let us go on. But first, another draught of the Medoc."

I broke and reached him a flagon of De Grâve.[11] He emptied it at a breath. His eyes flashed with a fierce light. He laughed and threw the bottle upward with a gesticulation I did not understand.

I looked at him in surprise. He repeated the movement—a grotesque one.

"You do not comprehend?" he said.

"Not I," I replied.

"Then you are not of the brotherhood."

"How?"

"You are not of the masons."[12]

8. Of gold (French).

9. "No one attacks me with impunity" (Latin).

10. Another type of wine cask.

11. Wine from the Graves region in France.

12. Freemasons.

"Yes, yes," I said; "yes, yes."

"You? Impossible! A mason?"

"A mason," I replied.

"A sign," he said.

"It is this," I answered, producing a trowel from beneath the folds of my *roquelaire*.

"You jest," he exclaimed, recoiling a few paces. "But let us proceed to the Amontillado."

"Be it so," I said, replacing the tool beneath the cloak, and again offering him my arm. He leaned upon it heavily. We continued our route in search of the Amontillado. We passed through a range of low arches, descended, passed on, and descending again, arrived at a deep crypt, in which the foulness of the air caused our flambeaux rather to glow than flame.

At the most remote end of the crypt there appeared another less spacious. Its walls had been lined with human remains, piled to the vault overhead, in the fashion of the great catacombs of Paris. Three sides of this interior crypt were still ornamented in this manner. From the fourth the bones had been thrown down, and lay promiscuously upon the earth, forming at one point a mound of some size. Within the wall thus exposed by the displacing of the bones, we perceived a still interior recess, in depth about four feet, in width three, in height six or seven. It seemed to have been constructed for no especial use within itself, but formed merely the interval between two of the colossal supports of the roof of the catacombs, and was backed by one of their circumscribing walls of solid granite.

It was in vain that Fortunato, uplifting his dull torch, endeavored to pry into the depth of the recess. Its termination the feeble light did not enable us to see.

"Proceed," I said; "herein is the Amontillado. As for Luchesi—"

"He is an ignoramus," interrupted my friend, as he stepped unsteadily forward, while I followed immediately at his heels. In an instant he had reached the extremity of the niche, and finding his progress arrested by the rock, stood stupidly bewildered. A moment more and I had fettered him to the granite. In its surface were two iron staples, distant from each other about two feet, horizontally. From one of these depended a short chain, from the other a padlock. Throwing the links about his waist, it was but the work of a few seconds to secure it. He was too much astounded to resist. Withdrawing the key I stepped back from the recess.

"Pass your hand," I said, "over the wall; you cannot help feeling the nitre. Indeed it is *very* damp. Once more let me *implore* you to return. No? Then I must positively leave you. But I must first render you all the little attentions in my power."

"The Amontillado!" ejaculated my friend, not yet recovered from his astonishment.

"True," I replied; "the Amontillado."

As I said these words I busied myself among the pile of bones of which I have before spoken. Throwing them aside, I soon uncovered a quantity of building stone and mortar. With these materials and with the aid of my trowel, I began vigorously to wall up the entrance of the niche.

I had scarcely laid the first tier of the masonry when I discovered that the intoxication of Fortunato had in a great measure worn off. The earliest indication I had of this was a low moaning cry from the depth of the recess. It was *not* the cry of a drunken man. There was then a long and obstinate silence. I laid the second tier, and the third, and the fourth; and then I heard the furious vibrations of the chain. The noise lasted for several minutes, during which, that I might hearken to it with the more satisfaction, I ceased my labors and sat down upon the bones. When at last the clanking subsided, I resumed the trowel, and finished without interruption the fifth, the sixth, and the seventh tier. The wall was now nearly upon a level with my breast. I again paused, and holding the flambeaux over the mason-work, threw a few feeble rays upon the figure within.

A succession of loud and shrill screams, bursting suddenly from the throat of the chained form, seemed to thrust me violently back. For a brief moment I hesitated—I trembled. Unsheathing my rapier,[13] I began to grope with it about the recess; but the thought of an instant reassured me. I placed my hand upon the solid fabric of the catacombs, and felt satisfied. I reapproached the wall. I replied to the yells of him who clamored. I re-echoed—I aided—I surpassed them in volume and in strength. I did this, and the clamorer grew still.

13. Sword.

It was now midnight, and my task was drawing to a close. I had completed the eighth, the ninth, and the tenth tier. I had finished a portion of the last and the eleventh; there remained but a single stone to be fitted and plastered in. I struggled with its weight; I placed it partially in its destined position. But now there came from out the niche a low laugh that erected the hairs upon my head. It was succeeded by a sad voice, which I had difficulty in recognizing as that of the noble Fortunato. The voice said—

"Ha! ha! ha!—he! he!—a very good joke indeed—an excellent jest. We will have many a rich laugh about it at the palazzo—he! he! he!—over our wine—he! he! he!"

"The Amontillado!" I said.

"He! he! he!—he! he! he!—yes, the Amontillado. But is it not getting late? Will not they be awaiting us at the palazzo, the Lady Fortunato and the rest? Let us be gone."

"Yes," I said, "let us be gone."

"*For the love of God, Montresor!*"

"Yes," I said, "for the love of God!"

But to these words I hearkened in vain for a reply. I grew impatient. I called aloud:

"Fortunato!"

No answer. I called again:

"Fortunato!"

No answer still. I thrust a torch through the remaining aperture and let it fall within. There came forth in return only a jingling of the bells. My heart grew sick—on account of the dampness of the catacombs. I hastened to make an end of my labor. I forced the last stone into its position; I plastered it up. Against the new masonry I re-erected the old rampart of bones. For the half of a century no mortal has disturbed them. *In pace requiescat!*[14]

1846

14. May he rest in peace! (Latin).

Katherine Anne Porter
1890–1980

"The Jilting of Granny Weatherall" alludes to Jesus' parable of the ten virgins. Ten virgins kept vigil for a bridegroom, who was delayed. Five were wise and took flasks of oil for their lamps, but five were foolish and brought no oil. They fell asleep, and when the cry went out that the groom was approaching, the foolish virgins had to go out to buy more oil. In their absence, the groom arrived, went in to the marriage feast with the wise virgins, and shut the doors. When the foolish virgins returned, they called through the door, but the lord replied, "Verily, I say unto you, I know you not." The bridegroom is typically interpreted as Christ during the Second Coming and as a warning always to be prepared for the Judgment Day. Granny's state of mind might make the story a bit difficult to untangle. Porter wrote the story using stream of consciousness. That technique always demands close attention from the reader, even more so here since Granny's consciousness is so distorting.

The Jilting of Granny Weatherall

She flicked her wrist neatly out of Doctor Harry's pudgy careful fingers and pulled the sheet up to her chin. The brat ought to be in knee breeches. Doctoring around the country with spectacles on his nose! "Get along now, take your schoolbooks and go. There's nothing wrong with me."

Doctor Harry spread a warm paw like a cushion on her forehead where the forked green vein danced and made her eyelids twitch. "Now, now, be a good girl, and we'll have you up in no time."

"That's no way to speak to a woman nearly eighty years old just because she's down. I'd have you respect your elders, young man."

"Well, Missy, excuse me." Doctor Harry patted her cheek. "But I've got to warn you, haven't I? You're a marvel, but you must be careful or you're going to be good and sorry."

"Don't tell me what I'm going to be. I'm on my feet now, morally speaking. It's Cornelia. I had to go to bed to get rid of her."

Her bones felt loose, and floated around in her skin, and Doctor

Harry floated like a balloon around the foot of the bed. He floated and pulled down his waistcoat and swung his glasses on a cord. "Well, stay where you are, it certainly can't hurt you."

"Get along and doctor your sick," said Granny Weatherall. "Leave a well woman alone. I'll call for you when I want you. . . . Where were you forty years ago when I pulled through milk-leg and double pneumonia? You weren't even born. Don't let Cornelia lead you on," she shouted, because Doctor Harry appeared to float up to the ceiling and out. "I pay my own bills, and I don't throw my money away on nonsense!"

She meant to wave good-by, but it was too much trouble. Her eyes closed of themselves, it was like a dark curtain drawn around the bed. The pillow rose and floated under her, pleasant as a hammock in a light wind. She listened to the leaves rustling outside the window. No, somebody was swishing newspapers: no, Cornelia and Doctor Harry were whispering together. She leaped broad awake, thinking they whispered in her ear.

"She was never like this, *never* like this!" "Well, what can we expect?" "Yes, eighty years old. . . ."

Well, and what if she was? She still had ears. It was like Cornelia to whisper around doors. She always kept things secret in such a public way. She was always being tactful and kind. Cornelia was dutiful; that was the trouble with her. Dutiful and good: "So good and dutiful," said Granny, "that I'd like to spank her." She saw herself spanking Cornelia and making a fine job of it.

"What'd you say, Mother?"

Granny felt her face tying up in hard knots.

"Can't a body think, I'd like to know?"

"I thought you might want something."

"I do. I want a lot of things. First off, go away and don't whisper."

She lay and drowsed, hoping in her sleep that the children would keep out and let her rest a minute. It had been a long day. Not that she was tired. It was always pleasant to snatch a minute now and then. There was always so much to be done, let me see: tomorrow.

Tomorrow was far away and there was nothing to trouble about. Things were finished somehow when the time came; thank God there was always a little margin over for peace: then a person could spread out the plan of life and tuck in the edges orderly. It was good to have everything clean and folded away, with the hair brushes and tonic bottles sitting straight on the white embroidered linen: the day started without fuss and the pantry shelves laid out with rows of jelly glasses and brown jugs and white stone-china jars with blue whirligigs and words painted on them: coffee, tea, sugar, ginger, cinnamon, allspice: and the bronze clock with the lion on top nicely dusted off. The dust that lion could collect in twenty-four hours! The box in the attic with all those letters tied up, well, she'd have to go through that tomorrow. All those letters—George's letters and John's letters and her letters to them both—lying around for the children to find afterwards made her uneasy. Yes, that would be tomorrow's business. No use to let them know how silly she had been once.

While she was rummaging around she found death in her mind and it felt clammy and unfamiliar. She had spent so much time preparing for death there was no need for bringing it up again. Let it take care of itself now. When she was sixty she had felt very old, finished, and went around making farewell trips to see her children and grandchildren, with a secret in her mind: This is the very last of your mother, children! Then she made her will and came down with a long fever. That was all just a notion like a lot of other things, but it was lucky too, for she had once for all got over the idea of dying for a long time. Now she couldn't be worried. She hoped she had better sense now. Her father had lived to be one hundred and two years old and had drunk a noggin of strong hot toddy on his last birthday. He told the reporters it was his daily habit, and he owed his long life to that. He had made quite a scandal and was very pleased about it. She believed she'd just plague Cornelia a little.

"Cornelia! Cornelia!" No footsteps, but a sudden hand on her cheek. "Bless you, where have you been?"

"Here, mother."

"Well, Cornelia, I want a noggin of hot toddy."

"Are you cold, darling?"

"I'm chilly, Cornelia. Lying in bed stops the circulation. I must have told you that a thousand times."

Well, she could just hear Cornelia telling her husband that Mother was getting a little childish and they'd have to humor her.

The thing that most annoyed her was that Cornelia thought she was deaf, dumb, and blind. Little hasty glances and tiny gestures tossed around her and over her head saying, "Don't cross her, let her have her way, she's eighty years old," and she sitting there as if she lived in a thin glass cage. Sometimes Granny almost made up her mind to pack up and move back to her own house where nobody could remind her every minute that she was old. Wait, wait, Cornelia, till your own children whisper behind your back!

In her day she had kept a better house and had got more work done. She wasn't too old yet for Lydia to be driving eighty miles for advice when one of the children jumped the track, and Jimmy still dropped in and talked things over: "Now, Mammy, you've a good business head, I want to know what you think of this? . . ." Old. Cornelia couldn't change the furniture around without asking. Little things, little things! They had been so sweet when they were little. Granny wished the old days were back again with the children young and everything to be done over. It had been a hard pull, but not too much for her. When she thought of all the food she had cooked, and all the clothes she had cut and sewed, and all the gardens she had made—well, the children showed it. There they were, made out of her, and they couldn't get away from that. Sometimes she wanted to see John again and point to them and say, Well, I didn't do so badly, did I? But that would have to wait. That was for tomorrow. She used to think of him as a man, but now all the children were older than their father, and he would be a child beside her if she saw him now. It seemed strange and there was something wrong in the idea. Why, he couldn't possibly recognize her. She had fenced in a hundred acres once, digging the post holes herself and clamping the wires with just a negro boy to help. That changed a woman. John would be looking for a young woman with the peaked Spanish comb in her hair and the painted fan. Digging post holes changed a woman. Riding country roads in the winter when women had their babies was another thing: sitting up nights with sick horses and sick negroes and sick children and hardly ever losing one. John, I hardly ever lost one of them! John would see that in a minute, that would be something he could understand, she wouldn't have to explain anything!

It made her feel like rolling up her sleeves and putting the whole place to rights again. No matter if Cornelia was determined to be everywhere at once, there were a great many things left undone on this place. She would start tomorrow and do them. It was good to be strong enough for everything, even if all you made melted and changed and slipped under your hands, so that by the time you finished you almost forgot what you were working for. What was it I set out to do? she asked herself intently, but she could not remember. A fog rose over the valley, she saw it marching across the creek swallowing the trees and moving up the hill like an army of ghosts. Soon it would be at the near edge of the orchard, and then it was time to go in and light the lamps. Come in, children, don't stay out in the night air.

Lighting the lamps had been beautiful. The children huddled up to her and breathed like little calves waiting at the bars in the twilight. Their eyes followed the match and watched the flame rise and settle in a blue curve, then they moved away from her. The lamp was lit, they didn't have to be scared and hang on to mother any more. Never, never, never more. God, for all my life I thank Thee. Without Thee, my God, I could never have done it. Hail, Mary, full of grace.

I want you to pick all the fruit this year and see that nothing is wasted. There's always someone who can use it. Don't let good things rot for want of using. You waste life when you waste good food. Don't let things get lost. It's bitter to lose things. Now, don't let me get to thinking, not when I am tired and taking a little nap before supper. . . .

The pillow rose about her shoulders and pressed against her heart and the memory was being squeezed out of it: oh, push down the pillow, somebody: it would smother her if she tried to hold it. Such a fresh breeze blowing and such a green day with no threats in it. But he had not come, just the same. What does a woman do when she has put on the white veil and set out the white cake for a man and he doesn't come? She tried to remember. No, I swear he never harmed me but in that. He never harmed me but in that . . . and what if he did? There was the day, the day, but a whirl of dark smoke rose and covered it, crept up and over into the bright field where everything was planted so carefully in orderly rows. That was hell, she knew hell when she saw it. For sixty years she had prayed against remembering him and against losing her soul in the deep pit of hell, and now the two things were mingled in one and the thought of him was a smoky cloud from hell that moved and crept in her head when she had just got rid of Doctor Harry and was trying to rest a minute. Wounded vanity, Ellen, said a sharp voice in the top of her mind. Don't let your wounded vanity get the upper hand of you. Plenty of girls get jilted. You were jilted, weren't you? Then stand up to it. Her eyelids wavered and let in streamers of blue-gray light like tissue paper over her eyes. She must get up and pull the shades down or she'd never sleep. She was in bed again and the shades were not down. How could that happen? Better turn over, hide from the light, sleeping in the light gave you nightmares. "Mother, how do you feel now?" and a stinging wetness on her forehead. But I don't like having my face washed in cold water!

Hapsy? George? Lydia? Jimmy? No, Cornelia, and her features were swollen and full of little puddles. "They're coming, darling, they'll all be here soon." Go wash your face, child, you look funny.

Instead of obeying, Cornelia knelt down and put her head on the pillow. She seemed to be talking but there was no sound. "Well, are you tongue-tied? Whose birthday is it? Are you going to give a party?"

Cornelia's mouth moved urgently in strange shapes. "Don't do that, you bother me, daughter."

"Oh, no, Mother. Oh, no. . . ."

Nonsense. It was strange about children. They disputed your every word. "No what, Cornelia?"

"Here's Doctor Harry."

"I won't see that boy again. He just left five minutes ago."

"That was this morning, Mother. It's night now. Here's the nurse."

"This is Doctor Harry, Mrs. Weatherall. I never saw you look so young and happy!"

"Ah, I'll never be young again—but I'd be happy if they'd let me lie in peace and get rested."

She thought she spoke up loudly, but no one answered. A warm weight on her forehead, a warm bracelet on her wrist, and a breeze went on whispering, trying to tell her something. A shuffle of leaves in the everlasting hand of God, He blew on them and they danced and rattled. "Mother, don't mind, we're going to give you a little hypodermic." "Look here, daughter, how do ants get in this bed? I saw sugar ants yesterday." Did you send for Hapsy too?

It was Hapsy she really wanted. She had to go a long way back through a great many rooms to find Hapsy standing with a baby on her arm. She seemed to herself to be Hapsy also, and the baby on Hapsy's arm was Hapsy and himself and herself, all at once, and there was no surprise in the meeting. Then Hapsy melted from within and turned flimsy as gray gauze and the baby was a gauzy shadow, and Hapsy came up close and said, "I thought you'd never come," and looked at her very searchingly and said, "You haven't changed a bit!" They leaned forward to kiss, when Cornelia began whispering from a long way off, "Oh, is there anything you want to tell me? Is there anything I can do for you?"

Yes, she had changed her mind after sixty years and she would like to see George. I want you to find George. Find him and be sure to tell him I forgot him. I want him to know I had my husband just the same and my children and my house like any other woman. A good house too and a good husband that I loved and fine children out of him. Better than I hoped for even. Tell him I was given back everything he took away and more. Oh, no, oh, God, no, there was something else besides the house and the man and the children. Oh, surely they were not all? What was it? Something not given back. . . . Her breath crowded down under her ribs and grew into a monstrous frightening shape with cutting edges; it bored up into her head, and the agony was unbelievable: Yes, John, get the Doctor now, no more talk, my time has come.

When this one was born it should be the last. The last. It should have been born first, for it was the one she had truly wanted. Everything came in good time. Nothing left out, left over. She was strong, in three days she would be as well as ever. Better. A woman needed milk in her to have her full health.

"Mother, do you hear me?"

"I've been telling you—"

"Mother, Father Connolly's here."

"I went to Holy Communion only last week. Tell him I'm not so sinful as all that."

"Father just wants to speak to you."

He could speak as much as he pleased. It was like him to drop in and inquire about her soul as if it were a teething baby, and then stay on for a cup of tea and a round of cards and gossip. He always had a funny story of some sort, usually about an Irishman who made his little mistakes and confessed them, and the point lay in some absurd thing he would blurt out in the confessional showing his struggles between native piety and original sin. Granny felt easy about her soul. Cornelia, where are your manners? Give Father Connolly a chair. She had her secret comfortable understanding with a few favorite saints who cleared a straight road to God for her. All as surely signed and sealed as the papers for the new Forty Acres. Forever . . . heirs and assigns forever. Since the day the wedding cake was not cut, but thrown out and wasted. The whole bottom dropped out of the world, and there she was blind and sweating with nothing under her feet and the walls falling away. His hand had caught her under the breast, she had not fallen, there was the freshly polished floor with the green rug on it, just as before. He had cursed like a sailor's parrot and said, "I'll kill him for you." Don't lay a hand on him, for my sake leave something to God. "Now, Ellen, you must believe what I tell you. . . ."

So there was nothing, nothing to worry about any more, except sometimes in the night one of the children screamed in a nightmare, and they both hustled out shaking and hunting for the matches and calling, "There, wait a minute, here we are!" John, get the doctor now, Hapsy's time has come. But there was Hapsy standing by the bed in a white cap. "Cornelia, tell Hapsy to take off her cap. I can't see her plain."

Her eyes opened very wide and the room stood out like a picture she had seen somewhere. Dark colors with the shadows rising towards the ceiling in long angles. The tall black dresser gleamed with nothing on it but John's picture, enlarged from a little one, with John's eyes very black when they should have been blue. You never saw him, so how do you know how he looked? But the man insisted the copy was perfect, it was very rich and handsome. For a picture, yes, but it's not my husband. The table by the bed had a linen cover and a candle and a crucifix. The light was blue from Cornelia's silk lampshades. No sort of light at all, just frippery. You had to live forty years with kerosene lamps to appreciate honest electricity. She felt very strong and she saw Doctor Harry with a rosy nimbus around him.

"You look like a saint, Doctor Harry, and I vow that's as near as you'll ever come to it."

"She's saying something."

"I heard you, Cornelia. What's all this carrying-on?"

"Father Connolly's saying—"

Cornelia's voice staggered and bumped like a cart in a bad road. It rounded corners and turned back again and arrived nowhere. Granny stepped up in the cart very lightly and reached for the reins, but a man sat beside her and she knew him by his hands, driving the cart. She did not look in his face, for she knew without seeing, but looked instead down the road where the trees leaned over and bowed to each other and a thousand birds were singing a Mass. She felt like singing too, but she put her hand in the bosom of her dress and pulled out a rosary, and Father Connolly murmured Latin in a very solemn voice and tickled her feet. My God, will you stop that nonsense? I'm a married woman. What if he did run away and leave me to face the priest by myself? I found another a whole world better. I wouldn't have exchanged my husband for anybody except St. Michael himself, and you may tell him that for me with a thank you in the bargain.

Light flashed on her closed eyelids, and a deep roaring shook her. Cornelia, is that lightning? I hear thunder. There's going to be a storm. Close all the windows. Call the children in. . . . "Mother, here we are, all of us." "Is that you, Hapsy?" "Oh, no, I'm Lydia. We drove as fast as we could." Their faces drifted above her, drifted away. The rosary fell out of her hands and Lydia put it back. Jimmy tried to help, their hands fumbled together, and Granny closed two fingers around Jimmy's thumb. Beads wouldn't do, it must be something alive. She was so amazed her thoughts ran round and round. So, my dear Lord, this is my death and I wasn't even thinking about it. My children have come to see me die. But I can't, it's not time. Oh, I always hated surprises. I wanted to give Cornelia the amethyst set—Cornelia, you're to have the amethyst set, but Hapsy's to wear it when she wants, and, Doctor Harry, do shut up. Nobody sent for you. Oh, my dear Lord, do wait a minute. I meant to do something about the Forty Acres, Jimmy doesn't need it and Lydia will later on, with that worthless husband of hers. I meant to finish the altar cloth and send six bottles of wine to Sister Borgia for her dyspepsia. I want to send six bottles of wine to Sister Borgia, Father Connolly, now don't let me forget.

Cornelia's voice made short turns and tilted over and crashed. "Oh, Mother, oh, Mother, oh, Mother. . . ."

"I'm not going, Cornelia. I'm taken by surprise. I can't go."

You'll see Hapsy again. What about her? "I thought you'd never come." Granny made a long journey outward, looking for Hapsy. What if I don't find her? What then? Her heart sank down and down, there was no bottom to death, she couldn't come to the end of it. The blue light from Cornelia's lampshade drew into a tiny point in the center of her brain, it flickered and winked like an eye, quietly it fluttered and dwindled. Granny lay curled down within herself, amazed and watchful, staring at the point of light that was herself; her body was now only a deeper mass of shadow in an endless darkness and this darkness would curl around the light and swallow it up. God, give a sign!

For the second time there was no sign. Again no bridegroom and the priest in the house. She could not remember any other sorrow because this grief wiped them all away. Oh, no, there's nothing more cruel than this—I'll never forgive it. She stretched herself with a deep breath and blew out the light.

1929

Leslie Marmon Silko

b. 1948

Silko is a Laguna Pueblo Indian from New Mexico. As "Yellow Woman" indicates, her writing derives from the lore and mythology of her tribe. This story comes from her book Storyteller, *which mixes poetry, Silko's personal family folklore, short stories, myths, and photographs. The poems that follow this story in that book recount two of the stories that the narrator's grandfather would have been fond of telling. In the first, Kochininako, the Yellow Woman, with whom the narrator of this story identifies herself, abandons her three children and husband to live with the Sun, who appears to her as a human being. In the second story, Kochininako goes looking for water to relieve her drought-stricken people. She is kidnapped by Buffalo Man and taken far to the east. Her husband, Arrowboy, comes after her, steals her back, and slays all the Buffalo People who follow them. In this way, Kochininako's people have enough food to get them through the summer, and they learn where to hunt buffalo in the future. But Kochininako grieves because she wanted to stay with Buffalo Man, so Arrowboy kills her to reunite her with her dead lover. Another poem begins "The Laguna people / always begin their stories / with 'humma-hah': / that means 'long ago.'" An important theme in "Yellow Woman" is the presence of "long ago" in the "here and now."*

Yellow Woman

My thigh clung to his with dampness, and I watched the sun rising up through the tamaracks and willows. The small brown water birds came to the river and hopped across the mud, leaving brown scratches in the alkali-white crust. They bathed in the river silently. I could hear the water, almost at our feet where the narrow fast channel bubbled and washed green ragged moss and fern leaves. I looked at him beside me, rolled in the red blanket on the white river sand. I cleaned the sand out of the cracks between my toes, squinting because the sun was above the willow trees. I looked at him for the last time, sleeping on the white river sand.

I felt hungry and followed the river south the way we had come the afternoon before, following our footprints that were already blurred by lizard tracks and bug trails. The horses were still lying down, and the black one whinnied when he saw me but he did not get up—maybe it was because the corral was made out of thick cedar branches and the horses had not yet felt the sun like I had. I tried to look beyond the pale red mesas to the pueblo. I knew it was there, even if I could not see it, on the sandrock hill above the river, the same river that moved past me now and had reflected the moon last night.

The horse felt warm underneath me. He shook his head and pawed the sand. The bay whinnied and leaned against the gate trying to follow, and I remembered him asleep in the red blanket beside the river. I slid off the horse and tied him close to the other horse, I walked north with the river again, and the white sand broke loose in footprints over footprints.

"Wake up."

He moved in the blanket and turned his face to me with his eyes still closed. I knelt down to touch him.

"I'm leaving."

He smiled now, eyes still closed. "You are coming with me, remember?" He sat up now with his bare dark chest and belly in the sun.

"Where?"

"To my place."

"And will I come back?"

He pulled his pants on. I walked away from him, feeling him behind me and smelling the willows.

"Yellow Woman," he said.

I turned to face him. "Who are you?" I asked.

He laughed and knelt on the low, sandy bank, washing his face in the river. "Last night you guessed my name, and you knew why I had come."

I stared past him at the shallow moving water and tried to remember the night, but I could only see the moon in the water and remember his warmth around me.

"But I only said that you were him and that I was Yellow Woman—I'm not really her—I have my own name and I come from the pueblo on the other side of the mesa. Your name is Silva and you are a stranger I met by the river yesterday afternoon."

He laughed softly. "What happened yesterday has nothing to do with what you will do today, Yellow Woman."

"I know—that's what I'm saying—the old stories about the ka'tsina spirit and Yellow Woman can't mean us."

My old grandpa liked to tell those stories best. There is one about Badger and Coyote who went hunting and were gone all day, and when the sun was going down they found a house. There was a girl living there alone, and she had light hair and eyes and she told them that they could sleep with her. Coyote wanted to be with her all night so he sent Badger into a prairie-dog hole, telling him he thought he saw something in it. As soon as Badger crawled in, Coyote blocked up the entrance with rocks and hurried back to Yellow Woman.

"Come here," he said gently.

He touched my neck and I moved close to him to feel his breathing and to hear his heart. I was wondering if Yellow Woman had known who she was—if she knew that she would become part of the stories. Maybe she'd had another name that her husband and relatives called her so that only the ka'tsina from the north and the storytellers would know her as Yellow Woman. But I didn't go on; I felt him all around me, pushing me down into the white river sand.

Yellow Woman went away with the spirit from the north and lived with him and his relatives. She was gone for a long time, but then one day she came back and she brought twin boys.

"Do you know the story?"

"What story?" He smiled and pulled me close to him as he said this. I was afraid lying there on the red blanket. All I could know was the way he felt, warm, damp, his body beside me. This is the way it happens in the stories, I was thinking, with no thought beyond the moment she meets the ka'tsina spirit and they go.

"I don't have to go. What they tell in stories was real only then, back in time immemorial, like they say."

He stood up and pointed at my clothes tangled in the blanket. "Let's go," he said.

I walked beside him, breathing hard because he walked fast, his hand around my wrist. I had stopped trying to pull away from him, because his hand felt cool and the sun was high, drying the river bed into alkali. I will see someone, eventually I will see someone, and then I will be certain that he is only a man—some man from nearby—and I will be sure that I am not Yellow Woman. Because she is from out of time past and I live now and I've been to school and there are highways and pickup trucks that Yellow Woman never saw.

It was an easy ride north on horseback. I watched the change from the cottonwood trees along the river to the junipers that brushed past us in the foothills, and finally there were only piñons, and when I looked up at the rim of the mountain plateau I could see pine trees growing on the edge. Once I stopped to look down, but the pale sandstone had disappeared and the river was gone and the dark lava hills were all around. He touched my hand, not speaking, but always singing softly a mountain song and looking into my eyes.

I felt hungry and wondered what they were doing at home now—my mother, my grandmother, my husband, and the baby. Cooking breakfast, saying, "Where did she go? maybe kidnapped." And Al going to the tribal police with the details: "She went walking along the river."

The house was made with black lava rock and red mud. It was high above the spreading miles of arroyos[1] and long mesas. I smelled a mountain smell of pitch and buck brush. I stood there beside the black horse, looking down on the small, dim country we had passed, and I shivered.

"Yellow Woman, come inside where it's warm." He lit a fire in the stove. It was an old stove with a round belly and an enamel coffeepot on top. There was only the stove, some faded Navajo blankets, and a bedroll and cardboard box. The floor was made of smooth adobe plaster, and there was one small window facing east. He pointed at the box.

"There's some potatoes and the frying pan." He sat on the floor with his arms around his knees pulling them close to his chest and he watched me fry the potatoes. I didn't mind him watching me because he was always watching me—he had been watching me since I came upon him sitting on the river bank trimming leaves from a willow twig with his knife. We ate from the pan and he wiped the grease from his fingers on his Levi's.

"Have you brought women here before?" He smiled and kept chewing, so I said, "Do you always use the same tricks?"

"What tricks?" He looked at me like he didn't understand.

"The story about being a ka'tsina from the mountains. The story about Yellow Woman."

Silva was silent; his face was calm.

"I don't believe it. Those stories couldn't happen now," I said.

He shook his head and said softly, "But someday they will talk about us, and they will say, 'Those two lived long ago when things like that happened.' "

He stood up and went out. I ate the rest of the potatoes and

1. Deep gulleys cut into the land by intermittent streams.

thought about things—about the noise the stove was making and the sound of the mountain wind outside. I remembered yesterday and the day before, and then I went outside.

I walked past the corral to the edge where the narrow trail cut through the black rim rock. I was standing in the sky with nothing around me but the wind that came down from the blue mountain peak behind me. I could see faint mountain images in the distance miles across the vast spread of mesas and valleys and plains. I wondered who was over there to feel the mountain wind on those sheer blue edges—who walks on the pine needles in those blue mountains.

"Can you see the pueblo?" Silva was standing behind me.

I shook my head. "We're too far away."

"From here I can see the world." He stepped out on the edge. "The Navajo reservation begins over there." He pointed to the east. "The Pueblo boundaries are over here." He looked below us to the south, where the narrow trail seemed to come from. "The Texans have their ranches over there, starting with that valley, the Concho Valley. The Mexicans run some cattle over there too."

"Do you ever work for them?"

"I steal from them," Silva answered. The sun was dropping behind us and the shadows were filling the land below. I turned away from the edge that dropped forever into the valleys below.

"I'm cold," I said, "I'm going inside." I started wondering about this man who could speak the Pueblo language so well but who lived on a mountain and rustled cattle. I decided that this man Silva must be Navajo, because Pueblo men didn't do things like that.

"You must be a Navajo."

Silva shook his head gently. "Little Yellow Woman," he said, "you never give up, do you? I have told you who I am. The Navajo people know me, too." He knelt down and unrolled the bedroll and spread the extra blankets out on a piece of canvas. The sun was down, and the only light in the house came from outside—the dim orange light from sundown.

I stood there and waited for him to crawl under the blankets.

"What are you waiting for?" he said, and I lay down beside him. He undressed me slowly like the night before beside the river—kissing my face gently and running his hands up and down my belly and legs. He took off my pants and then he laughed.

"Why are you laughing?"

"You are breathing so hard."

I pulled away from him and turned my back to him.

He pulled me around and pinned me down with his arms and chest. "You don't understand, do you, little Yellow Woman? You will do what I want."

And again he was all around me with his skin slippery against mine, and I was afraid because I understood that his strength could hurt me. I lay underneath him and I knew that he could destroy me. But later, while he slept beside me, I touched his face and I had a feeling—the kind of feeling for him that overcame me that morning along the river. I kissed him on the forehead and he reached out for me.

When I woke up in the morning he was gone. It gave me a strange feeling because for a long time I sat there on the blankets and looked around the little house for some object of his—some proof that he had been there or maybe that he was coming back. Only the blankets and the cardboard box remained. The .30-30 that had been leaning in the corner was gone, and so was the knife I had used the night before. He was gone, and I had my chance to go now. But first I had to eat, because I knew it would be a long walk home.

I found some dried apricots in the cardboard box, and I sat down on a rock at the edge of the plateau rim. There was no wind and the sun warmed me. I was surrounded by silence. I drowsed with apricots in my mouth, and I didn't believe that there were highways or railroads or cattle to steal.

When I woke up, I stared down at my feet in the black mountain dirt. Little black ants were swarming over the pine needles around my foot. They must have smelled the apricots. I thought about my family far below me. They would be wondering about me, because this had never happened to me before. The tribal police would file a report. But if old Grandpa weren't dead he would tell them what happened—he would laugh and say, "Stolen by a ka'tsina, a mountain spirit. She'll come home—they usually do." There are enough of them to handle things. My mother and grandmother will raise the baby like they raised me. Al will find someone else, and they will go on like before, except that there will be a story about the day I disappeared while I was walking along the river. Silva had come for me; he said he had. I did not decide to go. I just went. Moonflowers blossom in the sand hills before dawn, just as I followed him. That's what I was thinking as I wandered along the trail through the pine trees.

It was noon when I got back. When I saw the stone house I remembered that I had meant to go home. But that didn't seem important any more, maybe because there were little blue flowers growing in the meadow behind the stone house and the gray squirrels were playing in the pines next to the house. The horses were standing in the corral, and there was a beef carcass hanging on the shady side of a big pine in front of the house. Flies buzzed around the clotted blood that hung from the carcass. Silva was washing his hands in a bucket full of water. He must have heard me coming because he spoke to me without turning to face me.

"I've been waiting for you."

"I went walking in the big pine trees."

I looked into the bucket full of bloody water with brown-and-white animal hairs floating in it. Silva stood there letting his hand drip, examining me intently.

"Are you coming with me?"

"Where?" I asked him.

"To sell the meat in Marquez."

"If you're sure it's O.K."

"I wouldn't ask you if it wasn't," he answered.

He sloshed the water around in the bucket before he dumped it out and set the bucket upside down near the door. I followed him to the corral and watched him saddle the horses. Even beside the horses he looked tall, and I asked him again if he wasn't Navajo. He didn't say anything; he just shook his head and kept cinching up the saddle.

"But Navajos are tall."

"Get on the horse," he said, "and let's go."

The last thing he did before we started down the steep trail was to grab the .30-30 from the corner. He slid the rifle into the scabbard that hung from his saddle.

"Do they ever try to catch you?" I asked.

"They don't know who I am."

"Then why did you bring the rifle?"

"Because we are going to Marquez where the Mexicans live."

The trail leveled out on a narrow ridge that was steep on both sides like an animal spine. On one side I could see where the trail went around the rocky gray hills and disappeared into the southeast where the pale sandrock mesas stood in the distance near my home. On the other side was a trail that went west, and as I looked far into the distance I thought I saw the little town. But Silva said no, that I was looking in the wrong place, that I just thought I saw houses. After that I quit looking off into the distance; it was hot and the wildflowers were closing up their deep-yellow petals. Only the waxy cactus flowers bloomed in the bright sun, and I saw every color that a cactus blossom can be; the white ones and the red ones were still buds, but the purple and the yellow were blossoms, open full and the most beautiful of all.

Silva saw him before I did. The white man was riding a big gray horse, coming up the trail towards us. He was traveling fast and the gray horse's feet sent rocks rolling off the trail into the dry tumbleweeds. Silva motioned for me to stop and we watched the white man. He didn't see us right away, but finally his horse whinnied at our horses and he stopped. He looked at us briefly before he lapped the gray horse across the three hundred yards that separated us. He stopped his horse in front of Silva, and his young fat face was shadowed by the brim of his hat. He didn't look mad, but his small, pale eyes moved from the blood-soaked gunny sacks hanging from my saddle to Silva's face and then back to my face.

"Where did you get the fresh meat?" the white man asked.

"I've been hunting," Silva said, and when he shifted his weight in the saddle the leather creaked.

"The hell you have, Indian. You've been rustling cattle. We've been looking for the thief for a long time."

The rancher was fat, and sweat began to soak through his white cowboy shirt and the wet cloth stuck to the thick rolls of belly fat. He almost seemed to be panting from the exertion of talking, and he smelled rancid, maybe because Silva scared him.

Silva turned to me and smiled. "Go back up the mountain, Yellow Woman."

The white man got angry when he heard Silva speak in a language he couldn't understand. "Don't try anything, Indian. Just keep riding to Marquez. We'll call the state police from there."

The rancher must have been unarmed because he was very frightened and if he had a gun he would have pulled it out then. I turned my horse around and the rancher yelled, "Stop!" I looked at Silva for an instant and there was something ancient and dark—something I could feel in my stomach—in his eyes, and when I glanced at his hand I saw his finger on the trigger of the .30-30 that was still in the saddle scabbard. I slapped my horse across the flank and the sacks of raw meat swung against my knees as the horse leaped up the trail. It was hard to keep my balance, and once I thought I felt the saddle slipping backward; it was because of this that I could not look back.

I didn't stop until I reached the ridge where the trail forked. The horse was breathing deep gasps and there was a dark film of sweat on its neck. I looked down in the direction I had come from, but I couldn't see the place. I waited. The wind came up and pushed warm air past me. I looked up at the sky, pale blue and full of thin clouds and fading vapor trails left by jets.

I think four shots were fired—I remember hearing four hollow explosions that reminded me of deer hunting. There could have been more shots after that, but I couldn't have heard them because my horse was running again and the loose rocks were making too much noise as they scattered around his feet.

Horses have a hard time running downhill, but I went that way instead of uphill to the mountain because I thought it was safer. I felt better with the horse running southeast past the round gray hills that were covered with cedar trees and black lava rock. When I got to the plain in the distance I could see the dark green patches of tamaracks that grew along the river; and beyond the river I could see the beginning of the pale sandrock mesas. I stopped the horse and looked back to see if anyone was coming; then I got off the horse and turned the horse around, wondering if it would go back to its corral under the pines on the mountain. It looked back at me for a moment and then plucked a mouthful of green tumbleweeds before it trotted back up the trail with its ears pointed forward, carrying its head daintily to one side to avoid stepping on the dragging reins. When the horse disappeared over the last hill, the gunny sacks full of meat were still swinging and bouncing.

I walked toward the river on a wood-hauler's road that I knew would eventually lead to the paved road. I was thinking about waiting beside the road for someone to drive by, but by the time I got to the pavement I had decided it wasn't very far to walk if I followed the river back the way Silva and I had come.

The river water tasted good, and I sat in the shade under a cluster of silvery willows. I thought about Silva, and I felt sad at leaving him; still, there was something strange about him, and I tried to figure it out all the way back home.

I came back to the place on the river bank where he had been sitting the first time I saw him. The green willow leaves that he had trimmed from the branch were still lying there, wilted in the sand. I saw the leaves and I wanted to go back to him—to kiss him and to touch him—but the mountains were too far away now. And I told myself, because I believe it, he will come back sometime and be waiting again by the river.

I followed the path up from the river into the village. The sun was getting low, and I could smell supper cooking when I got to the screen door of my house. I could hear their voices inside—my mother was telling my grandmother how to fix the Jell-O and my husband, Al, was playing with the baby. I decided to tell them that some Navajo had kidnapped me, but I was sorry that old Grandpa wasn't alive to hear my story because it was the Yellow Woman stories he liked to tell best.

1974

John Steinbeck

1902–1968

Steinbeck wrote "The Chrysanthemums" in the early years of the Great Depression, and he published it in 1937, while he was writing his acclaimed novel The Grapes of Wrath, *which criticizes the American economy and politics. But this story seems less political than personal. Steinbeck claimed that it was "designed to strike without the reader's knowledge. I mean he reads it casually and after it is finished feels that something profound has happened to him although he does not know what nor how."*

The Chrysanthemums

The high grey-flannel fog of winter closed off the Salinas Valley from the sky and from all the rest of the world. On every side it sat like a lid on the mountains and made of the great valley a closed pot. On the broad, level land floor the gang ploughs bit deep and left the black earth shining like metal where the shares had cut. On the foot-hill ranches across the Salinas River, the yellow stubble fields seemed to be bathed in pale cold sunshine, but there was no sunshine in the valley now in December. The thick willow scrub along the river flamed with sharp and positive yellow leaves.

It was a time of quiet and of waiting. The air was cold and tender. A light wind blew up from the southwest so that the farmers were mildly hopeful of a good rain before long; but fog and rain do not go together.

Across the river, on Henry Allen's foot-hill ranch there was little work to be done, for the hay was cut and stored and the orchards were ploughed up to receive the rain deeply when it should come. The cattle on the higher slopes were becoming shaggy and rough-coated.

Elisa Allen, working in her flower garden, looked down across the yard and saw Henry, her husband, talking to two men in business suits. The three of them stood by the tractor-shed, each man with one foot on the side of the little Fordson. They smoked cigarettes and studied the machine as they talked.

Elisa watched them for a moment and then went back to her work. She was thirty-five. Her face was lean and strong and her eyes were as clear as water. Her figure looked blocked and heavy in her gardening costume, a man's black hat pulled low down over her eyes, clod-hopper shoes, a figured print dress almost completely covered by a big corduroy apron with four big pockets to hold the snips, the trowel and scratcher, the seeds and the knife she worked with. She wore heavy leather gloves to protect her hands while she worked.

She was cutting down the old year's chrysanthemum stalks with a pair of short and powerful scissors. She looked down toward the men by the tractor-shed now and then. Her face was eager and mature and handsome; even her work with the scissors was overeager, over-powerful. The chrysanthemum stems seemed too small and easy for her energy.

She brushed a cloud of hair out of her eyes with the back of her glove, and left a smudge of earth on her cheek in doing it. Behind her stood the neat white farmhouse with red geraniums close-banked around it as high as the windows. It was a hard-swept-looking little house, with hard-polished windows, and a clean mud-mat on the front steps.

Elisa cast another glance toward the tractor-shed. The strangers were getting into their Ford coupé. She took off a glove and put her strong fingers down into the forest of new green chrysanthemum sprouts that were growing around the old roots. She spread the leaves and looked down among the close-growing stems. No aphids were there, no sow bugs or snails or cutworms. Her terrier fingers destroyed such pests before they could get started.

Elisa started at the sound of her husband's voice. He had come near quietly, and he leaned over the wire fence that protected her flower garden from cattle and dogs and chickens.

"At it again," he said. "You've got a strong new crop coming."

Elisa straightened her back and pulled on the gardening glove again. "Yes. They'll be strong this coming year." In her tone and on her face there was a little smugness.

"You've got a gift with things," Henry observed. "Some of those yellow chrysanthemums you had this year were ten inches across. I wish you'd work out in the orchard and raise some apples that big."

Her eyes sharpened. "Maybe I could do it, too. I've a gift with things, all right. My mother had it. She could stick anything in the ground and make it grow. She said it was having planters' hands that knew how to do it."

"Well, it sure works with flowers," he said.

"Henry, who were those men you were talking to?"

"Why, sure, that's what I came to tell you. They were from the

Western Meat Company. I sold those thirty head of three-year-old steers. Got nearly my own price, too."

"Good," she said. "Good for you."

"And I thought," he continued, "I thought how it's Saturday afternoon, and we might go into Salinas for dinner at a restaurant, and then to a picture show—to celebrate, you see."

"Good," she repeated. "Oh, yes. That will be good."

Henry put on his joking tone. "There's fights tonight. How'd you like to go to the fights?"

"Oh, no," she said breathlessly. "No, I wouldn't like fights."

"Just fooling, Elisa. We'll go to a movie. Let's see. It's two now. I'm going to take Scotty and bring down those steers from the hill. It'll take us maybe two hours. We'll go in town about five and have dinner at the Cominos Hotel. Like that?"

"Of course I'll like it. It's good to eat away from home."

"All right, then. I'll go get up a couple of horses."

She said: "I'll have plenty of time to transplant some of these sets, I guess."

She heard her husband calling Scotty down by the barn. And a little later she saw the two men ride up the pale yellow hillside in search of the steers.

There was a little square sandy bed kept for rooting the chrysanthemums. With her trowel she turned the soil over and over, and smoothed it and patted it firm. Then she dug ten parallel trenches to receive the sets. Back at the chrysanthemum bed she pulled out the little crisp shoots, trimmed off the leaves of each one with her scissors and laid it on a small orderly pile.

A squeak of wheels and plod of hoofs came from the road. Elisa looked up. The country road ran along the dense bank of willows and cottonwoods that bordered the river, and up this road came a curious vehicle, curiously drawn. It was an old spring-wagon, with a round canvas top on it like the cover of a prairie schooner. It was drawn by an old bay horse and a little grey-and-white burro. A big stubble-bearded man sat between the cover flaps and drove the crawling team. Underneath the wagon, between the hind wheels, a lean and rangy mongrel dog walked sedately. Words were painted on the canvas, in clumsy, crooked letters. "Pots, pans, knives, sisors, lawn mores, Fixed." Two rows of articles, and the triumphantly definitive "Fixed" below. The black paint had run down in little sharp points beneath each letter.

Elisa, squatting on the ground, watched to see the crazy, loose-jointed wagon pass by. But it didn't pass. It turned into the farm road in front of her house, crooked old wheels skirling and squeaking. The rangy dog darted from between the wheels and ran ahead. Instantly the two ranch shepherds flew out at him. Then all three stopped, and with stiff and quivering tails, with taut straight legs, with ambassadorial dignity, they slowly circled, sniffing daintily. The caravan pulled up to Elisa's wire fence and stopped. Now the newcomer dog, feeling out-numbered, lowered his tail and retired under the wagon with raised hackles and bared teeth.

The man on the wagon seat called out: "That's a bad dog in a fight when he gets started."

Elisa laughed. "I see he is. How soon does he generally get started?"

The man caught up her laughter and echoed it heartily. "Sometimes not for weeks and weeks," he said. He climbed stiffly down, over the wheel. The horse and the donkey drooped like unwatered flowers.

Elisa saw that he was a very big man. Although his hair and beard were greying, he did not look old. His worn black suit was wrinkled and spotted with grease. The laughter had disappeared from his face and eyes the moment his laughing voice ceased. His eyes were dark, and they were full of the brooding that gets in the eyes of teamsters and of sailors. The calloused hands he rested on the wire fence were cracked, and every crack was a black line. He took off his battered hat.

"I'm off my general road, ma'am," he said. "Does this dirt road cut over across the river to the Los Angeles highway?"

Elisa stood up and shoved the thick scissors in her apron pocket. "Well, yes, it does, but it winds around and then fords the river. I don't think your team could pull through the sand."

He replied with some asperity: "It might surprise you what them beasts can pull through."

"When they get started?" she asked.

He smiled for a second. "Yes. When they get started."

"Well," said Elisa, "I think you'll save time if you go back to the Salinas road and pick up the highway there."

He drew a big finger down the chicken wire and made it sing. "I ain't in any hurry, ma'am. I go from Seattle to San Diego and back every year. Takes all my time. About six months each way. I aim to follow nice weather."

Elisa took off her gloves and stuffed them in the apron pocket with the scissors. She touched the under edge of her man's hat, searching for fugitive hairs. "That sounds like a nice kind of way to live," she said.

He leaned confidentially over the fence. "Maybe you noticed the writing on my wagon. I mend pots and sharpen knives and scissors. You got any of them things to do?"

"Oh, no," she said quickly. "Nothing like that." Her eyes hardened with resistance.

"Scissors is the worst thing," he explained. "Most people just ruin scissors trying to sharpen 'em, but I know how. I got a special tool. It's a little bobbit kind of thing, and patented. But it sure does the trick."

"No. My scissors are all sharp."

"All right, then. Take a pot," he continued earnestly, "a bent pot, or a pot with a hole. I can make it like new so you don't have to buy no new ones. That's a saving for you."

"No," she said shortly. "I tell you I have nothing like that for you to do."

His face fell to an exaggerated sadness. His voice took on a whining undertone. "I ain't had a thing to do today. Maybe I won't have no supper tonight. You see I'm off my regular road. I know folks on the highway clear from Seattle to San Diego. They save their things for me to sharpen up because they know I do it so good and save them money."

"I'm sorry," Elisa said irritably. "I haven't anything for you to do."

His eyes left her face and fell to searching the ground. They roamed about until they came to the chrysanthemum bed where she had been working. "What's them plants, ma'am?"

The irritation and resistance melted from Elisa's face. "Oh, those are chrysanthemums, giant whites and yellows. I raise them every year, bigger than anybody around here."

"Kind of a long-stemmed flower? Looks like a quick puff of colored smoke?" he asked.

"That's it. What a nice way to describe them."

"They smell kind of nasty till you get used to them," he said.

"It's a good bitter smell," she retorted, "not nasty at all."

He changed his tone quickly. "I like the smell myself."

"I had ten-inch blooms this year," she said.

The man leaned farther over the fence. "Look. I know a lady down the road a piece, has got the nicest garden you ever seen. Got nearly every kind of flower but no chrysanthemums. Last time I was mending a copper-bottom washtub for her (that's a hard job but I do it good), she said to me: 'If you ever run acrost some nice chrysanthemums I wish you'd try to get me a few seeds.' That's what she told me."

Elisa's eyes grew alert and eager. "She couldn't have known much about chrysanthemums. You *can* raise them from seed, but it's much easier to root the little sprouts you see here."

"Oh," he said. "I s'pose I can't take none to her, then."

"Why yes you can," Elisa cried. "I can put some in damp sand, and you can carry them right along with you. They'll take root in the pot if you keep them damp. And then she can transplant them."

"She'd sure like to have some, ma'am. You say they're nice ones?"

"Beautiful," she said. "Oh, beautiful." Her eyes shone. She tore off the battered hat and shook out her dark pretty hair. "I'll put them in a flowerpot, and you can take them right with you. Come into the yard."

While the man came through the picket gate Elisa ran excitedly along the geranium-bordered path to the back of the house. And she returned carrying a big red flower-pot. The gloves were forgotten now. She kneeled on the ground by the starting bed and dug up the sandy soil with her fingers and scooped it into the bright new flower-pot. Then she picked up the little pile of shoots she had prepared. With her strong fingers she pressed them into the sand and tamped around them with her knuckles. The man stood over her. "I'll tell you what to do," she said. "You remember so you can tell the lady."

"Yes, I'll try to remember."

"Well, look. These will take root in about a month. Then she must set them out, about a foot apart in good rich earth like this, see?" She lifted a handful of dark soil for him to look at. "They'll grow fast and tall. Now remember this. In July tell her to cut them down, about eight inches from the ground."

"Before they bloom?" he asked.

"Yes, before they bloom." Her face was tight with eagerness. "They'll grow right up again. About the last of September the buds will start."

She stopped and seemed perplexed. "It's the budding that takes the most care," she said hesitantly. "I don't know how to tell you." She looked deep into his eyes, searchingly. Her mouth opened a little, and she seemed to be listening. "I'll try to tell you," she said. "Did you ever hear of planting hands?"

"Can't say I have, ma'am."

"Well, I can only tell you what it feels like. It's when you're picking off the buds you don't want. Everything goes right down into your fingertips. You watch your fingers work. They do it themselves. You can feel how it is. They pick and pick the buds. They never make a mistake. They're with the plant. Do you see? Your fingers and the plant. You can feel that, right up your arm. They know. They never make a mistake. You can feel it. When you're like that you can't do anything wrong. Do you see that? Can you understand that?"

She was kneeling on the ground looking up at him. Her breast swelled passionately.

The man's eyes narrowed. He looked away self-consciously.

"Maybe I know," he said. "Sometimes in the night in the wagon there—"

Elisa's voice grew husky. She broke in on him: "I've never lived as you do, but I know what you mean. When the night is dark—why, the stars are sharp-pointed, and there's quiet. Why, you rise up and up! Every pointed star gets driven into your body. It's like that. Hot and sharp and—lovely."

Kneeling there, her hand went out toward his legs in the greasy black trousers. Her hesitant fingers almost touched the cloth. Then her hand dropped to the ground. She crouched low like a fawning dog.

He said. "It's nice, just like you say. Only when you don't have no dinner it ain't."

She stood up then, very straight, and her face was ashamed. She held the flower-pot out to him and placed it gently in his arms. "Here. Put it in your wagon, on the seat, where you can watch it. Maybe I can find something for you to do."

At the back of the house she dug in the can pile and found two old and battered aluminum saucepans. She carried them back and gave them to him. "Here, maybe you can fix these."

His manner changed. He became professional. "Good as new I can fix them." At the back of his wagon he set a little anvil, and out of an oily tool-box dug a small machine hammer. Elisa came through the gate to watch him while he pounded out the dents in the kettles. His mouth grew sure and knowing. At a difficult part of the work he sucked his underlip.

"You sleep right in the wagon?" Elisa asked.

"Right in the wagon, ma'am. Rain or shine I'm dry as a cow in there."

"It must be nice," she said. "It must be very nice. I wish women could do such things."

"It ain't the right kind of a life for a woman."

Her upper lip raised a little, showing her teeth. "How do you know? How can you tell?" she said.

"I don't know, ma'am," he protested. "Of course I don't know. Now here's your kettles, done. You don't have to buy no new ones."

"How much?"

"Oh, fifty cents'll do. I keep my prices down and my work good. That's why I have all them satisfied customers up and down the highway."

Elisa brought him a fifty-cent piece from the house and dropped it in his hand. "You might be surprised to have a rival some time. I can sharpen scissors, too. And I can beat the dents out of little pots. I could show you what a woman might do."

He put his hammer back in the oily box and shoved the little anvil out of sight. "It would be a lonely life for a woman, ma'am, and a scarey life, too, with animals creeping under the wagon all night." He climbed over the single-tree, steadying himself with a hand on the burro's white rump. He settled himself in the seat, picked up the lines. "Thank you kindly ma'am," he said. "I'll do like you told me; I'll go back and catch the Salinas road."

"Mind," she called, "if you're long in getting there, keep the sand damp."

"Sand, ma'am? . . . Sand? Oh, sure. You mean around the chrysanthemums. Sure I will." He clucked his tongue. The beasts leaned luxuriously into their collars. The mongrel dog took his place between the back wheels. The wagon turned and crawled out the entrance road and back the way it had come, along the river.

Elisa stood in front of her wire fence watching the slow progress of the caravan. Her shoulders were straight, her head thrown back, her eyes half-closed, so that the scene came vaguely into them. Her lips moved silently, forming the words "Good-bye—good-bye." Then she whispered: "That's a bright direction. There's a glowing there." The sound of her whisper startled her. She shook herself free and looked about to see whether anyone had been listening. Only the dogs had heard. They lifted their heads toward her from their sleeping in the dust, and then stretched out their chins and settled asleep again. Elisa turned and ran hurriedly into the house.

In the kitchen she reached behind the stove and felt the water tank. It was full of hot water from the noonday cooking. In the bathroom she tore off her soiled clothes and flung them into the corner. And then she scrubbed herself with a little block of pumice, legs and thighs, loins and chest and arms, until her skin was scratched and red. When she had dried herself she stood in front of a mirror in her bedroom and looked at her body. She tightened her stomach and threw out her chest. She turned and looked over her shoulders at her back.

After a while she began to dress, slowly. She put on her newest underclothing and her nicest stockings and the dress which was the symbol of her prettiness. She worked carefully on her hair, pencilled her eyebrows and rouged her lips.

Before she was finished she heard the little thunder of hoofs and the shouts of Henry and his helper as they drove the red steers into the corral. She heard the gate bang shut and set herself for Henry's arrival.

His step sounded on the porch. He entered the house calling: "Elisa, where are you?"

"In my room, dressing. I'm not ready. There's hot water for your bath. Hurry up. It's getting late."

When she heard him splashing in the tub, Elisa laid his dark suit on the bed, and shirt and socks and tie beside it. She stood his polished shoes on the floor beside the bed. Then she went to the porch and sat primly and stiffly down. She looked toward the river road where the willow-line was still yellow with frosted leaves so that under the high grey fog they seemed a thin band of sunshine. This was the only color in the grey afternoon. She sat unmoving for a long time. Her eyes blinked rarely.

Henry came banging out of the door, shoving his tie inside his vest as he came. Elisa stiffened and her face grew tight. Henry stopped short and looked at her. "Why—why, Elisa. You look so nice!"

"Nice? You think I look nice? What do you mean by 'nice'?"

Henry blundered on. "I don't know. I mean you look different, strong and happy."

"I am strong? Yes, strong. What do you mean 'strong'?"

He looked bewildered. "You're playing some kind of a game," he said helplessly. "It's a kind of a play. You look strong enough to break a calf over your knee, happy enough to eat it like a watermelon."

For a second she lost her rigidity. "Henry! Don't talk like that. You didn't know what you said." She grew complete again. "I'm strong," she boasted. "I never knew before how strong."

Henry looked down toward the tractor shed, and when he brought his eyes back to her, they were his own again. "I'll get out the car. You can put on your coat while I'm starting."

Elisa went into the house. She heard him drive to the gate and idle down his motor, and then she took a long time to put on her hat. She pulled it here and pressed it there. When Henry turned the motor off she slipped into her coat and went out.

The little roadster bounced along on the dirt road by the river, raising the birds and driving the rabbits into the brush. Two cranes flapped heavily over the willow-line and dropped into the river-bed.

Far ahead on the road Elisa saw a dark speck. She knew.

She tried not to look as they passed it, but her eyes would not obey. She whispered to herself sadly: "He might have thrown them off the road. That wouldn't have been much trouble, not very much. But he kept the pot," she explained. "He had to keep the pot. That's why he couldn't get them off the road."

The roadster turned a bend and she saw the caravan ahead. She swung full around toward her husband so she could not see the little covered wagon and the mis-matched team as the car passed them.

In a moment it was over. The thing was done. She did not look back.

She said loudly, to be heard above the motor: "It will be good, tonight, a good dinner."

"Now you've changed again," Henry complained. He took one hand from the wheel and patted her knee. "I ought to take you in to dinner oftener. It would be good for both of us. We get so heavy out on the ranch."

"Henry," she asked, "could we have wine at dinner?"

"Sure we could. Say! That will be fine."

She was silent for a while; then she said: "Henry, at those prize-fights, do the men hurt each other very much?"

"Sometimes a little, not often. Why?"

"Well, I've read how they break noses, and blood runs down their chests. I've read how the fighting gloves get heavy and soggy with blood."

He looked around at her. "What's the matter, Elisa? I didn't know you read things like that." He brought the car to a stop, then turned to the right over the Salinas River bridge.

"Do any women ever go to the fights?" she asked.

"Oh, sure, some. What's the matter, Elisa? Do you want to go? I don't think you'd like it, but I'll take you if you really want to go."

She relaxed limply in the seat. "Oh, no. No. I don't want to go. I'm sure I don't." Her face was turned away from him. "It will be enough if we can have wine. It will be plenty." She turned up her coat collar so he could not see that she was crying weakly—like an old woman.

1937

Paul Theroux
b. 1941

It might be strange to think of this selection as a story, because it doesn't have a plot or a central character. But it is definitely fiction. There are no Creech people; there is no memory priest; no one is eaten. It was first published in Harper's *in 1998, then in Theroux's collection* Fresh Air Fiend: Travel Writings, 1985–2000, *and again in the anthology* Flash Fiction Forward: 80 Very Short Stories *in 2006. In* Fresh Air Fiend *the story is one among many in a section called "Unspeakable Rituals and Outlandish Beliefs," all of which Theroux makes up. He claims that some rites are "uniquely unpleasant" while others mirror "practices we believe to be peculiar to our own lives." Theroux does not say into which category "The Memory Priest" falls.*

The Memory Priest of the Creech People

One person alone, always a man, serves as the memory for all the dates and names and events of the Creech, the hill-dwelling aboriginals of south-central Sumatra. This person possesses an entire history of the people and may spend as much as a week, day and night, reciting the various genealogies.

This Memory Priest reminds the Creech of who they are and what they have done. He is their entertainment and their historian, their memory and mind and imagination. He keeps the Creech amused and informed. The Creech have no chief or headman. The Memory Priest serves as the sole authority.

The Memory Priest is awarded his title at birth. As soon as he is able to talk he is given to understand that he is the repository of all the Creech lore.

His is not an easy career. He must memorize great lists of family names and must be able to recite all the events that took place from the moment of his birth.

The Creech are mostly placid, though they are subject to odd fits of violence. Biting themselves in order to show remorse is not unknown, and clawing their own faces is common. They are also untruthful and unreliable, prone to thieving, gossiping, gambling, and sudden spasms of the most aggressive behavior.

What the Memory Priest knows, the immensity of his storehouse of facts, is nothing compared with the one fact that he does not know, a secret that is withheld from him: After thirty years have passed, and he is old by Creech standards (possibly toothless, almost certainly wrinkled and shrunken), a meeting is convened. He recites the Creech history, and at the conclusion of this he is put to death. He is finally roasted and eaten by every member of the Creech, in a ritual known as the Ceremony of Purification.

The next male child born to a Creech woman is designated Memory Priest and elevated; history begins once again. Nothing that has taken place before his birth has any reality, all quarrels are settled, all debts nullified.

So the Memory Priest, now an infant, soon a man, learns his role, believing that history begins with him and never aware that at a specified moment his life will end. Yet it is the death of the Memory Priest that the Creech people live for and whisper about, the wiping out of all debts, all crimes, all shame and failure. They eagerly anticipate the amnesia his death will bring. Throughout his life, though he is unaware of it, he is less a supreme authority than a convenient receptacle into which all the ill-assorted details of the Creech are tossed. Secretly, he is mocked for not knowing that it will all end in oblivion, at the time of his certain death.

1998

John Updike

b. 1932

"A & P" has spurred many contradictory interpretations, and no doubt its ambiguity contributes to its consistent popularity (it is one of the most often anthologized stories in North America). Some critics compare Sammy's final vision to the dark epiphany at the end of Joyce's "Araby." Some see Sammy's gesture as a triumphant rejection of American middle-class values. Others think he acquiesces to crass materialism by envying the girls' class status. It seems that Updike wanted to leave the story open-ended. In an early draft, the story did not end where it does now. Sammy walked home and

drove to the water, ultimately idling his youth away at the beach waiting for the girls, who never reappear.

A & P

In walks these three girls in nothing but bathing suits. I'm in the third checkout slot, with my back to the door, so I don't see them until they're over by the bread. The one that caught my eye first was the one in the plaid green two-piece. She was a chunky kid, with a good tan and a sweet broad soft-looking can with those two crescents of white just under it, where the sun never seems to hit, at the top of the backs of her legs. I stood there with my hand on a box of HiHo crackers trying to remember if I rang it up or not. I ring it up again and the customer starts giving me hell. She's one of these cash-register-watchers, a witch about fifty with rouge on her cheekbones and no eyebrows, and I know it made her day to trip me up. She'd been watching cash registers for fifty years and probably never seen a mistake before.

By the time I got her feathers smoothed and her goodies into a bag—she gives me a little snort in passing, if she'd been born at the right time they would have burned her over in Salem[1]—by the time I get her on her way the girls had circled around the bread and were coming back, without a pushcart, back my way along the counters, in the aisle between the checkouts and the Special bins. They didn't even have shoes on. There was this chunky one, with the two-piece—it was bright green and the seams on the bra were still sharp and her belly was still pretty pale so I guessed she just got it (the suit)—there was this one, with one of those chubby berry-faces, the lips all bunched together under her nose, this one, and a tall one, with black hair that hadn't quite frizzed right, and one of these sunburns right across under the eyes, and a chin that was too long—you know, the kind of girl other girls think is very "striking" and "attractive" but never quite makes it, as they very well know, which

1. A city in Massachusetts, famous for the witch trials of 1692.

is why they like her so much—and then the third one, that wasn't quite so tall. She was the queen. She kind of led them, the other two peeking around and making their shoulders round. She didn't look around, not this queen, she just walked straight on slowly, on these long white primadonna legs. She came down a little hard on her heels, as if she didn't walk in bare feet that much, putting down her heels and then letting the weight move along to her toes as if she was testing the floor with every step, putting a little deliberate extra action into it. You never know for sure how girls' minds work (do you really think it's a mind in there or just a little buzz like a bee in a glass jar?) but you got the idea she had talked the other two into coming here with her, and now she was showing them how to do it, walk slow and hold yourself straight.

She had on a kind of dirty-pink—beige maybe, I don't know—bathing suit with a little nubble all over it and, what got me, the straps were down. They were off her shoulders looped loose around the cool tops of her arms, and I guess as a result the suit had slipped a little on her, so all around the top of the cloth there was this shining rim. If it hadn't been there you wouldn't have known there could have been anything whiter than those shoulders. With the straps pushed off, there was nothing between the top of the suit and the top of her head except just *her*, this clean bare plane of the top of her chest down from the shoulder bones like a dented sheet of metal tilted in the light. I mean, it was more than pretty.

She had a sort of oaky hair that the sun and salt had bleached, done up in a bun that was unravelling, and a kind of prim face. Walking into the A & P with your straps down, I suppose it's the only kind of face you *can* have. She held her head so high her neck, coming up out of those white shoulders, looked kind of stretched, but I didn't mind. The longer her neck was, the more of her there was.

She must have felt in the corner of her eye me and over my shoulder Stokesie in the second slot watching, but she didn't tip. Not this queen. She kept her eyes moving across the racks, and stopped, and turned so slow it made my stomach rub the inside of my apron, and buzzed to the other two, who kind of huddled against her for relief, and then they all three of them went up the cat-and-dog-food-breakfast-cereal-macaroni-rice-raisins-seasonings-spreads-spaghetti-soft-drinks-crackers-and-cookies aisle. From the third slot I look straight up this aisle to the meat counter, and I watched them all the way. The fat one with the tan sort of fumbled with the cookies, but on second thought she put the package back. The sheep pushing their carts down the aisle—the girls were walking against the usual traffic (not that we have one-way signs or anything)—were pretty hilarious. You could see them, when Queenie's white shoulders dawned on them, kind of jerk, or hop, or hiccup, but their eyes snapped back to their own baskets and on they pushed. I bet you could set off dynamite in an A & P and the people would by and large keep reaching and checking oatmeal off their lists and muttering "Let me see, there was a third thing, began with A, asparagus, no, ah, yes, applesauce!" or whatever it is they do mutter. But there was no doubt, this jiggled them. A few houseslaves in pin curlers even looked around after pushing their carts past to make sure what they had seen was correct.

You know, it's one thing to have a girl in a bathing suit down on the beach, where what with the glare nobody can look at each other much anyway, and another thing in the cool of the A & P, under the fluorescent lights, against all those stacked packages, with her feet paddling along naked over our checker-board green-and-cream rubber-tile floor.

"Oh Daddy," Stokesie said beside me. "I feel so faint."

"Darling," I said. "Hold me tight." Stokesie's married, with two babies chalked up on his fuselage already, but as far as I can tell that's the only difference. He's twenty-two, and I was nineteen this April.

"Is it done?" he asks, the responsible married man finding his voice. I forgot to say he thinks he's going to be manager some sunny day, maybe in 1990 when it's called the Great Alexandrov and Petrooshki Tea Company or something.[2]

What he meant was, our town is five miles from a beach, with a big summer colony out on the Point, but we're right in the middle of town, and the women generally put on a shirt or shorts or something

2. In other words, after the United States has taken over by the Soviet Union. This story was written in the midst of the Cold War. The Bay of Pigs invasion of Cuba, for example, was in 1961, and the Cuban missile crisis in October 1962.

before they get out of the car into the street. And anyway these are usually women with six children and varicose veins mapping their legs and nobody, including them, could care less. As I say, we're right in the middle of town, and if you stand at our front doors you can see two banks and the Congregational church and the newspaper store and three real-estate offices and about twenty-seven old free-loaders tearing up Central Street because the sewer broke again. It's not as if we're on the Cape;[3] we're north of Boston and there's people in this town haven't seen the ocean for twenty years.

The girls had reached the meat counter and were asking McMahon something. He pointed, they pointed, and they shuffled out of sight behind a pyramid of Diet Delight peaches. All that was left for us to see was old McMahon patting his mouth and looking after them sizing up their joints. Poor kids, I began to feel sorry for them, they couldn't help it.

Now here comes the sad part of the story, at least my family says it's sad, but I don't think it's so sad myself. The store's pretty empty, it being Thursday afternoon, so there was nothing much to do except lean on the register and wait for the girls to show up again. The whole store was like a pinball machine and I didn't know which tunnel they'd come out of. After a while they come around out of the far aisle, around the light bulbs, records at discount of the Caribbean Six or Tony Martin Sings or some such gunk you wonder they waste the wax on, six-packs of candy bars, and plastic toys done up in cellophane that fall apart when a kid looks at them anyway. Around they come, Queenie still leading the way, and holding a little gray jar in her hand. Slots Three through Seven are unmanned and I could see her wondering between Stokes and me, but Stokesie with his usual luck draws an old party in baggy gray pants who stumbles up with four giant cans of pineapple juice (what do these bums *do* with all that pineapple juice? I've often asked myself) so the girls come to me. Queenie puts down the jar and I take it into my fingers icy cold. Kingfish Fancy Herring Snacks in Pure Sour Cream: 49¢. Now her hands are empty, not a ring or a bracelet; bare as God made them, and I wonder where the money's

3. Cape Cod, Massachusetts, a seaside resort area where dress is usually informal.

coming from. Still with that prim look she lifts a folded dollar bill out of the hollow at the center of her nubbled pink top. The jar went heavy in my hand. Really, I thought that was so cute.

Then everybody's luck begins to run out. Lengel comes in from haggling with a truck full of cabbages on the lot and is about to scuttle into that door marked MANAGER behind which he hides all day when the girls touch his eye. Lengel's pretty dreary, teaches Sunday school and the rest, but he doesn't miss that much. He comes over and says, "Girls, this isn't the beach."

Queenie blushes, though maybe it's just a brush of sunburn I was noticing for the first time, now that she was so close. "My mother asked me to pick up a jar of herring snacks." Her voice kind of startled me, the way voices do when you see the people first, coming out so flat and dumb yet kind of tony, too, the way it ticked over "pick up" and "snacks." All of a sudden I slid right down her voice into her living room. Her father and the other men were standing around in ice-cream coats and bow ties and the women were in sandals picking up herring snacks on toothpicks off a big glass plate and they were all holding drinks the color of water with olives and sprigs of mint in them. When my parents have somebody over they get lemonade and if it's a real racy affair Schlitz in tall glasses with "They'll Do It Every Time" cartoons stencilled on.[4]

"That's all right," Lengel said. "But this isn't the beach." His repeating this struck me as funny as if it had just occurred to him, and he had been thinking all these years the A & P was a great big dune and he was the head lifeguard. He didn't like my smiling—as I say he doesn't miss much—but he concentrates on giving the girls that sad Sunday-school-superintendent stare.

Queenie's blush is no sunburn now, and the plump one in plaid, that I liked better from the back—a really sweet can—pipes up, "We weren't doing any shopping. We just came in for the one thing."

"That makes no difference," Lengel tells her and I could see from the way his eyes went that he hadn't noticed she was wearing a two-piece before. "We want you decently dressed when you come in here."

"We *are* decent," Queenie says suddenly her lower lip pushing, getting sore now that she remembers her place, a place from which

4. "They'll Do It Every Time" was a comic that appeared in daily newspapers.

the crowd that runs the A & P must look pretty crummy. Fancy Herring Snacks flashed in her very blue eyes.

"Girls, I don't want to argue with you. After this come in here with your shoulders covered. It's our policy." He turns his back. That's policy for you. Policy is what the kingpins want. What the others want is juvenile delinquency.

All this while, the customers had been showing up with their carts but, you know, sheep, seeing a scene, they had all bunched up on Stokesie, who shook open a paper bag as gently as peeling a peach, not wanting to miss a word. I could feel in the silence everybody getting nervous, most of all Lengel, who asks me, "Sammy, have you rung up their purchase?"

I thought and said "No" but it wasn't about that I was thinking. I go through the punches, 4, 9, GROC, TOT—it's more complicated than you think, and after you do it often enough, it begins to make a little song, that you hear words to, in my case "Hello (*bing*) there, you (*gung*) hap-py *pee*-pul (*splat*)!"—the *splat* being the drawer flying out. I uncrease the bill, tenderly as you may imagine, it just having come from between the two smoothest scoops of vanilla I had ever known there were, and pass a half and a penny into her narrow pink palm, and nestle the herrings in a bag and twist its neck and hand it over, all the time thinking.

The girls, and who'd blame them, are in a hurry to get out, so I say "I quit" to Lengel quick enough for them to hear, hoping they'll stop and watch me, their unsuspected hero. They keep right on going, into the electric eye; the door flies open and they flicker across the lot to their car, Queenie and Plaid and Big Tall Goony-Goony (not that as raw material she was so bad), leaving me with Lengel and a kink in his eyebrow.

"Did you say something, Sammy?"

"I said I quit."

"I thought you did."

"You didn't have to embarrass them."

"It was they who were embarassing us."

I started to say something that came out. "Fiddle-de-do." It's a saying of my grandmother's, and I know she would have been pleased.

"I don't think you know what you're saying," Lengel said.

"I know you don't," I said. "But I do." I pull the bow at the back of my apron and start shrugging it off my shoulders. A couple of customers that had been heading for my slot begin to knock against each other, liked scared pigs in a chute.

Lengel sighs and begins to look very patient and old and gray. He's been a friend of my parents for years. "Sammy, you don't want to do this to your Mom and Dad," he tells me. It's true, I don't. But it seems to me that once you begin a gesture it's fatal not to go through with it. I fold the apron, "Sammy" stitched in red on the pocket, and put it on the counter, and drop the bow tie on top of it. The bow tie is theirs, if you've ever wondered. "You'll feel this for the rest of your life," Lengel says, and I know that's true, too, but remembering how he made that pretty girl blush makes me so scrunchy inside I punch the No Sale tab and the machine whirs "pee-pul" and the drawer splats out. One advantage to this scene taking place in summer, I can follow this up with a clean exit, there's no fumbling around getting your coat and galoshes, I just saunter into the electric eye in my white shirt that my mother ironed the night before, and the door heaves itself open, and outside the sunshine is skating around on the asphalt.

I look around for my girls, but they're gone, of course. There wasn't anybody but some young married screaming with her children about some candy they didn't get by the door of a powder-blue Falcon station wagon. Looking back in the big windows, over the bags of peat moss and aluminum lawn furniture stacked on the pavement, I could see Lengel in my place in the slot, checking the sheep through. His face was dark gray and his back stiff, as if he's just had an injection of iron, and my stomach kind of fell as I felt how hard the world was going to be to me hereafter.

1962

Hannah Voskuil

b. 1975

According to Voskuil, this story began as an exercise in reverse narrative structure, or telling a story backwards. It is an example of the technique that William Faulkner uses in a more amplified and complex fashion in "A Rose for Emily." Despite this reversal and despite the story's brevity, all of the elements of plot discussed in the Introduction are present. You can analyze this short short story the same way you analyze the longer stories in this volume. It originally appeared in Quarterly West *magazine, and subsequently in* Flash Fiction Forward.

Currents

Gary drank single malt in the night, out on the porch that leaned toward the ocean. His mother, distracted, had shut off the floodlights and he did not protest against the dark.

Before that, his mother, Josey, tucked in her two shivering twelve-year-old granddaughters.

"I want you both to go swimming first thing tomorrow. Can't have two seals like you afraid of the water."

Before that, one of the girls held the hand of a wordless Filipino boy. His was the first hand she'd ever held. They were watching the paramedics lift the boy's dead brother into an ambulance.

At this time, the other girl heaved over a toilet in the cabana.

Before that, the girl who would feel nauseated watched as the drowned boy's hand slid off the stretcher and bounced along the porch rail. Nobody placed the hand back on the stretcher, and it bounced and dragged and bounced.

Before that, Gary saw the brown hair sink and resurface as the body bobbed. At first he mistook it for seaweed.

Before that, thirty-five people struggled out of the water at the Coast Guard's command. A lifeguard shouted over Jet Ski motors about the increasing strength of the riptide.

Before that, the thirty-five people, including Gary and the two girls, formed a human chain and trolled the waters for the body of a Filipino boy. The boy had gone under twenty minutes earlier, and never come back up.

Before that, a lifeguard sprinted up the beach, shouting for volunteers. The two girls, resting lightly on their sandy bodyboards, stood up to help.

Before that, a Filipino boy pulled on the torpid lifeguard's ankle and gestured desperately at the waves. My brother, he said.

Before that, it was a simple summer day.

2004

Alice Walker

b. 1944

Much of Walker's inspiration for "Everyday Use" came from her own life in rural Georgia. Walker, like Maggie, grew up scarred and self-conscious: she was blinded in one eye by a BB gun at the age of eight. She also grew up poor, with a mother who made all her children's clothes, canned food in the summer, and made quilts to get through the winter. Her mother had an artist's soul, and she grew flowers that were famous in three counties. "Everyday Use" substitutes quilts for flowers. Walker was once transfixed by an old quilt she saw in the Smithsonian—throwaway rag pieces sewn together into an image of Christ's crucifixion. Its author was an anonymous black woman who lived in the nineteenth century. Walker found in quilts, then, a rich and ready-made symbol representing the unrecorded tragedies and triumphs of black women like her mother.

Everyday Use

for your grandmamma

I will wait for her in the yard that Maggie and I made so clean and wavy yesterday afternoon. A yard like this is more comfortable than most people know. It is not just a yard. It is like an extended living room. When the hard clay is swept clean as a floor and the fine sand around the edges lined with tiny, irregular grooves, anyone can come and sit and look up into the elm tree and wait for the breezes that never come inside the house.

Maggie will be nervous until after her sister goes: she will stand hopelessly in corners, homely and ashamed of the burn scars down her arms and legs, eying her sister with a mixture of envy and awe. She thinks her sister has held life always in the palm of one hand, that "no" is a word the world never learned to say to her.

You've no doubt seen those TV shows where the child who has "made it" is confronted, as a surprise, by her own mother and father, tottering in weakly from backstage. (A pleasant surprise, of course: What would they do if parent and child came on the show only to curse out and insult each other?) On TV mother and child embrace and smile into each other's faces. Sometimes the mother and father weep, the child wraps them in her arms and leans across the table to tell how she would not have made it without their help. I have seen these programs.

Sometimes I dream a dream in which Dee and I are suddenly brought together on a TV program of this sort. Out of a dark and soft-seated limousine I am ushered into a bright room filled with many people. There I meet a smiling, gray, sporty man like Johnny Carson who shakes my hand and tells me what a fine girl I have. Then we are on the stage and Dee is embracing me with tears in her eyes. She pins on my dress a large orchid, even though she has told me once that she thinks orchids are tacky flowers.

In real life I am a large, big-boned woman with rough, man-working hands. In the winter I wear flannel nightgowns to bed and overalls during the day. I can kill and clean a hog as mercilessly as a man. My fat keeps me hot in zero weather. I can work outside all day, breaking ice to get water for washing; I can eat pork liver cooked over the open fire minutes after it comes steaming from the hog. One winter I knocked a bull calf straight in the brain between the eyes with a sledge hammer and had the meat hung up to chill before nightfall. But of course all this does not show on television. I am the way my daughter would want me to be: a hundred pounds lighter, my skin like an uncooked barley pancake. My hair glistens in the hot bright lights. Johnny Carson has much to do to keep up with my quick and witty tongue.

But that is a mistake. I know even before I wake up. Who ever knew a Johnson with a quick tongue? Who can even imagine me looking a strange white man in the eye? It seems to me I have talked to them always with one foot raised in flight, with my head turned in whichever way is farthest from them. Dee, though. She would always look anyone in the eye. Hesitation was no part of her nature.

"How do I look, Mama?" Maggie says, showing just enough of her thin body enveloped in pink skirt and red blouse for me to know she's there, almost hidden by the door.

"Come out into the yard," I say.

Have you ever seen a lame animal, perhaps a dog run over by some careless person rich enough to own a car, sidle up to someone who is ignorant enough to be kind to them? That is the way my Maggie walks. She has been like this, chin on chest, eyes on ground, feet in shuffle, ever since the fire that burned the other house to the ground.

Dee is lighter than Maggie, with nicer hair and a fuller figure. She's a woman now, though sometimes I forget. How long ago was it that the other house burned? Ten, twelve years? Sometimes I can still hear the flames and feel Maggie's arms sticking to me, her hair smoking and her dress falling off her in little black papery flakes. Her eyes seemed stretched open, blazed open by the flames reflected in them. And Dee. I see her standing off under the sweet gum tree she used to dig gum out of; a look of concentration on her face as she watched the last dingy gray board of the house fall in toward the red-hot brick chimney. Why don't you do a dance around the ashes? I'd wanted to ask her. She had hated the house that much.

I used to think she hated Maggie, too. But that was before we raised the money, the church and me, to send her to Augusta to school. She used to read to us without pity; forcing words, lies, other folks' habits, whole lives upon us two, sitting trapped and ignorant underneath her voice. She washed us in a river of make-believe, burned us with a lot of knowledge we didn't necessarily need to know. Pressed us to her with the serious way she read, to shove us away at just the moment, like dimwits, we seemed about to understand.

Dee wanted nice things. A yellow organdy dress to wear to her graduation from high school; black pumps to match a green suit she'd made from an old suit somebody gave me. She was determined to stare down any disaster in her efforts. Her eyelids would not flicker for minutes at a time. Often I fought off the temptation to shake her. At sixteen she had a style of her own: and knew what style was.

I never had an education myself. After second grade the school was closed down. Don't ask me why: in 1927 colored asked fewer questions than they do now. Sometimes Maggie reads to me. She stumbles along good naturedly but can't see well. She knows she is not bright. Like good looks and money, quickness passed her by. She will marry John Thomas (who has mossy teeth in an earnest face) and then I'll be free to sit here and I guess just sing church songs to myself. Although I never was a good singer. Never could carry a tune. I was always better at a man's job. I used to love to milk till I was hooked[1] in the side in '49. Cows are soothing and slow and don't bother you, unless you try to milk them the wrong way.

I have deliberately turned my back on the house. It is three rooms, just like the one that burned, except the roof is tin; they don't make shingle roofs any more. There are no real windows, just some holes cut in the sides, like the portholes in a ship, but not round and not square, with rawhide holding the shutters up on the outside. This house is in a pasture, too, like the other one. No doubt when Dee sees it she will want to tear it down. She wrote me once that no matter where we "choose" to live, she will manage to come see us. But she will never bring her friends. Maggie and I thought about this and Maggie asked me, "Mama, when did Dee ever *have* any friends?"

1. I.e., gored by the horn of a cow.

She had a few. Furtive boys in pink shirts hanging about on washday after school. Nervous girls who never laughed. Impressed with her they worshiped the well-turned phrase, the cute shape, the scalding humor that erupted like bubbles in lye. She read to them.

When she was courting Jimmy T she didn't have much time to pay to us, but turned all her faultfinding power on him. He *flew* to marry a cheap city girl from a family of ignorant flashy people. She hardly had time to recompose herself.

When she comes I will meet—but there they are!

Maggie attempts to make a dash for the house, in her shuffling way, but I stay her with my hand. "Come back here," I say. And she stops and tries to dig a well in the sand with her toe.

It is hard to see them clearly through the strong sun. But even the first glimpse of leg out of the car tells me it is Dee. Her feet were always neat-looking, as if God himself had shaped them with a certain style. From the other side of the car comes a short, stocky man. Hair is all over his head a foot long and hanging from his chin like a kinky mule tail. I hear Maggie suck in her breath. "Uhnnnh," is what it sounds like. Like when you see the wriggling end of a snake just in front of your foot on the road. "Uhnnnh."

Dee next. A dress down to the ground, in this hot weather. A dress so loud it hurts my eyes. There are yellows and oranges enough to throw back the light of the sun. I feel my whole face warming from the heat waves it throws out. Earrings gold, too, and hanging down to her shoulders. Bracelets dangling and making noises when she moves her arm up to shake the folds of the dress out of her armpits. The dress is loose and flows, and as she walks closer, I like it. I hear Maggie go "Uhnnnh" again. It is her sister's hair. It stands straight up like the wool on a sheep. It is black as night and around the edges are two long pigtails that rope about like small lizards disappearing behind her ears.

"Wa-su-zo-Tean-o!" she says, coming on in that gliding way the dress makes her move. The short stocky fellow with the hair to his navel is all grinning and he follows up with "Asalamalakim,[2] my

2. Transliteration of a Muslim greeting; literally, "Peace be with you." "Wa-su-zo-Tean-o" is a similar rendering of an African salutation.

mother and sister!" He moves to hug Maggie but she falls back, right up against the back of my chair. I feel her trembling there and when I look up I see the perspiration falling off her chin.

"Don't get up," says Dee. Since I am stout it takes something of a push. You can see me trying to move a second or two before I make it. She turns, showing white heels through her sandals, and goes back to the car. Out she peeks next with a Polaroid. She stoops down quickly and lines up picture after picture of me sitting there in front of the house with Maggie cowering behind me. She never takes a shot without making sure the house is included. When a cow comes nibbling around the edge of the yard she snaps it and me and Maggie *and* the house. Then she puts the Polaroid in the back seat of the car, and comes up and kisses me on the forehead.

Meanwhile Asalamalakim is going through motions with Maggie's hand. Maggie's hand is as limp as a fish, and probably as cold, despite the sweat, and she keeps trying to pull it back. It looks like Asalamalakim wants to shake hands but wants to do it fancy. Or maybe he don't know how people shake hands. Anyhow, he soon gives up on Maggie.

"Well," I say. "Dee."

"No, Mama," she says. "Not 'Dee,' Wangero Leewanika Kemanjo!"

"What happened to 'Dee'?" I wanted to know.

"She's dead," Wangero said. "I couldn't bear it any longer, being named after the people who oppress me."

"You know as well as me you was named after your aunt Dicie," I said. Dicie is my sister. She named Dee. We called her "Big Dee" after Dee was born.

"But who was *she* named after?" asked Wangero.

"I guess after Grandma Dee," I said.

"And who was she named after?" asked Wangero.

"Her mother," I said, and saw Wangero was getting tired. "That's about as far back as I can trace it," I said. Though, in fact, I probably could have carried it back beyond the Civil War through the branches.

"Well," said Asalamalakim, "there you are."

"Uhnnnh," I heard Maggie say.

"There I was not," I said, "before 'Dicie' cropped up in our family, so why should I try to trace it that far back?"

He just stood there grinning, looking down on me like somebody inspecting a Model A car. Every once in a while he and Wangero sent eye signals over my head.

"How do you pronounce this name?" I asked.

"You don't have to call me by it if you don't want to," said Wangero.

"Why shouldn't I?" I asked. "If that's what you want us to call you, we'll call you."

"I know it might sound awkward at first," said Wangero.

"I'll get used to it," I said. "Ream it out again."

Well, soon we got the name out of the way. Asalamalakim had a name twice as long and three times as hard. After I tripped over it two or three times he told me to just call him Hakim-a-barber. I wanted to ask him was he a barber, but I didn't really think he was, so I didn't ask.

"You must belong to those beef-cattle peoples down the road," I said. They said "Asalamalakim" when they met you, too, but they didn't shake hands. Always too busy: feeding the cattle, fixing the fences, putting up salt-lick shelters, throwing down hay. When the white folks poisoned some of the herd the men stayed up all night with rifles in their hands. I walked a mile and a half just to see the sight.

Hakim-a-barber said, "I accept some of their doctrines, but farming and raising cattle is not my style." (They didn't tell me, and I didn't ask, whether Wangero (Dee) had really gone and married him.)

We sat down to eat and right away he said he didn't eat collards and pork was unclean. Wangero, though, went on through the chitlins and corn bread, the greens and everything else. She talked a blue streak over the sweet potatoes. Everything delighted her. Even the fact that we still used the benches her daddy made for the table when we couldn't afford to buy chairs.

"Oh, Mama!" she cried. Then turned to Hakim-a-barber. "I never knew how lovely these benches are. You can feel the rump prints," she said running her hands underneath her and along the bench. Then she gave a sigh and her hand closed over Grandma

Dee's butter dish. "That's it!" she said. "I knew there was something I wanted to ask you if I could have." She jumped up from the table and went over in the corner where the churn stood, the milk in it clabber[3] by now. She looked at the churn and looked at it.

"This churn top is what I need," she said. "Didn't Uncle Buddy whittle it out of a tree you all used to have?"

"Yes," I said.

"Uh huh," she said happily. "And I want the dasher,[4] too."

"Uncle Buddy whittle that, too?" asked the barber.

Dee (Wangero) looked up at me.

"Aunt Dee's first husband whittled the dash," said Maggie so low you almost couldn't hear her. "His name was Henry, but they called him Stash."

"Maggie's brain is like an elephant's," Wangero said, laughing. "I can use the churn top as a centerpiece for the alcove table," she said, sliding a plate over the churn, "and I'll think of something artistic to do with the dasher."

When she finished wrapping the dasher the handle stuck out. I took it for a moment in my hands. You didn't even have to look close to see where hands pushing the dasher up and down to make butter had left a kind of sink in the wood. In fact, there were a lot of small sinks; you could see where thumbs and fingers had sunk into the wood. It was beautiful light yellow wood, from a tree that grew in the yard where Big Dee and Stash had lived.

After dinner Dee (Wangero) went to the trunk at the foot of my bed and started rifling through it. Maggie hung back in the kitchen over the dishpan. Out came Wangero with two quilts. They had been pieced by Grandma Dee and then Big Dee and me had hung them on the quilt frames on the front porch and quilted them. One was in the Lone Star pattern. The other was Walk Around the Mountain. In both of them were scraps of dresses Grandma Dee had worn fifty and more years ago. Bits and pieces of Grandpa Jarrell's Paisley shirts. And one teeny faded blue piece, about the size of a penny matchbox, that was from Great Grandpa Ezra's uniform that he wore in the Civil War.

3. Curdled.
4. A device for stirring the cream in a churn.

"Mama," Wangero said sweet as a bird. "Can I have these old quilts?"

I heard something fall in the kitchen, and a minute later the kitchen door slammed.

"Why don't you take one or two of the others?" I asked. "These old things was just done by me and Big Dee from some tops your grandma pieced before she died."

"No," said Wangero. "I don't want those. They are stitched around the borders by machine."

"That'll make them last better," I said.

"That's not the point," said Wangero. "These are all pieces of dresses Grandma used to wear. She did all this stitching by hand. Imagine!" She held the quilts securely in her arms, stroking them.

"Some of the pieces, like those lavender ones, come from old clothes her mother handed down to her," I said, moving up to touch the quilts. Dee (Wangero) moved back just enough so that I couldn't reach the quilts. They already belonged to her.

"Imagine!" she breathed again, clutching them closely to her bosom.

"The truth is," I said, "I promised to give them quilts to Maggie, for when she marries John Thomas."

She gasped like a bee had stung her.

"Maggie can't appreciate these quilts!" she said. "She'd probably be backward enough to put them to everyday use."

"I reckon she would," I said. "God knows I been saving 'em for long enough with nobody using 'em. I hope she will!" I didn't want to bring up how I had offered Dee (Wangero) a quilt when she went away to college. Then she had told me they were old-fashioned, out of style.

"But they're *priceless*!" she was saying now, furiously; for she has a temper. "Maggie would put them on the bed and in five years they'd be in rags. Less than that!"

"She can always make some more," I said. "Maggie knows how to quilt."

Dee (Wangero) looked at me with hatred. "You just will not understand. The point is these quilts, *these* quilts!"

"Well," I said, stumped. "What would *you* do with them?"

"Hang them," she said. As if that was the only thing you *could* do with quilts.

Maggie by now was standing in the door. I could almost hear the sound her feet made as they scraped over each other.

"She can have them, Mama," she said, like somebody used to never winning anything, or having anything reserved for her. "I can 'member Grandma Dee without the quilts."

I looked at her hard. She had filled her bottom lip with checkerberry snuff and it gave her a face a kind of dopey, hangdog look. It was Grandma Dee and Big Dee who taught her how to quilt herself. She stood there with her scarred hands hidden in the folds of her skirt. She looked at her sister with something like fear but she wasn't mad at her. This was Maggie's portion. This was the way she knew God to work.

When I looked at her like that something hit me in the top of my head and ran down to the soles of my feet. Just like when I'm in church and the spirit of God touches me and I get happy and shout. I did something I never had done before: hugged Maggie to me, then dragged her on into the room, snatched the quilts out of Miss Wangero's hands and dumped them into Maggie's lap. Maggie just sat there on my bed with her mouth open.

"Take one or two of the others," I said to Dee.

But she turned without a word and went out to Hakim-a-barber.

"You just don't understand," she said, as Maggie and I came out to the car.

"What don't I understand?" I wanted to know.

"Your heritage," she said. And then she turned to Maggie, kissed her, and said, "You ought to try to make something of yourself, too, Maggie. It's really a new day for us. But from the way you and Mama still live you'd never know it."

She put on some sunglasses that hid everything above the tip of her nose and her chin.

Maggie smiled; maybe at the sunglasses. But a real smile, not scared. After we watched the car dust settle I asked Maggie to bring me a dip of snuff. And then the two of us sat there just enjoying, until it was time to go in the house and go to bed.

1973

Eudora Welty
1909–2001

Once, upon going out in the woods to keep a landscape painter company, Welty, a white writer from Mississippi, witnessed an old woman bent on some selfless errand crossing her field of vision. The woman appeared from and disappeared again into the woods. This simple event was the inspiration for "A Worn Path." That anecdote as well as the story's title tells us where to focus our attention. Welty often explained how she was continually bombarded with the same question from teachers and students alike: Is Phoenix Jackson's grandson really dead? Her answer: "Phoenix is alive." The story is told from Phoenix's unreliable point of view, but hers is the only perspective we have, and, Welty insisted, Phoenix's was the only point of view that Welty herself had.

A Worn Path

It was December—a bright frozen day in the early morning. Far out in the country there was an old Negro woman with her head tied in a red rag, coming along a path through the pinewoods. Her name was Phoenix Jackson. She was very old and small and she walked slowly in the dark pine shadows, moving a little from side to side in her steps, with the balanced heaviness and lightness of a pendulum in a grandfather clock. She carried a thin, small cane made from an umbrella, and with this she kept tapping the frozen earth in front of her. This made a grave and persistent noise in the still air, that seemed meditative like the chirping of a solitary little bird.

She wore a dark striped dress reaching down to her shoe tops, and an equally long apron of bleached sugar sacks, with a full pocket: all neat and tidy, but every time she took a step she might have fallen over her shoelaces, which dragged from her unlaced shoes. She looked straight ahead. Her eyes were blue with age. Her skin had a pattern all its own of numberless branching wrinkles and as though a whole little tree stood in the middle of her forehead, but a golden color ran underneath, and the two knobs of her cheeks were illumined by a yellow burning under the dark. Under the red rag her hair came down on her neck in the frailest of ringlets, still black, and with an odor like copper.

Now and then there was a quivering in the thicket. Old Phoenix said, "Out of my way, all you foxes, owls, beetles, jack rabbits, coons and wild animals! . . . Keep out from under these feet, little bob-whites. . . . Keep the big wild hogs out of my path. Don't let none of those come running my direction. I got a long way." Under her small black-freckled hand her cane, limber as a buggy whip, would switch at the brush as if to rouse up any hiding things.

On she went. The woods were deep and still. The sun made the pine needles almost too bright to look at, up where the wind rocked. The cones dropped as light as feathers. Down in the hollow was the mourning dove—it was not too late for him.

The path ran up a hill. "Seem like there is chains about my feet, time I get this far," she said, in the voice of argument old people keep to use with themselves. "Something always take a hold of me on this hill—pleads I should stay."

After she got to the top she turned and gave a full, severe look behind her where she had come. "Up through pines," she said at length. "Now down through oaks."

Her eyes opened their widest, and she started down gently. But before she got to the bottom of the hill a bush caught her dress.

Her fingers were busy and intent, but her skirts were full and long, so that before she could pull them free in one place they were caught in another. It was not possible to allow the dress to tear. "I in the thorny bush," she said. "Thorns, you doing your appointed work. Never want to let folks pass, no sir. Old eyes thought you was a pretty little *green* bush."

Finally, trembling all over, she stood free, and after a moment dared to stoop for her cane.

"Sun so high!" she cried, leaning back and looking, while the thick tears went over her eyes. "The time getting all gone here."

At the foot of this hill was a place where a log was laid across the creek.

"Now comes the trial," said Phoenix.

Putting her right foot out, she mounted the log and shut her eyes. Lifting her skirt, leveling her cane fiercely before her, like a festival figure in some parade, she began to march across. Then she opened her eyes and she was safe on the other side.

"I wasn't as old as I thought," she said.

But she sat down to rest. She spread her skirts on the bank around her and folded her hands over her knees. Up above her was a tree in a pearly cloud of mistletoe. She did not dare to close her eyes, and when a little boy brought her a plate with a slice of marble-cake on it she spoke to him. "That would be acceptable," she said. But when she went to take it there was just her own hand in the air.

So she left that tree, and had to go through a barbed-wire fence. There she had to creep and crawl, spreading her knees and stretching her fingers like a baby trying to climb the steps. But she talked loudly to herself: she could not let her dress be torn now, so late in the day, and she could not pay for having her arm or her leg sawed off if she got caught fast where she was.

At last she was safe through the fence and risen up out in the clearing. Big dead trees, like black men with one arm, were standing in the purple stalks of the withered cotton field. There sat a buzzard.

"Who you watching?"

In the furrow she made her way along.

"Glad this not the season for bulls," she said, looking sideways, "and the good Lord made his snakes to curl up and sleep in the winter. A pleasure I don't see no two-headed snake coming around that tree, where it come once. It took a while to get by him, back in the summer."

She passed through the old cotton and went into a field of dead corn. It whispered and shook and was taller than her head. "Through the maze now," she said, for there was no path.

Then there was something tall, black, and skinny there, moving before her.

At first she took it for a man. It could have been a man dancing in the field. But she stood still and listened, and it did not make a sound. It was as silent as a ghost.

"Ghost," she said sharply, "who be you the ghost of? For I have heard of nary death close by."

But there was no answer—only the ragged dancing in the wind.

She shut her eyes, reached out her hand, and touched a sleeve. She found a coat and inside that an emptiness, cold as ice.

"You scarecrow," she said. Her face lighted. "I ought to be shut up for good," she said with laughter. "My senses is gone. I too old. I the oldest people I ever know. Dance, old scarecrow," she said, "while I dancing with you."

She kicked her foot over the furrow, and with mouth drawn down, shook her head once or twice in a little strutting way. Some husks blew down and whirled in streamers about her skirts.

Then she went on, parting her way from side to side with the cane, through the whispering field. At last she came to the end, to a wagon track where the silver grass blew between the red ruts. The quail were walking around like pullets, seeming all dainty and unseen.

"Walk pretty," she said. "This the easy place. This the easy going."

She followed the track, swaying through the quiet bare fields, through the little strings of trees silver in their dead leaves, past cabins silver from weather, with the doors and windows boarded shut, all like old women under a spell sitting there. "I walking in their sleep," she said, nodding her head vigorously.

In a ravine she went where a spring was silently flowing through a hollow log. Old Phoenix bent and drank. "Sweet-gum makes the water sweet," she said, and drank more. "Nobody know who made this well, for it was here when I was born."

The track crossed a swampy part where the moss hung as white as lace from every limb. "Sleep on, alligators, and blow your bubbles." Then the track went into the road.

Deep, deep the road went down between the high green-colored banks, Overhead the live-oaks met, and it was as dark as a cave.

A black dog with a lolling tongue came up out of the weeds by the ditch. She was meditating, and not ready, and when he came at her she only hit him a little with her cane. Over she went in the ditch, like a little puff of milkweed.

Down there, her senses drifted away. A dream visited her, and she reached her hand up, but nothing reached down and gave her a pull. So she lay there and presently went to talking. "Old woman," she said to herself, "that black dog come up out of the weeds to stall you off, and now there he sitting on his fine tail, smiling at you."

A white man finally came along and found her—a hunter, a young man, with his dog on a chain.

"Well, Granny!" he laughed. "What are you doing there?"

"Lying on my back like a June-bug waiting to be turned over, mister," she said, reaching up her hand.

He lifted her up, gave her a swing in the air, and set her down. "Anything broken, Granny?"

"No sir, them old dead weeds is springy enough," said Phoenix, when she had got her breath. "I thank you for your trouble."

"Where do you live, Granny?" he asked, while the two dogs were growling at each other.

"Away back yonder, sir, behind the ridge. You can't even see it from here."

"On your way home?"

"No sir, I going to town."

"Why, that's too far! That's as far as I walk when I come out myself, and I get something for my trouble." He patted the stuffed bag he carried, and there hung down a little closed claw. It was one of the bob-whites, with its beak hooked bitterly to show it was dead. "Now you go on home, Granny!"

"I bound to go to town, mister," said Phoenix. "The time come around."

He gave another laugh, filling the whole landscape. "I know you old colored people! Wouldn't miss going to town to see Santa Claus!"

But something held old Phoenix very still. The deep lines in her face went into a fierce and different radiation. Without warning, she had seen with her own eyes a flashing nickel fall out of the man's pocket onto the ground.

"How old are you, Granny?" he was saying.

"There's no telling, mister," she said, "no telling."

Then she gave a little cry and clapped her hands and said, "Git on away from here, dog! Look! Look at that dog!" She laughed as if in admiration. "He ain't scared of nobody. He a big black dog." She whispered, "Sic him!"

"Watch me get rid of that cur," said the man. "Sic him, Pete! Sic him!"

Phoenix heard the dogs fighting, and heard the man running and throwing sticks. She even heard a gunshot. But she was slowly bending forward by that time, further and further forward, the lid stretched down over her eyes, as if she were doing this in her sleep. Her chin was lowered almost to her knees. The yellow palm of her hand came out from the fold of her apron. Her fingers slid down and along the ground under the piece of money with the grace and care they would have in lifting an egg from under a setting hen. Then she slowly straightened up, she stood erect, and the nickel was in her apron pocket. A bird flew by. Her lips moved. "God watching me the whole time. I come to stealing."

The man came back, and his own dog panted about them. "Well, I scared him off that time," he said, and then he laughed and lifted his gun and pointed it at Phoenix.

She stood straight and faced him.

"Doesn't the gun scare you?" he said, still pointing it.

"No, sir, I seen plenty go off closer by, in my day, and for less than what I done," she said, holding utterly still.

He smiled, and shouldered the gun. "Well, Granny," he said, "you must be a hundred years old, and scared of nothing. I'd give you a dime if I had any money with me. But you take my advice and stay home, and nothing will happen to you."

"I bound to go on my way, mister," said Phoenix. She inclined her head in the red rag. Then they went in different directions, but she could hear the gun shooting again and again over the hill.

She walked on. The shadows hung from the oak trees to the road like curtains. Then she smelled wood-smoke, and smelled the river, and she saw a steeple and the cabins on their steep steps. Dozens of little black children whirled around her. There ahead was Natchez[1] shining. Bells were ringing. She walked on.

In the paved city it was Christmas time. There were red and green electric lights strung and crisscrossed everywhere, and all turned on in the daytime. Old Phoenix would have been lost if she had not distrusted her eyesight and depended on her feet to know where to take her.

She paused quietly on the sidewalk where people were passing by.

1. A city in southwestern Mississippi, on the Mississippi River.

A lady came along in the crowd, carrying an armful of red-, green- and silver-wrapped presents; she gave off perfume like the red roses in hot summer, and Phoenix stopped her.

"Please, missy, will you lace up my shoe?" She held up her foot.

"What do you want, Grandma?"

"See my shoe," said Phoenix. "Do all right for out in the country, but wouldn't look right to go in a big building."

"Stand still then, Grandma," said the lady. She put her packages down on the sidewalk beside her and laced and tied both shoes tightly.

"Can't lace 'em with a cane," said Phoenix. "Thank you, missy. I doesn't mind asking a nice lady to tie up my shoe, when I gets out on the street."

Moving slowly and from side to side, she went into the big building, and into the tower of steps, where she walked up and around and around until her feet knew to stop.

She entered a door, and there she saw nailed up on the wall the document that had been stamped with the gold seal and framed in the gold frame, which matched the dream that was hung up in her head.

"Here I be," she said. There was a fixed and ceremonial stiffness over her body.

"A charity case, I suppose," said an attendant who sat at the desk before her.

But Phoenix only looked above her head. There was a sweat on her face, the wrinkles in her skin shone like a bright net.

"Speak up, Grandma," the woman said. "What's your name? We must have your history, you know. Have you been here before? What seems to be the trouble with you?"

Old Phoenix only gave a twitch to her face as if a fly were bothering her.

"Are you deaf?" cried the attendant.

But then the nurse came in.

"Oh, that's just old Aunt Phoenix," she said. "She doesn't come for herself—she has a little grandson. She makes these trips just as regular as clockwork. She lives away back off the Old Natchez Trace."[2] She

2. An old Native American trail running from Natchez to Nashville, Tennessee.

bent down. "Well, Aunt Phoenix, why don't you just take a seat? We won't keep you standing after your long trip." She pointed.

The old woman sat down, bolt upright in the chair.

"Now, how is the boy?" asked the nurse.

Old Phoenix did not speak.

"I said, how is the boy?"

But Phoenix only waited and stared straight ahead, her face very solemn and withdrawn into rigidity.

"Is his throat any better?" asked the nurse. "Aunt Phoenix, don't you hear me? Is your grandson's throat any better since the last time you came for the medicine?"

With her hands on her knees, the old woman waited, silent, erect and motionless, just as if she were in armor.

"You mustn't take up our time this way, Aunt Phoenix," the nurse said. "Tell us quickly about your grandson, and get it over. He isn't dead, is he?"

At last there came a flicker and then a flame of comprehension across her face, and she spoke.

"My grandson. It was my memory had left me. There I sat and forgot why I made my long trip."

"Forgot?" The nurse frowned. "After you came so far?"

Then Phoenix was like an old woman begging a dignified forgiveness for waking up frightened in the night. "I never did go to school, I was too old at the Surrender,"[3] she said in a soft voice. "I'm an old woman without an education. It was my memory fail me. My little grandson, he is just the same, and I forgot it in the coming."

"Throat never heals, does it?" said the nurse, speaking in a loud, sure voice to old Phoenix. By now she had a card with something written on it, a little list. "Yes. Swallowed lye. When was it?—January—two-three years ago—"

Phoenix spoke unmasked now. "No, missy, he not dead, he just the same. Every little while his throat begin to close up again, and he not able to swallow. He not get his breath. He not able to help

3. The surrender of the Confederate general Robert E. Lee (1807–1870) to General Ulysses S. Grant (1822–1885) of the Union on April 9, 1865, which ended the American Civil War and slavery. Most Southern states had made it illegal to educate slaves, so Reconstruction opened the first schools for African Americans in the South in generations.

himself. So the time come around, and I go on another trip for the soothing medicine."

"All right. The doctor said as long as you came to get it, you could have it," said the nurse. "But it's an obstinate case."

"My little grandson, he sit up there in the house all wrapped up, waiting by himself," Phoenix went on. "We is the only two left in the world. He suffer and it don't seem to put him back at all. He got a sweet look. He going to last. He wear a little patch quilt and peep out holding his mouth open like a little bird. I remembers so plain now. I not going to forget him again, no, the whole enduring time. I could tell him from all the others in creation."

"All right." The nurse was trying to hush her now. She brought her a bottle of medicine. "Charity," she said, making a check mark in a book.

Old Phoenix held the bottle close to her eyes, and then carefully put it into her pocket.

"I thank you," she said.

"It's Christmas time, Grandma," said the attendants. "Could I give you a few pennies out of my purse?"

"Five pennies is a nickel," said Phoenix stiffly.

"Here's a nickel," said the attendant.

Phoenix rose carefully and held out her hand. She received the nickel and then fished the other nickel out of her pocket and laid it beside the new one. She stared at her palm closely, with her head on one side.

Then she gave a tap with her cane on the floor.

"This is what come to me to do," she said. "I going to the store and buy my child a little windmill they sells, made out of paper. He going to find it hard to believe there such a thing in the world. I'll march myself back where he waiting, holding it straight up in this hand."

She lifted her free hand, gave a little nod, turned around, and walked out of the doctor's office. Then her slow step began on the stairs, going down.

1941

Edith Wharton
1862–1937

"Roman Fever" depends on a surprise, ironic ending for its startling effect on the reader. But perhaps more important than the conflict between Mrs. Slade and Mrs. Ansley are the themes that reveal themselves repeatedly throughout the story. One is "the warm current of human communion" from which Mrs. Slade feels cut off. Another resides in the enveloping action: Wharton published "Roman Fever" in 1934, but the story is set in the mid-1920s. Though Mrs. Ansley and Mrs. Slade are considerably younger than Wharton herself, still they've lived to witness a revolution in social manners—accelerated by World War I—that parallels and amplifies the ever-present gap between generations. It is more than the years that separates them from their children. The landscape spread out beneath this café perched on the Janiculum Hill in Rome—the vast ruins, even the Colosseum itself—is all symbolic.

Roman Fever

I

From the table at which they had been lunching two American ladies of ripe but well-cared-for middle age moved across the lofty terrace of the Roman restaurant and, leaning on its parapet, looked first at each other, and then down on the outspread glories of the Palatine and the Forum,[1] with the same expression of vague but benevolent approval.

As they leaned there a girlish voice echoed up gaily from the stairs leading to the court below. "Well, come along, then," it cried, not to them but to an invisible companion, "and let's leave the young things to their knitting"; and a voice as fresh laughed back; "Oh, look here, Babs, not actually knitting—" "Well, I mean figuratively," rejoined the first. "After all, we haven't left our poor parents much else to do . . ." and at that point the turn of the stairs engulfed the dialogue.

1. Ancient ruins in Rome.

The two ladies looked at each other again, this time with a tinge of smiling embarrassment, and the smaller and paler one shook her head and coloured slightly.

"Barbara!" she murmured, sending an unheard rebuke after the mocking voice in the stairway.

The other lady, who was fuller, and higher in colour, with a small determined nose supported by vigorous black eyebrows, gave a good-humoured laugh. "That's what our daughters think of us!"

Her companion replied by a deprecating gesture. "Not of us individually. We must remember that. It's just the collective modern idea of Mothers. And you see—" Half guiltily she drew from her handsomely mounted black hand-bag a twist of crimson silk run through by two fine knitting needles. "One never knows," she murmured. "The new system has certainly given us a good deal of time to kill; and sometimes I get tired just looking—even at this." Her gesture was now addressed to the stupendous scene at their feet.

The dark lady laughed again, and they both relapsed upon the view, contemplating it in silence, with a sort of diffused serenity which might have been borrowed from the spring effulgence of the Roman skies. The luncheon-hour was long past, and the two had their end of the vast terrace to themselves. At its opposite extremity a few groups, detained by a lingering look at the outspread city, were gathering up guide-books and fumbling for tips. The last of them scattered, and the two ladies were alone on the air-washed height.

"Well, I don't see why we shouldn't just stay here," said Mrs. Slade, the lady of the high colour and energetic brows. Two derelict basketchairs stood near, and she pushed them into the angle of the parapet, and settled herself in one, her gaze upon the Palatine. "After all, it's still the most beautiful view in the world."

"It always will be, to me," assented her friend Mrs. Ansley, with so slight a stress on the "me" that Mrs. Slade, though she noticed it, wondered if it were not merely accidental, like the random underlinings of old-fashioned letter writers.

"Grace Ansley was always old-fashioned," she thought; and added aloud, with a retrospective smile: "It's a view we've both been familiar with for a good many years. When we first met here we were younger than our girls are now. You remember?"

"Oh, yes, I remember," murmured Mrs. Ansley, with the same undefinable stress.—"There's that head-waiter wondering," she interpolated. She was evidently far less sure than her companion of herself and of her rights in the world.

"I'll cure him of wondering," said Mrs. Slade, stretching her hand toward a bag as discreetly opulent-looking as Mrs. Ansley's. Signing to the head-waiter, she explained that she and her friend were old lovers of Rome, and would like to spend the end of the afternoon looking down on the view—that is, if it did not disturb the service? The head-waiter, bowing over her gratuity, assured her that the ladies were most welcome, and would be still more so if they would condescend to remain for dinner. A full moon night, they would remember . . .

Mrs. Slade's black brows drew together, as though references to the moon were out-of-place and even unwelcome. But she smiled away her frown as the head-waiter retreated. "Well, why not? We might do worse. There's no knowing, I suppose, when the girls will be back. Do you even know back from *where*? I don't!"

Mrs. Ansley again coloured slightly. "I think those young Italian aviators we met at the Embassy invited them to fly to Tarquinia[2] for tea. I suppose they'll want to wait and fly back by moonlight."

"Moonlight—moonlight! What a part it still plays. Do you suppose they're as sentimental as we were?"

"I've come to the conclusion that I don't in the least know what they are," said Mrs. Ansley. "And perhaps we didn't know much more about each other."

"No; perhaps we didn't."

Her friend gave her a shy glance. "I never should have supposed you were sentimental, Alida."

"Well, perhaps I wasn't." Mrs. Slade drew her lids together in retrospect; and for a few moments the two ladies, who had been intimate since childhood, reflected how little they knew each other. Each one, of course, had a label ready to attach to the other's name; Mrs. Delphin Slade, for instance, would have told herself, or any one who asked her, that Mrs. Horace Ansley, twenty-five years ago, had

2. Ancient Etruscan town northeast of Rome.

been exquisitely lovely—no, you wouldn't believe it, would you? . . . though, of course, still charming, distinguished . . . Well, as a girl she had been exquisite; far more beautiful than her daughter Barbara, though certainly Babs, according to the new standards at any rate, was more effective—had more *edge*, as they say. Funny where she got it, with those two nullities as parents. Yes; Horace Ansley was—well, just the duplicate of his wife. Museum specimens of old New York. Good-looking, irreproachable, exemplary. Mrs. Slade and Mrs. Ansley had lived opposite each other—actually as well as figuratively—for years. When the drawing-room curtains in No. 20 East 73rd Street were renewed, No. 23, across the way, was always aware of it. And of all the movings, buyings, travels, anniversaries, illnesses—the tame chronicle of an estimable pair. Little of it escaped Mrs. Slade. But she had grown bored with it by the time her husband made his big *coup* in Wall Street, and when they bought in upper Park Avenue had already begun to think: "I'd rather live opposite a speak-easy[3] for a change; at least one might see it raided." The idea of seeing Grace raided was so amusing that (before the move) she launched it at a woman's lunch. It made a hit, and went the rounds—she sometimes wondered if it had crossed the street, and reached Mrs. Ansley. She hoped not, but didn't much mind. Those were the days when respectability was at a discount, and it did the irreproachable no harm to laugh at them a little.

A few years later, and not many months apart, both ladies lost their husbands. There was an appropriate exchange of wreaths and condolences, and a brief renewal of intimacy in the half-shadow of their mourning; and now, after another interval, they had run across each other in Rome, at the same hotel, each of them the modest appendage of a salient daughter. The similarity of their lot had again drawn them together, lending itself to mild jokes, and the mutual confession that, if in old days it must have been tiring to "keep up" with daughters, it was now, at times, a little dull not to.

No doubt, Mrs. Slade reflected, she felt her unemployment more than poor Grace ever would. It was a big drop from being the wife of Delphin Slade to being his widow. She had always regarded her-

3. A place where alcoholic beverages are illegally sold, especially such a place during Prohibition.

self (with a certain conjugal pride) as his equal in social gifts, as contributing her full share to the making of the exceptional couple they were: but the difference after his death was irremediable. As the wife of the famous corporation lawyer, always with an international case or two on hand, every day brought its exciting and unexpected obligation: the impromptu entertaining of eminent colleagues from abroad, the hurried dashes on legal business to London, Paris or Rome, where the entertaining was so handsomely reciprocated; the amusement of hearing in her wake: "What, that handsome woman with the good clothes and the eyes is Mrs. Slade—*the* Slade's wife? Really? Generally the wives of celebrities are such frumps."

Yes; being *the* Slade's widow was a dullish business after that. In living up to such a husband all her faculties had been engaged; now she had only her daughter to live up to, for the son who seemed to have inherited his father's gifts had died suddenly in boyhood. She had fought through that agony because her husband was there, to be helped and to help; now, after the father's death, the thought of the boy had become unbearable. There was nothing left but to mother her daughter; and dear Jenny was such a perfect daughter that she needed no excessive mothering. "Now with Babs Ansley I don't know that I *should* be so quiet," Mrs. Slade sometimes half-enviously reflected; but Jenny, who was younger than her brilliant friend, was that rare accident, an extremely pretty girl who somehow made youth and prettiness seem as safe as their absence. It was all perplexing—and to Mrs. Slade a little boring. She wished that Jenny would fall in love—with the wrong man, even; that she might have to be watched, out-manoeuvred, rescued. And instead, it was Jenny who watched her mother, kept her out of draughts, made sure that she had taken her tonic . . .

Mrs. Ansley was much less articulate than her friend, and her mental portrait of Mrs. Slade was slighter, and drawn with fainter touches. "Alida Slade's awfully brilliant; but not as brilliant as she thinks," would have summed it up; though she would have added, for the enlightenment of strangers, that Mrs. Slade had been an extremely dashing girl; much more so than her daughter, who was pretty, of course, and clever in a way, but had none of her mother's—well, "vividness," some one had once called it. Mrs. Ansley would take up current words like this, and cite them in quotation marks, as unheard-of audacities. No; Jenny was not like her mother. Sometimes Mrs. Ansley thought Alida Slade was disappointed; on the whole she had had a sad life. Full of failures and mistakes; Mrs. Ansley had always been rather sorry for her . . .

So these two ladies visualized each other, each through the wrong end of her little telescope.

II

For a long time they continued to sit side by side without speaking. It seemed as though, to both, there was a relief in laying down their somewhat futile activities in the presence of the vast Memento Mori[4] which faced them. Mrs. Slade sat quite still, her eyes fixed on the golden slope of the Palace of the Cæsars,[5] and after a while Mrs. Ansley ceased to fidget with her bag, and she too sank into meditation. Like many intimate friends, the two ladies had never before had occasion to be silent together, and Mrs. Ansley was slightly embarrassed by what seemed, after so many years, a new stage in their intimacy, and one with which she did not yet know how to deal.

Suddenly the air was full of that deep clangour of bells which periodically covers Rome with a roof of silver. Mrs. Slade glanced at her wrist-watch. "Five o'clock already," she said, as though surprised.

Mrs. Ansley suggested interrogatively: "There's bridge at the Embassy at five." For a long time Mrs. Slade did not answer. She appeared to be lost in contemplation, and Mrs. Ansley thought the remark had escaped her. But after a while she said, as if speaking out of a dream: "Bridge, did you say? Not unless you want to . . . But I don't think I will, you know."

"Oh, no," Mrs. Ansley hastened to assure her. "I don't care to at all. It's so lovely here; and so full of old memories, as you say." She settled herself in her chair, and almost furtively drew forth her knit-

4. Any object serving as a reminder of death; loosely, "remember, you must die" (Latin).
5. On the Palatine Hill.

ting. Mrs. Slade took sideway note of this activity, but her own beautifully cared-for hands remained motionless on her knee.

"I was just thinking," she said slowly, "what different things Rome stands for to each generation of travellers. To our grandmothers, Roman fever; to our mothers, sentimental dangers—how we used to be guarded!—to our daughters, no more dangers than the middle of Main Street. They don't know it—but how much they're missing!"

The long golden light was beginning to pale, and Mrs. Ansley lifted her knitting a little closer to her eyes. "Yes; how we were guarded!"

"I always used to think," Mrs. Slade continued, "that our mothers had a much more difficult job than our grandmothers. When Roman fever stalked the streets it must have been comparatively easy to gather in the girls at the danger hour; but when you and I were young, with such beauty calling us, and the spice of disobedience thrown in, and no worse risk than catching cold during the cool hour after sunset, the mothers used to be put to it to keep us in—didn't they?"

She turned again toward Mrs. Ansley, but the latter had reached a delicate point in her knitting. "One, two, three—slip two; yes, they must have been," she assented, without looking up.

Mrs. Slade's eyes rested on her with a deepened attention. "She can knit—in the face of *this*! How like her . . ."

Mrs. Slade leaned back, brooding, her eyes ranging from the ruins which faced her to the long green hollow of the Forum, the fading glow of the church fronts beyond it, and the outlying immensity of the Colosseum.[6] Suddenly she thought: "It's all very well to say that our girls have done away with sentiment and moonlight. But if Babs Ansley isn't out to catch that young aviator—the one who's a Marchese[7]—then I don't know anything. And Jenny has no chance beside her. I know that too. I wonder if that's why Grace Ansley likes the two girls to go everywhere together? My poor Jenny as a foil—!" Mrs. Slade gave a hardly audible laugh, and at the sound Mrs. Ansley dropped her knitting.

6. Ruined Roman amphitheater famous for its gladiatorial combats and hallowed by thousands of Christian martyrs.

7. A marquis, a nobleman ranking below a duke and above an earl or count.

"Yes—?"

"I—oh, nothing. I was only thinking how your Babs carries everything before her. That Campolieri boy is one of the best matches in Rome. Don't look so innocent, my dear—you know he is. And I was wondering, ever so respectfully, you understand . . . wondering how two such exemplary characters as you and Horace had managed to produce anything quite so dynamic." Mrs. Slade laughed again, with a touch of asperity.

Mrs. Ansley's hands lay inert across her needles. She looked straight out at the great accumulated wreckage of passion and splendour at her feet. But her small profile was almost expressionless. At length she said: "I think you overrate Babs, my dear."

Mrs. Slade's tone grew easier. "No; I don't. I appreciate her. And perhaps envy you. Oh, my girl's perfect; if I were a chronic invalid I'd—well, I think I'd rather be in Jenny's hands. There must be times . . . but there! I always wanted a brilliant daughter . . . and never quite understood why I got an angel instead."

Mrs. Ansley echoed her laugh in a faint murmur. "Babs is an angel too."

"Of course—of course! But she's got rainbow wings. Well, they're wandering by the sea with their young men; and here we sit . . . and it all brings back the past a little too acutely."

Mrs. Ansley had resumed her knitting. One might almost have imagined (if one had known her less well, Mrs. Slade reflected) that, for her also, too many memories rose from the lengthening shadows of those august ruins. But no; she was simply absorbed in her work. What was there for her to worry about? She knew that Babs would almost certainly come back engaged to the extremely eligible Campolieri. "And she'll sell the New York house, and settle down near them in Rome, and never be in their way . . . she's much too tactful. But she'll have an excellent cook, and just the right people in for bridge and cocktails . . . and a perfectly peaceful old age among her grandchildren."

Mrs. Slade broke off this prophetic flight with a recoil of self-disgust. There was no one of whom she had less right to think unkindly than of Grace Ansley. Would she never cure herself of envying her? Perhaps she had begun too long ago.

She stood up and leaned against the parapet, filling her troubled eyes with the tranquillizing magic of the hour. But instead of tranquillizing her the sight seemed to increase her exasperation. Her gaze turned toward the Colosseum. Already its golden flank was drowned in purple shadow, and above it the sky curved crystal clear, without light or colour. It was the moment when afternoon and evening hang balanced in mid-heaven.

Mrs. Slade turned back and laid her hand on her friend's arm. The gesture was so abrupt that Mrs. Ansley looked up, startled.

"The sun's set. You're not afraid, my dear?"

"Afraid—"

"Of Roman fever or pneumonia? I remember how ill you were that winter. As a girl you had a very delicate throat, hadn't you?"

"Oh, we're all right up here. Down below, in the Forum, it does get deathly cold, all of a sudden . . . but not here."

"Ah, of course you know because you had to be so careful." Mrs. Slade turned back to the parapet. She thought: "I must make one more effort not to hate her." Aloud she said: "Whenever I look at the Forum from up here, I remember that story about a great-aunt of yours, wasn't she? A dreadfully wicked great-aunt?"

"Oh, yes; Great-aunt Harriet. The one who was supposed to have sent her young sister out to the Forum after sunset to gather a night-blooming flower for her album. All our great-aunts and grand-mothers used to have albums of dried flowers."

Mrs. Slade nodded. "But she really sent her because they were in love with the same man—"

"Well, that was the family tradition. They said Aunt Harriet confessed it years afterward. At any rate, the poor little sister caught the fever and died. Mother used to frighten us with the story when we were children."

"And you frightened *me* with it, that winter when you and I were here as girls. The winter I was engaged to Delphin."

Mrs. Ansley gave a faint laugh. "Oh, did I? Really frightened you? I don't believe you're easily frightened."

"Not often; but I was then. I was easily frightened because I was too happy. I wonder if you know what that means?"

"I—yes . . . " Mrs. Ansley faltered.

"Well, I suppose that was why the story of your wicked aunt made such an impression on me. And I thought: 'There's no more

Roman fever, but the Forum is deathly cold after sunset—especially after a hot day. And the Colosseum's even colder and damper.' "

"The Colosseum—?"

"Yes. It wasn't easy to get in, after the gates were locked for the night. Far from easy. Still, in those days it could be managed; it *was* managed, often. Lovers met there who couldn't meet elsewhere. You knew that?"

"I—I daresay. I don't remember."

"You don't remember? You don't remember going to visit some ruins or other one evening, just after dark, and catching a bad chill? You were supposed to have gone to see the moon rise. People always said that expedition was what caused your illness."

There was a moment's silence; then Mrs. Ansley rejoined: "Did they? It was all so long ago."

"Yes. And you got well again—so it didn't matter. But I suppose it struck your friends—the reason given for your illness, I mean—because everybody knew you were so prudent on account of your throat, and your mother took such care of you . . . You *had* been out late sight-seeing, hadn't you, that night?"

"Perhaps I had. The most prudent girls aren't always prudent. What made you think of it now?"

Mrs. Slade seemed to have no answer ready. But after a moment she broke out: "Because I simply can't bear it any longer—!"

Mrs. Ansley lifted her head quickly. Her eyes were wide and very pale. "Can't bear what?"

"Why—your not knowing that I've always known why you went."

"Why I went—?"

"Yes. You think I'm bluffing, don't you? Well, you went to meet the man I was engaged to—and I can repeat every word of the letter that took you there."

While Mrs. Slade spoke Mrs. Ansley had risen unsteadily to her feet. Her bag, her knitting and gloves, slid in a panic-stricken heap to the ground. She looked at Mrs. Slade as though she were looking at a ghost.

"No, no—don't," she faltered out.

"Why not? Listen, if you don't believe me. 'My one darling, things can't go on like this. I must see you alone. Come to the

Colosseum immediately after dark tomorrow. There will be somebody to let you in. No one whom you need fear will suspect'—but perhaps you've forgotten what the letter said?"

Mrs. Ansley met the challenge with an unexpected composure. Steadying herself against the chair she looked at her friend, and replied: "No; I know it by heart too."

"And the signature? 'Only *your* D.S.' Was that it? I'm right, am I? That was the letter that took you out that evening after dark?"

Mrs. Ansley was still looking at her. It seemed to Mrs. Slade that a slow struggle was going on behind the voluntarily controlled mask of her small quiet face. "I shouldn't have thought she had herself so well in hand," Mrs. Slade reflected, almost resentfully. But at this moment Mrs. Ansley spoke. "I don't know how you knew. I burnt that letter at once."

"Yes; you would, naturally—you're so prudent!" The sneer was open now. "And if you burnt the letter you're wondering how on earth I know what was in it. That's it, isn't it?"

Mrs. Slade waited, but Mrs. Ansley did not speak.

"Well, my dear, I know what was in that letter because I wrote it!"

"You wrote it?"

"Yes."

The two women stood for a minute staring at each other in the last golden light. Then Mrs. Ansley dropped back into her chair. "Oh," she murmured, and covered her face with her hands.

Mrs. Slade waited nervously for another word or movement. None came, and at length she broke out: "I horrify you."

Mrs. Ansley's hands dropped to her knee. The face they uncovered was streaked with tears. "I wasn't thinking of you. I was thinking—it was the only letter I ever had from him!"

"And I wrote it. Yes; I wrote it! But I was the girl he was engaged to. Did you happen to remember that?"

Mrs. Ansley's head drooped again. "I'm not trying to excuse myself . . . I remembered . . ."

"And still you went?"

"Still I went."

Mrs. Slade stood looking down on the small bowed figure at her side. The flame of her wrath had already sunk, and she wondered why she had ever thought there would be any satisfaction in inflicting so purposeless a wound on her friend. But she had to justify herself.

"You do understand? I'd found out—and I hated you, hated you. I knew you were in love with Delphin—and I was afraid; afraid of you, of your quiet ways, your sweetness . . . your . . . well, I wanted you out of the way, that's all. Just for a few weeks; just till I was sure of him. So in a blind fury I wrote that letter . . . I don't know why I'm telling you now."

"I suppose," said Mrs. Ansley slowly, "it's because you've always gone on hating me."

"Perhaps. Or because I wanted to get the whole thing off my mind." She paused. "I'm glad you destroyed the letter. Of course I never thought you'd die."

Mrs. Ansley relapsed into silence, and Mrs. Slade, leaning above her, was conscious of a strange sense of isolation, of being cut off from the warm current of human communion. "You think me a monster!"

"I don't know . . . It was the only letter I had, and you say he didn't write it?"

"Ah, how you care for him still!"

"I cared for that memory," said Mrs. Ansley.

Mrs. Slade continued to look down on her. She seemed physically reduced by the blow—as if, when she got up, the wind might scatter her like a puff of dust. Mrs. Slade's jealousy suddenly leapt up again at the sight. All these years the woman had been living on that letter. How she must have loved him, to treasure the mere memory of its ashes! The letter of the man her friend was engaged to. Wasn't it she who was the monster?

"You tried your best to get him away from me, didn't you? But you failed; and I kept him. That's all."

"Yes. That's all."

"I wish now I hadn't told you. I'd no idea you'd feel about it as you do; I thought you'd be amused. It all happened so long ago, as you say; and you must do me the justice to remember that I had no reason to think you'd ever taken it seriously. How could I, when you were married to Horace Ansley two months afterward? As soon as you could get out of bed your mother rushed you off to Florence and married you. People were rather surprised—they wondered at its being done so quickly; but I thought I knew. I had an idea you did it out of *pique*—to be able to say you'd got ahead of Delphin and me. Girls have such silly reasons for doing the most serious things. And your marrying so soon convinced me that you'd never really cared.

"Yes. I suppose it would," Mrs. Ansley assented.

The clear heaven overhead was emptied of all its gold. Dusk spread over it, abruptly darkening the Seven Hills.[8] Here and there lights began to twinkle through the foliage at their feet. Steps were coming and going on the deserted terrace—waiters looking out of the doorway at the head of the stairs, then reappearing with trays and napkins and flasks of wine. Tables were moved, chairs straightened. A feeble string of electric lights flickered out. Some vases of faded flowers were carried away, and brought back replenished. A stout lady in a dust-coat suddenly appeared, asking in broken Italian if any one had seen the elastic band which held together her tattered Baedeker.[9] She poked with her stick under the table at which she had lunched, the waiters assisting.

The corner where Mrs. Slade and Mrs. Ansley sat was still shadowy and deserted. For a long time neither of them spoke. At length Mrs. Slade began again: "I suppose I did it as a sort of joke—"

"A joke?"

"Well, girls are ferocious sometimes, you know. Girls in love especially. And I remember laughing to myself all that evening at the idea that you were waiting around there in the dark, dodging out of sight, listening for every sound, trying to get in—. Of course I was upset when I heard you were so ill afterward."

Mrs. Ansley had not moved for a long time. But now she turned slowly toward her companion. "But I didn't wait. He'd arranged everything. He was there. We were let in at once," she said.

Mrs. Slade sprang up from her leaning position. "Delphin there?

8. Group of hills on which the ancient city of Rome was built.
9. Guidebook.

They let you in?—Ah, now you're lying!" She burst out with violence.

Mrs. Ansley's voice grew clearer, and full of surprise. "But of course he was there. Naturally he came—"

"Came? How did he know he'd find you there? You must be raving!"

Mrs. Ansley hesitated, as though reflecting. "But I answered the letter. I told him I'd be there. So he came."

Mrs. Slade flung her hands up to her face. "Oh, God—you answered! I never thought of your answering . . ."

"It's odd you never thought of it, if you wrote the letter."

"Yes. I was blind with rage."

Mrs. Ansley rose, and drew her fur scarf about her. "It is cold here. We'd better go . . . I'm sorry for you," she said, as she clasped the fur about her throat.

The unexpected words sent a pang through Mrs. Slade. "Yes; we'd better go." She gathered up her bag and cloak. "I don't know why you should be sorry for me," she muttered.

Mrs. Ansley stood looking away from her toward the dusky secret mass of the Colosseum. "Well—because I didn't have to wait that night."

Mrs. Slade gave an unquiet laugh. "Yes; I was beaten there. But I oughtn't to begrudge it to you, I suppose. At the end of all these years. After all, I had everything; I had him for twenty-five years. And you had nothing but that one letter that he didn't write."

Mrs. Ansley was again silent. At length she turned toward the door of the terrace. She took a step, and turned back, facing her companion.

"I had Barbara," she said, and began to move ahead of Mrs. Slade toward the stairway.

1934

Virginia Woolf
1882–1941

"The New Dress" was originally intended to be part of a novel, Mrs. Dalloway, *which concludes with the party depicted here. This story was one of several other outtakes, so to speak, that presented the party from a variety of perspectives. (These stories were first published years after Woolf's death in a collection called* Mrs. Dalloway's Party.*) Nearly all of Woolf's fiction explores how human beings experience life—not in the way generally represented in stories and novels, but through the membrane of an intensely personal perspective. This perspective, which Woolf described as a "semi-transparent envelope," is thickened by our individual psyches, by the limitations of our senses, by our memories, emotions, etc., so that a thing (a dress, for example) or an event (such as a party) can never be described objectively; reality is always experienced subjectively and thus can only be truthfully represented subjectively. Woolf adopted the stream-of-consciousness type of narration in order to avoid what she considered the false objectivity of conventional third-person narrators. Woolf also described particularly heightened experiences, what she called "moments of being," during which a person can transcend the limitations of normal perspective and perceive reality more directly, more intensely, with greater insight into the harmony of things.*

The New Dress

Mabel had her first serious suspicion that something was wrong as she took her cloak off and Mrs. Barnet, while handing her the mirror and touching the brushes and thus drawing her attention, perhaps rather markedly, to all the appliances for tidying and improving hair, complexion, clothes, which existed on the dressing-table, confirmed the suspicion—that it was not right, not quite right, which growing stronger as she went upstairs and springing at her, with conviction as she greeted Clarissa Dalloway, she went straight to the far end of the room, to a shaded corner where a looking-glass hung and looked. No! It was not *right*.

And at once the misery which she always tried to hide, the profound dissatisfaction—the sense she had had, ever since she was a child, of being inferior to other people—set upon her, relentlessly, remorselessly, with an intensity which she could not beat off, as she would when she woke at night at home, by reading Borrow or Scott; for oh these men, oh these women, all were thinking—"What's Mabel wearing? What a fright she looks! What a hideous new dress!"—their eyelids flickering as they came up and then their lids shutting rather tight. It was her own appalling inadequacy; her cowardice; her mean, water-sprinkled blood that depressed her. And at once the whole of the room where, for ever so many hours, she had planned with the little dressmaker how it was to go, seemed sordid, repulsive; and her own drawing-room so shabby, and herself, going out, puffed up with vanity as she touched the letters on the hall table and said: "How dull!" to show off—all this now seemed unutterably silly, paltry, and provincial. All this had been absolutely destroyed, shown up, exploded, the moment she came into Mrs. Dalloway's drawing-room.

What she had thought that evening when, sitting over the teacups, Mrs. Dalloway's invitation came, was that, of course, she could not be fashionable. It was absurd to pretend it even—fashion meant cut, meant style, meant thirty guineas at least—but why not be original? Why not be herself, anyhow? And, getting up, she had taken that old fashion book of her mother's, a Paris fashion book of the time of the Empire, and had thought how much prettier, more dignified, and more womanly they were then, and so set herself—oh, it was foolish—trying to be like them, pluming herself in fact, upon being modest and old-fashioned, and very charming, giving herself up, no doubt about it, to an orgy of self-love, which deserved to be chastised, and so rigged herself out like this.

But she dared not look in the glass. She could not face the whole horror—the pale yellow, idiotically old-fashioned silk dress with its long skirt and its high sleeves and its waist and all the things that looked so charming in the fashion book, but not on her, not among all these ordinary people. She felt like a dressmaker's dummy standing there, for young people to stick pins into.

"But, my dear, it's perfectly charming!" Rose Shaw said, looking her up and down with that little satirical pucker of the lips which she expected—Rose herself being dressed in the height of fashion, precisely like everybody else, always.

We are all like flies trying to crawl over the edge of the saucer, Mabel thought, and repeated the phrase as if she were crossing herself, as if she were trying to find some spell to annul this pain, to make this agony endurable. Tags of Shakespeare, lines from books she had read ages ago, suddenly came to her when she was in agony, and she repeated them over and over again. "Flies trying to crawl," she repeated. If she could say that over often enough and make herself see the flies, she would become numb, chill, frozen, dumb. Now she could see flies crawling slowly out of a saucer of milk with their wings stuck together; and she strained and strained (standing in front of the looking-glass, listening to Rose Shaw) to make herself see Rose Shaw and all the other people there as flies, trying to hoist themselves out of something, or into something, meagre, insignificant, toiling flies. But she could not see them like that, not other people. She saw herself like that—she was a fly, but the others were dragonflies, butterflies, beautiful insects, dancing, fluttering, skimming, while she alone dragged herself up out of the saucer. (Envy and spite, the most detestable of the vices, were her chief faults.)

"I feel like some dowdy, decrepit, horribly dingy old fly," she said, making Robert Haydon stop just to hear her say that, just to reassure herself by furbishing up a poor weak-kneed phrase and so showing how detached she was, how witty, that she did not feel in the least out of anything. And, of course, Robert Haydon answered something, quite polite, quite insincere, which she saw through instantly, and said to herself, directly he went (again from some book), "Lies, lies, lies!" For a party makes things either much more real, or much less real, she thought; she saw in a flash to the bottom of Robert Haydon's heart; she saw through everything. She saw the truth. *This* was true, this drawing-room, this self, the other false. Miss Milan's little workroom was really terribly hot, stuffy, sordid. It smelt of clothes and cabbage cooking; and yet, when Miss Milan put the glass in her hand, and she looked at herself with the dress on, finished, an extraordinary bliss shot through her heart. Suffused with light, she sprang into existence. Rid of cares and wrinkles, what she had dreamed of herself was there—a beautiful woman.

Just for a second (she had not dared look longer, Miss Milan wanted to know about the length of the skirt), there looked at her, framed in the scrolloping mahogany, a grey-white, mysteriously smiling, charming girl, the core of herself, the soul of herself; and it was not vanity only, not only self-love that made her think it good, tender, and true. Miss Milan said the skirt could not well be longer; if anything the skirt, said Miss Milan, puckering her forehead, considering with all her wits about her, must be shorter; and she felt, suddenly, honestly, full of love for Miss Milan, much, much fonder of Miss Milan than of anyone in the whole world, and could have cried for pity that she should be crawling on the floor with her mouth full of pins, and her face red and her eyes bulging—that one human being should be doing this for another, and she saw them all as human beings merely, and herself going off to her party, and Miss Milan pulling the cover over the canary's cage, or letting him pick a hemp-seed from between her lips, and the thought of it, of this side of human nature and its patience and its endurance and its being content with such miserable, scanty, sordid, little pleasures filled her eyes with tears.

And now the whole thing had vanished. The dress, the room, the love, the pity, the scrolloping looking-glass, and the canary's cage—all had vanished, and here she was in a corner of Mrs. Dalloway's drawing-room, suffering tortures, woken wide awake to reality.

But it was all so paltry, weak-blooded, and petty-minded to care so much at her age with two children, to be still so utterly dependent on people's opinions and not have principles or convictions, not to be able to say as other people did, "There's Shakespeare! There's death! We're all weevils in a captain's biscuit"—or whatever it was that people did say.

She faced herself straight in the glass; she pecked at her left shoulder; she issued out into the room, as if spears were thrown at her yellow dress from all sides. But instead of looking fierce or tragic, as Rose Shaw would have done—Rose would have looked like Boadicea—she looked foolish and self-conscious, and simpered like a schoolgirl and slouched across the room, positively slinking, as if she were a beaten mongrel, and looked at a picture, an engraving. As if one went to a party to look at a picture! Everybody knew why she did it—it was from shame, from humiliation.

"Now the fly's in the saucer," she said to herself, "right in the middle, and can't get out, and the milk," she thought, rigidly staring at the picture, 'is sticking its wings together.'

"It's so old-fashioned," she said to Charles Burt, making him stop (which by itself he hated) on his way to talk to someone else.

She meant, or she tried to make herself think that she meant, that it was the picture and not her dress, that was old-fashioned. And one word of praise, one word of affection from Charles would have made all the difference to her at the moment. If he had only said, "Mabel, you're looking charming to-night!" it would have changed her life. But then she ought to have been truthful and direct. Charles said nothing of the kind, of course. He was malice itself. He always saw through one, especially if one were feeling particularly mean, paltry, or feeble-minded.

"Mabel's got a new dress!" he said, and the poor fly was absolutely shoved into the middle of the saucer. Really, he would like her to drown, she believed. He had no heart, no fundamental kindness, only a veneer of friendliness. Miss Milan was much more real, much kinder. If only one could feel that and stick to it, always. "Why," she asked herself—replying to Charles much too pertly, letting him see that she was out of temper, or "ruffled" as he called it ("Rather ruffled?" he said and went on to laugh at her with some woman over there)—"Why," she asked herself, "can't I feel one thing always, feel quite sure that Miss Milan is right, and Charles wrong and stick to it, feel sure about the canary and pity and love and not be whipped all round in a second by coming into a room full of people?" It was her odious, weak, vacillating character again, always giving at the critical moment and not being seriously interested in conchology, etymology, botany, archaeology, cutting up potatoes and watching them fructify like Mary Dennis, like Violet Searle.

Then Mrs. Holman, seeing her standing there, bore down upon her. Of course a thing like a dress was beneath Mrs. Holman's notice, with her family always tumbling downstairs or having the scarlet fever. Could Mabel tell her if Elmthorpe was ever let for August and September? Oh, it was a conversation that bored her unutterably—it made her furious to be treated like a house agent or a messenger boy, to be made use of. Not to have value, that was it, she thought, trying to grasp something hard, something real, while she tried to answer sensibly about the bathroom and the south aspect and the hot water to the top of the house; and all the time she could see little bits of her yellow dress in the round looking-glass which made them all the size of boot-buttons or tadpoles; and it was amazing to think how much humiliation and agony and self-loathing and effort and passionate ups and downs of feeling were contained in a thing the size of a threepenny bit. And what was still odder, this thing, this Mabel Waring, was separate, quite disconnected; and though Mrs. Holman (the black button) was leaning forward and telling her how her eldest boy had strained his heart running, she could see her too, quite detached in the looking-glass, and it was impossible that the black dot, leaning forward, gesticulating, should make the yellow dot, sitting solitary, self-centred, feel what the black dot was feeling, yet they pretended.

"So impossible to keep boys quiet"—that was the kind of thing one said.

And Mrs. Holman, who could never get enough sympathy and snatched what little there was greedily, as if it were her right (but she deserved much more for there was her little girl who had come down this morning with a swollen knee-joint), took this miserable offering and looked at it suspiciously, grudgingly, as if it were a halfpenny when it ought to have been a pound and put it away in her purse, must put up with it, mean and miserly though it was, times being hard, so very hard; and on she went, creaking, injured Mrs. Holman, about the girl with the swollen joints. Ah, it was tragic, this greed, this clamour of human beings, like a row of cormorants, barking and flapping their wings for sympathy—it was tragic, could one have felt it and not merely pretended to feel it!

But in her yellow dress to-night she could not wring out one drop more; she wanted it all, all for herself. She knew (she kept on looking into the glass, dipping into that dreadfully showing-up blue pool) that she was condemned, despised, left like this in a backwater, because of her being like this, a feeble, vacillating creature; and it seemed to her that the yellow dress was a penance which she had deserved, and if she had been dressed like Rose Shaw, in lovely, clinging green with a ruffle of swansdown, she would have deserved that; and she thought that there was no escape for her—none whatever. But it was not her fault altogether, after all. It was being one of a family of ten; never having money enough, always skimping and paring; and her mother carrying great cans, and the linoleum worn on the stair edges, and one sordid little domestic tragedy after another—nothing catastrophic, the sheep farm failing, but not utterly; her eldest brother marrying beneath him but not very much—there was no romance, nothing extreme about them all. They petered out respectably in seaside resorts; every watering-place had one of her aunts even now asleep in some lodging with the front windows not quite facing the sea. That was like them—they had to squint at things always. And she had done the same—she was just like her aunts. For all her dreams of living in India, married to some hero like Sir Henry Lawrence, some empire builder (still the sight of a native in a turban filled her with romance), she had failed utterly. She had married Hubert, with his safe, permanent underling's job in the Law Courts, and they managed tolerably in a smallish house, without proper maids, and hash when she was alone or just bread and butter, but now and then—Mrs. Holman was off, thinking her the most dried-up, unsympathetic twig she had ever met, absurdly dressed, too, and would tell everyone about Mabel's fantastic appearance—now and then, thought Mabel Waring, left alone on the blue sofa, punching the cushion in order to look occupied, for she would not join Charles Burt and Rose Shaw, chattering like magpies and perhaps laughing at her by the fireplace—now and then, there did come to her delicious moments, reading the other night in bed, for instance, or down by the sea on the sand in the sun, at Easter—let her recall it—a great tuft of pale sand-grass standing all twisted like a shock of spears against the sky, which was blue like a smooth china egg, so firm, so hard, and then the melody of the waves—"Hush, hush," they said, and the children's shouts paddling—yes, it was a divine moment, and there she lay, she felt, in the hand of the Goddess who was the world; rather a hard-hearted, but very beautiful Goddess, a little lamb laid on the altar (one did think these silly things, and it didn't matter so long as one never said them). And also with Hubert sometimes she had quite unexpectedly—carving the mutton for Sunday lunch, for no reason, opening a letter, coming into a room—divine moments, when she said to herself (for she would never say this to anybody else), "This is it. This has happened. This is it!" And the other way about it was equally surprising—that is, when everything was arranged—music, weather, holidays, every reason for happiness was there—then nothing happened at all. One wasn't happy. It was flat, just flat, that was all.

Her wretched self again, no doubt! She had always been a fretful, weak, unsatisfactory mother, a wobbly wife, lolling about in a kind of twilight existence with nothing very clear or very bold, or more one thing than another, like all her brothers and sisters, except perhaps Herbert—they were all the same poor water-veined creatures who did nothing. Then in the midst of this creeping, crawling life, suddenly she was on the crest of a wave. That wretched fly—where had she read the story that kept coming into her mind about the fly and the saucer?—struggled out. Yes, she had those moments. But now that she was forty, they might come more and more seldom. By degrees she would cease to struggle any more. But that was deplorable! That was not to be endured! That made her feel ashamed of herself!

She would go to the London Library tomorrow. She would find some wonderful, helpful, astonishing book, quite by chance, a book by a clergyman, by an American no one had ever heard of; or she would walk down the Strand and drop, accidentally, into a hall where a miner was telling about the life in the pit, and suddenly she would become a new person. She would wear a uniform; she would be called Sister Somebody; she would never give a thought to clothes again. And for ever after she would be perfectly clear about Charles Burt and Miss Milan and this room and that room; and it would be always, day after day, as if she were lying in the sun or carving the mutton. It would be it!

So she got up from the blue sofa, and the yellow button in the looking-glass got up too, and she waved her hand to Charles and Rose to show them she did not depend on them one scrap, and the yellow button moved out of the looking-glass, and all the spears were gathered into her breast as she walked towards Mrs. Dalloway and said "Good night."

"But it's too early to go," said Mrs. Dalloway, who was always so charming.

"I'm afraid I must," said Mabel Waring. "But," she added in her weak, wobbly voice which only sounded ridiculous when she tried to strengthen it, "I have enjoyed myself enormously."

"I have enjoyed myself," she said to Mr. Dalloway, whom she met on the stairs.

"Lies, lies, lies!" she said to herself, going downstairs, and "Right in the saucer!" she said to herself as she thanked Mrs. Barnet for helping her and wrapped herself, round and round, in the Chinese cloak she had worn these twenty years.

1944

✶

Biographical Sketches

Chinua Achebe (*b. 1930*) Achebe was born in Ogidi, an Igbo-speaking town in eastern Nigeria. His father was a Christian churchman. He was educated in English at church schools, at Government College in Umuahia, and at University College in Ibadan. In 1953 he received his B.A. from London University and then studied broadcasting at the British Broadcasting Corporation. He worked for a time at the Nigerian Broadcasting Corporation in Lagos. After the Nigerian civil war, he moved to the United States. Since 1990 he has been Charles P. Stevenson Jr. Professor of Languages and Literature at Bard College. Achebe is known mainly for his essays, short stories, and novels. A volume of his poetry was joint winner of the Commonwealth Poetry Prize in 1972.

Sherman Alexie (*b. 1966*) Alexie grew up on the Spokane Indian Reservation in Washington; he was the first in his family to go to college—first Gonzaga and then Washington State University. Shortly out of college he published two books of poetry; his first book of short stories, *The Lone Ranger and Tonto Fistfight in Heaven*, appeared to critical acclaim in 1993. Material from that book provided the basis of a film collaboration with Chris Eyre, *Smoke Signals*, which won awards at the Sundance Film Festival and was picked up by Miramax for national distribution. In the late 1990s, Alexie began an adjunct career as a standup comedian. His latest collection of stories, *Ten Little Indians*, was published in 2003.

James Baldwin (*1924–1987*) Baldwin grew up the oldest of nine children in a poor household in Harlem, New York City. Bookish from his earliest school days, he was encouraged by one of his junior high school teachers, the poet Countee Cullen, and graduated from a predominantly white high school in the Bronx in 1942. He trained to be a Pentecostal minister, but by 1943 he was living in bohemian Greenwich Village in Manhattan and began his career as a writer, publishing essays and articles and winning two prestigious fellowships, one arranged by his friend, the writer Richard Wright. The other financed his move to France, which became his lifelong refuge from the difficulties confronting black homosexuals in the United States. In 1953 he published his first novel, *Go Tell It on the Mountain*, based on his Harlem experiences, and followed it up in 1956 with *Giovanni's Room*, which examined frankly the sexuality of its gay protagonist. He published over twenty books—poetry, essays, fiction, plays—most dealing with sexual and racial politics and the influence of these on personal identity.

T. Coraghessan Boyle (*b. 1948*) Boyle is a graduate of the M.F.A. program at the University of Iowa (1974) and went on to earn a Ph.D. in nineteenth-century British literature three years later. He's published nearly twenty works of fiction and won dozens of literary awards and honors.

Raymond Carver (*1938–1988*) Carver was born in Clatskanie, Oregon, and grew up in Yakima, Washington. His father worked on the railroad and in the lumber mills and, like Carver, was an alcoholic. His mother worked as a waitress and a retail clerk. Their marriage was tumultuous. Carver was married at nineteen and had two children by the time he was twenty. His marriage, like that of his parents, was notable for its turmoil, and he was frequently hospitalized for acute alcoholism. While supporting his family by working menial jobs, Carver took classes at Chico State in California with the novelist John Gardner, and eventually transferred to and graduated from Humboldt State College and the Iowa Writer's Workshop. He was a Guggenheim Fellow in 1979 and was twice awarded grants from the National Endowment for the Arts. He also won *Poetry* magazine's Levinson Prize and was elected to the American Academy of Arts and Letters. Though he spent most of his life in California, he lived in Port Angeles, Washington, during the ten years before he died of cancer.

John Cheever (*1912–1982*) Cheever's formal education ended when he was expelled from Thayer Academy at the age of seventeen for smoking, and soon thereafter his father, who had left the family a few years before, lost all his money in the stock market crash of 1929. Cheever wrote his first short story about his expulsion, titling it "Expelled," and Malcolm Cowley, who was to become a lifelong friend, published the story in the *New Republic*. After travel in Europe, Cheever returned to America, where he settled in New York City and became friends with such writers as John Dos Passos, e. e. cummings, James Agee, and James Farrell. He lived in poverty in New York as he established himself as a writer. After serving in the Pacific in World War II, he married and had three children. He wrote about the manners and morals of middle-class urban and suburban America and was known primarily as a prolific short story writer until his first novel won the National Book Award in 1958. *The Stories of John Cheever* won the Pulitzer Prize in 1978.

Anton Chekhov (*1860–1904*) Born in the small town of Taganrog in Russia, Chekhov began writing short stories while attending medical school at the University of Moscow. He began practicing medicine in 1884, while at the same time writing short stories, comic sketches, and plays to support his family. Chekhov's first big success was the Moscow Art Theater's production of his play *The Seagull* in 1897. Chekhov eventually left medicine to write full time. In early 1897, he suffered a lung hemorrhage and was forced to spend most of his time in the Crimea for the sake of his health, though he still occasionally traveled to Moscow to participate in the productions of his plays. He died of tuberculosis in a German health resort at the age of forty-four.

Kate Chopin (*1851–1904*) Chopin was born Katherine O'Flaherty in St. Louis, Missouri, to an Irish immigrant father and a Catholic mother of French heritage. Her father, a successful businessman, died in a train wreck when she was only four. She grew up in the company of strong, loving women: her mother, grandmother, and great-grandmother. When she entered the St. Louis Academy of the Sacred Heart, she had already read a great deal of English and French literature. Chopin moved to Louisiana after her marriage to Oscar Chopin in 1870. After her husband's death in 1884, Chopin returned to St. Louis with her six children and lived there with her mother and then, after her mother's death, on her own. She began writing and soon earned a national reputation as a writer of local-color fiction. She is best known for her short stories and her novel *The Awakening*.

Stephen Crane (*1871–1900*) The son of a Methodist minister and a mother who was a social reformer, Crane rebelled against his parents by rejecting all religious and social traditions. At Syracuse University, he distinguished himself more as a baseball player than as a scholar, and he was unsure about what to do with his life when he graduated. But by 1891, he had found an occupation: he wanted to write. He wrote for several newspapers but never lasted long at any of them. Until the syndicated publication of *The Red Badge of Courage*, which he regarded as a "pot-boiler," he lived a life of extreme privation. The same newspaper that syndicated the novel hired him to work as a roving reporter in the West and Mexico, where he gathered material for his writing. His first volume of poetry, *The Black Riders and Other Lines*, earned praise from critics but not from the general public. In 1897 he moved to England, where he befriended some of the age's finest writers, including Henry James and Joseph Conrad. He died of tuberculosis at the age of twenty-eight.

Louise Erdrich (*b. 1954*) Part Chippewa and part German-American, Erdrich entered Dartmouth College the same year that it opened its now famous Native American Studies department. She earned a master's degree from Johns Hopkins and published her first novel, *Love Medicine*, in 1984. She's published nine other novels, three books of poetry, and children's stories, including a novel, *The Birchbark House*, something of a response to *Little House on the Prairie*.

William Faulkner (*1897–1962*) Faulkner was born to an old Mississippi family: his great-grandfather was a local legend, having been a colonel in the Civil War, a lawyer, a railroad builder, a financier, a politician, and a writer, who was shot and killed by a rival in 1889. After dropping out of high school in 1915, Faulkner drifted about the country working in various capacities. Though he never saw active service during his stint in the British Royal Flying Corps, he returned to Mississippi with what he claimed was a war wound. After beginning to write, he went to New Orleans and met Sherwood Anderson, who helped him develop his writing style and get his work published. His early novels and short stories were not very popular. His reputation as a writer was established only after the 1946 publication of *The Portable Faulkner*, edited by Malcolm Cowley. He was awarded the Nobel Prize in 1950 and died of a heart attack in 1962, at the age of sixty-five.

Gabriel García Márquez (*b. 1928*) Born in Aracataca, Colombia, García Márquez lived with his maternal grandparents until he was eight, when his parents took him in after his grandfather died and his grandmother's eyesight had deteriorated. He studied law half-heartedly at the Universidad Nacional and the Universidad de Cartagena, spending more of his time on literature than the law. He finally abandoned the law in 1950 and supported himself by working as a journalist in Latin America, Europe, and the United States. His first published work was *Leaf Storm* (1955). In 1967 he published what is still his most famous novel, *One Hundred Years of Solitude*, which chronicles six generations of a Colombian family and uses their town as a microcosm of Latin America. Within a week of its publication, all eight thousand copies had been sold, and the book was gaining García Márquez international acclaim. He won the Nobel Prize for Literature in 1982. García Márquez currently lives in Mexico City.

Charlotte Perkins Gilman (*1860–1935*) Gilman was born in Hartford, Connecticut, to a father who was a minor literary figure and to a mother whose family had lived in Rhode Island since the middle of the seventeenth century. After Gilman's father deserted the family, her mother moved back to Rhode Island, where she raised her two children on her own. Gilman's childhood was lonely. Later, she supported herself for some time as a governess, an art teacher, and a designer of greeting cards. After marrying the artist Charles Stetson, Gilman became severely depressed. Convinced that her marriage was threatening her sanity, she moved with her daughter to California and in 1892 divorced her husband. Her husband then married her best friend, the writer Grace Ellery Channing, and Gilman sent her daughter to live with them, for which she was widely criticized in the press. She pursued a double career, as a writer and as a lecturer on women, labor, and social organization.

Nathaniel Hawthorne (*1804–1864*) Hawthorne was born in Salem, Massachusetts, and descended from Puritan immigrants, one of whom had been a judge in the Salem witch trials. His father, a sea captain, died in 1808, and his mother's family took responsibility for his education. He attended Bowdoin College, after which he returned to Salem and dedicated himself to writing. He had difficulty getting his early works published, and only a few of his novels and short stories found their way into print. Soon after the publication of his *Twice-Told Tales* in 1837, he became engaged and went to work at the Boston Custom House to save enough money for his marriage. He abandoned his writing for years, convinced that it was the product of his loneliness, but after losing his post as surveyor of the Port of Salem in 1846, he returned to his old craft, writing *The Scarlet Letter* and *The House of Seven Gables*, among other works.

Ernest Hemingway *(1899–1961)* Hemingway was born and raised in Oak Park, Illinois, one of six children. Most of his summers were spent in the family's cottage in northern Michigan, where many of his stories are set. After graduating from high school, Hemingway went to work on the *Kansas City Star*. When the United States entered World War I, Hemingway, unable to join the army because of an eye problem, joined the ambulance corps. He returned from the war a decorated hero. In 1920 he married and went to Paris, where he met Gertrude Stein, Sherwood Anderson, Ezra Pound, and F. Scott Fitzgerald, and worked at becoming a writer. After the 1926 publication of his first novel, *The Sun Also Rises*, he became an international celebrity. His first marriage broke up not long afterward, and over the course of his life he remarried three times. He was awarded a Pulitzer Prize in 1953 and a Nobel Prize in 1954. After being hospitalized several times for depression and paranoia, he killed himself in 1961.

O. Henry *(1862–1910)* Born William Sidney Porter in Greensboro, North Carolina, Henry grew up in the South during the post–Civil War depression. He left school at the age of fifteen and eventually moved to Texas, where he was married. He joined the *Houston Post* as a reporter and columnist when his humorous weekly, *The Rolling Stone*, failed. In 1895, he fled to Honduras to escape prosecution for embezzlement, but he was convicted when he returned to Texas in 1897 to be with his dying wife. In 1898, he entered a penitentiary at Columbus, Ohio. During his three years in prison, he wrote short stories to support his daughter. His first work, "Whistling Dick's Christmas Stocking," which appeared in *McClure's Magazine* in 1899, was a huge success. After being released from prison, he moved to New York City and began writing full time. Ten collections of his works have been published, three posthumously, and over six hundred of his short stories were published during his lifetime. In 1918, the O. Henry Memorial Award, which gives awards annually for the best magazine stories, was established in his honor.

James Joyce *(1882–1941)* Joyce was born in Dublin, Ireland, to a feckless father who drifted steadily down the financial and social scale over the course of his life. Joyce was educated at a series of Jesuit institutions, including Clongowes Wood College, Belvedere College, and University College, in Dublin. He was very religious in his youth, but during his last year at Belvedere College he began turning away from Catholicism. He refused to become involved in any of the nationalist activities of his fellow students, choosing instead to live a life of exile. In 1904 he moved to the Continent, where he lived in Paris, Trieste, and Zurich and was supported by a series of patrons. His works include a series of stories entitled *Dubliners*; *A Portrait of the Artist as a Young Man*; *Ulysses*, which was banned for a dozen years in the United States; and *Finnegans Wake*.

Franz Kafka (*1883–1924*) Born in Prague to a middle-class Jewish family, Kafka attended a prestigious German high school and went on to earn a degree in law in 1906. He held a position in the civil service for many years, working for the Workers' Accident Insurance Organization. Though he never married, he was engaged twice to the same woman and lived with an actress in Berlin for some time before dying of tuberculosis in Vienna. Before his death, he directed his friend Max Brod to destroy his three novels and his numerous unfinished manuscripts. Brod disobeyed Kafka's instructions, and Kafka's work subsequently became known all over the world. His three novels are *The Trial, The Castle*, and *America*. His stories have been collected in English translation in three volumes: *The Great Wall of China, The Penal Colony*, and *The Complete Stories*.

Jamaica Kincaid (*b. 1949*) Kincaid was born Elaine Potter Richardson on Antigua in the Caribbean in 1949. She moved to New York when she was seventeen to work as a nanny, and she attended the New School and Franconia College. She was a staff writer at *The New Yorker* from 1976 to 1995, which is where she started publishing her stories, the first one, "Girl," in 1978. Her first collection, *At the Bottom of the River*, was published in 1983. In addition to fiction, she's written four books of essays, including a book on gardening.

D. H. Lawrence (*1885–1930*) Lawrence was born in the mining village of Eastwood, Nottinghamshire, in England. His mother was better educated and more genteel than her husband, who was a miner, and she struggled to have her children grow up to be like her. Lawrence was aware of the struggle between his parents and sided with his mother during his youth and his father later in his life. After the death of an elder brother, though, he became the center of his mother's emotional life, a place he found suffocating. After graduating from a Nottingham high school he had attended on scholarship, he worked as a clerk and a teacher. He earned a teacher's certificate at Nottingham University College. The publication of a group of his poems in the *English Review* in 1909 helped earn him a reputation as a promising young writer. He taught school in the suburb of Croyburg, England, until 1912, when he moved to Germany with Frieda von Richthofen, who was eventually divorced by her husband. In 1914, she and

Lawrence married. He lived in Italy, Australia, Mexico, and the south of France, where he died of tuberculosis. His three greatest novels are *Sons and Lovers, The Rainbow*, and *Women in Love.*

Beth Lordan (*b. 1948*) Beth Lordan is a late bloomer. She returned to school to earn her undergraduate degree at the age of thirty-seven, and her first novel, *August Heat*, was published in 1987, the same year she graduated with a master's degree from Cornell University. Since 1991, she's been teaching creative writing at Southern Illinois University, Carbondale. She's published two collections of stories, *And Both Shall Row* and *But Come Ye Back.*

Bobbie Ann Mason (*b. 1940*) Bobbie Ann Mason grew up on a dairy farm in Western Kentucky, and most of her fiction is rooted in this rural landscape. She graduated from the University of Kentucky in 1968, worked as a journalist in New York, and earned a Ph.D. in English from the University of Connecticut in 1972. She taught college briefly in Pennsylvania, but in 1978 she started writing full time, eventually getting her break with *The New Yorker* in 1980. "Shiloh" was among her first published stories, and it was the title piece in her first volume of stories, published in 1982. Her 1985 novel *In Country* recounts the lives of a family coping with the aftermath of the Vietnam War, and she has subsequently published two novels and another two collections of stories. She moved back to Kentucky in 1990.

James Alan McPherson (*b. 1943*) Born in Savannah, Georgia, McPherson received his B.A. from Morris Brown College, his LL.B. from Harvard University Law School, and his M.F.A. from the University of Iowa. His literary career began when he received first prize in the *Atlantic Monthly* short story contest in 1965, and in 1969 his first collection of short stories, *Hue and Cry*, was published. Since then he has received numerous fellowships and awards for his fiction. He has taught English at the University of California-Santa Cruz, Harvard University, Morgan State University, and the University of Virginia, and has been a professor of English at the University of Iowa since 1981.

Herman Melville (*1819–1891*) After a three-year clerkship in a bank, from which he escaped at the age of seventeen, Melville took to the sea as a cabin boy on a trans-Atlantic voyage. Four years later he embarked on a four-year journey to the South Seas, which began with arduous service on a New England whaler. Leaving that life, he wandered through a jungle in the Marquesas Islands until he met up with some native people with whom he lived an atavistic, sort of captive existence. After that, he made his way to Tahiti, where he worked at a variety of jobs. The long adventure concluded in Boston after a year's service on a frigate in the United States Navy. These rich experiences formed the bulk of his subjects in his imaginative fiction, beginning in 1846 with the publication of the novel *Typee.* The pinnacle of his career was the publication of *Moby Dick* five years later. During this productive phase of his life, which lasted a little more than a decade, he and Nathaniel Hawthorne formed one of the more notable friendships in American letters. After 1857, he published no more fiction (the famous novella *Billy Budd* was written at the end of his life but published decades later). He did write and publish three volumes of poetry, the first in 1866, *Battle-Pieces and Aspects of the War.*

Joyce Carol Oates (*b. 1938*) Oates describes her childhood in Lockport, New York, as having been "a daily scramble for existence." After receiving a typewriter as a gift at age fourteen, she began to write "novel after novel," continuing to do so throughout high school and college. While at Syracuse University on scholarship, she won the prestigious *Mademoiselle* fiction contest. After graduating as valedictorian of her class, she earned an M.A. in English at the University of Wisconsin. Between 1968 and 1978, Oates taught at the University of Windsor in Canada. At the same time, she published two or three new books each year. Oates has taught at Princeton University since 1978, where she is Roger S. Berlind Distinguished Professor of the Humanities. She and her husband also operate a small press and publish a literary magazine, *The Ontario Review.* She has received the National Book Award and has been nominated twice for the Nobel Prize in Literature.

Tim O'Brien (*b. 1946*) O'Brien is from Worthington, Minnesota. He graduated from Macalester College in 1968 with a B.A. in political science. He had intended to join the State Department, but he was drafted, so instead, served in Vietnam as an infantry foot soldier, even though he opposed the war. He returned from the war—where his division was involved in the My Lai massacre of 1968—with a Purple Heart. After Vietnam he did graduate work at Harvard but left to work as an intern at the *Washington Post.* Just as he was accepting a job as a national affairs reporter at the *Post,* his memoir, *If I Die in a Combat Zone, Box Me Up and Send Me Home,* was published. After a year as a reporter, O'Brien left the newspaper and dedicated himself full time to fiction writing. His novels have won the National Book Award and have been nominated for both the National Book Critics Circle Award and the Pulitzer Prize.

Flannery O'Connor (*1925–1964*) O'Connor lived with her mother in Milledgeville, Georgia, for most of her life. She began to suffer from disseminated lupus in 1950, but managed to halt the progress of the rare disease with injections of a cortisone derivative. The cortisone weakened her bones so much that from 1955 on she was forced to rely on crutches to get around, but she refused to indulge in self-pity or to restrict her activities. O'Connor wrote, traveled, and lectured until 1964, when the lupus reactivated and killed her. She wrote two novels, *Wise Blood* and *The Violent Bear It Away*, as well as numerous short stories.

Frank O'Connor (*1903–1966*) Born Michael O'Donovan in Cork, Ireland, O'Connor was the only child of a poor couple. His father was an alcoholic whose tyranny drove O'Connor to cling to his mother. O'Connor joined the Irish Volunteers and fought on the Republican side in the Irish Civil War. After the war he worked as a teacher, as a librarian, and in business, all the while writing under a pseudonym. He was director of the Abbey Theatre until the death of W. B. Yeats, and he lectured at Harvard University, Northwestern University, and Trinity College in Dublin. O'Connor published hundreds of short stories, translations of Irish poetry, novels, plays, criticism, a biography, and two autobiographies. His works include *Guests of a Nation*, *An Only Child*, and *The Saint and Mary Kate*.

Tillie Olsen (*1913–2007*) Olsen was the daughter of political refugees who fled from Russia to the United States during the czarist repression that followed the Revolution of 1905. She was born in Omaha, Nebraska, and dropped out of school at sixteen to help support her family during the Depression. She began writing her first novel, *Yonnondio*, at nineteen. During this period she was married, had a child, and then was abandoned by her husband. She put the book aside in 1937, a year after remarrying. She returned to writing only after her youngest daughter began school in 1953. During the 1950s she wrote the four stories collected in *Tell Me a Riddle*, which established her reputation when the book was published in paperback in 1961. In 1974, she published the unfinished *Yonnondio*. *Silences*, a collection of essays, appeared in 1978.

Edgar Allan Poe (*1809–1849*) Poe lived a remarkably melodramatic life. His mother, Elizabeth Arnold, was an actress and a teenage widow when she married his father, David Poe, an alcoholic actor who soon abandoned his family. Poe was born in Boston, and his mother died less than two years later. A young merchant named John Allan took Poe in and educated him at good schools in England and Virginia. After a quarrel with Allan, Poe went to look up his paternal relatives in Baltimore and ended up joining the army. Poe and Allan reconciled, and Allan helped Poe get admitted to West Point. There, he ruined his chance of becoming Allan's heir by getting expelled for missing classes and roll calls. After leaving West Point, he went to live in poverty with his relatives. He soon fell in love with and secretly married his thirteen-year-old cousin Virginia. Desperate for income, he took a position at the *Southern Literary Messenger.* There and at other publications, he flourished as a writer and an editor, but drinking and depression eventually ruined his career. Though the exact circumstances of his death are unknown, it is clear that his death was linked to, if not caused by, his alcoholism.

Katherine Anne Porter (*1890–1980*) Born Callie Porter in Indian Creek, Texas, Porter changed her name to Katherine Anne when she began to write. Her mother died when she was not quite two years old, and her father subsequently moved the family to his mother's home in Kyle, Texas. His mother cared for his four children until her death nine years later. Porter married in order to leave home but soon divorced her husband and started living on her own and working as a writer. Between 1918 and 1924 Porter lived primarily in Mexico, where she wrote and participated in revolutionary political activities. One of her short stories, "Flowering Judas," made her famous upon its publication in 1929, and the publication of each of her subsequent works was looked upon as a literary event. In 1931 Porter moved to Europe on a Guggenheim Fellowship, living in Berlin, Paris, and Basel before returning to the United States in 1936. In all, she wrote four books of stories and one novel, *Ship of Fools.* After the publication of her *Collected Stories*, she won the National Book Award, the Pulitzer Prize, the Gold Medal for Fiction from the National Institute of Arts and Letters, and election to the American Academy of Arts and Letters.

Leslie Marmon Silko (*b. 1948*) Born in New Mexico to parents of Laguna Pueblo, Plains Indian, Mexican, and white heritage, Silko considers her mixed heritage an important part of her identity and addresses it in much of her work. She attended Catholic schools, earned a B.A. from the University of New Mexico, and worked toward a law degree in a program for Native Americans. She left law school in order to become a teacher and a writer and has published short stories, poems, and novels. She is a leading figure among Native American writers.

John Steinbeck (*1902–1968*) Born and raised in the Salinas Valley, not far from San Francisco, Steinbeck was the son of the county treasurer and a former schoolteacher. He scoured his family's library for reading material in his youth, thereby becoming familiar with the work of such authors as Milton, Dostoevsky, Flaubert, George Eliot, and Hardy. Steinbeck enrolled at Stanford University after graduating from high school. He left college in 1925 and spent five years reading, writing, and traveling. After marrying in 1933, for the first of three times, he moved to Pacific Grove, California, and wrote while living in a house his father bought him and on the allowance his father provided. His third novel, *Tortilla Flat*, published in 1935, proved to be a success. He achieved further acclaim with some of his other works, including *In Dubious Battle, Of Mice and Men*, and *The Grapes of Wrath*. He won the Nobel Prize in 1963.

Paul Theroux (*b. 1941*) Theroux was born in Massachusetts and graduated from the University of Massachusetts in 1963. He joined the Peace Corps, was stationed in Malawi, was expelled from the Corps for his connections to a coup attempt in that country, and eventually took a teaching position in Uganda. His first novel, *Waldo*, was published in 1967, and was followed by more than three dozen novels, essays, and travel writing, much of it having to do with Africa or the Far East. After a life of many international addresses, he lives now in Hawaii and Cape Cod.

John Updike (*b. 1932*) Born in Shillington, Pennsylvania, an only child, Updike graduated from Harvard University in 1954. After spending a year studying in England, he returned to the United States and went to work for *The New Yorker*, where his first stories appeared and to which he still contributes regularly. He later moved to Ipswich, Massachusetts, with his wife and children to pursue the "solitary trade" of writing, as he called it. By 1958 he had published six books of poetry, a play, a great deal of prose, and a novel, *The Poorhouse Fair*. His four "Rabbit" novels, which star Harry "Rabbit" Angstrom, an ex–high school basketball star, are generally considered his best works of longer fiction.

Hannah Voskuil (*b. 1975*) Growing up in a navy family, Voskuil spent her childhood in California, Illinois, and Virginia. She earned a B.A. from Middlebury College in Vermont and an M.F.A. from Emerson College in Boston. She has been a fiction reader for *Ploughshares* literary magazine for many years and has published short stories in magazines and anthologies. Voskuil lives with her husband in Berkeley, California.

Alice Walker (*b. 1944*) Walker was born in Eatonton, Georgia, the eighth child of sharecroppers. At the age of eight, her brother accidentally shot her in the right eye with a BB gun, which caused her to lose the sight in that eye. Because the injury disfigured her face, she had an isolated childhood and spent her time reading, writing, and carefully observing the people around her. In 1961, Walker entered Spelman College, where she joined the civil rights movement. Two years later, she transferred to Sarah Lawrence College and began writing poetry. She published her first book of poetry in 1968 and her first novel in 1970. Her most famous work is *The Color Purple*, an epistolary novel that won a National Book Critics Circle Award nomination in 1982 and both the American Book Award and the Pulitzer Prize in 1983. She has been involved with the feminist movement, the anti-apartheid movement, the antinuclear movement, and the campaign against female genital mutilation. Alice Walker started her own publishing company, Wild Trees Press, in 1984. She currently lives in Northern California.

Eudora Welty (*1909–2001*) Welty was raised in Jackson, Mississippi, in comfortable circumstances. She attended the Mississippi State College for Women, graduated from the University of Wisconsin, and took a course in advertising at the Columbia University School of Business. She returned to Mississippi in 1931 and worked as a radio writer, a newspaper reporter, and then a photographer for the Works Progress Administration, writing all the while. She published her first story, "Death of a Traveling Salesman," in a small magazine in 1936. During the next two years, she published six stories in the *Southern Review*. Katherine Anne Porter was a mentor to Welty and wrote the introduction to her first book of stories, *A Curtain of Green*. Her first novel, *The Robber Bridgegroom*, was published in 1942. Welty went on to win the O. Henry Memorial Award for short fiction in both 1942 and 1943. She later won the Pulitzer Prize for her 1972 novel, *The Optimist's Daughter*.

Edith Wharton (*1862–1937*) Wharton was raised in an old and wealthy family in New York City. She was educated by tutors and governesses, often while in Europe with her family. She began writing as a young girl, managing to complete a thirty-thousand-word novella by age fifteen and to have two poems published, one in the *Atlantic Monthly*, by age sixteen. She married Edward Wharton, a Bostonian who was sixteen years her senior, in 1885. Their marriage was unhappy, but she did not seek a divorce until 1913, doing so then on the grounds of her husband's infidelity. Wharton began to dedicate herself fully to a career as an author in the late 1890s. With her 1905 novel, *The House of Mirth*, she became known as a serious and successful author. She went on to publish such works as *Ethan Frome, Summer*, and *The Age of Innocence*, as well as an autobiography, *A Backward Glance*. For her writing, she won the Pulitzer Prize and became the first woman to be awarded a gold medal by the National Institute of Arts and Letters.

Virginia Woolf (*1882–1941*) Woolf grew up in an intellectual household, but her childhood was marred by the untimely deaths of her mother and stepsister, and the sexual abuse she suffered from her stepbrothers contributed to her lifelong struggle with mental illness. Woolf ranged freely in her father's library, but keenly felt the injustice that gave her brothers a Cambridge education while denying her access to any university. When her father, Leslie Stephen, died in 1904, she and her siblings set up house in the Bloomsbury section of London, a bohemian part of town made more bohemian by the Stephens' Thursday night salons. The core of these gatherings were her brothers' Cambridge friends and included some of England's leading intellects: painters, writers, economists, diplomats. Influenced by the radical ethics of the Cambridge philosopher G. E. Moore, the Bloomsbury group (as this loose association came to be called) helped define the *modern* era that arose after World War I. Virginia married Leonard Woolf, and in 1917 they founded the Hogarth Press, a small company that published its first books from their living room. T. S. Eliot, John Maynard Keynes, and Sigmund Freud were among the authors they brought to the British public. Woolf published her first novel in 1915, but it was *Jacob's Room* in 1922 that brought the experimental style of writers like James Joyce to England. She published several stream-of-consciousness novels in the next two decades, as well as several influential essays, including *A Room of One's Own*, which is one of the inspirations of the modern women's movement. Sensing a recurrence of her mental illness in 1941, Woolf drowned herself.

✶

Glossary

allegory a narrative in which certain abstractions, such as sin, faith, loyalty, and mercy, are made concrete, usually by being personified. Allegory is a type of symbolism.

antagonist the person against whom the protagonist of a story struggles.

atmosphere the mood that pervades a story, usually established through descriptions of setting.

climax the point in the plot when the conflict reaches its highest tension; the conflict is resolved at the climax.

complication the incident that introduces conflict into a state of relative equilibrium. The complication sets the events of a story in motion.

conflict the struggle between the protagonist and some opposing person (antagonist) or force.

conventional symbol an object carrying symbolic meaning only within the context of a particular culture. For example, the maple leaf is a conventional symbol of Canada. That meaning is bestowed on the object by Canadians.

denouement (see **resolution**)

dynamic character a character who undergoes some fundamental change over the course of a story. A change in a character's material conditions does not make the character dynamic. The change must pertain to the person's character.

editorializing a narrator's intrusion into a story to direct the reader's interpretation.

enveloping action the wider social or historical events surrounding the narrower personal struggles of the characters in a story. For example, the Anglo-Irish War is the enveloping action of "Guests of the Nation."

epiphany a sudden manifestation of some truth, usually conveyed through mundane and otherwise meaningless events, dialogue, or details. Epiphany can refer to sudden insights experienced by either a character or the readers.

equilibrium the state of relative peace both before the protagonist comes into conflict with some opposing force and after the conflict is resolved.

first-person narrator a narrator who appears in the story, either as a participant or merely as an observer. A first-person narrator is a character in the story.

first-person observer a first-person narrator who witnesses the action from its fringes. This narrator is a minor character who does not significantly influence the course of the plot.

first-person participant a first-person narrator who is involved in the events he or she relates. Often a first-person participant is the protagonist of the story.

in medias res the technique of beginning a story by relating events well beyond the complication. The conflict is already well under way, sometimes even near its climax. The earlier incidents of plot are divulged through flashbacks or by some other method.

limited omniscience a third-person narrator who knows more than a first-person narrator could know, but whose knowledge is still limited, usually to the thoughts of one or a few characters.

literary symbol an object carrying symbolic meaning only within the context of a particular work of literature.

motif any word, phrase, idea, object, or situation that recurs throughout a work or that is common to works within a subgenre.

narrator the persona telling the story.

omniscient narrator a third-person narrator from whom no information is hidden. An omniscent narrator knows the thoughts of all characters.

plot the sequence of events in a story. Complication, rising action, climax, and resolution are all elements of plot; though these elements follow that order chronologically, a story might vary their sequence.

point of view the perspective from which a story is told. Each narrator has his or her particular perspective. By defining the narrator as thoroughly as possible, you will define the story's point of view.

projection a technique of narration by which the emotional state of a character colors the description of the setting.

protagonist the character whom the story is about. Often, but not always, readers are led to sympathize with the protagonist as he or she struggles through the conflict. Usually, the protagonist is a dynamic character, and his or her character at the resolution is different than it was at point of complication.

resolution the part of the story after the climax has ended the conflict. Since the conflict has been resolved, the resolution returns the story to a state of equilibrium.

reversal a condition somtimes suffered by a protagonist (especially in tragedy) in which the climax brings about a dramatic change in fortune, usually a change from real or figurative prosperity to a state of poverty.

rising action incidents in the plot between the complication and the climax; usually these incidents raise the reader's sense of tension.

setting the locale in which the story takes place.

static character a character who does not change throughout the course of a story.

stream of consciousness a technique of narration that attempts to reproduce the succession of thoughts, sensory impressions, memories, and so on, that pass through a character's mind.

symbol an object that represents something other than itself. The object might represent another thing or things, or it might represent some abstraction or a range of abstractions. For example, a barbecue in a backyard might represent the American dream.

sympathetic character a character whom the reader likes.

theme what the story is about on an abstract level. For example, love, revenge, friendship, mortality, and the like.

third-person narrator a narrator who does not appear as a character in the story. Often, a third-person narrator has no persona, and the writer expects readers to accept his or her narration as objective fact undistorted by personal perspective.

universal symbol an object carrying symbolic meaning in the context of various cultures. For example, the setting sun symbolizes death in many cultures.

unreliable narrator a narrator whose point of view clearly distorts the story he or she is relating.

✶

Permissions Acknowledgments

Chinua Achebe: "Uncle Ben's Choice" from *Girls at War and Other Stories*. Copyright © Chinua Achebe. Reprinted by permission of the author.

Sherman Alexie: "What You Pawn I Will Redeem" from *Ten Little Indians*. Originally published in *The New Yorker*. Copyright © 2003 by Sherman Alexie. Used by permission of Grove/Atlantic, Inc.

James Baldwin: "Sonny's Blues." Originally published in *Partisan Review*. Collected in *Going to Meet the Man* by James Baldwin. Copyright © 1965 by James Baldwin. Copyright renewed. Published by Vintage Books. Reprinted by arrangement with the James Baldwin Estate.

T. Coraghessan Boyle: "Tooth and Claw" from *Tooth and Claw* by T. Coraghessan Boyle, copyright © 2005 by T. Coraghessan Boyle. Used by permission of Viking Penguin, a division of Penguin Group (USA), Inc.

Raymond Carver: "Cathedral" from *Cathedral* by Raymond Carver, copyright © 1981, 1982, 1983 by Raymond Carver. Used by permission of Alfred A. Knopf, a division of Random House, Inc.

John Cheever: "The Swimmer" from *The Stories of John Cheever* by John Cheever, copyright © 1978 by John Cheever. Used by permission of Alfred A. Knopf, a division of Random House, Inc.

Anton Chekhov: "In Exile," from *Anton Chekhov: Selected Stories* by Anton Chekhov, translated by Ann Dunnigan, copyright © 1960 by Ann Dunnigan. Used by permission of Dutton Signet, a division of Penguin Group (USA), Inc.

Louise Erdrich: "I'm a Mad Dog Biting Myself for Sympathy." First published in *Granta* (34: Death of a Harvard Man) pages 137–141. Copyright © 1990 by Louise Erdrich, permission of The Wylie Agency.

William Faulkner: "A Rose for Emily" from *Collected Stories of William Faulkner* (New York: Random House, 1950). Reprinted by permission.

Gabriel García Márquez: All pages from "A Very Old Man with Enormous Wings" from *Leaf Storm and Other Stories* by Gabriel García Márquez. Translated by Gregory Rabassa. Copyright © 1971 by Gabriel García Márquez. Reprinted by permission of HarperCollins Publishers.

Ernest Hemingway: "Hills Like White Elephants." Reprinted with the permission of Scribner, an imprint of Simon & Schuster Adult Publishing Group, from *The Short Stories of Ernest Hemingway*. Copyright © 1927 by Charles Scribner's Sons. Copyright renewed 1955 by Ernest Hemingway.

Franz Kafka: "A Hunger Artist," edited by Nahum N. Glatzer, from *Franz Kafka: The Complete Stories* by Franz Kafka, edited by Nahum N. Glatzer, copyright © 1946, 1947, 1948, 1949, 1954, 1958, 1971 by Shocken Books. Used by permission of Schocken Books, a division of Random House, Inc.

Jamaica Kincaid: "Girl" from *At the Bottom of the River* by Jamaica Kincaid. Copyright © 1983 by Jamaica Kincaid. Reprinted by permission of Farrar, Straus and Giroux, LLC.

Beth Lordan: "Digging" from *But Come Ye Back* by Beth Lordan. Copyright © 2003 by Beth Lordan. Reprinted by permission of HarperCollins Publishers.

Bobbie Ann Mason: "Shiloh" from *Shiloh and Other Stories* by Bobbie Ann Mason. Originally published in *The New Yorker*. Copyright © 1982 by Bobbie Ann Mason. Reprinted by permission of International Creative Management.

James Alan McPherson: "A Loaf of Bread" from *Elbow Room*. Reprinted by permission of the author.

Joyce Carol Oates: "Where Are You Going, Where Have You Been?" Copyright © 1970 Ontario Review. Reprinted by permission of John Hawkins & Associates, Inc.

Tim O'Brien: "The Things They Carried" from *The Things They Carried* by Tim O'Brien. Copyright © 1990 by Tim O'Brien. Reprinted by permission of Houghton Mifflin Company. All rights reserved.

Flannery O'Connor: "A Good Man Is Hard to Find" from *A Good Man Is Hard to Find and Other Stories*, copyright © 1953 by Flannery O'Connor and renewed 1981 by Regina O'Connor, reprinted by permission of Harcourt, Inc.

Frank O'Connor: "Guests of the Nation," from *The Collected Stories of Frank O'Connor* by Frank O'Connor, copyright © 1931 by Frank O'Connor; copyright renewed 1981 by Harriet O'Donovan Sheehy, Executrix of the Estate of Frank O'Connor. Used by permission of Alfred A. Knopf, a division of Random House, Inc. and by arrangement with The Estate of Frank O'Connor and Writers House, LLC, acting as agent for the proprietor.

Tillie Olsen: "I Stand Here Ironing" from *Tell Me a Riddle*. Reprinted by permission of the Elaine Markson Literary Agency.

Katherine Anne Porter: "The Jilting of Granny Weatherall" from *Flowering Judas and Other Stories*, copyright © 1930 and renewed 1958 by Katherine Anne Porter, reprinted by permission of Harcourt, Inc.

Leslie Marmon Silko: "Yellow Woman," Copyright © 1981 by Leslie Marmon Silko. Reprint from *Storyteller* by Leslie Marmon Silko, published by Seaver Books, New York, New York. Reprinted by permission of Seaver Books.

John Steinbeck: "The Chrysanthemums," copyright © 1937, renewed © 1965 by John Steinbeck, from *The Long Valley* by John Steinbeck. Used by permission of Viking Penguin, a division of Penguin Group (USA), Inc.

Paul Theroux: "The Memory Priest of the Creech People." First published in *Harpers* (1998). Copyright © 1998 by Paul Theroux, permission of The Wylie Agency.

John Updike: "A & P," from *Pigeon Feathers and Other Stories* by John Updike, copyright © 1962 and renewed by 1990 by John Updike. Used by permission of Alfred A. Knopf, a division of Random House, Inc.

Hannah Voskuil: "Currents" from *Quarterly West*, 57 (Winter 2004). Reprinted by permission of the author.

Alice Walker: "Everyday Use" from *In Love & Trouble: Stories of Black Women*, copyright © 1973 by Alice Walker, reprinted by permission of Harcourt, Inc.